MR SPONGE'S
SPORTING TOUR

Mr Sponge's
Sporting Tour

Robert S. Surtees

NONSUCH

First published 1853
Copyright © in this edition 2006
Nonsuch Publishing Limited

Nonsuch Publishing Limited
The Mill, Brimscombe Port, Stroud, Gloucestershire, GL5 2QG
www.nonsuch-publishing.com

Nonsuch Publishing is an imprint of Tempus Publishing Group

For comments or suggestions, please email the editor of this series at:
classics@tempus-publishing.com

British Library Cataloguing in Publication Data.
A catalogue record for this book is available from the British Library.

ISBN 1-84588-212-1
ISBN-13 (from January 2007) 978-1-84588-212-9

Typesetting and origination by Nonsuch Publishing Limited
Printed in Great Britain by Oaklands Book Services Limited

Contents

INTRODUCTION TO THE MODERN EDITION

ROBERT SMITH SURTEES WAS BORN in 1805, the second son of Anthony Surtees, the squire of Hamsterley Hall in County Durham, a family which had long been established in the area. He was educated at Durham grammar school before being becoming a solicitor's articled clerk in 1822. He moved to London and practised law, but his heart was not really in it, country sports, and in particular hunting, being of far more interest to him. He attempted to combine his love of equestrian activities by publishing a treatise on the law as it related to horses, called *The Horseman's Manual*, in 1831. In the same year he was one of the founders of the *New Sporting Magazine*, which he edited for the next five years. In was in the pages of this publication that he developed his genius for comic writing, creating the character of John Jorrocks, the Cockney grocer.

Jorrocks is the antithesis of a conventional Master of Fox Hounds: a self-made tradesman from the East End of London, he is invited to become master of the Handley Cross pack because of his money and his exploits with 'the Surrey.' However, the refined hunting fraternity of Handley Cross are totally unprepared for the rather blunt, vulgar manners of Jorrocks and his wife. He featured in the *New Sporting Magazine* between 1832 and 1834, stories which were collected into book form as *Jorrocks' Jaunts and Jollities* in 1838, with illustrations by Hablot K Browne ('Phiz,' who drew for *Punch* and illustrated several of Charles Dickens' novels). He reappeared in *Handley Cross* (serialised in the *New Sporting Magazine* 1838–39) and *Hillingdon Hall* (serialised

1843–44); both of these stories were later reprinted in book form, with illustrations by John Leech (who also drew for *Punch*).

When Surtees' elder brother died in 1831, he became the heir of Hamsterley Hall; he finally gave up the law in 1835, resigned as editor of the *New Sporting Magazine* in 1836 and returned to County Durham, where he was able to indulge his love of country pursuits. When his father died in 1838 he succeeded him as squire, and seemed to find fulfilment in the life of a country gentleman. He became heavily involved in local affairs and politics, and kept his own pack of hounds from 1838–40. He stood for Parliament (unsuccessfully), served as a Justice of the Peace for County Durham and as an officer in the Durham Militia and was High Sheriff of the county in 1856. However, he continued to 'scribble,' as he termed it, producing three further (non-Jorrocks) hunting novels: *Hawbuck Grange* (1847), *Mr Sponge's Sporting Tour* (1853) and *Mr Facey Romford's Hounds* (1864) and two 'society' novels (*ie* with slightly less emphasis on hunting, although by no means devoid of it) *"Ask Mamma"* (1857–58) and *"Plain or Ringlets?"* (1859–60); *Young Tom Hall*, sub-titled 'His Heartaches and Horses,' remained unfinished at his death.

In 1841 Surtees married Elizabeth Jane Fenwick, daughter of Addison Fenwick, of Bishopwearmouth; they had a son, Anthony, and two daughters, Elizabeth Anne and Eleanor, the latter of whom married John Prendergast Vereker, later 5th Viscount Gort, in 1885. He died in 1864.

Mr Sponge's Sporting Tour was, during Surtees' lifetime, his most successful book. The first of his works to be illustrated by Leech (Surtees had originally asked William Makepeace Thackeray to do so, but he declined, citing an inability to draw horses, and recommended Leech instead), it follows the freeloading chancer 'Soapey' Sponge through English fox-hunting society. Surtees describes him as a 'characterless character', whose time 'may be shortly described as having been spent in hunting all the winter, and in talking about it all the summer. With this popular sport he combined the diversion of fortune-hunting'. Like John Jorrocks, he is a character who does not fit naturally into fox-hunting society, he has 'a jerky, twitchy, uneasy sort of air, that too plainly showed that he was not the natural, or what the lower orders call the *real* gentleman.' Although not quite at the bottom of the social scale, Sponge was not born 'with a silver spoon in his mouth,' which is always a disadvantage for someone with a love of an expensive occupation, such as hunting. He therefore contrives to keep a roof over him and a horse under him by tricking people into buying horses for much more than they are worth, and taking advantage of the hospitality of his friends and acquaintances: 'his dexterity in getting into people's houses was only equalled by the difficulty in getting him out again'.

However, part of 'Soapey' Sponge's skill lies in concealing his lack of money and breeding. In terms of fortune-hunting, itself a necessary activity for him if he wishes to maintain his lifestyle in the long term, he must contrive to appear the very opposite, to which end he 'knew there were places where a man can follow up the effect produced by a red coat in the morning to great advantage in the evening' and that 'hunting men … are all supposed to be rich, and as very few ladies are aware that a horse can't hunt every day in the week, they just class the whole 'genus' fourteen-horse power men, ten-horse power men, five-horse power men, two-horse power men, together, typing them in a bunch, label it 'very rich,' and proceed to take measures accordingly.' He encounters the ideal combination in the Jawleyfords of Jawleyford Court, for example, where he takes up a casual invitation to visit, that was never meant seriously, and finds there two daughters; he erroneously believes their father to be rich, and the Jawleyfords all believe the same of him.

Like all of Surtees' stories, *Mr Sponge's Sporting Tour* is filled with a plethora of memorable characters, most of whom sport amusing and apposite names: Lord Scattercash and the Earl of Scamperdale, Mr Frostyface and Mr Puffington, Robert Foozle and Lucy Glitters. His descriptions of country life and hunting are detailed and full of enthusiasm, but he does not take matters too seriously, displaying a dry wit and an appreciation of human absurdities. Although in the later twentieth and early twenty-first centuries hunting has become a controversial activity, during the middle of the nineteenth century it was a perfectly natural thing to do in the countryside, and, uncomplicated by animal rights activists and hunt saboteurs, Mr Sponge's equestrian escapades still bring joy to modern readers.

PREFACE

THE AUTHOR GLADLY AVAILS HIMSELF of the convenience of a Preface for stating that it will be seen at the close of the work why he makes such a characterless character as Mr. Sponge the hero of his tale.

He will be glad if it serves to put the rising generation on their guard against specious, promiscuous acquaintance, and trains them on to the noble sport of hunting, to the exclusion of its mercenary, illegitimate off-shoots.

November 1852

I

OUR HERO

IT WAS A MURKY OCTOBER day that the hero of our tale, Mr. Sponge, or Soapey Sponge, as his good-natured friends call him, was seen mizzling along Oxford Street, wending his way to the West. Not that there was anything unusual in Sponge being seen in Oxford Street, for when in town his daily perambulations consist of a circuit, commencing from the Bantam Hotel in Bond Street into Piccadilly, through Leicester Square, and so on to Aldridge's, in St. Martin's Lane, thence by Moore's sporting-print shop, and on through some of those ambiguous and tortuous streets that, appearing to lead all ways at once and none in particular, land the explorer, sooner or later, on the south side of Oxford Street.

Oxford Street acts to the north part of London what the Strand does to the south: it is sure to bring one up, sooner or later. A man can hardly get over either of them without knowing it. Well, Soapey having got into Oxford Street, would make his way at a squarey, in-kneed, duck-toed, sort of pace, regulated by the bonnets, the vehicles, and the equestrians he met to criticize; for of women, vehicles, and horses, he had voted himself a consummate judge. Indeed, he had fully established in his own mind that Kiddey Downey and he were the only men in London who *really* knew anything about horses, and fully impressed with that conviction, he would halt, and stand, and stare, in a way that with any other man would have been considered impertinent. Perhaps it was impertinent in Soapey—we don't mean to say it wasn't—but he had done it so long, and was of so sporting a gait and cut, that he felt himself somewhat privileged. Moreover, the majority of horsemen are so satisfied with the animals they bestride, that they cock up their jibs and ride along with a 'find any fault with either me or my horse, if you can' sort of air.

Thus Mr. Sponge proceeded leisurely along, now nodding to this man, now jerking his elbow to that, now smiling on a phaeton, now sneering at a 'bus. If he did not look in at Shackell's or Bartley's, or any of the dealers on the line, he was always to be found about half-past five at Cumberland Gate, from whence he would strike leisurely down the Park, and after coming to a long check at Rotten Row rails, from whence he would pass all the cavalry in the Park in review, he would wend his way back to the Bantam, much in the style he had come. This was his summer proceeding.

Mr. Sponge had pursued this enterprising life for some 'seasons'—ten at least—and supposing him to have begun at twenty or one-and-twenty, he would be about thirty at the time we have the pleasure of introducing him to our readers—a period of life at which men begin to suspect they were not quite so wise at twenty as they thought. Not that Mr. Sponge had any particular indiscretions to reflect upon, for he was tolerably sharp, but he felt that he might have made better use of his time, which may be shortly described as having been spent in hunting all the winter, and in talking about it all the summer. With this popular sport he combined the diversion of fortune-hunting, though we are concerned to say that his success, up to the period of our introduction, had not been commensurate with his deserts. Let us, however, hope that brighter days are about to dawn upon him.

Having now introduced our hero to our male and female friends, under his interesting pursuits of fox and fortune-hunter, it becomes us to say a few words as to his qualifications for carrying them on.

Mr. Sponge was a good-looking, rather vulgar-looking man. At a distance—say ten yards—his height, figure, and carriage gave him somewhat of a commanding appearance, but this was rather marred by a jerky, twitchy, uneasy sort of air, that too plainly showed he was not the natural, or what the lower orders call the *real* gentleman. Not that Sponge was shy. Far from it. He never hesitated about offering to a lady after a three days' acquaintance, or in asking a gentleman to take him a horse in over-night, with whom he might chance to come in contact in the hunting-field. And he did it all in such a cool, off-hand, matter-of-course sort of way, that people who would have stared with astonishment if anybody else had hinted at such a proposal, really seemed to come into the humour and spirit of the thing, and to look upon it rather as a matter of course than otherwise. Then his dexterity in getting into people's houses was only equalled by the difficulty of getting him out again, but this we must waive for the present in favour of his portraiture.

In height, Mr. Sponge was above the middle size—five feet eleven or so—with a well borne up, not badly shaped, closely cropped oval head, a tolerably good, but somewhat receding forehead, bright hazel eyes, Roman nose, with carefully tended whiskers, reaching the corners of a well-formed mouth, and thence descending in semicircles into a vast expanse of hair beneath the chin.

Having mentioned Mr. Sponge's groomy gait and horsey propensities, it were almost needless to say that his dress was in the sporting style— you saw what he was by his clothes. Every article seemed to be made to defy the utmost rigour of the elements. His hat (Lincoln and Bennett) was hard and heavy. It sounded upon an entrance-hall table like a drum. A little magical loop in the lining explained the cause of its weight. Somehow, his hats were never either old or new—not that he bought them second-hand, but when he got a new one he took its 'long-coat' off, as he called it, with a singeing lamp, and made it look as if it had undergone a few probationary showers.

When a good London hat recedes to a certain point, it gets no worse; it is not like a country-made thing that keeps going and going until it declines into a thing with no sort of resemblance to its original self. Barring its weight and hardness, the Sponge hat had no particular character apart from the Sponge head. It was not one of those punty ovals or Cheshire-cheese flats, or curly-sided things that enables one to say who is in a house and who is not, by a glance at the hats in the entrance, but it was just a quiet, round hat, without anything remarkable, either in the binding, the lining, or the band, but still it was a very becoming hat when Sponge had it on. There is a great deal of character in hats. We have seen hats that bring the owners to the recollection far more forcibly than the generality of portraits. But to our hero.

That there may be a dandified simplicity in dress, is exemplified every day by our friends the Quakers, who adorn their beautiful brown Saxony coats with little inside velvet collars and fancy silk buttons, and even the severe order of sporting costume adopted by our friend Mr.

Sponge is not devoid of capability in the way of tasteful adaptation. This Mr. Sponge chiefly showed in promoting a resemblance between his neck-cloths and waistcoats. Thus, if he wore a cream-coloured cravat, he would have a buff-coloured waistcoat, if a striped waistcoat, then the starcher would be imbued with somewhat of the same colour and pattern. The ties of these varied with their texture. The silk ones terminated in a sort of coaching fold, and were secured by a golden fox-head pin, while the striped starchers, with the aid of a pin on each side, just made a neat, unpretending tie in the middle, a sort of miniature of the flagrant, flyaway, Mile-End ones of aspiring youth of the present day. His coats were of the single-breasted cut-away order, with pockets outside, and generally either Oxford mixture or some dark colour, that required you to place him in a favourable light to say what it was.

His waistcoats, of course, were of the most correct form and material, generally either pale buff, or buff with a narrow stripe, similar to the undress vests of the servants of the Royal Family, only with the pattern run across instead of lengthways, as those worthies mostly have theirs, and made with good honest step collars, instead of the make-believe roll collars they sometimes convert their upright ones into. When in deep thought, calculating, perhaps, the value of a passing horse, or considering whether he should have beefsteaks or lamb chops for dinner, Sponge's thumbs would rest in the arm-holes of his waistcoat; in which easy, but not very elegant, attitude he would sometimes stand until all trace of the idea that elevated them had passed away from his mind.

In the trouser line he adhered to the close-fitting costume of former days; and many were the trials, the easings, and the alterings, ere he got a pair exactly to his mind. Many were the customers who turned away on seeing his manly figure filling the swing mirror in 'Snip and Sneiders', a monopoly that some tradesmen might object to, only Mr. Sponge's trousers being admitted to be perfect 'triumphs of the art,' the more such a walking advertisement was seen in the shop the better. Indeed, we believe it would have been worth Snip and Co.'s while to have let him have them for nothing. They were easy without being tight, or rather they looked tight without being so; there wasn't a bag, a wrinkle, or a crease that there shouldn't be, and strong and storm-defying as they seemed, they were yet as soft and as supple as a lady's glove. They looked more as if his legs had been blown in them than as if such irreproachable garments were the work of man's hands. Many were the nudges, and many the 'look at this chap's trousers,' that were given by ambitious men emulous of his appearance as he passed along, and many were the turnings round to examine their faultless fall upon his radiant boot. The boots, perhaps, might come in for a little of the glory, for they were beautifully soft and cool-looking to the foot, easy without being loose, and he preserved the lustre of their polish, even up to the last moment of his walk. There never was a better man for getting through dirt, either on foot or horseback, than our friend.

To the frequenters of the 'corner,' it were almost superfluous to mention that he is a constant attendant. He has several volumes of 'catalogues,' with the prices the horses have brought set down in the margins, and has a rare knack at recognizing old friends, altered, disguised, or disfigured as they may be—'I've seen that rip before,' he will say, with a knowing shake of the head, as some woebegone devil goes, best leg foremost, up to the hammer, or, 'What! is that old beast back? why he's here every day.' No man can impose upon Soapy with a horse. He can detect the rough-coated plausibilities of the straw-yard equally with the metamorphosis of the clipper or singer. His practised eye is not to be imposed upon either by the blandishments of the bang-tail, or the bereavements of the dock. Tattersall will hail him from his rostrum with—'Here's a horse will suit you, Mr. Sponge! cheap, good, and handsome! come and buy him.' But it is needless describing him here, for every out-of-place groom and dog-stealer's man knows him by sight.

II

MR. BENJAMIN BUCKRAM

Having dressed and sufficiently described our hero to enable our readers to form a general idea of the man, we have now to request them to return to the day of our introduction. Mr. Sponge had gone along Oxford Street at a somewhat improved pace to his usual wont—had paused for a shorter period in the "bus' perplexed 'Circus,' and pulled up seldomer than usual between the Circus and the limits of his stroll. Behold him now at the Edgeware Road end, eyeing the 'buses with a wanting-a-ride like air, instead of the contemptuous sneer he generally adopts towards those uncouth productions. Red, green blue, drab, cinnamon-colour, passed and crossed, and jostled, and stopped, and blocked, and the cads telegraphed, and winked, and nodded, and smiled, and slanged, but Mr. Sponge regarded them not. He had a sort of "bus' panorama in his head, knew the run of them all, whence they started, where they stopped, where they watered, where they changed, and, wonderful to relate, had never been entrapped into a sixpenny fare when he meant to take a threepenny one. In cab and "bus' geography there is not a more learned man in London.

Mark him as he stands at the corner. He sees what he wants, it's the chequered one with the red and blue wheels that the Bayswater ones have got between them, and that the St. John's Wood and two Western Railway ones are trying to get into trouble by crossing. What a row! how the ruffians whip, and stamp, and storm, and all but pick each other's horses' teeth with their poles, how the cads gesticulate, and the passengers imprecate! now the bonnets are out of the windows, and the row increases. Six coachmen cutting and storming, six cads sawing the air, sixteen ladies in flowers screaming, six-and-twenty sturdy passengers swearing they will 'fine them all,' and Mr. Sponge is the only cool person in the scene. He doesn't rush into the throng and 'jump in,' for fear the 'bus should extricate itself and drive on without him; he doesn't make confusion worse, confounded by intimating his behest; he doesn't soil his bright boots by stepping off the kerb-stone; but, quietly waiting the evaporation of the steam, and the disentanglement of the vehicles, by the smallest possible sign in the world, given at the opportune moment, and a steady adhesion to the flags, the 'bus is obliged either to 'come to,' or lose the fare, and he steps quietly in, and squeezes along to the far end, as though intent on going the whole hog of the journey.

Away they rumble up the Edgeware Road; the gradual emergence from the brick and mortar of London being marked as well by the telling out of passengers as by the increasing distances between the houses. First, it is all close huddle with both. Austere iron railings guard the subterranean kitchen areas, and austere looks indicate a desire on the part of the passengers to guard their own pockets; gradually little gardens usurp the places of the cramped areas, and, with their humanizing appearance, softer looks assume the place of frowning *anti* swell-mob ones.

Presently a glimpse of green country or of distant hills may be caught between the wider spaces of the houses, and frequent settings down increase the space between the passengers; gradually conservatories appear and conversation strikes up; then come the exclusiveness of villas, some detached and others running out at last into real pure green fields studded with trees and picturesque pot-houses, before one of which latter a sudden wheel round and a jerk announces the journey done. The last passenger (if there is one) is then unceremoniously turned loose upon the country.

Our readers will have the kindness to suppose our hero, Mr. Sponge, shot out of an omnibus at the sign of the Cat and Compasses, in the full rurality of grass country, sprinkled with fallows and turnip-fields. We should state that this unwonted journey was a desire to pay a visit to Mr. Benjamin Buckram, the horse-dealer's farm at Scampley, distant some mile and a half from where he was set down, a space that he now purposed travelling on foot.

Mr. Benjamin Buckram was a small horse-dealer—small, at least, when he was buying, though great when he was selling. It would do a youngster good to see Ben filling the two capacities. He dealt in second-hand, that is to say, past mark of mouth horses; but on the present occasion, Mr. Sponge sought his services in the capacity of a letter rather than a seller of horses. Mr. Sponge wanted to job a couple of plausible-looking horses, with the option of buying them, provided he (Mr. Sponge) could sell them for more than he would have to give Mr. Buckram, exclusive of the hire. Mr. Buckram's job price, we should say, was as near twelve pounds a month, containing twenty-eight days, as he could screw, the hirer, of course, keeping the animals.

Scampley is one of those pretty little suburban farms, peculiar to the north and north-west side of London—farms varying from fifty to a hundred acres of well-manured, gravelly soil; each farm with its picturesque little buildings, consisting of small, honey-suckled, rose-entwined brick houses, with small, flat, pantiled roofs, and lattice-windows; and, hard by, a large haystack, three times the size of the house, or a desolate barn, half as big as all the rest of the buildings. From the smallness of the holdings, the farmhouses are dotted about as thickly, and at such varying distances from the roads, as to look like inferior 'villas,' falling out of rank; most of them have a half-smart, half-seedy sort of look.

The rustics who cultivate them, or rather look after them, are neither exactly town nor country. They have the clownish dress and boorish gait of the regular 'chaws,' with a good deal of the quick, suspicious, sour sauciness of the low London resident. If you can get an answer from them at all, it is generally delivered in such a way as to show that the answerer thinks you are what they call 'chaffing them,' asking them what you know.

These farms serve the double purpose of purveyors to the London stables, and hospitals for sick, overworked, or unsaleable horses. All the great job-masters and horse-dealers have these retreats in the country, and the smaller ones pretend to have, from whence, in due course, they can draw any sort of an animal a customer may want, just as little cellarless wine-merchants can get you any sort of wine from real establishments—if you only give them time.

There was a good deal of mystery about Scampley. It was sometimes in the hands of Mr. Benjamin Buckram, sometimes in the hands of his assignees, sometimes in those of his cousin, Abraham Brown, and sometimes John Doe and Richard Roe were the occupants of it.

Mr. Benjamin Buckram, though very far from being one, had the advantage of looking like a respectable man. There was a certain plump, well-fed rosiness about him, which, aided by a bright-coloured dress, joined to a continual fumble in the pockets of his drab trousers, gave him the air of a 'well-to-do-in-the-world' sort of man. Moreover, he sported a velvet collar to his blue coat, a more imposing ornament than it appears at first sight. To be sure, there are two sorts of velvet collars—the legitimate velvet collar, commencing with the coat, and the adopted velvet collar, put on when the cloth one gets shabby.

Buckram's was always the legitimate velvet collar, new from the first, and, we really believe, a permanent velvet collar, adhered to in storm and in sunshine, has a very money-making impression on the world. It shows a spirit superior to feelings of paltry economy, and we think a person would be much more excusable for being victimized by a man with a good velvet collar to his coat, than by one exhibiting that spurious sign of gentility—a horse and gig.

The reader will now have the kindness to consider Mr. Sponge arriving at Scampley.

'Ah, Mr. Sponge!' exclaimed Mr. Buckram, who, having seen our friend advancing up the little twisting approach from the road to his house through a little square window almost blinded with Irish ivy, out of which he was in the habit of contemplating the arrival of his occasional lodgers, Doe and Roe. 'Ah, Mr. Sponge!' exclaimed he, with well-assumed gaiety; 'you should have been here yesterday; sent away two sich osses—perfect 'unters—the werry best I do think I ever saw in my life; either would have bin the werry oss for your money. But come in, Mr. Sponge, sir, come in,' continued he, backing himself through a little sentry-box of a green portico, to a narrow passage which branched off into little rooms on either side.

As Buckram made this retrograde movement, he gave a gentle pull to the wooden handle of an old-fashioned wire bell-pull in the midst of a buggy, four-in-hand, and other whips, hanging in the entrance, a touch that was acknowledged by a single tinkle of the bell in the stable-yard.

They then entered the little room on the right, whose walls were decorated with various sporting prints chiefly illustrative of steeple-chases, with here and there a stunted fox-brush, tossing about as a duster. The ill-ventilated room reeked with the effluvia of stale smoke, and the faded green baize of a little round table in the centre was covered with filbert-shells and empty ale-glasses. The whole furniture of the room wasn't worth five pounds.

Mr. Sponge, being now on the dealing tack, commenced in the poverty-stricken strain adapted to the occasion. Having deposited his hat on the floor, taken his left leg up to nurse, and given his hair a backward rub with his right hand, he thus commenced:

'Now, Buckram,' said he, 'I'll tell you how it is. I'm deuced hard-up—regularly in Short's Gardens. I lost eighteen 'undred on the Derby, and seven on the Leger, the best part of my year's income, indeed; and I just want to hire two or three horses for the season, with the option of buying, if I like; and if you supply me well, I may be the means of bringing grist to your mill; you twig, eh?'

'Well, Mr. Sponge,' replied Buckram, sliding several consecutive half-crowns down the incline plane of his pocket. 'Well, Mr. Sponge, I shall be happy to do my best for you. I wish you'd come yesterday, though, as I said before, I jest had two of the neatest nags—a bay and a grey—not that colour makes any matter to a judge like you; there's no sounder sayin' than that a good oss is not never of a bad colour; only to a young gemman, you know, it's well to have 'em smart, and the ticket, in short; howsomever, I must do the best I can for you, and if there's nothin' in that tickles your fancy, why, you must give me a few days to see if I can arrange an exchange with some other gent; but the present is like to be a werry haggiwatin' season; had more happlications for osses nor ever I remembers, and I've been a dealer now, man and boy, turned of eight-and-thirty years; but young gents is whimsical, and it was a young 'un wot got these, and there's no sayin' but he mayn't like them—indeed, one's rayther difficult to ride—that's to say, the grey, the neatest of the two, and he *may* come back, and if so, you shall have him; and a safer, sweeter oss was never seen, or one more like to do credit to a gent: but you knows what an oss is, Mr. Sponge, and can do justice to me, and I should like to put summut good into your hands—*that* I should.'

With conversation, or rather with balderdash, such as this, Mr. Buckram beguiled the few minutes necessary for removing the bandages, hiding the bottles, and stirring up the cripples about to be examined, and the heavy flap of the coach-house door announcing that all was ready, he forthwith led the way through a door in a brick wall into a little three-sides of a square yard, formed of stables and loose boxes, with a dilapidated dovecote above a pump in the centre; Mr. Buckram, not growing corn, could afford to keep pigeons.

III

PETER LEATHER

NOTHING BESPEAKS THE CHARACTER OF a dealer's trade more than the servants and hangers-on of the establishment. The civiler in manner, and the better they are 'put on,' the higher the standing of the master, and the better the stamp of the horses.

Those about Mr. Buckram's were of a very shady order. Dirty-shirted, sloggering, baggy-breeched, slangey-gaitered fellows, with the word 'gin' indelibly imprinted on their faces. Peter Leather, the head man, was one of the fallen angels of servitude. He had once driven a duke—the Duke of Dazzleton—having nothing whatever to do but dress himself and climb into his well-indented richly-fringed throne, with a helper at each horse's head to 'let go' at a nod from his broad-laced, three-cornered hat. Then having got in his cargo (or rubbish, as he used to call them), he would start off at a pace that was truly terrific, cutting out this vehicle, shooting past that, all but grazing a third, anathematizing the 'buses, and abusing the draymen. We don't know how he might be with the queen, but he certainly drove as though he thought nobody had any business in the street while the Duchess of Dazzleton wanted it. The duchess liked going fast, and Peter accommodated her. The duke jobbed his horses and didn't care about pace, and so things might have gone on very comfortably, if Peter one afternoon hadn't run his pole into the panel of a very plain but very neat yellow barouche, passing the end of New Bond Street, which having nothing but a simple crest—a stag's head on the panel—made him think it belonged to some bulky cit, taking the air with his rib, but who, unfortunately, turned out to be no less a person than Sir Giles Nabem, Knight, the great police magistrate, upon one of whose myrmidons in plain clothes, who came to the rescue, Peter committed a most violent assault, for which unlucky casualty his worship furnished him with rotatory occupation for his fat calves in the 'H. of C.,' as the clerk shortly designated the House of Correction. Thither Peter went, and *in lieu* of his lace-bedaubed coat, gold-gartered plushes, stockings, and buckled shoes, he was dressed up in a suit of tight-fitting yellow and black-striped worsteds, that gave him the appearance of a wasp without wings. Peter Leather then tumbled regularly down the staircase of servitude, the greatness of his fall being occasionally broken by landing in some inferior place. From the Duke of Dazzleton's, or rather from the treadmill, he went to the Marquis of Mammon, whom he very soon left because he wouldn't wear a second-hand wig. From the marquis he got hired to the great Irish Earl of Coarsegab, who expected him to wash the carriage, wait at table, and do other incidentals never contemplated by a London coachman. Peter threw this place up with indignation on being told to take the letters to the post. He then lived on his 'means' for a while, a thing that is much finer in theory than in practice, and having about exhausted his substance and placed the bulk of his apparel in safe keeping, he condescended to take a place as job coachman in a livery-stable—a 'horses let by the hour, day, or month' one, in which he enacted as many characters, at least made as many different appearances, as the late Mr. Mathews used to do in his celebrated 'At Homes.' One day Peter would be seen ducking under the mews' entrance in one of those greasy, painfully well-brushed hats, the certain precursors of soiled linen and seedy, most seedy-covered buttoned coats, that would puzzle a conjuror to say whether they were black, or grey, or olive, or invisible green turned visible brown. Then another day he might be seen in old Mrs. Gadabout's sky-blue livery, with a tarnished, gold-laced hat, nodding over his nose; and on a third he would shine forth in Mrs. Major-General Flareup's cockaded one, with a worsted shoulder-knot, and a much over-daubed, light, drab livery coat, with crimson inexpressibles, so tight as to astonish a beholder how he ever got into them. Humiliation, however, has its limits as well as other things; and Peter having been invited to descend from his box—alas! a regular country patent leather one, and invest himself in a Quaker-collared blue coat, with a red vest, and a pair of blue trousers with a broad red stripe down the sides, to drive the Honourable old Miss Wrinkleton, of Harley Street, to Court in a 'one oss pianoforte-case,' as he called a Clarence, he could stand it no longer, and, chucking the nether garments into the fire, he rushed frantically up the area-steps, mounted his box, and quilted the old crocodile of a horse all the way home, accompanying each cut with an imprecation such as '*me* make a guy of myself!' (whip) '*me* put on sich things!' (whip, whip) '*me* drive down Sin Jimses-street!' (whip, whip, whip), '*I'd* see her —— fust!' (whip, whip, whip), cutting at the old horse just as if he was laying it into Miss Wrinkleton, so that by the time he got home he had established a considerable lather on the old nag, which his master resenting, a row ensued, the sequel of which may readily be imagined. After assisting Mrs. Clearstarch, the Kilburn laundress, in getting in and taking out her washing, for a few weeks, chance at last landed him at Mr. Benjamin Buckram's, from whence he is now about to be removed to become our hero Mr. Sponge's Sancho Panza, in his fox-hunting, fortune-hunting career, and disseminate in remote parts his doctrines of the real honour and dignity of servitude. Now to the inspection.

Peter Leather, having a peep-hole as well as his master, on seeing Mr. Sponge arrive, had given himself an extra rub over, and covered his dirty shirt with a clean, well-tied, white kerchief, and a whole coloured scarlet waistcoat, late the property of one of his noble employers, in hopes that Sponge's visit might lead to something. Peter was about sick of the suburbs, and thought, of course, that he couldn't be worse off than where he was.

'Here's Mr. Sponge what wants some osses,' observed Mr. Buckram, as Leather met them in the middle of the little yard, and brought his right arm round with a sort of military swing to his forehead; 'what 'ave we in?' continued Buckram, with the air of a man with so many horses that he didn't know what were in and what were out.

'Vy we 'ave Rumbleton in,' replied Leather, thoughtfully, stroking down his hair as he spoke, 'and we 'ave Jack o'Lanthorn in, and we 'ave the Camel in, and there's the little Hirish oss with the sprig tail—Jack-a-Dandy, as I calls him, and the Flyer will be in to-night, he's just out a hairing, as it were, with old Mr. Callipash.'

'Ah, Rumbleton won't do for Mr. Sponge,' observed Buckram, thoughtfully, at the same time letting go a tremendous avalanche of silver down his trouser pocket, 'Rumbleton won't do,' repeated he, 'nor Jack-a-Dandy nouther.'

'Why, I wouldn't commend neither on 'em,' replied Peter, taking his cue from his master, 'only ven you axes me vot there's in, you knows vy I must give you a *cor*-rect answer, in course.'

'In course,' nodded Buckram.

Leather and Buckram had a good understanding in the lying line, and had fallen into a sort of tacit arrangement that if the former was staunch about the horses he was at liberty to make the best terms he could for himself. Whatever Buckram said, Leather swore to, and they had established certain signals and expressions that each understood.

'I've an unkimmon nice oss,' at length observed Mr. Buckram, with a scrutinizing glance at Sponge, 'and an oss in hevery respect werry like your work, but he's an oss I'll candidly state, I wouldn't put in every one's 'ands, for, in the fust place, he's werry walueous, and in the second, he requires an ossman to ride; howsomever, as I knows that you *can* ride, and if you doesn't mind taking my 'ead man,' jerking his elbow at Leather, 'to look arter him, I wouldn't mind 'commodatin' on you, prowided we can 'gree upon terms.'

'Well, let's see him,' interrupted Sponge, 'and we can talk about terms after.'

'Certainly, sir, certainly,' replied Buckram, again letting loose a reaccumulated rush of silver down his pocket. 'Here, Tom! Joe! Harry! where's Sam?' giving the little tinkler of a bell a pull as he spoke.

'Sam be in the straw 'ouse,' replied Leather, passing through a stable into a wooden projection beyond, where the gentleman in question was enjoying a nap.

'Sam!' said he, 'Sam!' repeated he, in a louder tone, as he saw the object of his search's nose popping through the midst of the straw.

'What now?' exclaimed Sam, starting up, and looking wildly around; 'what now?' repeated he, rubbing his eyes with the backs of his hands.

'Get out Ercles,' said Leather, *sotto voce*.

The lad was a mere stripling—some fifteen or sixteen, years, perhaps—tall, slight, and neat, with dark hair and eyes, and was dressed in a brown jacket—a real boy's jacket, without laps, white cords, and top-boots. It was his business to risk his neck and limbs at all hours of the day, on all sorts of horses, over any sort of place that any person chose to require him to put a horse at, and this he did with the daring pleasure of youth as yet undaunted by any serious fall. Sam now bestirred himself to get out the horse. The clambering of hoofs presently announced his approach.

Whether Hercules was called Hercules on account of his amazing strength, or from a fanciful relationship to the famous horse of that name, we know not; but his strength and his colour would favour either supposition. He was an immense, tall, powerful, dark brown, sixteen hands horse, with an arched neck and crest, well set on, clean, lean head, and loins that looked as if they could shoot a man into the next county. His condition was perfect. His coat lay as close and even as satin, with cleanly developed muscle, and altogether he looked as hard as a cricket-ball. He had a famous switch tail, reaching nearly to his hocks, and making him look less than he would otherwise have done.

Mr. Sponge was too well versed in horse-flesh to imagine that such an animal would be in the possession of such a third-rate dealer as Buckram, unless there was something radically wrong about him, and as Sam and Leather were paying the horse those stable attentions that always precede a show out, Mr. Sponge settled in his own mind that the observation about his requiring a horseman to ride him, meant that he was vicious. Nor was he wrong in his anticipations, for not all Leather's whistlings, or Sam's endearings and watchings, could conceal the sunken, scowling eye, that as good as said, 'you'd better keep clear of me.'

Mr. Sponge, however, was a dauntless horseman. What man dared he dared, and as the horse stepped proudly and freely out of the stable, Mr. Sponge thought he looked very like a hunter. Nor were Mr. Buckram's laudations wanting in the animal's behalf.

'There's an 'orse!' exclaimed he, drawing his right hand out of his trouser pocket, and flourishing it towards him. 'If that 'orse were down in Leicestersheer,' added he, 'he'd fetch three 'under'd guineas. Sir Richard would 'ave him in a minnit—*that he would*!' added he, with a stamp of his foot as he saw the animal beginning to set up his back and wince at the approach of the lad. (We may here mention by way of parenthesis, that Mr. Buckram had brought him out of Warwicksheer for thirty pounds, where the horse had greatly distinguished himself, as well by kicking off sundry scarlet swells in the gaily thronged streets of Leamington, as by running away with divers others over the wide-stretching grazing grounds of Southam and Dunchurch.)

But to our story. The horse now stood staring on view: fire in his eye, and vigour in his every limb. Leather at his head, the lad at his side. Sponge and Buckram a little on the left.

'W—h—o—a—a—y, my man, w—h—o—a—a—y,' continued Mr. Buckram, as a liberal show of the white of the eye was followed by a little wince and hoist of the hind quarters on the nearer approach of the lad.

'Look sharp, boy,' said he, in a very different tone to the soothing one in which he had just been addressing the horse. The lad lifted up his leg for a hoist. Leather gave him one as quick as thought, and led on the horse as the lad gathered up his reins. They then made for a large field at the back of the house, with leaping-bars, hurdles, 'on and offs,' 'ins and outs,' all sorts of fancy leaps scattered about. Having got him fairly in, and the lad having got himself fairly settled in the saddle he gave the horse a touch with the spur as Leather let go his head, and after a desperate plunge or two started off at a gallop.

'He's fresh,' observed Mr. Buckram confidentially to Mr. Sponge, 'he's fresh—wants work, in short—short of work—wouldn't put every one on him—wouldn't put one o' your timid cocknified chaps on him, for if ever he were to get the hupper 'and, vy I doesn't know as 'ow that we might get the hupper 'and o' him, agen, but the playful rogue knows ven he's got a workman on his back—see how he gives to the lad though he's only fifteen, and not strong of his hage nouther,' continued Mr. Buckram, 'and I guess if he had sich a consternation of talent as you on his back, he'd wery soon be as quiet as a lamb—not that he's wicious—far from it, only play—full of play, I may say, though to be sure, if a man gets spilt it don't argufy much whether it's done from play or from wice.'

During this time the horse was going through his evolutions, hopping over this thing, popping over that, making as little of everything as practice makes them do.

Having gone through the usual routine, the lad now walked the glowing-coated, snorting horse back to where the trio stood. Mr. Sponge again looked him over, and still seeing no exception to take to him, bid the lad get off and lengthen the stirrups for him to take a ride. That was the difficulty. The first two minutes always did it. Mr. Sponge, however, nothing daunted, borrowed Sam's spurs, and making Leather hold the horse by the head till he got well into the saddle, and then lead him on a bit; he gave the animal such a dig in both sides as fairly threw him off his guard, and made him start away at a gallop, instead of standing and delivering, as was his wont.

Away Mr. Sponge shot, pulling him about, trying all his paces, and putting him at all sorts of leaps.

Emboldened by the nerve and dexterity displayed by Mr. Sponge, Mr. Buckram stood meditating a further trial of his equestrian ability, as he watched him bucketing 'Ercles' about. Hercules had 'spang-hewed' so many triers, and the hideous contraction of his resolute back had deterred so many from mounting, that Buckram had begun to fear he would have to place him in the only remaining school for incurables, the 'bus. Hack-horse riders are seldom great horsemen. The very fact of their being hack-horse riders shows they are little accustomed to horses, or they would not give the fee-simple of an animal for a few weeks' work.

'I've a wonderful clever little oss,' observed Mr. Buckram, as Sponge returned with a slack-rein and a satisfied air on the late resolute animal's back. 'Little I can 'ardly call 'im,' continued Mr. Buckram, 'only he's low; but you knows that the 'eight of an oss has nothin' to do with his size. Now this is a perfect dray-oss in miniature. An 'Arrow gent, lookin' at him t'other day christen'd him "Multum in Parvo." But though he's so *ter-men*-dous strong, he has the knack o' goin', specially in deep; and if you're not a-goin' to Sir Richard, but into some o' them plough sheers (shires), I'd 'commend him to you.'

'Let's have a look at him,' replied Mr. Sponge, throwing his right leg over Hercules' head and sliding from the saddle on to the ground, as if he were alighting from the quietest shooting pony in the world.

All then was hurry, scurry, and scamper to get this second prodigy out. Presently he appeared. Multum in Parvo certainly was all that Buckram described him. A long, low, clean-headed, clean-necked, big-hocked, chestnut, with a long tail, and great, large, flat white legs, without mark or blemish upon them. Unlike Hercules, there was nothing indicative of vice or mischief about him. Indeed, he was rather a sedate, meditative-looking animal; and, instead of the watchful, arms'-length sort of way Leather and Co. treated Hercules, they jerked and punched Parvo about as if he were a cow.

Still Parvo had his foibles. He was a resolute, head-strong animal, that would go his own way in spite of all the pulling and hauling in the world. If he took it into his obstinate head to turn into a particular field, into it he would be; or against the gate-post he would bump the rider's leg in a way that would make him remember the difference of opinion between them. His was not a fiery, hot-headed spirit, with object or reason for its guide, but just a regular downright pig-headed sort of stupidity, that nobody could account for. He had a mouth like a bull, and would walk clean through a gate sometimes rather than be at the trouble of rising to leap it; at other times he would hop over it like a bird. He could not beat Mr. Buckram's men, because they were always on the look-out for objects of contention with sharp spur rowels, ready to let into his sides the moment he began to stop; but a weak or a timid man on his back had no more chance than he would on an elephant. If the horse chose to carry him into the midst of the hounds at the meet, he would have him in—nay, he would think nothing of upsetting the master himself in the middle of the pack. Then the provoking part was, that the obstinate animal, after having done all the mischief, would just set to to eat as if nothing had happened. After rolling a sportsman in the mud, he would repair to the nearest hay-stack or grassy bank, and be caught. He was now ten years old, or a *leetle* more perhaps, and very wicked years some of them had been. His adventures, his sellings and his returning, his lettings and his unlettings, his bumpings and spillings, his smashings and crashings, on the road, in the field, in single and in double harness, would furnish a volume of themselves; and in default of a more able historian, we purpose blending his future fortune with that of 'Ercles,' in the service of our hero Mr. Sponge, and his accomplished groom, and undertaking the important narration of them ourselves.

IV

LAVERICK WELLS

WE TRUST OUR OPENING CHAPTERS will have enabled our readers to embody such a Sponge in their mind's eye as will assist them in following us through the course of his peregrinations. We do not profess to have drawn such a portrait as will raise the same sort of Sponge in the minds of all, but we trust we have given such a general outline of style, and indication of character, as an ordinary knowledge of the world will enable them to imagine a good, pushing, free-and-easy sort of man, wishing to be a gentleman without knowing how.

Far more difficult is the task of conveying to our readers such information as will enable them to form an idea of our hero's ways and means. An accommodating world—especially the female portion of it—generally attribute ruin to the racer, and fortune to the fox-hunter; but though Mr. Sponge's large losses on the turf, as detailed by him to Mr. Buckram on the occasion of their deal or 'job,' would bring him in the category of the unfortunates; still that representation was nearly, if not altogether, fabulous. That Mr. Sponge might have lost a trifle on the great races of the year, we don't mean to deny, but that he lost such a sum as eighteen hundred on the Derby, and seven on the Leger, we are in a condition to contradict, for the best of all possible reasons, that he hadn't it to lose. At the same time we do not mean to attribute falsehood to Mr. Sponge—quite the contrary—it is no uncommon thing for merchants and traders—men who 'talk in thousands,' to declare that they lost twenty thousand by this, or forty thousand by that, simply meaning that they didn't make it, and if Mr. Sponge, by taking the longest of the long odds against the most wretched of the outsiders, might have won

the sums he named, he surely had a right to say he lost them when he
didn't get them.

It never does to be indigenously poor, if we may use such a
term, and when a man gets to the end of his tether, he must have
something or somebody to blame rather than his own extravagance
or imprudence, and if there is no 'rascally lawyer' who has bolted with
his title-deeds, or fraudulent agent who has misappropriated his funds,
why then, railroads, or losses on the turf, or joint-stock banks that
have shut up at short notice, come in as the scapegoats. Very willing
hacks they are, too, railways especially, and so frequently ridden, that
it is no easy matter to discriminate between the real and the fictitious
loser.

But though we are able to contradict Mr. Sponge's losses on the turf,
we are sorry we are not able to elevate him to the riches the character
of a fox-hunter generally inspires. Still, like many men of whom the
common observation is, 'nobody knows how he lives,' Mr. Sponge
always seemed well-to-do in the world. There was no appearance
of want about him. He always hunted: sometimes with five horses,
sometimes with four, seldom with less than three, though at the period
of our introduction he had come down to two. Nevertheless, those two,
provided he could but make them 'go,' were well calculated to do the
work of four. And hack horses, of all sorts, it may be observed, generally
do double the work of private ones; and if there is one man in the world
better calculated to get the work out of them than another, that man
most assuredly is Mr. Sponge. And this reminds us, that we may as well
state that his bargain with Buckram was a sort of jobbing deal. He had
to pay ten guineas a month for each horse, with a sort of sliding scale
of prices if he chose to buy—the price of 'Ercles' (the big brown) being
fixed at fifty, inclusive of hire at the end of the first month, and gradually
rising according to the length of time he kept him beyond that; while,
'Multum in Parvo,' the resolute chestnut, was booked at thirty, with the
right of buying at five more, a contingency that Buckram little expected.
He, we may add, had got him for ten, and dear he thought him when
he got him home.

The world was now all before Mr. Sponge where to choose; and not
being the man to keep hack horses to look at, we must be setting him
a-going.

'Leicesterscheer swells,' as Mr. Buckram would call them, with their fourteen hunters and four hacks, will smile at the idea of a man going from home to hunt with only a couple of 'screws,' but Mr. Sponge knew what he was about, and didn't want any one to counsel him. He knew there were places where a man can follow up the effect produced by a red coat in the morning to great advantage in the evening; and if he couldn't hunt every day in the week, as he could have wished, he felt he might fill up his time perhaps quite as profitably in other ways. The ladies, to do them justice, are never at all suspicious about men—on the 'nibble'—always taking it for granted, they are 'all they could wish,' and they know each other so well, that any cautionary hint acts rather in a man's favour than otherwise. Moreover, hunting men, as we said before, are all supposed to be rich, and as very few ladies are aware that a horse can't hunt every day in the week, they just class the whole 'genus' fourteen-horse power men, ten-horse power men, five-horse power men, two-horse power men, together, and tying them in a bunch, label it 'very rich,' and proceed to take measures accordingly.

Let us now visit one of the 'strongholds' of fox and fortune-hunting.

A sudden turn of a long, gently rising, but hitherto uninteresting road, brings the posting traveller suddenly upon the rich, well-wooded, beautifully undulating vale of Fordingford, whose fine green pastures are brightened with occasional gleams of a meandering river, flowing through the centre of the vale. In the far distance, looking as though close upon the blue hills, though in reality several miles apart, sundry spires and taller buildings are seen rising above the grey mists towards which a straight, undeviating, matter-of-fact line of railway passing up the right of the vale, directs the eye. This is the famed Laverick Wells, the resort, as indeed all watering-places are, according to newspaper accounts, of

Knights and dames, And all that wealth and lofty lineage claim.

At the period of which we write, however, 'Laverick Wells' was in great feather—it had never known such times. Every house, every lodging, every hole and corner was full, and the great hotels, which more resemble Lancashire cotton-mills than English hostelries, were sending away applicants in the most offhand, indifferent way.

The Laverick Wells hounds had formerly been under the management of the well-known Mr. Thomas Slocdolager, a hard-riding, hard-bitten, hold-harding sort of sportsman, whose whole soul was in the thing, and who would have ridden over his best friend in the ardour of the chase.

In some countries such a creature may be considered an acquisition, and so long as he reigned at the Wells, people made the best they could of him, though it was painfully apparent to the livery-stable keepers, and others, who had the best interest of the place at heart, that such a red-faced, gloveless, drab-breeched, mahogany-booted buffer, who would throw off at the right time, and who resolutely set his great stubbly-cheeked face against all show meets and social intercourse in the field, was not exactly the man for a civilized place. Whether time might have enlightened Mr. Slocdolager as to the fact, that continuous killing of foxes, after fatiguingly long runs, was not the way to the hearts of the Laverick Wells sportsmen, is unknown, for on attempting to realize as fine a subscription as ever appeared upon paper, it melted so in the process of collection, that what was realized was hardly worth his acceptance; saying so, in his usual blunt way, that if he hunted a country at his own expense he would hunt one that wasn't encumbered with fools, he just stamped his little wardrobe into a pair of old black saddle-bags, and rode out of town without saying 'tar, tar,' good-bye, carding, or P.P.C.-ing anybody.

This was at the end of a season, a circumstance that considerably mitigated the inconvenience so abrupt a departure might have occasioned, and as one of the great beauties of Laverick Wells is that it is just as much in vogue in summer as in winter, the inhabitants consoled themselves with the old aphorism, that there is as 'good fish in the sea as ever came out of it,' and cast about in search of some one to supply his place at as small cost to themselves as possible. In a place so replete with money and the enterprise of youth, little difficulty was anticipated, especially when the old bait of 'a name' being all that was wanted, 'an ample subscription,' to defray all expenses figuring in the background, was held out.

V

MR. WAFFLES

AMONG A HOST OF MOST meritorious young men—(any of whom would get up behind a bill for five hundred pounds without looking to see that it wasn't a thousand)—among a host of most meritorious young men who made their appearance at Laverick Wells towards the close of Mr. Slocdolager's reign, was Mr. Waffles; a most enterprising youth, just on the verge of arriving of age, and into the possession of a very considerable amount of charming ready money.

Were it not that a 'proud aristocracy,' as Sir Robert Peel called them, have shown that they can get over any little deficiency of birth if there is sufficiency of cash, we should have thought it necessary to make the best of Mr. Waffles' pedigree, but the tide of opinion evidently setting the other way, we shall just give it as we had it, and let the proud aristocracy reject him if they like. Mr. Waffles' father, then, was either a great grazier or a great brazier—which, we are unable to say, 'for a small drop of ink having fallen,' not 'like dew,' but like a black beetle, on the first letter of the word in our correspondent's communication, it may do for either—but in one of which trades he made a 'mint of money,' and latish on in life married a lady who hitherto had filled the honourable office of dairymaid in his house; she was a fine handsome woman and a year or two after the birth of this their only child, he departed this life, nearer eighty than seventy, leaving an 'inconsolable,' &c., who unfortunately contracted matrimony with a master pork-butcher, before she got the fine flattering white monument up, causing young Waffles to be claimed for dry-nursing by that expert matron, the High Court of Chancery; who, of course, had him properly educated—where, it is immaterial to relate, as we shall step on till we find him at college.

Our friend, having proved rather too vivacious for the Oxford dons, had been recommended to try the effects of the Laverick Wells, or any other waters he liked, and had arrived with a couple of hunters and a hack, much to the satisfaction of the neighbouring master of hounds and his huntsman; for Waffles had ridden over and maimed more hounds to his own share, during the two seasons he had been at Oxford, than that gentleman had been in the habit of appropriating to the use of the whole university. Corresponding with that gentleman's delight at getting rid of him was Mr. Slocdolager's dismay at his appearance, for fully satisfied that Oxford was the seat of fox-hunting as well as of all the other arts and sciences, Mr. Waffles undertook to enlighten him and his huntsman on the mysteries of their calling, and 'Old Sloc,' as he was called, being a very silent man, while Mr. Waffles was a very noisy one. Sloc was nearly talked deaf by him.

Mr. Waffles was just in the heyday of hot, rash, youthful indiscretion and extravagance. He had not the slightest idea of the value of money, and looked at the fortune he was so closely approaching as perfectly inexhaustible. His rooms, the most spacious and splendid at that most spacious and splendid hotel, the 'Imperial,' were filled with a profusion of the most useless but costly articles. Jewellery without end, pictures innumerable, pictures that represented all sorts of imaginary sums of money, just as they represented all sorts of imaginary scenes, but whose real worth or genuineness would never be tested till the owner wanted to 'convert them.'

Mr. Waffles was a 'pretty man.' Tall, slim, and slight, with long curly light hair, pink and white complexion, visionary whispers, and a tendency to moustache that could best be seen sideways. He had light blue eyes; while his features generally were good, but expressive of little beyond great good-humour. In dress, he was both smart and various; indeed, we feel a difficulty in fixing him in any particular costume, so frequent and opposite were his changes. He had coats of every cut and colour. Sometimes he was the racing man with a bright-button'd Newmarket brown cut-away, and white-cord trousers, with drab cloth-boots; anon, he would be the officer, and shine forth in a fancy forage cap, cocked jauntily over a profusion of well-waxed curls, a richly braided surtout, with military overalls strapped down over highly varnished boots, whose hypocritical heels would sport a pair of large rowelled long-necked, ringing, brass spurs. Sometimes he was a Jack tar, with a little glazed hat, a once-round tie, a checked shirt, a blue jacket, roomy trousers, and broad-stringed pumps; and, before the admiring ladies had well digested him in that dress, he would be seen cantering away on a long-tailed white barb, in a pea-green duck-hunter, with cream-coloured leather and rose-tinted tops. He was:

All things by turns, and nothing long.

Such was the gentleman elected to succeed the silent, matter-of-fact Mr. Slocdolager in the important office of Master of the Laverick Wells Hunt; and whatever may be the merits of either—upon which we pass no opinion—it cannot be denied that they were essentially different. Mr. Slocdolager was a man of few words, and not at all a ladies' man. He could not even talk when he was crammed with wine, and though he could hold a good quantity, people soon found out they might just as well pour it into a jug as down his throat, so they gave up asking him out. He was a man of few coats, as well as of few words; one on, and one off, being the extent of his wardrobe. His scarlet was growing plum-colour, and the rest of his hunting costume has been already glanced at. He lodged above Smallbones, the veterinary surgeon, in a little back street, where he lived in the quietest way, dining when he came in from hunting,—dressing, or rather changing, only when he was wet, hunting each fox again over his brandy-and-water, and bundling off to bed long before many of his 'field' had left the dining-room. He was little better than a better sort of huntsman.

Waffles, as we said before, had made himself conspicuous towards the close of Mr. Slocdolager's reign, chiefly by his dashing costume, his reckless riding, and his off-hand way of blowing up and slanging people.

Indeed, a stranger would have taken him for the master, a delusion that was heightened by his riding with a formidable-looking sherry-case, in the shape of a horn, at his saddle. Save when engaged in sucking this, his tongue was never at fault. It was jabber, jabber, jabber; chatter, chatter, chatter; prattle, prattle, prattle; occasionally about something, oftener about nothing, but in cover or out, stiff country or open, trotting or galloping, wet day or dry, good scenting day or bad, Waffles' clapper never was at rest. Like all noisy chaps, too, he could not bear any one to make a noise but himself. In furtherance of this, he called in the aid of his Oxfordshire rhetoric. He would halloo *at* people, designating them by some peculiarity that he thought he could wriggle out of, if necessary, instead of attacking them by name. Thus, if a man spoke, or placed himself where Waffles thought he ought not to be (that is to say, anywhere but where Waffles was himself), he would exclaim, 'Pray, sir, hold your tongue!—you, sir!—no, sir, not you—the man that speaks as if he had a brush in his throat!'—or, '*Do* come away, sir!—you, sir!—the man in the mushroom-looking hat!'—or, 'that gentleman in the parsimonious boots!' looking at some one with very narrow tops.

Still, he was a rattling, good-natured, harum-scarum fellow; and masterships of hounds, memberships of Parliament—all expensive unmoney-making offices,—being things that most men are anxious to foist upon their friends, Mr. Waffles' big talk and interference in the field procured him the honour of the first refusal. Not that he was the man to refuse, for he jumped at the offer, and, as he would be of age before the season came round, and would have got all his money out of Chancery, he disdained to talk about a subscription, and boldly took the hounds as his own. He then became a very important personage at Laverick Wells.

He had always been a most important personage among the ladies, but as the men couldn't marry him, those who didn't want to borrow money of him, of course, ran him down. It used to be, 'Look at that dandified ass, Waffles, I declare the sight of him makes me sick'; or, 'What a barber's apprentice that fellow is, with his ringlets all smeared with Macassar.'

Now it was Waffles this, Waffles that, 'Who dines with Waffles?' 'Waffles is the best fellow under the sun! By Jingo, I know no such man as Waffles!' '*Most deserving* young man!'

In arriving at this conclusion, their judgement was greatly assisted by the magnificent way he went to work. Old Tom Towler, the whip, who had toiled at his calling for twenty long years on fifty pounds and what he could 'pick up,' was advanced to a hundred and fifty, with a couple of men under him. Instead of riding worn-out, tumble-down, twenty-pound screws, he was mounted on hundred-guinea horses, for which the dealers were to have a couple of hundred, *when they were paid*. Everything was in the same proportion.

Mr. Waffles' succession to the hunt made a great commotion among the fair—many elegant and interesting young ladies, who had been going on the pious tack against the Reverend Solomon Winkeyes, the popular bachelor preacher of St. Margaret's, teaching in his schools, distributing his tracts, and collecting the penny subscriptions for his clothing club, now took to riding in fan-tailed habits and feathered hats, and talking about leaping and hunting, and riding over rails. Mr. Waffles had a pound of hat-strings sent him in a week, and muffatees innumerable. Some, we are sorry to say, worked him cigar-cases. He, in return, having expended a vast of toil and ingenuity in inventing a 'button,' now had several dozen of them worked up into brooches, which he scattered about with a liberal hand. It was not one of your matter-of-fact story-telling buttons—a fox with 'TALLY-HO,' or a fox's head grinning in grim death—making a red coat look like a miniature butcher's shamble, but it was one of your queer-twisting lettered concerns, that may pass either for a military button or a naval button, or a club button, or even for a livery button. The letters, two W's, were so skilfully entwined, that even a compositor—and compositors are people who can read almost anything—would have been puzzled to decipher it. The letters were gilt, riveted on steel, and the wearers of the button-brooches were very soon dubbed by the non-recipients, 'Mr. Waffles' sheep.'

A fine button naturally requires a fine coat to put it on, and many were the consultations and propositions as to what it should be. Mr. Slocdolager had done nothing in the decorative department, and many thought the failure of funds was a good deal attributable to that fact. Mr. Waffles was not the man to lose an opportunity of adding another costume to his wardrobe, and after an infinity of trouble, and trials of almost all the colours of the rainbow, he at length settled the following uniform, which, at least, had the charm of novelty to recommend it. The morning, or hunt-coat, was to be scarlet, with a cream-coloured collar and cuffs; and the evening, or dress coat, was to be cream-colour, with a scarlet collar and cuffs, and scarlet silk facings and linings, looking as if the wearer had turned the morning one inside out. Waistcoats, and other articles of dress, were left to the choice of the wearer, experience having proved that they are articles it is impossible to legislate upon with any effect.

The old ladies, bless their disinterested hearts, alone looked on the hound freak with other than feelings of approbation.

They thought it a pity he should take them. They wished he mightn't injure himself—hounds were expensive things—led to habits of irregularity—should be sorry to see such a nice young man as Mr. Waffles led astray—not that it would make any difference to them, *but*—(looking significantly at their daughters). No fox had been hunted by more hounds than Waffles had been by the ladies; but though he had chatted and prattled with fifty fair maids—any one of whom he might have found difficult to resist, if 'pinned' single-handed by, in a country house, yet the multiplicity of assailants completely neutralized each other, and verified the truth of the adage that there is 'safety in a crowd.'

If pretty, lisping Miss Wordsworth thought she had shot an arrow home to his heart over night, a fresh smile and dart from little Mary Ogleby's dark eyes extracted it in the morning, and made him think of her till the commanding figure and noble air of the Honourable Miss Letitia Amelia Susannah Jemimah de Jenkins, in all the elegance of first-rate millinery and dressmakership, drove her completely from his mind, to be in turn displaced by some one more bewitching. Mr. Waffles was reputed to be made of money, and he went at it as though he thought it utterly impossible to get through it. He was greatly aided in his endeavours by the fact of its being all in the funds—a great convenience to the spendthrift. It keeps him constantly in cash, and enables him to 'cut and come again,' as quick as ever he likes. Land is not half so accommodating; neither is money on mortgage. What with time spent in investigating a title, or giving notice to 'pay in,' an industrious man wants a second loan by the time, or perhaps before, he gets the first. Acres are not easy of conversion, and the mere fact of wanting to sell implies a deficiency somewhere. With money in the funds, a man has nothing to do but lodge a power of attorney with his broker, and write up for four or five thousand pounds, just as he would write to his bootmaker for four or five pairs of boots, the only difference being, that in all probability the money would be down before the boots. Then, with money in the funds, a man keeps up his credit to the far end—the last thousand telling no more tales than the first, and making just as good a show.

We are almost afraid to say what Mr. Waffles' means were, but we really believe, at the time he came of age, that he had £100,000 in the funds, which were nearly at 'par'—a term expressive of each hundred being worth a hundred, and not eighty-nine or ninety pounds as is now the case, which makes a considerable difference in the melting. Now a real *bona fide* £100,000 always counts as three in common parlance, which latter sum would yield a larger income than gilds the horizon of the most mercenary mother's mind, say ten thousand a-year, which we believe is generally allowed to be 'v—a—a—ry handsome.'

No wonder, then, that Mr. Waffles was such a hero. Another great recommendation about him was, that he had not had time to be much plucked. Many of the young men of fortune that appear upon town have lost half their feathers on the race-course or the gaming-table before the ladies get a chance at them; but here was a nice, fresh-coloured youth, with all his downy verdure full upon him. It takes a vast quantity of clothes, even at Oxford prices, to come to a thousand pounds, and if we allow four or five thousand for his other extravagances, he could not have done much harm to a hundred thousand.

Our friend, soon finding that he was 'cock of the walk,' had no notion of exchanging his greatness for the nothingness of London, and, save going up occasionally to see about opening the flood-gates of his fortune, he spent nearly the whole summer at Laverick Wells. A fine season it was, too—the finest season the Wells had ever known. When at length the long London season closed, there was a rush of rank and fashion to the English watering-places, quite unparalleled in the 'recollection of the oldest inhabitants.' There were blooming widows in every stage of grief and woe, from the becoming cap to the fashionable corset and ball flounce—widows who would never forget the dear deceased, or think of any other man—*unless he had at least five thousand a year*. Lovely girls, who didn't care a farthing if the man was 'only handsome'; and smiling mammas 'egging them on,' who would look very different when they came to the horrid £ s. d. And this mercantile expression leads us to the observation that we know nothing so dissimilar as a trading town and a watering-place. In the one, all is bustle, hurry, and activity; in the other, people don't seem to know what to do to get through the day. The city and west-end present somewhat of the contrast, but not to the extent of manufacturing or sea-port towns and watering-places. Bathing-places are a shade better than watering-places in the way of occupation, for people can sit staring at the sea, counting the ships, or polishing their nails with a shell, whereas at watering-places, they have generally little to do but stare at and talk of each other, and mark the progress of the day, by alternately drinking at the wells, eating at the hotels, and wandering between the library and the railway station. The ladies get on better, for where there are ladies there are always fine shops, and what between turning over the goods, and sweeping the streets with their trains, making calls, and arranging partners for balls, they get through their time very pleasantly; but what is 'life' to them is often death to the men.

VI

LAVERICK WELLS

THE FLATTERING ACCOUNTS MR. SPONGE read in the papers of the distinguished company assembled at Laverick Wells, together with details of the princely magnificence of the wealthy commoner, Mr. Waffles, who appeared to entertain all the world at dinner after each day's hunting made Mr. Sponge think it would be a very likely place to suit him. Accordingly, thither he despatched Mr. Leather with the redoubtable horses by the road, intending to follow in as many hours by the rail as it took them days to trudge on foot.

Railways have helped hunting as well as other things, and enables a man to glide down into the grass 'sheers,' as Mr. Buckram calls them, with as little trouble, and in as short a time almost, as it took him to accomplish a meet at Croydon, or at the Magpies at Staines. But to our groom and horses.

Mr. Sponge was too good a judge to disfigure the horses with the miserable, pulpy, weather-bleached job-saddles and bridles of 'livery,' but had them properly turned out with well-made, slightly-worn London ones of his own, and nice, warm brown woollen rugs, below broadly bound, blue-and-white-striped sheeting, with richly braided lettering, and blue and white cordings. A good saddle and bridle makes a difference of ten pounds in the looks of almost any horse. There is no need because a man rides a hack horse to proclaim it to all the world; a fact that few hack horse letters seem to be aware of. Perhaps, indeed, they think to advertise them by means of their inferior appointments.

Leather, too, did his best to keep up appearances, and turned out in a very stud-groomish-looking, basket-button'd, brown cutaway, with a clean striped vest, ample white cravat, drab breeches and boots, that looked as though they had brushed through a few bullfinches; and so they had, but not with Leather's legs in them, for he had bought them second-hand of a pad groom in distress. His hands were encased in cat's-skin sable gloves, showing that he was a gentleman who liked to be comfortable. Thus accoutred, he rode down Broad Street at Laverick Wells, looking like a fine, faithful old family servant, with a slight scorbutic affection of the nose. He had everything correctly arranged in true sporting marching order. The collar-shanks were neatly coiled under the headstalls, the clothing tightly rolled and balanced above the little saddle-bags on the led horse, 'Multum in Parvo's' back, with the story-telling whip sticking through the roller.

Leather arrived at Laverick Wells just as the first shades of a November night were drawing on, and anxious mammas and careful *chaperons* were separating their fair charges from their respective admirers and the dreaded night air, leaving the streets to the gaslight men and youths 'who love the moon.' The girls having been withdrawn, licentious youths linked arms, and bore down the broad *pave*, quizzing this person, laughing at that, and staring the pin-stickers and straw-chippers out of countenance.

'Here's an arrival!' exclaimed one. 'Dash my buttons, who have we here?' asked another, as Leather hove in sight. 'That's not a bad looking horse,' observed a third. 'Bid him five pounds for it for me,' rejoined a fourth.

'I say, old Bardolph! who do them 'ere quadrupeds belong to?' asked one, taking a scented cigar out of his mouth.

Leather, though as impudent a dog as any of them, and far more than a match for the best of them at a tournament of slang, being on his preferment, thought it best to be civil, and replied, with a touch of his hat, that they were 'Mr. Sponge's.'

'Ah! old sponge biscuits!—I know him!' exclaimed a youth in a Tweed wrapper.' My father married his aunt. Give my love to him, and tell him to breakfast with me at six in the morning—he! he! he!'

'I say, old boy, that copper-coloured quadruped hasn't got all his shoes on before,' squeaked a childish voice, now raised for the first time.

'That's intended, gov'nor,' growled Leather, riding on, indignant at the idea of any one attempting to 'sell him' with such an old stable joke. So Leather passed on through the now splendidly lit up streets, the large plate-glass windowed shops, radiant with gas, exhibiting rich, many-coloured velvets, silver gauzes, ribbons without end, fancy flowers, elegant shawls labelled 'Very chaste,' 'Patronized by Royalty,' 'Quite the go!' and white kid-gloves in such profusion that there seemed to be a pair for every person in the place.

Mr. Leather established himself at the 'Eclipse Livery and Bait Stables,' in Pegasus Street, or Peg Street, as it is generally called, where he enacted the character of stud-groom to perfection, doing nothing himself, but seeing that others did his work, and strutting consequentially with the corn-sieves at feeding time.

After Leather's long London experience, it is natural to suppose that he would not be long in falling in with some old acquaintance at a place like the 'Wells,' and the first night fortunately brought him in contact with a couple of grooms who had had the honour of his acquaintance when in all the radiance of his glass-blown wigged prosperity as body-coachman to the Duke of Dazzleton, and who knew nothing of the treadmill, or his subsequent career. This introduction served with his own easy assurance, and the deference country servants always pay to London ones, at once to give him standing, and it is creditable to the etiquette of servitude to say, that on joining the 'Mutton Chop and Mealy Potato Club,' at the Cat and Bagpipes, on the second night after his arrival, the whole club rose to receive him on entering, and placed him in the post of honour, on the right of the president.

He was very soon quite at home with the whole of them, and ready to tell anything he knew of the great families in which he had lived. Of course, he abused the duke's place, and said he had been obliged to give him 'hup' at last, 'bein' quite an unpossible man to live with; indeed, his only wonder was, that he had been able to put hup with him so long.' The duchess was a 'good cretur,' he said, and, indeed, it was mainly on her account that he stayed, but as to the duke, he was—everything that was bad, in short.

Mr. Sponge, on the other hand, had no reason to complain of the colours in which his stud-groom painted him. Instead of being the shirtless strapper of a couple of vicious hack hunters. Leather made himself out to be the general superintendent of the opulent owner of a large stud. The exact number varied with the number of glasses of grog

Leather had taken, but he never had less than a dozen, and sometimes as many as twenty hunters under his care. These, he said, were planted all over the kingdom; some at Melton, to ''unt with the Quorn'; some at Northampton, to ''unt with the Pytchley'; some at Lincoln, to ''unt with Lord 'Enry'; and some at Louth, to ''unt with'—he didn't know who. What a fine flattering, well-spoken world this is, when the speaker can raise his own consequence by our elevation! One would think that 'envy, hatred, malice, and all uncharitableness' had gone to California. A weak-minded man might have his head turned by hearing the description given of him by his friends. But hear the same party on the running-down tack!—when either his own importance is not involved, or dire offence makes it worth his while 'to cut off his nose to spite his face.' No one would recognize the portrait then drawn as one of the same individual.

Mr. Leather, as we said before, was in the laudatory strain, but, like many indiscreet people, he overdid it. Not content with magnifying the stud to the liberal extent already described, he must needs puff his master's riding, and indulge in insinuations about 'showing them all the way,' and so on. Now nothing 'aggravates' other grooms so much as this sort of threat, and few things travel quicker than these sort of vapourings to their masters' ears. Indeed, we can only excuse the lengths to which Leather went, on the ground of his previous coaching career not having afforded him a due insight into the delicacies of the hunting stable; it being remembered that he was only now acting as stud-groom for the first time. However, be that as it may, he brewed up a pretty storm, and the longer it raged the stronger it became.

''Ord dash it!' exclaimed young Spareneck, the steeple-chase rider, bursting into Scorer's billiard-room in the midst of a full gathering, who were looking on at a grand game of poule, ''Ord dash it! there's a fellow coming who swears by Jove that he'll take the shine out of us all, "cut us all down!"'

'I'll play him for what he likes!' exclaimed the cool, coatless Captain Macer, striking his ball away for a cannon.

'Hang your play!' replied Spareneck; 'you're always thinking of play— it's hunting I'm talking of,' bringing his heavy, silver-mounted jockey-whip a crack down his leg.

'You don't say so!' exclaimed Sam Shortcut, who had been flattered into riding rather harder than he liked, and feared his pluck might be put to the test.

'What a ruffian!'—(puff)—observed Mr. Waffles, taking his cigar from his mouth as he sat on the bench, dressed as a racket-player, looking on at the game, 'he shalln't ride roughshod over us.'

'That he shalln't!' exclaimed Caingey Thornton, Mr. Waffles's premier toady, and constant trencherman.

'I'll ride him!' rejoined Mr. Spareneck, jockeying his arms, and flourishing his whip as if he was at work, adding: 'his old brandy-nosed, frosty-whiskered trumpeter of a groom says he's coming down by the five o'clock train. I vote we go and meet him—invite him to a steeple-chase by moonlight.'

'I vote we go and see him, at all events,' observed Frank Hoppey, laying down his cue and putting on his coat, adding, 'I should like to see a man bold enough to beard a whole hunt—especially such a hunt as *ours*.'

'Finish the game first,' observed Captain Macer, who had rather the best of it.

'No, leave the balls as they are till we come back,' rejoined Ned Stringer; 'we shall be late. See, it's only ten *to*, now,' continued he, pointing to the timepiece above the fire; whereupon there was a putting away of cues, hurrying on of coats, seeking of hats, sorting of sticks, and a general desertion of the room for the railway station.

VII

OUR HERO ARRIVES
AT LAVERICK WELLS

Punctual to the moment, the railway train, conveying the redoubtable genius, glid into the well-lighted, elegant little station of Laverick Wells, and out of a first-class carriage emerged Mr. Sponge, in a 'down the road' coat, carrying a horse-sheet wrapper in his hand. So small and insignificant did the station seem after the gigantic ones of London, that Mr. Sponge thought he had wasted his money in taking a first-class ticket, seeing there was no one to know. Mr. Leather, who was in attendance, having received him hat in hand, with all the deference due to the master of twenty hunters, soon undeceived him on that point. Having eased him of his wrapper, and inquired about his luggage, and despatched a porter for a fly, they stood together over the portmanteau and hat-box till it arrived.

'How are the horses?' asked Sponge.

'Oh, the osses be nicely, sir,' replied Leather; 'they travelled down uncommon well, and I've had 'em both removed sin they com'd, so either on 'em is fit to go i' the mornin' that you think proper.'

'Where are the hounds?' asked our hero.

''Ounds be at Whirleypool Windmill,' replied Leather, 'that's about five miles off.'

'What sort of country is it?' inquired Sponge.

'It be a stiffish country from all accounts, with a good deal o' water jumpin'; that is to say, the Liffey runs twistin' and twinin' about it like a H'Eel.'

'Then I'd better ride the brown, I think,' observed Sponge, after a pause: 'he has size and stride enough to cover anything, if he will but face water.'

'I'll warrant him for that,' replied Leather; 'only let the Latchfords well into him, and he'll go.'

'Are there many hunting-men down?' inquired our friend casually.

'Great many,' replied Leather, 'great many; some good 'ands among 'em too; at least to say their grums, though I never believe all these jockeys say. There be some on 'em 'ere now,' observed Leather, in an undertone, with a wink of his roguish eye, and jerk of his head towards where a knot of them stood eyeing our friend most intently.

'Which?' inquired Sponge, looking about the thinly peopled station.

'There,' replied Leather, 'those by the book-stall. That be Mr. Waffles,' continued he, giving his master a touch in the ribs as he jerked his portmanteau into a fly, 'that be Mr. Waffles,' repeated he, with a knowing leer.

'Which?' inquired Mr. Sponge eagerly.

'The gent in the green wide-awake 'at, and big-button'd overcoat,' replied Leather, 'jest now a speakin' to the youth in the tweed and all tweed; that be Master Caingey Thornton, as big a little blackguard as any in the place—lives upon Waffles, and yet never has a good word to say for him, no, nor for no one else—and yet to 'ear the little devil a-talkin' to him, you'd really fancy he believed there wasn't not never sich another man i' the world as Waffles—not another sich rider—not another sich racket-player—not another sich pigeon-shooter—not another sich fine chap altogether.'

'Has Thornton any horses?' asked Sponge.

'Not he,' replied Leather, 'not he, nor the gen'lman next him nouther—he, in the pilot coat, with the whip sticking out of the pocket, nor the one in the coffee-coloured 'at, nor none on 'em in fact'; adding, 'they all live on Squire Waffles—breakfast with him—dine with him—drink with him—smoke with him—and if any on 'em 'appen to 'ave an 'orse, why they sell to him, and so ride for nothin' themselves.'

'A convenient sort of gentleman,' observed Mr. Sponge, thinking he, too, might accommodate him.

The fly-man now touched his hat, indicative of a wish to be off, having a fare waiting elsewhere. Mr. Sponge directed him to proceed to the Brunswick Hotel, while, accompanied by Leather, he proceeded on foot to the stables.

Mr. Leather, of course, had the valuable stud under lock and key, with every crevice and air-hole well stuffed with straw, as if they had been the most valuable horses in the world. Having produced the ring-key from his pocket, Mr. Leather opened the door, and having got his master in, speedily closed it, lest a breath of fresh air might intrude. Having lighted a lucifer, he turned on the gas, and exhibited the blooming-coated horses, well littered in straw, showing that he was not the man to pay four-and-twenty shillings a week for nothing. Mr. Sponge stood eyeing them for some seconds with evident approbation.

'If any one asks you about the horses, you can say they are *mine*, you know,' at length observed he casually, with an emphasis on the mine.

'In course,' replied Leather.

'I mean, you needn't say anything about their being *jobs*,' observed Sponge, fearing Leather mightn't exactly 'take.'

'You trust me,' replied Leather, with a knowing wink and a jerk of his elbow against his master's side; 'you trust me,' repeated he, with a look as much as to say, 'we understand each other.'

'I've hadded a few to them, indeed,' continued Leather, looking to see how his master took it.

'Have you?' observed Mr. Sponge inquiringly.

'I've made out that you've as good as twenty, one way or another,' observed Leather; 'some 'ere, some there, all over in fact, and that you jest run about the country, and 'unt with 'oever comes h'uppermost.'

'Well, and what's the upshot of it all?' inquired Mr. Sponge, thinking his groom seemed wonderfully enthusiastic in his interest.

'Why, the hupshot of it is,' replied Leather, 'that the men are all mad, and the women all wild to see you. I hear at my club, the Mutton Chop and Mealy Potato Club, which is frequented by flunkies as well as grums, that there's nothin' talked of at dinner or tea, but the terrible rich stranger that's a comin', and the gals are all pulling caps, who's to have the first chance.'

'Indeed,' observed Mr. Sponge, chuckling at the sensation he was creating.

'The Miss Shapsets, there be five on 'em, have had a game at fly loo for you,' continued Leather, 'at least so their little maid tells me.'

'Fly *what*?' inquired Mr. Sponge.

'Fly loo,' repeated Leather, 'fly loo.'

Mr. Sponge shook his head. For once he was not 'fly.'

'You see,' continued Leather, in explanation, 'their father is one of them tight-laced candlestick priests wot abhors all sorts of wice and himmorality, and won't stand card playin', or gamblin', or nothin' o' that sort, so the young ladies when they want to settle a point, who's to be married first, or who's to have the richest 'usband, play fly loo. 'Sposing it's at breakfast time, they all sit quiet and sober like round the table, lookin' as if butter wouldn't melt in their mouths, and each has a lump o' sugar on her plate, or by her cup, or somewhere, and whoever can 'tice a fly to come to her sugar first, wins the wager, or whatever it is they play for.'

'Five on 'em,' as Leather said, being a hopeless number to extract any good from, Mr. Sponge changed the subject by giving orders for the morrow.

Mr. Sponge's appearance being decidedly of the sporting order, and his horses maintaining the character, did not alleviate the agitated minds of the sporting beholders, ruffled as they were with the threatening, vapouring insinuations of the coachman-groom, Peter Leather. There is nothing sets men's backs up so readily, as a hint that any one is coming to take the 'shine' out of them across country. We have known the most deadly feuds engendered between parties who never spoke to each other by adroit go-betweens reporting to each what the other said, or, perhaps, did not say, but what the 'go-betweens' knew would so rouse the British lion as to make each ride to destruction if necessary.

'He's a varmint-looking chap,' observed Mr. Waffles, as the party returned from the railway station; 'shouldn't wonder if he can go—dare say he'll try—shouldn't wonder if he's floored—awfully stiff country this for horses that are not used to it—most likely his are Leicestershire nags, used to fly—won't do here. If he attempts to take some of our big banked bullfinches in his stride, with a yawner on each side, will get into grief.'

'Hang him,' interrupted Caingey Thornton, 'there are good men in all countries.'

'So there are!' exclaimed Mr. Spareneck, the steeple-chase rider.

'I've no notion of a fellow lording it, because he happens to come out of Leicestershire,' rejoined Mr. Thornton.

'Nor I!' exclaimed Mr. Spareneck.

'Why doesn't he stay in Leicestershire?' asked Mr. Hoppey, now raising his voice for the first time—adding, 'Who asked him here?'

'Who, indeed?' sneered Mr. Thornton.

In this mood our friends arrived at the Imperial Hotel, where there was always a dinner the day before hunting—a dinner that, somehow, was served up in Mr. Waffles's rooms, who was allowed the privilege of paying for all those who did not pay for themselves; rather a considerable number, we believe.

The best of everything being good enough for the guests, and profuse liberality the order of the day, the cloth generally disappeared before a contented audience, whatever humour they might have set down in. As the least people can do who dine at an inn and don't pay their own shot, is to drink the health of the man who does pay, Mr. Waffles was always lauded and applauded to the skies—such a master—such a sportsman—such knowledge—such science—such a pattern-card. On this occasion the toast was received with extra enthusiasm, for the proposer, Mr. Caingey Thornton, who was desperately in want of a mount, after going the rounds of the old laudatory course, alluded to the threatened vapourings of the stranger, and expressed his firm belief that he would 'meet with his match,' a 'taking of the bull by the horns,' that met with very considerable favour from the wine-flushed party, the majority of whom, at that moment, made very 'small,' in their own minds, of the biggest fence that ever was seen.

There is nothing so easy as going best pace over the mahogany.

Mr. Waffles, who was received with considerable applause, and patting of the table, responded to the toast in his usual felicitous style, assuring the company that he lived but for the enjoyment of their charming society, and that all the money in the world would be useless, if he hadn't Laverick Wells to spend it in. With regard to the vapourings of a 'certain gentleman,' he thought it would be very odd if some of them could not take the shine out of him, observing that 'Brag' was a good dog, but 'Holdfast' was a better, with certain other sporting similes and phrases, all indicative of showing fight. The steam is soon got up after dinner, and as they were all of the same mind, and all agreed that a gross insult had been offered to the hunt in general, and themselves in particular, the only question was, how to revenge it. At last they hit upon it. Old

Slocdolager, the late master of the hunt, had been in the habit of having Tom Towler, the huntsman, to his lodgings the night before hunting, where, over a glass of gin-and-water, they discussed the doings of the day, and the general arrangements of the country.

Mr. Waffles had had him in sometimes, though for a different purpose—at least, in reality for a different purpose, though he always made hunting the excuse for sending for him, and that purpose was, to try how many silver foxes' heads full of port wine Tom could carry off without tumbling, and the old fellow being rather liquorishly inclined, had never made any objection to the experiment. Mr. Waffles now wanted him, to endeavour, under the mellowing influence of drink, to get him to enter cordially into what he knew would be distasteful to the old sportsman's feelings, namely, to substitute a 'drag' for the legitimate find and chase of the fox. Fox-hunting, though exciting and exhilarating at all times, except, perhaps, when the 'fallows are flying,' and the sportsman feels that in all probability, the further he goes the further he is left behind—Fox-hunting, we say, though exciting and exhilarating, does not, when the real truth is spoken, present such conveniences for neck-breaking, as people, who take their ideas from Mr. Ackermann's print-shop window, imagine. That there are large places in most fences is perfectly true; but that there are also weak ones is also the fact, and a practised eye catches up the latter uncommonly quick. Therefore, though a madman may ride at the big places, a sane man is not expected to follow; and even should any one be tempted so to do, the madman having acted pioneer, will have cleared the way, or at all events proved its practicability for the follower.

In addition to this, however, hounds having to smell as they go, cannot travel at the ultra steeple-chase pace, so opposed to 'looking before you leap,' and so conducive to danger and difficulty, and as going even at a fair pace depends upon the state of the atmosphere, and the scent the fox leaves behind, it is evident that where mere daring hard riding is the object, a fox-hunt cannot be depended upon for furnishing the necessary accommodation. A drag-hunt is quite a different thing. The drag can be made to any strength; enabling hounds to run as if they were tied to it, and can be trailed so as to bring in all the dangerous places in the country with a certain air of plausibility, enabling a man to look round and exclaim, as he crams at a bullfinch or brook, 'he's leading us over a most desperate country—never saw such fencing in all my life!' Drag-hunting, however, as we said before, is not popular with sportsmen, certainly not with huntsmen, and though our friends with their wounded feelings determined to have one, they had yet to smooth over old Tom to get him to come into their views. That was now the difficulty.

VIII

OLD TOM TOWLER

THERE ARE FEW MORE DIFFICULT persons to identify than a huntsman in undress, and of all queer ones perhaps old Tom Towler was the queerest. Tom in his person furnished an apt illustration of the right appropriation of talent and the fitness of things, for he would neither have made a groom, nor a coachman, nor a postillion, nor a footman, nor a ploughman, nor a mechanic, nor anything we know of, and yet he was first-rate as a huntsman. He was too weak for a groom, too small for a coachman, too ugly for a postillion, too stunted for a footman, too light for a ploughman, too useless-looking for almost anything.

Any one looking at him in 'mufti' would exclaim, 'what an unfortunate object!' and perhaps offer him a penny, while in his hunting habiliments lords would hail him with, 'Well, Tom, how are you?' and baronets ask him 'how he was?' Commoners felt honoured by his countenance, and yet, but for hunting, Tom would have been wasted—a cypher—an inapplicable sort of man. Old Tom, in his scarlet coat, black cap, and boots, and Tom in his undress—say, shirt-sleeves, shorts, grey stockings and shoes, bore about the same resemblance to each other that a three months dead jay nailed to a keeper's lodge bears to the bright-plumaged bird when flying about. On horseback, Tom was a cockey, wiry-looking, keen-eyed, grim-visaged, hard-bitten little fellow, sitting as though he and his horse were all one, while on foot he was the most shambling, scambling, crooked-going crab that ever was seen. He was a complete mash of a man. He had been scalped by the branch of a tree, his nose knocked into a thing like a button by the kick of a horse, his teeth sent down his throat by a fall, his collar-bone fractured, his left leg broken and his right arm ditto, to say nothing of damage to his ribs, fingers, and feet, and having had his face scarified like pork by repeated brushings through strong thorn fences.

But we will describe him as he appeared before Mr. Waffles, and the gentlemen of the Laverick Wells Hunt, on the night of Mr. Sponge's arrival. Tom's spirit being roused at hearing the boastings of Mr. Leather, and thinking, perhaps, his master might have something to say, or thinking, perhaps, to partake of the eleemosynary drink generally going on in large houses of public entertainment, had taken up his quarters in the bar of the 'Imperial,' where he was attentively perusing the 'meets' in *Bell's Life*, reading how the Atherstone met at Gopsall, the Bedale at Hornby, the Cottesmore at Tilton Wood, and so on, with an industry worthy of a better cause; for Tom neither knew country, nor places, nor masters, nor hounds, nor huntsmen, nor anything, though he still felt an interest in reading where they were going to hunt. Thus he sat with a quick ear, one of the few undamaged organs of his body, cocked to hear if Tom Towler was asked for; when a waiter dropping his name from the landing of the staircase to the hall porter, asking if anybody had seen anything of him, Tom folded up his paper, put it in his pocket, and passing his hand over the few straggling bristles yet sticking about his bald head, proceeded, hat in hand, upstairs to his master's room.

His appearance called forth a round of view halloos! Who-hoops! Tally-ho's! Hark forwards! amidst which, and the waving of napkins, and general noises, Tom proceeded at a twisting, limping, halting, sideways sort of scramble up the room. His crooked legs didn't seem to have an exact understanding with his body which way they were to go; one, the right one, being evidently inclined to lurch off to the side, while the left one went stamp, stamp, stamp, as if equally determined to resist any deviation.

At length he reached the top of the table, where sat his master, with the glittering Fox's head before him. Having made a sort of scratch bow, Tom proceeded to stand at ease, as it were, on the left leg, while he placed the late recusant right, which was a trifle shorter, as a prop behind. No one, to look at the little wizen'd old man in the loose dark frock, baggy striped waistcoat, and patent cord breeches, extending below where the calves of his bow legs ought to have been, would have supposed that it was the noted huntsman and dashing rider, Tom Towler, whose name was celebrated throughout the country. He might have been a village tailor, or sexton, or barber; anything but a hero.

'Well, Tom,' said Mr. Waffles, taking up the Fox's head, as Tom came to anchor by his side, 'how are you?'

'Nicely, thank you, sir,' replied Tom, giving the bald head another sweep.

Mr. Waffles.—'What'll you drink?'

Tom.—'Port, if you please, sir.'

'There it is for you, then,' said Mr. Waffles, brimming the Fox's head, which held about the third of a bottle (an inn bottle at least), and handing it to him.

'Gentlemen all,' said Tom, passing his sleeve across his mouth, and casting a side-long glance at the company as he raised the cup to drink their healths.

He quaffed it off at a draught.

'Well, Tom, and what shall we do to-morrow?' asked Mr. Waffles, as Tom replaced the Fox's head, nose uppermost, on the table.

'Why, we must draw Ribston Wood fust, I s'pose,' replied Tom, 'and then on to Bradwell Grove, unless you thought well of tryin' Chesterton Common on the road, or—'

'Aye, aye,' interrupted Waffles, 'I know all that; but what I want to know is, whether we can make sure of a run. We want to give this great metropolitan swell a benefit. You know who I mean?'

'The gen'leman as is com'd to the Brunswick, I 'spose,' replied Tom; 'at least as *is* comin', for I've not heard that he's com'd yet.'

'Oh, but he *has*,' replied Mr. Waffles, 'and I make no doubt will be out to-morrow.'

'S—o—o,' observed Tom, in a long drawled note.

'Well, now! do you think you can engage to give us a run?' asked Mr. Waffles, seeing his huntsman did not seem inclined to help him to his point.

'I'll do my best,' replied Tom, cautiously running the many contingencies through his mind.

'Take another drop of something,' said Mr. Waffles, again raising the Fox's head. 'What'll you have?'

'Port, if you please,' replied Tom.

'There,' said Mr. Waffles, handing him another bumper; 'drink to Fox-hunting.'

'Fox-huntin',' said old Tom, quaffing off the measure, as before. A flush of life came into his weather-beaten face, just as a glow of heat enlivens a blacksmith's hearth, after a touch of the bellows.

'You must never let this bumptious cock beat us,' observed Mr. Waffles.

'No—o—o,' replied Tom, adding, 'there's no fear of that.'

'But he swears he *will*!' exclaimed Mr. Caingey Thornton. 'He swears there isn't a man shall come within a field of him.'

'Indeed,' observed Tom, with a twinkle of his little bright eyes.

'I tell you what, Tom,' observed Mr. Waffles, 'we must sarve him out, somehow.'

'Oh! he'll sarve hissel' out, in all probability,' replied Tom; carelessly adding, 'these boastin' chaps always do.'

'Couldn't we contrive something,' asked Mr. Waffles, 'to draw him out?'

Tom was silent. He was a hunting huntsman, not a riding one.

'Have a glass of something,' said Mr. Waffles, again appealing to the Fox's head.

'Thank you, sir, I've had a glass,' replied Tom, sinking the second one.

'What will you have?' asked Mr. Waffles.

'Port, if you please,' replied Tom.

'Here it is,' rejoined Mr. Waffles, again handing him the measure.

Up went the cup, over went the contents; but Tom set it down with a less satisfied face than before. He had had enough. The left leg prop, too, gave way, and he was nearly toppling on the table.

Having got a chair for the dilapidated old man, they again essayed to get him into their line, with better success than before. Having plied him well with port, they now plied him well with the stranger, and what with the one and the other, and a glass or two of brandy-and-water, Tom became very tractable, and it was ultimately arranged that they should have a drag over the very stiffest parts of the country, wherein all who liked should take part, but that Mr. Caingey Thornton and Mr. Spareneck should be especially deputed to wait upon Mr. Sponge, and lead him into mischief. Of course it was to be a 'profound secret,' and equally, of course, it stood a good chance of being kept, seeing how many were in it, the additional number it would have to be communicated to before it could be carried out, and the happy state old Tom was in for arranging matters. Nevertheless, our friends at the 'Imperial' congratulated themselves on their success; and after a few minutes spent in discussing old Tom on his withdrawal, the party broke up, to array themselves in the splendid dress uniform of the 'Hunt,' to meet again at Miss Jumpheavy's ball.

IX

THE MEET—THE FIND, AND THE FINISH

Early to bed and early to rise being among Mr. Sponge's maxims, he was enjoying the view of the pantiles at the back of his hotel shortly after daylight the next morning, a time about as difficult to fix in a November day as the age of a lady of a 'certain age.' It takes even an expeditious dresser ten minutes or a quarter of an hour extra the first time he has to deal with boots and breeches; and Mr. Sponge being quite a pattern card in his peculiar line, of course took a good deal more to get himself 'up'.

An accustomed eye could see a more than ordinary stir in the streets that morning. Riding-masters and their assistants might be seen going along with strings of saddled and side-saddled screws; flys began to roll at an earlier hour, and natty tigers to kick about in buckskins prior to departing with hunters, good, bad, and indifferent.

Each man had told his partner at Miss Jumpheavy's ball of the capital trick they were going to play the stranger; and a desire to see the stranger, far more than a desire to see the trick, caused many fair ones to forsake their downy couches who had much better have kept them.

The world is generally very complaisant with regard to strangers, so long as they *are* strangers, generally making them out to be a good deal better than they really are, and Mr. Sponge came in for his full share of stranger credit. They not only brought all the twenty horses Leather said he had scattered about to Laverick Wells, but made him out to have a house in Eaton Square, a yacht at Cowes, and a first-rate moor in Scotland, and some said a peerage in expectancy. No wonder that he 'drew,' as theatrical people say.

Let us now suppose him breakfasted, and ready for a start.

He was 'got up' with uncommon care in the most complete style of the severe order of sporting costume. It being now the commencement of the legitimate hunting season—the first week in November—he availed himself of the privileged period for turning out in everything new. Rejecting the now generally worn cap, he adhered to the heavy, close-napped hat, described in our opening chapter, whose connexion with his head, or back, if it came off, was secured by a small black silk cord, hooked through the band by a fox's tooth, and anchored to a button inside the haven of his low coat-collar. His neck was enveloped in the ample folds of a large white silk cravat, tied in a pointing diamond tie, and secured with a large silver horse-shoe pin, the shoe being almost large enough for the foot of a young donkey.

His low, narrow-collared coat was of the infinitesimal order; that is to say, a coat, and yet as little of a coat as possible—very near a jacket, in fact. The seams, of course, were outside, and were it not for the extreme strength and evenness of the sewing and the evident intention of the thing, an ignorant person might have supposed that he had had his coat turned. A double layer of cloth extended the full length of the outside of the sleeves, much in the fashion of the stage-coachmen's greatcoats in former times; and instead of cuffs, the sleeves were carried out to the ends of the fingers, leaving it to the fancy of the wearer to sport a long cuff or a short cuff, or no cuff at all—just as the weather dictated. Though the coat was single-breasted, he had a hole made on the button side, to enable him to keep it together by means of a miniature snaffle, instead of a button. The snaffle passed across his chest, from whence the coatee, flowing easily back, displayed the broad ridge and furrow of a white cord waistcoat, with a low step collar, the vest reaching low down his figure, with large flap pockets and a nick out in front, like a coachman's. Instead of buttons, the waistcoat was secured with foxes' tusks and catgut loops, while a heavy curb chain, passing from one pocket to the other, raised the impression that there was a watch in one and a bunch of seals in the other. The waistcoat was broadly bound with white binding, and, like the coat, evinced great strength and powers of resistance. His breeches were of a still broader furrow than the waistcoat, looking as if the ploughman had laid two ridges into one. They came low down the leg, and were met by a pair of well-made, well put on, very brown topped boots, a colour then unknown at Laverick Wells. His spurs were bright and heavy, with formidable necks and rowels, whose slightest touch would make a horse wince, and put him on his good behaviour.

Nor did the great slapping brown horse, Hercules, turn out less imposingly than his master. Leather, though not the man to work himself, had a very good idea of work, and right manfully he made the helpers at the Eclipse livery and bait stables strap and groom his horses. Hercules was a fine animal. It did not require a man to be a great judge of a horse to see that. Even the ladies, though perhaps they would rather have had him a white or a cream colour, could not but admire his nut-brown muzzle, his glossy coat, his silky mane, and the elegant way in which he carried his flowing tail. His step was delightful to look at—so free, so accurate, and so easy. And that reminds us that we may as well be getting Mr. Sponge up—a feat of no easy accomplishment. Few hack hunters are without their little peculiarities. Some are runaways—some kick—some bite—some go tail first on the road—some go tail first at their fences—some rush as if they were going to eat them, others baulk them altogether—and few, very few, give satisfaction. Those that do, generally retire from the public stud to the private one. But to our particular quadruped, 'Hercules.'

Mr. Sponge was not without his misgivings that, regardless of being on his preferment, the horse might exhibit more of his peculiarity than would forward his master's interests, and, independently of the disagreeableness of being kicked off at the cover side, not being always compensated for by falling soft, Mr. Sponge thought, as the meet was not far off, and he did not sport a cover hack, it would look quite as well to ride his horse quietly on as go in a fly, provided always he could accomplish the mount—the mount—like the man walking with his head under his arm—being the first step to everything.

Accordingly, Mr. Leather had the horse saddled and accoutred as quietly as possible—his warm clothing put over the saddle immediately, and everything kept as much in the usual course as possible, so that the noble animal's temper might not be ruffled by unaccustomed trouble or unusual objects. Leather having seen that the horse could not eject Mr. Sponge even in trousers, had little fear of his dislodging him in boots and breeches; still it was desirable to avoid all unseemly contention, and maintain the high character of the stud, by which means Leather felt that his own character and consequence would best be maintained. Accordingly, he refrained from calling in the aid of any of the stable assistants, preferring for once to do a little work himself, especially when the rider was up to the trick, and not 'a gent' to be cajoled into 'trying a horse.' Mr. Sponge, punctual to his time, appeared at the stable, and after much patting, whistling, so—so—ing, my man, and general ingratiation, the redoubtable nag was led out of the stable into a well-littered straw-yard, where, though he might be gored by a bull if he fell, the 'eyes of England' at all events would not witness the floorer. Horses, however, have wonderful memories and discrimination. Though so differently attired to what he was on the occasion of his trial, the horse seemed to recognize Mr. Sponge, and independently of a few snorts as he was led out, and an indignant stamp or two of his foot as it was let down, after Mr. Sponge was mounted he took things very quietly.

'Now,' said Leather, in an undertone, patting the horse's arched neck, 'I'll give you a hint; they're a goin' to run a drag to try what he's made on, so be on the look-out.'

'How do you know?' asked Mr. Sponge, in surprise, drawing his reins as he spoke.

'*I know*,' replied Mr. Leather with a wink.

Just then the horse began to plunge, and paw, and give symptoms of uneasiness, and not wishing to fret or exhibit his weak points, Mr. Sponge gave him his head, and passing through the side-gate was presently in the street. He didn't exactly understand it, but having full confidence in his horsemanship, and believing the one he was on required nothing but riding, he was not afraid to take his chance.

Not being the man to put his candle under a bushel, Mr. Sponge took the principal streets on his way out of town. We are not sure that he did not go rather out of his way to get them in, but that is neither here nor there, seeing he was a stranger who didn't know the way. What a sensation his appearance created as the gallant brown stepped proudly and freely up Coronation Street, showing his smart, clean, well-put-on head up and down on the unrestrained freedom of the snaffle.

'Oh, d—n it, there he is!' exclaimed Mr. Spareneck, jumping up from the breakfast-table, and nearly sweeping the contents off by catching the cloth with his spur.

'Where?' exclaimed half-a-dozen voices, amid a general rush to the windows.

'What a fright!' exclaimed little Miss Martindale, whispering into Miss Beauchamp's ear: 'I'm sure anybody may have him for me,' though she felt in her heart that he was far from bad looking.

'I wonder how long he's taken to put on that choker,' observed Mr. Spareneck, eyeing him intently, not without an inward qualm that he had set himself a more difficult task than he imagined, to 'cut him down,' especially when he looked at the noble animal he bestrode, and the masterly way he sat him.

'What a pair of profligate boots,' observed Captain Whitfield, as our friend now passed his lodgings.

'It would be the duty of a right-thinking man to ride over a fellow in such a pair,' observed his friend, Mr. Cox, who was breakfasting with him.

'Ride over a fellow in such a pair!' exclaimed Whitfield. 'No well-bred horse would face such things, I should think.'

'He seems to think a good deal of himself!' observed Mr. Cox, as Sponge cast an admiring eye down his shining boot.

'Shouldn't wonder,' replied Whitfield; 'perhaps he'll have the conceit taken out of him before night.'

'Well, I hope you'll be in time, old boy!' exclaimed Mr. Waffles to himself, as looking down from his bedroom window, he espied Mr. Sponge passing up the street on his way to cover. Mr. Waffles was just out of bed, and had yet to dress and breakfast.

One man in scarlet sets all the rest on the fidget, and without troubling to lay 'that or that' together, they desert their breakfasts, hurry to the stables, get out their horses and rattle away, lest their watches should be wrong or some arrangement made that they are ignorant of. The hounds too, were on, as was seen as well by their footmarks, as by the bob, bob, bobbing of sundry black caps above the hedges, on the Borrowdon road as the huntsman and whips proceeded at that pleasant post-boy trot, that has roused the wrath of so many riders against horses that they could not get to keep in time.

Now look at old Tom, cocked jauntily on the spicey bay and see what a different Tom he is to what he was last night. Instead of a battered, limping, shabby-looking little old man, he is all alive and rises to the action of his horse, as though they were all one. A fringe of grey hair protrudes beneath his smart velvet cap, which sets off a weather-beaten but keen and expressive face, lit up with little piercing black eyes. See how chirpy and cheery he is; how his right arm keeps rising and falling with his whip, beating responsive to the horse's action with the butt-end against his thigh. His new scarlet coat imparts a healthy hue to his face, and good boots and breeches hide the imperfections of his bad legs. His hounds seem to partake of the old man's gaiety, and gather round his horse or frolic forward on the grassy sidings of the road, till, getting almost out of earshot, a single 'yooi doit!—Arrogant!'—or 'here again, Brusher!' brings them cheerfully back to whine and look in the old man's face for applause. Nor is he chary of his praise. 'G—oood betch!—Arrogant!—g—oood betch!' says he, leaning over his horse's shoulder towards her, and jerking his hand to induce her to proceed forward again. So the old man trots gaily on, now making of his horse, now coaxing a hound, now talking to a 'whip,' now touching or taking off his cap as he passes a sportsman, according to the estimation in which he holds him.

As the hounds reach Whirleypool Windmill, there is a grand rush of pedestrians to meet them. First comes a velveteen-jacketed, leather-legginged keeper, with whom Tom (albeit suspicious of his honesty) thinks it prudent to shake hands; the miller and he, too, greet; and forthwith a black bottle with a single glass make their appearance, and pass current with the company. Then the earth-stopper draws nigh, and, resting a hand on Tom's horse's shoulder, whispers confidentially in his ear. The pedestrian sportsman of the country, too, has something to say; also a horse-breaker; while groups of awe-stricken children stand staring at the mighty Tom, thinking him the greatest man in the world.

Railways and fox-hunting make most people punctual, and in less than five minutes from the halting of the hounds by the Windmill, the various roads leading up to it emit dark-coated grooms, who, dismounting, proceed to brush off the mud sparks, and rectify any little derangement the horses or their accoutrements may have contracted on the journey. Presently Mr. Sponge, and such other gentlemen as have ridden their own horses on, cast up, while from the eminence the road to Laverick Wells is distinctly traceable with scarlet coats and flys, with furs and flaunting feathers. Presently the foremost riders begin to canter up the hill, when

All around is gay: men, horses, dogs. And in each smiling countenance appears fresh blooming health and universal joy.

Then the ladies mingle with the scene, some on horseback, some in flys, all chatter and prattle as usual, some saying smart things, some trying, all making themselves as agreeable as possible, and of course as captivating. Some were in ecstasies at dear Miss Jumpheavy's ball—she was such a *nice* creature—such a charming ball, and so well managed, while others were anticipating the delights of Mrs. Tom Hoppey's, and some again were asking which was Mr. Sponge. Then up went the eye-glasses, while Mr. Sponge sat looking as innocent and as killing as he could. 'Dear me!' exclaimed one, 'he's younger than I thought.' 'That's him, is it?' observed another; 'I saw him ride up the street'; while the propriety-playing ones praised his horse, and said it was a beauty.

The hounds, which they all had come to see, were never looked at.

Mr. Waffles, like many men with nothing to do, was most unpunctual. He never seemed to know what o'clock it was, and yet he had a watch, hung in chains, and gewgaws, like a lady's chatelaine. Hunting partook of the general confusion. He did not profess to throw off till eleven, but it was often nearly twelve before he cast up. Then he would come up full tilt, surrounded by 'scarlets,' like a general with his staff; and once at the meet, there was a prodigious hurry to begin, equalled only by the eagerness to leave off. On this auspicious day he hove in sight, coming best pace along the road, about twenty minutes before twelve, with a more numerous retinue than usual. In dress, Mr. Waffles was the light, butterfly order of sportsman—once-round tie, French polish, paper boots, and so on. On this occasion he sported a shirt-collar with three or four blue lines, and then a white space followed by three or more blue lines, the whole terminating in blue spots about the size of fourpenny pieces at the points; a once-round blue silk tie, with white spots and flying ends. His coat was a light, jackety sort of thing, with little pockets behind, something in the style of Mr. Sponge's (a docked dressing-gown), but wanting the outside seaming, back strapping, and general strength that characterized Mr. Sponge's. His waistcoat, of course, was a worked one—heart's-ease mingled with foxes' heads, on a true blue ground, the gift of—we'll not say who—his leathers were of the finest doe-skin, and his long-topped, pointed-toed boots so thin as to put all idea of wet or mud out of the question.

Such was the youth who now cantered up and took off his cap to the rank, beauty, and fashion, assembled at Whirleypool Windmill. He then proceeded to pay his respects in detail. At length, having exhausted his 'nothings,' and said the same thing over again in a dozen different ways to a dozen different ladies, he gave a slight jerk of the head to Tom Towler, who forthwith whistled his hounds together, and attended by the whips, bustled from the scene.

Epping Hunt, in its most palmy days, could not equal the exhibition that now took place. Some of the more lively of the horses, tired of waiting, perhaps pinched by the cold, for most of them were newly-clipped, evinced their approbation of the move, by sundry squeals and capers, which being caught by others in the neighbourhood, the infection quickly spread, and in less than a minute there was such a scene of rocking, and rearing, and kicking, and prancing, and neighing and shooting over heads, and rolling over tails, and hanging on by manes, mingled with such screamings from the ladies in the flys, and such hearty-sounding kicks against splash boards and fly bottoms, from sundry of the vicious ones in harness, as never was witnessed. One gentleman, in a bran-new scarlet, mounted on a flourishing piebald, late the property of Mr. Batty, stood pawing and fighting the air, as if in the saw-dust circle, his unfortunate rider clinging round his neck, expecting to have the beast back over upon him. Another little wiry chestnut, with abundance of rings, racing martingale, and tackle generally, just turned tail on the crowd and ran off home as hard as ever he could lay legs to the ground; while a good steady bay cob, with a barrel like a butt, and a tail like a hearth-brush, having selected the muddiest, dirtiest place he could find, deliberately proceeded to lie down, to the horror of his rider, Captain Greatgun, of the royal navy, who, feeling himself suddenly touch mother earth, thought he was going to be swallowed up alive, and was only awoke from the delusion by the shouts of the foot people, telling him to get clear of his horse before he began to roll.

Hercules would fain have joined the truant set, and, at the first commotion, up went his great back, and down went his ears, with a single lash out behind that meant mischief, but Mr. Sponge was on the alert, and just gave him such a dig with his spurs as restored order, without exposing anything that anybody could take notice of.

The sudden storm was quickly lulled. The spilt ones scrambled up; the loose riders got tighter hold of their horses; the screaming fair ones sank languidly in their carriages; and the late troubled ocean of equestrians fell into irregular line *en route* for the cover.

Bump, bump, bump; trot, trot, trot; jolt, jolt, jolt; shake, shake, shake; and carriages and cavalry got to Ribston Wood somehow or other. It is a long cover on a hillside, from which parties, placing themselves in the green valley below, can see hounds 'draw,' that is to say, run through with their noses to the ground, if there are any men foolish enough to believe that ladies care for seeing such things. However, there they were.

'Eu leu, in!' cries old Tom, with a wave of his arm, finding he can no longer restrain the ardour of the pack as they approach, and thinking to save his credit, by appearing to direct. 'Eu leu, in!' repeats he, with a heartier cheer, as the pack charge the rotten fence with a crash that echoes through the wood. The whips scuttle off to their respective points, gentlemen feel their horses' girths, hats are thrust firmly on the head, and the sherry and brandy flasks begin to be drained.

'Tally ho!' cries a countryman at the top of the wood, hoisting his hat on a stick. At the magic sound, fear comes over some, joy over others, intense anxiety over all. What commotion! What indecision! What confusion! 'Which way?—Which way?' is the cry.

'Twang, twang, twang,' goes old Tom's horn at the top of the wood, whither he seems to have flown, so quick has he got there.

A dark-coated gentleman on a good family horse solves the important question—'Which way?'—by diving at once into the wood, crashing along till he comes to a cross-road that leads to the top, when the scene opening to 'open fresh fields and pastures new,' discloses divers other sections struggling up in long drawn files, following other leaders, all puffing, and wheezing and holding on by the manes, many feeling as if they had had enough already—'Quick!' is the word, for the tail-hounds are flying the fence out of the first field over the body of the pack, which are running almost mute at best pace beyond, looking a good deal smaller than is agreeable to the eyes of a sportsman.

'F—o—o—r—rard!' screams old Tom, flying the fence after them, followed by jealous jostling riders in scarlet and colours, some anxious, some easy, some wanting to be at it, some wanting to look as if they did, some wishing to know if there was anything on the far side.

Now Tom tops another fence, rising like a rocket and dropping like a bird; still 'F—o—o—r—rard!' is the cry—away they go at racing pace.

The field draws out like a telescope, leaving the largest portion at the end, and many—the fair and fat ones in particular—seeing the hopelessness of the case, pull up their horses, while yet on an eminence that commands a view. Fifteen or twenty horsemen enter for the race, and dash forward, though the hounds rather gain on old Tom, and the further they go the smaller the point of the telescope becomes. The pace is awful; many would give in but for the ladies. At the end of a mile or so, the determined ones show to the front, and the spirters and 'make-believes' gladly avail themselves of their pioneering powers.

Mr. Sponge, who got well through the wood, has been going at his ease, the great striding brown throwing the large fields behind him with ease, and taking his leaps safely and well. He now shows to the front, and old Tom, who is still 'F—o—o—r—rarding' to his hounds, either rather falls back to the field or the field draws upon him. At all events they get together somehow. A belt of Scotch fir plantation, with a stiffish fence on each side, tries their mettle and the stoutness of their hats: crash they get through it, the noise they make among the thorns and rotten branches resembling the outburst of a fire. Several gentlemen here decline under cover of the trees.

'F—o—o—r—rard!' screams old Tom, as he dives through the stiff fence and lands in the field outside the plantation. He might have saved his breath, for the hounds were beating him as it was. Mr. Sponge bores through the same place, little aided, however, by anything old Tom has done to clear the way for him, and the rest follow in his wake.

The field is now reduced to six, and two of the number, Mr. Spareneck and Caingey Thornton, become marked in their attention to our hero. Thornton is riding Mr. Waffles' crack steeple-chaser 'Dare-Devil,' and Mr. Spareneck is on a first-rate hunter belonging to the same gentleman, but they have not been able to get our friend Sponge into grief. On the contrary, his horse, though lathered, goes as strong as ever, and Mr. Sponge, seeing their design, is as careful of him as possible, so as not to lose ground. His fine, strong, steady seat, and quiet handling, contrasts well with Thornton's rolling bucketing style, who has already begun to ply a heavy cutting whip, in aid of his spurs at his fences, accompanied with a half frantic 'g—u—r—r—r along!' and inquires of the horse if he thinks he stole him?

The three soon get in front; fast as they go, the hounds go faster, and fence after fence is thrown behind them, just as a girl throws her skipping-rope.

Tom and the whips follow, grinning with their tongues in their cheeks, Tom still screeching 'F—o—o—o—rard!—F—o—o—o—rard!' at intervals.

A big stone wall, built with mortar, and coped with heavy blocks of stone, is taken by the three abreast, for which they are rewarded by a gallop up Stretchfurrow pasture, from the summit of which they see the hounds streaming away to a fine grass country below, with pollard willows dotted here and there in the bottom.

'Water!' says our friend Sponge to himself, wondering whether Hercules would face it. A desperate black bullfinch, so thick that they could hardly see through it, is shirked by consent, for a gate which a countryman opens, and another fence or two being passed, the splashing of some hounds in the water, and the shaking of others on the opposite bank, show that, as usual, the willows are pretty true prophets.

Caingey, grinning his coarse red face nearly double, and getting his horse well by the head, rams in the spurs, and flourishes his cutting whip high in air, with a 'g—u—u—ur along! do you think I'—the 'stole you' being lost under water just as Sponge clears the brook a little lower down. Spareneck then pulls up.

When Nimrod had Dick Christian under water in the Whissendine in his Leicestershire run, and someone more humane than the rest of the field observed, as they rode on,

'But he'll be drowned.'

'Shouldn't wonder,' exclaimed another.

'But the pace,' Nimrod added, 'was too good to inquire.'

Such, however, was not the case with our watering-place cock, Mr. Sponge. Independently of the absurdity of a man risking his neck for the sake of picking up a bunch of red herrings, Mr. Sponge, having beat everybody, could afford a little humanity, more especially as he rode his horse on sale, and there was now no one left to witness the further prowess of the steed. Accordingly, he availed himself of a heavy, newly-ploughed fallow, upon which he landed as he cleared the brook, for pulling up, and returned just as Mr. Spareneck, assisted by one of the whips, succeeded in landing Caingey on the taking-off side. Caingey was not a pretty boy at the best of times—none but the most partial parents could think him one—and his clumsy-featured, short, compressed face, and thick, lumpy figure, were anything but improved by a sort of pea-green net-work of water-weeds with which he arose from his bath. He was uncommonly well soaked, and had to be held up by the heels to let the water run out of his boots, pockets, and clothes. In this undignified position he was found by Mr. Waffles and such of the field as had ridden the line.

'Why, Caingey, old boy! you look like a boiled porpoise with parsley sauce!' exclaimed Mr. Waffles, pulling up where the unfortunate youth was spluttering and getting emptied like a jug. 'Confound it!' added he, as the water came gurgling out of his mouth, 'but you must have drunk the brook dry.'

Caingey would have censured his inhumanity, but knowing the imprudence of quarrelling with his bread and butter, and also aware of the laughable, drowned-rat figure he must then be cutting, he thought it best to laugh, and take his change out of Mr. Waffles another time. Accordingly, he chuckled and laughed too, though his jaws nearly refused their office, and kindly transferred the blame of the accident from the horse to himself.

'He didn't put on steam enough,' he said.

Meanwhile, old Tom, who had gone on with the hounds, having availed himself of a well-known bridge, a little above where Thornton went in, for getting over the brook, and having allowed a sufficient time to elapse for the proper completion of the farce, was now seen rounding the opposite hill, with his hounds clustered about his horse, with his mind conning over one of those imaginary runs that experienced huntsmen know so well how to tell, when there is no one to contradict them.

Having quartered his ground to get at his old friend the bridge again, he just trotted up with well-assumed gaiety as Caingey Thornton spluttered the last piece of green weed out from between his great thick lips.

'Well, Tom!' exclaimed Mr. Waffles, 'what have you done with him?'

'Killed him, sir,' replied Tom, with a slight touch of his cap, as though 'killing' was a matter of every-day occurrence with them.

'Have you, indeed!' exclaimed Mr. Waffles, adopting the lie with avidity.

'Yes, sir,' said Tom gravely; 'he was nearly beat afore he got to the brook. Indeed, I thought Vanquisher would have had him in it; but, however, he got through, and the scent failed on the fallow, which gave him a chance; but I held them on to the hedgerow beyond, where they hit it off like wildfire, and they never stopped again till they tumbled him over at the back of Mr. Plummey's farm-buildings, at Shapwick. I've got his brush,' added Tom, producing a much tattered one from his pocket, 'if you'd like to have it?'

'Thank you, no—yes—no,' replied Waffles, not wanting to be bothered with it; 'yet stay,' continued he, as his eye caught Mr. Sponge, who was still on foot beside his vanquished friend; 'give it to Mr. What-de-ye-call-'em,' added he, nodding towards our hero.

'Sponge,' observed Tom, in an undertone, giving the brush to his master.

'Mr. Sponge, will you do me the favour to accept the brush?' asked Mr. Waffles, advancing with it towards him; adding, 'I am sorry this unlucky bather should have prevented your seeing the end.'

Mr. Sponge was a pretty good judge of brushes, and not a bad one of camphire; but if this one had smelt twice as strong as it did—indeed, if it had dropped to pieces in his hand, or the moths had flown up in his face, he would have pocketed it, seeing it paved the way to what he wanted—an introduction.

'I'm very much obliged, I'm sure,' observed he, advancing to take it—'very much obliged, indeed; been an extremely good run, and fast.'

'Very fair—very fair,' observed Mr. Waffles, as though it were nothing in their way; 'seven miles in twenty minutes, I suppose, or something of that sort.'

'*One*-and-twenty,' interposed Tom, with a laudable anxiety for accuracy.

'Ah! one-and-twenty,' rejoined Mr. Waffles. 'I thought it would be somewhere thereabouts. Well, I suppose we've all had enough,' added he, 'may as well go home and have some luncheon, and then a game at billiards, or rackets, or something. How's the old water-rat?' added he, turning to Thornton, who was now busy emptying his cap and mopping the velvet.

The water-rat was as well as could be expected, but did not quite like the new aspect of affairs. He saw that Mr. Sponge was a first-rate horseman, and also knew that nothing ingratiated one man with another so much as skill and boldness in the field. It was by that means, indeed, that he had established himself in Mr. Waffles' good graces—an ingratiation that had been pretty serviceable to him, both in the way of meat, drink, mounting, and money. Had Mr. Sponge been, like himself, a needy, penniless adventurer, Caingey would have tried to have kept him out by some of those plausible, admonitory hints, that poverty makes men so obnoxious to; but in the case of a rich, flourishing individual, with such an astonishing stud as Leather made him out to have, it was clearly Caingey's policy to knock under and be subservient to Mr. Sponge also. Caingey, we should observe, was a bold, reckless rider, never seeming to care for his neck, but he was no match for Mr. Sponge, who had both skill and courage.

Caingey being at length cleansed from his weeds, wiped from his mud, and made as comfortable as possible under the circumstances, was now hoisted on to the renowned steeple-chase horse again, who had scrambled out of the brook on the taking-off side, and, after meandering the banks for a certain distance, had been caught by the bridle in the branch of a willow—Caingey, we say, being again mounted, Mr. Sponge also, without hindrance from the resolute brown horse, the first whip put himself a little in advance, while old Tom followed with the hounds, and the second whip mingled with the now increasing field, it being generally understood (by the uninitiated, at least) that hounds have no business to go home so long as any gentleman is inclined for a scurrey, no matter whether he has joined early or late. Mr. Waffles, on the contrary, was very easily satisfied, and never took the shine off a run with a kill by risking a subsequent defeat. Old Tom, though keen when others were keen, was not indifferent to his comforts, and soon came into the way of thinking that it was just as well to get home to his mutton-chops at two or three o'clock, as to be groping his way about bottomless bye-roads on dark winter nights.

As he retraced his steps homeward, and overtook the scattered field of the morning, his talent for invention, or rather stretching, was again called into requisition.

'What have you done with him, Tom?' asked Major Bouncer, eagerly bringing his sturdy collar-marked cob alongside of our huntsman.

'Killed him, sir,' replied Tom, with the slightest possible touch of the cap. (Bouncer was no tip.)

'Indeed!' exclaimed Bouncer, gaily, with that sort of sham satisfaction that most people express about things that can't concern them in the least. 'Indeed! I'm deuced glad of that! Where did you kill him?'

'At the back of Mr. Plummey's farm-buildings, at Shapwick,' replied Tom; adding, 'but, my word, he led us a dance afore we got there—up to Ditchington, down to Somerby, round by Temple Bell Wood, cross Goosegreen Common, then away for Stubbington Brooms, skirtin' Sanderwick Plantations, but scarce goin' into 'em, then by the round hill at Camerton, leavin' great Heatherton to the right, and so straight on to Shapwick, where we killed, with every hound up—'

'God bless me!' exclaimed Bouncer, apparently lost in admiration, though he scarcely knew the country; 'God bless me!' repeated he, 'what a run! The finest run that ever was seen.'

'Nine miles in twenty-five minutes,' replied Tom, tacking on a little both for time and distance.

'B-o-y JOVE!' exclaimed the major.

Having shaken hands with, and congratulated Mr. Waffles most eagerly and earnestly, the major hurried off to tell as much as he could remember to the first person he met, just as the cheese-bearer at a christening looks out for some one to give the cheese to. The cheese-getter on this occasion was Doctor Lotion, who was going to visit old Jackey Thompson, of Woolleyburn. Jackey being then in a somewhat precarious state of health, and tolerably advanced in life, without any very self-evident heir, was obnoxious to the attentions of three distinct litters of cousins, some one or other of whom was constantly 'baying him.' Lotion, though a sapient man, and somewhat grinding in his practice, did not profess to grind old people young again, and feeling he could do very little for the body corporate, directed his attention to amusing Jackey's mind, and anything in the shape of gossip was extremely acceptable to the doctor to retail to his patient. Moreover,

Jackey had been a bit of a sportsman, and was always extremely happy to see the hounds—*on anybody's land but his own.*

So Lotion got primed with the story, and having gone through the usual routine of asking his patient how he was, how he had slept, looking at his tongue, and reporting on the weather, when the old posing question, 'What's the news?' was put, Lotion replied, as he too often had to reply, for he was a very slow hand at picking up information.

'Nothin' particklar, I think, sir,' adding, in an off-hand sort of way, 'you've heard of the greet run, I s'pose, sir?'

'Great run!' exclaimed the octogenarian, as if it was a matter of the most vital importance to him; 'great run, sir; no, sir, not a word!'

The doctor then retailed it.

Old Jackey got possessed of this one idea—he thought of nothing else. Whoever came, he out with it, chapter and verse, with occasional variations. He told it to all the 'cousins in waiting'; Jackey Thompson, of Carrington Ford; Jackey Thompson, of Houndesley; Jackey Thompson, of the Mill; and all the Bobs, Bills, Sams, Harrys, and Peters, composing the respective litters;—forgetting where he got it from, he nearly told it back to Lotion himself. We sometimes see old people affected this way—far more enthusiastic on a subject than young ones. Few dread the aspect of affairs so much as those who have little chance of seeing how they go.

But to the run. The cousins reproduced the story according to their respective powers of exaggeration. One tacked on two miles, another ten, and so it went on and on, till it reached the ears of the great Mr. Seedeyman, the mighty WE of the country, as he sat in his den penning his 'stunners' for his market-day *Mercury*. It had then distanced the great sea-serpent itself in length, having extended over thirty-three miles of country, which Mr. Seedeyman reported to have been run in one hour and forty minutes.

Pretty good going, we should say.

X

THE FEELER

Bag fox-hunts, be they ever so good, are but unsatisfactory things; drag runs are, beyond all measure, unsatisfactory. After the best-managed bag fox-hunt, there is always a sort of suppressed joy, a deadly liveliness in the field. Those in the secret are afraid of praising it too much, lest the secret should ooze out, and strangers suppose that all their great runs are with bag foxes, while the mere retaking of an animal that one has had in hand before is not calculated to arouse any very pleasurable emotions. Nobody ever goes frantic at seeing an old donkey of a deer handed back into his carriage after a canter.

Our friends on this occasion soon exhausted what they had to say on the subject.

'That's a nice horse of yours,' observed Mr. Waffles to Mr. Sponge, as the latter, on the strength of the musty brush, now rode alongside the master of the hounds.

'I think he is,' replied Sponge, rubbing some of the now dried sweat from his shoulder and neck; 'I think he is; I like him a good deal better to-day than I did the first time I rode him.'

'What, he's a new one, is he?' asked Mr. Waffles, taking a scented cigar from his mouth, and giving a steady sidelong stare at the horse.

'Bought him in Leicestershire,' replied Sponge. 'He belonged to Lord Bullfrog, who didn't think him exactly up to his weight.'

'Up to his weight!' exclaimed Mr. Caingey Thornton, who had now ridden up on the other side of his great patron, 'why, he must be another Daniel Lambert.'

'Rather so,' replied Mr. Sponge; 'rides nineteen stun.'

'What a monster!' exclaimed Thornton, who was of the pocket order.

'I thought he didn't go fast enough at his fences the first time I rode him,' observed Mr. Sponge, drawing the curb slightly so as to show the horse's fine arched neck to advantage; 'but he went quick enough to-day, in all conscience,' added he.

'He did *that*,' observed Mr. Thornton, now bent on a toadying match. 'I never saw a finer lepper.'

'He flew many feet beyond the brook,' observed Mr. Spareneck, who, thinking discretion was the better part of valour, had pulled up on seeing his comrade Thornton blobbing about in the middle of it, and therefore was qualified to speak to the fact.

So they went on talking about the horse, and his points, and his speed, and his action, very likely as much for want of something to say, or to keep off the subject of the run, as from any real admiration of the animal.

The true way to make a man take a fancy to a horse is to make believe that you don't want to sell him—at all events, that you are easy about selling. Mr. Sponge had played this game so very often, that it came quite natural to him. He knew exactly how far to go, and having expressed his previous objection to the horse, he now most handsomely made the *amende honorable* by patting him on the neck, and declaring that he really thought he should keep him.

It is said that every man has his weak or 'do-able' point, if the sharp ones can but discover it. This observation does not refer, we believe, to men with an innocent *penchant* for play, or the turf, or for buying pictures, or for collecting china, or for driving coaches and four, all of which tastes proclaim themselves sooner or later, but means that the most knowing, the most cautious, and the most careful, are all to be come over, somehow or another.

There are few things more surprising in this remarkable world than the magnificent way people talk about money, or the meannesses they will resort to in order to get a little. We hear fellows flashing and talking in hundreds and thousands, who will do almost anything for a five-pound note. We have known men pretending to hunt countries at their own expense, and yet actually 'living out of the hounds.' Next to the accomplishment of that—apparently almost impossible feat—comes the dexterity required for living by horse-dealing.

A little lower down in the scale comes the income derived from the profession of a 'go-between'—the gentleman who can buy the horse cheaper than you can. This was Caingey Thornton's trade. He was always lurking about people's stables talking to grooms and worming out secrets—whose horse had a cough, whose was a wind-sucker, whose was lame after hunting, and so on—and had a price current of every horse in the place—knew what had been given, what the owners asked, and had a pretty good guess what they would take.

Waffles would have been an invaluable customer to Thornton if the former's groom, Mr. Figg, had not been rather too hard with his 'reg'lars.' He insisted on Caingey dividing whatever he got out of his master with him. This reduced profits considerably; but still, as it was a profession that did not require any capital to set up with, Thornton could afford to be liberal, having only to tack on to one end to cut off at the other.

After the opening Sponge gave as they rode home with the hounds, Thornton had no difficulty in sounding him on the subject.

'You'll not think me impertinent, I hope,' observed Caingey, in his most deferential style, to our hero when they met at the News'-room the next day—'you'll not think me impertinent, I hope; but I think you said as we rode home, yesterday, that you didn't altogether like the brown horse you were on?'

'*Did I?*' replied Mr. Sponge, with apparent surprise; 'I think you must have misunderstood me.'

'Why, no; it wasn't exactly that,' rejoined Mr. Thornton, 'but you said you liked him better than you did, I think?'

'Ah! I believe I did say something of the sort,' replied Sponge casually—'I believe I did say something of the sort; but he carried me so well that I thought better of him. The fact was,' continued Mr. Sponge, confidentially, 'I thought him rather too light-mouthed; I like a horse that bears more on the hand.'

'Indeed!' observed Mr. Thornton; 'most people think a light mouth a recommendation.'

'I know they do,' replied Mr. Sponge, 'I know they do; but I like a horse that requires a little riding. Now this is too much of a made horse—too much of what I call an old man's horse, for me. Bullfrog, whom I bought him of, is very fat—eats a great deal of venison and turtle—all sorts of good things, in fact—and can't stand much tewing in the saddle; now, I rather like to feel that I am on a horse, and not in an arm-chair.'

'He's a fine horse,' observed Mr. Thornton.

'So he ought,' replied Mr. Sponge; 'I gave a hatful of money for him—two hundred and fifty golden sovereigns, and not a guinea back. Bullfrog's the biggest screw I ever dealt with.'

That latter observation was highly encouraging to Thornton. It showed that Mr. Sponge was not one of your tight-laced dons, who take offence at the mere mention of 'drawbacks,' but, on the contrary, favoured the supposition that he would do the 'genteel,' should he happen to be a seller.

'Well, if you should feel disposed to part with him, perhaps you will have the kindness to let me know,' observed Mr. Thornton; adding, 'he's not for myself, of course, but I think I know a man he would suit, and who would be inclined to give a good price for him.'

'I will,' replied Mr. Sponge; 'I will,' repeated he, adding, 'if I *were* to sell him, I wouldn't take a farthing under three 'underd for him—three 'underd *guineas*, mind, *not punds*.'

'That's a vast sum of money,' observed Mr. Thornton.

'Not a bit on't,' replied Mr. Sponge. 'He's worth it all, and a great deal more. Indeed, I haven't said, mind that, I'll take that for him; all I've said is, that I wouldn't take less.'

'Just so,' replied Mr. Thornton.

'He's a horse of high character,' observed Mr. Sponge. 'Indeed he has no business out of Leicestershire; and I don't know what set my fool of a groom to bring him here.'

'Well, I'll see if I can coax my friend into giving what you say,' observed Mr. Thornton.

'Nay, never mind coaxing,' replied Mr. Sponge, with the utmost indifference; 'never mind coaxing; if he's not anxious, my name's "easy." Only mind ye, if I ride him again, and he carries me as he did yesterday, I shall clap on another fifty. A horse of that figure can't be dear at any price,' added he. 'Put him in a steeple-chase, and you'd get your money back in ten minutes, and a bagful to boot.'

'True,' observed Mr. Thornton, treasuring that fact up as an additional inducement to use to his friend.

So the amiable gentlemen parted.

XI

THE DEAL,
AND THE DISASTER

IF PEOPLE ARE INCLINED TO deal, bargains can very soon be struck at idle watering-places, where anything in the shape of occupation is a godsend, and bargainers know where to find each other in a minute. Everybody knows where everybody is.

'Have you seen Jack Sprat?'

'Oh yes; he's just gone into Muddle's Bazaar with Miss Flouncey, looking uncommon sweet.' Or—

'Can you tell me where I shall find Mr. Slowman?'

Answer.—'You'll find him at his lodgings, No. 15, Belvidere Terrace, till a quarter before seven. He's gone home to dress, to dine with Major and Mrs. Holdsworthy, at Grunton Villa, for I heard him order Jenkins's fly at that time.'

Caingey Thornton knew exactly when he would find Mr. Waffles at Miss Lollypop's, the confectioner, eating ices and making love to that very interesting much-courted young lady. True to his time, there was Waffles, eating and eyeing the cherry-coloured ribbons, floating in graceful curls along with her raven-coloured ringlets, down Miss Lollypop's nice fresh plump cheeks.

After expatiating on the great merits of the horse, and the certainty of getting all the money back by steeple-chasing him in the spring, and stating his conviction that Mr. Sponge would not take any part of the purchase-money in pictures or jewellery, or anything of that sort, Mr. Waffles gave his consent to deal, on the terms the following conversation shows.

'My friend will give you your price, if you wouldn't mind taking his cheque and keeping it for a few months till he's into funds,' observed Mr. Thornton, who now sought Mr. Sponge out at the billiard-room.

'Why,' observed Mr. Sponge, thoughtfully, 'you know horses are always ready money.'

'True,' replied Thornton; 'at least that's the theory of the thing; only my friend is rather peculiarly situated at present.'

'I suppose Mr. Waffles is your man?' observed Mr. Sponge, rightly judging that there couldn't be two such flats in the place.

'Just so,' said Mr. Thornton.

'I'd rather take his "stiff" than his cheque,' observed Mr. Sponge, after a pause. 'I could get a bit of stiff *done*, but a cheque, you see—especially a post-dated one—is always objected to.'

'Well, I dare say that will make no difference,' observed Mr. Thornton, '"stiff," if you prefer it—say three months; or perhaps you'll give us four?'

'Three's long enough, in all conscience,' replied Mr. Sponge, with a shake of the head, adding, 'Bullfrog made me pay down on the nail.'

'Well, so be it, then,' assented Mr. Thornton; 'you draw at three months, and Mr. Waffles will accept, payable at Coutts's.'

After so much liberality, Mr. Caingey expected that Mr. Sponge would have hinted at something handsome for him; but all Sponge said was, 'So be it,' too, as he walked away to buy a bill-stamp.

Mr. Waffles was more considerate, and promised him the first mount on his new purchase, though Caingey would rather have had a ten, or even a five-pound note.

Towards the hour of ten on that eventful day, numerous gaitered, trousered, and jacketed grooms began to ride up and down the High Street, most of them with their stirrups crossed negligently on the pommels of the saddles, to indicate that their masters were going to ride the horses, and not them. The street grew lively, not so much with people going to hunt, as with people coming to see those who were. Tattered Hibernians, with rags on their backs and jokes on their lips; young English *chevaliers d'industrie*, with their hands ready to dive into anybody's pockets but their own; stablemen out of place, servants loitering on their errands, striplings helping them, ladies'-maids with novels or three-corner'd notes, and a good crop of beggars.

'What, Spareneck, do you ride the grey to-day? I thought you'd done Gooseman out of a mount,' observed Ensign Downley, as a line of scarlet-coated youths hung over the balcony of the Imperial Hotel, after breakfast and before mounting for the day.

Spareneck.—'No, that's for Tuesday. He wouldn't stand one to-day. What do you ride?'

Downley.—'Oh, I've a hack, one of Screwman's, Perpetual Motion they call him, because he never gets any rest. That's him, I believe, with the lofty-actioned hind-legs,' added he, pointing to a weedy string-halty bay passing below, high in bone and low in flesh.

'Who's o' the gaudy chestnut?' asked Caingey Thornton, who now appeared, wiping his fat lips after his second glass of *eau de vie*.

'That's Mr. Sponge's,' replied Spareneck in a low tone, knowing how soon a man catches his own name.

'A deuced fine horse he is, too,' observed Caingey, in a louder key; adding, 'Sponge has the finest lot of horses of any man in England—in the world, I may say.'

Mr. Sponge himself now rose from the breakfast table, and was speedily followed by Mr. Waffles and the rest of the party, some bearing sofa-pillows and cushions to place on the balustrades, to loll at their ease, in imitation of the Coventry Club swells in Piccadilly. Then our friends smoked their cigars, reviewed the cavalry, and criticised the ladies who passed below in the flys on their way to the meet.

'Come, old Bolter!' exclaimed one, 'here's Miss Bussington coming to look after you—got her mamma with her, too—so you may as well knock under at once, for she's determined to have you.'

'A devil of a woman the old un is, too,' observed Ensign Downley; 'she nearly frightened Jack Simpers of ours into fits, by asking what he meant after dancing three dances with her daughter one night.'

'My word, but Miss Jumpheavy must expect to do some execution to-day with that fine floating feather and her crimson satin dress and ermine,' observed Mr. Waffles, as that estimable lady drove past in her Victoria phaeton. 'She looks like the Queen of Sheba herself. But come, I suppose,' he added, taking a most diminutive Geneva watch out of his waistcoat-pocket, 'we should be going. See! there's your nag kicking up a shindy,' he said to Caingey Thornton, as the redoubtable brown was led down the street by a jean-jacketed groom, kicking and lashing out at everything he came near.

'I'll kick him,' observed Thornton, retiring from the balcony to the brandy-bottle, and helping himself to a pretty good-sized glass. He then extricated his large cutting whip from the confusion of whips with which it was mixed, and clonk, clonk, clonked downstairs to the door.

'Multum in Parvo' stopped the doorway, across whose shoulder Leather passed the following hints, in a low tone of voice, to Mr. Sponge, as the latter stood drawing on his dogskin gloves, the observed, as he flattered himself, of all observers.

'Mind now,' said Leather, 'this oss as a will of his own; though he seems so quiet like, he's not always to be depended on; so be on the look-out for squalls.'

Sponge, having had a glass of brandy, just mounted with the air of a man thoroughly at home with his horse, and drawing the rein, with a slight feel of the spur, passed on from the door to make way for the redoubtable Hercules. Hercules was evidently not in a good humour. His ears were laid back, and the rolling white eye showed mischief. Sponge saw all this, and turned to see whether Thornton's clumsy, wash-ball seat, would be able to control the fractious spirit of the horse.

'Whoay!' roared Thornton, as his first dive at the stirrup missed, and was answered by a hearty kick out from the horse, the 'whoay' being given in a very different tone to the gentle, coaxing style of Mr. Buckram and his men. Had it not been for the brandy within and the lookers-on without, there is no saying but Caingey would have declined the horse's further acquaintance. As it was, he quickly repeated his attempt at the stirrup with the same sort of domineering 'whoay,' adding, as he landed in the saddle and snatched at the reins, 'Do you think I stole you?'

Whatever the horse's opinion might be on that point, he didn't seem to care to express it, for finding kicking alone wouldn't do, he immediately commenced rearing too, and by a desperate plunge, broke away from the groom, before Thornton had either got him by the head or his feet in the stirrups. Three most desperate bounds he gave, rising at the bit as though he would come back over if the hold was not relaxed, and the fourth effort bringing him to the opposite kerb-stone, he up again with such a bound and impetus that he crashed right through Messrs. Frippery and Flummery's fine plate-glass window, to the terror

and astonishment of their elegant young counter-skippers, who were busy arranging their ribbons and finery for the day. Right through the window Hercules went, switching through book muslins and bareges as he would through a bullfinch, and attempting to make his exit by a large plate-glass mirror against the wall of the cloak-room beyond, which he dashed all to pieces with his head. Worse remains to be told. 'Multum in Parvo,' seeing his old comrade's hind-quarters disappearing through the window, just took the bit between his teeth, and followed, in spite of Mr. Sponge's every effort to turn him; and when at length he got him hauled round, the horse was found to have decorated himself with a sky-blue *visite* trimmed with Honiton lace, which he wore like a charger on his way to the Crusades, or a steed bearing a knight to the Eglinton tournament.

Quick as it happened, and soon as it was over, all Laverick Wells seemed to have congregated in the street as our heroes rode out of the folding glass-doors.

XII

AN OLD FRIEND

ABOUT A FORTNIGHT AFTER THE above catastrophe, and as the recollection of it was nearly effaced by Miss Jumpheavy's abduction of Ensign Downley, our friend, Mr. Waffles, on visiting his stud at the four o'clock stable-hour, found a most respectable, middle-aged, rosy-gilled, better-sort-of-farmer-looking man, straddling his tight drab-trousered legs, with a twisted ash plant propping his chin, behind the redoubtable Hercules. He had a brand-new hat on, a velvet-collared blue coat with metal buttons, that anywhere but in the searching glare and contrast of London might have passed for a spic-and-span new one; a small, striped, step-collared toilanette vest; and the aforesaid drab trousers, in the right-hand pocket of which his disengaged hand kept fishing up and slipping down an avalanche of silver, which made a pleasant musical accompaniment to his monetary conversation. On seeing Mr. Waffles, the stranger touched his hat, and appeared to be about to retire, when Mr. Figg, the stud-groom, thus addressed his master:

'This be Mr. Buckram, sir, of London, sir; says he knows our brown 'orse, sir.'

'Ah, indeed,' observed Mr. Waffles, taking a cigar from his mouth; 'knows no good of him, I should think. What part of London do you live in, Mr. Buckram?' asked he.

'Why, I doesn't exactly live in London, my lord—that's to say, sir—a little way out of it, you know—have a little hindependence of my own, you understand.'

'Hang it, how should I understand anything of the sort—never set eyes on you before,' replied Mr. Waffles.

The half-crowns now began to descend singly in the pocket, keeping up a protracted jingle, like the notes of a lazy, undecided musical snuff-box. By the time the last had dropped, Mr. Buckram had collected himself sufficiently to resume.

Taking the ash-plant away from his mouth, with which he had been barricading his lips, he observed—

'I know'd that oss when Lord Bullfrog had him,' nodding his head at our old friend as he spoke.

'The deuce you did!' observed Mr. Waffles; 'where was that?'

'In Leicestersheer,' replied Mr. Buckram. 'I have a haunt as lives at Mount Sorrel; she has a little hindependence of her own, and I goes down 'casionally to see her—in fact, I believes I'm her *hare*. Well, I was down there just at the beginnin' of the season, the 'ounds met at Kirby Gate—a mile or two to the south, you know, on the Leicester road—it was the fust day of the season, in fact—and there was a great crowd, and I was one; and havin' a heye for an oss, I was struck with this one, you understand, bein' as I thought, a 'ticklar nice 'un. Lord Bullfrog's man was a ridin' of him, and he kept him outside the crowd, showin' off his pints, and passin' him backwards and forwards under people's noses, to 'tract the notish of the nobs—parsecutin, what I call—and I see'd Mr. Sponge struck—I've known Mr. Sponge many years, and a 'ticklar nice gent he is—well, Mr. Sponge pulled hup, and said to the grum, "Who's o' that oss?" "My Lor' Bullfrog's, sir," said the man. "He's a deuced nice 'un," observed Mr. Sponge, thinkin', as he was a lord's, he might praise 'im, seein', in all probability, he weren't for sale. "He is *that*," said the grum, patting him on the neck, as though he were special fond on him. "Is my lord out?" asked Mr. Sponge. "No, sir; he's not come down yet," replied the man, "nor do I know when he will come. He's been down at Bath for some time 'sociatin' with the aldermen o' Bristol and has thrown up a vast o' bad flesh—two stun' sin' last season—and he's afeared this oss won't be able to carry 'im, and so he writ to me to take 'im out to-day, to show 'im." "He'd carry *me*, I think," said Mr. Sponge, making hup his mind on the moment, jist as he makes hup his mind to ride at a fence—not that I think it's a good plan for a gent to show that he's sweet on an oss, for they're sure to make him pay for it. Howsomever, that's nouther here nor there. Well, jist as Mr. Sponge said this, Sir Richard driv' hup, and havin' got his oss, away we trotted to the goss jist below, and the next thing I see'd was Mr. Sponge leadin' the 'ole field on this werry nag. Well, I heard no more till I got to Melton, for I didn't go to my haunt's at Mount Sorrel that night, and I saw little of the run, for my oss was rather puffy, livin' principally on chaff, bran mashes, swedes, and soft food; and when I got to Melton, I heard 'ow Mr. Sponge had bought this oss,' Mr. Buckram nodding his head at the horse as he spoke, 'and 'ow that he'd given the matter o' two 'under'd—or I'm not sure it weren't two 'under'd-and-fifty guineas for 'im, and—'

'Well,' interrupted Mr. Waffles, tired of his verbosity, 'and what did they say about the horse?'

'Why,' continued Mr. Buckram, thoughtfully, propping his chin up with his stick, and drawing all the half-crowns up to the top of his pocket again, 'the fust 'spicious thing I heard was Sir Digby Snaffle's grum, Sam, sayin' to Captain Screwley's bat-man grum, jist afore the George Inn door,—

"'Well, Jack, Tommy's sold the brown oss!"

"'N—O—O—R!" exclaimed Jack, starin' 'is eyes out, as if it were unpossible.

"'He '*as* though," said Sam.

"'Well, then, I 'ope the gemman's fond o' walkin'," exclaimed Jack, bustin' out a laughin' and runnin' on.

'This rayther set me a thinkin',' continued Mr. Buckram, dropping a second half-crown, which jinked against the nest-egg one left at the bottom, 'and fearin' that Mr. Sponge had fallen 'mong the Philistines— which I was werry concerned about, for he's a real nice gent, but thoughtless, as many young gents are who 'ave plenty of tin—I made it my business to inquire 'bout this oss; and if he *is* the oss that I saw in Leicestersheer, and I 'ave little doubt about it (dropping two consecutive half-crowns as he spoke), though I've not seen him out, I—'

'Ah! well, I bought him of Mr. Sponge, who said he got him from Lord Bullfrog,' interrupted Mr. Waffles.

'Ah! then he *is* the oss, in course,' said Mr. Buckram, with a sort of mournful chuck of the chin; 'he *is* the oss,' repeated he; 'well, then, he's a dangerous hanimal,' added he, letting slip three half-crowns.

'What does he do?' asked Mr. Waffles.

'Do!' repeated Mr. Buckram, 'Do! he'll do for anybody.'

'Indeed,' responded Mr. Waffles; adding, 'how could Mr. Sponge sell me such a brute?'

'I doesn't mean to say, mind ye,' observed Mr. Buckram, drawing back three half-crowns, as though he had gone that much too far,—'I doesn't mean to say, mind, that he's wot you call a mistiched, runaway, rear-backwards-over-hanimal—but I mean to say he's a difficultish oss to ride—himpetuous—and one that, if he got the hupper 'and, would be werry likely to try and keep the hupper 'and—you understand me?' said he, eyeing Mr. Waffles intently, and dropping four half-crowns as he spoke.

'I'm tellin' you nothin' but the truth,' observed Mr. Buckram, after a pause, adding, 'in course it's nothin' to me, only bein' down here on a visit to a friend, and 'earin' that the oss were 'ere, I made bold to look in to see whether it was 'im or no. No offence, I 'opes,' added he, letting go the rest of the silver, and taking the prop from under his chin, with an obeisance as if he was about to be off.

'Oh, no offence at all,' rejoined Mr. Waffles, 'no offence—rather the contrary. Indeed, I'm much obliged to you for telling me what you have done. Just stop half a minute,' added he, thinking he might as well try and get something more out of him. While Mr. Waffles was considering his next question, Mr. Buckram saved him the trouble of thinking by 'leading the gallop' himself.

'I believe 'im to be a *good* oss, and I believe 'im to be a *bad* oss,' observed Mr. Buckram, sententiously. 'I believe that oss, with a bold rider on his back, and well away with the 'ounds, would beat most osses goin', but it's the start that's the difficulty with him; for if, on the other 'and, he don't incline to go, all the spurrin', and quiltin', and leatherin' in the world won't make 'im. It'll be a mercy o' Providence if he don't cut out work for the crowner some day.'

'Hang the brute!' exclaimed Mr. Waffles, in disgust; 'I've a good mind to have his throat cut.'

'Nay,' replied Mr. Buckram, brightening up, and stirring the silver round and round in his pocket like a whirlpool, 'nay,' replied he, 'he's fit for summat better nor that.'

'Not much, I think,' replied Mr. Waffles, pouting with disgust. He now stood silent for a few seconds.

'Well, but what did they mean by hoping Mr. Sponge was fond of walking?' at length asked he.

'Oh, vy,' replied Mr. Buckram, gathering all the money up again, 'I believe it was this 'ere,' beginning to drop them to half-minute time, and talking very slowly; 'the oss, I believe, got the better of Lord Bullfrog one day, somewhere a little on this side of Thrussinton—that, you know, is where Sir 'Arry built his kennels—between Mount Sorrel and Melton in fact—and havin' got his Lordship off, who, I should tell you, is an uncommon fat 'un, he wouldn't let him on again, and he 'ad to lead him the matter of I don't know 'ow many miles'; Mr. Buckram letting go the whole balance of silver in a rush, as if to denote that it was no joke.

'The brute!' observed Mr. Waffles, in disgust, adding, 'Well, as you seem to have a pretty good opinion of him, suppose you buy him; I'll let you have him cheap.'

''Ord bless you—my lord—that's to say, sir!' exclaimed Buckram, shrugging up his shoulders, and raising his eyebrows as high as they would go, 'he'd be of no use to me, none votsomever—shouldn't know what to do with him—never do for 'arness—besides, I 'ave a werry good machiner as it is—at least, he sarves my turn, and that's everything, you know. No, sir, no,' continued he, slowly and thoughtfully, dropping the silver to half-minute time; 'no, sir, no; if I might make free with a gen'leman o' your helegance,' continued he, after a pause, 'I'd say, sell 'im to a post-master or a buss-master, or some sich cattle as those, but I doesn't think I'd put 'im into the 'ands of no gen'leman, that's to say if I were *you*, at least,' added he.

'Well, then, will you speculate on him yourself for the buss-masters?' asked Mr. Waffles, tired alike of the colloquy and the quadruped.

'Oh, vy, as to that,' replied Mr. Buckram, with an air of the most perfect indifference, 'vy, as to that—not bein' nouther a post-master nor a buss-master—but 'aving, as I said before, a little hindependence o' my own, vy, I couldn't in course give such a bountiful price as if I could turn 'im to account at once; but if it would be any 'commodation to you,' added he, working the silver up into full cry, 'I wouldn't mind givin' you the with (worth) of 'im—say, deductin' expenses hup to town, and standin' at livery afore I finds a customer—expenses hup to town,' continued Mr. Buckram, muttering to himself in apparent calculation, 'standin' at livery—three-and-sixpence a night, grum, and so on—I wouldn't mind,' continued he briskly, 'givin' of you twenty pund for 'im—if you'd throw me back a sov.,' continued he, seeing Mr. Waffles' brow didn't contract into the frown he expected at having such a sum offered for his three-hundred-guinea horse.

In the course of an hour, that wonderful invention of modern times,—the Electric Telegraph—conveyed the satisfactory words 'All right' to our friend Mr. Sponge, just as he was sitting down to dinner in a certain sumptuously sanded coffee-room in Conduit Street, who forthwith sealed and posted the following ready-written letter:

Bantam Hotel, Bond Street.

Sir,

I have been greatly surprised and hurt to hear that you have thought fit to impeach my integrity, and insinuate that I had taken you in with the brown horse. Such insinuations touch one in a tender point—one's self-respect. The bargain, I may remind you, was of your own seeking, and I told you at the time I knew nothing of the horse, having only ridden him once, and I also told you where I got him. To show how unjust and unworthy your insinuations have been, I have now to inform you that, having ascertained that Lord Bullfrog knew he was vicious, I insisted on his lordship taking him back, and have only to add that, on my receiving him from you, I will return you your bill.

I am, Sir, your obedient servant,
H. SPONGE.

To W. WAFFLES, Esq., Imperial Hotel, Laverick Wells.

Mr. Waffles was a good deal vexed and puzzled when he got this letter. He had parted with the horse, who was gone no one knew where, and Mr. Waffles felt that he had used a certain freedom of speech in speaking of the transaction. Mr. Sponge having left Laverick Wells, had, perhaps, led him a little astray with his tongue—slandering an absent man being generally thought a pretty safe game; it now seemed Mr. Waffles was all wrong, and might have had his money back if he had not been in such a hurry to part with the horse. Like a good many people, he thought he had best eat up his words, which he did in the following manner:

Imperial Hotel, Laverick Wells.

DEAR MR. SPONGE,

You are quite mistaken in supposing that I ever insinuated anything against *you* with regard to the horse. I said *he* was a beast, and it seems Lord Bullfrog admits it. However, never mind anything more about him, though I am equally obliged to you for the trouble you have taken. The fact is, I have parted with him.

We are having capital sport; never go out but we kill, sometimes a brace, sometimes a leash of foxes. Hoping you are recovered from the effects of your ride through the window, and will soon rejoin us, believe me, dear Mr. Sponge,

Yours very sincerely,
W. WAFFLES.

To which Mr. Sponge shortly after rejoined as follows:

Bantam Hotel, Bond Street.

DEAR WAFFLES,

Yours to hand—I am glad to receive a disclaimer of any unworthy imputations respecting the brown horse. Such insinuations are only for horse-dealers, not for men of high gentlemanly feeling.

I am sorry to say we have not got out of the horse as I hoped. Lord Bullfrog, who is a most cantankerous fellow, insists upon having him back, according to the terms of my letter; I must therefore trouble you to hunt him up, and let us accommodate his lordship with him again. If you will say where he is, I may very likely know some one who can assist us in getting him. You will excuse this trouble, I hope, considering that it was to serve you that I moved in the matter, and insisted on returning him to his lordship, at a loss of £50 to myself, having only given £250 for him.

I remain, dear Waffles,
Yours sincerely,
H. SPONGE.

To W. WAFFLES, Esq., Imperial Hotel, Laverick Wells.

Laverick Wells.

DEAR SPONGE,

I'm afraid Bullfrog will have to make himself happy without his horse, for I hav'n't the slightest idea where he is. I sold him to a cockneyfied, countryfied sort of a man, who said he had a small "hindependence of his own"—somewhere, I believe, about London. He didn't give much for him, as you may suppose, when I tell you he paid for him chiefly in silver. If I were you, I wouldn't trouble myself about him.

Yours very truly,
W. WAFFLES.

To H. SPONGE, Esq.

Our hero addressed Mr. Waffles again, in the course of a few days, as follows:

DEAR WAFFLES,

I am sorry to say Bullfrog won't be put off without the horse. He says I insisted on his taking him back, and now he insists on having him. I have had his lawyer, Mr. Chousam, of the great firm of Chousam, Doem, and Co., of Throgmorton Street, at me, who says his lordship will play old gooseberry with us if we don't return him by Saturday. Pray put on all steam, and look him up.

Yours in haste,
H. SPONGE.

To W. WAFFLES, Esq.

Mr. Waffles did put on all steam, and so successfully that he ran the horse to ground at our friend Mr. Buckram's. Though the horse was in the box adjoining the house, Mr. Buckram declared he had sold him to go to 'Hireland'; to what county he really couldn't say, nor to what hunt; all he knew was, the gentleman said he was a 'captin,' and lived in a castle.

Mr. Waffles communicated the intelligence to Sponge, requesting him to do the best he could for him, who reported what his 'best' was in the following letter:

DEAR WAFFLES,

My lawyer has seen Chousam, and deuced stiff he says he was. It seems Bullfrog is indignant at being accused of a "do"; and having got me in the wrong box, by not being able to return the horse as claimed, he meant to work me. At first Chousam would hear of nothing but "l—a—w." Bullfrog's wounded honour could only be salved that way. Gradually, however, we diverged from l—a—w to L—s.—d.; and the upshot of it is, that he will advise his lordship to take £250 and be done with it. It's a bore; but I did it for the best, and shall be glad now to know your wishes on the subject. Meanwhile, I remain,

Yours very truly,
H. SPONGE.

To W. WAFFLES, Esq.

Formerly a remittance by post used to speak for itself. The tender-fingered clerks could detect an enclosure, however skilfully folded. Few people grudged double postage in those days. Now one letter is so much like another, that nothing short of opening them makes one any wiser. Mr. Sponge received Mr. Waffles' answer from the hands of the waiter with the sort of feeling that it was only the continuation of their correspondence. Judge, then, of his delight, when a nice, clean, crisp promissory note, on a five-shilling stamp, fell quivering to the floor. A few lines, expressive of Mr. Waffles' gratitude for the trouble our hero had taken, and hopes that it would not be inconvenient to take a note at two months, accompanied it. At first Mr. Sponge was overjoyed. It would set him up for the season. He thought how he'd spend it. He had half a mind to go to Melton. There were no heiresses there, or else he would. Leamington would do, only it was rather expensive. Then he thought he might as well have done Waffles a little more.

'Confound it!' exclaimed Sponge, 'I don't do myself justice! I'm too much of a gentleman! I should have had five 'under'd—such an ass as Waffles deserves to be done!'

XIII

A NEW SCHEME

OUR FRIEND SOAPEY WAS NOW in good feather; he had got a large price for his good-for-nothing horse, with a very handsome bonus for not getting him back, making him better off than he had been for some time. Gentlemen of his calibre are generally extremely affluent in everything except cash. They have bills without end—bills that nobody will touch, and book debts in abundance—book debts entered with metallic pencils in curious little clasped pocket-books, with such utter disregard of method that it would puzzle an accountant to comb them into anything like shape.

It is true, what Mr. Sponge got from Mr. Waffles were bills—but they were good bills, and of such reasonable date as the most exacting of the Jew tribe would 'do' for twenty per cent. Mr. Sponge determined to keep the game alive, and getting Hercules and Multum in Parvo together again, he added a showy piebald hack, that Buckram had just got from some circus people who had not been able to train him to their work.

The question now was, where to manoeuvre this imposing stud—a problem that Mr. Sponge quickly solved.

Among the many strangers who rushed into indiscriminate friendship with our hero at Laverick Wells, was Mr. Jawleyford, of Jawleyford Court, in ——shire. Jawleyford was a great humbug. He was a fine, off-hand, open-hearted, cheery sort of fellow, who was always delighted to see you, would start at the view, and stand with open arms in the middle of the street, as though quite overjoyed at the meeting. Though he never gave dinners, nor anything where he was, he asked everybody, at least

everybody who did give them, to visit him at Jawleyford Court. If a man
was fond of fishing, he must come to Jawleyford Court, he must, indeed;
he would take no refusal, he wouldn't leave him alone till he promised.
He would show him such fishing—no waters in the world to compare
with his. The Shannon and the Tweed were not to be spoken of in the
same day as his waters in the Swiftley.

Shooting, the same way. 'By Jove! are you a shooter? Well, I'm delighted
to hear it. Well, now, we shall be at home all September, and up to the
middle of October, and you must just come to us at your own time, and
I will give you some of the finest partridge and pheasant shooting you
ever saw in your life; Norfolk can show nothing to what I can. Now, my
good fellow, say the word; do say you'll come, and then it will be a settled
thing, and I shall look forward to it with such pleasure!'

He was equally magnanimous about hunting, though, like a good
many people who have 'had their hunts,' he pretended that his day was
over, though he was a most zealous promoter of the sport. So he asked
everybody who did hunt to come and see him; and what with his hearty,
affable manner, and the unlimited nature of his invitations, he generally
passed for a deuced hospitable, good sort of fellow, and came in for no
end of dinners and other entertainments for his wife and daughters,
of which he had two—daughters, we mean, not wives. His time was
about up at Laverick Wells when Mr. Sponge arrived there; nevertheless,
during the few days that remained to them, Mr. Jawleyford contrived to
scrape a pretty intimate acquaintance with a gentleman whose wealth
was reported to equal, if it did not exceed, that of Mr. Waffles himself.
The following was the closing scene between them:

'Mr. Sponge,' said he, getting our hero by both hands in Culeyford's
Billiard Room, and shaking them as though he could not bear the idea
of separation; 'my dear Mr. Sponge,' added he, 'I grieve to say we're
going to-morrow; I had hoped to have stayed a little longer, and to
have enjoyed the pleasure of your most agreeable society.' (This was
true; he would have stayed, only his banker wouldn't let him have any
more money.) 'But, however, I won't say adieu,' continued he; 'no, I
won't say adieu! I live, as you perhaps know, in one of the best hunting
countries in England—my Lord Scamperdale's—Scamperdale and I are
like brothers; I can do whatever I like with him—he has, I may say, the
finest pack of hounds in the world; his huntsman, Jack Frostyface, I really

believe, cannot be surpassed. Come, then, my dear fellow,' continued Mr. Jawleyford, increasing the grasp and shake of the hands, and looking most earnestly in Sponge's face, as if deprecating a refusal; 'come, then, my dear fellow, and see us; we will do whatever we can to entertain and make you comfortable. Scamperdale shall keep our side of the country till you come; there are capital stables at Lucksford, close to the station, and you shall have a stall for your hack at Jawleyford, and a man to look after him, if you like; so now, don't say nay—your time shall be ours—we shall be at home all the rest of the winter, and I flatter myself, if you once come down, you will be inclined to repeat your visit; at least, I hope so.'

There are two common sayings; one, 'that birds of a feather flock together'; the other, 'that two of a trade never agree'; which often seem to us to contradict each other in the actual intercourse of life. Humbugs certainly have the knack of drawing together, and yet they are always excellent friends, and will vouch for the goodness of each other in a way that few straightforward men think it worth their while to adopt with regard to indifferent people. Indeed, humbugs are not always content to defend their absent brother humbugs when they hear them abused, but they will frequently lug each other in neck and crop, apparently for no other purpose than that of proclaiming what excellent fellows they are, and see if anybody will take up the cudgels against them.

Mr. Sponge, albeit with a considerable cross of the humbug himself, and one who perfectly understood the usual worthlessness of general invitations, was yet so taken with Mr. Jawleyford's hail-fellow-well-met, earnest sort of manner, that, adopting the convenient and familiar solution in such matters, that there is no rule without an exception, concluded that Mr. Jawleyford was the exception, and really meant what he said.

Independently of the attractions offered by hunting, which were both strong and cogent, we have said there were two young ladies, to whom fame attached the enormous fortunes common in cases where there is a large property and no sons. Still Sponge was a wary bird, and his experience of the worthlessness of most general invitations made him think it just possible that it might not suit Mr. Jawleyford to receive him now, at the particular time he wanted to go; so after duly considering the case, and also the impressive nature of the invitation, so recently given, too, he determined not to give Jawleyford the chance of refusing him, but just to say he was coming, and drop down upon him before he could say 'no.' Accordingly, he penned the following epistle:

> Bantam Hotel, Bond-street, London.
>
> DEAR JAWLEYFORD,
>
> I purpose being with you to-morrow, by the express train, which I see, by Bradshaw, arrives at Lucksford a quarter to three. I shall only bring two hunters and a hack, so perhaps you could oblige me by taking them in for the short time I shall stay, as it would not be convenient for me to separate them. Hoping to find Mrs. Jawleyford and the young ladies well, I remain, dear sir,
>
> Yours very truly,
> H. SPONGE.
>
> To — JAWLEYFORD, Esq., Jawleyford Court, Lucksford.

'Curse the fellow!' exclaimed Jawleyford, nearly choking himself with a fish bone, as he opened and read the foregoing at breakfast. 'Curse the fellow!' he repeated, stamping the letter under foot, as though he would crush it to atoms. 'Who ever saw such a piece of impudence as that!'

'What's the matter, my dear?' inquired Mrs. Jawleyford, alarmed lest it was her dunning jeweller writing again.

'Matter!' shrieked Jawleyford, in a tone that sounded through the thick wall of the room, and caused the hobbling old gardener on the terrace to peep in at the heavy-mullioned window. 'Matter!' repeated he, as though he had got his *coup de grace*; 'look there,' added he, handing over the letter.

'Oh, my dear,' rejoined Mrs. Jawleyford soothingly, as soon as she saw it was not what she expected. 'Oh, my dear, I'm sure there's nothing to make you put yourself so much out of the way.' 'No!' roared Jawleyford, determined not to be done out of his grievance. 'No!' repeated he; 'do you call that nothing?'

'Why, nothing to make yourself unhappy about,' replied Mrs. Jawleyford, rather pleased than otherwise; for she was glad it was not from Rings, the jeweller, and, moreover, hated the monotony of

Jawleyford Court, and was glad of anything to relieve it. If she had had her own way, she would have gadded about at watering-places all the year round.

'Well,' said Jawleyford, with a toss of the head and a shrug of resignation, 'you'll have me in gaol; I see that.'

'Nay, my dear J.,' rejoined his wife, soothingly; 'I'm sure you've plenty of money.'

'Have I!' ejaculated Jawleyford. 'Do you suppose, if I had, I'd have left Laverick Wells without paying Miss Bustlebey, or given a bill at three months for the house-rent?'

'Well, but, my dear, you've nothing to do but tell Mr. Screwemtight to get you some money from the tenants.'

'Money from the tenants!' replied Mr. Jawleyford. 'Screwemtight tells me he can't get another farthing from any man on the estate.'

'Oh, pooh!' said Mrs. Jawleyford; 'you're far too good to them. I always say Screwemtight looks far more to their interest than he does to yours.'

Jawleyford, we may observe, was one of the rather numerous race of paper-booted, pen-and-ink landowners. He always dressed in the country as he would in St. James's Street, and his communications with his tenantry were chiefly confined to dining with them twice a year in the great entrance-hall, after Mr. Screwemtight had eased them of their cash in the steward's room. Then Mr. Jawleyford would shine forth the very impersonification of what a landlord ought to be. Dressed in the height of the fashion, as if by his clothes to give the lie to his words, he would expatiate on the delights of such meetings of equality; declare that, next to those spent with his family, the only really happy moments of his life were those when he was surrounded by his tenantry; he doated on the manly character of the English farmer. Then he would advert to the great antiquity of the Jawleyford family, many generations of whom looked down upon them from the walls of the old hall; some on their war-steeds, some armed *cap-à-pie*, some in court-dresses, some in Spanish ones, one in a white dress with gold brocade breeches and a hat with an enormous plume, old Jawleyford (father of the present one) in the Windsor uniform, and our friend himself, the very prototype of what then stood before them. Indeed, he had been painted in the act of addressing his hereditary chawbacons in the hall in which the picture was suspended. There he stood, with his bright auburn hair (now rather badger-pied, perhaps, but still very passable by candlelight)—his bright auburn hair, we say, swept boldly off his lofty forehead, his hazy grey eyes flashing with the excitement of drink and animation, his left hand reposing on the hip of his well-fitting black pantaloons, while the right one, radiant with rings, and trimmed with upturned wristband, sawed the air, as he rounded off the periods of the well-accustomed saws.

Jawleyford, like a good many people, was very hospitable when in full fig—two soups, two fishes, and the necessary concomitants; but he would see any one far enough before he would give him a dinner merely because he wanted one. That sort of ostentatious banqueting has about brought country society in general to a deadlock. People tire of the constant revision of plate, linen, and china.

Mrs. Jawleyford, on the other hand, was a very rough-and-ready sort of woman, never put out of her way; and though she constantly preached the old doctrine that girls 'are much better single than married,' she was always on the look-out for opportunities of contradicting her assertions.

She was an Irish lady, with a pedigree almost as long as Jawleyford's, but more compressible pride, and if she couldn't get a duke, she would take a marquis or an earl, or even put up with a rich commoner.

The perusal, therefore, of Sponge's letter, operated differently upon her to what it did upon her husband, and though she would have liked a little more time, perhaps, she did not care to take him as they were. Jawleyford, however, resisted violently. It would be most particularly inconvenient to him to receive company at that time. If Mr. Sponge had gone through the whole three hundred and sixty-five days in the year, he could not have hit upon a more inconvenient one for him. Besides, he had no idea of people writing in that sort of a way, saying they were coming, without giving him the chance of saying no. 'Well, but, my dear, I dare say you asked him,' observed Mrs. Jawleyford.

Jawleyford was silent, the scene in the billiard-room recurring to his mind.

'I've often told you, my dear,' continued Mrs. Jawleyford, kindly, 'that you shouldn't be so free with your invitations if you don't want people to come; things are very different now to what they were in the old coaching and posting days, when it took a day and a night and half the next day to get here, and I don't know how much money besides. You might then invite people with safety, but it is very different now, when they have nothing to do but put themselves into the express train and whisk down in a few hours.'

'Well, but, confound him, I didn't ask his horses,' exclaimed Jawleyford; 'nor will I have them either,' continued he, with a jerk of the head, as he got up and rang the bell, as though determined to put a stop to that at all events.

'Samuel,' said he, to the dirty page of a boy who answered the summons, 'tell John Watson to go down to the Railway Tavern directly, and desire them to get a three-stalled stable ready for a gentleman's horses that are coming to-day—a gentleman of the name of Sponge,' added he, lest any one else should chance to come and usurp them—'and tell John to meet the express train, and tell the gentleman's groom where it is.'

XIV

JAWLEYFORD COURT

TRUE TO A MINUTE, THE hissing engine drew the swiftly gliding train beneath the elegant and costly station at Lucksford—an edifice presenting a rare contrast to the wretched old red-tiled, five-windowed house, called the Red Lion, where a brandy-faced blacksmith of a landlord used to emerge from the adjoining smithy, to take charge of any one who might arrive per coach for that part of the country. Mr. Sponge was quickly on the platform, seeing to the detachment of his horse-box.

Just as the cavalry was about got into marching order, up rode John Watson, a ragamuffin-looking gamekeeper, in a green plush coat, with a very tarnished laced hat, mounted on a very shaggy white pony, whose hide seemed quite impervious to the visitations of a heavily-knotted dogwhip, with which he kept saluting his shoulders and sides.

'Please, sir,' said he, riding up to Mr. Sponge, with a touch of the old hat, 'I've got you a capital three-stall stable at the Railway Tavern, here,' pointing to a newly built brick house standing on the rising ground.

'Oh! but I'm going to Jawleyford Court,' responded our friend, thinking the man was the 'tout' of the tavern.

'Mr. Jawleyford don't take in horses, sir,' rejoined the man, with another touch of the hat.

'He'll take in *mine*,' observed Mr. Sponge, with an air of authority.

'Oh, I beg pardon, sir,' replied the keeper, thinking he had made a mistake; 'it was Mr. Sponge whose horses I had to bespeak stalls for,' touching his hat profusely as he spoke.

'Well, *this* be Mister Sponge,' observed Leather, who had been listening attentively to what passed.

''Deed!' said the keeper, again turning to our hero with an 'I beg pardon, sir, but the stable *is* for you then, sir—for Mr. Sponge, sir.'

'How do you know that?' demanded our friend.

''Cause Mr. Spigot, the butler, says to me, says he, "Mr. Watson," says he—my name's Watson, you see,' continued the speaker, sawing away at his hat, 'my name's Watson, you see, and I'm the head gamekeeper. "Mr. Watson," says he, "you must go down to the tavern and order a three-stall stable for a gentleman of the name of Sponge, whose horses are a comin' to-day"; and in course I've come 'cordingly,' added Watson. 'A *three*-stall'd stable!' observed Mr. Sponge, with an emphasis.

'A three-stall'd stable,' repeated Mr. Watson.

'Confound him, but he said he'd take in a hack at all events,' observed Sponge, with a sideway shake of the head; 'and a hack he *shall* take in, too,' he added. 'Are your stables full at Jawleyford Court?' he asked.

''Ord bless you, no, sir,' replied Watson with a leer; 'there's nothin' in them but a couple of weedy hacks and a pair of old worn-out carriage-horses.'

'Then I can get this hack taken in, at all events,' observed Sponge, laying his hand on the neck of the piebald as he spoke.

'Why, as to that,' replied Mr. Watson, with a shake of the head, 'I can't say nothin'.'

'I must, though,' rejoined Sponge, tartly; 'he *said* he'd take in my hack, or I wouldn't have come.'

'Well, sir,' observed the keeper, 'you know best, sir.'

'Confounded screw!' muttered Sponge, turning away to give his orders to Leather. 'I'll *work* him for it,' he added. 'He sha'n't get rid of *me* in a hurry—at least, not unless I can get a better billet elsewhere.'

Having arranged the parting with Leather, and got a cart to carry his things, Mr. Sponge mounted the piebald, and put himself under the guidance of Watson to be conducted to his destination. The first part of the journey was performed in silence, Mr. Sponge not being particularly well pleased at the reception his request to have his horses taken in had met with. This silence he might perhaps have preserved throughout had it not occurred to him that he might pump something out of the servant about the family he was going to visit.

'That's not a bad-like old cob of yours,' he observed, drawing rein so as to let the shaggy white come alongside of him.

'He belies his looks, then,' replied Watson, with a grin of his cadaverous face, 'for he's just as bad a beast as ever looked through a bridle. It's a parfect disgrace to a gentleman to put a man on such a beast.'

Sponge saw the sort of man he had got to deal with, and proceeded accordingly.

'Have you lived long with Mr. Jawleyford?' he asked.

'No, nor will I, if I can help it,' replied Watson, with another grin and another touch of the old hat. Touching his hat was about the only piece of propriety he was up to.

'What, he's not a brick, then?' asked Sponge.

'Mean man,' replied Watson with a shake of the head; 'mean man,' he repeated. 'You're nowise connected with the fam'ly, I s'pose?' he asked with a look of suspicion lest he might be committing himself.

'No,' replied Sponge; 'no; merely an acquaintance. We met at Laverick Wells, and he pressed me to come and see him.'

'Indeed!' said Watson, feeling at ease again.

'Who did you live with before you came here?' asked Mr. Sponge, after a pause.

'I lived many years—the greater part of my life, indeed—with Sir Harry Swift. *He* was a *real* gentleman now, if you like—a free, open-handed gentleman—none of your close-shavin', cheese-parin' sort of gentlemen, or imitation gentlemen, as I calls them, but a man who knew what was due to good servants and gave them it. We had good wages, and all the proper "reglars." Bless you, I could sell a new suit of clothes there every year, instead of having to wear the last keeper's cast-offs, and a hat that would disgrace anything but a flay-crow. If the linin' wasn't stuffed full of gun-waddin' it would be over my nose,' he observed, taking it off and adjusting the layer of wadding as he spoke.

'You should have stuck to Sir Harry,' observed Mr. Sponge.

'I did,' rejoined Watson. 'I did, I stuck to him to the last. I'd have been with him now, only he couldn't get a manor at Boulogne, and a keeper was of no use without one.'

'What, he went to Boulogne, did he?' observed Mr. Sponge.

'Aye, the more's the pity,' replied Watson. 'He was a gentleman, every inch of him,' he added, with a shake of the head and a sigh, as if recurring to more prosperous times. 'He was what a gentleman ought to be,' he continued, 'not one of your poor, pryin', inquisitive critturs, what's always fancyin' themselves cheated. I ordered everything in my department, and paid for it too; and never had a bill disputed or even commented on. I might have charged for a ton of powder, and never had nothin' said.'

'Mr. Jawleyford's not likely to find his way to Boulogne, I suppose?' observed Mr. Sponge.

'Not he!' exclaimed Watson, 'not he!—safe bird—*very*.'

'He's rich, I suppose?' continued Sponge, with an air of indifference.

'Why, *I* should say he was; though others say he's not,' replied Watson, cropping the old pony with the dog-whip, as it nearly fell on its nose. 'He can't fail to be rich, with all his property; though they're desperate hands for gaddin' about; always off to some waterin'-place or another, lookin' for husbands, I suppose. I wonder,' he continued, 'that gentlemen can't settle at home, and amuse themselves with coursin' and shootin'.' Mr. Watson, like many servants, thinking that the bulk of a gentleman's income should be spent in promoting the particular sport over which they preside.

With this and similar discourse, they beguiled the short distance between the station and the Court—a distance, however, that looked considerably greater after the flying rapidity of the rail. But for these occasional returns to *terra firma*, people would begin to fancy themselves birds. After rounding a large but gently swelling hill, over the summit of which the road, after the fashion of old roads, led, our traveller suddenly looked down upon the wide vale of Sniperdown, with Jawleyford Court glittering with a bright open aspect, on a fine, gradual elevation, above the broad, smoothly gliding river. A clear atmosphere, indicative either of rain or frost, disclosed a vast tract of wild, flat, ill-cultivated-looking country to the south, little interrupted by woods or signs of population; the whole losing itself, as it were, in an indistinct grey outline, commingling with the fleecy white clouds in the distance.

'Here we be,' observed Watson, with a nod towards where a tarnished red-and-gold flag floated, or rather flapped lazily in the winter's breeze, above an irregular mass of towers, turrets, and odd-shaped chimneys.

Jawleyford Court was a fine old mansion, partaking more of the character of a castle than a Court, with its keep and towers, battlements, heavily grated mullioned windows, and machicolated gallery. It stood, sombre and grey, in the midst of gigantic but now leafless sycamores—

trees that had to thank themselves for being sycamores; for, had they
been oaks, or other marketable wood, they would have been made into
bonnets or shawls long before now. The building itself was irregular,
presenting different sorts of architecture, from pure Gothic down to some
even perfectly modern buildings; still, viewed as a whole, it was massive
and imposing; and as Mr. Sponge looked down upon it, he thought
far more of Jawleyford and Co. than he did as the mere occupants of
a modest, white-stuccoed, green-verandahed house, at Laverick Wells.
Nor did his admiration diminish as he advanced, and, crossing by a
battlemented bridge over the moat, he viewed the massive character of
the buildings rising grandly from their rocky foundation. An imposing,
solemn-toned old clock began striking four, as the horsemen rode under
the Gothic portico, whose notes re-echoed and reverberated, and at last
lost themselves among the towers and pinnacles of the building. Sponge,
for a moment, was awe-stricken at the magnificence of the scene, feeling
that it was what he would call 'a good many cuts above him'; but he
soon recovered his wonted impudence.

'He *would* have me,' thought he, recalling the pressing nature of the
Jawleyford invitation.

'If you'll hold my nag,' said Watson, throwing himself off the shaggy
white, 'I'll ring the bell,' added he, running up a wide flight of steps to
the hall-door. A riotous peal announced the arrival.

XV

THE JAWLEYFORD
ESTABLISHMENT

THE LOUD PEAL OF THE Jawleyford Court door-bell, announcing Mr. Sponge's arrival, with which we closed the last chapter, found the inhabitants variously engaged preparing for his reception.

Mrs. Jawleyford, with the aid of a very indifferent cook, was endeavouring to arrange a becoming dinner; the young ladies, with the aid of a somewhat better sort of maid, were attractifying themselves, each looking with considerable jealousy on the efforts of the other; and Mr. Jawleyford was trotting from room to room, eyeing the various pictures of himself, wondering which was now the most like, and watching the emergence of curtains, carpets, and sofas from their brown holland covers.

A gleam of sunshine seemed to reign throughout the mansion; the long-covered furniture appearing to have gained freshness by its retirement, just as a newly done-up hat surprises the wearer by its goodness; a few days, however, soon restores the defects of either.

All these arrangements were suddenly brought to a close by the peal of the door-bell, just as the little stage-tinkle of a theatre stops preparation, and compels the actors to stand forward as they are. Mrs. Jawleyford threw aside her silk apron, and took a hasty glance of her face in the old eagle-topped mirror in the still-room; the young ladies discarded their coarse dirty pocket-handkerchiefs, and gently drew elaborately fringed ones through their taper fingers to give them an air of use, as they took a hasty review of themselves in the swing mirrors;

the housemaid hurried off with a whole armful of brown holland; and Jawleyford threw himself into attitude in an elaborately carved, richly cushioned, easy-chair, with a Disraeli's *Life of Lord George Bentinck* in his hand. But Jawleyford's thoughts were far from his book. He was sitting on thorns lest there might not be a proper guard of honour to receive Mr. Sponge at the entrance.

Jawleyford, as we said before, was not the man to entertain unless he could do it 'properly'; and, as we all have our pitch-notes of propriety up to which we play, we may state that Jawleyford's note was a butler and two footmen. A butler and two footmen he looked upon as perfectly indispensable to receiving company. He chose to have two footmen to follow the butler, who followed the gentleman to the spacious flight of steps leading from the great hall to the portico, as he mounted his horse. The world is governed a good deal by appearances. Mr. Jawleyford started life with two most unimpeachable Johns. They were nearly six feet high, heads well up, and legs that might have done for models for a sculptor. They powdered with the greatest propriety, and by two o'clock each day were silk-stockinged and pumped in full-dress Jawleyford livery: sky-blue coats with massive silver *aiguillettes*, and broad silver seams down the front and round their waistcoat-pocket flaps; silver garters at their crimson plush breeches' knees: and thus attired, they were ready to turn out with the butler to receive visitors, and conduct them back to their carriages. Gradually they came down in style, but not in number, and, when Mr. Sponge visited Mr. Jawleyford, he had a sort of out-of-door man-of-all-work who metamorphosed himself into a second footman at short notice.

'My dear Mr. Sponge!—I am delighted to see you!' exclaimed Mr. Jawleyford, rising from his easy-chair, and throwing his Disraeli's *Bentinck* aside, as Mr. Spigot, the butler, in a deep, sonorous voice, announced our worthy friend. 'This is, indeed, most truly kind of you,' continued Jawleyford, advancing to meet him; and getting our friend by both hands, he began working his arms up and down like the under man in a saw-pit. 'This is, indeed, most truly kind,' he repeated; 'I assure you I shall never forget it. It's just what I like—it's just what Mrs. Jawleyford likes—it's just what we *all* like—coming without fuss or ceremony. Spigot!' he added, hailing old Pomposo as the latter was slowly withdrawing, thinking what a humbug his master was—'Spigot!' he repeated in a louder voice; 'let the ladies know Mr. Sponge is here. Come to the fire, my dear fellow,' continued Jawleyford, clutching his guest by the arm, and drawing him towards where an ample grate of indifferent coals was crackling and spluttering beneath a magnificent old oak mantelpiece of the richest and costliest carved work. 'Come to the fire, my dear fellow,' he repeated, 'for you feel cold; and I don't wonder at it, for the day is cheerless and uncomfortable, and you've had a long ride. Will you take anything before dinner?'

'What time do you dine?' asked Mr. Sponge, rubbing his hands as he spoke.

'Six o'clock,' replied Mr. Jawleyford, 'six o'clock—say six o'clock—not particular to a moment—days are short, you see—days are short.'

'I think I should like a glass of sherry and a biscuit, then,' observed Mr. Sponge.

And forthwith the bell was rung, and in due course of time Mr. Spigot arrived with a tray, followed by the Miss Jawleyfords, who had rather expected Mr. Sponge to be shown into the drawing-room to them, where they had composed themselves very prettily; one working a parrot in chenille, the other with a lapful of crochet.

The Miss Jawleyfords—Amelia and Emily—were lively girls; hardly beauties—at least, not sufficiently so to attract attention in a crowd; but still, girls well calculated to 'bring a man to book,' in the country. Mr. Thackeray, who bound up all the home truths in circulation, and many that exist only in the inner chambers of the heart, calling the whole 'Vanity Fair,' says, we think (though we don't exactly know where to lay hand on the passage), that it is not your real striking beauties who are the most dangerous—at all events, that do the most execution—but sly, quiet sort of girls, who do not strike the beholder at first sight, but steal insensibly upon him as he gets acquainted. The Miss Jawleyfords were of this order. Seen in plain morning gowns, a man would meet them in the street, without either turning round or making an observation, good, bad, or indifferent; but in the close quarters of a country house, with all the able assistance of first-rate London dresses, well-flounced and set out, each bent on doing the agreeable, they became dangerous. The Miss Jawleyfords were uncommonly well got up, and Juliana, their mutual maid, deserved great credit for the impartiality she displayed in arraying them. There wasn't a halfpenny's worth of choice as to which was the best. This was the more creditable to the maid, inasmuch as the dresses—sea-green glaces—were rather dashed; and the worse they looked, the likelier they would be to become her property. Half-dashed dresses, however, that would look rather seedy by contrast, come out very fresh in the country, especially in winter, when day begins to close in at four. And here we may observe, what a dreary time is that which intervenes between the arrival of a guest and the dinner hour, in the dead winter months in the country. The English are a desperate people for overweighting their conversational powers. They have no idea of penning up their small talk, and bringing it to bear in generous flow upon one particular hour; but they keep dribbling it out throughout the live-long day, wearying their listeners without benefiting themselves—just as a careless waggoner scatters his load on the road. Few people are insensible to the advantage of having their champagne brisk, which can only be done by keeping the cork in; but few ever think of keeping the cork of their own conversation in. See a Frenchman—how light and buoyant he trips into a drawing-room, fresh from the satisfactory scrutiny of the looking-glass, with all the news, and jokes, and tittle-tattle of the day, in full bloom! How sparkling and radiant he is, with something smart and pleasant to say to every one! How thoroughly happy and easy he is; and what a contrast to phlegmatic John Bull, who stands with his great red fists doubled, looking as if he thought whoever spoke to him would be wanting him to endorse a bill of exchange! But, as we said before, the dread hour before dinner is an awful time in the country—frightful when there are two hours, and never a subject in common for the company to work upon. Laverick Wells and their mutual acquaintance was all Sponge and Jawleyford's stock-in-trade; and that was a very small capital to begin upon, for they had been there together too short a time to make much of a purse of conversation. Even the young ladies, with their inquiries after the respective flirtations—how Miss Sawney and Captain Snubnose were 'getting on'? and whether the rich Widow Spankley was likely to bring Sir Thomas Greedey to book?—failed to make up a conversation; for Sponge knew little of the ins and outs of these matters, his attention having been more directed to Mr. Waffles than any one else. Still, the mere questions, put in a playful, womanly way, helped the time on, and prevented things coming to that frightful deadlock of silence, that causes an involuntary inward exclamation of

'How *am I* to get through the time with this man?' There are people who seem to think that sitting and looking at each other constitutes society. Women have a great advantage over men in the talking way; they have always something to say. Let a lot of women be huddled together throughout the whole of a livelong day, and they will yet have such a balance of conversation at night, as to render it necessary to convert a bedroom into a clearing-house, to get rid of it. Men, however, soon get high and dry, especially before dinner; and a host ought to be at liberty to read the Riot Act, and disperse them to their bedrooms, till such times as they wanted to eat and drink.

A most scientifically sounded gong, beginning low, like distant thunder, and gradually increasing its murmur till it filled the whole mansion with its roar, at length relieved all parties from the labour of further efforts; and, looking at his watch, Jawleyford asked Mrs. Jawleyford, in an innocent, indifferent sort of way, which was Mr. Sponge's room; though he had been fussing about it not long before, and dusting the portrait of himself in his green-and-gold yeomanry uniform, with an old pocket-handkerchief.

'The crimson room, my dear,' replied the well-drilled Mrs. Jawleyford; and Spigot coming with candles, Jawleyford preceded 'Mr. Sponge' up a splendid richly carved oak staircase, of such gradual and easy rise that an invalid might almost have been drawn up it in a garden-chair.

Passing a short distance along a spacious corridor, Mr. Jawleyford presently opened a door to the right, and led the way into a large gloomy room, with a little newly lighted wood fire crackling in an enormous grate, making darkness visible, and drawing the cold out of the walls. We need scarcely say it was that terrible room—the best; with three creaking, ill-fitting windows, and heavy crimson satin-damask furniture, so old as scarcely to be able to sustain its own weight. 'Ah! here you are,' observed Mr. Jawleyford, as he nearly tripped over Sponge's luggage as it stood by the fire. 'Here you are,' repeated he, giving the candle a flourish, to show the size of the room, and draw it back on the portrait of himself above the mantelpiece. 'Ah! I declare here's an old picture of myself,' said he, holding the candle up to the face, as if he hadn't seen it for some time—'a picture that was done when I was in the Bumperkin yeomanry,' continued he, passing the light before the facings. 'That was considered a good likeness at the time,' said he, looking affectionately at it, and feeling his nose to see if it was still the same size. 'Ours was a capital corps—one of the best, if not the very best in the service. The inspecting officer always spoke of it in the highest possible terms—especially of *my* company, which really was just as perfect as anything my Lord Cardigan, or any of your crack disciplinarians, can produce. However, never mind,' continued he, lowering the candle, seeing Mr. Sponge didn't enter into the spirit of the thing; 'you'll be wanting to dress. You'll find hot water on the table yonder,' pointing to the far corner of the room, where the outline of a jug might just be descried; 'there's a bell in the bed if you want anything; and dinner will be ready as soon as you are dressed. You needn't make yourself very fine,' added he, as he retired; 'for we are only ourselves: hope we shall have some of our neighbours to-morrow or next day, but we are rather badly off for neighbours just here—at least, for short-notice neighbours.' So saying, he disappeared through the dark doorway.

The latter statement was true enough, for Jawleyford, though apparently such a fine open-hearted, sociable sort of man, was in reality a very quarrelsome, troublesome fellow. He quarrelled with all his neighbours in succession, generally getting through them every two or three years; and his acquaintance were divided into two classes—the best and the worst fellows under the sun. A stranger revising Jawleyford after an absence of a year or two, would very likely find the best fellows of former days transformed into the worst ones of that. Thus, Parson Hobanob, that pet victim of country caprice, would come in and go out of season like lamb or asparagus; Major Moustache and Jawleyford would be as 'thick as thieves' one day, and at daggers drawn the next; Squire Squaretoes, of Squaretoes House, and he, were continually kissing or cutting; and even distance—nine miles of bad road, and, of course, heavy tolls—could not keep the peace between lawyer Seedywig and him. What between rows and reconciliations, Jawleyford was always at work.

XVI

THE DINNER

Notwithstanding Jawleyford's recommendation to the contrary, Mr. Sponge made himself an uncommon swell. He put on a desperately stiff starcher, secured in front with a large gold fox-head pin with carbuncle eyes; a fine, fancy-fronted shirt, with a slight tendency to pink, adorned with mosaic-gold-tethered studs of sparkling diamonds (or French paste, as the case might be); a white waistcoat with fancy buttons; a blue coat with bright plain ones, and a velvet collar, black tights, with broad black-and-white Cranbourne-alley-looking stockings (socks rather), and patent leather pumps with gilt buckles—Sponge was proud of his leg. The young ladies, too, turned out rather smart, for Amelia, finding that Emily was going to put on her new yellow watered silk, instead of a dyed satin she had talked of, made Juliana produce her broad-laced blue satin dress out of the wardrobe in the green dressing-room, where it had been laid away in an old tablecloth; and bound her dark hair with a green-beaded wreath, which Emily met by crowning herself with a chaplet of white roses.

Thus attired, with smiles assumed at the door, the young ladies entered the drawing-room in the full fervour of sisterly animosity. They were very much alike in size, shape, and face. They were tallish and full-figured. Miss Jawleyford's features being rather more strongly marked, and her eyes a shade darker than her sister's; while there was a sort of subdued air about her—the result, perhaps, of enlarged intercourse with the world—or maybe of disappointments. Emily's eyes sparkled and glittered, without knowing perhaps why.

Dinner was presently announced. It was of the imposing order that people give their friends on a first visit, as though their appetites were larger on that day than on any other. They dined off plate; the sideboards glittered with the Jawleyford arms on cups, tankards, and salvers; 'Brecknel and Turner's' flamed and swealed in profusion on the table; while every now and then an expiring lamp on the sideboards or brackets proclaimed the unwonted splendour of the scene, and added a flavour to the repast not contemplated by the cook. The room, which was large and lofty, being but rarely used, had a cold, uncomfortable feel; and, if it hadn't been for the looks of the thing, Jawleyford would, perhaps, as soon that they had dined in the little breakfast parlour. Still there was everything very smart; Spigot in full fig, with a shirt frill nearly tickling his nose, an acre of white waistcoat, and glorious calves swelling within his gauze-silk stockings. The improvised footman went creaking about, as such gentlemen generally do.

The style was perhaps better than the repast: still they had turtle-soup (Shell and Tortoise, to be sure, but still turtle-soup); while the wines were supplied by the well-known firm of 'Wintle & Co.' Jawleyford sank where he got it, and pretended that it had been 'ages' in his cellar: 'he really had such a stock that he thought he should never get through it'—to wit, two dozen old port at 36s. a dozen, and one dozen at 48s.; two dozen pale sherry at 36s., and one dozen brown ditto at 48s.; three bottles of Bucellas, of the 'finest quality imported,' at 38s. a dozen; Lisbon 'rich and dry,' at 32s.; and some marvellous creaming champagne at 48s., in which they were indulging when he made the declaration: 'don't wait of me, my dear Mr. Sponge!' exclaimed Jawleyford, holding up a long needle-case of a glass with the Jawleyford crests emblazoned about; 'don't wait of me, pray,' repeated he, as Spigot finished dribbling the froth into Sponge's glass; and Jawleyford, with a flourishing bow and waive of his empty needle-case, drank Mr. Sponge's very good health, adding, 'I'm *extremely* happy to see you at Jawleyford Court.'

It was then Jawleyford's turn to have a little froth; and having sucked it up with the air of a man drinking nectar, he set down his glass with a shake of the head, saying:

'There's no such wine as that to be got now-a-days.'

'Capital wine!—Excellent!' exclaimed Sponge, who was a better judge of ale than of champagne. 'Pray, where might you get it?'

'Impossible to say!—Impossible to say!' replied Jawleyford, throwing up his hands with a shake, and shrugging his shoulders. 'I have such a stock of wine as is really quite ridiculous.'

'*Quite* ridiculous,' thought Spigot, who, by the aid of a false key, had been through the cellar.

Except the 'Shell and Tortoise' and 'Wintle,' the estate supplied the repast. The carp was out of the home-pond; the tench, or whatever it was, was out of the mill-pond; the mutton was from the farm; the carrot-and-turnip-and-beet-bedaubed stewed beef was from ditto; while the garden supplied the vegetables that luxuriated in the massive silver side-dishes. Watson's gun furnished the old hare and partridges that opened the ball of the second course; and tarts, jellies, preserves, and custards made their usual appearances. Some first-growth Chateaux Margaux 'Wintle,' again at 66s., in very richly cut decanters accompanied the old 36s. port; and apples, pears, nuts, figs, preserved fruits, occupied the splendid green-and-gold dessert set. Everything, of course, was handed about—an ingenious way of tormenting a person that has 'dined.' The ladies sat long, Mrs. Jawleyford taking three glasses of port (when she could get it); and it was a quarter to eight when they rose from the table.

Jawleyford then moved an adjournment to the fire; which Sponge gladly seconded, for he had never been warm since he came into the house, the heat from the fires seeming to go up the chimneys. Spigot set them a little round table, placing the port and claret upon it, and bringing them a plate of biscuits *in lieu* of the dessert. He then reduced the illumination on the table, and extinguished such of the lamps as had not gone out of themselves. Having cast an approving glance around, and seen that they had what he considered right, he left them to their own devices.

'Do you drink port or claret, Mr. Sponge?' asked Jawleyford, preparing to push whichever he preferred over to him.

'I'll take a little port, *first*, if you please,' replied our friend—as much as to say, 'I'll finish off with claret.'

'You'll find that very good, I expect,' said Mr. Jawleyford, passing the bottle to him; 'it's '20 wine—very rare wine to get now—was a very rich fruity wine, and was a long time before it came into drinking. Connoisseurs would give any money for it.'

'It has still a good deal of body,' observed Sponge, turning off a glass and smacking his lips, at the same time holding the glass up to the candle to see the oily mark it made on the side.

'Good sound wine—good sound wine,' said Mr. Jawleyford. 'Have plenty lighter, if you like.' The light wine was made by watering the strong.

'Oh no, thank you,' replied Mr. Sponge, 'oh no, thank you. I like good strong military port.'

'So do I,' said Mr. Jawleyford, 'so do I; only unfortunately it doesn't like me—am obliged to drink claret. When I was in the Bumperkin yeomanry we drank nothing but port.' And then Jawleyford diverged into a long rambling dissertation on messes and cavalry tactics, which nearly sent Mr. Sponge asleep.

'Where did you say the hounds are to-morrow?' at length asked he, after Mr. Jawleyford had talked himself out.

'To-morrow,' repeated Mr. Jawleyford, thoughtfully, 'to-morrow—they don't hunt to-morrow—not one of their days—next day. Scrambleford Green—Scrambleford Green—no, no, I'm wrong—Dundleton Tower—Dundleton Tower.'

'How far is that from here?' asked Mr. Sponge.

'Oh, ten miles—say ten miles,' replied Mr. Jawleyford. It was sometimes ten, and sometimes fifteen, depending upon whether Mr. Jawleyford wanted the party to go or not. These elastic places, however, are common in all countries—to sight-seers as well as to hunters. 'Close by—close by,' one day. 'Oh! a lo-o-ng way from here,' another.

It is difficult, for parties who have nothing in common, to drive a conversation, especially when each keeps jibbing to get upon a private subject of his own. Jawleyford was all for sounding Sponge as to where he came from, and the situation of his property; for as yet, it must be remembered, he knew nothing of our friend, save what he had gleaned at Laverick Wells, where certainly all parties concurred in placing him high on the list of 'desirables,' while Sponge wanted to talk about hunting, the meets of the hounds, and hear what sort of a man Lord Scamperdale was. So they kept playing at cross-purposes, without either getting much out of the other. Jawleyford's intimacy with Lord Scamperdale seemed to have diminished with propinquity, for he now no longer talked of him—'Scamperdale this, and Scamperdale that—Scamperdale, with whom he could do anything he liked'; but he called him 'My Lord Scamperdale,' and spoke of him in a reverent and becoming way. Distance often lends boldness to the tongue, as the poet Campbell says it:

Lends enchantment to the view,
And robes the mountain in its azure hue.

There are few great men who haven't a dozen people, at least, who 'keep them right,' as they call it. To hear some of the creatures talk, one would fancy a lord was a lunatic as a matter of course.

Spigot at last put an end to their efforts by announcing that 'tea and coffee were ready!' just as Mr. Sponge buzzed his bottle of port. They then adjourned from the gloom of the large oak-wainscoted dining-room, to the effulgent radiance of the well-lit, highly gilt, drawing-room, where our fair friends had commenced talking Mr. Sponge over as soon as they retired from the dining-room.

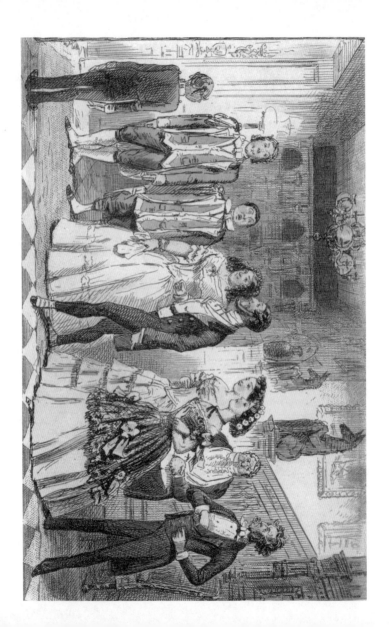

XVII

The Tea

'AND WHAT DO YOU THINK of *him*?' asked mamma.

'Oh, I think he's very well,' replied Emily gaily.

'I should say he was very *toor*-lerable,' drawled Miss Jawleyford, who reckoned herself rather a judge, and indeed had had some experience of gentlemen.

'*Tolerable*, my dear!' rejoined Mrs. Jawleyford, 'I should say he's very well—rather *distingué*, indeed.'

'I shouldn't say *that*,' replied Miss Jawleyford; 'his height and figure are certainly in his favour, but he isn't quite my idea of a gentleman. He is evidently on good terms with himself; but I should say, if it wasn't for his forwardness, he'd be awkward and uneasy.'

'He's a fox-hunter, you know,' observed Emily.

'Well, but I don't know that that should make him different to other people,' rejoined her sister. 'Captain Curzon, and Mr. Lancaster, and Mr. Preston, were all fox-hunters; but they didn't stare, and blurt, and kick their legs about, as this man does.'

'Oh, you are so fastidious!' rejoined her mamma; 'you must take men as you find them.'

'I wonder where he lives?' observed Emily, who was quite ready to take our friend as he was.

'I wonder where he *does* live?' chimed in Mrs. Jawleyford, for the suddenness of the descent had given them no time for inquiry. 'Somebody said Manchester,' observed Miss Jawleyford drily.

'So much the better,' observed Mrs. Jawleyford, 'for then he is sure to have plenty of money.'

'Law, ma! but you don't s'pose pa would ever allow such a thing,' retorted Miss, recollecting her papa's frequent exhortations to them to look high.

'If he's a landowner,' observed Mrs. Jawleyford 'we'll soon find him out in *Burke*. Emily, my dear,' added she, 'just go into your pa's room, and bring me the *Commoners*—you'll find it on the large table between the *Peerage* and the *Wellington Despatches*.'

Emily tripped away to do as she was bid. The fair messenger presently returned, bearing both volumes, richly bound and lettered, with the Jawleyford crests studded down the backs, and an immense coat of arms on the side.

A careful search among the S's produced nothing in the shape of Sponge.

'Not likely, I should think,' observed Miss Jawleyford, with a toss of her head, as her mamma announced the fact.

'Well, never mind,' replied Mrs. Jawleyford, seeing that only one of the girls could have him, and that one was quite ready; 'never mind, I dare say I shall be able to find out something from himself,' and so they dropped the subject.

In due time in swaggered our hero, himself, kicking his legs about as men in tights or tops generally do.

'May I give you tea or coffee?' asked Emily, in the sweetest tone possible, as she raised her finely turned gloveless arm towards where the glittering appendages stood on the large silver tray.

'Neither, thank you,' said Sponge, throwing himself into an easy-chair beside Mrs. Jawleyford. He then crossed his legs, and cocking up a toe for admiration, began to yawn.

'You feel tired after your journey?' observed Mrs. Jawleyford.

'No, I'm not,' said Sponge, yawning again—a good yawn this time.

Miss Jawleyford looked significantly at her sister—a long pause ensued. 'I knew a family of your name,' at length observed Mrs. Jawleyford, in the simple sort of way women begin pumping men. 'I knew a family of your name,' repeated she, seeing Sponge was half asleep—'the Sponges of Toadey Hall. Pray are they any relation of yours?'

'Oh—ah—yes,' blurted Sponge: 'I suppose they are. The fact is—the—haw—Sponges—haw—are a rather large family—haw. Meet them almost everywhere.'

'You don't live in the same county, perhaps?' observed Mrs. Jawleyford.

'No, we don't,' replied he, with a yawn.

'Is yours a good hunting country?' asked Jawleyford, thinking to sound him in another way.

'No; a devilish bad 'un,' replied Sponge, adding with a grunt, 'or I wouldn't be here.'

'Who hunts it?' asked Mr. Jawleyford.

'Why, as to that—haw,'—replied Sponge, stretching out his arms and legs to their fullest extent, and yawning most vigorously—'why, as to that, I can hardly say which you would call my country, for I have to do with so many; but I should say, of all the countries I am—haw—connected with—haw—Tom Scratch's is the worst.'

Mr. Jawleyford looked at Mrs. Jawleyford as a counsel who thinks he has made a grand hit looks at a jury before he sits down, and said no more.

Mrs. Jawleyford looked as innocent as most jurymen do after one of these forensic exploits.—Mr. Sponge beginning his nasal recreations, Mrs. Jawleyford motioned the ladies off to bed—Mr. Sponge and his host presently followed.

XVIII

THE EVENING'S REFLECTIONS

'WELL, I THINK HE'LL DO,' said our friend to himself, as having reached his bedroom, in accordance with modern fashion, he applied a cedar match to the now somewhat better burnt-up fire, for the purpose of lighting a cigar—a cigar! in the state-bedroom of Jawleyford Court. Having divested himself of his smart blue coat and white waistcoat, and arrayed himself in a grey dressing-gown, he adjusted the loose cushions of a recumbent chair, and soused himself into its luxurious depths for a 'think over.'

'He has money,' mused Sponge, between the copious whiffs of the cigar, 'splendid style he lives in, to be sure' (puff), continued he, after another long draw, as he adjusted the ash at the end of the cigar. 'Two men in livery' (puff), 'one out, can't be done for nothing' (puff). 'What a profusion of plate, too!' (whiff)—'declare I never' (puff) 'saw such' (whiff, puff) 'magnificence in the whole course of my' (whiff, puff) 'life.'

The cigar being then well under way, he sucked and puffed and whiffed in an apparently vacant stupor, his legs crossed, and his eyes fixed on a projecting coal between the lower bars, as if intent on watching the alternations of flame and gas; though in reality he was running all the circumstances through his mind, comparing them with his past experience, and speculating on the probable result of the present adventure.

He had seen a good deal of service in the matrimonial wars, and was entitled to as many bars as the most distinguished peninsular veteran. No woman with money, or the reputation of it, ever wanted an offer while he was in the way, for he would accommodate her at the second or third interview: and always pressed for an immediate fulfilment, lest the 'cursed lawyers' should interfere and interrupt their felicity. Somehow or other, the 'cursed lawyers' always had interfered; and as sure as they walked in, Mr. Sponge walked out. He couldn't bear the idea of their coarse, inquisitive inquiries. He was too much of a gentleman!

> Love, light as air, at sight of human ties
> Spreads his light wings and in a moment flies.

So Mr. Sponge fled, consoling himself with the reflection that there was no harm done, and hoping for 'better luck next time.'

He roved from flower to flower like a butterfly, touching here, alighting there, but always passing away with apparent indifference. He knew if he couldn't square matters at short notice, he would have no better chance with an extension of time; so, if he saw things taking the direction of inquiry he would just laugh the offer off, pretend he was only feeling his way—saw he was not acceptable—sorry for it—and away he would go to somebody else. He looked upon a woman much in the light of a horse; if she didn't suit one man, she would another, and there was no harm in trying. So he puffed and smoked, and smoked and puffed—gliding gradually into wealth and prosperity.

A second cigar assisted his comprehension considerably—just as a second bottle of wine not only helps men through their difficulties, but shows them the way to unbounded wealth. Many of the bright railway schemes of former days, we make no doubt, were concocted under the inspiring influence of the bottle. Sponge now saw everything as he wished. All the errors of his former days were apparent to him. He saw how indiscreet it was confiding in Miss Trickery's cousin, the major; why the rich widow at Chesterfield had *chasséed* him; and how he was done out of the beautiful Miss Rainbow, with her beautiful estate, with its lake, its heronry, and its perpetual advowson. Other mishaps he also considered.

Having disposed of the past, he then turned his attention to the future. Here were two beautiful girls apparently full of money, between whom there wasn't the toss-up of a halfpenny for choice. Most exemplary parents, too, who didn't seem to care a farthing about money.

He then began speculating on what the girls would have. 'Great house—great establishment—great estate, doubtless. Why, confound it,' continued he, casting his heavy eye lazily around, 'here's a room as big as a field in a cramped country! Can't have less than fifty thousand a-piece, I should say, at the least. Jawleyford, to be sure, is young,' thought he; 'may live a long time' (puff). 'If Mrs. J. were to die (Curse—the cigar's burnt my lips'), added he, throwing the remnant into the fire, and rolling out of the chair to prepare for turning into bed.

If any one had told Sponge that there was a rich papa and mamma on the look-out merely for amiable young men to bestow their fair daughters upon, he would have laughed them to scorn, and said, 'Why, you fool, they are only laughing at you'; or 'Don't you see they are playing you off against somebody else?' But our hero, like other men, was blind where he himself was concerned, and concluded that he was the exception to the general rule.

Mr. and Mrs. Jawleyford had their consultation too.

'Well,' said Mr. Jawleyford, seating himself on the high wire fender immediately below a marble bust of himself on the mantelpiece; 'I think he'll do.'

'Oh, no doubt,' replied Mrs. Jawleyford, who never saw any difficulty in the way of a match; 'I should say he is a very nice young man,' continued she.

'Rather brusque in his manner, perhaps,' observed Jawleyford, who was quite the 'lady' himself. 'I wonder what he was?' added he, fingering away at his whiskers.

'He's rich, I've no doubt,' replied Mrs. Jawleyford.

'What makes you think so?' asked her loving spouse.

'I don't know,' replied Mrs. Jawleyford; 'somehow I feel certain he is—but I can't tell why—all fox-hunters are.'

'I don't know that,' replied Jawleyford, who knew some very poor ones. 'I should like to know what he has,' continued Jawleyford musingly, looking up at the deeply corniced ceiling as if he were calculating the chances among the filagree ornaments of the centre.

'A hundred thousand, perhaps,' suggested Mrs. Jawleyford, who only knew two sums—fifty and a hundred thousand.

'That's a vast amount of money,' replied Jawleyford, with a slight shake of the head.

'Fifty at least, then,' suggested Mrs. Jawleyford, coming down half-way at once.

'Well, if he has that, he'll do,' rejoined Jawleyford, who also had come down considerably in his expectations since the vision of his railway days, at whose bright light he had burnt his fingers.

'He was said to have an immense fortune—I forget how much—at Laverick Wells,' observed Mrs. Jawleyford.

'Well, we'll see,' said Jawleyford, adding, 'I suppose either of the girls will be glad enough to take him?'

'Trust them for that,' replied Mrs. Jawleyford, with a knowing smile and nod of the head: 'trust them for that,' repeated she. 'Though Amelia does turn up her nose and pretend to be fine, rely upon it she only wants to be sure that he's worth having.'

'Emily seems ready enough, at all events,' observed Jawleyford.

'She'll never get the chance,' observed Mrs. Jawleyford. 'Amelia is a very prudent girl, and won't commit herself, but she knows how to manage the men.'

'Well, then,' said Jawleyford, with a hearty yawn, 'I suppose we may as well go to bed.'

So saying, he took his candle and retired.

XIX

The Wet Day

When the dirty slip-shod housemaid came in the morning with her blacksmith's-looking tool-box to light Mr. Sponge's fire, a riotous winter's day was in the full swing of its gloomy, deluging power. The wind howled, and roared, and whistled, and shrieked, playing a sort of æolian harp amongst the towers, pinnacles, and irregular castleisations of the house; while the old casements rattled and shook, as though some one were trying to knock them in.

'Hang the day!' muttered Sponge from beneath the bedclothes. 'What the deuce is a man to do with himself on such a day as this, in the country?' thinking how much better he would be flattening his nose against the coffee-room window of the Bantam, or strolling through the horse-dealers' stables in Piccadilly or Oxford Street.

Presently the overnight chair before the fire, with the picture of Jawleyford in the Bumperkin yeomanry, as seen through the parted curtains of the spacious bed, recalled his overnight speculations, and he began to think that perhaps he was just as well where he was. He then 'backed' his ideas to where he had left off, and again began speculating on the chances of his position. 'Deuced fine girls,' said he, 'both of 'em: wonder what he'll give 'em down?'—recurring to his overnight speculations, and hitting upon the point at which he had burnt his lips with the end of the cigar—namely, Jawleyford's youth, and the possibility of his marrying again if Mrs. Jawleyford were to die. 'It won't do to raise up difficulties for one's self, however,' mused he; so, kicking off the bedclothes, he raised himself instead, and making for a window, began to gaze upon his expectant territory.

It was a terrible day; the ragged, spongy clouds drifted heavily along, and the lowering gloom was only enlivened by the occasional driving rush of the tempest. Earth and sky were pretty much the same grey, damp, disagreeable hue.

'Well,' said Sponge to himself, having gazed sufficiently on the uninviting landscape, 'it's just as well it's not a hunting day—should have got terribly soused. Must get through the time as well as I can—girls to talk to—house to see. Hope I've brought my *Mogg*,' added he, turning to his portmanteau, and diving for his *Ten Thousand Cab Fares*. Having found the invaluable volume, his almost constant study, he then proceeded to array himself in what he considered the most captivating apparel; a new wide-sleeved dock-tail coatee, with outside pockets placed very low, faultless drab trousers, a buff waistcoat, with a cream-coloured once-round silk tie, secured by red cornelian cross-bars set in gold, for a pin. Thus attired, with *Mogg* in his pocket, he swaggered down to the breakfast-room, which he hit off by means of listening at the doors till he heard the sound of voices within.

Mrs. Jawleyford and the young ladies were all smiles and smirks, and there were no symptoms of Miss Jawleyford's *hauteur* perceptible. They all came forward and shook hands with our friend most cordially. Mr. Jawleyford, too, was all flourish and compliment; now tilting at the weather, now congratulating himself upon having secured Mr. Sponge's society in the house.

That leisurely meal of protracted ease, a country-house breakfast, being at length accomplished, and the ladies having taken their departure, Mr. Jawleyford looked out on the terrace, upon which the angry rain was beating the standing water into bubbles, and observing that there was no chance of getting out, asked Mr. Sponge if he could amuse himself in the house.

'Oh yes,' replied he, 'got a book in my pocket.'

'Ah, I suppose—the *New Monthly*, perhaps?' observed Mr. Jawleyford.

'No,' replied Sponge.

'Dizzey's *Life of Bentinck*, then, I dare say,' suggested Jawleyford; adding, 'I'm reading it myself.'

'No, nor that either,' replied Sponge, with a knowing look; 'a much more useful work, I assure you,' added he, pulling the little purple-backed volume out of his pocket, and reading the gilt letters on the back: '*Mogg's Ten Thousand Cab Fares*. Price one shilling!'

'Indeed,' exclaimed Mr. Jawleyford, 'well, I should never have guessed that.'

'I dare say not,' replied Sponge, 'I dare say not, it's a book I never travel without. It's invaluable in town, and you may study it to great advantage in the country. With *Mogg* in my hand, I can almost fancy myself in both places at once. Omnibus guide,' added he, turning over the leaves, and reading, 'Acton five, from the end of Oxford Street and the Edger Road—see Ealing; Edmonton seven, from Shoreditch Church—"Green Man and Still" Oxford Street—Shepherd's Bush and Starch Green, Bank, and Whitechapel—Tooting—Totteridge— Wandsworth; in short, every place near town. Then the cab fares are truly invaluable; you have ten thousand of them here,' said he, tapping the book, 'and you may calculate as many more for yourself as ever you like. Nothing to do but sit in an arm-chair on a wet day like this, and say, If from the Mile End turnpike to the "Castle" on the Kingsland Road is so much, how much should it be to the "Yorkshire Stingo," or Pine-Apple-Place, Maida Vale? And you measure by other fares till you get as near the place you want as you can, if it isn't set down in black and white to your hand in the book.'

'Just so,' said Jawleyford, 'just so. It must be a very useful work indeed, very useful work. I'll get one—I'll get one. How much did you say it was—a guinea? a guinea?'

'A shilling,' replied Sponge, adding, 'you may have mine for a guinea if you like.'

'By Jove, what a day it is!' observed Jawleyford, turning the conversation, as the wind dashed the hard sleet against the window like a shower of pebbles. 'Lucky to have a good house over one's head, in such weather; and, by the way, that reminds me, I'll show you my new gallery and collection of curiosities—pictures, busts, marbles, antiques, and so on; there'll be fires on, and we shall be just as well there as here.' So saying, Jawleyford led the way through a dark, intricate, shabby passage, to where a much-gilded white door, with a handsome crimson curtain over it, announced the entrance to something better. 'Now,' said Mr. Jawleyford, bowing as he threw open the door, and motioned, or rather flourished, his guest to enter—'now,' said he, 'you shall see what you shall see.'

Mr. Sponge entered accordingly, and found himself at the end of a gallery fifty feet by twenty, and fourteen high, lighted by skylights and small windows round the top. There were fires in handsome Caen-stone chimney-pieced fireplaces on either side, a large timepiece and an organ at the far end, and sundry white basins scattered about, catching the drops from the skylights.

'Hang the rain!' exclaimed Jawleyford, as he saw it trickling over a river scene of Van Goyen's (gentlemen in a yacht, and figures in boats), and drip, drip, dripping on to the head of an infant Bacchus below.

'He wants an umbrella, that young gentleman,' observed Sponge, as Jawleyford proceeded to dry him with his handkerchief.

'Fine thing,' observed Jawleyford, starting off to a side, and pointing to it; 'fine thing—Italian marble—by Frère—cost a vast sum of money—was offered three hundred for it. Are you a judge of these things?' asked Jawleyford; 'are you a judge of these things?'

'A little,' replied Sponge, 'a little'; thinking he might as well see what his intended father-in-law's personal property was like.

'There's a beautiful thing!' observed Jawleyford, pointing to another group. 'I picked that up for a mere nothing—twenty guineas—worth two hundred at least. Lipsalve, the great picture-dealer in Gammon Passage, offered me Murillo's "Adoration of the Virgin and Shepherds," for which he showed me a receipt for a hundred and eighty-five, for it.'

'Indeed!' replied Sponge, 'what is it?'

'It's a Bacchanal group, after Poussin, sculptured by Marin. I bought it at Lord Breakdown's sale; it happened to be a wet day—much such a day as this—and things went for nothing. This you'll know, I presume?' observed Jawleyford, laying his hand on a life-size bust of Diana, in Italian marble.

'No, I don't,' replied Sponge.

'No!' exclaimed Jawleyford; 'I thought everybody had known this: this is my celebrated "Diana," by Noindon—one of the finest things in the world. Louis Philippe sent an agent over to this country expressly to buy it.'

'Why didn't you sell it him?' asked Sponge.

'Didn't want the money,' replied Jawleyford, 'didn't want the money. In addition to which, though a king, he was a bit of a screw, and we couldn't agree upon terms. This,' observed Jawleyford, 'is a vase of the

Cinque Cento period—a very fine thing; and this,' laying his hand on the crown of a much frizzed, barber's-window-looking bust, 'of course you know?'

'No, I don't,' replied Sponge.

'No!' exclaimed Jawleyford, in astonishment.

'No,' repeated Sponge.

'Look again, my dear fellow; you *must* know it,' observed Jawleyford.

'I suppose it's meant for you,' at last replied Sponge, seeing his host's anxiety.

'*Meant*! my dear fellow; why, don't you think it like?'

'Why, there's a resemblance, certainly,' said Sponge, 'now that one knows. But I shouldn't have guessed it was you.'

'Oh, my dear Mr. Sponge!' exclaimed Jawleyford, in a tone of mortification, 'Do you *really* mean to say you don't think it like?'

'Why, yes, it's like,' replied Sponge, seeing which way his host wanted it; 'it's like, certainly; the want of expression in the eye makes such a difference between a bust and a picture.'

'True,' replied Jawleyford, comforted—'true,' repeated he, looking affectionately at it; 'I should say it was very like—like as anything can be. You are rather too much above it there, you see; sit down here,' continued he, leading Sponge to an ottoman surrounding a huge model of the column in the Place Vendome, that stood in the middle of the room—'sit down here now, and look, and say if you don't think it like?'

'Oh, *very* like,' replied Sponge, as soon as he had seated himself. 'I see it now, directly; the mouth is yours to a T.'

'And the chin. It's my chin, isn't it?' asked Jawleyford.

'Yes; and the nose, and the forehead, and the whiskers, and the hair, and the shape of the head, and everything. Oh! I see it now as plain as a pikestaff,' observed Sponge.

'I thought you would,' rejoined Jawleyford comforted—'I thought you would; it's generally considered an excellent likeness—so it should, indeed, for it cost a vast amount of money—fifty guineas! to say nothing of the lotus-leafed pedestal it's on. That's another of me,' continued Jawleyford, pointing to a bust above the fireplace, on the opposite side of the gallery; 'done some years since—ten or twelve, at least—not so like as this, but still like. That portrait up there, just above the "Finding of Moses," by Poussin,' pointing to a portrait of himself attitudinizing, with his hand on his hip, and frock-coat well thrown back, so as to show his figure and the silk lining to advantage, 'was done the other day, by a very rising young artist; though he has hardly done me justice, perhaps—particularly in the nose, which he's made far too thick and heavy; and the right hand, if anything, is rather clumsy; otherwise the colouring is good, and there is a considerable deal of taste in the arrangement of the background, and so on.'

'What book is it you are pointing to?' asked Sponge.

'It's not a book,' replied Mr. Jawleyford, 'it's a plan—a plan of this gallery, in fact. I am supposed to be giving the final order for the erection of the very edifice we are now in.'

'And a very handsome building it is,' observed Sponge, thinking he would make it a shooting-gallery when he got it.

'Yes, it's a handsome thing in its way,' assented Jawleyford; 'better if it had been water-tight, perhaps,' added he, as a big drop splashed upon the crown of his head.

'The contents must be very valuable,' observed Sponge.

'Very valuable,' replied Jawleyford. 'There's a thing I gave two hundred and fifty guineas for—that vase. It's of Parian marble, of the Cinque Cento period, beautifully sculptured in a dance of Bacchanals, arabesques, and chimera figures; it was considered cheap. Those fine monkeys in Dresden china, playing on musical instruments, were forty; those bronzes of scaramouches on ormolu plinths were seventy; that ormolu clock, of the style of Louis Quinze, by Le Roy, was eighty; those Sèvres vases were a hundred—mounted, you see, in ormolu, with lily candelabra for ten lights. The handles,' continued he, drawing Sponge's attention to them, 'are very handsome—composed of satyrs holding festoons of grapes and flowers, which surround the neck of the vase; on the sides are pastoral subjects, painted in the highest style—nothing can be more beautiful or more chaste.'

'Nothing,' assented Sponge.

'The pictures I should think are most valuable,' observed Jawleyford. 'My friend Lord Sparklebury said to me the last time he was here—he's now in Italy, increasing his collection—"Jawleyford, old boy," said he, for we are very intimate—just like brothers, in fact; "Jawleyford, old boy, I wonder whether your collection or mine would fetch most money, if they were Christie-&-Manson'd." "Oh, your lordship," said I, "your Guidos, and Ostades, and Poussins, and Velasquez, are not to be surpassed." "True," replied his lordship, "they are fine—very fine; but you have the Murillos. I'd like to give you a good round sum," added he, "to pick out half-a-dozen pictures out of your gallery." Do you understand pictures?' continued Jawleyford, turning short on his friend Sponge.

'A little,' replied Sponge, in a tone that might mean either yes or no—a great deal or nothing at all.

Jawleyford then took him and worked him through his collection—talked of light and shade, and tone, and depth of colouring, tints, and pencillings; and put Sponge here and there and everywhere to catch the light (or rain, as the case might be); made him convert his hand into an opera-glass, and occasionally put his head between his legs to get an upside-down view—a feat that Sponge's equestrian experience made him pretty well up to. So they looked, and admired, and criticized, till Spigot's all-important figure came looming up the gallery and announced that luncheon was ready.

'Bless me!' exclaimed Jawleyford, pulling a most diminutive Geneva watch, hung with pencils, pistol-keys, and other curiosities, out of his pocket; 'Bless me, who'd have thought it? One o'clock, I declare! Well, if this doesn't prove the value of a gallery on a wet day. I don't know what does. However,' said he, 'we must tear ourselves away for the present, and go and see what the ladies are about.'

If ever a man may be excused for indulging in luncheon, it certainly is on a pouring wet day (when he eats for occupation), or when he is making love; both which excuses Mr. Sponge had to offer, so he just sat down and ate as heartily as the best of the party, not excepting his host himself, who was an excellent hand at luncheon.

Jawleyford tried to get him back to the gallery after luncheon, but a look from his wife intimated that Sponge was wanted elsewhere, so he quietly saw him carried off to the music-room; and presently the notes of the 'grand piano,' and full clear voices of his daughters, echoing along the passage, intimated that they were trying what effect music would have upon him.

When Mrs. Jawleyford looked in about an hour after, she found Mr. Sponge sitting over the fire with his *Mogg* in his hand, and the young ladies with their laps full of company-work, keeping up a sort of crossfire of conversation in the shape of question and answer. Mrs. Jawleyford's company making matters worse, they soon became tediously agreeable.

In course of time, Jawleyford entered the room, with:

'My dear Mr. Sponge, your groom has come up to know about your horse to-morrow. I told him it was utterly impossible to think of hunting, but he says he must have his orders from you. I should say,' added Jawleyford, 'it is *quite* out of the question—madness to think of it; much better in the house, in such weather.'

'I don't know that,' replied Sponge, 'the rain's come down, and though the country will ride heavy, I don't see why we shouldn't have sport after it.'

'But the glass is falling, and the wind's gone round the wrong way; the moon changed this morning—everything, in short, indicates continued wet,' replied Jawleyford. 'The rivers are all swollen, and the low grounds under water; besides, my dear fellow, consider the distance—consider the distance; sixteen miles, if it's a yard.'

'What, Dundleton Tower!' exclaimed Sponge, recollecting that Jawleyford had said it was only ten the night before.

'Sixteen miles, and bad road,' replied Jawleyford.

'The deuce it is!' muttered Sponge; adding, 'Well, I'll go and see my groom, at all events.' So saying, he rang the bell as if the house was his own, and desired Spigot to show him the way to his servant.

Leather, of course, was in the servants' hall, refreshing himself with cold meat and ale, after his ride up from Lucksford.

Finding that he had ridden the hack up, he desired Leather to leave him there. 'Tell the groom I *must* have him put up,' said Sponge; 'and you ride the chestnut on in the morning. How far is it to Dundleton Tower?' asked he.

'Twelve or thirteen miles, they say, from here,' replied Leather; 'nine or ten from Lucksford.'

'Well, that'll do,' said Sponge; 'you tell the groom here to have the hack saddled for me at nine o'clock, and you ride Multum in Parvo quietly on, either to the meet or till I overtake you.'

'But how am I to get back to Lucksford?' asked Leather, cocking up a foot to show how thinly he was shod.

'Oh, just as you can,' replied Sponge; 'get the groom here to set you down with his master's hacks. I dare say they haven't been out to-day, and it'll do them good.'

So saying, Mr. Sponge left his valuable servant to do the best he could for himself.

Having returned to the music-room, with the aid of an old county map, Mr. Sponge proceeded to trace his way to Dundleton Tower; aided, or rather retarded, by Mr. Jawleyford, who kept pointing out all sorts of difficulties, till, if Mr. Sponge had followed his advice, he would have made eighteen or twenty miles of the distance. Sponge, however, being used to scramble about strange countries, saw the place was to be accomplished in ten or eleven. Jawleyford was sure he would lose himself, and Sponge was equally confident that he wouldn't.

At length the glad sound of the gong put an end to all further argument; and the inmates of Jawleyford Court retired, candle in hand, to their respective apartments, to adorn for a repetition of the yesterday's spread, with the addition of the Rev. Mr. Hobanob's company, to say grace, and praise the 'Wintle.'

An appetiteless dinner was succeeded by tea and music, as before.

The three elegant French clocks in the drawing-room being at variance, one being three-quarters of an hour before the slowest, and twenty minutes before the next, Mr. Hobanob (much to the horror of Jawleyford) having nearly fallen asleep with his Sèvres coffee-cup in his hand, at last drew up his great silver watch by its jack-chain, and finding it was a quarter past ten, prepared to decamp—taking as affectionate a leave of the ladies as if he had been going to China. He was followed by Mr. Jawleyford, to see him pocket his pumps, and also by Mr. Sponge, to see what sort of a night it was.

The sky was clear, stars sparkled in the firmament, and a young crescent moon shone with silvery brightness o'er the scene.

'That'll do,' said Sponge, as he eyed it; 'no haze there. Come,' added he to his papa-in-law, as Hobanob's steps died out on the terrace, 'you'd better go to-morrow.'

'Can't,' replied Jawleyford; 'go next day, perhaps—Scrambleford Green—better place—much. You may lock up,' said he, turning to Spigot, who, with both footmen, was in attendance to see Mr. Hobanob off; 'you may lock up, and tell the cook to have breakfast ready at nine precisely.'

'Oh, never mind about breakfast for me,' interposed Sponge, 'I'll have some tea or coffee and chops, or boiled ham and eggs, or whatever's going, in my bedroom,' said he; 'so never mind altering your hour for me.'

'Oh, but my dear fellow, we'll all breakfast together,' (Jawleyford had no notion of standing two breakfasts), 'we'll all breakfast together,' said he; 'no trouble, I assure you—rather the contrary. Say half-past eight— half-past eight. Spigot! to a minute, mind.'

And Sponge, seeing there was no help for it, bid the ladies good night, and tumbled off to bed with little expectation of punctuality.

XX

THE F.H.H.

NOR WAS SPONGE WRONG IN his conjecture, for it was a quarter to nine ere Spigot appeared with the massive silver urn, followed by the train-band bold, bearing the heavy implements of breakfast. Then, though the young ladies were punctual, smiling, and affable as usual, Mrs. Jawleyford was absent, and she had the keys; so it was nearly nine before Mr. Sponge got his fork into his first mutton chop. Jawleyford was not exactly pleased; he thought it didn't look well for a young man to prefer hunting to the society of his lovely and accomplished daughters. Hunting was all very well occasionally, but it did not do to make a business of it. This, however, he kept to himself.

'You'll have a fine day, my dear Mr. Sponge,' said he, extending a hand, as he found our friend brown-booted and red-coated, working away at the breakfast.

'Yes,' said Sponge, munching away for hard life. In less than ten minutes, he managed to get as much down as, with the aid of a knotch of bread that he pocketed, he thought would last him through the day; and, with a hasty *adieu*, he hurried off to find the stables, to get his hack. The piebald was saddled, bridled, and turned round in the stall; for all servants that are worth anything like to further hunting operations. With the aid of the groom's instructions, who accompanied him out of the courtyard, Sponge was enabled to set off at a hard canter, cheered by the groom's observation, that 'he thought he would be there in time.' On, on he went; now speculating on a turn; now pulling a scratch map he had made on a bit of paper out of his waistcoat-pocket; now inquiring the name of any place he saw of any person he met. So he proceeded for five or six miles without much difficulty; the road, though not all turnpike, being mainly over good sound township ones, it was at the village of Swineley, with its chubby-towered church and miserable hut-like cottages, that his troubles were to begin. He had two sharp turns to make—to ride through a straw-yard, and leap over a broken-down wall at the corner of a cottage—to get into Swaithing Green Lane, and so cut off an angle of two miles. The road then became a bridle one, and was, like all bridle ones, very plain to those who know them, and very puzzling to those who don't. It was evidently a little-frequented road; and what with looking out for footmarks (now nearly obliterated by the recent rains) and speculating on what queer corners of the fields the gates would be in, Mr. Sponge found it necessary to reduce his pace to a very moderate trot. Still he had made good way; and supposing they gave a quarter-of-an-hour's law, and he had not been deceived as to distance, he thought he should get to the meet about the time. His horse, too, would be there, and perhaps Lord Scamperdale might give a little extra law on that account. He then began speculating on what sort of a man his lordship was, and the probable nature of his reception. He began to wish that Jawleyford had accompanied him, to introduce him. Not that Sponge was shy, but still he thought that Jawleyford's presence would do him good.

Lord Scamperdale's hunt was not the most polished in the world. The hounds and the horses were a good deal better bred than the men. Of course his lordship gave the *tone* to the whole; and being a coarse, broad, barge-built sort of man, he had his clothes to correspond, and looked like a drayman in scarlet. He wore a great round flat-brimmed hat, which being adopted by the hunt generally, procured it the name of the 'F.H.H.,' or 'Flat Hat Hunt.' Our readers, we dare say, have noticed it figuring away, in the list of hounds during the winter, along with the 'H.H.s,' 'V.W.H.s,' and other initialized packs. His lordship's clothes were of the large, roomy, baggy, abundant order, with great pockets, great buttons, and lots of strings flying out. Instead of tops, he sported leather leggings, which at a distance gave him the appearance of riding with his trousers up to his knees. These the hunt too adopted; and his 'particular,' Jack (Jack Spraggon), the man whom he mounted, and who was made much in his own mould, sported, like his patron, a pair of great broad-rimmed, tortoise-shell spectacles of considerable power. Jack was always at his lordship's elbow; and it was 'Jack' this, 'Jack' that, 'Jack' something, all day long. But we must return to Mr. Sponge, whom we left working his way through the intricate fields. At last he got through them, and into Red Pool Common, which, by leaving the windmill to the right, he cleared pretty cleverly, and entered upon a district still wilder and drearier than any he had traversed. Peewits screamed and hovered over land that seemed to grow little but rushes and water-grasses, with occasional heather. The ground poached and splashed as he went; worst of all, time was nearly up.

In vain Sponge strained his eyes in search of Dundleton Tower. In vain he fancied every high, sky-line-breaking place in the distance was the much-wished-for spot. Dundleton Tower was no more a tower than it was a town, and would seem to have been christened by the rule of contrary, for it was nothing but a great flat open space, without object or incident to note it.

Sponge, however, was not destined to see it.

As he went floundering along through an apparently interminable and almost bottomless lane, whose sunken places and deep ruts were filled with clayey water, which played the very deuce with the cords and brown boots, the light note of a hound fell on his ear, and almost at the same instant, a something that he would have taken for a dog had it not been for the note of the hound, turned, as it were, from him, and went in a contrary direction.

Sponge reined in the piebald, and stood transfixed. It was, indeed, the fox!—a magnificent full-brushed fellow, with a slight tendency to grey along the back, and going with the light spiry ease of an animal full of strength and running.

'I wish I mayn't ketch it,' said Sponge to himself, shuddering at the idea of having headed him.

It was, however, no time for thinking. The cry of hounds became more distinct—nearer and nearer they came, fuller and more melodious; but, alas! it was no music to Sponge. Presently the cheering of hunters was heard—'For—rard! For—rard!' and anon the rate of a whip farther back. Another second, and hounds, horses, and men were in view, streaming away over the large pasture on the left.

There was a high, straggling fence between Sponge and the field, thick enough to prevent their identifying him, but not sufficiently high to screen him altogether. Sponge pulled round the piebald, and gathered himself together like a man going to be shot. The hounds came tearing in full cry to where he was; there was a breast-high scent, and every one seemed to have it. They charged the fence at a wattled pace a few yards below where he sat, and flying across the deep dirty lane, dashed full cry into the pasture beyond.

'Hie back!' cried Sponge. 'Hie back!' trying to turn them; but instead of the piebald carrying him in front of the pack, as Sponge wanted, he took to rearing, and plunging, and pawing the air. The hounds meanwhile dashed jealously on without a scent, till first one and then another feeling ashamed, gave in; and at last a general lull succeeded the recent joyous cry. Awful period! terrible to any one, but dreadful to a stranger! Though Sponge was in the road, he well knew that no one has any business anywhere but with hounds, when a fox is astir.

'Hold hard!' was now the cry, and the perspiring riders and lathered steeds came to a standstill.

'Twang—twang—twang,' went a shrill horn; and a couple of whips, singling themselves out from the field, flew over the fence to where the hounds were casting.

'Twang—twang—twang,' went the horn again.

Meanwhile Sponge sat enjoying the following observations, which a westerly wind wafted into his ear.

'Oh, d—n me! that man in the lane's headed the fox,' puffed one.

'Who is it?' gasped another.

'Tom Washball!' exclaimed a third.

'Heads more foxes than any man in the country,' puffed a fourth.

'Always nicking and skirting,' exclaimed a fifth.

'Never comes to the meet,' added a sixth.

'Come on a cow to-day,' observed another.

'Always chopping and changing,' added another; 'he'll come on a giraffe next.'

Having commenced his career with the 'F.H.H.' so inauspiciously and yet escaped detection, Mr. Sponge thought of letting Tom Washball enjoy the honours of his *faux-pas*, and of sneaking quietly home as soon as the hounds hit off the scent; but unluckily, just as they were crossing the lane, what should heave in sight, cantering along at his leisure, but the redoubtable Multum in Parvo, who, having got rid of old Leather by bumping and thumping his leg against a gate-post, was enjoying a line of his own.

'Whoay!' cried Sponge, as he saw the horse quickening his pace to have a shy at the hounds as they crossed. 'Who—o—a—y!' roared he, brandishing his whip, and trying to turn the piebald round; but no, the brute wouldn't answer the bit, and dreading lest, in addition to heading the fox, he should kill 'the best hound in the pack,' Mr. Sponge threw himself off, regardless of the mud-bath in which he lit, and caught the runaway as he tried to dart past.

'For-rard!—for-rard!—for-rard!' was again the cry, as the hounds hit off the scent; while the late pausing, panting sportsmen tackled vigorously with their steeds, and swept onward like the careering wind.

Mr. Sponge, albeit somewhat perplexed, had still sufficient presence of mind to see the necessity of immediate action; and though he had so lately contemplated beating a retreat, the unexpected appearance of Parvo altered the state of affairs.

'Now or never,' said he, looking first at the disappearing field, and then for the non-appearing Leather. 'Hang it! I may as well see the run,' added he; so hooking the piebald on to an old stone gate-post that stood in the ragged fence, and lengthening a stirrup-leather, he vaulted into the saddle, and began lengthening the other as he went.

It was one of Parvo's going days; indeed, it was that that old Leather and he had quarrelled about—Parvo wanting to follow the hounds, while Leather wanted to wait for his master. And Parvo had the knack of going, as well as the occasional inclination. Although such a drayhorse-looking animal, he could throw the ground behind him amazingly; and the deep-holding clay in which he now found himself was admirably suited to his short, powerful legs and enormous stride. The consequence was, that he was very soon up with the hindmost horsemen. These he soon passed, and was presently among those who ride hard when there is nothing to stop them. Such time as these sportsmen could now spare from looking out ahead was devoted to Sponge, whom they eyed with the utmost astonishment, as if he had dropped from the clouds.

A stranger—a real out-and-out stranger—had not visited their remote regions since the days of poor Nimrod. 'Who could it be?' But 'the pace,' as Nimrod used to say, 'was too good to inquire.' A little farther on, and Sponge drew upon the great guns of the hunt—the men who ride *to* hounds, and not *after* them; the same who had criticized him through the fence—Mr. Wake, Mr. Fossick, Parson Blossomnose, Mr. Fyle, Lord Scamperdale, Jack himself, and others. Great was their astonishment at the apparition, and incoherent the observations they dropped as they galloped on.

'It isn't Wash, after all,' whispered Fyle into Blossomnose's ear, as they rode through a gate together.

'No-o-o,' replied the nose, eyeing Sponge intently.

'What a coat!' whispered one.

'Jacket,' replied the other.

'Lost his brush,' observed a third, winking at Sponge's docked tail.

'He's going to ride over us all,' snapped Mr. Fossick, whom Sponge passed at a hand-canter, as the former was blobbing and floundering about the deep ruts leading out of a turnip-field.

'He'll catch it just now,' said Mr. Wake, eyeing Sponge drawing upon his lordship and Jack, as they led the field as usual. Jack being at a respectful distance behind his great patron, espied Sponge first; and having taken a good stare at him through his formidable spectacles, to satisfy himself that it was nobody he knew—a stare that Sponge returned as well as a man without spectacles can return the stare of one with—Jack spurred his horse up to his lordship, and rising in his stirrups, shot into his ear—

'Why, here's the man on the cow!' adding, 'it isn't Washey.'

'Who the deuce is it then?' asked his lordship, looking over his left shoulder, as he kept galloping on in the wake of his huntsman.

'Don't know,' replied Jack; 'never saw him before.'

'Nor I,' said his lordship, with an air as much as to say, 'It makes no matter.'

His lordship, though well mounted, was not exactly on the sort of horse for the country they were in; while Mr. Sponge, in addition to being on the very animal for it, had the advantage of the horse having gone the first part of the run without a rider: so Multum in Parvo, whether Mr. Sponge wished it or not, insisted on being as far forward as he could get. The more Sponge pulled and hauled, the more determined the horse was; till, having thrown both Jack and his lordship in the rear, he made for old Frostyface, the huntsman, who was riding well up to the still-flying pack.

'HOLD HARD, sir! For God's sake, hold hard!' screamed Frosty, who knew by intuition there was a horse behind, as well as he knew there was a man shooting in front, who, in all probability, had headed the fox.

'HOLD HARD, sir!' roared he, as, yawning and boring and shaking his head, Parvo dashed through the now yelping scattered pack, making straight for a stiff new gate, which he smashed through, just as a circus pony smashes through a paper hoop.

'Hoo-ray!' shouted Jack Spraggon, on seeing the hounds were safe. 'Hoo-ray for the tailor!'

'Billy Button, himself!' exclaimed his lordship, adding, 'never saw such a thing in my life!'

'Who the deuce is he?' asked Blossomnose, in the full glow of pulling-five-year-old exertion.

'Don't know,' replied Jack, adding, 'he's a shaver, whoever he is.'

Meanwhile the frightened hounds were scattered right and left.

'I'll lay a guinea he's one of those confounded waiting chaps,' observed Fyle, who had been handled rather roughly by one of the tribe, who had dropped 'quite promiscuously' upon a field where he was, just as Sponge had done with Lord Scamperdale's.

'Shouldn't wonder,' replied his lordship, eyeing Sponge's vain endeavours to turn the chestnut, and thinking how he would 'pitch into him' when he came up. 'By Jove,' added his lordship, 'if the fellow had taken the whole country round, he couldn't have chosen a worse spot for such an exploit; for there never *is* any scent over here. See! not a hound can own it. Old Harmony herself throws up.

The whips again are in their places, turning the astonished pack to Frostyface, who sets off on a casting expedition. The field, as usual, sit looking on; some blessing Sponge; some wondering who he was; others looking what o'clock it is; some dismounting and looking at their horses' feet.

'Thank you, Mr. Brown Boots!' exclaimed his lordship, as, by dint of bitting and spurring, Sponge at length worked the beast round, and came sneaking back in the face of the whole field. 'Thank you, Mr. Brown Boots,' repeated he, taking off his hat and bowing very low. 'Very much ob*leg*ed to you, Mr. Brown Boots. Most particklarly ob*leg*ed to you, Mr. Brown Boots,' with another low bow. 'Hang'd ob*leg*ed to you,

Mr. Brown Boots! D—n you, Mr. Brown Boots!' continued his lordship, looking at Sponge as if he would eat him.

'Beg pardon, sir,' blurted Sponge; 'my horse—'

'Hang your horse!' screamed his lordship; 'it wasn't your horse that headed the fox, was it?'

'Beg pardon—couldn't help it; I—'

'Couldn't help it. Hang your helps—you're *always* doing it, sir. You could stay at home, sir—I s'pose, sir—couldn't you, sir? eh, sir?'

Sponge was silent.

'See, sir!' continued his lordship, pointing to the mute pack now following the huntsman, 'you've lost us our fox, sir—yes, sir, lost us our fox, sir. D'ye call that nothin', sir? If you don't, *I* do, you perpendicular-looking Puseyite pig-jobber! By Jove! you think because I'm a lord, and can't swear, or use coarse language, that you may do what you like—but I'll take my hounds home, sir—yes, sir, I'll take my hounds home, sir.' So saying, his lordship roared HOME to Frostyface; adding, in an undertone to the first whip, 'bid him go to Furzing-field gorse.'

XXI

A COUNTRY DINNER-PARTY

'WELL, WHAT SPORT?' ASKED JAWLEYFORD, as he encountered his exceedingly dirty friend crossing the entrance hall to his bedroom on his return from his day, or rather his non-day, with the 'Flat Hat Hunt.'

'Why, not much—that's to say, nothing particular—I mean, I've not had any,' blurted Sponge.

'But you've had a run?' observed Jawleyford, pointing to his boots and breeches, stained with the variation of each soil.

'Ah, I got most of that going to cover,' replied Sponge; 'country's awfully deep, roads abominably dirty!' adding, 'I wish I'd taken your advice, and stayed at home.'

'I wish you had,' replied Jawleyford, 'you'd have had a most excellent rabbit-pie for luncheon. However, get changed, and we will hear all about it after.' So saying, Jawleyford waved an *adieu*, and Sponge stamped away in his dirty water-logged boots.

'I'm afraid you are very wet, Mr. Sponge,' observed Amelia in the sweetest tone, with the most loving smile possible, as our friend, with three steps at a time, bounded upstairs, and nearly butted her on the landing, as she was on the point of coming down.

'I am that,' exclaimed Sponge, delighted at the greeting; 'I am that,' repeated he, slapping his much-stained cords; 'dirty, too,' added he, looking down at his nether man.

'Hadn't you better get changed as quick as possible?' asked Amelia, still keeping her position before him.

'Oh! all in good time,' replied Sponge, 'all in good time. The sight of you warms me more than a fire would do'; adding, 'I declare you look quite bewitching, after all the roughings and tumblings about out of doors.'

'Oh! you've not had a fall, have you?' exclaimed Amelia, looking the picture of despair; 'you've not had a fall, have you? Do send for the doctor, and be bled.'

Just then a door along the passage to the left opened; and Amelia, knowing pretty well who it was, smiled and tripped away, leaving Sponge to be bled or not, as he thought proper.

Our hero then made for his bedroom, where, having sucked off his adhesive boots, and divested himself of the rest of his hunting attire, he wrapped himself up in his grey flannel dressing-gown, and prepared for parboiling his legs and feet, amid agreeable anticipations arising out of the recent interview, and occasional references to his old friend *Mogg*, whenever he did not see his way on the matrimonial road as clearly as he could wish. 'She'll have me, that's certain,' observed he.

'Curse the water! how hot it is!' exclaimed he, catching his foot up out of the bath, into which he had incautiously plunged it without ascertaining the temperature of the water. He then sluiced it with cold, and next had to add a little more hot; at last he got it to his mind, and lighting a cigar, prepared for uninterrupted enjoyment.

'Gad!' said he, 'she's by no means a bad-looking girl' (whiff). 'Devilish good-looking girl' (puff); 'good head and neck, and carries it well too' (puff)—'capital eye' (whiff), 'bright and clear' (puff); 'no cataracts there. She's all good together' (whiff, puff, whiff). 'Nice size, too,' continued he, 'and well set up (whiff, puff, whiff); 'straight as a dairy maid' (puff); 'plenty of substance—grand thing, substance' (puff). 'Hate a weedy woman—fifteen two and a half—that's to say, five feet four's plenty of height for a woman' (puff). 'Height of a woman has nothing to do with her size' (whiff). 'Wish she hadn't run off (puff); 'would like to have had a little more talk with her' (whiff, puff). 'Women never look so well as when one comes in wet and dirty from hunting' (puff). He then sank silently back in the easy-chair and whiffed and puffed all sorts of fantastic clouds and columns and corkscrews at his leisure. The cigar being finished, and the water in the foot-bath beginning to get cool, he emptied the remainder of the hot into it, and lighting a fresh cigar, began speculating on how the match was to be accomplished.

The lady was safe, that was clear; he had nothing to do but 'pop.' That he would do in the evening, or in the morning, or any time—a man living in the house with a girl need never be in want of an opportunity. That preliminary over, and the usual answer 'Ask papa' obtained, then came the question, how was the old boy to be managed?—for men with marriageable daughters are to all intents and purposes 'old boys,' be their ages what they may.

He became lost in reflection. He sat with his eyes fixed on the Jawleyford portrait above the mantelpiece, wondering whether he was the amiable, liberal, hearty, disinterested sort of man he appeared to be, indifferent about money, and only wanting unexceptionable young men for his daughters; or if he was a worldly minded man, like some he had met, who, after giving him every possible encouragement, sent him to the right-about like a servant. So Sponge smoked and thought, and thought and smoked, till the water in the foot-bath again getting cold, and the shades of night drawing on, he at last started up like a man determined to awake himself, and poking a match into the fire, lighted the candles on the toilet-table, and proceeded to adorn himself. Having again got himself into the killing tights and buckled pumps, with a fine flower-fronted shirt, ere he embarked on the delicacies and difficulties of the starcher, he stirred the little pittance of a fire, and, folding himself in his dressing-gown, endeavoured to prepare his mind for the calm consideration of all the minute bearings of the question by a little more *Mogg*. In idea he transferred himself to London, now fancying himself standing at the end of Burlington Arcade, hailing a Fulham or Turnham Green 'bus; now wrangling with a conductor for charging him sixpence when there was a pennant flapping at his nose with the words "ALL THE WAY 3D." upon it; now folding the wooden doors of a hansom cab in Oxford Street, calculating the extreme distance he could go for an eightpenny fare: until at last he fell into a downright vacant sort of reading, without rhyme or reason, just as one sometimes takes a read of a directory or a dictionary—"Conduit Street, George Street, to or from the Adelphi Terrace, Astley's Amphitheatre, Baker Street, King Street, Bryanston Square any part, Covent Garden Theatre, Foundling Hospital, Hatton Garden," and so on, till the thunder of the gong aroused him to a recollection of his duties. He then up and at his neckcloth.

"Ah, well," said he, reverting to his lady love, as he eyed himself intently in the glass while performing the critical operation, "I'll just sound the old gentleman after dinner—one can do that sort of thing better over one's wine, perhaps, than at any other time: looks less formal, too," added he, giving the cravat a knowing crease at the side; "and if it doesn't seem to take, one can just pass it off as if it was done for somebody else—some young gentleman at Laverick Wells, for instance."

So saying, he on with his white waistcoat, and crowned the conquering suit with a blue coat and metal buttons. Returning his *Mogg* to his dressing-gown pocket, he blew out the candles and groped his way downstairs in the dark.

In passing the dining-room, he looked in (to see if there were any champaign-glasses set, we believe), when he saw that he should not have an opportunity of sounding his intended papa-in-law after dinner, for he found the table laid for twelve, and a great display of plate, linen, and china.

He then swaggered on to the drawing-room, which was in a blaze of light. The lively Emily had stolen a march on her sister, and had just entered, attired in a fine new pale yellow silk dress with a point-lace berthe and other adornments.

High words had ensued between the sisters as to the meanness of Amelia in trying to take her *beau* from her, especially after the airs Amelia had given herself respecting Sponge; and a minute observer might have seen the slight tinge of red on Emily's eyelids denoting the usual issue of such scenes. The result was, that each determined to do the best she could for herself; and free trade being proclaimed, Emily proceeded to dress with all expedition, calculating that, as Mr. Sponge had come in wet, he would, very likely dress at once and appear in the drawing-room in good time. Nor was she out in her reckoning, for she had hardly enjoyed an approving glance in the mirror ere our hero came swaggering in, twitching his arms as if he hadn't got his wristbands adjusted, and working his legs as if they didn't belong to him.

"Ah, my dear Miss Emley!" exclaimed he, advancing gaily towards her with extended hand, which she took with all the pleasure in the world; adding, "and how have you been?"

"Oh, pretty well, thank you," replied she, looking as though she would have said, "As well as I can be without you."

Sponge, though a consummate judge of a horse, and all the minutiae connected with them, was still rather green in the matter of woman; and having settled in his own mind that Amelia should be his choice, he concluded that Emily knew all about it, and was working on her sister's account, instead of doing the agreeable for herself. And there it is where elder sisters have such an advantage over younger ones. They are always shown, or contrive to show themselves, first; and if a man once makes up his mind that the elder one will do, there is an end of the matter; and it is neither a deeper shade or two of blue, nor a brighter tinge of brown, nor a little smaller foot, nor a more elegant waist, that will make him change for a younger sister. The younger ones immediately become sisters in the men's minds, and retire, or are retired, from the field—"scratched," as Sponge would say.

Amelia, however, was not going to give Emily a chance; for, having dressed with all the expedition compatible with an attractive toilet—a lavender-coloured satin with broad black lace flounces, and some heavy jewellery on her well-turned arms, she came sidling in so gently as almost to catch Emily in the act of playing the agreeable. Turning the sidle into a stately sail, with a haughty sort of sneer and toss of the head to her sister, as much as to say, 'What are you doing with my man?'—a sneer that suddenly changed into a sweet smile as her eye encountered Sponge's—she just motioned him off to a sofa, where she commenced a *sotto voce* conversation in the engaged-couple style.

The plot then began to thicken. First came Jawleyford, in a terrible stew.

'Well, this is too bad!' exclaimed he, stamping and flourishing a scented note, with a crest and initials at the top. 'This is too bad,' repeated he; 'people accepting invitations, and then crying off at the last moment.'

'Who is it can't come, papa—the Foozles?' asked Emily.

'No—Foozles be hanged,' sneered Jawleyford; 'they always come—*the Blossomnoses!*' replied he, with an emphasis.

'The Blossomnoses!' exclaimed both girls, clasping their hands and looking up at the ceiling.

'What, all of them?' asked Emily.

'All of them,' rejoined Jawleyford.

'Why, that's four,' observed Emily.

'To be sure it is,' replied Jawleyford; 'five, if you count them by appetites; for old Blossom always eats and drinks as much as two people.'

'What excuse do they give?' asked Amelia.

'Carriage-horse taken suddenly ill,' replied Jawleyford; 'as if that's any excuse when there are post-horses within half a dozen miles.'

'He wouldn't have been stopped hunting for want of a horse, I dare say,' observed Amelia.

'I dare say it's all a lie,' observed Jawleyford; adding, 'however, the invitation shall go for a dinner, all the same.'

The denunciation was interrupted by the appearance of Spigot, who came looming up the spacious drawing-room in the full magnificence of black shorts, silk stockings, and buckled pumps, followed by a sheepish-looking, straight-haired, red apple-faced young gentleman, whom he announced as Mr. Robert Foozle. Robert was the hope of the house of Foozle; and it was fortunate his parents were satisfied with him, for few other people were. He was a young gentleman who shook hands with everybody, assented to anything that anybody said, and in answering a question, wherein indeed his conversation chiefly consisted, he always followed the words of the interrogation as much as he could. For instance: 'Well, Robert, have you been at Dulverton to-day?' Answer, 'No, I've not been at Dulverton to-day.' Question, 'Are you going to Dulverton to-morrow?' Answer, 'No, I'm not going to Dulverton to-morrow.' Having shaken hands with the party all round, and turned to the fire to warm his red fists, Jawleyford having stood at 'attention' for such time as he thought Mrs. Foozle would be occupied before the glass in his study arranging her head-gear, and seeing no symptoms of any further announcement, at last asked Foozle if his papa and mamma were not coming.

'No, my papa and mamma are not coming,' replied he.

'Are you sure?' asked Jawleyford, in a tone of excitement.

'Quite sure,' replied Foozle, in the most matter-of-course voice.

'The deuce!' exclaimed Jawleyford, stamping his foot upon the soft rug, adding, 'it never rains but it pours!'

'Have you any note, or anything?' asked Mrs. Jawleyford, who had followed Robert Foozle into the room.

'Yes, I have a note,' replied he, diving into the inner pocket of his coat, and producing one. The note was a letter—a letter from Mrs. Foozle to Mrs. Jawleyford, three sides and crossed; and seeing the magnitude thereof, Mrs. Jawleyford quietly put it into her reticule, observing, 'that she hoped Mr. and Mrs. Foozle were well?'

'Yes, they are well,' replied Robert, notwithstanding he had express orders to say that his papa had the toothache, and his mamma the earache.

Jawleyford then gave a furious ring at the bell for dinner, and in due course of time the party of six proceeded to a table for twelve. Sponge pawned Mrs. Jawleyford off upon Robert Foozle, which gave Sponge the right to the fair Amelia, who walked off on his arm with a toss of her head at Emily, as though she thought him the finest, sprightliest man under the sun. Emily followed, and Jawleyford came sulking in alone, sore put out at the failure of what he meant for *the* grand entertainment.

Lights blazed in profusion; lamps more accustomed had now become better behaved; and the whole strength of the plate was called in requisition, sadly puzzling the unfortunate cook to find something to put upon the dishes. She, however, was a real magnanimous-minded woman, who would undertake to cook a lord mayor's feast—soups, sweets, joints, entrees, and all.

Jawleyford was nearly silent during the dinner; indeed, he was too far off for conversation, had there been any for him to join in; which was not the case, for Amelia and Sponge kept up a hum of words, while Emily worked Robert Foozle with question and answer, such as:

"Were your sisters out to-day?"

"Yes, my sisters were out to-day."

"Are your sisters going to the Christmas ball?"

"Yes, my sisters are going to the Christmas ball," &c. &c.

Still, nearly daft as Robert was, he was generally asked where there was anything going on; and more than one young la—but we will not tell about that, as he has nothing to do with our story.

By the time the ladies took their departure, Mr. Jawleyford had somewhat recovered from the annoyance of his disappointment; and as they retired he rang the bell, and desired Spigot to set in the horse-shoe table, and bring a bottle of the "green seal," being the colour affixed on the bottles of a four-dozen hamper of port ("curious old port at 48s.") that had arrived from "Wintle & Co." by rail (goods train of course) that morning.

"There!" exclaimed Jawleyford, as Spigot placed the richly cut decanter on the horse-shoe table. "There!" repeated he, drawing the green curtain as if to shade it from the fire, but in reality to hide the dullness the recent shaking had given it; "that wine," said he, "is a quarter of a century in bottle, at the very least."

'Indeed,' observed Sponge: 'time it was drunk.'

'A quarter of a century?' gaped Robert Foozle.

'Quarter of a century, if it's a day,' replied Jawleyford, smacking his lips as he set down his glass after imbibing the precious beverage.

'Very fine,' observed Sponge; adding, as he sipped off his glass, 'it's odd to find such old wine so full-bodied.'

'Well, now tell us all about your day's proceedings,' said Jawleyford, thinking it advisable to change the conversation at once. 'What sport had you with my lord?'

'Oh, why, I really can't tell you much,' drawled Sponge, with an air of bewilderment. 'Strange country—strange faces—nobody I knew, and—'

'Ah, true,' replied Jawleyford, 'true. It occurred to me after you were gone, that perhaps you might not know any one. Ours, you see, is rather an out-of-the-way country; few of our people go to town, or indeed anywhere else; they are all tarry-at-home birds. But they'd receive you with great politeness, I'm sure—if they knew you came from here, at least,' added he.

Sponge was silent, and took a great gulp of the dull 'Wintle,' to save himself from answering.

'Was my Lord Scamperdale out?' asked Jawleyford, seeing he was not going to get a reply.

'Why, I can really hardly tell you that,' replied Sponge. 'There were two men out, either of whom might be him; at least, they both seemed to take the lead, and—and—' he was going to say 'blow up the people,' but he thought he might as well keep that to himself.

'Stout, hale-looking men, dressed much alike, with great broad tortoise-shell-rimmed spectacles on?' asked Jawleyford.

'Just so,' replied Sponge.

'Ah, you are right, then,' rejoined Jawleyford; 'it would be my lord.'

'And who was the other?' inquired our friend.

'Oh, that Jack Spraggon,' replied Jawleyford, curling up his nose, as if he was going to be sick; 'one of the most odious wretches under the sun.

I really don't know any man that I have so great a dislike to, so utter a contempt for, as that Jack, as they call him.'

'What is he?' asked Sponge.

'Oh, just a hanger-on of his lordship's; the creature has nothing—nothing whatever; he lives on my lord—eats his venison, drinks his claret, rides his horses, bullies those his lordship doesn't like to tackle with, and makes himself generally useful.'

'He seems a man of that sort,' observed Sponge, as he thought over the compliment he had received.

'Well, who else had you out, then?' asked Jawleyford. 'Was Tom Washball there?'

'No,' replied Sponge: '*he* wasn't out, I know.'

'Ah, that's unfortunate,' observed Jawleyford, helping himself and passing the bottle. 'Tom's a capital fellow—a perfect gentleman—great friend of mine. If he'd been out you'd have had nothing to do but mention my name, and he'd have put you all right in a minute. Who else was there, then?' continued he.

'There was a tall man in black, on a good-looking young brown horse, rather rash at his fences, but a fine style of goer.'

'What!' exclaimed Jawleyford, 'man in drab cords and jack-boots, with the brim of his hat rather turning upwards?'

'Just so,' replied Sponge; 'and a double ribbon for a hat-string.'

'That's Master Blossomnose,' observed Jawleyford, scarcely able to contain his indignation. 'That's Master Blossomnose,' repeated he, taking a back hand at the port in the excitement of the moment. 'More to his credit if he were to stay at home and attend to his parish,' added Jawleyford; meaning, it would have been more to his credit if he had fulfilled his engagement to him that evening, instead of going out hunting in the morning.

The two then sat silent for a time, Sponge seeing where the sore place was, and Robert Foozle, as usual, seeing nothing. 'Ah, well,' observed Jawleyford, at length breaking silence, 'it was unfortunate you went this morning. I did my best to prevent you—told you what a long way it was, and so on. However, never mind, we will put all right to-morrow. His lordship, I'm sure, will be most happy to see you. So help yourself,' continued he, passing the 'Wintle,' 'and we will drink his health and success to fox-hunting.'

Sponge filled a bumper and drank his lordship's health, with the accompaniment as desired; and turning to Robert Foozle, who was doing likewise, said, 'Are you fond of hunting?'

'Yes, I'm fond of hunting,' replied Foozle.

'But you *don't* hunt, you know, Robert,' observed Jawleyford.

'No, I don't hunt,' replied Robert.

The 'green seal' being demolished, Jawleyford ordered a bottle of the 'other,' attributing the slight discoloration (which he did not discover until they had nearly finished the bottle) to change of atmosphere in the outer cellar. Sponge tackled vigorously with the new-comer, which was better than the first; and Robert Foozle, drinking as he spoke, by pattern, kept filling away, much to Jawleyford's dissatisfaction, who was compelled to order a third. During the progress of its demolition, the host's tongue became considerably loosened. He talked of hunting and the charms of the chase—of the good fellowship it produced: and expatiated on the advantages it was of to the country in a national point of view, promoting as it did a spirit of manly enterprise, and encouraging our unrivalled breed of horses; both of which he looked upon as national objects, well worthy the attention of enlightened men like himself.

Jawleyford was a great patron of the chase; and his keeper, Watson, always had a bag-fox ready to turn down when my lord's hounds met there. Jawleyford's covers were never known to be drawn blank. Though they had been shot in the day before, they always held a fox the next—if a fox was wanted.

Sponge being quite at home on the subjects of horses and hunting, lauded all his papa-in-law's observations up to the skies; occasionally considering whether it would be advisable to sell him a horse, and thinking, if he did, whether he should let him have one of the three he had down, or should get old Buckram to buy some quiet screw that would stand a little work and yield him (Sponge) a little profit, and yet not demolish the great patron of English sports. The more Jawleyford drank, the more energetic he became, and the greater pleasure he anticipated from the meet of the morrow. He docked the lord, and spoke of 'Scamperdale' as an excellent fellow—a real, good, hearty, honest Englishman—a man that 'the more you knew the more you liked'; all of which was very encouraging to Sponge. Spigot at length appeared to read the tea and coffee riot-act, when Jawleyford determined not to be done out of another bottle, pointing to the nearly emptied decanter, said to Robert Foozle, 'I suppose you'll not take any more wine?' To which Robert replied, 'No, I'll not take any more wine.' Whereupon, pushing out his chair and throwing away his napkin, Jawleyford arose and led the way to the drawing-room, followed by Sponge and this entertaining young gentleman.

A round game followed tea; which, in its turn, was succeeded by a massive silver tray, chiefly decorated with cold water and tumblers; and as the various independent clocks in the drawing-room began chiming and striking eleven, Mr. Jawleyford thought he would try to get rid of Foozle by asking him if he hadn't better stay all night.

'Yes, I think I'd better stay all night,' replied Foozle.

'But won't they be expecting you at home, Robert?' asked Jawleyford, not feeling disposed to be caught in his own trap.

'Yes, they'll be expecting me at home,' replied Foozle.

'Then, perhaps you had better not alarm them by staying,' suggested Jawleyford.

'No, perhaps I'd better not alarm them by staying,' repeated Foozle. Whereupon they all rose, and wishing him a very good night, Jawleyford handed him over to Spigot, who transferred him to one footman, who passed him to another, to button into his leather-headed shandridan.

After talking Robert over, and expatiating on the misfortune it would be to have such a boy, Jawleyford rang the bell for the banquet of water to be taken away; and ordering breakfast half-an-hour earlier than usual, our friends went to bed.

XXII

THE F.H.H. AGAIN

GENTLEMEN UNACCUSTOMED TO PUBLIC HUNTING often make queer figures of themselves when they go out. We have seen them in all sorts of odd dresses, half fox-hunters half fishermen, half fox-hunters, half sailors, with now and then a good sturdy cross of the farmer.

Mr. Jawleyford was a cross between a military dandy and a squire. The green-and-gold Bumperkin foraging-cap, with the letters 'B.Y.C.' in front, was cocked jauntily on one side of his badger-pyed head, while he played sportively with the patent leather strap—now, toying with it on his lip, now dropping it below his chin, now hitching it up on to the peak. He had a tremendously stiff stock on—so hard that no pressure made it wrinkle, and so high that his pointed gills could hardly peer above it. His coat was a bright green cut-away—made when collars were worn very high and very hollow, and when waists were supposed to be about the middle of a man's back, Jawleyford's back buttons occupying that remarkable position. These, which were of dead gold with a bright rim, represented a hare full stretch for her life, and were the buttons of the old Muggeridge hunt—a hunt that had died many years ago from want of the necessary funds (£80) to carry it on. The coat, which was single-breasted and velvet-collared, was extremely swallow-tailed, presenting a remarkable contrast to the barge-built, roomy roundabouts of the members of the Flat Hat Hunt; the collar rising behind, in the shape of a Gothic arch, exhibited all the stitchings and threadings incident to that department of the garment.

But if Mr. Jawleyford's coat went to 'hare,' his waistcoat was fox and all 'fox.' On a bright blue ground he sported such an infinity of 'heads,' that there is no saying that he would have been safe in a kennel of unsteady hounds. One thing, to be sure, was in his favour—namely, that they were just as much like cats' heads as foxes'. The coat and waistcoat were old stagers, but his nether man was encased in rhubarb-coloured tweed pantaloons of the newest make—a species of material extremely soft and comfortable to wear, but not so well adapted for roughing it across country. These had a broad brown stripe down the sides, and were shaped out over the foot of his fine French-polished paper boots, the heels of which were decorated with long-necked, ringing spurs. Thus attired, with a little silver-mounted whip which he kept flourishing about, he encountered Mr. Sponge in the entrance-hall, after breakfast. Mr. Sponge, like all men who are 'extremely natty' themselves, men who wouldn't have a button out of place if it was ever so, hardly knew what to think of Jawleyford's costume. It was clear he was no sportsman; and then came the question, whether he was of the privileged few who may do what they like, and who can carry off any kind of absurdity. Whatever uneasiness Sponge felt on that score, Jawleyford, however, was quite at his ease, and swaggered about like an *aide-de-camp* at a review.

'Well, we should be going, I suppose,' said he, drawing on a pair of half-dirty, lemon-coloured kid gloves, and sabreing the air with his whip.

'Is Lord Scamperdale punctual?' asked Sponge.

'Tol-lol,' replied Jawleyford, 'tol-lol.'

'He'll wait for *you*, I suppose?' observed Sponge, thinking to try Jawleyford on that infallible criterion of favour.

'Why, if he knew I was coming, I dare say he would,' replied Jawleyford slowly and deliberately, feeling it was now no time for flashing. 'If he knew I was coming I dare say he would,' repeated he; 'indeed, I make no doubt he would: but one doesn't like putting great men out of their way; besides which, it's just as easy to be punctual as otherwise. When I was in the Bumperkin—'

'But your horse is on, isn't it?' interrupted Sponge; 'he'll see your horse there, you know.'

'Horse on, my dear fellow!' exclaimed Jawleyford, 'horse on? No, certainly not. How should I get there myself, if my horse was on?'

'Hack, to be sure,' replied Sponge, striking a light for his cigar.

'Ah, but then I should have no groom to go with me,' observed Jawleyford, adding, 'one must make a certain appearance, you know. But come, my dear Mr. Sponge,' continued he, laying hold of our hero's arm, 'let us get to the door, for that cigar of yours will fumigate the whole house; and Mrs. Jawleyford hates the smell of tobacco.'

Spigot, with his attendants in livery, here put a stop to the confab by hurrying past, drawing the bolts, and throwing back the spacious folding doors, as if royalty or Daniel Lambert himself were 'coming out.'

The noise they made was heard outside; and on reaching the top of the spacious flight of steps, Sponge's piebald in charge of a dirty village lad, and Jawleyford's steeds with a sky-blue groom, were seen scuttling under the portico, for the owners to mount. The Jawleyford cavalry was none of the best; but Jawleyford was pleased with it, and that is a great thing. Indeed, a thing had only to be Jawleyford's, to make Jawleyford excessively fond of it.

'There!' exclaimed he, as they reached the third step from the bottom. 'There!' repeated he, seizing Sponge by the arm, 'that's what I call shape. You don't see such an animal as that every day,' pointing to a not badly formed, but evidently worn-out, over-knee'd bay, that stood knuckling and trembling for Jawleyford to mount.

'One of the "has beens," I should say,' replied Sponge, puffing a cloud of smoke right past Jawleyford's nose; adding, 'It's a pity but you could get him four new legs.'

'Faith, I don't see that he wants anything of the sort,' retorted Jawleyford, nettled as well at the smoke as the observation.

'Well, where "ignorance is bliss," &c.,' replied Sponge, with another great puff, which nearly blinded Jawleyford. 'Get on, and let's see how he goes,' added he, passing on to the piebald as he spoke.

Mr. Jawleyford then mounted; and having settled himself into a military seat, touched the old screw with the spur, and set off at a canter. The piebald, perhaps mistaking the portico for a booth, and thinking it was a good place to exhibit it, proceeded to die in the most approved form; and not all Sponge's 'Come-up's' or kicks could induce him to rise before he had gone through the whole ceremony. At length, with a mane full of gravel, a side well smeared, and a 'Wilkinson & Kidd' sadly scratched, the *ci-devant* actor arose, much to the relief of the village lad, who having indulged in a gallop as he brought him from Lucksford, expected his death would be laid at his door. No sooner was he up, than, without waiting for him to shake himself, Mr. Soapey vaulted into the saddle, and seizing him by the head, let in the Latchfords in a style that satisfied the hack he was not going to canter in a circle. Away he went, best pace; for like all Mr. Sponge's horses, he had the knack of going, the general difficulty being to get them to go the way they were wanted.

Sponge presently overtook Mr. Jawleyford, who had been brought up by a gate, which he was making sundry ineffectual Briggs-like passes and efforts to open; the gate and his horse seeming to have combined to prevent his getting through. Though an expert swordsman, he had never been able to accomplish the art of opening a gate, especially one of those gingerly balanced spring-snecked things that require to be taken at the nick of time, or else they drop just as the horse gets his nose to them.

'Why aren't you here to open the gate?' asked Jawleyford, snappishly, as the blue boy bustled up as his master's efforts became more hopeless at each attempt.

The lad, like a wise fellow, dropped from his horse, and opening it with his hands, ran it back on foot.

Jawleyford and Sponge then rode through.

Canter, canter, canter, went Jawleyford, with an arm akimbo, head well up, legs well down, toes well pointed, as if he were going to a race, where his work would end on arriving, instead of to a fox-hunt, where it would only begin.

'You are rather hard on the old nag, aren't you?' at length asked Sponge, as, having cleared the rushy, swampy park, they came upon the macadamized turnpike, and Jawleyford selected the middle of it as the scene of his further progression.

'Oh, no!' replied Jawleyford, tit-tup-ing along with a loose rein, as if he was on the soundest, freshest-legged horse in the world; 'oh no! my horses are used to it.' 'Well, but if you mean to hunt him,' observed Sponge, 'he'll be blown before he gets to cover.'

'Get him in wind, my dear fellow,' replied Jawleyford, 'get him in wind,' touching the horse with the spur as he spoke.

'Faith, but if he was as well on his legs as he is in his wind, he'd not be amiss,' rejoined Sponge.

So they cantered and trotted, and trotted and cantered away, Sponge thinking he could afford pace as well as Jawleyford. Indeed, a horse has only to become a hack, to be able to do double the work he was ever supposed to be capable of.

But to the meet.

Scrambleford Green was a small straggling village on the top of a somewhat high hill, that divided the vale in which Jawleyford Court was situated from the more fertile one of Farthinghoe, in which Lord Scamperdale lived.

It was one of those out-of-the-way places at which the meet of the hounds, and a love feast or fair, consisting of two fiddlers (one for each public-house), a few unlicensed packmen, three or four gingerbread stalls, a drove of cows and some sheep, form the great events of the year among a people who are thoroughly happy and contented with that amount of gaiety. Think of that, you 'used up' young gentlemen of twenty, who have exhausted the pleasures of the world! The hounds did not come to Scrambleford Green often, for it was not a favourite meet; and when they did come, Frosty and the men generally had them pretty much to themselves. This day, however, was the exception; and Old Tom Yarnley, whom age had bent nearly double, and who hobbled along on two sticks, declared that never in the course of his recollection, a period extending over the best part of a century, had he seen such a 'sight of red coats' as mustered that morning at Scrambleford Green. It seemed as if there had been a sudden rising of sportsmen. What brought them all out? What brought Mr. Puffington, the master of the Hanby hounds, out? What brought Blossomnose again? What Mr. Wake, Mr. Fossick, Mr. Fyle, who had all been out the day before? Reader, the news had spread throughout the country that there was a great writer down; and they wanted to see what he would say of them—they had come to sit for their portraits, in fact. There was a great gathering, at least for the Flat Hat Hunt, who seldom mustered above a dozen. Tom Washball came, in a fine new coat and new flat-fliped hat with a broad binding; also Mr. Sparks, of Spark Hall; Major Mark; Mr. Archer, of Cheam Lodge; Mr. Reeves, of Coxwell Green; Mr. Bliss, of Boltonshaw; Mr. Joyce, of Ebstone; Dr. Capon, of Calcot; Mr. Dribble, of Hook; Mr. Slade, of Three-Burrow Hill; and several others. Great was the astonishment of each as the other cast up.

'Why, here's Joe Reeves!' exclaimed Blossomnose. 'Who'd have thought of seeing you?'

'And who'd have thought of seeing *you*?' rejoined Reeves, shaking hands with the jolly old nose.

'Here's Tom Washball in time for once, I declare!' exclaimed Mr. Fyle, as Mr. Washball cantered up in apple-pie order.

'Wonders will never cease!' observed Fossick, looking Washy over.

So the field sat in a ring about the hounds in the centre of which, as usual, were Jack and Lord Scamperdale, looking with their great tortoise-shell-rimmed spectacles, and short grey whiskers trimmed in a curve up to their noses, like a couple of horned owls in hats.

'Here's the man on the cow!' exclaimed Jack, as he espied Sponge and Jawleyford rising the hill together, easing their horses by standing in their stirrups and holding on by their manes.

'You don't say so!' exclaimed Lord Scamperdale, turning his horse in the direction Jack was looking, and staring for hard life too. 'So there is, I declare!' observed he. 'And who the deuce is this with him?'

'That ass Jawleyford, as I live!' exclaimed Jack, as the blue-coated servant now hove in sight.

'So it is!' said Lord Scamperdale; 'the confounded humbug!'

'This boy'll be after one of the young ladies,' observed Jack; 'not one of the writing chaps we thought he was.'

'Shouldn't wonder,' replied Lord Scamperdale; adding, in an undertone, 'I vote we have a rise out of old Jaw. I'll let you in for a good thing—you shall dine with him.'

'Not I,' replied Jack.

'You *shall*, though,' replied his lordship firmly.

'Pray don't!' entreated Jack.

'By the powers, if you don't,' rejoined his lordship, 'you shall not have a mount out of me for a month.'

While this conversation was going on, Jawleyford and Sponge, having risen the hill, had resumed their seats in the saddle, and Jawleyford, setting himself in attitude, tickled his horse with his spur, and proceeded to canter becomingly up to the pack; Sponge and the groom following a little behind.

'Ah, Jawleyford, my dear fellow!' exclaimed Lord Scamperdale, putting his horse on a few steps to meet him as he came flourishing up. 'Ah, Jawleyford, my dear fellow, I'm delighted to see you,' extending a hand as he spoke. 'Jack, here, told me that he saw your flag flying as he passed, and I said what a pity it was but I'd known before; for Jawleyford, said I, is a real good fellow, one of the best fellows I know, and has asked me to dine so often that I'm almost ashamed to meet him; and it would have been such a nice opportunity to have volunteered a visit, the hounds being here, you see.'

'Oh, that's so kind of your lordship!' exclaimed Jawleyford, quite delighted—'that's so kind of your lordship—that's just what I like!—that's just what Mrs. Jawleyford likes!—that's just what we all like!—coming without fuss or ceremony, just as my friend Mr. Sponge, here, does. By the way, will your lordship give me leave to introduce my friend Mr. Sponge—my Lord Scamperdale.' Jawleyford suiting the action to the word, and manoeuvring the ceremony.

'Ah, I made Mr. Sponge's acquaintance yesterday,' observed his lordship drily, giving a sort of servants' touch of his hat as he scrutinized our friend through his formidable glasses, adding, 'To tell you the truth,' addressing himself in an undertone to Sponge, 'I took you for one of those nasty writing chaps, who I 'bominate. But,' continued his lordship, returning to Jawleyford. 'I'll tell you what I said about the dinner. Jack, here, told me the flag was flying; and I said I only wished I'd known before, and I would certainly have proposed that Jack and I should dine with you, either to-day or to-morrow; but unfortunately I'd engaged myself to my Lord Barker's not five minutes before.'

'Ah, my lord!' exclaimed Jawleyford, throwing out his hand and shrugging his shoulders as if in despair, 'you tantalize me—you do indeed. You should have come, or said nothing about it. You distress me—you do indeed.'

'Well, I'm wrong, perhaps,' replied his lordship, patting Jawleyford encouragingly on the shoulder; 'but, however, I'll tell you what,' said he, 'Jack here's not engaged, and he shall come to you.'

'Most happy to see Mr.—ha—hum—haw—Jack—that's to say, Mr. Spraggon,' replied Jawleyford, bowing very low, and laying his hand on his heart, as if quite overpowered at the idea of the honour.

'Then, that's a bargain. Jack,' said his lordship, looking knowingly round at his much disconcerted friend; 'you dine and stay all night at Jawleyford Court tomorrow! and mind,' added he, 'make yourself 'greeable to the girls—ladies, that's to say.'

'Couldn't your lordship arrange it so that we might have the pleasure of seeing you both on some future day?' asked Jawleyford, anxious to avert the Jack calamity. 'Say next week,' continued he; 'or suppose you meet at the Court?'

'Ha—he—hum. Meet at the Court,' mumbled his lordship—'meet at the Court—ha—he—ha—hum—no;—got no foxes.'

'Plenty of foxes, I assure you, my lord!' exclaimed Jawleyford. 'Plenty of foxes!' repeated he.

'We never find them, then, somehow,' observed his lordship, drily; 'at least, none but those three-legged beggars in the laurels at the back of the stables.'

'Ah! that will be the fault of the hounds,' replied Jawleyford; 'they don't take sufficient time to draw—run through the covers too quickly.'

'Fault of the hounds be hanged!' exclaimed Jack, who was the champion of the pack generally. 'There's not a more patient, painstaking pack in the world than his lordship's.'

'Ah—well—ah—never mind that,' replied his lordship, 'Jaw and you can settle that point over your wine tomorrow; meanwhile, if your friend Mr. What's-his-name here, 'll get his horse,' continued his lordship, addressing himself to Jawleyford, but looking at Sponge, who was still on the piebald, 'we'll throw off.'

'Thank you, my lord,' replied Sponge; 'but I'll mount at the cover side,' Sponge not being inclined to let the Flat Hat Hunt field see the difference of opinion that occasionally existed between the gallant brown and himself.

'As you please,' rejoined his lordship, 'as you please,' jerking his head at Frostyface, who forthwith gave the office to the hounds; whereupon all was commotion. Away the cavalcade went, and in less than five minutes the late bustling village resumed its wonted quiet; the old man on sticks, two crones gossiping at a door, a rag-or-anything-else-gatherer going about with a donkey, and a parcel of dirty children tumbling about on the green, being all that remained on the scene. All the able-bodied men had followed the hounds. Why the hounds had ever climbed the long hill seemed a mystery, seeing that they returned the way they came.

Jawleyford, though sore disconcerted at having 'Jack' pawned upon him, stuck to my lord, and rode on his right with the air of a general. He felt he was doing his duty as an Englishman in thus patronizing the

hounds—encouraging a manly spirit of independence, and promoting
our unrivalled breed of horses. The post-boy trot at which hounds travel,
to be sure, is not well adapted for dignity; but Jawleyford nourished and
vapoured as well as he could under the circumstances, and considering
they were going down hill. Lord Scamperdale rode along, laughing in
his sleeve at the idea of the pleasant evening Jack and Jawleyford would
have together, occasionally complimenting Jawleyford on the cut and
condition of his horse, and advising him to be careful of the switching
raspers with which the country abounded, and which might be fatal to
his nice nutmeg-coloured trousers. The rest of the 'field' followed, the
fall of the ground enabling them to see 'how thick Jawleyford was with
my lord.' Old Blossomnose, who, we should observe, had slipped away
unperceived on Jawleyford's arrival, took a bird's-eye view from the rear.
Naughty Blossom was riding the horse that ought to have gone in the
'chay' to Jawleyford Court.

XXIII

THE GREAT RUN

OUR HERO HAVING INVEIGLED THE brown under lee of an out-house as the field moved along, was fortunate enough to achieve the saddle without disclosing the secrets of the stable; and as he rejoined the throng in all the pride of shape, action, and condition, even the top-sawyers. Fossick, Fyle, Bliss, and others, admitted that Hercules was not a bad-like horse; while the humbler-minded ones eyed Sponge with a mixture of awe and envy, thinking what a fine trade literature must be to stand such a horse.

'Is your friend What's-his-name, a workman?' asked Lord Scamperdale, nodding towards Sponge as he trotted Hercules gently past on the turf by the side of the road along which they were riding.

'Oh, no,' replied Jawleyford, tartly. 'Oh, no—gentleman, man of property—'

'I did not mean was he a mechanic,' explained his lordship drily, 'but a workman; a good 'un across country, in fact.' His lordship working his arms as if he was going to set-to himself.

'Oh, a first-rate man!—first-rate man!' replied Jawleyford; 'beat them all at Laverick Wells.'

'I thought so,' observed his lordship; adding to himself, 'then Jack shall take the conceit out of him.'

'Jack!' halloaed he over his shoulder to his friend, who was jogging a little behind; 'Jack!' repeated he, 'that Mr. Something—'

'*Sponge!*' observed Jawleyford, with an emphasis.

'That Mr. Sponge,' continued his lordship, 'is a stranger in the country: have the kindness to take *care* of him. You know what I mean?'

'Just so,' replied Jack; 'I'll take care of him.'

'Most polite of your lordship, I'm sure,' said Jawleyford, with a low bow, and laying his hand on his breast. 'I can assure you I shall never forget the marked attention I have received from your lordship this day.'

'Thank you for nothing,' grunted his lordship to himself.

Bump, bump; trot, trot; jabber, jabber, on they went as before.

They had now got to the cover, Tickler Gorse, and ere the last horsemen had reached the last angle of the long hill, Frostyface was rolling about on foot in the luxuriant evergreen; now wholly visible, now all but overhead, like a man buffeting among the waves of the sea. Save Frosty's cheery voice encouraging the invisible pack to 'wind him!' and 'rout him out!' an injunction that the shaking of the gorse showed they willingly obeyed, and an occasional exclamation from Jawleyford, of 'Beautiful! beautiful!—never saw better hounds!—can't be a finer pack!' not a sound disturbed the stillness of the scene. The waggoners on the road stopped their wains, the late noisy ploughmen leaned vacantly on their stilts, the turnip-pullers stood erect in the air, and the shepherds' boys deserted the bleating flocks;—all was life and joy and liberty— 'Liberty, equality, and foxhunt-ity!'

'Yo—i—cks, wind him! Y—o—o—icks! rout him out!' went Frosty; occasionally varying the entertainment with a loud crack of his heavy whip, when he could get upon a piece of rising ground to clear the thong.

'Tally-ho!' screamed Jawleyford, hoisting the Bumperkin Yeomanry cap in the air. 'Tally-ho!' repeated he, looking triumphantly round, as much as to say, 'What a clever boy am I!'

'Hold your noise!' roared Jack, who was posted a little below. 'Don't you see it's a hare?' added he, amidst the uproarious mirth of the company.

'I haven't your great staring specs on, or I should have seen he hadn't a tail,' retorted Jawleyford, nettled at the tone in which Jack had addressed him.

'Tail be—!' replied Jack, with a sneer; 'who but a tailor would call it a tail?'

Just then a light low squeak of a whimper was heard in the thickest part of the gorse, and Frostyface cheered the hound to the echo. 'Hoick to, Pillager! H—o—o—ick!' screamed he, in a long-drawn note, that thrilled through every frame, and set the horses a-capering.

Ere Frosty's prolonged screech was fairly finished, there was such an outburst of melody, and such a shaking of the gorse-bushes, as plainly showed there was no safety for Reynard in cover; and great was the bustle and commotion among the horsemen. Mr. Fossick lowered his hat-string and ran the fox's tooth through the buttonhole; Fyle drew his girths; Washball took a long swig at his hunting-horn-shaped monkey; Major Mark and Mr. Archer threw away their cigar ends; Mr. Bliss drew on his dogskin gloves; Mr. Wake rolled the thong of his whip round the stick, to be better able to encounter his puller; Mr. Sparks got a yokel to take up a link of his curb; George Smith and Joe Smith looked at their watches; Sandy McGregor, the factor, filled his great Scotch nose with Irish snuff, exclaiming, as he dismissed the balance from his fingers by a knock against his thigh, 'Oh, my mon, aw think this tod will gie us a ran!' while Blossomnose might be seen stealing gently forward, on the far side of a thick fence, for the double purpose of shirking Jawleyford and getting a good start.

In the midst of these and similar preparations for the fray, up went a whip's cap at the low end of the cover; and a volley of 'Tallyhos' burst from our friends, as the fox, whisking his white-tipped brush in the air, was seen stealing away over the grassy hill beyond. What a commotion was there! How pale some looked! How happy others!

'Sing out, Jack! for heaven's sake, sing out!' exclaimed Lord Scamperdale; an enthusiastic sportsman, always as eager for a run as if he had never seen one. 'Sing out, Jack; or, by Jove, they'll override 'em at starting!'

'HOLD HARD, gentlemen,' roared Jack, clapping spurs into his grey, or rather, into his lordship's grey, dashing in front, and drawing the horse across the road to stop the progression of the field. 'HOLD HARD, *one minute!*' repeated Jack, standing erect in his stirrups, and menacing them with his whip (a most formidable one). 'Whatever you do, *pray* let them get away! *Pray* don't spoil your own sport! Pray remember they're his lordship's hounds!—that they cost him five-and-twenty under'd—two thousand five under'd a year! And where, let me ax, with wheat down to nothing, would you get another, if he was to throw up?'

As Jack made this inquiry, he took a hurried glance at the now pouring-out pack; and seeing they were safe away, he wiped the foam from his mouth on his sleeve, dropped into his saddle, and, catching his horse short round by the head, clapped spurs into his sides, and galloped away, exclaiming:

'Now, ye tinkers, we'll all start fair!'

Then there was such a scrimmage! such jostling and elbowing among the jealous ones; such ramming and cramming among the eager ones; such pardon-begging among the polite ones; such spurting of ponies, such clambering of cart-horses. All were bent on going as far as they could—all except Jawleyford, who sat curvetting and prancing in the patronizing sort of way gentlemen do who encourage hounds for the sake of the manly spirit the sport engenders, and the advantage hunting is of in promoting our unrivalled breed of horses.

His lordship having slipped away, horn in hand, under pretence of blowing the hounds out of cover, as soon as he set Jack at the field, had now got a good start, and, horse well in hand, was sailing away in their wake.

'F-o-o-r-r-ard!' screamed Frostyface, coming up alongside of him, holding his horse—a magnificent thoroughbred bay—well by the head, and settling himself into his saddle as he went.

'F-o-r-rard!' screeched his lordship, thrusting his spectacles on to his nose.

'Twang—twang—twang,' went the huntsman's deep-sounding horn.

'T'weet—t'weet—t'weet,' went his lordship's shriller one.

'In for a stinger, my lurd,' observed Jack, returning his horn to the case.

'Hope so,' replied his lordship, pocketing his.

They then flew the first fence together.

'F-o-r-r-ard!' screamed Jack in the air, as he saw the hounds packing well together, and racing with a breast-high scent.

'F-o-r-rard!' screamed his lordship, who was a sort of echo to his huntsman, just as Jack Spraggon was echo to his lordship.

'He's away for Gunnersby Craigs,' observed Jack, pointing that way, for they were a good ten miles off.

'Hope so,' replied his lordship, for whom the distance could never be too great, provided the pace corresponded.

'F-o-o-r-rard!' screamed Jack.

'F-o-r-rard!' screeched his lordship.

So they went flying and 'forrarding' together; none of the field— thanks to Jack Spraggon—being able to overtake them.

'Y-o-o-nder he goes!' at last cried Frosty, taking off his cap as he viewed the fox, some half-mile ahead, stealing away round the side of Newington Hill.

'Tallyho!' screeched his lordship, riding with his flat hat in the air, by way of exciting the striving field to still further exertion.

'He's a good 'un!' exclaimed Frosty, eyeing the fox's going.

'He is that!' replied his lordship, staring at him with all his might.

Then they rode on, and were presently rounding Newington Hill themselves, the hounds packing well together, and carrying a famous head.

His lordship now looked to see what was going on behind.

Scrambleford Hill was far in the rear. Jawleyford and the boy in blue were altogether lost in the distance. A quarter of a mile or so this way were a couple of dots of horsemen, one on a white, the other on a dark colour—most likely Jones, the keeper, and Farmer Stubble, on the foaly mare. Then, a little nearer, was a man in a hedge, trying to coax his horse after him, stopping the way of two boys in white trousers, whose ponies looked like rats. Again, a little nearer, were some of the persevering ones—men who still hold on in the forlorn hopes of a check—all dark-coated, and mostly trousered. Then came the last of the red-coats—Tom Washball, Charley Joyce, and Sam Sloman, riding well in the first flight of second horsemen—his lordship's pad-groom, Mr. Fossick's man in drab with a green collar, Mr. Wake's in blue, also a lad in scarlet and a flat hat, with a second horse for the huntsman. Drawing still nearer came the ruck—men in red, men in brown, men in livery, a farmer or two in fustian, all mingled together; and a few hundred yards before these, and close upon his lordship, were the élite of the field—five men in scarlet and one in black. Let us see who they are. By the powers, Mr. Sponge is first!—Sponge sailing away at his ease, followed by Jack, who is staring at him through his great lamps, longing to launch out at him, but as yet wanting an excuse; Sponge having ridden with judgement—judgement, at least, in everything except in having taken the lead of Jack. After Jack comes old black-booted Blossomnose; and Messrs. Wake, Fossick, and Fyle, complete our complement of five. They are all riding steadily and well; all very irate, however, at the stranger for going before them, and ready to back Jack in anything he may say or do.

On, on they go; the hounds still pressing forward, though not carrying quite so good a head as before. In truth, they have run four miles in twenty minutes; pretty good going anywhere except upon paper, where they always go unnaturally fast. However, there they are, still pressing on, though with considerably less music than before.

After rounding Newington Hill, they got into a wilder and worse sort of country, among moorish, ill-cultivated land, with cold unwholesome-looking fallows. The day, too, seemed changing for the worse; a heavy black cloud hanging overhead. The hounds were at length brought to their noses.

His lordship, who had been riding all eyes, ears, and fears, foresaw the probability of this; and pulling-to his horse, held up his hand, the usual signal for Jack to 'sing out' and stop the field. Sponge saw the signal, but, unfortunately, Hercules didn't; and tearing along with his head to the ground, resolutely bore our friend not only past his lordship, but right on to where the now stooping pack were barely feathering on the line.

Then Jack and his lordship sang out together.

'*Hold hard!*' screeched his lordship, in a dreadful state of excitement.

'HOLD HARD!' thundered Jack.

Sponge *was* holding hard—hard enough to split the horse's jaws, but the beast would go on, notwithstanding.

'By the powers, he's among 'em again!' shouted his lordship, as the resolute beast, with his upturned head almost pulled round to Sponge's knee, went star-gazing on like the blind man in Regent Street. 'Sing out. Jack! sing out! for heaven's sake, sing out,' shrieked his lordship, shutting his eyes, as he added, 'or he'll kill every man jack of them.'

'NOW, SUR!' roared Jack, 'can't you steer that 'ere aggravatin' quadruped of yours?'

'Oh, you pestilential son of a pontry-maid!' screeched his lordship, as Brilliant ran yelping away from under Sponge's horse's feet. 'Sing out. Jack! sing out!' gasped his lordship again.

'Oh, you scandalous, hypocritical, rusty-booted, numb-handed son of a puffing corn-cutter, why don't you turn your attention to feeding hens, cultivating cabbages, or making pantaloons for small folk, instead of killing hounds in this wholesale way?' roared Jack; an inquiry that set him foaming again.

'Oh, you unsightly, sanctified, idolatrous, Bagnigge-Wells coppersmith, you think because I'm a lord, and can't swear or use coarse language, that you may do what you like; rot you, sir, I'll present you with a testimonial! I'll settle a hundred a year upon you if you'll quit the country. By the

powers, they're away again!' added his lordship, who, with one eye on
Sponge and the other on the pack, had been watching Frosty lifting them
over the bad scenting-ground, till, holding them on to a hedgerow beyond,
they struck the scent on good sound pasture, and went away at score, every
hound throwing his tongue, and filling the air with joyful melody. Away
they swept like a hurricane. 'F-o-o-rard!' was again the cry.

'Hang it. Jack,' exclaimed Lord Scamperdale, laying his hand on his
double's shoulder, as they galloped alongside of each other, 'Hang it, Jack,
see if you can't sarve out this unrighteous, mahogany-booted, rattle-
snake. *Do* if you die for it!—I'll bury your remainders genteelly—patent
coffin with brass nails, all to yourself—put Frosty and all the fellows in
black, and raise a white marble monument to your memory, declaring
you were the most spotless virtuous man under the sun.'

'Let me off dining with Jaw, and I'll do my best,' replied Jack.

'Done!' screamed his lordship, flourishing his right arm in the air, as
he flew over a great stone wall.

A good many of the horses and sportsmen too had had enough before
the hounds checked; and the quick way Frosty lifted them and hit off the
scent, did not give them much time to recruit. Many of them now sat
hat in hand, mopping, and puffing, and turning their red perspiring faces
to the wind. 'Poough,' gasped one, as if he was going to be sick; 'Puff,'
went another; 'Oh! but it's 'ot!' exclaimed a third, pulling off his limp
neckcloth; 'Wonder if there's any ale hereabouts,' cried a fourth; 'Terrible
run!' observed a fifth; 'Ten miles at least,' gasped another. Meanwhile the
hounds went streaming on; and it is wonderful how soon those who
don't follow are left hopelessly in the rear.

Of the few that did follow, Mr. Sponge, however, was one. Nothing
daunted by the compliments that had been paid him, he got Hercules
well in hand; and the horse dropping again on the bit, resumed his place
in front, going as strong and steadily as ever. Thus he went, throwing
the mud in the faces of those behind, regardless of the oaths and
imprecations that followed, Sponge knowing full well they would do the
same by him if they could.

'All jealousy,' said Sponge, spurring his horse. 'Never saw such a jealous
set of dogs in my life.'

An accommodating lane soon presented itself, along which they all
pounded, with the hounds running parallel through the enclosures on

the left, Sponge sending such volleys of pebbles and mud in his rear as made it advisable to keep a good way behind him. The line was now apparently for Firlingham Woods; but on nearing the thatched cottage on Gasper Heath, the fox, most likely being headed, had turned short to the right; and the chase now lay over Sheeplow Water meadows, and so on to Bolsover brick-fields, when the pack again changed from hunting to racing, and the pace for a time was severe. His lordship having got his second horse at the turn, was ready for the tussle, and plied away vigorously, riding, as usual, with all his heart, with all his mind, with all his soul, and with all his strength; while Jack, still on the grey, came plodding diligently along in the rear, saving his horse as much as he could. His lordship charged a stiff flight of rails in the brick-fields; while Jack, thinking to save his, rode at a weak place in the fence, a little higher up, and in an instant was soused overhead in a clay-hole.

'Duck under, Jack! duck under!' screamed his lordship, as Jack's head rose to the surface. 'Duck under! you'll have it full directly!' added he, eyeing Sponge and the rest coming up.

Sponge, however, saw the splash, and turning a little lower down, landed safe on sound ground; while poor Blossomnose, who was next, went floundering overhead also. But the pace was too good to stop to fish them out.

'Dash it,' said Sponge, looking at them splashing about, 'but that was a near go for me!'

Jack being thus disposed of, Sponge, with increased confidence, rose in his stirrups, easing the redoubtable Hercules; and patting him on the shoulder, at the same time that he gave him the gentlest possible touch of the spur, exclaimed, 'By the powers, we'll show these old Flat Hats the trick!' He then commenced humming:

> Mister Sponge, the raspers taking,
> Sets the junkers' nerves a shaking;

and riding cheerfully on, he at length found himself on the confines of a wild rough-looking moor, with an undulating range of hills in the distance.

Frostyface and Lord Scamperdale here, for the first time, diverged from the line the hounds were running, and made for the neck of a smooth, flat, rather inviting-looking piece of ground, instead of crossing it. Sponge, thinking to get a niche, rode to it; and the 'deeper and deeper still' sort of flounder his horse made soon let him know that he was in a bog. The impetuous Hercules rushed and reared onwards as if to clear the wide expanse; and alighting still lower, shot Sponge right overhead in the middle.

'*That's* cooked *your* goose!' exclaimed his lordship, eyeing Sponge and his horse floundering about in the black porridge-like mess.

'Catch my horse!' hallooed Sponge to the first whip, who came galloping up as Hercules was breasting his way out again.

'Catch him yourself,' grunted the man, galloping on.

A peat-cutter, more humane, received the horse as he emerged from the black sea, exclaiming, as the now-piebald Sponge came lobbing after on foot, 'Ah, sir! but ye should niver set tee to ride through sic a place as that!'

Sponge, having generously rewarded the man with a fourpenny piece for catching his horse and scraping the thick of the mud off him, again mounted, and cantered round the point he should at first have gone; but his chance was out—the farther he went, the farther he was left behind; till at last, pulling up, he stood watching the diminishing pack, rolling like marbles over the top of Rotherjade Hill, followed by his lordship hugging his horse round the neck as he went, and the huntsman and whips leading and driving theirs up before them.

'Nasty jealous old beggar!' said Sponge, eyeing his lessening lordship disappearing over the hill, too. Sponge then performed the sickening ceremony of turning away from hounds running; not but that he might have plodded on on the line, and perhaps seen or heard what became of the fox, but Sponge didn't hunt on those terms. Like a good many other gentlemen, he would be first, or nowhere.

If it was any consolation to him, he had plenty of companions in misfortune. The line was dotted with horsemen back to the brick-fields. The first person he overtook wending his way home in the discontented, moody humour of a thrown-out man, was Mr. Puffington, master of the Hanby hounds; at whose appearance at the meet we expressed our surprise.

Neighbouring masters of hounds are often more or less jealous of each other. No man in the master-of-hound world is too insignificant for censure. Lord Scamperdale *was* an undoubted sportsman; while poor Mr. Puffington thought of nothing but how to be thought one.

Hearing the mistaken rumour that a great writer was down, he thought that his chance of immortality was arrived; and, ordering his best horse, and putting on his best apparel, had braved the jibes and sneers of Jack and his lordship for the purpose of scraping acquaintance with the stranger. In that he had been foiled: there was no time at the meet to get introduced, neither could he get jostled beside Sponge in going down to the cover; while the quick find, the quick get away, followed by the quick thing we have described, were equally unfavourable to the undertaking. Nevertheless, Mr. Puffington had held on beyond the brick-fields; and had he but persevered a little farther, he would have had the satisfaction of helping Mr. Sponge out of the bog.

Sponge now, seeing a red coat a little before, trotted on, and quickly overtook a fine nippy, satin-stocked, dandified looking gentleman, with marvellously smart leathers and boots—a great contrast to the large, roomy, bargemanlike costume of the members of the Flat Hat Hunt.

'You're not hurt, I hope?' exclaimed Mr. Puffington, with well-feigned anxiety, as he looked at Mr. Sponge's black-daubed clothes.

'Oh, no!' replied Sponge. 'Oh, no!—fell soft—fell soft. More dirt, less hurt—more dirt, less hurt.'

'Why, you've been in a bog!' exclaimed Mr. Puffington, eyeing the much-stained Hercules.

'Almost over head,' replied Sponge. 'Scamperdale saw me going, and hadn't the grace to halloa.'

'Ah, that's like him,' replied Mr. Puffington, 'that's like him: there's nothing pleases him so much as getting fellows into grief.'

'Not very polite to a stranger,' observed Mr. Sponge.

'No, it isn't,' replied Mr. Puffington, 'no, it isn't; far from it indeed—far from it; but, low be it spoken,' added he, 'his lordship is only a roughish sort of customer.'

'So he is,' replied Mr. Sponge, who thought it fine to abuse a nobleman.

'The fact is,' said Mr. Puffington, 'these Flat Hat chaps are all snobs. They think there are no such fine fellows as themselves under the sun; and if ever a stranger looks near them, they make a point of being as rude and disagreeable to him as they possibly can. This is what they call keeping the hunt select.' 'Indeed,' observed Mr. Sponge, recollecting how they had complimented him, adding, 'they seem a queer set.'

'There's a fellow they call "Jack,"' observed Mr. Puffington, 'who acts as a sort of bulldog to his lordship, and worries whoever his lordship sets him upon. He got into a clay-hole a little farther back, and a precious splashing he was making, along with the chaplain, old Blossomnose.'

'Ah, I saw him,' observed Mr. Sponge.

'You should come and see *my* hounds,' observed Mr. Puffington.

'What are they?' asked Sponge.

'The Hanby,' replied Mr. Puffington.

'Oh! then you are Mr. Puffington,' observed Sponge, who had a sort of general acquaintance with all the hounds and masters—indeed, with all the meets of all the hounds in the kingdom—which he read in the weekly lists in *Bell's Life*, just as he read *Mogg's Cab Fares*. 'Then you are Mr. Puffington?' observed Sponge.

'The same,' replied the stranger.

'I'll have a look at you,' observed Sponge, adding, 'do you take in horses?'

'Yours, of course,' replied Mr. Puffington, bowing; adding something about great public characters, which Sponge didn't understand.

'I'll be down upon you, as the extinguisher said to the rushlight,' observed Mr. Sponge.

'Do,' said Mr. Puffington; 'come before the frost. Where are you staying now?'

'I'm at Jawleyford's,' replied our friend.

'Indeed!—Jawleyford's, are you?' repeated Mr. Puffington. 'Good fellow, Jawleyford—gentleman, Jawleyford. How long do you stay?'

'Why, I haven't made up my mind,' replied Sponge. 'Have no thoughts of budging at present.'

'Ah, well—good quarters,' said Mr. Puffington, who now smelt a rat; 'good quarters—nice girls—fine fortune—fine place, Jawleyford Court. Well, book me for the next visit,' added he. 'I will,' said Sponge, 'and no mistake. What do they call your shop?'

'Hanby House,' replied Mr. Puffington; 'Hanby House—anybody can tell you where Hanby House is.'

'I'll not forget,' said Mr. Sponge, booking it in his mind, and eyeing his victim.

'I'll show you a fine pack of hounds,' said Mr. Puffington; 'far finer animals than those of old Scamperdale's—steady, true hunting hounds, that won't go a yard without a scent—none of your jealous, flashy, frantic devils, that will tear over half a township without one, and are always looking out for "halloas" and assistance—'

Mr. Puffington was interrupted in the comparison he was about to draw between his lordship's hounds and his, by arriving at the Bolsover brick-fields, and seeing Jack and Blossomnose, horse in hand, running to and fro, while sundry countrymen blobbed about in the clay-hole they had so recently occupied. Tom Washball, Mr. Wake, Mr. Fyle, Mr. Fossick, and several dark-coated horsemen and boys were congregated around. Jack had lost his spectacles, and Blossomnose his whip, and the countrymen were diving for them.

'Not hurt, I hope?' said Mr. Puffington, in the most dandified tone of indifference, as he rode up to where Jack and Blossomnose were churning the water in their boots, stamping up and down, trying to get themselves warm.

'Hurt be hanged!' replied Jack, who had a frightful squint, that turned his eyes inside out when he was in a passion: 'hurt be hanged!' said he; 'might have been drownded, for anything you'd have cared.'

'I should have been sorry for that,' replied Mr. Puffington, adding, 'the Flat Hat Hunt could ill afford to lose so useful and ornamental a member.'

'I don't know what the Flat Hat Hunt can afford to lose,' spluttered Jack, who hadn't got all the clay out of his mouth; 'but I know they can afford to do without the company of certain gentlemen who shall be nameless,' said he, looking at Sponge and Puffington as he thought, but in reality showing nothing but the whites of his eyes. 'I told you so,' said Puffington, jerking his head towards Jack, as Sponge and he turned their horses' heads to ride away; 'I told you so,' repeated he; 'that's a specimen of their style'; adding, 'they are the greatest set of ruffians under the sun.'

The new acquaintances then jogged on together as far as the cross-roads at Stewley, when Puffington, having bound Sponge in his own recognizance to come to him when he left Jawleyford Court, pointed him out his way, and with a most hearty shake of the hands the new-made friends parted.

XXIV

LORD SCAMPERDALE
AT HOME

WE FEAR OUR FAIR FRIENDS will expect something gay from the above heading—lamps and flambeaux outside, fiddlers, feathers, and flirters in. Nothing of the sort, fair ladies—nothing of the sort. Lord Scamperdale 'at home' simply means that his lordship was not out hunting, that he had got his dirty boots and breeches off, and dry tweeds and tartans on.

Lord Scamperdale was the eighth earl; and, according to the usual alternating course of great English families—one generation living and the next starving—it was his lordship's turn to live; but the seventh earl having been rather unreasonable in the length of his lease, the present earl, who during the lifetime of his father was Lord Hardup, had contracted such parsimonious habits, that when he came into possession he could not shake them off; and but for the fortunate friendship of Abraham Brown, the village blacksmith, who had given his young idea a sporting turn, entering him with ferrets and rabbits, and so training him on with terriers and rat-catching, badger-baiting and otter-hunting, up to the noble sport of fox-hunting itself, in all probability his lordship would have been a regular miser. As it was, he did not spend a halfpenny upon anything but hunting; and his hunting, though well, was still economically done, costing him some couple of thousand a year, to which, for the sake of euphony, Jack used to add an extra five hundred; 'two thousand five under'd a year, five-and-twenty under'd a year,' sounding better, as Jack thought, and more imposing, than a couple of thousand, or two thousand, a year. There were few days on which Jack didn't inform the field what the hounds cost his lordship, or rather what they didn't cost him.

Woodmansterne, his lordship's principal residence, was a fine place. It stood in an undulating park of 800 acres, with its church, and its lakes, and its heronry, and its decoy, and its racecourse, and its varied grasses of the choicest kinds, for feeding the numerous herds of deer, so well known at Temple Bar and Charing Cross as the Woodmansterne venison. The house was a modern edifice, built by the sixth earl, who, having been a 'liver,' had run himself aground by his enormous outlay on this Italian structure, which was just finished when he died. The fourth earl, who, we should have stated, was a 'liver' too, was a man of *vertu*—a great traveller and collector of coins, pictures, statues, marbles, and curiosities generally—things that are very dear to buy, but oftentimes extremely cheap when sold; and, having collected a vast quantity from all parts of the world (no easy feat in those days), he made them heirlooms, and departed this life, leaving the next earl the pleasure of contemplating them. The fifth earl, having duly starved through life, then made way for the sixth; who, finding such a quantity of valuables stowed away, as he thought, in rather a confined way, sent to London for a first-rate architect. Sir Thomas Squareall (who always posted with four horses), who forthwith pulled down the old brick-and-stone Elizabethan mansion, and built the present splendid Italian structure, of the finest polished stone, at an expense of—furniture and all—say £120,000; Sir Thomas's estimates being £30,000. The seventh earl, of course, they starved; and the present lord, at the age of forty-three, found himself in possession of house, and coins, and curiosities; and, best of all, of some £90,000 in the funds, which had quietly rolled up during the latter part of his venerable parent's existence. His lordship then took counsel with himself—first, whether he should marry or remain single; secondly, whether he should live or starve. Having considered the subject with all the attention a limited allowance of brains permitted, he came to the resolution that the second proposition depended a good deal upon the first; 'for,' said he to himself, 'if I marry, my lady, perhaps, may *make* me live; and therefore,' said he, 'perhaps I'd better remain single.' At all events, he came to the determination not to marry in a hurry; and until he did, he felt there was no occasion for him to inconvenience himself by living. So he had the house put away in brown holland, the carpets rolled up, the pictures covered, the statues shrouded in muslin, the cabinets of curiosities locked, the plate secured, the china closeted, and everything arranged with the greatest care against the time, which he put before him in the distance like a target, when he should marry and begin to live.

At first, he gave two or three great dinners a year, about the height of the fruit season, and when it was getting too ripe for carriage to London by the old coaches—when a grand airing of the state-rooms used to take place, and ladies from all parts of the county used to sit shivering with their bare shoulders, all anxious for the honours of the head of the table. His lordship always held out that he was a marrying man; but even if he hadn't been, they would have come all the same, an unmarried man being always clearly on the cards; and though he was stumpy, and clumsy, and ugly, with as little to say for himself as could well be conceived, they all agreed that he was a most engaging, attractive man—quite a pattern of a man. Even on horseback, and in his hunting clothes, in which he looked far the best, he was only a coarse, square, bull-headed looking man, with hard, dry, round, matter-of-fact features, that never looked young, and yet somehow never got old. Indeed, barring the change from brown to grey of his short stubbly whiskers, which he trained with great care into a curve almost on to his cheek-bone, he looked very little older at the period of which we are writing than he did a dozen years before, when he was Lord Hardup. These dozen years, however, had brought him down in his doings.

The dinners had gradually dwindled away altogether, and he had had all the large tablecloths and napkins rough-dried and locked away against he got married; an event that he seemed more anxious to provide for the more unlikely it became. He had also abdicated the main body of the mansion, and taken up his quarters in what used to be the steward's room; into which he could creep quietly by a side door opening from the outer entrance, and so save frequent exposure to the cold and damp of the large cathedral-like hall beyond. Through the steward's room was what used to be the muniment room, which he converted into a bedroom for himself; and a little farther along the passage was another small chamber, made out of what used to be the plate-room, whereof

Jack, or whoever was in office, had the possession. All three rooms were furnished in the roughest, coarsest, homeliest way—his lordship wishing to keep all the good furniture against he got married. The sitting-room, or parlour, as his lordship called it, had an old grey drugget for a carpet, an old round black mahogany table on castors, that the last steward had ejected as too bad for him, four semi-circular wooden-bottomed walnut smoking-chairs; an old spindle-shanked sideboard, with very little middle, over which swung a few bookshelves, with the termination of their green strings surmounted by a couple of foxes' brushes. Small as the shelves were, they were larger than his lordship wanted—two books, one for Jack and one for himself, being all they contained; while the other shelves were filled with hunting-horns, odd spurs, knots of whipcord, piles of halfpence, lucifer-match boxes, gun-charges, and such-like miscellaneous articles.

His lordship's fare was as rough as his furniture. He was a great admirer of tripe, cow-heel, and delicacies of that kind; he had tripe twice a week—boiled one day, fried another. He was also a great patron of beefsteaks, which he ate half-raw, with slices of cold onion served in a saucer with water.

It was a beefsteak-and-batter-pudding day on which the foregoing run took place; and his lordship and Jack, having satisfied nature off their respective dishes—for they only had vegetables in common—and having finished off with some very strong Cheshire cheese, wheeled their chairs to the fire, while Bags the butler cleared the table and placed it between them. They were dressed in full suits of flaming large-check red-and-yellow tartans, the tartan of that noble clan the 'Stunners,' with black-and-white Shetland hose and red slippers. His lordship and Jack had related their mutual adventures by cross visits to each other's bedrooms while dressing: and, dinner being announced by the time they were ready, they had fallen to, and applied themselves diligently to the victuals, and now very considerately unbuttoned their many-pocketed waistcoats and stuck out their legs, to give it a fair chance of digesting. They seldom spoke much until his lordship had had his nap, which he generally took immediately after dinner; but on this particular night he sat bending forward in his chair, picking his teeth and looking at his toes, evidently ill at ease in his mind. Jack guessed the cause, but didn't say anything. Sponge, he thought, had beat him.

At length his lordship threw himself back in his chair, and stretching his little queer legs out before him, began to breathe thicker and thicker, till at last he got the melody up to a grunt. It was not the fine generous snore of a sleep that he usually enjoyed, but short, fitful, broken naps, that generally terminated in spasmodic jerks of the arms or legs. These grew worse, till at last all four went at once, like the limbs of a Peter Waggey, when, throwing himself forward with a violent effort, he awoke; and finding his horse was not a-top of him, as he thought, he gave vent to his feelings in the following ejaculations:

'Oh, Jack, I'm onhappy!' exclaimed he. 'I'm distressed!' continued he. 'I'm wretched!' added he, slapping his knees. 'I'm perfectly *miserable*!' he concluded, with a strong emphasis on the 'miserable.'

'What's the matter?' asked Jack, who was half-asleep himself.

'Oh, that Mister Something!—he'll be the death of me!' observed his lordship.

'I thought so,' replied Jack; 'what's the chap been after now?'

'I dreamt he'd killed old Lablache—best hound I have,' replied his lordship.

'He be——,' grunted Jack.

'Ah, it's all very well for you to say "he be this" and "he be that," but I can tell you what, that fellow is going to be a very awkward customer—a terrible thorn in my side.'

'Humph!' grunted Jack, who didn't see how.

'There's mischief about that fellow,' continued his lordship, pouring himself out half a tumbler of gin, and filling it up with water. 'There's mischief about the fellow. I don't like his looks—I don't like his coat—I don't like his boots—I don't like anything about him. I'd rather see the back of him than the front. He must be got rid of,' added his lordship.

'Well, I did my best to-day, I'm sure,' replied Jack. 'I was deuced near wanting the patent coffin you were so good as to promise me.'

'You did your work well,' replied his lordship; 'you did your work well; and you shall have my other specs till I can get you a new pair from town; and if you'll serve me again, I'll remember you in my will—I'll leave you something handsome.'

'I'm your man,' replied Jack.

'I never was so bothered with a fellow in my life,' observed his lordship. 'Captain Topsawyer was bad enough, and always pressed far too close on the hounds, but he would pull up at a check; but this rusty-booted 'bomination seems to think the hounds are kept for him to ride over. He must be got rid of somehow,' repeated his lordship; 'for we shall have no peace while he's here.'

'If he's after either of the Jawley girls, he'll be bad to shake off,' observed Jack.

'That's just the point,' replied his lordship, quaffing off his gin with the air of a man most thoroughly thirsty; 'that's just the point,' repeated he, setting down his tumbler. 'I think if he is, I could cook his goose for him.'

'How so?' asked Jack, drinking off his glass.

'Why, I'll tell you,' replied his lordship, replenishing his tumbler, and passing the old gilt-labelled blue bottle over to Jack; 'you see, Frosty's a cunning old file, picks up all the news and gossip of the country when he's out at exercise with the hounds, or in going to cover—knows everything!—who licks his wife, and whose wife licks him—who's after such a girl, and so on—and he's found out somehow that this Mr. What's-his-name isn't the man of metal he's passing for.'

'Indeed,' exclaimed Jack, raising his eyebrows, and squinting his eyes inside out; Jack's opinion of a man being entirely regulated by his purse.

'It's a fact,' said his lordship, with a knowing shake of his head. 'As we were toddling home with the hounds, I said to Frosty, "I hope that Mr. Something's comfortable in his bath"—meaning Gobblecow Bog, which he rode into. "Why," said Frosty, "it's no great odds what comes of such rubbage as that." Now, Frosty, you know, in a general way, is a most polite, fair-spoken man, specially before Christmas, when he begins to look for the tips; and as we are not much troubled with strangers, thanks to your sensible way of handling them, I thought Frosty would have made the most of this natural son of Dives, and been as polite to him as possible. However, he was evidently no favourite of Frosty's. So I just asked—not that one likes to be familiar with servants, you know, but still this brown-booted beggar is enough to excite one's curiosity and make any one go out of one's way a little—so I just asked Frosty what he knew about him. "All over the left," said Frosty, jerking his thumb back over his shoulder, and looking as knowing as a goose with one eye; "all over the left," repeated he. "What's over the left?" said I. "Why, this Mr. Sponge,"

said he. "How so?" asked I. "Why," said Frosty, "he's come gammonin'
down here that he's a great man—full of money, and horses, and so on;
but it's all my eye, he's no more a great man than I am."'

'The deuce!' exclaimed Jack, who had sat squinting and listening
intently as his lordship proceeded. 'Well, now, hang me, I thought he was
a snob the moment I saw him,' continued he; Jack being one of those
clever gentlemen who know everything after they are told.

"'Well, how do you know, Jack?" said I to Frosty. "Oh, I knows,"
replied he, as if he was certain about it. However, I wasn't satisfied
without knowing too; and, as we kept jogging on, we came to the old
Coach and Horses, and I said to Jack, "We may as well have a drop of
something to warm us." So we halted, and had glasses of brandy apiece,
whips and all; and then, as we jogged on again, I just said to Jack casually,
"Did you say it was Mr. Blossomnose told you about old Brown Boots?"
"No—Blossomnose—no," replied he, as if Blossom never had anything
half so good to tell; "it was a young woman," said he, in an undertone,
"who told me, and she had it from old Brown Boots's groom."'

'Well, that's good,' observed Jack, diving his hands into the very bottom
of his great tartan trouser pockets, and shooting his legs out before him;
'well, that's good,' repeated he, falling into a sort of reverie.

'Well, but what can we make of it?' at length inquired he, after a long
pause, during which he ran the facts through his mind, and thought they
could not be much ruder to Sponge than they had been. 'What can
we make of it?' said he. 'The fellow can ride, and we can't prevent him
hunting; and his having nothing only makes him less careful of his neck.'

'Why, that was just what I thought,' replied Lord Scamperdale, taking
another tumbler of gin; 'that was just what I thought—the fellow can
ride, and we can't prevent him; and just as I settled that in my sleep, I
thought I saw him come staring along, with his great brown horse's
head in the air, and crash right a-top of old Lablache. But I see my way
clearer with him now. But help yourself,' continued his lordship, passing
the gin-bottle over to Jack, feeling that what he had to say required a
little recommendation. 'I think I can turn Frosty's information to some
account.'

'I don't see how,' observed Jack, replenishing his glass.

'*I* do, though,' replied his lordship, adding, 'but I must have your
assistance.'

'Well, anything in moderation,' replied Jack, who had had to turn his hand to some very queer jobs occasionally.

'I'll tell you what *I* think,' observed his lordship. 'I think there are two ways of getting rid of this haughty Philistine—this unclean spirit—this 'bomination of a man. I think, in the first place, if old Chatterbox knew that he had nothing, he would very soon bow him out of Jawleyford Court; and in the second, that we might get rid of him by buying his horses.'

'Well,' replied Jack, 'I don't know but you're right. Chatterbox would soon wash his hands of him, as he has done of many promising young gentlemen before, if he has nothing; but people differ so in their ideas of what nothing consists of.'

Jack spoke feelingly, for he was a gentleman who was generally spoken of as having nothing a year, paid quarterly; and yet he was in the enjoyment of an annuity of sixty pounds.

'Oh, why, when I say he has nothing,' replied Lord Scamperdale, 'I mean that he has not what Jawleyford, who is a bumptious sort of an ass, would consider sufficient to make him a fit match for one of his daughters. He may have a few hundreds a year, but Jaw, I'm sure, will look at nothing under thousands.'

'Oh, certainly not,' said Jack, 'there's no doubt about that.'

'Well, then, you see, I was thinking,' observed Lord Scamperdale, eyeing Jack's countenance, 'that if you would dine there to-morrow, as we fixed—'

'Oh, dash it! I couldn't do that,' interrupted Jack, drawing himself together in his chair like a horse refusing a leap; 'I couldn't do that—I couldn't dine with Jaw, not at no price.'

'Why not?' asked Lord Scamperdale; 'he'll give you a good dinner— *fricassées*, and all sorts of good things; far finer fare than you have here.'

'That may all be,' replied Jack, 'but I don't want none of his food. I hate the sight of the fellow, and detest him fresh every time I see him. Consider, too, you said you'd let me off if I sarved out Sponge; and I'm sure I did my best. I led him over some awful places, and then what a ducking I got! My ears are full of water still,' added he, laying his head on one side to try to run it out.

'You did well,' observed Lord Scamperdale—'you did well, and I fully intended to let you off, but then I didn't know what a beggar I had to deal with. Come, say you'll go, that's a good fellow.'

'Couldn't,' replied Jack, squinting frightfully.

'You'll *oblige* me,' observed Lord Scamperdale.

'Ah, well, I'd do anything to oblige your lordship,' replied Jack, thinking of the corner in the will. 'I'd do anything to oblige your lordship: but the fact is, sir, I'm not prepared to go. I've lost my specs— I've got no swell clothes—I can't go in the Stunner tartan,' added he, eyeing his backgammon-board-looking chest, and diving his hands into the capacious pockets of his shooting-jacket.

'I'll manage all that,' replied his lordship; 'I've got a pair of splendid silver-mounted spectacles in the Indian cabinet in the drawing-room, that I've kept to be married in. I'll lend them to you, and there's no saying but you may captivate Miss Jawleyford in them. Then, as to clothes, there's my new damson-coloured velvet waistcoat with the steel buttons, and my fine blue coat with the velvet collar, silk facings, and our button on it; altogether I'll rig you out and make you such a swell as there's no saying but Miss Jawleyford'll offer to you, by way of consoling herself for the loss of Sponge.'

'I'm afraid you'll have to make a settlement for me, then,' observed our friend.

'Well, you are a good fellow, Jack,' said his lordship, 'and I'd as soon make one on you as on any one.'

'I s'pose you'll send me on wheels?' observed Jack.

'In course,' replied his lordship. 'Dog-cart—name behind—Right Honourable the Earl of Scamperdale—lad with cockade—everything genteel'; adding, 'by Jove, they'll take you for me!'

Having settled all these matters, and arranged how the information was to be communicated to Jawleyford, the friends at length took their block-tin candlesticks, with their cauliflower-headed candles, and retired to bed.

XXV

MR. SPRAGGON'S EMBASSY
TO JAWLEYFORD COURT

WHEN MR. SPONGE RETURNED, ALL dirtied and stained, from the chase, he found his host sitting in an arm-chair over the study fire, dressing-gowned and slippered, with a pocket-handkerchief tied about his head, shamming illness, preparatory to putting off Mr. Spraggon. To be sure, he played rather a better knife and fork at dinner than is usual with persons with that peculiar ailment; but Mr. Sponge, being very hungry, and well attended to by the fair—moreover, not suspecting any ulterior design—just ate and jabbered away as usual, with the exception of omitting his sick papa-in-law in the round of his observations. So the dinner passed over.

'Bring me a tumbler and some hot water and sugar,' said Mr. Jawleyford, pressing his head against his hand, as Spigot, having placed some bottle ends on the table, and reduced the glare of light, was preparing to retire. 'Bring me some hot water and sugar,' said he; 'and tell Harry he will have to go over to Lord Scamperdale's, with a note, the first thing in the morning.'

The young ladies looked at each other, and then at mamma, who, seeing what was wanted, looked at papa, and asked, 'if he was going to ask Lord Scamperdale over?' Amelia, among her many 'presentiments,' had long enjoyed one that she was destined to be Lady Scamperdale.

'No—*over*—no,' snapped Jawleyford; 'what should put that in your head?'

'Oh, I thought as Mr. Sponge was here, you might think it a good time to ask him.'

'His lordship knows he can come when he likes,' replied Jawleyford, adding, 'it's to put that Mr. John Spraggon off, who thinks he may do the same.'

'Mr. Spraggon!' exclaimed both the young ladies. 'Mr. Spraggon!— what should set him here?'

'What, indeed?' asked Jawleyford.

'Poor man! I dare say there's no harm in him,' observed Mrs. Jawleyford, who was always ready for anybody.

'No good either,' replied Jawleyford—'at all events, we'll be just as well without him. You know him, don't you?' added he, turning to Sponge—'great coarse man in spectacles.'

'Oh yes, I know him,' replied Sponge; 'a great ruffian he is, too,' added he.

'One ought to be in robust health to encounter such a man,' observed Jawleyford, 'and have time to get a man or two of the same sort to meet him. *We* can do nothing with such a man. I can't understand how his lordship puts up with such a fellow.'

'Finds him useful, I suppose,' observed Mr. Sponge.

Spigot presently appeared with a massive silver salver, bearing tumblers, sugar, lemon, nutmeg, and other implements of negus.

'Will you join me in a little wine-and-water?' asked Jawleyford, pointing to the apparatus and bottle ends, 'or will you have a fresh bottle?—plenty in the cellar,' added he, with a flourish of his hand, though he kept looking steadfastly at the negus-tray.

'Oh—why—I'm afraid—I doubt—I think I should hardly be able to do justice to a bottle single-handed,' replied Sponge. 'Then have negus,' said Jawleyford; 'you'll find it very refreshing; medical men recommend it after violent exercise in preference to wine. But pray have wine if you prefer it.'

'Ah—well, I'll finish off with a little negus, perhaps,' replied Sponge, adding, 'meanwhile the ladies, I dare say, would like a little wine.'

'The ladies drink white wine—sherry,' rejoined Jawleyford, determined to make a last effort to save his port. 'However, you can have a bottle of port to yourself, you know.'

'Very well,' said Sponge.

'One condition I must attach,' said Mr. Jawleyford, 'which is, that you *finish* the bottle. Don't let us have any waste, you know.'

'I'll do my best,' said Sponge, determined to have it; whereupon Mr. Jawleyford growled the word 'Port' to the butler, who had been witnessing his master's efforts to direct attention to the negus. Thwarted in his endeavour, Jawleyford's headache became worse, and the ladies, seeing how things were going, beat a precipitate retreat, leaving our hero to his fate.

'I'll leave a note on my writing-table when I go to bed,' observed Jawleyford to Spigot, as the latter was retiring after depositing the bottle; 'and tell Harry to start with it early in the morning, so as to get to Woodmansterne about breakfast—nine o'clock, or so, at latest,' added he.

'Yes, sir,' replied Spigot, withdrawing with an air.

Sponge then wanted to narrate the adventures of the day; but, independently of Jawleyford's natural indifference for hunting, he was too much out of humour at being done out of his wine to lend a willing ear; and after sundry 'hums,' 'indeeds,' 'sos,' &c., Sponge thought he might as well think the run over to himself as trouble to put it into words, whereupon a long silence ensued, interrupted only by the tinkling of Jawleyford's spoon against his glass, and the bumps of the decanter as Sponge helped himself to his wine.

At length Jawleyford, having had as much negus as he wanted, excused himself from further attendence, under the plea of increasing illness, and retired to his study to concoct his letter to Jack.

At first he was puzzled how to address him. If he had been Jack Spraggon, living in old Mother Nipcheese's lodgings at Starfield, as he was when Lord Scamperdale took him by the hand, he would have addressed him as 'Dear Sir,' or perhaps in the third person, 'Mr. Jawleyford presents his compliments to Mr. Spraggon,' &c.; but, as my lord's right-hand man, Jack carried a certain weight, and commanded a certain influence, that he would never have acquired of himself.

Jawleyford spoilt three sheets of cream-laid satin-wove note-paper (crested and ciphered) before he pleased himself with a beginning. First he had it 'Dear Sir,' which he thought looked too stiff; then he had it 'My dear Sir,' which he thought looked too loving; next he had it 'Dear Spraggon,' which he considered as too familiar; and then he tried 'Dear Mr. Spraggon,' which he thought would do. Thus he wrote:

DEAR MR. SPRAGGON,—

I am sorry to be obliged to put you off; but since I came in from hunting I have been attacked with influenza, which will incapacitate me from the enjoyment of society at least for two or three days. I therefore think the kindest thing I can do is to write to put you off; and, in the hopes of seeing both you and my lord at no distant day.

I remain, dear sir, yours sincerely,

CHARLES JAMES JAWLEYFORD,

Jawleyford Court.

To JOHN SPRAGGON, ESQ.,

&c. &c. &c.

This he sealed with the great seal of Jawleyford Court—a coat of arms containing innumerable quarterings and heraldic devices. Having then refreshed his memory by looking through a bundle of bills, and selected the most threatening of the lawyers' letters to answer the next day, he proceeded to keep up the delusion of sickness, by retiring to sleep in his dressing-room. Our readers will now have the kindness to accompany us to Lord Scamperdale's: time, the morning after the foregoing. 'Love me, love my dog,' being a favourite saying of his lordship's, he fed himself, his friends, and his hounds, on the same meal. Jack and he were busy with two great basins full of porridge, which his lordship diluted with milk, while Jack stirred his up with hot dripping, when the put-off note arrived. His lordship was still in a complete suit of the great backgammon-board-looking red-and-yellow Stunner tartan: but as Jack was going from home, he had got himself into a pair of his lordship's yellow-ochre leathers and new top-boots, while he wore the Stunner jacket and waistcoat to save his lordship's Sunday green cutaway with metal buttons, and canary-coloured waistcoat. His lordship did not eat his porridge with his usual appetite, for he had had a disturbed night, Sponge having appeared to him in his dreams in all sorts of forms and predicaments; now jumping a-top of him—now upsetting Jack—now riding over Frostyface—now

crashing among his hounds; and he awoke, fully determined to get rid
of him by fair means or foul. Buying his horses did not seem so good a
speculation as blowing his credit at Jawleyford Court, for, independently
of disliking to part with his cash, his lordship remembered that there
were other horses to get, and he should only be giving Sponge the means
of purchasing them. The more, however, he thought of the Jawleyford
project, the more satisfied he was that it would do; and Jack and he were
in a sort of rehearsal, wherein his lordship personated Jawleyford, and was
showing Jack (who was only a clumsy diplomatist) how to draw up to
the subject of Sponge's pecuniary deficiencies, when the dirty old butler
came with Jawleyford's note.

'What's here?' exclaimed his lordship, fearing from its smartness, that it
was from a lady. 'What's here?' repeated he, as he inspected the direction.
'Oh, it's for *you*!' exclaimed he, chucking it over to Jack, considerably
relieved by the discovery.

'*Me*!' replied Jack. 'Who can be writing to me?' said he, squinting his
eyes inside out at the seal. He opened it: 'Jawleyford Court,' read he.
'Who the deuce can be writing to me from Jawleyford Court when
I'm going there?'

'A put-off, for a guinea!' exclaimed his lordship.

'Hope so,' muttered Jack.

'Hope *not*,' replied his lordship.

'It is!' exclaimed Jack, reading, 'Dear Mr. Spraggon,' and so on.

'The humbug!' muttered Lord Scamperdale, adding, 'I'll be bound he's
got no more influenza than I have.'

'Well,' observed Jack, sweeping a red cotton handkerchief, with which
he had been protecting his leathers, off into his pocket, 'there's an end
of that.'

'Don't go so quick,' replied his lordship, ladling in the porridge.

'Quick!' retorted Jack; 'why, what can you do?'

'*Do*! why, *go* to be sure,' replied his lordship.

'How can I go,' asked Jack, 'when the sinner's written to put me off?'

'Nicely,' replied his lordship, 'nicely. I'll just send word back by the
servant that you had started before the note arrived, but that you shall
have it as soon as you return; and you just cast up there as if nothing had
happened.' So saying, his lordship took hold of the whipcord-pull and
gave the bell a peal.

'There's no beating you,' observed Jack.

Bags now made his appearance again.

'Is the servant here that brought this note?' asked his lordship, holding it up.

'Yes, *me* lord,' replied Bags.

'Then tell him to tell his master, with my compliments, that Mr. Spraggon had set off for Jawleyford Court before it came, but that he shall have it as soon as he returns—you understand?'

'Yes, *me* lord,' replied Bags, looking at Jack supping up the fat porridge, and wondering how the lie would go down with Harry, who was then discussing his master's merits and a horn of small beer with the lad who was going to drive Jack.

Jawleyford Court was twenty miles from Woodmansterne as the crow flies, and any distance anybody liked to call it by the road. The road, indeed, would seem to have been set out with a view of getting as many hills and as little level ground over which a traveller could make play as possible; and where it did not lead over the tops of the highest hills, it wound round their bases, in such little, vexatious, up-and-down, wavy dips as completely to do away with all chance of expedition. The route was not along one continuous trust, but here over a bit of turnpike and there over a bit of turnpike, with ever and anon long interregnums of township roads, repaired in the usual primitive style with mud and soft field-stones, that turned up like flitches of bacon. A man would travel from London to Exeter by rail in as short a time, and with far greater ease, than he would drive from Lord Scamperdale's to Jawleyford Court. His lordship being aware of this fact, and thinking, moreover, it was no use trashing a good horse over such roads, had desired Frostyface to put an old spavined grey mare, that he had bought for the kennel, into the dog-cart, and out of which, his lordship thought, if he could get a day's work or two, she would come all the cheaper to the boiler.

'That's a good-shaped beast,' observed his lordship, as she now came hitching round to the door; 'I really think she would make a cover hack.'

'Sooner you ride her than me,' replied Jack, seeing his lordship was coming the dealer over him—praising the shape when he could say nothing for the action.

'Well, but she'll take you to Jawleyford Court as quick as the best of them,' rejoined his lordship, adding, 'the roads are wretched, and Jaw's stables are a disgrace to humanity—might as well put a horse in a cellar.'

'Well,' observed Jack, retiring from the parlour window to his little den along the passage, to put the finishing touch to his toilet—the green cutaway and buff waistcoat, which he further set off with a black satin stock—'Well,' said he, 'needs must when a certain gentleman drives.'

He presently reappeared full fig, rubbing a fine new eight-and-sixpenny flat-brimmed hat round and round with a substantial puce-coloured bandana. 'Now for the specs!' exclaimed he, with the gaiety of a man in his Sunday's best, bound on a holiday trip. 'Now for the silver specs!' repeated he.

'Ah, true,' replied his lordship; 'I'd forgot the specs.' (He hadn't, only he thought his silver-mounted ones would be safer in his keeping than in Jack's.) 'I'd forgot the specs. However, never mind, you shall have these,' said he, taking his tortoise-shell-rimmed ones off his nose and handing them to Jack.

'You promised me the silver ones,' observed our friend Jack, who wanted to be smart.

'Did I?' replied his lordship; 'I declare I'd forgot. Ah yes, I believe I did,' added he, with an air of sudden enlightenment—'the pair upstairs; but how the deuce to get at them I don't know, for the key of the Indian cabinet is locked in the old oak press in the still-room, and the key of the still-room is locked away in the linen-press in the green lumber-room at the top of the house, and the key of the green lumber-room is in a drawer at the bottom of the wardrobe in the Star-Chamber, and the—'

'Ah, well; never mind,' grunted Jack, interrupting the labyrinth of lies. 'I dare say these will do—I dare say these will do,' putting them on; adding, 'Now, if you'll lend me a shawl for my neck, and a mackintosh, my name shall be *Walker*.'

'Better make it *Trotter*,' replied his lordship, 'considering the distance you have to go.'

'Good,' said Jack, mounting and driving away.

'It will be a blessing if we get there,' observed Jack to the liveried stable-lad, as the old bag of bones of a mare went hitching and limping away.

'Oh, she can go when she's warm,' replied the lad, taking her across the ears with the point of the whip. The wheels followed merrily over the sound, hard road through the park, and the gentle though almost imperceptible fall of the ground giving an impetus to the vehicle, they bowled away as if they had four of the soundest, freshest legs in the world before them, instead of nothing but a belly-band between them and eternity.

When, however, they cleared the noble lodge and got upon the unscraped mud of the Deepdebt turnpike, the pace soon slackened, and, instead of the gig running away with the old mare, she was fairly brought to her collar. Being a game one, however, she struggled on with a trot, till at length, turning up the deeply spurlinged, clayey bottomed cross-road between Rookgate and Clamley, it was all she could do to drag the gig through the holding mire. Bump, bump, jolt, jolt, creak, creak, went the vehicle. Jack, now diving his elbow into the lad's ribs, the lad now diving his into Jack's; both now threatening to go over on the same side, and again both nearly chucked on to the old mare's quarters. A sharp, cutting sleet, driving pins and needles directly in their faces, further disconcerted our travellers. Jack felt acutely for his new eight-and-sixpenny hat, it being the only article of dress he had on of his own.

Long and tedious as was the road, weak and jaded as was the mare, and long as Jack stopped at Starfield, he yet reached Jawleyford Court before the messenger Harry.

As our friend Jawleyford was stamping about his study anathematizing a letter he had received from the solicitor to the directors of the Doembrown and Sinkall Railway, informing him that they were going to indulge in the winding-up act, he chanced to look out of his window just as the contracted limits of a winter's day were drawing the first folds of night's muslin curtain over the landscape, when he espied a gig drawn by a white horse, with a dot-and-go-one sort of action, hopping its way up the slumpey avenue.

'That's Buggins the bailiff,' exclaimed he to himself, as the recollection of an unanswered lawyer's letter flashed across his mind; and he was just darting off to the bell to warn Spigot not to admit any one, when the lad's cockade, standing in relief against the sky-line, caused him to pause and gaze again at the unwonted apparition.

'Who the deuce can it be?' asked he of himself, looking at his watch, and seeing it was a quarter-past four. 'It surely can't be my lord, or that Jack Spraggon coming after all?' added he, drawing out a telescope and opening a lancet-window.

'Spraggon, as I live!' exclaimed he, as he caught Jack's harsh, spectacled features, and saw him titivating his hair and arranging his collar and stock as he approached.

'Well, that beats everything!' exclaimed Jawleyford, burning with rage as he fastened the window again.

He stood for a few seconds transfixed to the spot, not knowing what on earth to do. At last resolution came to his aid, and, rushing upstairs to his dressing-room, he quickly divested himself of his coat and waistcoat, and slipped on a dressing-gown and night-cap. He then stood, door in hand, listening for the arrival. He could just hear the gig grinding under the portico, and distinguish Jack's gruff voice saying to the servant from the top of the steps, 'We'll start *directly* after breakfast, mind.' A tremendous peal of the bell immediately followed, convulsing the whole house, for nobody had seen the vehicle approaching, and the establishment had fallen into the usual state of undress torpor that intervenes between calling hours and dinner-time.

The bell not being answered as quickly as Jack expected, he just opened the door himself; and when Spigot arrived, with such a force as he could raise at the moment, Jack was in the act of 'peeling' himself, as he called it.

'What time do we dine?' asked he, with the air of a man with the *entrée*.

'Seven o'clock, my lord—that's to say, sir—that's to say, my lord,' for Spigot really didn't know whether it was Jack or his master.

'Seven o'clock!' muttered Jack. 'What the deuce is the use of dinin' at such an hour as that in winter?'

Jack and my lord always dined as soon as they got home from hunting. Jack, having got himself out of his wraps, and run his bristles backwards with a pocket-comb, was ready for presentation.

'What name shall I enounce?' asked Mr. Spigot, fearful of committing himself before the ladies.

'MISTER SPRAGGON, to be sure,' exclaimed Jack, thinking, because he knew who he was, that everybody else ought to know too.

Spigot then led the way to the music-room.

The peal at the bell had caused a suppressed commotion in the apartment. Buried in the luxurious depths of a well-cushioned low chair, Mr. Sponge sat, *Mogg* in hand, with a toe cocked up, now dipping leisurely into his work—now whispering something sweet into Amelia's ear, who sat with her crochet-work at his side; while Emily played the piano, and Mrs. Jawleyford kept in the background, in the discreet way mothers do when there is a little business going on. The room was in that happy state of misty light that usually precedes the entrance of candles—a light that no one likes to call darkness, lest their eyes might be supposed to be failing. It is a convenient light, however, for a timid stranger, especially where there are not many footstools set to trip him up—an exemption, we grieve to say, not accorded to every one.

Though Mr. Spraggon was such a cool, impudent fellow with men, he was the most awkward, frightened wretch among ladies that ever was seen. His conversation consisted principally of coughing. 'Hem!'— cough—'yes, mum,'—hem—cough, cough—'the day,'—hem—cough— 'mum, is'—hem—cough—'very,'—hem—cough—'mum, cold.' But we will introduce him to our family circle.

'MR. SPRAGGON!' exclaimed Spigot, in a tone equal to the one in which Jack had announced himself in the entrance; and forthwith there was such a stir in the twilit apartment—such suppressed exclamations of:

'Mr. Spraggon!—Mr. Spraggon! What can bring him here?'

Our traveller's creaking boots and radiant leathers eclipsing the sombre habiliments of Mr. Spigot, Mrs. Jawleyford quickly rose from her Pembroke writing-desk, and proceeded to greet him.

'My daughters I think you know, Mr. Spraggon; also Mr. Sponge? Mr. Spraggon,' continued she, with a wave of her hand to where our hero was ensconced in his form, in case they should not have made each other's speaking acquaintance.

The young ladies rose, and curtsied prettily; while Mr. Sponge gave a sort of backward hitch of his head as he sat in his chair, as much as to say, 'I know as much of Mr. Spraggon as I want.'

'Tell your master Mr. Spraggon is here,' added Mrs. Jawleyford to Spigot, as that worthy was leaving the room. 'It's a cold day, Mr. Spraggon; won't you come near the fire?' continued Mrs. Jawleyford, addressing our friend, who had come to a full stop just under the chandelier in the centre of the room. 'Hem—cough—hem—thank ye, mum,' muttered Jack. 'I'm not—hem—cough—cold, thank ye, mum.' His face and hands were purple notwithstanding.

'How is my Lord Scamperdale?' asked Amelia, who had a strong inclination to keep in with all parties.

'Hem—cough—hem—my lord—that's to say, my lady—hem—cough—I mean to say, my lord's pretty well, thank ye,' stuttered Jack.

'Is he coming?' asked Amelia.

'Hem—cough—hem—my lord's—hem—not well—cough—no—hem—I mean to say—hem—cough—my lord's gone—hem—to dine—cough—hem—with his—cough—friend Lord Bubbley Jock—hem—cough—I mean Barker—cough.'

Jack and Lord Scamperdale were so in the habit of calling his lordship by this nickname, that Jack let it slip, or rather cough out, inadvertently.

In due time Spigot returned, with 'Master's compliments, and he was very sorry, but he was so unwell that he was quite unable to see any one.'

'Oh, dear!' exclaimed Mrs. Jawleyford.

'Poor pa!' lisped Amelia.

'What a pity!' observed Mr. Sponge.

'I must go and see him,' observed Mrs. Jawleyford, hurrying off.

'Hem—cough—hem—hope he's not much—hem—damaged?' observed Jack.

The old lady being thus got rid of, and Jawleyford disposed of—apparently for the night—Mr. Spraggon felt more comfortable, and presently yielded to Amelia's entreaties to come near the fire and thaw himself. Spigot brought candles, and Mr. Sponge sat moodily in his chair, alternately studying *Mogg's Cab Fares*—'Old Bailey, Newgate Street, to or from the Adelphi, the Terrace, 1*s*. 6*d*.; Admiralty, 2*s*.'; and so on; and hazarding promiscuous sidelong sort of observations, that might be taken up by Jack or not, as he liked. He seemed determined to pay Mr. Jack off for his out-of-door impudence. Amelia, on the other hand, seemed desirous of making up for her suitor's rudeness, and kept talking to Jack with an assiduity that perfectly astonished her sister, who had always heard her speak of him with the utmost abhorrence.

Mrs. Jawleyford found her husband in a desperate state of excitement, his influenza being greatly aggravated by Harry having returned very drunk, with the mare's knees desperately broken 'by a fall,' as Harry hiccuped out, or by his 'throwing her down,' as Jawleyford declared. Horses *fall* with their masters, servants *throw* them down. What a happiness it is when people can send their servants on errands by coaches or railways, instead of being kept on the fidget all day, lest a fifty-pound horse should be the price of a bodkin or a basket of fish!

Amelia's condescension quite turned Jack's head; and when he went upstairs to dress, he squinted at his lordship's best clothes, all neatly laid out for him on the bed, with inward satisfaction at having brought them.

'Dash me!' said he, 'I really think that girl has a fancy for me.' Then he examined himself minutely in the glass, brushed his whiskers up into a curve on his cheeks, the curves almost corresponding with the curve of his spectacles above; then he gave his bristly, porcupine-shaped head a backward rub with a sort of thing like a scrubbing-brush. 'If I'd only had the silver specs,' thought he, 'I should have done.'

He then began to dress; an operation that, ever and anon was interrupted by the outburst of volleys of smoke from the little spluttering, smouldering fire in the little shabby room Jawleyford insisted on having him put into.

Jack tried all things—opening the window and shutting the door, shutting the window and opening the door; but finding that, instead of curing it, he only produced the different degrees of comparison—bad, worse, worst—he at length shut both, and applied himself vigorously to dressing. He soon got into his stockings and pumps, also his black Saxony trousers; then came a fine black laced fringe cravat, and the damson-coloured velvet waistcoat with the cut-steel buttons.

'Dash me, but I look pretty well in this!' said he, eyeing first one side and then the other as he buttoned it. He then stuck a chased and figured fine gold brooch, with two pendant tassel-drops, set with turquoise and agates, that he had abstracted from his lordship's dressing-case, into his, or rather his lordship's finely worked shirt-front, and crowned the toilet with his lordship's best new blue coat with velvet collar, silk facings, and the Flat Hat Hunt button—'a striding fox,' with the letters 'F.H.H.' below.

'Who shall say Mr. Spraggon's not a gentleman?' said he, as he perfumed one of his lordship's fine coronetted cambric handkerchiefs with lavender-water. Scent, in Jack's opinion, was one of the criterions of a gentleman.

Somehow Jack felt quite differently towards the house of Jawleyford; and though he did not expect much pleasure in Mr. Sponge's company, he thought, nevertheless, that the ladies and he—Amelia and he, at least—would get on very well. Forgetting that he had come to eject Sponge on the score of insufficiency, he really began to think he might be a very desirable match for one of them himself.

'The Spraggons are a most respectable family,' said he, eyeing himself in the glass. 'If not very handsome, at all events, very genteel,' added he, speaking of himself in particular. So saying, he adorned himself with his spectacles and set off to explore his way downstairs. After divers mistakes, he at length found himself in the drawing-room, where the rest of the party being assembled, they presently proceeded to dinner.

Jack's amended costume did not produce any difference in Mr. Sponge's behaviour, who treated him with the utmost indifference. In truth, Sponge had rather a large balance against Jack for his impudence to him in the field. Nevertheless, the fair Amelia continued her attentions, and talked of hunting, occasionally diverging into observations on Lord Scamperdale's fine riding and manly character and appearance, in the roundabout way ladies send their messages and compliments to their friends.

The dinner was flat. Jawleyford had stopped the champagne tap, though the needle-case glasses stood to tantalize the party till about the time that the beverage ought to have been flowing, when Spigot took them off. The flatness then became flatter. Nevertheless, Jack worked away in his usual carnivorous style, and finished by paying his respects to all the sweets, jellies, and things in succession. He never got any of these, he said, at 'home,' meaning at Lord Scamperdale's—Amelia thought, if she was 'my lady,' he would not get any meat there either.

At length Jack finished; and having discussed cheese, porter, and red herrings, the cloth was drawn, and a hard-featured dessert, consisting principally of apples, followed. The wine having made a couple of melancholy circuits, the strained conversation about came to a full stop, and Spigot having considerately placed the little round table, as if to keep the peace between them, the ladies left the male worthies to discuss their port and sherry together. Jack, according to Woodmansterne fashion, unbuttoned his waistcoat, and stuck his legs out before him—an example that Mr. Sponge quickly followed, and each assumed an attitude that as good as said 'I don't care twopence for you.' A dead silence then prevailed, interrupted only by the snap, snap, snapping of Jack's toothpick against his chair-edge, when he was not busy exploring his mouth with it. It seemed to be a match which should keep silence longest. Jack sat squinting his eyes inside out at Sponge, while Sponge pretended to be occupied with the fire. The wine being with Sponge, and at length wanting some, he was constrained to make the first move, by passing it over to Jack, who helped himself to port and sherry simultaneously—a glass of sherry after dinner (in Jack's opinion) denoting a gentleman. Having smacked his lips over that, he presently turned to the glass of port. He checked his hand in passing it to his mouth, and bore the glass up to his nose.

'Corked, by Jove!' exclaimed he, setting the glass down on the table with a thump of disgust.

It is curious what unexpected turns things sometimes take in the world, and how completely whole trains of well-preconcerted plans are often turned aside by mere accidents such as this. If it hadn't been for the corked bottle of port, there is no saying but these two worthies would have held a Quakers' meeting without the 'spirit' moving either of them.

'Corked, by Jove!' exclaimed Jack.

'It is!' rejoined Sponge, smelling at his half-emptied glass.

'Better have another bottle,' observed Jack.

'Certainly,' replied Sponge, ringing the bell. 'Spigot, this wine's corked,' observed Sponge, as old Pomposo entered the room.

'Is it?' said Spigot, with the most perfect innocence, though he knew it came out of the corked batch. 'I'll bring another bottle,' added he, carrying it off as if he had a whole pipe at command, though in reality he had but another out. This fortunately was less corked than the first; and Jack having given an approving smack of his great thick lips, Mr. Sponge took it on his judgement, and gave a nod to Spigot, who forthwith took his departure.

'Old trick that,' observed Jack, with a shake of the head, as Spigot shut the door.

'Is it?' observed Mr. Sponge, taking up the observation, though in reality it was addressed to the fire.

'Noted for it,' replied Jack, squinting at the sideboard, though he was staring intently at Sponge to see how he took it.

'Well, I thought we had a bottle with a queer smatch the other night,' observed Sponge.

'Old Blossomnose corked half a dozen in succession one night,' replied Jack.

(He had corked three, but Jawleyford re-corked them, and Spigot was now reproducing them to our friends.)

Although they had now got the ice broken, and entered into something like a conversation, it nevertheless went on very slowly, and they seemed to weigh each word before it was uttered. Jack, too, had time to run his peculiar situation through his mind, and ponder on his mission from Lord Scamperdale—on his lordship's detestation of Mr. Sponge, his anxiety to get rid of him, his promised corner in his will, and his lordship's hint about buying Sponge's horses if he could not get rid of him in any other way.

Sponge, on his part, was thinking if there was any possibility of turning Jack to account.

It may seem strange to the uninitiated that there should be prospect of gain to a middle-man in the matter of a horse-deal, save in the legitimate trade of auctioneers and commission stable-keepers; but we are sorry to say we have known men calling themselves gentlemen, who have not thought it derogatory to accept a 'trifle' for their good offices in the cause. 'I can buy cheaper than you,' they say, 'and we may as well divide the trifle between us.'

That was Mr. Spraggon's principle, only that the word 'trifle' inadequately conveys his opinion on the point; Jack's notion being that a man was entitled to £5 per cent. as of right, and as much more as he could get.

It was not often that Jack got a 'bite' at my lord, which, perhaps, made him think it the more incumbent on him not to miss an opportunity. Having been told, of course he knew exactly the style of man he had to deal with in Mr. Sponge—a style of men of whom there is never any difficulty in asking if they will sell their horses, price being the only consideration. They are, indeed, a sort of unlicensed horse-dealers, from whose presence few hunts are wholly free. Mr. Spraggon thought if he could get Sponge to make it worth his while to get my lord to buy his horses, the—whatever he might get—would come in very comfortably to pay his Christmas bills.

By the time the bottle drew to a close, our friends were rather better friends, and seemed more inclined to fraternize. Jack had the advantage of Sponge, for he could stare, or rather squint, at him without Sponge knowing it. The pint of wine apiece—at least, as near a pint apiece as Spigot could afford to let them have—somewhat strung Jack's nerves as well as his eyes, and he began to show more of the pupils and less of the whites than he did. He buzzed the bottle with such a hearty good will as settled the fate of another, which Sponge rang for as a matter of course. There was but the rejected one, which, however. Spigot put into a different decanter, and brought in with such an air as precluded either of them saying a word in disparagement of it.

'Where are the hounds next week?' asked Sponge, sipping away at it.

'Monday, Larkhall Hill; Tuesday, the cross-roads by Dallington Burn; Thursday, the Toll-bar at Whitburrow Green; Saturday, the kennels,' replied Jack.

'Good places?' asked Sponge.

'Monday's good,' replied Jack; 'draw Thorney Gorse—sure find; second draw, Barnlow Woods, and home by Loxley, Padmore, and so on.'

'What sort of a place is Tuesday?'

'Tuesday?' repeated Jack. 'Tuesday! Oh, that's the cross-roads. Capital place, unless the fox takes to Rumborrow Craigs, or gets into Seedywood Forest, when there's an end of it—at least, an end of everything except pulling one's horse's legs off in the stiff clayey rides. It's a long way from here, though,' observed Jack.

'How far?' asked Sponge.

'Good twenty miles,' replied Jack. 'It's sixteen from us; it'll be a good deal more from here.'

'His lordship will lay out overnight, then?' observed Sponge.

'Not he,' replied Jack. 'Takes better care of his sixpences than that. Up in the dark, breakfast by candlelight, grope our ways to the stable, and blunder along the deep lanes, and through all the by-roads in the country—get there somehow or another.'

'Keen hand!' observed Sponge.

'Mad!' replied Jack.

They then paid their mutual respects to the port.

'He hunts there on Tuesdays,' observed Jack, setting down his glass, 'so that he may have all Wednesday to get home in, and be sure of appearing on Thursday. There's no saying where he may finish with a cross-roads' meet.'

By the time the worthies had finished the bottle, they had got a certain way into each other's confidence. The hint Lord Scamperdale had given about buying Sponge's horses still occupied Jack's mind; and the more he considered the subject, and the worth of a corner in his lordship's will, the more sensible he became of the truth of the old adage, that 'a bird in the hand is worth two in the bush.' 'My lord,' thought Jack, 'promises fair, but it is *but* a chance, and a remote one. He may live many years—as long, perhaps longer, than me. Indeed, he puts me on horses that are anything but calculated to promote longevity. Then he may marry a wife who may eject me, as some wives do eject their husbands' agreeable friends; or he may change his mind, and leave me nothing after all.'

All things considered, Jack came to the conclusion that he should not be doing himself justice if he did not take advantage of such fair opportunities as chance placed in his way, and therefore he thought he might as well be picking up a penny during his lordship's life, as be waiting for a contingency that might never occur. Mr. Jawleyford's indisposition preventing Jack making the announcement he was sent to do, made it incumbent on him, as he argued, to see what could be done with the alternative his lordship had proposed—namely, buying Sponge's horses. At least, Jack salved his conscience over with the old plea of duty; and had come to that conclusion as he again helped himself to the last glass in the bottle.

'Would you like a little claret?' asked Sponge, with all the hospitality of a host.

'No, hang your claret!' replied Jack.

'A little brandy, perhaps?' suggested Sponge.

'I shouldn't mind a glass of brandy,' replied Jack, 'by way of a nightcap.'

Spigot, at this moment entering to announce tea and coffee, was interrupted in his oration by Sponge demanding some brandy.

'Sorry,' replied Spigot, pretending to be quite taken by surprise, 'very sorry, sir—but, sir—master, sir—bed, sir—disturb him, sir.'

'Oh, dash it, never mind that!' exclaimed Jack; 'tell him Mr. Sprag—Sprag—Spraggon' (the bottle of port beginning to make Jack rather inarticulate)—'tell him Mr. Spraggon wants a little.'

'Durstn't disturb him, sir,' responded Spigot, with a shake of his head; 'much as my place, sir, is worth, sir.'

'Haven't you a little drop in your pantry, think you?' asked Sponge.

'The *cook* perhaps has,' replied Mr. Spigot, as if it was quite out of his line.

'Well, go and ask her,' said Sponge; 'and bring some hot water and things, the same as we had last night, you know.'

Mr. Spigot retired, and presently returned, bearing a tray with three-quarters of a bottle of brandy, which he impressed upon their minds was the 'cook's *own*.'

'I dare say,' hiccuped Jack, holding the bottle up to the light.

'Hope she wasn't using it herself,' observed Sponge.

'Tell her we'll (hiccup) her health,' hiccuped Jack, pouring a liberal potation into his tumbler.

'That'll be all you'll *do*, I dare say,' muttered Spigot to himself, as he sauntered back to his pantry.

'Does Jaw stand smoking?' asked Jack, as Spigot disappeared.

'Oh, I should think so,' replied Sponge; 'a friend like you, I'm sure, would be welcome'—Sponge thinking to indulge in a cigar, and lay the blame on Jack.

'Well, if you think so,' said Jack, pulling out his cigar-case, or rather his lordship's, and staggering to the chimney-piece for a match, though there was a candle at his elbow, 'I'll have a pipe.'

'So'll I,' said Sponge, 'if you'll give me a cigar.' 'Much yours as mine,' replied Jack, handing him his lordship's richly embroidered case with coronets and ciphers on either side, the gift of one of the many would-be Lady Scamperdales.

'Want a light!' hiccuped Jack, who had now got a glow-worm end to his.

'Thanks,' said Sponge, availing himself of the friendly overture.

Our friends now whiffed and puffed away together—whiffing and puffing where whiffing and puffing had never been known before. The brandy began to disappear pretty quickly; it was better than the wine.

'That's a n—n—nice—ish horse of yours,' stammered Jack, as he mixed himself a second tumbler.

'Which?' asked Sponge.

'The bur—bur—brown,' spluttered Jack.

'He is *that*,' replied Sponge; 'best horse in this country by far.'

'The che—che—chest—nut's not a ba—ba—bad un. I dare say,' observed Jack.

'No, he's not,' replied Sponge; 'a deuced good un.'

'I know a man who's rayther s—s—s—sweet on the b—b—br—brown,' observed Jack, squinting frightfully.

Sponge sat silent for a few seconds, pretending to be wrapt up in his 'sublime tobacco.'

'Is he a buyer, or just a jawer?' he asked at last.

'Oh, a *buyer*,' replied Jack.

'I'll *sell*,' said Sponge, with a strong emphasis on the sell.

'How much?' asked Jack, sobering with the excitement.

'Which?' asked Sponge.

'The brown,' rejoined Jack.

'Three hundred,' said Sponge; adding, 'I gave two for him.'

'Indeed!' said Jack.

A long pause then ensued, Jack thinking whether he should put the question boldly as to what Sponge would give him for effecting a sale, or should he beat about the bush a little. At last he thought it would be most prudent to beat about the bush, and see if Sponge would make an offer.

'Well,' said Jack, 'I'll s—s—s—see what I can do.'

'That's a good fellow,' said Sponge; adding, 'I'll remember you, if you do.'

'I dare say I can s—s—s—sell them both, for that matter,' observed Jack, encouraged by the promise.

'Well,' replied Sponge, 'I'll take the same for the chestnut; there isn't the toss-up of a halfpenny for choice between them.'

'Well,' said Jack, 'we'll s—s—s—see them next week.'

'Just so,' said Sponge.

'You r—r—ride well up to the h—h—hounds,' continued Jack; 'and let his lordship s—s—see w—w—what they can do.'

'I will,' said Sponge, wishing he was at work.

'Never mind his rowing,' observed Jack; 'he c—c—can't help it.'

'Not I,' replied Sponge, puffing away at his cigar.

When men once begin to drink brandy-and-water (after wine) there's an end of all note of time. Our friends—for we 'may now call them so,' sat sip, sip, sipping—mix, mix, mixing; now strengthening, now weakening, now warming, now flavouring, till they had not only finished the hot water but a large jug of cold, that graced the centre of the table between two frosted tumblers, and had nearly got through the brandy, too.

'May as well fi—fi—fin—nish the bottle,' observed Jack, holding it up to the candle. 'Just a thi—thi—thim—bleful apiece,' added he, helping himself to about three-quarters of what there was.

'You've taken your share,' observed Sponge, as the bottle suspended payment before he got half the quantity that Jack had.

'Sque—ee—eze it,' replied Jack, suiting the action to the word, and working away at an exhausted lemon.

At length they finished.

'Well, I s'pose we may as well go and have some tea,' observed Jack.

'It's not announced yet,' said Sponge, 'but I make no doubt it will be ready.'

So saying, the worthies rose, and, after sundry bumps and certain irregularities of course, they each succeeded in reaching the door. The passage lamp had died out and filled the corridor with its fragrance. Sponge, however, knew the way, and the darkness favored the adjustment of cravats and the fingering of hair. Having got up a sort of drunken simper, Sponge opened the drawing-room door, expecting to find smiling ladies in a blaze of light. All, however, was darkness, save the expiring embers in the grate. The tick, tick, tick, ticking of the clocks sounded wonderfully clear.

'Gone to bed!' exclaimed Sponge.

'WHO-HOOP!' shrieked Jack, at the top of his voice.

'What's smatter, gentlemen?—What's smatter?' exclaimed Spigot rushing in, rubbing his eyes with one hand, and holding a block tin candlestick in the other.

'Nothin',' replied Jack, squinting his eyes inside out; adding, 'get me a devilled—' (hiccup).

'Don't know how to do them here, sir,' snapped Spigot.

'Devilled turkey's leg though you do, you rascal!' rejoined Jack, doubling his fists and putting himself in posture.

'Beg pardon, sir,' replied Spigot, 'but the cook, sir, is gone to bed, sir. Do you know, sir, what o'clock it is, sir?'

'No,' replied Jack.

'What time is it?' asked Sponge.

'Twenty minutes to two,' replied Spigot, holding up a sort of pocket warming-pan, which he called a watch.

'The deuce!' exclaimed Sponge.

'Who'd ha' thought it?' muttered Jack.

'Well, then, I suppose we may as well go to bed,' observed Sponge.

'S'pose so,' replied Jack; 'nothin' more to get.'

'Do you know your room?' asked Sponge.

'To be sure I do,' replied Jack; 'don't think I'm d—d—dr—drunk, do you?'

'Not likely,' rejoined Sponge.

Jack then commenced a very crab-like ascent of the stairs, which fortunately were easy, or he would never have got up. Mr. Sponge, who still occupied the state apartments, took leave of Jack at his own door, and Jack went bumping and blundering on in search of the branch passage leading to his piggery. He found the green baize door that usually distinguishes the entrance to these secondary suites, and was presently lurching along its contracted passage. As luck would have it, however, he got into his host's dressing-room, where that worthy slept; and when Jawleyford jumped up in the morning, as was his wont, to see what sort of a day it was, he trod on Jack's face, who had fallen down in his clothes alongside of the bed, and Jawleyford broke Jack's spectacles across the bridge of his nose.

'Rot it!' roared Jack, jumping up, 'don't ride over a fellow that way!' When, shaking himself to try whether any limbs were broken, he found he was in his dress clothes instead of in the roomy garments of the Flat Hat Hunt. 'Who are you? where am I? what the deuce do you mean by breaking my specs?' he exclaimed, squinting frightfully at his host.

'My dear sir,' exclaimed Mr. Jawleyford, from the top of his night-shirt, 'I'm very sorry, but—'

'Hang your *buts*! you shouldn't ride so near a man!' exclaimed Jack, gathering up the fragments of his spectacles; when, recollecting himself, he finished by saying, 'Perhaps I'd better go to my own room.'

'Perhaps you had,' replied Mr. Jawleyford, advancing towards the door to show him the way.

'Let me have a candle,' said Jack, preparing to follow.

'Candle, my dear fellow! why, it's broad daylight,' replied his host.

'Is it?' said Jack, apparently unconscious of the fact. 'What's the hour?'

'Five minutes to eight,' replied Jawleyford, looking at a timepiece.

When Jack got into his own den he threw himself into an old invalid chair, and sat rubbing the fractured spectacles together as if he thought they would unite by friction, though in reality he was endeavouring to run the overnight's proceedings through his mind. The more he thought of Amelia's winning ways, the more satisfied he was that he had made an impression, and then the more vexed he was at having his spectacles broken: for though he considered himself very presentable without them, still he could not but feel that they were a desirable addition. Then, too, he had a splitting headache; and finding that breakfast was not till ten and might be a good deal later, all things considered, he determined to be off and follow up his success under more favourable auspices. Considering that all the clothes he had with him were his lordship's, he thought it immaterial which he went home in, so to save trouble he just wrapped himself up in his mackintosh and travelled in the dress ones he had on.

It was fortunate for Mr. Sponge that he went, for, when Jawleyford smelt the indignity that had been offered to his dining-room, he broke out in such a torrent of indignation as would have been extremely unpleasant if there had not been some one to lay the blame on. Indeed, he was not particularly gracious to Mr. Sponge as it was; but that arose as much from certain dark hints that had worked their way from the servants' hall into 'my lady's chamber' as to our friend's pecuniary resources and prospects. Jawleyford began to suspect that Sponge might not be quite the great 'catch' he was represented.

Beyond, however, putting a few searching questions—which Mr. Sponge skilfully parried—advising his daughters to be cautious, lessening the number of lights, and lowering the scale of his entertainments

generally, Mr. Jawleyford did not take any decided step in the matter. Mr.
Spraggon comforted Lord Scamperdale with the assurance that Amelia
had no idea of Sponge, who he made no doubt would very soon be
out of the country—and his lordship went to church and prayed most
devoutly for him to go.

XXVI

MR. AND MRS. SPRINGWHEAT

'LORD SCAMPERDALE'S FOXHOUNDS MEET ON Monday at Larkhall Hill,' &c. &c.—*County Paper.*

The Flat Hat Hunt had relapsed into its wonted quiet, and 'Larkhall Hill' saw none but the regular attendants, men without the slightest particle of curve in their hats—hats, indeed, that looked as if the owners sat upon them when they hadn't them on their heads. There was Fyle, and Fossick, and Blossomnose, and Sparks, and Joyce, and Capon, and Dribble, and a few others, but neither Washball nor Puffington, nor any of the holiday birds.

Precisely at ten, my lord, and his hounds, and his huntsman, and his whips, and his Jack, trotted round Farmer Springwheat's spacious back premises, and appeared in due form before the green rails in front. 'Pride attends us all,' as the poet says; and if his lordship had ridden into the yard, and halloaed out for a glass of home-brewed, Springwheat would have trapped every fox on his farm, and the blooming Mrs. Springwheat would have had an interminable poultry-bill against the hunt; whereas, simply by 'making things pleasant'—that is to say, coming to breakfast—Springwheat saw his corn trampled on, nay, led the way over it himself, and Mrs. Springwheat saw her Dorkings disappear without a murmur—unless, indeed, an inquiry when his lordship would be coming could be considered in that light.

Larkhall Hill stood in the centre of a circle, on a gentle eminence, commanding a view over a farm whose fertile fields and well-trimmed fences sufficiently indicated its boundaries, and looked indeed as if all the good of the country had come up to it. It was green and luxuriant even in winter, while the strong cane-coloured stubbles showed what a crop there had been. Turnips as big as cheeses swelled above the ground. In a little narrow dell, whose existence was more plainly indicated from the house by several healthy spindling larches shooting up from among the green gorse, was the cover—an almost certain find, with the almost equal certainty of a run from it. It occupied both sides of the sandy, rabbit-frequented dell, through which ran a sparkling stream, and it possessed the great advantage to foot-people of letting them see the fox found. Larkhall Hill was, therefore, a favourite both with horse and foot. So much good—at all events, so much well-farmed land would seem to justify a better or more imposing-looking house, the present one consisting, exclusive of the projecting garret ones in the Dutch tile roof, of the usual four windows and a door, that so well tell their own tale; passage in the middle, staircase in front, parlour on the right, best ditto on the left, with rooms to correspond above. To be sure, there was a great depth of house to the back; but this in no way contributed to the importance of the front, from which point alone the Springwheats chose to have it contemplated. If the back arrangements could have been divided, and added to the sides, they would have made two very good wings to the old red brick rose-entwined mansion. Having mentioned that its colour was red, it is almost superfluous to add that the door and rails were green.

This was a busy morning at Larkhall Hill. It was the first day of the season of my lord's hounds meeting there, and the handsome Mrs. Springwheat had had as much trouble in overhauling the china and linen, and in dressing the children, preparatory to breakfast, as Springwheat had had in collecting knives and forks, and wine-glasses and tumblers for his department of the entertainment, to say nothing of looking after his new tops and cords. 'The Hill,' as the country people call it, was 'full fig'; and a bright, balmy winter's day softened the atmosphere, and felt as though a summer's day had been shaken out of its place into winter. It is not often that the English climate is accommodating enough to lend its aid to set off a place to advantage.

Be that, however, as it may, things looked smiling both without and within. Mrs. Springwheat, by dint of early rising and superintendence, had got things into such a state of forwardness as to be able to adorn herself with a little jaunty cap—curious in microscopic punctures and cherry-coloured ribbon interlardments—placed so far back on her finely-shaped head as to proclaim beyond all possibility of cavil that it was there for ornament, and not for the purpose of concealing the liberties of time with her well-kept, clearly parted, raven-black hair. Liberties of time, forsooth! Mrs. Springwheat was in the heighday of womanhood; and though she had presented Springwheat with twins three times in succession, besides an eldest son, she was as young, fresh-looking, and finely figured as she was the day she was married. She was now dressed in a very fine French grey merino, with a very small crochet-work collar, and, of course, capacious muslin sleeves. The high flounces to her dress set off her smart waist to great advantage.

Mrs. Springwheat had got everything ready, and herself too, by the time Lord Scamperdale's second horseman rode into the yard and demanded a stall for his horse. Knowing how soon the balloon follows the pilot, she immediately ranged the Stunner-tartan-clad children in the breakfast-room; and as the first whip's rate sounded as he rode round the corner, she sank into an easy-chair by the fire, with a lace-fringed kerchief in the one hand and the *Mark Lane Express* in the other.

'Halloa! Springey!' followed by the heavy crack of a whip, announced the arrival of his lordship before the green palings; and a loud view halloa burst from Jack, as the object of inquiry was seen dancing about the open-windowed room above, with his face all flushed with the exertion of pulling on a very tight boot.

'Come in, my lord! pray, come in! The missis is below!' exclaimed Springwheat, from the window; and just at the moment the pad-groom emerged from the house, and ran to his lordship's horse's head.

His lordship and Jack then dismounted, and gave their hacks in charge of the servant; while Wake, and Fyle, and Archer, who were also of the party, scanned the countenances of the surrounding idlers, to see in whose hands they had best confide their nags.

In Lord Scamperdale stamped, followed by his train-band bold, and Maria, the maid, being duly stationed in the passage, threw open the parlour door on the left, and discovered Mrs. Springwheat sitting in attitude.

'Well, my lady, and how are you?' exclaimed his lordship, advancing gaily, and seizing both her pretty hands as she rose to receive him. 'I declare, you look younger and prettier every time I see you.'

'Oh! my lord,' simpered Mrs. Springwheat, 'you gentlemen are always so complimentary.'

'Not a bit of it!' exclaimed his lordship, eyeing her intently through his silver spectacles, for he had been obliged to let Jack have the other pair of tortoiseshell-rimmed ones. 'Not a bit of it,' repeated his lordship. 'I always tell Jack you are the handsomest woman in Christendom; don't I, Jack?' inquired his lordship, appealing to his factotum.

'Yes, my lord,' replied Jack, who always swore to whatever his lordship said.

'By Jove!' continued his lordship, with a stamp of his foot, 'if I could find such a woman I'd marry her to-morrow. Not such women as you to pick up every day. And what a lot of pretty pups!' exclaimed his lordship, starting back, pretending to be struck with the row of staring, black-haired, black-eyed, half-frightened children. 'Now, that's what I call a good entry,' continued his lordship, scrutinizing them attentively, and pointing them out to Jack; 'all dogs—all boys I mean!' added he.

'No, my lord,' replied Mrs. Springwheat, laughing, 'these are girls,' laying her hand on the heads of two of them, who were now full giggle at the idea of being taken for boys.

'Well, they're devilish handsome, anyhow,' replied his lordship, thinking he might as well be done with the inspection.

Springwheat himself now made his appearance, as fine a sample of a man as his wife was of a woman. His face was flushed with the exertion of pulling on his tight boots, and his lordship felt the creases the hooks had left as he shook him by the hand.

'Well, Springey,' said he, 'I was just asking your wife after the new babby.'

'Oh, thank you, my lord,' replied Springey, with a shake of his curly head; 'thank you, my lord; no new babbies, my lord, with wheat below forty, my lord.'

'Well, but you've got a pair of new boots, at all events,' observed his lordship, eyeing Springwheat's refractory calves bagging over the tops of them.

''Deed have I!' replied Springwheat; 'and a pair of uncommon awkward tight customers they are,' added he, trying to move his feet about in them.

'Ah! you should always have a chap to wear your boots a few times before you put them on yourself,' observed his lordship. 'I never have a pair of tight uns,' added he; 'Jack here always does the needful by mine.'

'That's all very well for lords,' replied Mr. Springwheat; 'but us farmers wear out our boots fast enough ourselves, without anybody to help us.'

'Well, but I s'pose we may as well fall to,' observed his lordship, casting his eye upon the well-garnished table. 'All these good things are meant to eat, I s'pose,' added he: 'cakes, and sweets, and jellies without end: and as to your sideboard,' said he, turning round and looking at it, 'it's a match for any Lord Mayor's. A round of beef, a ham, a tongue, and is that a goose or a turkey?'

'A turkey, my lord,' replied Springwheat; 'home-fed, my lord.'

'Ah, home-fed, indeed!' ejaculated his lordship, with a shake of the head: 'home-fed: wish I could feed at home. The man who said that

E'en from the peasant to the lord,
The turkey smokes on every board,

told a big un, for I'm sure none ever smokes on mine.'

'Take a little here to-day, then,' observed Mr. Springwheat, cutting deep into the white breast.

'I will,' replied his lordship, 'I will: and a slice of tongue, too,' added he.

'There are some hot sausingers comin',' observed Mr. Springwheat.

'You *don't* say so,' replied his lordship, apparently thunderstruck at the announcement. 'Well, I must have all three. By Jove, Jack!' said he, appealing to his friend, 'but you've lit on your legs coming here. Here's a breakfast fit to set before the Queen—muffins, and crumpets, and cakes. Let me advise you to make the best use of your time, for you have but twenty minutes,' continued his lordship, looking at his watch, 'and muffins and crumpets don't come in your way every day.'

''Deed they don't,' replied Jack, with a grin.

'Will your lordship take tea or coffee?' asked Mrs. Springwheat, who had now taken her seat at the top of the table, behind a richly chased equipage for the distribution of those beverages.

''Pon my word,' replied his lordship, apparently bewildered—''pon my word, I don't know what to say. Tea or coffee? To tell you the truth,

I was going to take something out of my black friend yonder,' nodding to where a French bottle like a tall bully was lifting its head above an encircling stand of liqueur-glasses.

'Suppose you have a little of what we call laced tea, my lord—tea with a dash of brandy in it?' suggested Mr. Springwheat.

'Laced tea,' repeated his lordship; 'laced tea: so I will,' said he. 'Deuced good idea—deuced good idea,' continued he, bringing the bottle and seating himself on Mrs. Springwheat's right, while his host helped him to a most plentiful plate of turkey and tongue. The table was now about full, as was the room; the guests just rolling in as they would to a public-house, and helping themselves to whatever they liked. Great was the noise of eating.

As his lordship was in the full enjoyment of his plateful of meat, he happened to look up, and, the space between him and the window being clear, he saw something that caused him to drop his knife and fork and fall back in his chair as if he was shot.

'My lord's ill!' exclaimed Mr. Springwheat, who, being the only man with his nose up, was the first to perceive it.

'Clap him on the back!' shrieked Mrs. Springwheat, who considered that an infallible recipe for the ailments of children.

'Oh, Mr. Spraggon!' exclaimed both, as they rushed to his assistance, 'what is the matter with my lord?'

'Oh, that Mister something!' gasped his lordship, bending forward in his chair, and venturing another glance through the window.

Sure enough, there was Sponge, in the act of dismounting from the piebald, and resigning it with becoming dignity to his trusty groom, Mr. Leather, who stood most respectfully—Parvo in hand—waiting to receive it.

Mr. Sponge, being of opinion that a red coat is a passport everywhere, having stamped the mud sparks off his boots at the door, swaggered in with the greatest coolness, exclaiming as he bobbed his head to the lady, and looked round at the company:

'What, grubbing away! grubbing away, eh?'

'Won't you take a little refreshment?' asked Mr. Springwheat, in the hearty way these hospitable fellows welcome everybody.

'Yes, I will,' replied Sponge, turning to the sideboard as though it were an inn. 'That's a monstrous fine ham,' observed he; 'why doesn't somebody cut it?'

'Let me help you to some, sir,' replied Mr. Springwheat, seizing the buck-handled knife and fork, and diving deep into the rich red meat with the knife.

Mr. Sponge having got two bountiful slices, with a knotch of home-made brown bread, and some mustard on his plate, now made for the table, and elbowed himself into a place between Mr. Fossick and Sparks, immediately opposite Mr. Spraggon.

'Good morning,' said he to that worthy, as he saw the whites of his eyes showing through his spectacles.

'Mornin',' muttered Jack, as if his mouth was either too full to articulate, or he didn't want to have anything to say to Mr. Sponge.

'Here's a fine hunting morning, my lord,' observed Sponge, addressing himself to his lordship, who sat on Jack's left.

'Here's a very fine hunting morning, my lord,' repeated Sponge, not getting an answer to his first assertion.

'Is it?' blurted his lordship, pretending to be desperately busy with the contents of his plate, though in reality his appetite was gone.

A dead pause now ensued, interrupted only by the clattering of knives and forks, and the occasional exclamations of parties in want of some particular article of food. A chill had come over the scene—a chill whose cause was apparent to every one, except the worthy host and hostess, who had not heard of Mr. Sponge's descent upon the country. They attributed it to his lordship's indisposition, and Mr. Springwheat endeavoured to cheer him up with the prospect of sport.

'There's a brace, if not a leash, of foxes in cover, my lord,' observed he, seeing his lordship was only playing with the contents of his plate.

'Is there?' exclaimed his lordship, brightening up: 'let's be at 'em!' added he, jumping up and diving under the side-table for his flat hat and heavy iron hammer-headed whip. 'Good morning, my dear Mrs. Springwheat,' exclaimed he, putting on his hat and seizing both her soft fat-fingered hands and squeezing them ardently. 'Good morning, my dear Mrs. Springwheat,' repeated he, adding, 'By Jove! if ever there was an angel in petticoats, you're her; I'd give a hundred pounds for such a wife as you! I'd give a thousand pounds for such a wife as you! By the powers! I'd give five thousand pounds for such a wife as you!' With which asseverations his lordship stamped away in his great clumsy boots, amidst the ill-suppressed laughter of the party.

'No hurry, gentlemen—no hurry,' observed Mr. Springwheat, as some of the keen ones were preparing to follow, and began sorting their hats, and making the mistakes incident to their being all the same shape. 'No hurry, sir—no hurry, sir,' repeated Springwheat, addressing Mr. Sponge specifically; 'his lordship will have a talk to his hounds yet, and his horse is still in the stable.'

With this assurance Mr. Sponge resumed his seat at the table, where several of the hungry ones were plying their knives and forks as if they were indeed breaking their fasts.

'Well, old boy, and how are you?' asked Sponge, as the whites of Jack's eyes again settled upon him, on the latter's looking up from his plateful of sausages.

'Nicely. How are you?' asked Jack.

'Nicely, too,' replied Sponge, in the laconic way men speak who have been engaged in some common enterprise—getting drunk, pelting people with rotten eggs, or anything of that sort.

'Jaw and the ladies well?' asked Jack, in the same strain.

'Oh, nicely,' said Sponge.

'Take a glass of cherry-brandy,' exclaimed the hospitable Mr. Springwheat: 'nothing like a drop of something for steadying the nerves.'

'Presently,' replied Sponge, 'presently; meanwhile I'll trouble the missis for a cup of coffee. Coffee without sugar,' said Sponge, addressing the lady.

'With pleasure,' replied Mrs. Springwheat, glad to get a little custom for her goods. Most of the gentlemen had been at the bottles and sideboard.

Springwheat, seeing Mr. Sponge, the only person who, as a stranger, there was any occasion for him to attend to, in the care of his wife, now slipped out of the room, and mounting his five-year-old horse, whose tail stuck out like the long horn of a coach, as his ploughman groom said, rode off to join the hunt.

'By the powers, but those are capital sarsingers!' observed Jack, smacking his lips and eating away for hard life. 'Just look if my lord's on his horse yet,' added he to one of the children, who had begun to hover round the table and dive their fingers into the sweets.

'No,' replied the child; 'he's still on foot, playing with the dogs.'

'Here goes, then,' said Jack, 'for another plate,' suiting the action to the word, and running with his plate to the sausage-dish.

'Have a hot one,' exclaimed Mrs. Springwheat, adding, 'it will be done in a minute.'

'No, thank ye,' replied Jack, with a shake of the head, adding, 'I might be done in a minute too.'

'He'll wait for you, I suppose?' observed Sponge, addressing Jack.

'Not so clear about that,' replied Jack, gobbling away; 'time and my lord wait for no man. But it's hardly the half-hour yet,' added he, looking at his watch.

He then fell to with the voracity of a hound after hunting. Sponge, too, made the most of his time, as did two or three others who still remained.

'Now for the jumping-powder!' at length, exclaimed Sponge, looking round for the bottle. 'What shall it be, cherry or neat?' continued he, pointing to the two. 'Cherry, for me,' replied Jack, squinting and eating away without looking up.

'I say *neat*,' rejoined Sponge, helping himself out of the French bottle.

'You'll be hard to hold after that,' observed Jack, as he eyed Sponge tossing it off.

'I hope my horse won't,' replied Sponge, remembering he was going to ride the resolute chestnut.

'You'll show us the way, I dare say,' observed Jack.

'Shouldn't wonder,' replied Sponge, helping himself to a second glass.

'What! at it again!' exclaimed Jack, adding, 'Take care you don't ride over my lord.'

'I'll take care of the old file,' said Sponge; 'it wouldn't do to kill the goose that lays the golden what-do-ye-call-'ems, you know—he, he, he!'

'No,' chuckled Jack; ''deed it wouldn't—must make the most of him.'

'What sort of a humour is he in to-day?' asked Sponge.

'Middlin',' replied Jack, 'middlin'; he'll abuse you most likely, but that you mustn't mind.'

'Not I,' replied Sponge, who was used to that sort of thing.

'You mustn't mind me, either,' observed Jack, sweeping the last piece of sausage into his mouth with his knife, and jumping up from the table.

'When his lordship rows, I row,' added he, diving under the side-table for his flat hat.

'Hark! there's the horn!' exclaimed Sponge, rushing to the window.

'So there is,' responded Jack, standing transfixed on one leg to the spot.

'By the powers, they're away!' exclaimed Sponge, as his lordship was seen hat in hand careering over the meadow, beyond the cover, with the tail hounds straining to overtake their flying comrades. Twang—twang—twang went Frostyface's horn; crack—crack—crack went the ponderous thongs of the whips; shouts, and yells, and yelps, and whoops, and halloas, proclaimed the usual wild excitement of this privileged period of the chase. All was joy save among the gourmands assembled at the door—they looked blank indeed.

'What a sell!' exclaimed Sponge, in disgust, who, with Jack, saw the hopelessness of the case.

'Yonder he goes!' exclaimed a lad, who had run up from the cover to see the hunt from the rising ground.

'Where?' exclaimed Sponge, straining his eyeballs.

'There!' said the lad, pointing due south. 'D'ye see Tommy Claychop's pasture? Now he's through the hedge and into Mrs. Starveland's turnip field, making right for Bramblebrake Wood on the hill.'

'So he is,' said Sponge, who now caught sight of the fox emerging from the turnips on to a grass field beyond.

Jack stood staring through his great spectacles, without deigning a word.

'What shall we do?' asked Sponge.

'Do?' replied Jack, with his chin still up; 'go home, I should think.'

'There's a man down!' exclaimed a groom, who formed one of the group, as a dark-coated rider and horse measured their length on a pasture.

'It's Mr. Sparks,' said another, adding, 'he's always rolling about.'

'Lor', look at the parson!' exclaimed a third, as Blossomnose was seen gathering his horse and setting up his shoulders preparatory to riding at a gate.

'Well done, old 'un!' roared a fourth, as the horse flew over it, apparently without an effort.

'Now for Tom!' cried several, as the second whip went galloping up on the line of the gate.

'Ah! he won't have it!' was the cry, as the horse suddenly stopped short, nearly shooting Tom over his head. 'Try him again—try him again—take a good run—that's him—there, he's over!' was the cry, as Tom flourished his arm in the air on landing.

'Look! there's old Tommy Baker, the rat-ketcher!' cried another, as a man went working his arms and legs on an old white pony across a fallow.

'Ah, Tommy! Tommy! you'd better shut up,' observed another: 'a pig could go as fast as that.'

And so they criticized the laggers.

'How did my lord get his horse?' asked Spraggon of the groom who had brought them on, who now joined the eye-straining group at the door.

'It was taken down to him at the cover,' replied the man. 'My lord went in on foot, and the horse went round the back way. The horse wasn't there half a minute before he was wanted; for no sooner were the hounds in at one end than out popped the fox at t'other. Sich a whopper!—biggest fox that ever was seen.'

'They are all the biggest foxes that ever were seen,' snapped Mr. Sponge. 'I'll be bound he was not a bit bigger than common.'

'I'll be bound not, either,' growled Mr. Spraggon, squinting frightfully at the man, adding, 'go, get me my hack, and don't be talking nonsense there.'

Our friends then remounted their hacks and parted company in very moderate humours, feeling fully satisfied that his lordship had done it on purpose.

XXVII

THE FINEST RUN
THAT EVER WAS SEEN

'HOO-RAY, JACK! HOO-RAY!' EXCLAIMED LORD Scamperdale, bursting into his sanctum where Mr. Spraggon sat in his hunting coat and slippers, spelling away at a second-hand copy of *Bell's Life* by the light of a melancholy mould candle. 'Hooray, Jack! hooray!' repeated he, waving that proud trophy, a splendid fox's brush, over his grizzly head.

His lordship was the picture of delight. He had had a tremendous run—the finest run that ever was seen! His hounds had behaved to perfection; his horse—though he had downed him three times—had carried him well, and his lordship stood with his crownless flat hat in his hand, and one coat lap in the pocket of the other—a grinning, exulting, self-satisfied specimen of a happy Englishman.

'Lor! what a sight you are!' observed Jack, turning the light of the candle upon his lordship's dirty person. 'Why, I declare you're an inch thick with mud,' he added, 'mud from head to foot,' he continued, working the light up and down.

'Never mind the mud, you old badger!' roared his lordship, still waving the brush over his head: 'never mind the mud, you old badger; the mud'll come off, or may stay on; but such a run as we've had does not come off every day.'

'Well, I'm glad you have had a run,' replied Jack. 'I'm glad you have had a run,' adding, 'I was afraid at one time that your day's sport was spoiled.'

'Well, do you know,' replied his lordship, 'when I saw that unrighteous snob, I was near sick. If it were possible for a man to faint, I should have thought I was going to do so. At first I thought of going home, taking the hounds away too; then I thought of going myself and leaving the hounds; then I thought if I left the hounds it would only make the sinful scaramouch more outrageous, and I should be sitting on pins and needles till they came home, thinking how he was crashing among them. Next I thought of drawing all the unlikely places in the country, and making a blank day of it. Then I thought that would only be like cutting off my nose to spite my face. Then I didn't know what on earth to do. At last, when I saw the critter's great pecker steadily down in his plate, I thought I would try and steal a march upon him, and get away with my fox while he was feeding; and, oh! how thankful I was when I looked back from Bramblebrake Hill, and saw no signs of him in the distance.'

'It wasn't likely you'd see him,' interrupted Jack, 'for he never got away from the front door. I twigged what you were after, and kept him up in talk about his horses and his ridin' till I saw you were fairly away.'

'You did well,' exclaimed Lord Scamperdale, patting Jack on the back; 'you did well, my old buck-o'-wax; and, by Jove! we'll have a bottle of port—a bottle of port, as I live,' repeated his lordship, as if he had made up his mind to do a most magnificent act.

'But what's happened to you behind?—what's happened to you behind?' asked Jack, as his lordship turned to the fire, and exhibited his docked tail.

'Oh, hang the coat!—it's neither here nor there,' replied his lordship; 'hat neither,' he added, exhibiting its crushed proportions. 'Old Blossomnose did the coat; and as to the hat, I did it myself—at least, old Daddy Longlegs and I did it between us. We got into a grass-field, of which they had cut a few roods of fence, just enough to tempt a man out of a very deep lane, and away we sailed, in the enjoyment of fine sound sward, with the rest of the field plunging and floundering, and holding and grinning, and thinking what fools they were for not following my example—when, lo and behold! I got to the bottom of the field, and found there was no way out—no chance of a bore through the great thick, high hedge, except at a branchy willow, where there was just enough room to squeeze a horse through, provided he didn't rise at the ditch on the far side. At first I was for getting off; indeed, had my right foot out of the stirrup, when the hounds dashed forrard with such energy—looking like running—and remembering the tremendous climb I should have to get on to old Daddy's back again, and seeing some of the nasty jealous chaps in the lane eyeing me through the fence, thinking how I was floored, I determined to stay where I was; and gathering the horse together, tried to squeeze through the hole. Well, he went shuffling and sliding down to it, as though he were conscious of the difficulty, and poked his head quietly past the tree, when, getting a sight of the ditch on the far side, he rose, and banged my head against the branch above, crushing my hat right over my eyes, and in that position he carried me through blindfold.'

'Indeed!' exclaimed Jack, turning his spectacles full upon his lordship, and adding, 'it's lucky he didn't crack your crown.'

'It is,' assented his lordship, feeling his head to satisfy himself that he had not done so.

'And how did you lose your tail?' asked Jack, having got the information about the hat.

'The tail! ah, the tail!' replied his lordship, feeling behind, where it wasn't; 'I'll tell you how that was: you see we went away like blazes from Springwheat's gorse—nice gorse it is, and nice woman he has for a wife—but, however, that's neither here nor there; what I was going to tell you about was the run, and how I lost my tail. Well, we got away like winking; no sooner were the hounds in on one side than away went the fox on the other. Not a soul shouted till he was clean gone; hats in the air was all that told his departure. The fox thus had time to run matters through his mind—think whether he should go to Ravenscar Craigs, or make for the main earths at Painscastle Grove. He chose the latter, doubtless feeling himself strong and full of running; and if we had chosen his ground for him he could not have taken us a finer line. He went as straight as an arrow through Bramblebrake Wood, and then away down the hill over those great enormous pastures to Haselbury Park, which he skirted, leaving Evercreech Green on the left, pointing as if for Dormston Dean. Here he was chased by a cur, and the hounds were brought to a momentary check. Frosty, however, was well up, and a hat being held up on Hothersell Hill, he clapped forrard and laid the hounds on beyond. We then viewed the fox sailing away over Eddlethorp Downs, still pointing for Painscastle Grove, with the Hamerton Brook lighting up here and there in the distance.

'The field, I should tell you, were fairly taken by surprise. There wasn't a man ready for a start; my horse had only just come down. Fossick was on foot, drawing his girths; Fyle was striking a light to smoke a cigar on his hack; Blossomnose and Capon's grooms were fistling and wisping their horses; Dribble, as usual, was all behind; and altogether there was such a scene of hurry and confusion as never was seen.

'As they came to the brook they got somewhat into line, and one saw who was there. Five or six of us charged it together, and two went under. One was Springwheat on his bay, who was somewhat pumped out; the other was said to be Hook. Old Daddy Longlegs skimmed it like a swallow, and, getting his hind-legs well under him, shot over the pastures beyond, as if he was going upon turf. The hounds all this time had been running, or rather racing, nearly mute. They now, however, began to feel for the scent; and, as they got upon the cold, bleak grounds above Somerton Quarries, they were fairly brought to their noses. Uncommon glad I was to see them; for ten minutes more, at the pace they had been going, would have shaken off every man Jack of us. As it was, it was bellows to mend; and Calcott's roarer roared as surely roarer never roared before. You could hear him half a mile off. We had barely time, however, to turn our horses to the wind, and ease them for a few moments, before the pace began to mend, and from a catching to a holding scent they again poured across Wallingburn pastures, and away to Roughacres Court. It was between these places that I got my head duntled into my hat,' continued his lordship, knocking the crownless hat against his mud-stained knee. 'However, I didn't care a button, though I'd not worn it above two years, and it might have lasted me a long time about home; but misfortunes seldom come singly, and I was soon to have another. The few of us that were left were all for the lanes, and very accommodating the one between Newton Bushell and the Forty-foot Bank was, the hounds running parallel within a hundred yards on the left for nearly a mile. When, however, we got to the old water-mill in the fields below, the fox made a bend to the left, as if changing his mind, and making for Newtonbroome Woods, and we were obliged to try the fortunes of war in the fields. The first fence we came to looked like nothing, and there was a weak place right in my line that I rode at, expecting the horse would easily bore through a few twigs that crossed the upper part of it. These, however, happened to be twisted, to stop the gap, and not having put on enough steam, they checked him as he rose, and brought him right down on his head in the broad ditch, on the far side. Old Blossomnose, who was following close behind, not making any allowance for falls, was in the air before I was well down, and his horse came with a forefoot, into my pocket, and tore the lap clean off by the skirt'; his lordship exhibiting the lap as he spoke.

'It's your new coat, too,' observed Jack, examining it with concern as he spoke.

''Deed, is it!' replied his lordship, with a shake of the head. ''Deed, is it! That's the consequence of having gone out to breakfast. If it had been to-morrow, for instance, I should have had number two on, or maybe number three,' his lordship having coats of every shade and grade, from stainless scarlet down to tattered mulberry colour.

'It'll mend, however,' observed his lordship, taking it back from Jack; 'it'll mend, however,' he said, fitting it round to the skirt as he spoke.

'Oh, nicely!' replied Jack; 'it's come off clean by the skirt. But what said Old Blossom?' inquired Jack.

'Oh, he was full of apologies and couldn't helps it as usual,' replied his lordship; 'he was down, too, I should tell you, with his horse on his left leg; but there wasn't much time for apologies or explanation, for the hounds were running pretty sharp, considering how long they had been at work, and there was the chance of others jumping upon us if we didn't get out of the way, so we both scrambled up as quick as we could and got into our places again.'

'Which way did you go, then?' asked Jack, who had listened with the attention of a man who knows every yard of the country.

'Well,' continued his lordship, casting back to where he got his fall, 'the fox crossed the Coatenburn township, picking all the plough and bad-scenting ground as he went, but it was of no use, his fate was sealed; and though he began to run short, and dodge and thread the hedge-rows, they hunted him yard by yard till he again made an effort for his life, and took over Mossingburn Moor, pointing for Penrose Tower on the hill. Here Frosty's horse, Little Jumper, declined, and we left him standing in the middle of the moor with a stiff neck, kicking and staring and looking mournfully at his flanks. Daddy Longlegs, too, had begun to sob, and in vain I looked back in hopes of seeing Jack-a-Dandy coming up. "Well," said I to myself, "I've got a pair of good strong boots on, and I'll finish the run on foot but I'll see it"; when, just at the moment, the pack broke from scent to view and rolled the fox up like a hedgehog amongst them.'

'Well done!' exclaimed Jack, adding, 'that was a run with a vengeance!'

'Wasn't it?' replied his lordship, rubbing his hands and stamping; 'the finest run that ever was seen—the finest run that ever was seen!'

'Why, it couldn't be less than twelve miles from point to point,' observed Jack, thinking it over.

'Not a yard,' replied his lordship, 'not a yard, and from fourteen to fifteen as the hounds ran.'

'It would be all that,' assented Jack. 'How long were you in doing it?' he asked.

'An hour and forty minutes,' replied his lordship; 'an hour and forty minutes from the find to the finish'; adding, 'I'll stick the brush and present it to Mrs. Springwheat.'

'It's to be hoped Springy's out of the brook,' observed Jack.

'To be hoped so,' replied his lordship, thinking, if he wasn't whether he should marry Mrs. Springwheat or not.

Well now, after all that, we fancy we hear our fair friends exclaim, 'Thank goodness, there's an end of Lord Scamperdale and his hunting; he has had a good run, and will rest quiet for a time; we shall now hear something of Amelia and Emily, and the doings at Jawleyford Court.' Mistaken lady! If you are lucky enough to marry an out-and-out fox-hunter, you will find that a good run is only adding fuel to the fire, only making him anxious for more. Lord Scamperdale's sporting fire was in full blaze. His bumps and his thumps, his rolls, and his scrambles, only brought out the beauties and perfections of the thing. He cared nothing for his hat-crown, no; nor for his coat-lap either. Nay, he wouldn't have cared if it had been made into a spencer.

'What's to-day? Monday,' said his lordship, answering himself. 'Monday,' he repeated; 'Monday—bubble-and-squeak, I guess—sooner it's ready the better, for I'm half-famished—didn't do half-justice to that nice breakfast at Springy's. That nasty brown-booted buffer completely threw me off my feed. By the way, what became of the chestnut-booted animal?'

'Went home,' replied Jack; 'fittest place for him.'

'Hope he'll stay there,' rejoined his lordship. 'No fear of his being at the roads to-morrow, is there?' 'None,' replied Jack. 'I told him it was quite an impossible distance from him, twenty miles at least.'

'That's grand!' exclaimed his lordship; 'that's grand! Then we'll have a rare, ding-dong hey-away pop. There'll be no end of those nasty, jealous, Puffington dogs out; and if we have half such a scent as we had to-day, we'll sew some of them up, we'll show 'em what hunting is. Now,' he added, 'if you'll go and get the bottle of port, I'll clean myself, and then we'll have dinner as quick as we can.'

XXVIII

THE FAITHFUL GROOM

W<small>E LEFT OUR FRIEND</small> M<small>R</small>. Sponge wending his way home moodily, after having lost his day at Larkhall Hill. Some of our readers will, perhaps, say, why didn't he clap on, and try to catch up the hounds at a check, or at all events rejoin them for an afternoon fox? Gentle reader! Mr. Sponge did not hunt on those terms; he was a front-rank or a 'nowhere' man, and independently of catching hounds up being always a fatiguing and hazardous speculation, especially on a fine-scenting day, the exertion would have taken more out of his horse than would have been desirable for successful display in a second run. Mr. Sponge, therefore, determined to go home.

As he sauntered along, musing on the mishaps of the chase, wondering how Miss Jawleyford would look, and playing himself an occasional tune with his spur against his stirrup, who should come trotting behind him but Mr. Leather on the redoubtable chestnut? Mr. Sponge beckoned him alongside. The horse looked blooming and bright; his eye was clear and cheerful, and there was a sort of springy graceful action that looked like easy going.

One always fancies a horse most with another man on him. We see all his good points without feeling his imperfections—his trippings, or startings, or snatchings, or borings, or roughness of action, and Mr. Sponge proceeded to make a silent estimate of Multum in Parvo's qualities as he trotted gently along on the grassy side of the somewhat wide road.

'By Jove! it's a pity but his lordship had seen him,' thought Sponge, as the emulation of companionship made the horse gradually increase his pace, and steal forward with the lightest, freest action imaginable.' If he was but all right,' continued Sponge, with a shake of the head, 'he would be worth any money, for he has the strength of a dray-horse, with the symmetry and action of a racer.'

Then Sponge thought he shouldn't have an opportunity of showing the horse till Thursday, for Jack had satisfied him that the next day's meet was quite beyond distance from Jawleyford Court.

'It's a bore,' said he, rising in his stirrups, and tickling the piebald with his spurs, as if he were going to set-to for a race. He thought of having a trial of speed with the chestnut, up a slip of turf they were now approaching; but a sudden thought struck him, and he desisted. 'These horses have done nothing to-day,' he said; 'why shouldn't I send the chestnut on for to-morrow?'

'Do you know where the cross-roads are?' he asked his groom.

'Cross-roads, cross-roads—what cross-roads?' replied Leather.

'Where the hounds meet to-morrow.'

'Oh, the cross-roads at Somethin' Burn,' rejoined Leather thoughtfully—'no, 'deed, I don't,' he added. 'From all 'counts, they seem to be somewhere on the far side of the world.'

That was not a very encouraging answer; and feeling it would require a good deal of persuasion to induce Mr. Leather to go in search of them without clothing and the necessary requirements for his horses, Mr. Sponge went trotting on, in hopes of seeing some place where he might get a sight of the map of the county. So they proceeded in silence, till a sudden turn of the road brought them to the spire and housetops of the little agricultural town of Barleyboll. It differed nothing from the ordinary run of small towns. It had a pond at one end, an inn in the middle, a church at one side, a fashionable milliner from London, a merchant tailor from the same place, and a hardware shop or two where they also sold treacle, Dartford gunpowder, pocket-handkerchiefs, sheep-nets, patent medicines, cheese, blacking, marbles, mole-traps, men's hats, and other miscellaneous articles. It was quite enough of a town, however, to raise a presumption that there would be a map of the county at the inn.

'We'll just put the horses up for a few minutes, I think,' said Sponge, turning into the stable-yard at the end of the Red Lion Hotel and Posting House, adding, 'I want to write a letter, and perhaps,' said he, looking at his watch, 'you may be wanting your dinner.'

Having resigned his horse to his servant, Mr. Sponge walked in, receiving the marked attention usually paid to a red coat. Mine host left his bar, where he was engaged in the usual occupation of drinking with customers for the 'good of the house.' A map of the county, of such liberal dimensions, was speedily produced, as would have terrified any one unaccustomed to distances and scales on which maps are laid down. For instance, Jawleyford Court, as the crow flies, was the same distance from the cross-roads at Dallington Burn as York was from London, in a map of England hanging beside it.

'It's a goodish way,' said Sponge, getting a lighter off the chimney-piece, and measuring the distances. 'From Jawleyford Court to Billingsborough Rise, say seven miles; from Billingsborough Rise to Downington Wharf, other seven; from Downington Wharf to Shapcot, which seems the nearest point, will be—say five or six, perhaps—nineteen or twenty in all. Well, that's my work,' he observed, scratching his head, 'at least, my hack's; and from here, home,' he continued, measuring away as he spoke, 'will be twelve or thirteen. Well, that's nothing,' he said. 'Now for the horse,' he continued, again applying the lighter in a different direction. 'From here to Hardington will be, say, eight miles; from Hardington to Bewley, other five; eight and five are thirteen; and there, I should say, he might sleep. That would leave ten or twelve miles for the morning; nothing for a hack hunter; 'specially such a horse as that, and one that's done nothing for I don't know how long.'

Altogether, Mr. Sponge determined to try it, especially considering that if he didn't get Tuesday, there would be nothing till Thursday; and he was not the man to keep a hack hunter standing idle.

Accordingly he sought Mr. Leather, whom he found busily engaged in the servants' apartment, with a cold round of beef and a foaming flagon of ale before him.

'Leather,' he said, in a tone of authority, 'I'll hunt to-morrow—ride the horse I should have ridden to-day.'

'Where at?' asked Leather, diving his fork into a bottle of pickles, and fishing out an onion.

'The cross-roads,' replied Sponge.

'The cross-roads be fifty miles from here!' cried Leather.

'Nonsense!' rejoined Sponge; 'I've just measured the distance. It's nothing of the sort.'

'How far do you make it, then?' asked Leather, tucking into the beef.

'Why, from here to Hardington is about six, and from Hardington to Bewley, four—ten in all,' replied Sponge. 'You can stay at Bewley all night, and then it is but a few miles on in the morning.'

'And whativer am I to do for clothin'?' asked Leather, adding, 'I've nothin' with me—nothin' nouther for oss nor man.'

'Oh, the ostler'll lend you what you want,' replied Sponge, in a tone of determination, adding, 'you can make shift for one night surely?'

'One night surely!' retorted Leather. 'D'ye think an oss can't be ruined in one night?—humph!'

'I'll risk it,' said Sponge.

'But I won't,' replied Leather, blowing the foam from the tankard, and taking a long swig at the ale. 'I thinks I knows my duty to my gov'nor better nor that,' continued he, setting it down. 'I'll not see his waluable 'unters stowed away in pigsties—not I, indeed.'

The fact was, Leather had an invitation to sup with the servants at Jawleyford Court that night, and he was not going to be done out of his engagement, especially as Mr. Sponge only allowed him two shillings a day for expenses wherever he was.

'Well, you're a cool hand, anyhow,' observed Mr. Sponge, quite taken by surprise.

'Cool 'and, or not cool 'and,' replied Leather, munching away, 'I'll do my duty to my master. I'm not one o' your coatless, characterless scamps wot 'ang about livery-stables ready to do anything they're bid. No sir, no,' he continued, pronging another onion; 'I have some regard for the hinterest o' my master. I'll do my duty in the station o' life in which I'm placed, and won't be 'fraid to face no man.' So saying, Mr. Leather cut himself a grand circumference of beef.

Mr. Sponge was taken aback, for he had never seen a conscientious livery-stable helper before, and did not believe in the existence of such articles. However, here was Mr. Leather assuming a virtue, whether he had it or not; and Mr. Sponge being in the man's power, of course durst not quarrel with him. It was clear that Leather would not go; and the question was, what should Mr. Sponge do? 'Why shouldn't I go myself?' he thought, shutting his eyes, as if to keep his faculties free from outward distraction. He ran the thing quickly over in his mind. 'What Leather can do, I can do,' he said, remembering that a groom never demeaned himself by working where there was an ostler. 'These things I have on will do quite well for to-morrow, at least among such rough-and-ready dogs as the Flat Hat men, who seem as if they had their clothes pitched on with a fork.'

His mind was quickly made up, and calling for pen, ink, and paper, he wrote a hasty note to Jawleyford, explaining why he would not cast up till the morrow; he then got the chestnut out of the stable, and desiring the ostler to give the note to Leather, and tell him to go home with his hack, he just rode out of the yard without giving Leather the chance of saying 'nay.' He then jogged on at a pace suitable to the accurate measurement of the distance.

The horse seemed to like having Sponge's red coat on better than Leather's brown, and champed his bit, and stepped away quite gaily.

'Confound it!' exclaimed Sponge, laying the rein on its neck, and leaning forward to pat him; 'it's a pity but you were always in this humour—you'd be worth a mint of money if you were.' He then resumed his seat in the saddle, and bethought him how he would show them the way on the morrow. 'If he doesn't beat every horse in the field, it shan't be my fault,' thought he; and thereupon he gave him the slightest possible touch with the spur, and the horse shot away up a strip of grass like an arrow.

'By Jove, but you *can* go!' said he, pulling up as the grass ran out upon the hard road.

Thus he reached the village of Hardington, which he quickly cleared, and took the well-defined road to Bewley—a road adorned with milestones and set out with a liberal horse-track at either side.

Day had closed ere our friend reached Bewley, but the children returning from school, and the country folks leaving their work, kept assuring him that he was on the right line, till the lights of the town, bursting upon him as he rounded the hill above, showed him the end of his journey.

The best stalls at the head inn—the Bull's Head—were all full, several trusty grooms having arrived with the usual head-stalls and rolls of clothing on their horses, denoting the object of their mission. Most of the horses had been in some hours, and were now standing well littered up with straw, while the grooms were in the tap talking over their masters, discussing the merits of their horses, or arguing whether Lord Scamperdale was mad or not. They had just come to the conclusion that his lordship was mad, but not incapable of taking care of his affairs, when the trampling of Sponge's horse's feet drew them out to see who was coming next. Sponge's red coat at once told his tale, and procured him the usual attention.

Mr. Leather's fear of the want of clothing for the valuable hunter proved wholly groundless, for each groom having come with a plentiful supply for his own horse, all the inn stock was at the service of the stranger. The stable, to be sure, was not quite so good as might be desired, but it was warm and water-tight, and the corn was far from bad. Altogether, Mr. Sponge thought he would do very well, and, having seen to his horse, proceeded to choose between beefsteaks and mutton chops for his own entertainment, and with the aid of the old country paper and some very questionable port, he passed the evening in anticipation of the sports of the morrow.

XXIX

THE CROSS-ROADS
AT DALLINGTON BURN

WHEN HIS LORDSHIP AND JACK mounted their hacks in the morning to go to the cross-roads at Dallington Burn, it was so dark that they could not see whether they were on bays or browns. It was a dull, murky day, with heavy spongy clouds overhead.

There had been a great deal of rain in the night, and the horses poached and squashed as they went. Our sportsmen, however, were prepared as well for what had fallen as for what might come; for they were encased in enormously thick boots, with baggy overalls, and coats and waistcoats of the stoutest and most abundant order. They had each a sack of a mackintosh strapped on to their saddle fronts. Thus they went blobbing and groping their way along, varying the monotony of the journey by an occasional spurt of muddy water up into their faces, or the more nerve-trying noise of a floundering stumble over a heap of stones by the roadside. The country people stared with astonishment as they passed, and the muggers and tinkers, who were withdrawing their horses from the farmers' fields, stood trembling, lest they might be the 'pollis' coming after them.

'I think it'll be a fine day,' observed his lordship, after they had bumped for some time in silence without its getting much lighter. 'I think it will be a fine day,' he said, taking his chin out of his great puddingy-spotted neckcloth, and turning his spectacled face up to the clouds.

'The want of light is its chief fault,' observed Jack, adding, 'it's deuced dark!'

'Ah, it'll get better of that,' observed his lordship. 'It's not much after eight yet,' he added, staring at his watch, and with difficulty making out that it was half-past. 'Days take off terribly about this time of year,' he observed; 'I've seen about Christmas when it has never been rightly light all day long.'

They then floundered on again for some time further as before.

'Shouldn't wonder if we have a large field,' at length observed Jack, bringing his hack alongside his lordship's.

'Shouldn't wonder if Puff himself was to come—all over brooches and rings as usual,' replied his lordship.

'And Charley Slapp, I'll be bund to say,' observed Jack. 'He a regular hanger-on of Puff's.'

'Ass, that Slapp,' said his lordship; 'hate the sight of him!'

'So do I,' replied Jack, adding, 'hate a hanger-on!'

'There are the hounds,' said his lordship, as they now approached Culverton Dean, and a line of something white was discernible travelling the zig-zagging road on the opposite side.

'Are they, think you?' replied Jack, staring through his great spectacles; 'are they, think you? It looks to me more like a flock of sheep.'

'I believe you're right,' said his lordship, staring too; 'indeed, I hear the dog. The hounds, however, can't be far ahead.'

They then drew into single file to take the broken horse-track through the steep woody dean.

'This is the longest sixteen miles I know,' observed Jack, as they emerged from it, and overtook the sheep.

'It is,' replied his lordship, spurring his hack, who was now beginning to lag: 'the fact is, it's eighteen,' he continued; 'only if I was to tell Frosty it was eighteen, he would want to lay overnight, and that wouldn't do. Besides the trouble and inconvenience, it would spoil the best part of a five-pund note; and five-pund notes don't grow upon gooseberry-bushes—at least, not in my garden.'

'Rather scarce in all gardens just now, I think,' observed Jack; 'at least, I never hear of anybody with one to spare.'

'Money's like snow,' said his lordship, 'a very meltable article; and talking of snow,' he said, looking up at the heavy clouds, 'I wish we mayn't be going to have some—I don't like the look of things overhead.'

'Heavy,' replied Jack; 'heavy: however, it's due about now.'

'Due or not due,' said his lordship, 'it's a thing one never wishes to come; anybody may have my share of snow that likes—frost, too.'

The road, or rather track, now passed over Blobbington Moor, and our friends had enough to do to keep their horses out of peat-holes and bogs, without indulging in conversation. At length they cleared the moor, and, pulling out a gap at the corner of the inclosures, cut across a few fields, and got on to the Stumpington turnpike.

'The hounds are here,' said Jack, after studying the muddy road for some time.

'They'll not be there long,' replied his lordship, 'for Grabtintoll Gate isn't far ahead, and we don't waste our substance on pikes.'

His lordship was right. The imprints soon diverged up a muddy lane on the right, and our sportsmen now got into a road so deep and bottomless as to put the idea of stones quite out of the question.

'Hang the road!' exclaimed his lordship, as his hack nearly came on his nose, 'hang the road!' repeated he, adding, 'if Puff wasn't such an ass, I really think I'd give him up the cross-road country.'

'It's bad to get at from us,' observed Jack, who didn't like such trashing distances.

'Ah! but it's a rare good country when you get to it,' replied his lordship, shortening his rein and spurring his steed.

The lane being at length cleared, the road became more practicable, passing over large pastures where a horseman could choose his own ground, instead of being bound by the narrow limits of the law. But though the road improved, the day did not; a thick fog coming drifting up from the south-east in aid of the general obscurity of the scene.

'The day's gettin' *wuss*,' observed Jack, snuffling and staring about.

'It'll blow over,' replied his lordship, who was not easily disheartened. 'It'll blow over,' repeated he, adding, 'often rare scents such days as these. But we must put on,' continued he, looking at his watch, 'for it's half-past, and we are a mile or more off yet.' So saying, he clapped spurs to his hack and shot away at a canter, followed by Jack at a long-drawn 'hammer and pincers' trot.

A hunt is something like an Assize circuit, where certain great guns show everywhere, and smaller men drop in here and there, snatching a day or a brief, as the case may be. Sergeant Bluff and Sergeant Huff rustle and wrangle in every court, while Mr. Meeke and Mr. Sneeke enjoy their frights on the forensic arenas of their respective towns, on behalf of simple neighbours, who look upon them as thorough Solomons. So with hunts. Certain men who seem to have been sent into the world for the express purpose of hunting, arrive at every meet, far and near, with a punctuality that is truly surprising, and rarely associated with pleasure.

If you listen to their conversation, it is generally a dissertation on the previous day's sport, with inquiries as to the nearest way to cover the next. Sometimes it is seasoned with censure of some other pack they have been seeing. These men are mounted and appointed in a manner that shows what a perfect profession hunting is with them. Of course, they come cantering to cover, lest any one should suppose they ride their horses on.

The 'Cross-roads' was like two hunts or two circuits joining, for it generally drew the picked men from each, to say nothing of outriggers and chance customers. The regular attendants of either hunt were sufficiently distinguishable as well by the flat hats and baggy garments of the one, as by the dandified, Jemmy Jessamy air of the other. If a lord had not been at the head of the Flat Hats, the Puffington men would have considered them insufferable snobs. But, to our day.

As usual, where hounds have to travel a long distance, the field were assembled before they arrived. Almost all the cantering gentlemen had cast up.

One cross-road meet being so much like another, it will not be worthwhile describing the one at Dallington Burn. The reader will have the kindness to imagine a couple of roads crossing an open common, with an armless sign-post on one side, and a rubble-stone bridge, with several of the coping-stones lying in the shallow stream below, on the other.

The country round about, if any country could have been seen, would have shown wild, open, and cheerless. Here a patch of wood, there a patch of heath, but its general aspect bare and unfruitful. The commanding outline of Beechwood Forest was not visible for the weather. Time now, let us suppose, half-past ten, with a full muster of horsemen and a fog making unwonted dullness of the scene—the old sign-pole being the most conspicuous object of the whole.

Hark! what a clamour there is about it. It's like a betting-post at Newmarket. How loud the people talk! What's the news? Queen Anne dead, or is there another French Revolution, or a fixed duty on corn? Reader, Mr. Puffington's hounds have had a run, and the Flat Hat men are disputing it.

'Nothing of the sort! nothing of the sort!' exclaims Fossick, 'I know every yard of the country, and you can't make more nor eight of it anyhow, if eight.'

'Well, but I've measured it on the map,' replied the speaker (Charley Slapp himself), 'and it's thirteen, if it's a yard.'

'Then the country's grown bigger since my day,' rejoins Fossick, 'for I was dropped at Stubgrove, which is within a mile of where you found, and I've walked, and I've ridden, and I've driven every yard of the distance, and you can't make it more than eight, if it's as much. Can you, Capon?' exclaimed Fossick, appealing to another of the 'flat brims,' whose luminous face now shone through the fog.

'No,' replied Capon, adding, 'not so much, I should say.'

Just then up trotted Frostyface with the hounds.

'Good morning, Frosty! good morning!' exclaim half-a-dozen voices, that it would be difficult to appropriate from the denseness of the fog. Frosty and the whips make a general salute with their caps.

'Well, Frosty, I suppose you've heard what a run we had yesterday?' exclaims Charley Slapp, as soon as Frosty and the hounds are settled.

'Had they, sir—had they?' replies Frosty, with a slight touch of his cap and a sneer. 'Glad to hear it, sir—glad to hear it. Hope they killed, sir—hope they killed!' with a still slighter touch of the cap.

'Killed, aye!—killed in the open just below Crabstone Green, in *your* country,' adding, 'It was one of your foxes, I believe.'

'Glad of it, sir—glad of it, sir,' replies Frosty. 'They wanted blood sadly—they wanted blood sadly. Quite welcome to one of our foxes, sir—*quite* welcome. That's a brace and a 'alf they've killed.'

'Brace and a ha-r-r-f!' drawls Slapp, in well-feigned disgust; 'brace and a ha-r-r-f!—why, it makes them ten brace, and six run to ground.'

'Oh, don't tell *me*,' retorts Frosty, with a shake of disgust; 'don't tell me. I knows better—I knows better. They'd only killed a brace since they began hunting up to yesterday. The rest were all cubs, poor things!—all cubs, poor things! Mr. Puffington's hounds are not the sort of animals to kill foxes: nasty, skirtin', flashy, jealous divils; always starin' about for holloas and assistance. I'll be d——d if I'd give eighteenpence for the 'ole lot on 'em.'

A loud guffaw from the Flat Hat men greeted this wholesale condemnation. The Puffington men looked unutterable things, and there is no saying what disagreeable comparisons might have been instituted (for the Puffingtonians mustered strong) had not his lordship and Jack cast up at the moment. Hats off and politeness was then the order of the day.

'Mornin',' said his lordship, with a snatch of his hat in return, as he pulled up and stared into the cloud-enveloped crowd; 'Mornin', Fyle; mornin', Fossick,' he continued, as he distinguished those worthies, as much by their hats as anything else. 'Where are the horses?' he said to Frostyface.

'Just beyond there, my lord,' replied the huntsman, pointing with his whip to where a cockaded servant was 'to-and-froing' a couple of hunters—a brown and a chestnut.

'Let's be doing,' said his lordship, trotting up to them and throwing himself off his hack like a sack. Having divested himself of his muddy overalls, he mounted the brown, a splendid sixteen-hands horse in tip-top condition, and again made for the field in all the pride of masterly equestrianism. A momentary gleam of sunshine shot o'er the scene; a jerk of the head acted as a signal to throw off, and away they all moved from the meet.

Thorneybush Gorse was a large eight-acre cover, formed partly of gorse and partly of stunted blackthorn, with here and there a sprinkling of Scotch firs. His lordship paid two pounds a year for it, having vainly tried to get it for thirty shillings, which was about the actual value of the land, but the proprietor claimed a little compensation for the trampling of horses about it; moreover, the Puffington men would have taken it at two pounds. It was a sure find, and the hounds dashed into it with a scent.

The field ranged themselves at the accustomed corner, both hunts full of their previous day's run. Frostyface's 'Yoicks, wind him!' 'Yoicks, push him up!' was drowned in a medley of voices.

A loud, clear, shrill 'TALLY-HO, AWAY!' from the far side of the cover caused all tongues to stop, and all hands to drop on the reins. Great was the excitement! Each hunt was determined to take the shine out of the other.

'Twang, twang, twang!' 'Tweet, tweet, tweet!' went his lordship's and Frostyface's horns, as they came bounding over the gorse to the spot, with the eager pack rushing at their horses' heels. Then as the hounds crossed the line of scent, there was such an outburst of melody in cover, and such gathering of reins and thrusting on of hats outside! The hounds dashed out of cover as if somebody was kicking them. A man in scarlet was seen flying through the fog, producing the usual hold-hardings. 'Hold hard, sir!' 'God bless you, hold hard, sir!' with inquiries as to 'who the chap was that was going to catch the fox.'

'It's Lumpleg!' exclaimed one of the Flat Hat men.

'No, it's not!' roared a Puffingtonite; 'Lumpleg's here.'

'Then it's Charley Slapp; he's always doing it,' rejoined the first speaker. 'Most jealous man in the world.'

'Is he!' exclaimed Slapp, cantering past at his ease on a thoroughbred grey, as if he could well afford to dispense with a start.

Reader! it was neither Lumpleg nor Slapp, nor any of the Puffington snobs, or Flat Hat swells, or Puffington swells, or Flat Hat snobs. It was our old friend Sponge; Monsieur Tonson again! Having arrived late, he had posted himself, unseen, by the cover side, and the fox had broke close to him. Unfortunately, he had headed him back, and a pretty kettle of fish was the result. Not only had he headed him back, but the resolute chestnut, having taken it into his head to run away, had snatched the bit between his teeth; and carried him to the far side of a field ere Sponge managed to manoeuvre him round on a very liberal semi-circle, and face the now flying sportsmen, who came hurrying on through the mist like a charge of yeomanry after a salute. All was excitement, hurry-scurry, and horse-hugging, with the usual spurring, elbowing, and exertion to get into places, Mr. Fossick considering he had as much right to be before Mr. Fyle as Mr. Fyle had to be before old Capon.

It apparently being all the same to the chestnut which way he went so long as he had his run, he now bore Sponge back as quickly as he had carried him away, and with yawning mouth, and head in the air, he dashed right at the coming horsemen, charging Lord Scamperdale full tilt as he was in the act of returning his horn to its case. Great was the collision! His lordship flew one way, his horse another, his hat a third, his whip a fourth, his spectacles a fifth; in fact, he was scattered all over. In an instant he lay the centre of a circle, kicking on his back like a lively turtle.

'Oh! I'm kilt!' he roared, striking out as if he was swimming, or rather floating. 'I'm kilt!' he repeated. 'He's broken my back—he's broken my legs—he's broken my ribs—he's broken my collar-bone—he's knocked my right eye into the heel of my left boot. Oh! will nobody catch him and kill him? Will nobody do for him? Will you see an English nobleman knocked about like a ninepin?' added his lordship, scrambling up to go in pursuit of Mr. Sponge himself, exclaiming, as he stood shaking his fist at him, 'Rot ye, sir! hangin's too good for ye! you should be condemned to hunt in Berwickshire the rest of your life!'

XXX

BOLTING THE BADGER

W HEN A MAN AND HIS horse differ seriously in public, and the man feels the horse has the best of it, it is wise for the man to appear to accommodate his views to those of the horse, rather than risk a defeat. It is best to let the horse go his way, and pretend it is yours. There is no secret so close as that between a rider and his horse.

Mr. Sponge, having scattered Lord Scamperdale in the summary way described in our last chapter, let the chestnut gallop away, consoling himself with the idea that even if the hounds did hunt, it would be impossible for him to show his horse to advantage on so dark and unfavourable a day. He, therefore, just let the beast gallop till he began to flag, and then he spurred him and made him gallop on his account. He thus took his change out of him, and arrived at Jawleyford Court a little after luncheon time.

Brief as had been his absence, things had undergone a great change. Certain dark hints respecting his ways and means had worked their way from the servants' hall to my lady's chamber, and into the upper regions generally. These had been augmented by Leather's, the trusty groom's, overnight visit, in fulfilment of his engagement to sup with the servants. Nor was Mr. Leather's anger abated by the unceremonious way Mr. Sponge rode off with the horse, leaving him to hear of his departure from the ostler. Having broken faith with him, he considered it his duty to be 'upsides' with him, and tell the servants all he knew about him. Accordingly he let out, in strict confidence of course, to Spigot, that so far from Mr. Sponge being a gentleman of 'fortin,' as he called it, with a dozen or two hunters planted here and there, he was nothing but the hirer of a couple of hacks, with himself as a job-groom, by the week.

Spigot, who was on the best of terms with the 'cook-housekeeper,' and had his clothes washed on the sly in the laundry, could not do less than communicate the intelligence to her, from whom it went to the lady's-maid, and thence circulated in the upper regions.

Juliana, the maid, finding Miss Amelia less indisposed to hear Mr. Sponge run down than she expected, proceeded to add her own observations to the information derived from Leather, the groom. 'Indeed, she couldn't say that she thought much of Mr. Sponge herself; his shirts were coarse, so were his pocket-handkerchiefs; and she never yet saw a real gent without a valet.'

Amelia, without any positive intention of giving up Mr. Sponge, at least not until she saw further, had nevertheless got an idea that she was destined for a much higher sphere. Having duly considered all the circumstances of Mr. Spraggon's visit to Jawleyford Court, conned over several mysterious coughs and half-finished sentences he had indulged in, she had about come to the conclusion that the real object of his mission was to negotiate a matrimonial alliance on behalf of Lord Scamperdale. His lordship's constantly expressed intention of getting married was well calculated to mislead one whose experience of the world was not sufficiently great to know that those men who are always talking about it are the least likely to get married, just as men who are always talking about buying horses are the men who never do buy them. Be that, however, as it may, Amelia was tolerably easy about Mr. Sponge. If he had money she could take him; if he hadn't, she could let him alone.

Jawleyford, too, who was more hospitable at a distance, and in imagination than in reality, had had about enough of our friend. Indeed, a man whose talk was of hunting, and his reading *Mogg* was not likely to have much in common with a gentleman of taste and elegance, as our friend set up to be. The delicate inquiry that Mrs. Jawleyford now made, as to 'whether he knew Mr. Sponge to be a man of fortune,' set him off at a tangent.

'ME know he's a man of fortune! *I* know nothing of his fortune. You asked him here, not ME,' exclaimed Jawleyford, stamping furiously.

'No, my dear,' replied Mrs. Jawleyford mildly; 'he asked himself, you know; but I thought, perhaps, you might have said something that—'

'ME say anything!' interrupted Jawleyford. '*I* never said anything—at least, nothing that any man with a particle of sense would think anything of,' continued he, remembering the scene in the billiard-room. 'It's one thing to tell a man, if he comes your way, you'll be glad to see him, and another to ask him to come bag and baggage, as this impudent Mr. Sponge has done,' added he.

'Certainly,' replied Mrs. Jawleyford, who saw where the shoe was pinching her bear.

'I wish he was off,' observed Jawleyford, after a pause. 'He bothers me excessively—I'll try and get rid of him by saying we are going from home.'

'Where can you say we are going to?' asked Mrs. Jawleyford.

'Oh, anywhere,' replied Jawleyford; 'he doesn't know the people about here: the Tewkesbury's, the Woolerton's, the Brown's—anybody.'

Before they had got any definite plan of proceeding arranged, Mr. Sponge returned from the chase. 'Ah, my dear sir!' exclaimed Jawleyford, half-gaily, half-moodily, extending a couple of fingers as Sponge entered his study: 'we thought you had taken French leave of us, and were off.'

Mr. Sponge asked if his groom had not delivered his note.

'No,' replied Jawleyford boldly, though he had it in his pocket; 'at least, not that I've seen. Mrs. Jawleyford, perhaps, may have got it,' added he.

'Indeed!' exclaimed Sponge; 'it was very idle of him.' He then proceeded to detail to Jawleyford what the reader already knows, how he had lost his day at Larkhall Hill, and had tried to make up for it by going to the cross-roads. 'Ah!' exclaimed Jawleyford, when he was done; 'that's a pity—great pity—monstrous pity—never knew anything so unlucky in my life.'

'Misfortunes will happen,' replied Sponge, in a tone of unconcern.

'Ah, it wasn't so much the loss of the hunt I was thinking of,' replied Jawleyford, 'as the arrangements we have made in consequence of thinking you were gone.'

'What are they?' asked Sponge.

'Why, my Lord Barker, a great friend of ours—known him from a boy—just like brothers, in short—sent over this morning to ask us all there—shooting party, charades, that sort of thing—and we accepted.'

'But that need make no difference,' replied Sponge; 'I'll go too.'

Jawleyford was taken aback. He had not calculated upon so much coolness.

'Well,' stammered he, 'that might do, to be sure; but—if—I'm not quite sure that I could take any one—'

'But if you're as thick as you say, you can have no difficulty,' replied our friend.

'True,' replied Jawleyford; 'but then we go a large party ourselves—two and two's four,' said he, 'to say nothing of servants; besides, his lordship mayn't have room—house will most likely be full.'

'Oh, a single man can always be put up; shake-down—anything does for him,' replied Sponge. 'But you would lose your hunting,' replied Jawleyford. 'Barkington Tower is quite out of Lord Scamperdale's country.'

'That doesn't matter,' replied Sponge, adding, 'I don't think I'll trouble his lordship much more. These Flat Hat gentlemen are not over and above civil, in my opinion.'

'Well,' replied Jawleyford, nettled at this thwarting of his attempt, 'that's for your consideration. However, as you've come, I'll talk to Mrs. Jawleyford, and see if we can get off the Barkington expedition.'

'But don't get off on my account,' replied Sponge. 'I can stay here quite well. I dare say you'll not be away long.'

This was worse still; it held out no hope of getting rid of him. Jawleyford therefore resolved to try and smoke and starve him out. When our friend went to dress, he found his old apartment, the state-room, put away, the heavy brocade curtains brown-hollanded, the jugs turned upside down, the bed stripped of its clothes and the looking-glass laid a-top of it.

The smirking housemaid, who was just rolling the fire-irons up in the hearth-rug, greeted him with a 'Please, sir, we've shifted you into the brown room, east,' leading the way to the condemned cell that 'Jack' had occupied, where a newly lit fire was puffing out dense clouds of brown smoke, obscuring even the gilt letters on the back of *Mogg's Cab Fares*, as the little volume lay on the toilet-table.

'What's happened now?' asked our friend of the maid, putting his arm round her waist, and giving her a hearty squeeze. 'What's happened now, that you've put me into this dog-hole?' asked he.

'Oh! I don't know,' replied she, laughing; 'I s'pose they're afraid you'll bring the old rotten curtains down in the other room with smokin'. Master's a sad old wife,' added she.

A great change had come over everything. The fare, the lights, the footmen, the everything, underwent grievous diminution. The lamps were extinguished, and the transparent wax gave way to Palmer's composites, under the mild influence of whose unsearching light the young ladies sported their dashed dresses with impunity. Competition between them, indeed, was about an end. Amelia claimed Mr. Sponge, should he be worth having, and should the Scamperdale scheme fail; while Emily, having her mamma's assurance that he would not do for either of them, resigned herself complacently to what she could not help.

Mr. Sponge, on his part, saw that all things portended a close. He cared nothing about the old willow-pattern set usurping the place of the Jawleyford-armed china; but the contents of the dishes were bad, and the wine, if possible, worse. Most palpable Marsala did duty for sherry, and the corked port was again in requisition. Jawleyford was no longer the brisk, cheery-hearted Jawleyford of Laverick Wells, but a crusty, fidgety, fire-stirring sort of fellow, desperately given to his *Morning Post*.

Worst of all, when Mr. Sponge retired to his den to smoke a cigar and study his dear cab fares, he was so suffocated with smoke that he was obliged to put out the fire, notwithstanding the weather was cold, indeed inclining to frost. He lit his cigar notwithstanding; and, as he indulged in it, he ran all the circumstances of his situation through his mind. His pressing invitation—his magnificent reception—the attention of the ladies—and now the sudden change everything had taken. He couldn't make it out, somehow; but the consequences were plain enough. 'The fellow's a humbug,' at length said he, throwing the cigar-end away, and turning into bed, when the information Watson the keeper gave him on arriving recurred to his mind, and he was satisfied that Jawleyford was a humbug. It was clear Mr. Sponge had made a mistake in coming; the best thing he could do now was to back out, and see if the fair Amelia would take it to heart. In the midst of his cogitations Mr. Puffington's pressing invitation occurred to his mind, and it appeared to be the very thing for him, affording him an immediate asylum within reach of the fair lady, should she be likely to die.

Next day he wrote to volunteer a visit.

Mr. Puffington, who was still in ignorance of our friend's real character, and still believed him to be a second 'Nimrod' out on a 'tour,' was overjoyed at his letter; and, strange to relate, the same post that brought his answer jumping at the proposal, brought a letter from Lord Scamperdale to Jawleyford, saying that, 'as soon as Jawleyford was *quite alone* (scored under) he would like to pay him a visit.' His lordship, we should inform the reader, notwithstanding his recent mishap, still held out against Jack Spraggon's recommendation to get rid of Mr. Sponge by buying his horses, and he determined to try this experiment first. His lordship thought at one time of entering into an explanation, telling Mr. Jawleyford the damage Sponge had done him, and the nuisance he was entailing upon him by harbouring him; but not being a great scholar, and several hard words turning up that his lordship could not well clear in the spelling, he just confined himself to a laconic, which, as it turned out, was a most fortunate course. Indeed, he had another difficulty besides the spelling, for the hounds having as usual had a great run after Mr. Sponge had floored him—knocked his right eye into the heel of his left boot, as he said—in the course of which run his lordship's horse had rolled over him on a road, he was like the railway people—unable to distinguish between capital and income—unable to say which were Sponge's bangs and which his own; so, like a hard cricket-ball sort of a man as he was, he just pocketed all, and wrote as we have described.

His lordship's and Mr. Puffington's letters diffused joy into a house that seemed likely to be distracted with trouble.

So then endeth our thirtieth chapter, and a very pleasant ending it is, for we leave everyone in perfect good humour and spirits, Sponge pleased at having got a fresh billet, Jawleyford delighted at the coming of the lord, and each fair lady practising in private how to sign her Christian name in conjunction with 'Scamperdale.'

XXXI

MR. PUFFINGTON; OR THE YOUNG MAN ABOUT TOWN

MR. PUFFINGTON TOOK THE MANGEYSTERNE, now the Hanby hounds, because he thought they would give him consequence. Not that he was particularly deficient in that article; but being a new man in the county, he thought that taking them would make him popular, and give him standing. He had no natural inclination for hunting, but seeing friends who had no taste for the turf take upon themselves the responsibility of stewardships, he saw no reason why he should not make a similar sacrifice at the shrine of Diana. Indeed, Puff was not bred for a sportsman. His father, a most estimable man, and one with whom we have spent many a convivial evening, was a great starch-maker at Stepney; and his mother was the daughter of an eminent Worcestershire stone-china maker. Save such ludicrous hunts as they might have seen on their brown jugs, we do not believe either of them had any acquaintance whatever with the chase. Old Puffington was, however, what a wise heir esteems a great deal more—an excellent man of business, and amassed mountains of money. To see his establishment at Stepney, one would think the whole world was going to be starched. Enormous dock-tailed dray-horses emerged with ponderous waggons heaped up to the very skies, while others would come rumbling in, laden with wheat, potatoes, and other starch-making ingredients. Puffington's blue roans were well known about town, and were considered the handsomest horses of the day; quite equal to Barclay and Perkin's piebalds.

Old Puffington was not like a sportsman. He was a little, soft, rosy, roundabout man, with stiff resolute legs that did not look as if they could be bent to a saddle. He was great, however, in a gig, and slouched like a sack.

Mrs. Puffington, *née* Smith, was a tall handsome woman, who thought a good deal of herself. When she and her spouse married, they lived close to the manufactory, in a sweet little villa replete with every elegance and convenience—a pond, which they called a lake—laburnums without end; a yew, clipped into a dock-tailed waggon-horse; standing for three horses and gigs, with an acre and half of land for a cow.

Old Puffington, however, being unable to keep those dearest documents of the British merchant, his balance-sheets, to himself, and Mrs. Puffington finding a considerable sum going to the 'good' every year, insisted, on the birth of their only child, our friend, upon migrating to the 'west,' as she called it, and at one bold stroke they established themselves in Heathcote Street, Mecklenburgh Square. Novelists had not then written this part down as 'Mesopotamia,' and it was quite as genteel as Harley or Wimpole Street are now. Their chief object then was to increase their wealth and make their only son 'a gentleman.' They sent him to Eton, and in due time to Christ Church, where, of course, he established a red coat to persecute Sir Thomas Mostyn's and the Duke of Beaufort's hounds, much to the annoyance of their respective huntsmen, Stephen Goodall and Philip Payne, and the aggravation of poor old Griff Lloyd.

What between the field and college, young Puffington made the acquaintance of several very dashing young sparks—Lord Firebrand, Lord Mudlark, Lord Deuceace, Sir Harry Blueun, and others, whom he always spoke of as 'Deuceace,' 'Blueun,' etc., in the easy style that marks the perfect gentleman. How proud the old people were of him! How they would sit listening to him, flashing, and telling how Deuceace and he floored a Charley, or Blueun and he pitched a snob out of the boxes into the pit.[1] This was in the old Tom-and-Jerry days, when fisticuffs were the fashion. One evening, after he had indulged us with a more than usual dose, and was leaving the room to dress for an eight o'clock dinner at Long's, 'Buzzer!' exclaimed the old man, clutching our arm, as the tears started to his eyes, 'Buzzer! that's an am*aa*zin' instance of a pop'lar man!' And certainly, if a large acquaintance is a criterion of popularity, young

Puffington, as he was then called, had his fair share. He once did us the honour—an honour we shall never forget—of walking down Bond Street with us, in the spring-tide of fashion, of a glorious summer's day, when you could not cross Conduit Street under a lapse of a quarter of an hour, and carriages seemed to have come to an interminable lock at the Piccadilly end of the street. In those days great people went about like great people, in handsome hammer-clothed, arms-emblazoned coaches, with plethoric three-corner-hatted coachmen, and gigantic, lace-bedizened, quivering-calved Johnnies, instead of rumbling along like apothecaries in pill-boxes, with a handle inside to let themselves out. Young men, too, dressed as if they were dressed—as if they were got up with some care and attention—instead of wearing the loose, careless, flowing, sack-like garments they do now.

We remember the day as if it were but yesterday; Puffington overtook us in Oxford Street, where we were taking our usual sauntering stare into the shop windows, and instead of shirking or slipping behind our back, he actually ran his arm up to the hilt in ours, and turned us into the middle of the flags, with an 'Ah, Buzzer, old boy, what are you doing in this debauched part of the town? Come along with me, and I'll show you Life!'

So saying he linked arms, and pursuing our course at a proper kill-time sort of pace, we were at length brought up at the end of Vere Street, along which there was a regular rush of carriages, cutting away as if they were going to a fire instead of to a finery shop.

Many were the smiles, and bows, and nods, and finger kisses, and bright eyes, and sweet glances, that the fair flyers shot at our friend as they darted past. We were lost in astonishment at the sight. 'Verily,' said we, 'but the old man was right. This *is* an am*aa*zin' instance of a pop'lar man.'

Young Puffington was then in the heyday of youth, about one-and-twenty or so, fair-haired, fresh-complexioned, slim, and standing, with the aid of high-heeled boots, little under six feet high. He had taken after his mother, not after old Tom Trodgers, as they called his papa. At length we crossed over Oxford Street, and taking the shady side of Bond Street, were quickly among the real swells of the world—men who crawled along as if life was a perfect burden to them—men with eye-glasses fixed and tasselled canes in their hands, scarcely less ponderous than those borne by the footmen. Great Heavens! but they were tight, and smart, and shiny; and Puffington was just as tight, and smart, and shiny as any of them. He was as much in his element here as he appeared to be out of it in Oxford Street. It might be prejudice, or want of penetration on our part, but we thought he looked as high-bred as any of them. They all seemed to know each other, and the nodding, and winking, and jerking, began as soon as we got across. Puff kindly acted as cicerone, or we should not have been aware of the consequence we were encountering.

'Well, Jemmy!' exclaimed a debauched-looking youth to our friend, 'how are you?—breakfasted yet?'

'Going to,' replied Puffington, whom they called Jemmy because his name was Tommy.

'That,' said he, in an undertone, 'is a *capital* fellow—Lord Legbail, eldest son of the Marquis of Loosefish—will be Lord Loosefish. We were at the Finish together till six this morning—such fun!—bonneted a Charley, stole his rattle, and broke an early breakfast-man's stall all to shivers.' Just then up came a broad-brimmed hat, above a confused mass of greatcoats and coloured shawls.

'Holloa, Jack!' exclaimed Mr. Puffington, laying hold of a mother-of-pearl button nearly as large as a tart-plate, 'not off yet?'

'Just going,' replied Jack, with a touch of his hat, as he rolled on, adding, 'want aught down the road?'

'What coachman is that?' asked we.

'*Coachman!*' replied Puff, with a snort. 'That's Jack Linchpin—Honourable Jack Linchpin—son of Lord Splinterbars—best gentleman coachman in England.'

So Puffington sauntered along, good morninging 'Sir Harrys' and 'Sir Jameses,' and 'Lord Johns' and 'Lord Toms,' till, seeing a batch of irreproachable dandies flattening their noses against the windows of the Sailors' Old Club, in whose eyes, he perhaps thought, our city coat and country gaiters would not find much favour, he gave us a hasty parting squeeze of the arm and bolted into Long's just as a mountainous hackney-coach was rumbling between us and them.

But to the old man. Time rolled on, and at length old Puffington paid the debt of nature—the only debt, by the way, that he was slow in discharging—and our friend found himself in possession, not only of the starch manufactory, but of a very great accumulation of consols—so great that, though starch is as inoffensive a thing as a man can well deal in, a thing that never obtrudes itself, or, indeed appears in a shop unless it is asked for—notwithstanding all this, and though it was bringing him in lots of money, our friend determined to 'cut the shop' and be done with trade altogether.

Accordingly, he sold the premises and goodwill, with all the stock of potatoes and wheat, to the foreman, old Soapsuds, at something below what they were really worth, rather than make any row in the way of advertising; and the name of 'Soapsuds, Brothers & Co.' reigns on the blue-and-whitey-brown parcel-ends, where formerly that of Puffington stood supreme.

It is a melancholy fact, which those best acquainted with London society can vouch for, that her 'swells' are a very ephemeral race. Take the last five-and-twenty years—say from the days of the Golden Ball and Pea-green Hayne down to those of Molly C——l and Mr. D-l-f-ld—and see what a succession of joyous—no, not joyous, but rattling, careless, dashing, sixty-percenting youths we have had.

And where are they all now? Some dead, some at Boulogne-sur-Mer, some in Denman Lodge, some perhaps undergoing the polite attentions of Mr. Commissioner Phillips, or figuring in Mr. Hemp's periodical publication of gentlemen 'who are wanted.'

In speaking of 'swells,' of course, we are not alluding to men with reference to their clothes alone, but to men whose dashing, and perhaps eccentric, exteriors are but indicative of their general system of extravagance. The man who rests his claims to distinction solely on his clothes will very soon find himself in want of society. Many things contribute to thin the ranks of our swells. Many, as we said before, outrun the constable. Some get fat, some get married, some get tired, and a few get wiser. There is, however, always a fine pushing crop coming on. A man like Puffington, who starts a dandy (in contradistinction to a swell), and adheres steadily to clothes—talking eternally of the cuts of coats or the ties of cravats—up to the sober age of forty, must be always falling back on the rising generation for society.

Puffington was not what the old ladies call a profligate young man. On the contrary, he was naturally a nice, steady young man; and only

indulged in the vagaries we have described because they were indulged in by the high-born and gay.

Tom and Jerry had a great deal to answer for in the way of leading soft-headed young men astray; and old Puffington having had the misfortune to christen our friend 'Thomas,' of course his companions dubbed him 'Corinthian Tom'; by which name he has been known ever since.

A man of such undoubted wealth could not be otherwise than a great favourite with the fair, and innumerable were the invitations that poured into his chambers in the Albany—dinner parties, evening parties, balls, concerts, boxes for the opera; and as each succeeding season drew to a close, invitations to those last efforts of the desperate, boating and whitebait parties.

Corinthian Tom went to them all—at least, to as many as he could manage—always dressing in the most exemplary way, as though he had been asked to show his fine clothes instead of to make love to the ladies. Manifold were the hopes and expectations that he raised. Puff could not understand that, though it is all very well to be 'an amaazin' instance of a pop'lar man' with the men, that the same sort of thing does not do with the ladies.

We have heard that there were six mammas, bowling about in their barouches, at the close of his second season, innuendoing, nodding, and hinting to their friends, 'that, &c.,' when there wasn't one of their daughters who had penetrated the rhinoceros-like hide of his own conceit. The consequence was that all these ladies, all their daughters, all the relations and connexions of this life, thought it incumbent upon them to 'blow' our friend Puff—proclaim how infamously he had behaved—all because he had danced three supper dances with one girl, brought another a fine bouquet from Covent Garden, walked a third away from her party at a picnic at Erith, begged the mamma of a fourth to take her to a Woolwich ball, sent a fifth a ticket for a Toxophilite meeting, and dangled about the carriage of the sixth at a review at the Scrubbs. Poor Puff never thought of being more than an amaazin' instance of a pop'lar man!

Not that the ladies' denunciations did the Corinthian any harm at first—old ladies know each other better than that; and each new mamma had no doubt but Mrs. Depecarde or Mrs. Mainchance, as the case might be, had been deceiving herself—'was always doing so, indeed; her ugly girls were not likely to attract any one—certainly not such an elegant man as Corinthian Tom.'

But as season after season passed away, and the Corinthian still played the old game—still went the old rounds—the dinner and ball invitations gradually dwindled away, till he became a mere stop-gap at the one, and a landing-place appendage at the other.

1.   Query, 'snob'?—Printer's Devil.

XXXII

THE MAN OF P-R-O-R-PERTY

A ND NOW BEHOLD MR. PUFFINGTON, fat, fair, and rather more than forty—Puffington, no longer the light limber lad who patronized us in Bond Street, but Puffington a plump, portly sort of personage, filling his smart clothes uncommonly full. Men no longer hailing him heartily from bay windows, or greeting him cheerily in short but familiar terms, but bowing ceremoniously as they passed with their wives, or perhaps turning down streets or into shops to avoid him. What is the last rose of summer to do under such circumstances? What, indeed, but retire into the country? A man may shine there long after he is voted a bore in town, provided none of his old friends are there to proclaim him. Country people are tolerant of twaddle, and slow of finding things out for themselves. Puff now turned his attention to the country, or rather to the advertisements of estates for sale, and immortal George Robins soon fitted him with one of his earthly paradises; a mansion replete with every modern elegance, luxury, and convenience, situated in the heart of the most lovely scenery in the world, with eight hundred acres of land of the finest quality, capable of growing forty bushels of wheat after turnips. In addition to the estate there was a lordship or reputed lordship to shoot over, a river to fish in, a pack of fox-hounds to hunt with, and the advertisements gave a sly hint as to the possibility of the property influencing the representation of the neighbouring borough of Swillingford, if not of returning the member itself.

This was Hanby House, and though the description undoubtedly partook of George's usual high-flown *couleur-de-rose* style, the manor being only a manor provided the owner sacrificed his interest in

Swillingford by driving off its poachers, and the river being only a river when the tiny Swill was swollen into one, still Hanby House was a very nice attractive sort of place, and seen in the rich foliage of its summer dress, with all its roses and flowering shrubs in full blow, the description was not so wide of the mark as Robins's descriptions usually were. Puff bought it, and became what he called 'a man of p-r-o-r-perty.' To be sure, after he got possession he found that it was only an acre here and there that would grow forty bushels of wheat after turnips, and that there was a good deal more to do at the house than he expected, the furniture of the late occupants having hidden many defects, added to which they had walked off with almost everything they could wrench down, under the name of fixtures; indeed, there was not a peg to hang up his hat when he entered. This, however, was nothing, and Puff very soon made it into one of the most perfect bachelor residences that ever was seen. Not but that it was a family house, with good nurseries and offices of every description; but Puff used to take a sort of wicked pleasure in telling the ladies who came trooping over with their daughters, pretending they thought he was from home, and wishing to see the elegant furniture, that there was nothing in the nurseries, which he was going to convert into billiard and smoking-rooms. This, and a few similar sallies, earned our friend the reputation of a wit in the country.

There was great rush of gentlemen to call upon him; many of the mammas seemed to think that first come would be first served, and sent their husbands over before he was fairly squatted. Various and contradictory were the accounts they brought home. Men are so stupid at seeing and remembering things. Old Mr. Muddle came back bemused with sherry, declaring that he thought Mr. Puffington was as old as he was (sixty-two), while Mrs. Mousetrap thought he wasn't more than thirty at the outside. She described him as 'painfully handsome.' Mr. Slowan couldn't tell whether the drawing-room furniture was chintz, or damask, or what it was; indeed, he wasn't sure that he was in the drawing-room at all; while Mr. Gapes insisted that the carpet was a Turkey carpet, whereas it was a royal cut pile. It might be that the smartness and freshness of everything confused the bucolic minds, little accustomed to wholesale grandeur.

Mr. Puffington quite eclipsed all the old country families with their 'company rooms' and put-away furniture. Then, when he began to grind about the country in his lofty mail-phaeton, with a pair of spanking, high-stepping bays, and a couple of arm-folded, lolling grooms, shedding his cards in return for their calls, there was such a talk, such a commotion, as had never been known before. Then, indeed, he was appreciated at his true worth.

'Mr. Puffington was here the other day,' said Mrs. Smirk to Mrs. Smooth, in the well-known 'great-deal-more-meant-than-said' style. 'Oh such a charming man! Such ease! such manners! such knowledge of high life!' Puff had been at his old tricks. He had resuscitated Lord Legbail, now Earl of Loosefish; imported Sir Harry Blueun from somewhere near Geneva, whither he had retired on marrying his mistress; and resuscitated Lord Mudlark, who had broken his neck many years before from his tandem in Piccadilly. Whatever was said, Puff always had a duplicate or illustration involving a nobleman. The great names might be rather far-fetched at times, to be sure, but when people are inclined to be pleased they don't keep putting that and that together to see how they fit, and whether they come naturally or are lugged in neck and heels, Puff's talk was very telling.

One great man to a house is the usual country allowance, and many are not very long in letting out who theirs are; but Puffington seemed to have the whole peerage, baronetage, and knightage at command. Old Mrs. Slyboots, indeed, thought that he must be connected with the peerage some way; his mother, perhaps, had been the daughter of a peer, and she gave herself an infinity of trouble in hunting through the 'matches'—with what success it is not necessary to say. The old ladies unanimously agreed that he was a most agreeable, interesting young man; and though the young ones did pretend to run him down among themselves, calling him ugly, and so on, it was only in the vain hope of dissuading each other from thinking of him.

Mr. Puffington still stuck to the 'am*aazin*' pop'lar man' character; a character that is not so convenient to support in the country as it is in town. The borough of Swillingford, as we have already intimated, was not the best conducted borough in the world; indeed, when we say that the principal trade of the place was poaching, our country readers will be able to form a very accurate opinion on that head. When Puff took possession of Hanby there was a fair show of pheasants about the house, and a good sprinkling of hares and partridges over the estate and manor generally; but refusing to prosecute the first poachers that were caught, the rest took the hint, and cleared everything off in a week, dividing the plunder among them. They also burnt his river and bagged his fine Dorking fowls, and all these feats being accomplished with impunity, they turned their attention to his fat sheep.

'Poacher' is only a mild term for 'thief.'

Puff was a perfect milch-cow in the way of generosity. He gave to everything and everybody, and did not seem to be acquainted with any smaller sum than a five-pound note; a five-pound note to replace Giles Jolter's cart-horse (that used to carry his own game for the poachers to the poulterers at Plunderstone)—five pounds to buy Dame Doubletongue another pig, though she had only just given three pounds for the one that died—five pounds towards the fire at farmer Scratchley's, though it had taken place two years before Puff came into the country, and Scratchley had been living upon it ever since—and sundry other five pounds to other equally deserving and amiable people. He put his name down for fifty to the Mangeysterne hounds without ever being asked; which reminds us that we ought to be directing our attention to that noble establishment.

It is hard to have to go behind the scenes of an ill-supported hunt, and we will be as brief and tender with the cripples as we can. The Mangeysterne hounds wanted that great ingredient of prosperity, a large nest-egg subscriber, to whom all others could be tributary—paying or not as might be convenient. The consequence was they were always up the spout. They were neither a scratch pack nor a regular pack, but something betwixt and between. They were hunted by a saddler, who found his own horses, and sometimes he had a whip and sometimes he hadn't. The establishment died as often as old Mantalini himself. Every season that came to a close was proclaimed to be their last, but somehow or other they always managed to scramble into existence on the approach of another. It is a way, indeed, that delicate packs have of recruiting their finances. Nevertheless, the Mangeysternes did look very like coming to an end about the time that Mr. Puffington bought Hanby House. The saddler huntsman had failed; John Doe had taken one of his screws, and Richard Roe the other, and anybody might have the hounds that liked: Puffington then turned up.

Great was the joy diffused throughout the Mangeysterne country when it transpired, through the medium of his valet, Louis Bergamotte, that 'his lor' had *beaucoup habit rouge*' in his wardrobe. Not only habit rouge, but habit blue and buff, that he used to sport with 'Old Beaufort' and the Badminton Hunt—coats that he certainly had no chance of ever getting into again, but still which he kept as memorials of the past—souvenirs of the days when he was young and slim. The bottle-conjurer could just as soon have got into his quart bottle as Puff could into the Beaufort coat at the time of which we are writing. The intelligence of their existence was quickly followed by the aforesaid fifty-pound cheque. A meeting of the Mangeysterne hunt was called at the sign of the Thirsty Freeman in Swillingford—Sir Charles Figgs, Knight—a large-promising but badly paying subscriber—in the chair, when it was proposed and carried unanimously that Mr. Puffington was eminently qualified for the mastership of the hunt, and that it be offered to him accordingly. Puff 'bit.' He recalled his early exploits with 'Mostyn and old Beaufort,' and resolved that the hunt had taken a right view of his abilities. In coming to this decision he, perhaps, was not altogether uninfluenced by a plausible subscription list, which seemed about equal to the ordinary expenses, supposing that any reliance could be placed on the figures and calculations of Sir Charles. All those, however, who have had anything to do with subscription lists—and in these days of universal testimonializing who has not?—well know that pounds upon paper and pounds in the pocket are very different things. Above all, Puff felt that he was a new man in the country, and that taking the hounds would give him weight.

The 'Mangeysterne dogs' then began to 'look up'; Mr. Puffington took to them in earnest; bought a 'Beckford,' and shortened his military stirrups to a hunting seat.

XXXIII

A SWELL HUNTSMAN

ONE EVENING THE RATTLE OF Puff's pole-chains brought, in addition to the usual rush of shirt-sleeved helpers, an extremely smart, dapper little man, who might be either a jockey or a gentleman, or both, or neither. He was a clean-shaved, close-trimmed, spruce little fellow; remarkably natty about the legs—indeed, all over. His close-napped hat was carefully brushed, and what little hair appeared below its slightly curved brim was of the pepper-and-salt mixture of—say, fifty years. His face, though somewhat wrinkled and weather-beaten, was bright and healthy; and there was a twinkle about his little grey eyes that spoke of quickness and watchful observation. Altogether, he was a very quick-looking little man—a sort of man that would know what you were going to say before you had well broke ground. He wore no gills; and his neatly tied starcher had a white ground with small black spots, about the size of currants. The slight interregnum between it and his step-collared striped vest (blue stripe on a canary-coloured ground) showed three golden foxes' heads, acting as studs to his well-washed, neatly plaited shirt; while a sort of careless turn back of the right cuff showed similar ornaments at his wrists. His single-breasted, cutaway coat was Oxford mixture, with a thin cord binding, and very natty light kerseymere mother-o'-pearl buttoned breeches, met a pair of bright, beautifully fitting, rose-tinted tops, that wrinkled most elegantly down to the Jersey-patterned spur. He was a remarkably well-got-up little man, and looked the horseman all over.

As he emerged from the stable, where he had been mastering the ins and outs of the establishment, learning what was allowed and what was not, what had not been found fault with and, therefore, might be

264   ROBERT S. SURTEES

presumed upon, and so on, he carried the smart dogskin leather glove of one hand in the other, while the fox's head of a massive silver-mounted jockey-whip peered from under his arm. On a ring round the fox's neck was the following inscription: 'FROM JACK BRAGG TO HIS COUSIN DICK.'

Mr. Puffington having drawn up his mail-phaeton, and thrown the ribbons to the active grooms at the horses' heads in the true coaching style, proceeded to descend from his throne, and had reached the ground ere he was aware of the presence of a stranger. Seeing him then, he made the sort of half-obeisance of a man that does not know whether he is addressing a gentleman or a servant, or, maybe, a scamp, going about with a prospectus. Puff had been bit in the matter of some maps in London, and was wary, as all people ought to be, of these birds.

The stranger came sidling up with a half-bow, half-touch of the hat, drawling out:

"Sceuuse me, sir—'sceuuse me, sir,' with another half-bow and another half-touch of the hat. 'I'm Mister Bragg, sir—Mister Richard Bragg, sir; of whom you have most likely heard.'

'Bragg—Richard Bragg,' repeated our friend, thoughtfully, while he scanned the man's features, and ran his sporting acquaintance through his mind's eye.

'Bragg, Bragg,' repeated he, without hitting him off.

'I was huntsman, sir, to my Lord Reynard, sir,' observed the stranger, with a touch of the hat to each 'sir.' 'Thought p'r'aps you might have known his ludship, sir. Before him, sir, I held office, sir, under the Duke of Downeybird, sir, of Downeybird Castle, sir, in Downeybirdshire, sir.'

'Indeed!' replied Mr. Puffington, with a half-bow and a smile of politeness.

'Hearing, sir, you had taken these Mangeysterne *dogs*, sir,' continued the stranger, with rather a significant emphasis on the word '*dogs*'— 'hearing, sir, you had taken these Mangeysterne *dogs*, sir, it occurred to me that possibly I might be useful to you, sir, in your new calling, sir; and if you were of the same opinion, sir, why, sir, I should be glad to negotiate a connexion, sir.'

'Hem!—hem!—hem!' coughed Mr. Puffington. 'In the way of a huntsman, do you mean?' afraid to talk of servitude to so fine a gentleman.

'Just so,' said Mr. Bragg, with a chuck of his head, 'just so. The fact is, though I'm used to the grass countries, sir, and could go to the Marquis of Maneylies, sir, to-morrow, sir, I should prefer a quiet place in a somewhat inferior country, sir, to a five-days-a-week one in the best. Five and six days a week, sir, is a terrible tax, sir, on the constitution, sir; and though, sir, I'm thankful to say, sir, I've pretty good 'ealth, sir, yet, sir, you know, sir, it don't do, sir, to take too great liberties with oneself, sir'; Mr. Bragg, sawing away at his hat as he spoke, measuring off a touch, as it were, to each 'sir,' the action becoming quick towards the end.

'Why, to tell you the truth,' said Puff, looking rather sheepish, 'to tell you the truth—I intended—I thought at least of—of—of—hunting them myself.'

'Ah! that's another pair of shoes altogether, as we say in France,' replied Bragg, with a low bow and a copious round of the hand to the hat. 'That's *another* pair of shoes altogether,' repeated he, tapping his boot with his whip.

'Why, I *thought* of it,' rejoined Puff, not feeling quite sure whether he could or not.

'Well,' said Mr. Bragg, drawing on his dogskin glove as if to be off.

'My friend Swellcove does it,' observed Puff.

'True,' replied Bragg, 'true; but my Lord Swellcove is one of a thousand. See how many have failed for one that has succeeded. Why, even my Lord Scamperdale was 'bliged to give it up, and no man rides harder than my Lord Scamperdale—always goes as if he had a spare neck in his pocket. But he couldn't 'unt a pack of 'ounds. Your gen'l'men 'untsmen are all very well on fine scentin' days when everything goes smoothly and well, and the 'ounds are tied to their fox, as it were; but see them in difficulties—a failing scent, 'ounds pressed upon by the field, fox chased by a dog, storm in the air, big brook to get over to make a cast. Oh, sir, sir, it makes even me, with all my acknowledged science and experience, shudder to think of the ordeal one undergoes!'

'Indeed,' exclaimed Mr. Puffington, staring, and beginning to think it mightn't be quite so easy as it looked.

'I don't wish, sir, to dissuade you, sir, from the attempt, sir,' continued Mr. Bragg; 'far from it, sir—for he, sir, who never makes an effort, sir, never risks a failure, sir, and in great attempts, sir, 'tis glorious to fail, sir';

Mr. Bragg sawing away at his hat as he spoke, and then sticking the fox-head handle of his whip under his chin.

Puff stood mute for some seconds.

'My Lord Scamperdale,' continued Mr. Bragg, scrutinizing our friend attentively, 'was as likely a man, sir, as ever I see'd, sir, to make an 'untsman, for he had a deal of ret (rat) ketchin' cunnin' about him, and, as I said before, didn't care one dim for his neck, but a more signal disastrous failure was never recognized. It was quite lamentable to witness his proceeding.'

'How?' asked Mr. Puffington.

'How, sir?' repeated Mr. Bragg; 'why, sir, in all wayses. He had no dog language, to begin with—he had little idea of making a cast—no science, no judgement, no manner—no nothin'—I'm dim'd if ever I see'd such a mess as he made.'

Puff looked unutterable things.

'He never did no good, in fact, till I fit him with Frostyface. *I* taught Frosty,' continued Mr. Bragg. 'He whipped in to me when I 'unted the Duke of Downeybird's 'ounds—nice, 'cute, civil chap he was—of all my pupils—and I've made some first-rate 'untsmen, I'm dim'd if I don't think Frostyface does me about as much credit as any on 'em. Ah, sir,' continued Mr. Bragg, with a shake of his head, 'take my word for it, sir, there's nothin' like a professional. S-c-e-u-s-e me, sir,' added he, with a low bow and a sort of military salute of his hat; 'but dim all gen'l'men 'untsmen, say I.'

Mr. Bragg had talked himself into several good places. Lord Reynard's and the Duke of Downeybird's among others. He had never been able to keep any beyond his third season, his sauce or his science being always greater than the sport he showed. Still, he kept up appearances, and was nothing daunted, it being a maxim of his that 'as one door closed another opened.'

Mr. Puffington's was the door that now opened for him.

What greater humiliation can a free-born Briton be subjected to than paying a man eighty or a hundred pounds a year, and finding him house, coals, and candles, and perhaps a cow, to be his master?

Such was the case with poor Mr. Puffington, and such, we grieve to say, is the case with nine-tenths of the men who keep hounds; with all, indeed, save those who can hunt themselves, or who are blest with an aspiring whip, ready to step into the huntsman's boots if he seems inclined to put them off in the field. How many portly butlers are kept in subjection by having a footman ready to supplant them. Of all cards in the servitude pack, however, the huntsman's is the most difficult one to play. A man may say, 'I'm dim'd if I won't clean my own boots or my own horse, before I'll put up with such a fellow's impudence'; but when it comes to hunting his own hounds, it is quite another pair of shoes, as Mr. Bragg would say.

Mr. Bragg regularly took possession of poor Puff, as regularly as a policeman takes possession of a prisoner. The reader knows the sort of feeling one has when a lawyer, a doctor, an architect, or any one whom we have called in to assist, takes the initiative, and treats one as a nonentity, pooh-poohing all one's pet ideas, and upsetting all one's well-considered arrangements.

Bragg soon saw he had a greenhorn to deal with, and treated Puff accordingly. If a 'perfect servant' is only to begot out of the establishments of the great, Mr. Bragg might be looked upon as a paragon of perfection, and now combined in his own person all the bad practices of all the places he had been in. Having 'accepted Mr. Puffington's situation,' as the elegant phraseology of servitude goes, he considered that Mr. Puffington had nothing more to do with the hounds, and that any interference in 'his department' was a piece of impertinence. Puffington felt like a man who has bought a good horse, but which he finds on riding is rather more of a horse than he likes. He had no doubt that Bragg was a good man, but he thought he was rather more of a gentleman than he required. On the other hand, Mr. Bragg's opinion of his master may be gleaned from the following letter which he wrote to his successor, Mr. Brick, at Lord Reynard's:

Hanby House, Swillingford.

DEAR BRICK,

If your old man is done daffling with your draft, I should like to have the pick of it. I'm with one Mr. Puffington, a city gent. His father was a great confectioner in the Poultry, just by the Mansion House, and made his money out of Lord Mares. I shall only stay with him till I can get myself suited in the rank of life in which

I have been accustomed to move; but in the meantime I consider
it necessary for my own credit to do things as they should be. You
know my sort of hound: good shoulders, deep chests, strong loins,
straight legs, round feet, with plenty of bone all over. I hate a weedy
animal; a small hound, light of bone, is only fit to hunt a kat in a
kitchen.

I shall also want a couple of whips—not fellows like waiters from
Crawley's hotel, but light, active *men*, not boys. I'll have nothin' to do
with boys; every boy requires a man to look arter him. No; a couple
of short, light, active men—say from five-and-twenty to thirty, with
bow-legs and good cheery voices, as nearly of the same make as
you can find them. I shall not give them a large wage, you know;
but they will have opportunities of improving themselves under me,
and qualifying themselves for high places. But mind, they *must be
steady*—I'll keep no unsteady servants; the first act of drunkenness,
with me, is the last.

I shall also want a second horseman; and here I wouldn't mind
a mute boy who could keep his elbows down and never touch
the curb; but he must be bred in the line; a huntsman's second
horseman is a critical article, and the sporting world must not
be put in mourning for Dick Bragg. The lad will have to clean
my boots, and wait at table when I have company—yourself, for
instance.

This is only a poor, rough, ungentlemanly sort of shire, as far as I
have seen it; and however they got on with the things I found that
they called hounds I can't for the life of me imagine. I understand
they went stringing over the country like a flock of wild geese.
However, I have rectified that in a manner by knocking all the fast
'uns and slow 'uns on the head; and I shall require at least twenty
couple before I can take the field. In your official report of what
your old file puts back, you'll have the kindness to cobble us up
good long pedigrees, and carry half of them at least back to the
Beaufort Justice. My man has got a crochet into his head about
that hound, and I'm dimmed if he doesn't think half the hounds in
England are descended from the Beaufort Justice. These hounds are
at present called the Mangeysternes, a very proper title, I should say,
from all I've seen and heard. That, however, must be changed; and

we must have a button struck, instead of the plain pewter plates the men have been in the habit of hunting in.

As to horses, I'm sure I don't know what we are to do in that line. Our pastrycook seems to think that a hunter, like one of his pa's pies, can be made and baked in a day. He talks of going over to Rowdedow Fair, and picking some up himself; but I should say a gentleman demeans himself sadly who interferes with the just prerogative of the groom. It has never been allowed I know in any place I have lived; nor do I think servants do justice to themselves or their order who submit to it. Howsomever the crittur has what Mr. Cobden would call the "raw material" for sport—that is to say, plenty of money—and I must see and apply it in such a way as will produce it. I'll do the thing as it should be, or not at all.

I hope your good lady is well—also all the little Bricks. I purpose making a little tower of some of the best kennels as soon as the drafts are arranged, and will spend a day or two with you, and see how you get on without me. Dear Brick,

Yours to the far end,
RICHARD BRAGG.

To BENJAMIN BRICK, Esq.,
Huntsman to the Right Hon. the Earl of Reynard,
Turkeypout Park.

P.S.—I hope your old man keeps a cleaner tongue in his head than he did when I was premier. I always say there was a good bargeman spoiled when they made him a lord.
R.B.

XXXIV

THE BEAUFORT JUSTICE

THERE IS NOTHING MORE INDICATIVE of real fine people than the easy indifferent sort of way they take leave of their friends. They never seem to care a farthing for parting.

Our friend Jawleyford was quite a man of fashion in this respect. He saw Sponge's preparations for departure with an unconcerned air, and a—'sorry you're going,' was all that accompanied an imitation shake, or rather touch of the hand, on leaving. There was no 'I hope we shall see you again soon,' or 'Pray look in if you are passing our way,' or 'Now that you've found your way here we hope you'll not be long in being back,' or any of those blarneyments that fools take for earnest and wise men for nothing. Jawleyford had been bit once, and he was not going to give Mr. Sponge a second chance. Amelia too, we are sorry to say, did not seem particularly distressed, though she gave him just as much of a sweet look as he squeezed her hand, as said, 'Now, if you *should* be a man of money, and my Lord Scamperdale does not make me my lady, you may,' &c.

There is an old saying, that it is well to be 'off with the old love before one is on with the new,' and Amelia thought it was well to be on with the new love before she was off with the old. Sponge, therefore, was to be in abeyance.

We mentioned the delight infused into Jawleyford Court by the receipt of Lord Scamperdale's letter, volunteering a visit, nor was his lordship less gratified at hearing in reply that Mr. Sponge was on the eve of departure, leaving the coast clear for his reception. His lordship was not only delighted at getting rid of his horror, but at proving the superiority of his judgement over that of Jack, who had always stoutly maintained that the only way to get rid of Mr. Sponge was by buying his horses.

'Well, that's *good*,' said his lordship, as he read the letter; 'that's *good*,' repeated he, with a hearty slap of his thigh. 'Jaw's not such a bad chap after all; worse chaps in the world than Jaw.' And his lordship worked away at the point till he very nearly got him up to be a good chap.

They say it never rains but it pours, and letters seldom come singly; at least, if they do they are quickly followed by others.

As Jack and his lordship were discussing their gin, after a repast of cow-heel and batter-pudding, Baggs entered with the old brown weather-bleached letter-bag, containing a county paper, the second-hand copy of *Bell's Life*, that his lordship and Frostyface took in between them, and a very natty 'thick cream-laid' paper note.

'That must be from a woman,' observed Jack, squinting ardently at the writing, as his lordship inspected the fine seal.

'Not far wrong,' replied his lordship. 'From a bitch of a fellow, at all events,' said he, reading the words 'Hanby House' in the wax.

'What can old Puffey be wanting now?' inquired Jack.

'Some bother about hounds, most likely,' replied his lordship, breaking the seal, adding, 'the thing's always amusing itself with playing at sportsman. Hang his impudence!' exclaimed his lordship, as he opened the note.

'What's happened now?' asked Jack.

'How d'ye think he begins?' asked his lordship, looking at his friend.

'Can't tell, I'm sure,' said Jack, squinting his eyes inside out.

'Dear Scamp!' exclaimed his lordship, throwing out his arms.

'Dear Scamp!' repeated Jack in astonishment. 'It must be a mistake. It must be dear Frost, not dear Scamp.'

'Dear Scamp is the word,' replied his lordship, again applying himself to the letter. 'Dear Scamp,' repeated he, with a snort, adding, 'the impudent button-maker! I'll dear Scamp him! "Dear Scamp, our friend Sponge!" Bo-o-y the powers, just fancy that!' exclaimed his lordship, throwing himself back in his chair, as if thoroughly overcome with disgust. '*Our friend Sponge*! the man who nearly knocked me into the middle of the week after next—the man who, first and last, has broken every bone in my skin—the man who I hate the sight of, and detest afresh every time I see—the 'bomination of all 'bominations; and then to call him our friend Sponge! "Our friend Sponge," continued his lordship, reading, "'is coming on a visit of inspection to my hounds, and I should be glad if you would meet him.'"

'Shouldn't wonder!' exclaimed Jack.

'*Meet him!*' snapped his lordship; 'I'd go ten miles to avoid him.'

"'Glad if you would meet him,'" repeated his lordship, returning to the letter, and reading as follows: "'If you bring a couple of nags or so we can put them up, and you may get a wrinkle or two from Bragg.'" A wrinkle or two from Bragg!' exclaimed his lordship, dropping the letter and rolling in his chair with laughter. 'A wrinkle or two from Bragg!—he—he—he—he! The idea of a wrinkle or two from Bragg!—haw—haw—haw—haw!

'That beats cockfightin',' observed Jack, squinting frightfully.

'Doesn't it?' replied his lordship. 'The man who's so brimful of science that he doesn't kill above three brace of foxes in a season.'

'Which Puff calls thirty,' observed Jack.

'Th-i-r-ty!' exclaimed his lordship, adding, 'I'll lay he'll not kill thirty in ten years.'

His lordship then picked the letter from the floor, and resumed where he had left off.

"'I expect you will meet Tom Washball, Lumpleg, and Charley Slapp.'"

'A very pretty party,' observed Jack, adding, 'Wouldn't be seen goin' to a bull-bait with any on 'em.'

'Nor I,' replied his lordship.

'Birds of a feather,' observed Jack.

'Just so,' said his lordship, resuming his reading.

"'I think I have a hound that may be useful to you—'" The devil you have!' exclaimed his lordship, grinding his teeth with disgust. 'Useful to *me*, you confounded haberdasher!—you hav'n't a hound in your pack that I'd take. "I think I have a hound that may be useful to you—'" repeated his lordship.

'A Beaufort Justice one, for a guinea!' interrupted Jack, adding, 'He got the name into his head at Oxford, and has been harping upon it ever since.'

"'I think I have a hound that may be useful to you—'" resumed his lordship, for the third time. "'It is Old Merriman, a remarkably stout, true line hunting hound; but who is getting slow for me—" Slow for you, you beggar!' exclaimed his lordship; 'I should have thought nothin' short of a wooden 'un would have been too slow for you. "He's a six-season hunter, and is by Fitzwilliam's Singwell out of his Darling. Singwell was by the Rutland Rallywood out of Tavistock's Rhapsody. Rallywood was by Old Lonsdale's—" Old Lonsdale's!—the snob!' sneered Lord Scamperdale—"'Old Lonsdale's Palafox, out of Anson's—" Anson's!—curse the fellow,' again muttered his lordship—"'out of Anson's Madrigal. Darling was by old Grafton's Bolivar, out of Blowzy. Bolivar was by the Brocklesby; that's Yarborough's—" That's Yarborough's!' sneered his lordship, 'as if one didn't know that as well as him—"by the Brocklesby; that's Yarborough's Marmion out of Petre's Matchless; and Marmion was by that undeniable hound, the—" the—what?' asked his lordship.

'Beaufort Justice, to be sure!' replied Jack.

"'The Beaufort Justice!"' read his lordship, with due emphasis.

'Hurrah!' exclaimed Jack, waving the dirty, egg-stained, mustardy copy of *Bell's Life* over his head. 'Hurrah! I told you so.'

'But hark to Justice!' exclaimed his lordship, resuming his reading. "'I've always been a great admirer of the Beaufort Justice blood—'"

'No doubt,' said Jack; 'it's the only blood you know.'

"'It was in great repute in the Badminton country in old Beaufort's time, with whom I hunted a great deal many years ago, I'm sorry to say. The late Mr. Warde, who, of course, was very justly partial to his own sort, had never any objection to breeding from this *Beaufort* Justice. He was of Lord Egremont's blood, by the New Forest Justice; Justice by Mr. Gilbert's Jasper; and Jasper bred by Egremont—" Oh, the hosier!' exclaimed his lordship; 'he'll be the death of me.'

'Is that all?' asked Jack, as his lordship seemed lost in meditation.

'All?—no!' replied he, starting up, adding, 'here's something about you.'

'Me!' exclaimed Jack.

"'If Mr. Spraggon is with you, and you like to bring him, I can manage to put him up, too,"' read his lordship. 'What think you of that?' asked his lordship, turning to our friend, who was now squinting his eyes inside out with anger.

'Think of it!' retorted Jack, kicking out his legs—'think of it!—why, I think he's a dim'd impittant feller, as Bragg would say.'

'So he is,' replied his lordship; 'treating my friend Jack so.'

'I've a good mind to go,' observed Jack, after a pause, thinking he might punish Puff, and try to do a little business with Sponge. 'I've a good mind to go,' repeated he; 'just by way of paying Master Puff off. He's a consequential jackass, and wants taking down a peg or two.'

'I think you may as well go and do it,' replied his lordship, after thinking the matter over; 'I think you may as well go and do it. Not that he'll be good to take the conceit out of, but you may vex him a bit; and also learn something of the movements of his friend Sponge. If he serves Puff out as he's sarved me,' continued his lordship, rubbing his ribs with his elbows, 'he'll very soon have enough of him.'

'Well,' said Jack, 'I really think it will be worth doing. I've never been at the beggar's shop, and they say he lives well.'

'*Well*, aye!' exclaimed his lordship; 'fat o' the land—dare say that man has fish and soup every day.'

'And wax-candles to read by, most likely,' observed Jack, squinting at the dim mutton-fats that Baggs now brought in.

'Not so grand as that,' observed his lordship, doubting whether any man could be guilty of such extravagance; 'composites, p'raps.'

It being decided that Jack should answer Mr. Puffington's invitation as well and saucily as he could, and a sheet of very inferior paper being at length discovered in the sideboard drawer, our friends forthwith proceeded to concoct it. Jack, having at length got all square, and the black-ink lines introduced below, dipped his pen in the little stone ink-bottle, and, squinting up at his lordship, said:

'How shall I begin?'

'Begin?' replied he. 'Begin—oh, let's see—begin—begin, "Dear Puff," to be sure.'

'That'll do,' said Jack, writing away.

('Dear Puff!' sneered our friend, when he read it; 'the idea of a fellow like that writing to a man of my p-r-o-r-perty that way.')

'Say "Scamp,"' continued his lordship, dictating again, '"is engaged, but I'll be with you at feeding-time."'

('Scamp's engaged,' read Puffington, with a contemptuous curl of the lip, 'Scamp's engaged: I like the impudence of a fellow like that calling noblemen nicknames.')

The letter concluded by advising Puffington to stick to the Beaufort

Justice blood, for there was nothing in the world like it. And now, having got both our friends booked for visits, we must yield precedence to the nobleman, and accompany him to Jawleyford Court.

XXXV

LORD SCAMPERDALE
AT JAWLEYFORD COURT

ALTHOUGH WE HAVE HITHERTO DEPICTED Lord Scamperdale either in his great uncouth hunting-clothes or in the flare-up red and yellow Stunner tartan, it must not be supposed that he had not fine clothes when he chose to wear them, only he wanted to save them, as he said, to be married in. That he had fine ones, indeed, was evident from the rig-out he lent Jack when that worthy went to Jawleyford Court, and, in addition to those which were of the evening order, he had an uncommonly smart Stultz frock-coat, with a velvet collar, facings, and cuffs, and a silk lining. Though so rough and ready among the men, he was quite the dandy among the ladies, and was as anxious about his appearance as a girl of sixteen. He got himself clipped and trimmed, and shaved with the greatest care, curving his whiskers high on to the cheekbones, leaving a great breadth of bare fallow below.

Baggs, the butler, was despatched betimes to Jawleyford Court with the dog-cart freighted with clothes, driven by a groom to attend to the horses, while his lordship mounted his galloping grey hack towards noon, and dashed through the country like a comet. The people, who were only accustomed to see him in his short, country-cut hunting-coats, baggy breeches, and shapeless boots, could hardly recognize the frock-coated, fancy-vested, military-trousered swell, as Lord Scamperdale. Even Titus Grabbington, the superintendent of police, declared that he wouldn't have known him but for his hat and specs. The latter, we need hardly say, were the silver ones—the pair that he would not let Jack have when he went to Jawleyford Court. So, his lordship went capering and careering along, avoiding, of course, all the turnpike-gates, of which he had a mortal aversion.

Jawleyford Court was in full dress to receive him—everything was full fig. Spigot appeared in buckled shorts and black silk stockings, while vases of evergreens and winter flowers mounted sentry on passage tables and landing-places. Everything bespoke the elegant presence of the fair.

To the credit of Dame Fortune, let us record that everything went smoothly and well. Even the kitchen fire behaved as it ought. Neither did Lord Scamperdale arrive before he was wanted, a very common custom with people unused to public visiting. He cast up just when he was wanted. His ring of the door-bell acted like the little tinkling bell at a theatre, sending all parties to their places, for the curtain to rise.

Spigot and his two footmen answered the summons, while his lordship's groom rushed out of a side-door, with his mouth full of cold meat, to take his hack.

Having given his flat hat to Spigot, his whip-stick to one footman, and his gloves to the other, he proceeded to the family *tableau* in the drawing-room.

Though his lordship lived so much by himself he was neither *gauche* nor stupid when he went into society. Unlike Mr. Spraggon, he had a tremendous determination of words to the mouth, and went best pace with his tongue instead of coughing and hemming, and stammering and stuttering—wishing himself 'well out of it,' as the saying is. His seclusion only seemed to sharpen his faculties and make him enjoy society more. He gushed forth like a pent-up fountain. He was not a bit afraid of the ladies—rather the contrary; indeed, he would make love to them all—all that were good-looking, at least, for he always candidly said that he 'wouldn't have anything to do with the ugly 'uns.' If anything, he was rather too vehement, and talked to the ladies in such an earnest, interested sort of way, as made even bystanders think there was 'something in it,' whereas, in point of fact, it was mere manner.

He began as soon as ever he got to Jawleyford Court—at least, as soon as he had paid his respects all round and got himself partially thawed at the fire; for the cold had struck through his person, his fine clothes being a poor substitute for his thick double-milled red coat, blankety waistcoat, and Jersey shirt.

There are some good-natured, well-meaning people in this world who think that fox-hunters can talk of nothing but hunting, and who put themselves to very serious inconvenience in endeavouring to get up a little conversation for them. We knew a bulky old boy of this sort, who invariably, after the cloth was drawn, and he had given each leg a kick out to see if they were on, commenced with, 'Well, I suppose, Mr. Harkington has a fine set of dogs this season?' 'A fine set of dogs this season!' What an observation! How on earth could any one hope to drive a conversation on the subject with such a commencement?

Some ladies are equally obliging in this respect. They can stoop to almost any subject that they think will procure them husbands. Music!— if a man is fond of music, they will sing themselves into his good graces in no time. Painting!—oh, they adore painting—though in general they don't profess to be great hands at it themselves. Balls, boating, archery, racing—all these they can take a lively interest in; or, if occasion requires, can go on the serious tack and hunt a parson with penny subscriptions for a clothing-club or soup-kitchen.

Fox-hunting!—we do not know that fox-hunting is so safe a speculation for young ladies as any of the foregoing. There are many pros and cons in the matter of the chase. A man may think—especially in these hard times, with 'wheat below forty,' as Mr. Springwheat would say—that it will be as much as he can do to mount himself. Again, he may not think a lady looks any better for running down with perspiration, and being daubed with mud. Above all, if he belongs to the worshipful company of Craners, he may not like for his wife to be seen beating him across country.

Still, there are many ways that young ladies may insinuate themselves into the good graces of sportsmen without following them into the hunting-field. Talking about their horses, above all admiring them, taking an interest in their sport, seeing that they have nice papers of sandwiches to take out with them, or recommending them to be bled when they come home with dirty faces after falls.

Miss Amelia Jawleyford, who was most elegantly attired in a sea-green silk dress with large imitation pearl buttons, claiming the usual privilege of seniority of birth, very soon led the charge against Lord Scamperdale.

'Oh, what a lovely horse that is you were riding,' observed she, as his lordship kept stooping with both his little red fists close into the bars of the grate.

'Isn't it!' exclaimed he, rubbing his hands heartily together. 'Isn't it!' repeated he, adding, 'that's what I call a clipper.'

'Why do you call it so?' asked she.

'Oh, I don't mean that clipper is its name,' replied he; 'indeed, we call her Cherry Bounce in the stable—but she's what they call a clipper—a good 'un to go, you know,' continued he, staring at the fair speaker through his great, formidable spectacles.

We believe there is nothing frightens a woman so much as staring at her through spectacles. A barrister in barnacles is a far more formidable cross-examiner than one without. But, to his lordship's back.

'Will he eat bread out of your hand?' asked Amelia, adding, 'I *should* so like a horse that would eat bread out of my hand.'

'Oh, yes; or cheese either,' replied his lordship, who was a bit of a wag, and as likely to try a horse with one as the other.

'Oh, how delightful! what a charming horse!' exclaimed Amelia, turning her fine eyes up to the ceiling.

'Are you fond of horses?' asked his lordship, smacking one hand against the other, making a noise like the report of a pistol.

'Oh, so fond!' exclaimed Amelia, with a start; for she hadn't got through her favourite, and, as she thought, most attractive attitude.

'Well, now, that's nice,' said his lordship, giving his other hand a similar bang, adding, 'I like a woman that's fond of horses.'

'Then 'Melia and you'll 'gree nicely,' observed Mrs. Jawleyford, who was always ready to give a helping hand to her own daughters, at least.

'I don't doubt it!' replied his lordship, with emphasis, and a third bang of his hand, louder if possible than before. 'And do *you* like horses?' asked his lordship, darting sharply round on Emily, who had been yielding, or rather submitting, to the precedence of her sister.

'Oh yes; and hounds, too!' replied she eagerly.

'And hounds, too!' exclaimed his lordship, with a start, and another hearty bang of the fist, adding, 'well, now, I like a woman that likes hounds.'

Amelia frowned at the unhandsome march her sister had stolen upon her. Just then in came Jawleyford, much to the annoyance of all parties. A host should never show before the dressing-bell rings.

When that glad sound was at length heard, the ladies, as usual, immediately withdrew; and of course the first thing Amelia did when she got to her room was to run to the glass to see how she had been looking: when, grievous to relate, she found an angry hot spot in the act of breaking out on her nose.

What a distressing situation for a young lady, especially one with a spectacled suitor. 'Oh, dear!' she thought, as she eyed it in the glass, 'it will look like Vesuvius itself through his formidable inquisitors.' Worst of all, it was on the side she would have next him at dinner, should he choose to sit with his back to the fire. However, there was no help for it, and the maid kindly assuring her, as she worked away at her hair, that it 'would never be seen,' she ceased to watch it, and turned her attention to her toilette. The fine, new broad-lace flounced, light-blue satin dress—a dress so much like a ball dress as to be only appreciable as a dinner one by female eyes—was again in requisition; while her fine arms were encircled with chains and armlets of various brilliance and devices. Thus attired, with a parting inspection of the spot, she swept downstairs, with as smart a bouquet as the season would afford. As luck would have it, she encountered his lordship himself wandering about the passage in search of the drawing-room, of whose door he had not made a sufficient observation on leaving. He too, was uncommonly smart, with the identical dress-coat Mr. Spraggon wore, a white waistcoat with turquoise buttons, a lace-frilled shirt, and a most extensive once-round Joinville. He had been eminently successful in accomplishing a tie that would almost rival the sticks farmers put upon truant geese to prevent their getting through gaps or under gates.

Well, Miss Amelia having come to his lordship's assistance, and eased him of his candle, now showed him into the drawing-room; and his hands being disengaged, like a true Englishman, he must be doing, and accordingly he commenced an attack on her bouquet.

'That's a fine nosegay!' exclaimed he, staring and rubbing his snub nose into the midst of it.

'Let me give you a piece,' replied Amelia, proceeding to detach some of the best.

'Do,' replied his lordship, banging one hand against the other, adding, 'I'll wear it next my heart of hearts.'

In sidled Miss Emily just as his lordship was adjusting it in his button-hole, and the inconstant man immediately chopped over to her.

'Well, now, that *is* a beautiful nosegay!' exclaimed he, turning upon her in precisely the same way, with a bang of the hand and a dive of his nose into Emily's.

She did not offer him any, and his lordship continued his attentions to her until Mrs. Jawleyford entered.

Dinner was presently announced; but his lordship, instead of choosing to sit with his back to the fire, took the single chair opposite, which gave him a commanding view of the young ladies. He did not, however, take any advantage of his position during the repast, neither did he talk much, his maxim being to let his meat stop his mouth. The preponderance of his observations, perhaps, were addressed to Amelia, though a watchful observer might have seen that the spectacles were oftener turned upon Emily. Up to the withdrawal of the cloth, however, there was no perceptible advantage on either side.

As his lordship settled to the sweets, at which he was a great hand at dessert, Amelia essayed to try her influence with the popular subject of a ball. 'I wish the members of your hunt would give us a ball, my lord,' observed she.

'Ah, hay, hum—ball,' replied he, ladling up the syrup of some preserved peaches that he had been eating; 'ball, ball, ball. No place to give it—no place to give it,' repeated he.

'Oh, give it in the town-hall, or the long room at the Angel,' replied she.

'Town-hall—long room at the Angel—Angel at the long room of the town-hall—oh, certainly, certainly, certainly,' muttered he, scraping away at the contents of his plate.

'Then, that's a bargain, mind,' observed Amelia significantly.

'Bargain, bargain, bargain—certainly,' replied he; 'and I'll lead off with you, or you'll lead off with me—whichever way it is—meanwhile, I'll trouble you for a piece of that gingerbread.'

Having supplied him with a most liberal slice, she resumed the subject of the ball.

'Then we'll fix it so,' observed she.

'Oh, fix it so, certainly—certainly fix it so,' replied his lordship, filling his mouth full of gingerbread.

'Suppose we have it on the day of the races?' continued Amelia.

'Couldn't be better,' replied his lordship; 'couldn't be better,' repeated he, eyeing her intently through his formidable specs.

His lordship was quite in the assenting humour, and would have agreed to anything—anything short of lending one a five-pound note.

Amelia was charmed with her success. Despite the spot on her nose, she felt she was winning.

His lordship sat like a target, shot at by all, but making the most of his time, both in the way of eating and staring between questions.

At length the ladies withdrew, and his lordship having waddled to the door to assist their egress, now availed himself of Jawleyford's invitation to occupy an arm-chair during the enjoyment of his 'Wintle.'

Whether it was the excellence of the beverage, or that his lordship was unaccustomed to wine-drinking, or that Jawleyford's conversation was unusually agreeable, we know not, but the summons to tea and coffee was disregarded, and when at length they did make their appearance, his lordship was what the ladies call rather elevated, and talked thicker than there was any occasion for. He was very voluble at first—told all how Sponge had knocked him about, how he detested him, and wouldn't allow him to come to the hunt ball, &c.; but he gradually died out, and at last fell asleep beside Mrs. Jawleyford on the sofa, with his little legs crossed, and a half-emptied coffee-cup in his hand, which Mr. Jawleyford and she kept anxiously watching, expecting the contents to be over the fine satin furniture every moment.

In this pleasant position they remained till he awoke himself with a hearty snore, and turned the coffee over on to the carpet. Fortunately there was little damage done, and, it being nearly twelve o'clock, his lordship waddled off to bed.

Amelia, when she came to think matters over in the retirement of her own room, was well satisfied with the progress she had made. She thought she only wanted the opportunity to capture him. Though she was most anxious for a good night in order that she might appear to advantage in the morning, sleep forsook her eyelids, and she lay awake long thinking what she would do when she was my lady—how she would warm Woodmansterne, and what a dashing equipage she would keep. At length she dropped off, just as she thought she was getting into her well-appointed chariot, showing a becoming portion of her elegantly turned ankles.

In the morning, she attired herself in her new light blue satin robe, corsage Albanaise, with a sort of three-quarter sleeves, and muslin under-ones—something, we believe, out of the last book of fashion. She also had her hair uncommonly well arranged, and sported a pair of clean primrose-coloured gloves. 'Now for victory,' said she, as she took a parting glance at herself in general, and the hot spot in particular.

Judge of her disgust on meeting her mamma on the staircase at learning that his lordship had got up at six o'clock, and had gone to meet his hounds on the other side of the county. That Baggs had boiled his oatmeal porridge in his bedroom, and his lordship had eaten it as he was dressing.

It may be asked, what was the maid about not to tell her.

The fact is, that ladies'-maids are only numb hands in all that relates to hunting, and though Juliana knew that his lordship was up, she thought he had gone to have his hunt before breakfast, just as the young gentlemen in the last place she lived in used to go and have a bathe.

Baggs, we may add, was a married man, and Juliana and he had not had much conversation.

XXXVI

MR. BRAGG'S
KENNEL MANAGEMENT

THE READER WILL NOW HAVE the kindness to consider that Mr.
Puffington has undergone his swell huntsman, Dick Bragg, for
three whole years, during which time it was difficult to say whether his
winter's service or his summer's impudence was most oppressive. Either
way, Mr. Puffington had had enough both of him and the honours of
hound-keeping. Mr. Bragg was not a judicious tyrant. He lorded it too
much over Mr. Puffington; was too fond of showing himself off, and
exposing his master's ignorance before the servants, and field. A stranger
would have thought that Mr. Bragg, and not 'Mr. Puff,' as Bragg called
him, kept the hounds. Mr. Puffington took it pretty quietly at first, Bragg
inundating him with what they did at the Duke of Downeybird's, Lord
Reynard's, and the other great places in which he had lived, till he almost
made Puff believe that such treatment was a necessary consequence
of hound-keeping. Moreover, the cost was heavy, and the promised
subscriptions were almost wholly imaginary; even if they had been paid,
they would not have covered a quarter of the expense Mr. Bragg ran
him to; and worst of all, there was an increasing, instead of a diminishing,
expenditure. Trust a servant for keeping things up to the mark.

All things, however, have an end, and Mr. Bragg began to get to the
end of Mr. Puff's patience. As Puff got older he got fonder of his five-
pound notes, and began to scrutinize bills and ask questions; to be, as Mr.
Bragg said, 'very little of the gentleman'; Bragg, however, being quite one
of your 'make-hay-while-the-sun-shines' sort, and knowing too well the

style of man to calculate on a lengthened duration of office, just put on the steam of extravagance, and seemed inclined to try how much he could spend for his master. His bills for draft hounds were enormous; he was continually chopping and changing his horses, often almost without consulting his master; he had a perfect museum of saddles and bridles, in which every invention and variety of bit was exhibited; and he had paid as much as twenty pounds to different 'valets' and grooms for invaluable recipes for cleaning leather breeches and gloves. Altogether, Bragg overdid the thing; and when Mr. Puffington, in the solitude of a winter's day, took pen, ink, and paper, and drew out a 'balance sheet,' he found that on the average of six brace of foxes to the season, they had cost him about three hundred pounds a head killing. It was true that Bragg always returned five or six and twenty brace; but that was as between Bragg and the public, as between Bragg and his master the smaller figure was the amount.

Mr. Puffington had had enough of it, and he now thought if he could get Mr. Sponge (who he still believed to be a sporting author on his travels) to immortalize him, he might retire into privacy, and talk of 'when *I* kept hounds,' 'when *I* hunted the country,' 'when *I* was master of hounds *I* did this, and *I* did that,' and fuss, and be important as we often see ex-masters of hounds when they go out with other packs. It was this erroneous impression with regard to Mr. Sponge that took our friend to the meet of Lord Scamperdale's hounds at Scrambleford Green, when he gave Mr. Sponge a general invitation to visit him before he left the country, an invitation that was as acceptable to Mr. Sponge on his expulsion from Jawleyford Court, as it was agreeable to Mr. Puffington—by opening a route by which he might escape from the penalty of hound-keeping, and the persecution of his huntsman.

The reader will therefore now have the kindness to consider Mr. Puffington in receipt of Mr. Sponge's note, volunteering a visit.

With gay and cheerful steps our friend hurried off to the kennel, to communicate the intelligence to Mr. Bragg of an intended honour that he inwardly hoped would have the effect of extinguishing that great sporting luminary.

Arriving at the kennel, he learned from the old feeder, Jack Horsehide, who, as usual, was sluicing the flags with water, though the weather was wet, that Mr. Bragg was in the house (a house that had been the

steward's in the days of the former owner of Hanby House). Thither
Mr. Puffington proceeded; and the front door being open he entered,
and made for the little parlour on the right. Opening the door without
knocking, what should he find but the swell huntsman, Mr. Bragg, full
fig, in his cap, best scarlet and leathers, astride a saddle-stand, sitting for
his portrait!

'*O, dim it!*' exclaimed Bragg, clasping the front of the stand as if it was
a horse, and throwing himself off, an operation that had the effect of
bringing the new saddle on which he was seated bang on the floor. 'O,
sc-e-e-use me, sir,' seeing it was his master, 'I thought it was my servant;
this, sir,' continued he, blushing and looking as foolish as men do when
caught getting their hair curled or sitting for their portraits, 'this, sir, is
my friend, Mr. Ruddle, the painter, sir—yes, sir—very talented young
man, sir—asked me to sit for my portrait, sir—is going to publish a series
of portraits of all the best huntsmen in England, sir.'

'And masters of hounds,' interposed Mr. Ruddle, casting a sheep's eye
at Mr. Puffington.

'And masters of hounds, sir,' repeated Mr. Bragg; 'yes, sir, and masters of
hounds, sir', Mr. Bragg being still somewhat flurried at the unexpected
intrusion.

'Ah, well,' interrupted Mr. Puffington, who was still eager about his
mission, 'we'll talk about that after. At present I'm come to tell you,'
continued he, holding up Mr. Sponge's note, 'that we must brush up a
little—going to have a visit of inspection from the great Mr. Sponge.'

'Indeed, sir!' replied Mr. Bragg, with the slightest possible touch of his
cap, which he still kept on. 'Mr. Sponge, sir!—indeed, sir—Mr. Sponge,
sir?—pray who may *he* be, sir?'

'Oh—why—hay—hum—haw—he's Mr. Sponge, you know—been
hunting with Lord Scamperdale, you know—great sportsman, in fact—
great authority, you know.' 'Indeed—great authority is he—indeed—
oh—yes—thinks so p'raps—sc-e-e-use me, sir, but des-say, sir, I've forgot
more, sir, than Mr. Sponge ever knew, sir.'

'Well, but you mustn't tell him so,' observed Mr. Puffington, fearful
that Bragg might spoil sport.

'Oh, tell him—no,' sneered Bragg, with a jerk of the head; 'tell him—
no; I'm not exactly such a donkey as that; on the contrary, I'll make
things pleasant, sir—sugar his milk for him, sir, in short, sir.'

'Sugar his milk!' exclaimed Mr. Puffington, who was only a matter-of-fact man; 'sugar his milk! I dare say he takes tea.'

'Well, then, sugar his tea,' replied Bragg, with a smile, adding, 'can 'commodate myself, sir, to circumstances, sir,' at the same time taking off his cap and setting a chair for his master.

'Thank you, but I'm not going to stay,' replied Mr. Puffington; 'I only came up to let you know who you had to expect, so that you might prepare, you know—have all on the square, you know—best horses—best hounds—best appearance in general, you know.'

'That I'll attend to,' replied Mr. Bragg, with a toss of the head—'that *I'll* attend to,' repeated he, with an emphasis on the *I'll*, as much as to say, 'Don't you meddle with what doesn't concern you.'

Mr. Puffington would fain have rebuked him for his impertinence, as indeed he often would fain have rebuked him; but Mr. Bragg had so overpowered him with science, and impressed him with the necessity of keeping him—albeit Mr. Puffington was sensible that he killed very few foxes—that, having put up with him so long, he thought it would never do to risk a quarrel, which might lose him the chance of getting rid of him and hounds altogether; therefore, Mr. Puffington, instead of saying, 'You conceited humbug, get out of this,' or indulging in any observations that might lead to controversy, said, with a satisfied, confidential nod of the head:

'I'm sure you will—I'm sure you will,' and took his departure, leaving Mr. Bragg, to remount the saddle-stand and take the remainder of his sitting.

XXXVII

MR. PUFFINGTON'S
DOMESTIC ARRANGEMENTS

Perhaps it was fortunate that Mr. Bragg did take the kennel management upon himself, or there is no saying but what with that and the house department, coupled with the usual fussiness of a bachelor, the Sponge visit might have proved too much for our master. The notice of the intended visit was short; and there were invitations to send out, and answers to get, bedrooms to prepare, and culinary arrangements to make—arrangements that people in town, with all their tradespeople at their elbows, can have no idea of the difficulty of effecting in the country. Mr. Puffington was fully employed.

In addition to the parties mentioned as asked in his note to Lord Scamperdale, viz. Washball, Charley Slapp, and Lumpleg, were Parson Blossomnose; Mr. Fossick of the Flat Hat Hunt, who declined—Mr. Crane of Crane Hall; Captain Guano, late of that noble corps the Spotted Horse Marines; and others who accepted. Mr. Spraggon was a sort of volunteer, at all events an undesired guest, unless his lordship accompanied him. It so happened that the least wanted guest was the first to arrive on the all-important day.

Lord Scamperdale, knowing our friend Jack was not over affluent, had no idea of spoiling him by too much luxury, and as the railway would serve a certain distance in the line of Hanby House, he despatched Jack to the Over-shoes-over-boots station with the dog-cart, and told him he would be sure to find a 'bus, or to get some sort of conveyance at the Squandercash station to take him up to Puffington's; at all events, his lordship added to himself, 'If he doesn't, it'll do him no harm to walk, and he can easily get a boy to carry his bag.'

The latter was the case; for though the station-master assured Jack, on his arrival at Squandercash, that there was a 'bus, or a mail gig, or a something to every other train, there was nothing in connexion with the one that brought him, nor would he undertake to leave his carpet-bag at Hanby House before breakfast-time the next morning.

Jack was highly enraged, and proceeded to squint his eyes inside out, and abuse all railways, and chairmen, and directors, and secretaries, and clerks, and porters, vowing that railways were the greatest nuisances under the sun—that they were a perfect impediment instead of a facility to travelling—and declared that formerly a gentleman had nothing to do but order his four horses, and have them turned out at every stage as he came up, instead of being stopped in the *ridicklous* manner he then was; and he strutted and stamped about the station as if he would put a stop to the whole line. His vehemence and big talk operated favourably on the Cockney station-master, who, thinking he must be a duke, or some great man, began to consider how to get him forwarded. It being only a thinly populated district—though there was a station equal to any mercantile emergency, indeed to the requirements of the whole county—he ran the resources of the immediate neighbourhood through his mind, and at length was obliged to admit—humbly and respectfully—that he really was afraid Martha Muggins's donkey was the only available article.

Jack fumed and bounced at the very mention of such a thing, vowing that it was a downright insult to propose it; and he was so bumptious that the station-master, who had nothing to gain by the transaction, sought the privacy of the electric telegraph office, and left him to vent the balance of his wrath upon the porters.

Of course, they could do nothing more than the king of their little colony had suggested; and finding there was no help for it, Mr. Spraggon at last submitted to the humiliation, and set off to follow young Muggins with his bag on the donkey, in his best top-boots, worn under his trousers—an unpleasant operation to any one, but especially to a man like Jack, who preferred wearing his tops out against the flaps of his friends' saddles, rather than his soles by walking upon them. However, necessity said yes; and cocking his flat hat jauntily on his head, he stuck a cheroot in his mouth, and went smoking and swaggering on, looking—

or rather squinting—bumptiously at everybody he met, as much as to say, 'Don't suppose I'm walking from necessity! I've plenty of tin.'

The third cheroot brought Jack and his suite within sight of Hanby House.

Mr. Puffington had about got through all the fuss of his preparations, arranged the billets of the guests and of those scarcely less important personages—their servants, allotted the stables, and rehearsed the wines, when a chance glance through the gaily furnished drawing-room window discovered Jack trudging up the trimly kept avenue.

'Here's that nasty Spraggon,' exclaimed he, eyeing Jack dragging his legs along, adding, 'I'll be bound to say he'll never think of wiping his filthy feet if I don't go to meet him.'

So saying, Puffington rushed to the entrance, and crowning himself with a white wide-awake, advanced cheerily to do so.

Jack, who was more used to 'cold shoulder' than cordial reception, squinted and stared with surprise at the unwonted warmth, so different to their last interview, when Jack was fresh out of his clay-hole in the Brick Fields; but not being easily put out of his way, he just took Puff as Puff took him. They talked of Scamperdale, and they talked of Frostyface, and the number of foxes he had killed, the price of corn, and the difference its price made in the keep of hounds and horses. Altogether they were very 'thick.'

'And how's our friend Sponge?' asked Puffington, as the conversation at length began to flag.

'Oh, he's nicely,' replied Jack, adding, 'hasn't he come yet?'

'Not that I've seen,' answered Puffington, adding, 'I thought, perhaps, you might come together.'

'No,' grunted Jack; 'he comes from Jawleyford's, you know; I'm from Woodmansterne.'

'We'll go and see if he's come,' observed Puffington, opening a door in the garden wall, into which he had manoeuvred Jack, communicating with the courtyard of the stable.

'Here are his horses,' observed Puffington, as Mr. Leather rode through the great gates on the opposite side, with the renowned hunters in full marching order.

'Monstrous fine animals they are,' said Jack, squinting intently at them.

'They are that,' replied Puffington.

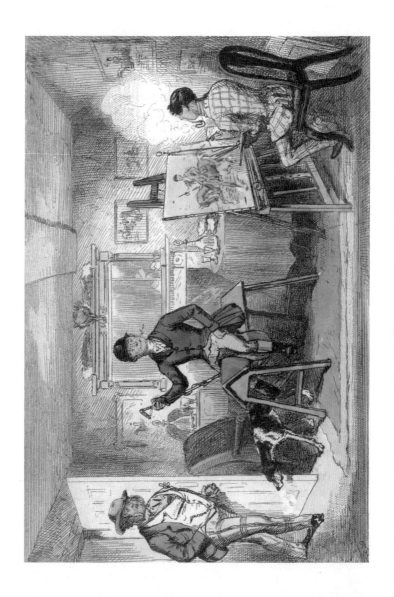

'Mr. Sponge seems a very pleasant, gentlemanly man,' observed Mr. Puffington.

'Oh, he is,' replied Jack.

'Can you tell me—can you inform me—that's to say, can you give me any idea,' hesitated Puffington, 'what is the usual practice—the usual course—the usual understanding as to the treatment of those sort of gentlemen?'

'Oh, the best of everything's good enough for them,' replied Jack, adding, 'just as it is with me.'

'Ah, I don't mean in the way of eating and drinking, but in the way of encouragement—in the way of a present, you know?' adding—'What did my lord do?' seeing Jack was slow at comprehension.

'Oh, my lord bad-worded him well,' replied Jack, adding, 'he didn't get much encouragement from him.'

'Ah, that's the worst of my lord,' observed Puffington; 'he's rather coarse—rather too indifferent to public opinion. In a case of this sort, you know, that doesn't happen every day, or, perhaps, more than once in a man's life, it's just as well to be favourably spoken of as not, you know'; adding, as he looked intently at Jack—'Do you understand me?'

Jack, who was tolerably quick at a chance, now began to see how things were, and to fathom Mr. Puffington's mistake. His ready imagination immediately saw there might be something made of it, so he prepared to keep up the delusion.

'Wh-o-o-y!' said he, straddling out his legs, clasping his hands together, and squinting steadily through his spectacles, to try and see, by Puffington's countenance, how much he would stand. 'W-h-o-o-y!' repeated he, 'I shouldn't think—though, mind, it's mere conjectur' on my part—that you couldn't offer him less than—twenty or five-and-twenty punds; or, say, from that to thirty,' continued Jack, seeing that Puff's countenance remained complacent under the rise.

'And that you think would be sufficient?' asked Puff, adding—'If one does the thing at all, you know, it's as well to do it handsomely.'

'True,' replied Jack, sticking out his great thick lips, 'true. I'm a great advocate for doing things handsomely. Many a row I have with my lord for thanking fellows, and saying he'll *remember* them instead of giving them sixpence or a shilling; but really I should say, if you were to give him forty or fifty pund—say a fifty—pund note, he'd be—'

The rest of the sentence was lost by the appearance of Mr. Sponge, cantering up the avenue on the conspicuous piebald. Mr. Puffington and Mr. Spraggon greeted him as he alighted at the door.

Sponge was quickly followed by Tom Washball; then came Charley Slapp and Lumpleg, and Captain Guano came in a gig. Mutual bows and bobs and shakes of the hand being exchanged, amid offers of 'anything before dinner' from the host, the guests were at length shown to their respective apartments, from which in due time they emerged, looking like so many bridegrooms.

First came the worthy master of the hounds himself, in his scarlet dress-coat, lined with white satin; Tom Washball, and Charley Slapp also sported Puff's uniform; while Captain Guano, who was proud of his leg, sported the uniform of the Muffington Hunt—a pea-green coat lined with yellow, and a yellow collar, white shorts with gold garters, and black silk stockings.

Spraggon had been obliged to put up with Lord Scamperdale's second-best coat, his lordship having taken the best one himself; but it was passable enough by candle-light, and the seediness of the blue cloth was relieved by a velvet collar and a new set of the Flat Hat Hunt buttons. Mr. Sponge wore a plain scarlet with a crimson velvet collar, and a bright fox on the frosted ground of a gilt button, with tights as before; and when Mr. Crane arrived he was found to be attired in a dress composed partly of Mr. Puffington's and partly of the Muggeridge Hunt uniform—the red coat of the former surmounting the white shorts and black stockings of the other. Altogether, however, they were uncommonly smart, and it is to be hoped that they appreciated each other.

The dinner was sumptuous. Puff, of course, was in the chair; and Captain Guano, coming last into the room, and being very fond of office, was vice. When men run to the 'noble science' of gastronomy, they generally outstrip the ladies in the art of dinner-giving, for they admit of no makeweight, or merely ornamental dishes, but concentrate the cook's energies on sterling and approved dishes. Everything men set on is meant to be eaten. Above all, men are not too fine to have the plate-warmer in the room, the deficiency of hot plates proving fatal to many a fine feast. It was evident that Puff prided himself on his table. His linen was the finest and whitest, his glass the most elegant and transparent, his plate the brightest, and his wines the most costly and *recherché*. Like many people, however, who are not much in the habit of dinner-giving, he was anxious and fussy, too intent upon making people comfortable to allow of their being so, and too anxious to get victuals and drink down their throats to allow of their enjoying either.

He not only produced a tremendous assortment of wines—Hock, Sauterne, Champagne, Barsack, Burgundy, but descended into endless varieties of sherries and Madeiras. These he pressed upon people, always insisting that the last sample was the best.

In these hospitable exertions Puffington was ably assisted by Captain Guano, who, being fond of wine, came in for a good quantity; first of all by asking everyone to take wine with him, and then in return every one asking him to do the same with them. The present absurd non-asking system was not then in vogue. The great captain, noisy and talkative at all times, began to be boisterous almost before the cloth was drawn.

Puffington was equally promiscuous with his after-dinner wines. He had all sorts of clarets, and 'curious old ports.' The party did not seem to have any objection to spoil their digestions for the next day, and took whatever he produced with great alacrity. Lengthened were the candle examinations, solemn the sips, and sounding the smacks that preceded the delivery of their Campbell-like judgements.

The conversation, which at first was altogether upon wine, gradually diverged upon sporting, and they presently brewed up a very considerable cry. Foremost among the noisy ones was Captain Guano. He seemed inclined to take the shine out of everybody.

'Oh! if they could but find a good fox that would give them a run of ten miles—say, ten miles—just ten miles would satisfy him—say, from Barnesley Wold to Chingforde Wood, or from Carleburg Clump to Wetherden Head. He was going to ride his famous horse Jack-a-Dandy—the finest horse that ever was foaled! No day too long for him—no pace too great for him—no fence too stiff for him—no brook too broad for him.'

Tom Washball, too, talked as if wearing a red coat was not the only purpose for which he hunted; and altogether they seemed to be an amazing, sporting, hard-riding set.

When at length they rose to go to bed, it struck each man as he followed his neighbour upstairs that the one before him walked very crookedly.

XXXVIII

A Day with
Puffington's Hounds

DAY DAWNED CHEERFULLY. IF THERE was rather more sun than the strict rules of Beckford prescribe, still sunshine is not a thing to quarrel with under any circumstances—certainly not for a gentleman to quarrel with who wants his place seen to advantage on the occasion of a meet of hounds. Everything at Hanby House was in apple-pie order. All the stray leaves that the capricious wintry winds still kept raising from unknown quarters, and whisking about the trim lawns, were hunted and caught, while a heavy roller passed over the Kensington gravel, pressing out the hoof and wheelmarks of the previous day. The servants were up betimes, preparing the house for those that were in it, and a *déjeuner à la fourchette* for chance customers, from without.

They were equally busy at the stable. Although Mr. Bragg did profess such indifference for Mr. Sponge's opinion, he nevertheless thought it might perhaps be as well to be condescending to the stranger. Accordingly, he ordered his whips to be on the alert, to tie their ties and put on their boots as they ought to be, and to hoist their caps becomingly on the appearance of our friend. Bragg, like a good many huntsmen, had a sort of tariff of politeness, that he indicated by the manner in which he saluted the field. To a lord, he made a sweep of his cap like the dome of St. Paul's; a baronet came in for about half as much; a knight, to a quarter. Bragg had also a sort of City or monetary tariff of politeness—a tariff that was oftener called in requisition than the 'Debrett' one, in Mr. Puffington's country. To a good 'tip' he vouchsafed as much cap as he gave to a lord; to a middling 'tip' he gave a sort of move that might either pass for a touch of the cap or a more comfortable adjustment of it to his head; a very small 'tip' had a forefinger to the peak; while he who gave nothing at all got a good stare or a good morning! or something of that sort. A man watching the arrival of the field could see who gave the fives, who the fours, who the threes, who the twos, who the ones, and who were the great o's.

But, to our day with Mr. Puffington's hounds.

Our overnight friends were not quite so brisk in the morning as the servants and parties outside. Puffington's 'mixture' told upon a good many of them. Washball had a headache, so had Lumpleg; Crane was seedy; and Captain Guano, sea-green. Soda-water was in great request.

There was a splendid breakfast, table and sideboard looking as if Fortnum and Mason or Morel had opened a branch establishment at Hanby House. Though the staying guests could not do much for the good things set out, they were not wasted, for the place was fairly taken by storm shortly before the advertised hour of meeting; and what at one time looked like a most extravagant supply, at another seemed likely to prove a deficiency. Each man helped himself to whatever he fancied, without waiting for the ceremony of an invitation, in the usual style of fox-hunting hospitality.

A few minutes before eleven, a 'gently, Rantaway,' accompanied by a slight crack of a whip, drew the seedy and satisfied parties to the oriel window, to see Mr. Bragg pass along with his hounds. They were gliding noiselessly over the green sward, Mr. Bragg rising in his stirrups, as spruce as a game-cock, with his thoroughbred bay gambolling and pawing with delight at the frolic of the hounds, some clustering around him, others shooting forward a little, as if to show how obediently they would return at his whistle. Mr. Bragg was known as the whistling huntsman, and was a great man for telegraphing and signalizing with his arms, boasting that he could make hounds so handy that they could do everything, except pay the turnpike-gates. At his appearance the men all began to shuffle to the passage and entrance-hall, to look for their hats and whips; and presently there was a great outpouring of red coats upon the lawn, all straddling and waddling, of course. Then Mr. Bragg, seeing an audience, with a slight whistle and wave of his right arm, wheeled his forces round, and trotted gaily towards where our guests had grouped themselves, within the light iron railing that separated the smooth slope from the field. As he reined in his horse, he gave his cap an aerial sweep, taking off perpendicularly, and finishing at his horse's ears—an example that was immediately followed by the whips, and also by Mr. Bragg's second horseman, Tom Stot.

'Good morning, Mister Bragg! Good morning, Mister Bragg!—Good morning, Mister Bragg!' burst from the assembled spectators: for Mr. Bragg was one of those people that one occasionally meets whom everybody 'Misters.' Mister Bragg, rising in his stirrups with a gracious smile, passed a very polite bow along the line.

'Here's a fine morning, Mr. Bragg,' observed Tom Washball, who thought it knowing to talk to servants.

'Y*as*, sir,' replied Bragg, 'y*as*,' with a slight inclination to cap; '*r-a-y*-ther more s*a*n, p'raps, than desirable,' continued he, raising his face towards the heavens; 'but still by no means a bad day, sir—no, sir—by no means a bad day, sir.'

'Hounds looking well,' observed Charley Slapp, between the whiffs of a cigar.

'Y*as*, sir,' said Bragg, 'y*as*,' looking around them with a self-satisfied smile; adding, 'so they ought, sir—so they ought; if *I* can't bring a pack out as they should be, don't know who can.'

'Why, here's our old Rummager, I declare!' exclaimed Spraggon, who, having vaulted the iron hurdles, was now among the pack. 'Why, here's our old Rummager, I declare!' repeated he, laying his whip on the head of a solemn-looking black and white hound, somewhat down in the toes, and looking as if he was about done.

'Sc-e-e-use me, sir,' replied Bragg, leaning over his horse's shoulder, and whispering into Jack's ear; 'sc-e-e-use me, sir, but *drop* that, sir, if you please, sir.'

'Drop what?' asked Jack, squinting through his great tortoiseshell-rimmed spectacles up into Bragg's face.

''Bout knowing of that 'ound, sir,' whispered Bragg; 'the fact is, sir—we call him Merryman, sir; master don't know I got him from you, sir.'

'O-o-o,' replied Jack, squinting, if possible, more frightfully than before.

'Ah, that's the hound I offered to Scamperdale,' observed Puffington, seeing the movement, and coming up to where Jack stood; 'that's the hound I offered to Scamperdale,' repeated he, taking the old dog's head between his hands. 'There's no better hound in the world than this,' continued he, patting and smoothing him; 'and no better *bred* hound either,' added he, rubbing the dog's sides with his whip.

'How is he bred?' asked Jack, who knew the hound's pedigree better than he did his own.

'Why, I got him from Reynard—no, I mean from Downeybird—the Duke, you know; but he was bred by Fitzwilliam—by his Singwell out of Darling. Singwell was by the Rutland Rallywood out of Tavistock Rhapsody; but to make a long story short, he's lineally descended from the Beaufort Justice.'

'Indeed!' exclaimed Jack hardly able to contain himself; 'that's undeniable blood.'

'Well, I'm glad to hear you say so,' replied Puffington. 'I'm glad to hear you say so, for you understand these things—no man better; and I confess I've a warm side to that Beaufort Justice blood.'

'Don't wonder at it,' replied Jack, laughing his waistcoat strings off.

'The great Mr. Warde,' continued Mr. Puffington, 'who was justly partial to his own sort, had never any objection to breeding from the Beaufort Justice.'

'No, nor nobody else that knew what he was about,' replied Jack, turning away to conceal his laughter.

'We should be moving, I think, sir,' observed Bragg, anxious to put an end to the conversation; 'we should be moving, I think, sir,' repeated he, with a rap of his forefinger against his cap peak. 'It's past eleven,' added he, looking at his gold watch, and shutting it against his cheek.

'What do you draw first?' asked Jack.

'Draw—draw—draw,' replied Puffington. 'Oh, we'll draw Rabbitborough Gorse—that's a new cover I've inclosed on my pro-o-r-perty.'

'Sc-e-e-use me, sir,' replied Bragg, with a smile, and another rap of the cap: 'sc-e-e-use me, sir, but I'm going to Hollyburn Hanger first.'

'Ah, well, Hollyburn Hanger,' replied Puffington, complacently; 'either will do very well.'

If Puff had proposed Hollyburn Hanger, Bragg would have said Rabbitborough Gorse.

The move of the hounds caused a rush of gentlemen to their horses, and there was the usual scramblings up, and fidgetings, and funkings, and who-o-hayings and drawing of girths, and taking up of curbs, and lengthening and shortening of stirrups.

Captain Guano couldn't get his stirrups to his liking anyhow. ''Ord hang these leathers,' roared he, clutching up a stirrup-iron; 'who the devil would ever have sent one out a-huntin' with a pair of new stirrup-leathers?'

'Hang you and the stirrup leathers,' growled the groom, as his master rode away; 'you're always wantin' sumfin to find fault with. I'm blowed if it arn't a disgrace to an oss to carry such a man,' added he, eyeing the chestnut fidgeting and wincing as the captain worked away at the stirrups.

Mr. Bragg trotted briskly on with the hounds, preceded by Joe Banks, the first whip, and having Jack Swipes, the second, and Tom Stot, riding together behind him, to keep off the crowd.

Thus the cavalcade swept down the avenue, crossed the Swillingford turnpike, and took through a well-kept field road, which speedily brought them to the cover—rough, broomy, brushwood-covered banks, of about three acres in extent, lying on either side of the little Hollyburn Brook, one of the tiny streams that in angry times helped to swell the Swill into a river.

'Dim all these foot people!' exclaimed Mr. Bragg, in well-feigned disgust, as he came in view, and found all the Swillingford snobs, all the tinkers and tailors, and cobblers and poachers, and sheep-stealers, all the scowling, rotten-fustianed, baggy-pocketed scamps of the country ranged round the cover, some with dogs, some with guns, some with snares, and all with sticks or staffs. 'Well, I'm dimmed if ever I seed sich a—' The rest of the speech being lost amidst the exclamations of: 'Ah! the hunds! the hunds! hoop! tally-o the hunds!' and a general rush of the ruffians to meet them.

Captain Guano, who had now come up, joined in the denunciation, inwardly congratulating himself on the probability that the first cover, at least, would be drawn blank. Tom Washball, who was riding a very troublesome tail-foremost grey, also censured the proceeding.

And Mr. Puffington, still an 'am*aa*izin' instance of a pop'lar man,' exclaimed, as he rode among them, 'Ah! my good fellows, I'd rather you'd come up and had some ale than disturbed the cover'; a hint that

the wily ones immediately took, rushing up to the house, and availing
themselves of the absence of the butler, who had followed the hounds,
to take a couple of dozen of his best fiddle-handled forks while the
footman was drawing them the ale.

The whips being duly signalled by Bragg to their points—Brick to the
north corner, Swipes to the south—and the field being at length drawn
up to his liking, Mr. Bragg looked at Mr. Puffington for his signal (the
only piece of interference he allowed him); at a nod Mr. Bragg gave a
wave of his cap, and the pack dashed into cover with a cry.

'Yo-o-icks—wind him! Yo-o-icks—pash him up!' cheered Bragg,
standing erect in his stirrups, eyeing the hounds spreading and sniffing
about, now this way, now that—now pushing through a thicket, now
threading and smelling along a meuse. 'Yo-o-icks—wind him! Yo-o-
icks—pash him up!' repeated he, cracking his whip, and moving slowly
on. He then varied the entertainment by whistling, in a sharp, shrill key,
something like the chirp of a sparrow-hawk.

Thus the hounds rummaged and scrimmaged for some minutes.

'No fox here,' observed Captain Guano, bringing his horse alongside
of Mr. Bragg's.

'Not so sure o' *that*,' replied Mr. Bragg, with a sneer, for he had a
great contempt for the captain. 'Not so sure o' that,' replied he, eyeing
Thunderer and Galloper feathering up the brook.

'Hang these stirrups!' exclaimed the captain, again attempting to adjust
them; adding, 'I declare I have no seat whatever in this saddle.'

'Nor in any other,' muttered Bragg. 'Yo-icks, Galloper! Yo-icks,
Thunderer! Ge-e-ntly, Warrior!' continued he, cracking his whip, as
Warrior pounced at a bunny.

The hounds were evidently on a scent, hardly strong enough to
own, but sufficiently indicated by their feathering, and the rush of their
comrades to the spot.

'A fox for a thousand!' exclaimed Mr. Bragg, eyeing them, and looking
at his watch.

'Oh, d—mn me! I've got one stirrup longer than another now!' roared
Captain Guano, trying the fresh adjustment. 'I've got one stirrup longer
than another!' added he, in a terrible pucker.

A low snatch of a whimper now proceeded from Galloper, and Bragg
cheered him to the echo. In another second a great banging brown

fox burst from among the broom, and dashed down the little dean. What noises, what exclamations rent the air! 'Talli-ho! talliho! talliho!' screamed a host of voices, in every variety of intonation, from the half-frantic yell of a party seeing him, down to the shout of a mere partaker of the epidemic. Shouting is very contagious. The horsemen gathered up their reins, pressed down their hats, and threw away their cigar-ends.

''Ord hang it!' roared Captain Guano, still fumbling at the leathers, 'I shall never be able to ride with stirrups in this state.'

'Hang your stirrups!' exclaimed Charley Slapp, shooting past him; adding, 'It was your *saddle* last time.'

Bragg's queer tootle of his horn, for he was full of strange blows, now sounded at the low end of the cover; and, having a pet line of gaps and other conveniences that he knew how to turn to on the minute, he soon shot so far ahead as to give him the appearance (to the slow 'uns) of having flown. Brick and Swipes quickly had all the hounds after him, and Stot, dropping his elbows, made for the road, to ride the second horse gently on the line. The field, as usual, divided into two parts, the soft riders and the hard ones—the soft riders going by the fields, the hard riders by the road. Messrs. Spraggon, Sponge, Slapp, Quilter, Rasper, Crasher, Smasher, and some half-dozen more, bustled after Bragg; while the worthy master, Mr. Puffington, Lumpleg, Washball, Crane, Guano, Shirker, and very many others, came pounding along the lane. There was a good scent, and the hounds shot across the Fleecyhaughwater Meadows, over the hill, to the village of Berrington Roothings, where, the fox having been chased by a cur, the hounds were brought to a check on some very bad scenting-ground, on the common, a little to the left of the village, at the end of a quarter of an hour or so. The road having been handy, the hard riders were there almost as soon as the soft ones; and there being no impediments on the common, they all pushed boldly on among the now stooping hounds.

'Hold hard, gentlemen!' exclaimed Mr. Bragg, rising in his stirrups and telegraphing with his right arm. 'Hold hard!—pray do!' added he, with little better success. 'Dim it, gen'lemen, hold hard!' added he, as they still pressed upon the pack. 'Have a little regard for a huntsman's raputation,' continued he. 'Remember that it rises and falls with the sport he shows'— exhortations that seemed to be pretty well lost upon the field, who began comparing notes as to their respective achievements, enlarging the leaps and magnifying the distance into double what they had been. Puffington and some of the fat ones sat gasping and mopping their brows.

Seeing there was not much chance of the hounds hitting off the scent by themselves, Mr. Bragg began telegraphing with his arm to the whippers-in, much in the manner of the captain of a Thames steamer to the lad at the engine, and forthwith they drove the pack on for our swell huntsman to make his cast. As good luck would have it, Bragg crossed the line of the fox before he had got half-through his circle, and away the hounds dashed, at a pace and with a cry that looked very like killing. Mr. Bragg was in ecstasies, and rode in a manner very contrary to his wont. All again was life, energy, and action; and even some who hoped there was an end of the thing, and that they might go home and say, as usual, 'that they had had a very good run, but not killed,' were induced to proceed.

Away they all went as before.

At the end of eighteen minutes more, the hounds ran into their fox in the little green valley below Mountnessing Wood, and Mr. Bragg had him stretched on the green with the pack baying about him, and the horses of the field-riders getting led about by the country people, while the riders stood glorying in the splendour of the thing. All had a direct interest in making it out as good as possible, and Mr. Bragg was quite ready to appropriate as much praise as ever they liked to give.

"Ord dim him,' said he, turning up the fox's grim head with his foot, 'but Mr. Bragg's an awkward customer for gen'lemen of your description.'

'You hunted him well!' exclaimed Charley Slapp, who was trumpeter general of the establishment.

'Oh, sir,' replied Bragg, with a smirk and a condescending bow, 'if Richard Bragg can't kill foxes, I don't know who can.'

Just then 'Puffington and Co.' hove in sight up the valley, their faces beaming with delight as the *tableau* before them told the tale. They hastened to the spot.

'How many brace is that?' asked Puffington, with the most matter-of-course air, as he trotted up, and reined in his horse outside the circle.

'Seventeen brace, your grace, I mean to say my lord, that's to say *sur*,' replied Bragg, with a strong emphasis on the *sur*, as if to say, 'I'm not used to you snobs of commoners.'

'Seventeen brace!' sneered Jack Spraggon to Sponge, adding, in a whisper, 'More like *seven* foxes.'

'And how many run to ground?' asked Puffington, alighting.

'Four brace,' replied Bragg, stooping to cut off the brush.

We were wrong in saying that Bragg only allowed Puff the privilege of nodding his head to say when he might throw off. He let him lead the 'lie gallop' in the kill department.

Mr. Puffington then presented Mr. Sponge with the brush, and the usual solemnities being observed, the sherry flasks were produced and drained, the biscuits munched, and, amidst the smoke of cigars, the ring broke up in great goodwill.

XXXIX

WRITING A RUN

THE FIRST FUMES OF EXCITEMENT over, after a run with a kill, the field begins to take things more coolly and veraciously, and ere long some of them begin to pick holes in the affair. The men of the hunt run it up, while those of the next hunt run it down. Added to this there are generally some cavilling, captious fellows in every field who extol a run to the master's face, and abuse it behind his back. So it was on the present occasion. The men of the hunt—Charley Slapp, Lumpleg, Guano, Crane, Washball, and others—lauded and magnified it into something magnificent; while Fossick, Fyle, Wake, Blossomnose, and others of the 'Flat Hat Hunt,' pronounced it a niceish thing—a pretty burst; and Mr. Vosper, who had hunted for five-and-twenty seasons without ever subscribing one farthing to hounds, always declaring that each season was 'his last,' or that he was going to confine himself entirely to some other pack, said it was nothing to make a row about, that he had seen fifty better things with the Tinglebury harriers, and never a word said.

'Well,' said Sponge to Spraggon, between the whiffs of a cigar, as they rode together; 'it wasn't so bad, was it?'

'Bad!—no,' squinted Jack, 'devilish good—for Puff, at least,' adding, 'I question he's had a better this season.'

'Well, we are in luck,' observed Tom Washball, riding up and joining them;' we are in luck to have a satisfactory thing with you great connoisseurs out.'

'A pretty thing enough,' replied Jack, 'pretty thing enough.'

'Oh, I don't mean to say it's equal to many we've had this season,' replied Washball; 'nothing like the Boughton Hill day, nor yet the

Hembury Forest one; but still, considering the meet and the state of the country—'

'Hout! the country's good enough,' growled Jack, who hated Washball; adding, 'a good fox makes any country good'; with which observation he sidled up to Sponge, leaving Washball in the middle of the road.

'That reminds me,' said Jack, *sotto voce* to Sponge, 'that the crittur wants his run puffed, and he thinks you can do it.'

'Me!' exclaimed Sponge, 'what's put that in his head?'

'Why, you see,' exclaimed Jack, 'the first time you came out with our hounds at Dundleton Tower, you'll remember—or rather, the first time we saw you, when your horse ran away with you—somebody, Fyle, I think it was, said you were a literary cove; and Puff, catchin' at the idea, has never been able to get rid of it since: and the fact is, he'd like to be flattered—he'd be uncommonly pleased if you were to "soft sawder" him handsomely.'

'*Me!*' exclaimed Sponge; 'bless your heart, man, I can't write anything—nothing fit to print, at least.'

'Hout, fiddle!' retorted Spraggon, 'you can write as well as any other man; see what lots of fellows write, and nobody ever finds fault.'

'But the spellin' bothers one,' replied Sponge, with a shake of his elbow and body, as if the idea was quite out of the question.

'Hang the spellin',' muttered Jack, 'one can always borrow a dictionary; or let the man of the paper—the editor, as they call him—smooth out the spellin'. You say at the end of your letter, that your hands are cold, or your hand aches with holdin' a pullin' horse, and you'll thank him to correct any inadvertencies—you needn't call them errors, you know.'

'But where's the use of it?' exclaimed Sponge; 'it'll do us no good, you know, praisin' Puff's pack, or himself, or anything about him.'

'That's just the point,' said Jack, 'that's just the point. I can make it answer both our purposes,' said he, with a nudge of the elbow, and an inside-out squint of his eyes.

'Oh, that's another matter,' replied our friend; 'if we can turn the thing to account, well and good—I'm your man for a shy.'

'We *can* turn it to account,' rejoined Jack; 'we *can* turn it to account—at least *I* can; but then you must do it. He wouldn't take it as any compliment from me. It's the stranger that sees all things in their true lights. D'ye understand?' asked he, eagerly.

'I twig,' replied Sponge.

'You write the account,' continued Jack, 'and I'll manage the rest.'

'You must help me,' observed Sponge.

'Certainly,' replied Jack; 'we'll do it together, and go halves in the plunder.'

'Humph,' mused Sponge: 'halves,' said he to himself. 'And what will you give me for my half?' asked he.

'Give you!' exclaimed Jack, brightening up. 'Give you! Let me see,' continued he, pretending to consider—'Puff's rich—Puff's a liberal fellow—Puff's a conceited beggar—mix it strong,' said Jack, 'and I'll give you ten pounds.'

'Make it twelve,' replied Sponge, after a pause.

If Jack had said twelve. Sponge would have asked fourteen.

'Couldn't,' said Jack, with a shake of the head; 'it really isn't with (worth) the money.'

The two then rode on in silence for some little distance.

'I'll tell you what I'll do,' said Jack, spurring his horse, and trotting up the space that the other had now shot ahead. 'I'll split the difference with you!'

'Well, give me the sov.,' said Sponge, holding out his hand for earnest.

'Why, I haven't a sov. upon me,' replied Jack; 'but, honour bright, I'll do what I say.'

'Give me eleven golden sovereigns for my chance,' repeated Sponge slowly, in order that there might be no mistake.

'Eleven golden sovereigns for your chance,' repeated Jack.

'Done!' replied Sponge.

'Done!' repeated Jack.

'Let's jog on and do it at once while the thing's fresh in our minds,' said Jack, working his horse into a trot.

Sponge did the same; and the grass-siding of Orlantire Parkwall favouring their design, they increased the trot to a canter. They soon passed the park's bounds, and entering upon one of those rarities—an unenclosed common, angled its limits so as to escape the side-bar, and turning up Farningham Green lane, came out upon the Kingsworth and Swillingford turnpike within sight of Hanby House.

'We'd better pull up and walk the horses gently in, p'raps,' observed

Sponge, reining his in.

'Ah! I was only wantin' to get home before the rest,' observed Jack, pulling up, too.

They then proceeded more leisurely together.

'We'd better get into one of our bedrooms to do it,' observed Jack, as they passed the lodge. 'Just so,' replied Sponge, adding, 'I dare say we shall want all the quiet we can get.'

'Oh, no!' said Jack; 'the thing's simple enough—met at such a place—found at such another—killed at so and so.'

'Well, I hope it will,' said Sponge, riding into the stable-yard, and resigning his steed to the care of his groom.

Jack did the same by Sponge's other horse, which he had been riding, and in reply to Leather's inquiry (who stood with his right hand ready, as if to shake hands with him), 'how the horse had carried him?' replied:

'Cursed ill,' and stamped away without giving him anything.

'Ah, *you're* a gen'leman, you are,' muttered Leather, as he led the horse away. 'Now, come!' exclaimed Jack to Sponge, 'come! let's get in before any of those bothersome fellows come'; adding, as he dived into a passage, 'I'll show you the back way.'

After passing a scullery, a root-house, and a spacious entrance-hall, upon a table in which stood the perpetual beer-jug and bread-basket, a green baize door let them into the regions of upper service, and passing the dashed carpets of the housekeeper's room and butler's pantry, a red baize door let them into the far side of the front entrance. Having deposited their hats and whips, they bounded up the richly carpeted staircase to their rooms.

Hanby House, as we have already said, was splendidly furnished. All the grandeur did not run to the entertaining rooms; but each particular apartment, from the state bedroom down to the smallest bachelor snuggery, was replete with elegance and comfort.

Like many houses, however, the bedrooms possessed every imaginable luxury except boot-jacks and pens that would write. In Sponge's room for instance, there were hip-baths, and foot-baths, a shower-bath, and hot and cold baths adjoining, and mirrors innumerable; an eight-day mantel-clock, by Moline of Geneva, that struck the hours, half-hours, and quarters: cut-glass toilet candlesticks, with silver sconces; an elegant zebra-wood cabinet; also a beautiful davenport of zebra-wood, with a plate glass

back, containing a pen rug worked on silver ground, an ebony match
box, a blue crystal, containing a sponge pen-wiper, a beautiful envelope-
case, a white-cornelian seal, with 'Hanby House' upon it, wax of all
colours, papers of all textures, envelopes without end—every imaginable
requirement of correspondence except a pen that would write. There *were*
pens, indeed—there almost always are—but they were miserable apologies
of things; some were mere crow-quills—sort of cover-hacks of pens,
while others were great, clumsy, heavy-heeled, cart-horse sort of things,
clotted up to the hocks with ink, or split all the way through—vexatious
apologies, that throw a person over just at the critical moment, when he
has got his sheet prepared and his ideas all ready to pour upon paper; then
splut—splut—splutter goes the pen, and away goes the train of thought.
Bold is the man who undertakes to write his letters in his bedroom with
country-house pens. But, to our friends. Jack and Sponge slept next door
to each other; Sponge, as we have already said, occupying the state-room,
with its canopy-topped bedstead, carved and panelled sides, and elegant
chintz curtains lined with pink, and massive silk-and-bullion tassels;
while Jack occupied the dressing-room, which was the state bedroom in
miniature, only a good deal more comfortable. The rooms communicated
with double doors, and our friends very soon effected a passage.

'Have you any 'baccy?' asked Jack, waddling in in his slippers, after
having sucked off his tops without the aid of a boot-jack.

'There's some in my jacket pocket,' replied Sponge, nodding to where
it hung in the wardrobe; 'but it won't do to smoke here, will it?' asked
he.

'Why not?' inquired Jack.

'Such a fine room,' replied Sponge, looking around.

'Oh, fine be hanged!' replied Jack, adding, as he made for the jacket,
'no place too fine for smokin' in.'

Having helped himself to one of the best cigars, and lighted it, Jack
composed himself cross-legged in an easy, spring, stuffed chair, while
Sponge fussed about among the writing implements, watering and
stirring up the clotted ink, and denouncing each pen in succession, as
he gave it the initiatory trial in writing the word 'Sponge.'

'Curse the pens!' exclaimed he, throwing the last bright crisp yellow
thing from him in disgust. 'There's not one among 'em that can go!—all
reg'larly stumped up.'

'Haven't you a penknife?' asked Jack, taking the cigar out of his mouth.

'Not I,' replied Sponge.

'Take a razor, then,' said Jack, who was good at an expedient.

'I'll take one of yours,' said Sponge, going into the dressing-room for one. 'Hang it, but you're rather too sharp,' exclaimed Jack, with a shake of his head.

'It's more than your razor 'll be when I'm done with it,' replied Sponge.

Having, at length, with the aid of Jack's razor, succeeded in getting a pen that would write, Mr. Sponge selected a sheet of best cream-laid satin paper, and, taking a cane-bottomed chair, placed himself at the table in an attitude for writing. Dipping the fine yellow pen in the ink, he looked in Jack's face for an idea. Jack, who had now got well advanced in the cigar, sat squinting through his spectacles at our scribe, though apparently looking at the top of the bed.

'Well?' said Sponge, with a look of inquiry.

'Well,' replied Jack, in a tone of indifference.

'How shall I begin?' asked Sponge, twirling the pen between his fingers, and spluttering the ink over the paper.

'Begin!' replied Jack, 'begin, oh, begin, just as you usually begin.'

'As a letter?' asked Sponge.

'I 'spose so,' replied Jack; 'how would you think?'

'Oh, I don't know,' replied Sponge. 'Will *you* try your hand?' added he, holding out the pen.

'Why, I'm busy just now, you see,' said he, pointing to his cigar, 'and that horse of yours' (Jack had ridden the redoubtable chestnut, Multum-in-Parvo, who had gone very well in the company of Hercules) 'pulled so confoundedly that I've almost lost the use of my fingers,' continued he, working away as if he had got the cramp in both hands; 'but I'll prompt you,' added he, 'I'll prompt you.'

'Why don't you begin then?' asked Sponge.

'Begin!' exclaimed Jack, taking the cigar from his lips; 'begin!' repeated he, 'oh, I'll begin directly—didn't know you were ready.'

Jack then threw himself back in his chair, and sticking out his little bandy legs, turned the whites of his eyes up to the ceiling, as if lost in meditation.

'Begin,' said he, after a pause, 'begin, "This splendid pack had a stunning run."'

'But we must put *what* pack first,' observed Sponge, writing the words 'Mr. Puffington's hounds' at the top of the paper. 'Well,' said he, writing on, 'this stunning pack had a splendid run.'

'No, not stunning *pack*,' growled Jack, '*splendid* pack—"this splendid pack had a stunning run."'

'Stop!' exclaimed Sponge, writing it down; 'well,' said he looking up, 'I've got it.'

'This stunning pack had a splendid run,' repeated Jack, squinting away at the ceiling.

'I thought you said *splendid* pack,' observed Sponge.

'So I did,' replied Jack.

'You said stunning just now,' rejoined he.

'Ah, that was a slip of the tongue,' said Jack. 'This splendid pack had a stunning run,' repeated Jack, appealing again to his cigar for inspiration; 'well, then,' said he, after a pause, 'you just go on as usual, you know,' continued he, with a flourish of his great red hand.

'As usual!' exclaimed Sponge, 'you don't s'pose one's pen goes of itself.'

'Why, no,' replied Jack, knocking the ashes off his cigar on to the arabesque-patterned tapestry carpet—'why, no, not exactly; but these things, you know, are a good deal matter of course; just describe what you saw, you know, and butter Puff well, that's the main point.'

'But you forget,' replied Sponge, 'I don't know the country, I don't know the people, I don't know anything at all about the run—I never once looked at the hounds.'

'That's nothin',' replied Jack, 'there'd be plenty like you in that respect. However,' continued he, gathering himself up in his chair as if for an effort, 'you can say—let me see what you can say—you can say, "this splendid pack had a stunning run from Hollyburn Hanger, the property of its truly popular master, Mr. Puffington," or—stop,' said Jack, checking himself, 'say, "the property of its truly popular and sporting master, Mr. Puffington." The cover's just as much mine as it's his,' observed Jack; 'it belongs to old Sir Timothy Tensthemain, who's vegetating at Boulogne-sur-Mer, but Puff says he'll buy it when it comes to the hammer, so we'll flatter him by considering it his already, just as we flatter him by calling him a sportsman—*sportsman!*' added Jack, with a sneer, 'he's just as much taste for the thing as a cow.'

'Well,' said Sponge, looking up, 'I've got "truly popular and sporting master, Mr. Puffington,"' adding, 'hadn't we better say something about the meet and the grand spread here before we begin with the run?'

'True,' replied Jack, after a long-drawn whiff and another adjustment of the end of his cigar; 'say that "a splendid field of well-appointed sportsmen"—'

'A splendid field of well-appointed sportsmen,' wrote Sponge.

'"Among whom we recognized several distinguished strangers and members of Lord Scamperdale's hunt." That means you and I,' observed Jack.

'"Of Lord Scamperdale's hunt—that means you and I"'—read Sponge, as he wrote it.

'But you're not to put in that; you're not to write "that means you and I," my man,' observed Jack.

'Oh, I thought that was part of the sentence,' replied Sponge.

'No, no,' said Jack; 'I meant to say that you and I were the distinguished strangers and members of Lord Scamperdale's hunt; but that's between ourselves, you know.'

'Good,' said Sponge; 'then I'll strike that out,' running his pen through the words 'that means you and I.' 'Now get on,' said he, appealing to Jack, adding, 'we've a deal to do yet.'

'Say,' said Jack, '"after partaking of the well-known profuse and splendid hospitality of Hanby House, they proceeded at once to Hollyburn Hanger, where a fine seasoned fox—though some said he was a bag one—"'

'Did they?' exclaimed Sponge, adding, 'well, I thought he went away rather queerly.'

'Oh, it was only old Bung, the brewer, who runs down every run he doesn't ride.'

'Well, never mind,' replied Sponge, 'we'll make the best of it, whatever it was'; writing away as he spoke, and repeating the words 'bag one' as he penned them.

'"Broke away,"' continued Jack:

'"In view of the whole field,"' added Sponge. 'Just so,' assented Jack.

'"Every hound scoring to cry, and making the"—the—the—what d'ye call the thing?' asked Jack.

'Country,' suggested Sponge.

'No,' replied Jack, with a shake of the head.

'Hill and dale?' tried Sponge again.

'Welkin!' exclaimed Jack, hitting it off himself—'"makin' the welkin ring with their melody!" makin' the welkin ring with their melody,' repeated he, with exultation.

'Capital!' observed Sponge, as he wrote it.

'Equal to Littlelegs,'[1] said Jack, squinting his eyes inside out.

'We'll make a grand thing of it,' observed Sponge.

'So we will,' replied Jack, adding, 'if we had but a book of po'try we'd weave in some lines here. You haven't a book o' no sort with you that we could prig a little po'try from?' asked he.

'No,' replied Sponge thoughtfully. 'I'm afraid not; indeed, I'm sure not. I've got nothin' but *Mogg's Cab Fares*.'

'Ah, that won't do,' observed Jack, with a shake of the head. 'But stay,' said he, 'there are some books over yonder,' pointing to the top of an Indian cabinet, and squinting in a totally different direction. 'Let's see what they are,' added he, rising, and stumping away to where they stood. *I Promessi Sposi*, read he off the back of one. 'What can that mean! Ah, it's Latin,' said he, opening the volume. *Contes à ma Fille*, read he off the back of another. 'That sounds like racin',' observed he, opening the volume, 'it's Latin too,' said he, returning it. 'However, never mind, we'll "sugar Puff's milk," as Mr. Bragg would say, without po'try.' So saying, Mr. Spraggon stumped back to his easy-chair. 'Well, now,' said he, seating himself comfortably in it, 'let's see where did we go first? "He broke at the lower end of the cover, and, crossing the brook, made straight for Fleecyhaugh Water Meadows, over which," you may say, "there's always a ravishing scent."' 'Have you got that?' asked Jack, after what he thought a sufficient lapse of time for writing it.

'"Ravishing scent,"' repeated Sponge as he wrote the words.

'Very good,' said Jack, smoking and considering. '"From there,"' continued he, '"he made a bit of a bend, as if inclining for the plantations at Winstead, but, changing his mind, he faced the rising ground, and crossing over nearly the highest part of Shillington Hill, made direct for the little village of Berrington Roothings below."'

'Stop!' exclaimed Sponge, 'I haven't got half that; I've only got to "the plantations at Winstead."' Sponge made play with his pen, and presently held it up in token of being done.

'Well,' pondered Jack, 'there was a check there. Say,' continued he, addressing himself to Sponge, '"Here the hounds came to a check."'

'Here the hounds came to a check,' wrote Sponge. 'Shall we say anything about distance?' asked he.

'P'raps we may as well,' replied Jack. 'We shall have to stretch it though a bit.'

'Let's see,' continued he; 'from the cover to Berrington Roothings over by Shillington Hill and Fleecyhaugh Water Meadows will be—say, two miles and a half or three miles at the most—call it four, well, four miles—say four miles in twelve minutes, twenty miles an hour,—too quick—four miles in fifteen minutes, sixteen miles an hour; no—I think p'raps it'll be safer to lump the distance at the end, and put in a place or two that nobody knows the name of, for the convenience of those who were not out.'

'But those who *were* out will blab, won't they?' asked Sponge.

'Only to each other,' replied Jack. 'They'll all stand up for the truth of it as against strangers. You need never be afraid of over-eggin' the puddin' for those that were out.'

'Well, then,' observed Sponge, looking at his paper to report progress, 'we've got the hounds to a check. "Here the hounds came to a check,"' read he. 'Ah! now, then,' said Jack, in a tone of disgust, 'we must say summut handsome of Bragg; and of all conceited animals under the sun, he certainly is the most conceited. I never saw such a man! How that unfortunate, infatuated master of his keeps him, I can't for the life of me imagine. *Master*! faith, Bragg's the *master*,' continued Jack, who now began to foam at the mouth. 'He laughs at old Puff to his face; yet it's wonderful the influence Bragg has over him. I really believe he has talked Puff into believing that there's not such another huntsman under the sun, and really he's as great a muff as ever walked. He can just dress the character, and that's all.' So saying Jack wiped his mouth on the sleeve of his red coat preparatory to displaying Mr. Bragg upon paper.

'Well, now we are at fault,' said Jack, motioning Sponge to resume; 'we are at fault; now say, "but Mr. Bragg, who had ridden gallantly on his favourite bay, as fine an animal as ever went, though somewhat past mark of mouth—" He *is* a good horse, at least *was*,' observed Jack, adding, 'I sold Puff him, he was one of old Sugarlip's,' meaning Lord Scamperdale's.

'Sure to be a good 'un, then,' replied Sponge, with a wink, adding, 'I wonder if he'd like to buy any more?'

'We'll talk about that after,' replied Jack, 'at present let us get on with our run.'

'Well,' said Sponge, 'I've got it: "Mr. Bragg, who had ridden gallantly on his favourite bay, as fine an animal as ever went, though somewhat past mark of mouth—"'

'"Was well up with his hounds,"' continued Jack, '"and with a gently, Rantipole! and a single wave of his arm, proceeded to make one of those scientific casts for which this eminent huntsman is so justly celebrated." Justly *celebrated*!' repeated Jack, spitting on the carpet with a hawk of disgust; 'the conceited self-sufficient bantam-cock never made a cast worth a copper, or rode a yard but when he thought somebody was looking at him.'

'I've got it,' said Sponge, who had plied his pen to good purpose.

'Justly celebrated,' repeated Jack, with a snort. 'Well, then, say, "Hitting off the scent like a workman"—big H, you know, for a fresh sentence—"they went away again at score, and passing by Moorlinch farm buildings, and threading the strip of plantation by Bexley Burn, he crossed Silverbury Green, leaving Longford Hutch to the right, and passing straight on by the gibbet at Harpen." Those are all bits of places, observed Jack, 'that none but the country folks know, indeed, I shouldn't have known them but for shootin' over them when old Bloss lived at the Green. Well, now, have you got all that?' asked he.

'"Gibbet at Harpen,"' read Sponge, as he wrote it.

'"Here, then, the gallant pack, breaking from scent to view,"' continued Jack, speaking slowly, '"ran into their fox in the open close upon Mountnessing Wood, evidently his point from the first, and into which a few more strides would have carried him. It was as fine a run as ever was seen, and the hunting of the hounds was the admiration of all who saw it. The distance couldn't have been less than"—than—what shall we say?' asked Jack.

'Ten, twelve miles, as the crow flies,' suggested Sponge.

'No,' said Jack,' that would be too much. Say ten'; adding, 'that will be four miles more than it was.'

'Never mind,' said Sponge, as he wrote it; 'folks like good measure with runs as well as ribbons.'

'Now we must butter old Puff,' observed Spraggon.

'What can we say for him?' asked Sponge; 'that he never went off the road?'

'No, by Jove!' said Jack; 'you'll spoil all if you do that: better leave it alone altogether than do that. Say, "the justly popular owner of this most celebrated pack, though riding good fourteen stone" (he rides far more,' observed Jack; 'at least sixteen; but it'll please him to make out that he *can* ride fourteen), "led the welters, on his famous chestnut horse, Tappey Lappey."'

'What shall we say about the rest?' asked Sponge; 'Lumpleg, Slapp, Guano, and all those?'

'Oh, say nothin',' replied Jack; 'we've nothin' to do with nobody but Puff, and we couldn't mention them without bringin' in our Flat Hat men too—Blossomnose, Fyle, Fossick, and so on. Besides, it would spoil all to say that Guano was up—people would say directly it couldn't have been much of a run if Guano was there. You might finish off,' observed Jack, after a pause, 'by saying that "after this truly brilliant affair, Mr. Puffington, like a thorough sportsman, and one who never trashes his hounds unnecessarily—unlike some masters," you may say, "who never know when to leave off" (that will be a hit at Old Scamp,' observed Jack, with a frightful squint), '"returned to Hanby House, where a distinguished party of sportsmen—" or, say, "a distinguished party of noblemen and gentlemen"—that'll please the ass more—"a large party of noblemen and gentlemen were partaking of his"—his—what shall we call it?'

'Grub!' said Sponge.

'No, no—summut genteel—his—his—his—"splendid hospitality!"' concluded Jack, waving his arm triumphantly over his head.

'Hard work, authorship!' exclaimed Sponge, as he finished writing, and threw down the pen.

'Oh, I don't know,' replied Jack, adding, 'I could go on for an hour.'

'Ah, *you*!—that's all very well,' replied Sponge, 'for you, squatting comfortably in your arm-chair: but consider me, toiling with my pen, bothered with the writing, and craning at the spelling.'

'Never mind, we've done it,' replied Jack, adding, 'Puff'll be as pleased as Punch. We've polished him off uncommon. That's just the sort of account to tickle the beggar. He'll go riding about the country, showing it to everybody, and wondering who wrote it.'

'And what shall we send it to?—the *Sporting Magazine*, or what?' asked Sponge.

'*Sporting Magazine*!—no,' replied Jack; 'wouldn't be out till next year—quick's the word in these railway times. Send it to a newspaper—*Bell's Life*, or one of the Swillingford papers. Either of them would be glad to put it in.'

'I hope they'll be able to read it,' observed Sponge, looking at the blotched and scrawled manuscript.

'Trust them for that,' replied Jack, adding, 'If there's any word that bothers them, they've nothing to do but look in the dictionary—these folks all have dictionaries, wonderful fellows for spellin'.'

Just then a little buttony page, in green and gold, came in to ask if there were any letters for the post; and our friends hastily made up their packet, directing it to the editor of the Swillingford 'GUIDE TO GLORY AND FREEMAN'S FRIEND'; words that in the hurried style of Mr. Sponge's penmanship looked very like 'GUIDE TO GROG, AND FREEMAN'S FRIEND.'

XL

A LITERARY BLOOMER

T IME WAS WHEN THE INDEPENDENT borough of Swillingford supported two newspapers, or rather two editors, the editor of the *Swillingford Patriot*, and the editor of the *Swillingford Guide to Glory*; but those were stirring days, when politics ran high and votes and corn commanded good prices. The papers were never very prosperous concerns, as may be supposed when we say that the circulation of the former at its best time was barely seven hundred, while that of the latter never exceeded a thousand.

They were both started at the reform times, when the reduction of the stamp-duty brought so many aspiring candidates for literary fame into the field, and for a time they were conducted with all the bitter hostility that a contracted neighbourhood, and a constant crossing by the editors of each other's path, could engender. The competition, too, for advertisements, was keen, and the editors were continually taunting each other with taking them for the duty alone. Æneas M'Quirter was the editor of the *Patriot*, and Felix Grimes that of the *Guide to Glory*.

M'Quirter, we need hardly say, was a Scotsman—a big, broad-shouldered Sawney—formidable in 'slacks,' as he called his trousers, and terrific in kilts; while Grimes was a native of Swillingford, an ex-schoolmaster and parish clerk, and now an auctioneer, a hatter, a dyer and bleacher, a paper-hanger, to which the wits said when he set up his paper, he added the trade of 'stainer.'

At first the rival editors carried on a 'war to the knife' sort of contest with one another, each denouncing his adversary in terms of the most unmeasured severity. In this they were warmly supported by a select

knot of admirers, to whom they read their weekly effusions at their
respective 'houses of call' the evening before publication. Gradually, the
fire of bitterness began to pale, and the excitement of friends to die out;
M'Quirter presently put forth a signal of distress. To accommodate 'a large
and influential number of its subscribers and patrons,' he determined to
publish on a Tuesday instead of on a Saturday as heretofore, whereupon
Mr. Grimes, who had never been able to fill a single sheet properly, now
doubled his paper, lowered his charge for advertisements, and hinted at
his intention of publishing an occasional supplement.

However exciting it may be for a time, parties soon tire of carrying
on a losing game for the mere sake of abusing each other, and Æneas
M'Quirter, not being behind the generality of his countrymen in
'canniness' and shrewdness of intellect, came to the conclusion that
it was no use doing so in this case, especially as the few remaining
friends who still applauded would be very sorry to subscribe anything
towards his losses. He therefore very quietly negotiated the sale of his
paper to the rival editor, and having concluded a satisfactory bargain,
he placed the bulk of his property in the poke of his plaid, and walked
out of Swillingford just as if bent on taking the air, leaving Mr. Grimes
in undisputed possession of both papers, who forthwith commenced
leading both Whig and Tory mind, the one on the Tuesday, the other
on the Saturday.

The pot and pipe companions of course saw how things were, but
the majority of the readers living in the country just continued to pin
their faith to the printed declarations of their oracles, while Grimes
kept up the delusion of sincerity by every now and then fulminating a
tremendous denunciation against his trimming, vacillating, inconsistent
opponent on the Tuesday, and then retaliating with equal vigour upon
himself on the Saturday. He wrote his own 'leaders,' both Whig and Tory,
the arguments of one side pointing out answers for the other. Sometimes,
he led the way for a triumphant refutal, while the general tone of the
articles was quite of the 'upset a ministry' style. Indeed, Grimes strutted
and swaggered as if the fate of the nation rested with him.

The papers themselves were not very flourishing-looking concerns,
the wide-spread paragraphs, the staring type, the catching advertisements,
forming a curious contrast to the close packing of *The Times*. The 'Gutta
Percha Company,' 'Locock's Female Pills,' 'Keating's Cough Lozenges,'

and the 'Triumphs of Medicine,' all with staring woodcuts and royal arms, occupied conspicuous places in every paper. A new advertisement was a novelty. However, the two papers answered a great deal better than either did singly, and any lack of matter was easily supplied from the magazines and new books. In this department, indeed, in the department of elegant light literature generally, Mr. Grimes was ably assisted by his eldest daughter, Lucy, a young lady of a certain age—say liberal thirty—an ardent Bloomer—with a considerable taste for sentimental poetry, with which she generally filled the poet's corner. This assistance enabled Grimes to look after his auctioneering, bleaching, and paper-hanging concerns, and it so happened that when the foregoing run arrived at the office he, having seen the next paper ready for press, had gone to Mr. Vosper's, some ten miles off, to paper his drawing-room, consequently the duties of deciding upon its publication devolved on the Bloomer. Now, she was a most refined, puritanical young woman, full of sentiment and elegance, with a strong objection to what she considered the inhumanities of the chase. At first she was for rejecting the article altogether, and had it been a run with the Tinglebury Harriers, or even, we believe, with Lord Scamperdale's hounds, she would have consigned it to the 'Balaam box,' but seeing it was with Mr. Puffington's hounds, whose house they had papered, and who advertised with them, she condescended to read it; and though her delicacy was shocked at encountering the word 'stunning' at the outset, and also at the term 'ravishing scent' farther on, she nevertheless sent the manuscript to the compositors, after making such alterations and corrections as she thought would fit it for eyes polite. The consequence was that the article appeared in the following form, though whether all the absurdities were owing to Miss Lucy's corrections, or the carelessness of the writer, or the printers, had anything to do with it, we are not able to say. The errors, some of them arising from the mere alteration or substitution of a letter, will strike a sporting more than a general reader. Thus it appeared in the middle of the third sheet of the *Swillingford Patriot*:

SPLENDID RUN WITH MR. PUFFINGTON'S HOUNDS.

This splendid pack had a superb run from Hollyburn Hanger, the property of its truly popular and sporting owner, Mr. Puffington. A splendid field of well-appointed sportsmen, among whom we recognized several distinguished strangers, and members of Lord Scamperdale's hunt, were present. After partaking of the well-known profuse and splendid hospitality of Hanby House, they proceeded at once to Hollyburn Hanger, where a fine seasonal fox, though some said he was a bay one, broke away in view of the whole pack, every hound scorning to cry, and making the welkin ring with their melody. He broke at the lower end of the cover, and crossing the brook, made straight for Fleecyhaugh Water Meadows, over which there is always an exquisite perfume; from there he made a slight bend, as if inclining for the plantations at Winstead, but changing his mind, he faced the rising ground, and crossing over nearly the highest point of Shillington Hill, made direct for the little village of Berrington Roothings below. Here the hounds came to a check, but Mr. Bragg, who had ridden gallantly on his favourite bay, as fine an animal as ever went, though somewhat past work of mouth, was well up with his hounds, and with a 'gentle rantipole!' and a single wave of his arm, proceeded to make one of those scientific rests for which this eminent huntsman is so justly celebrated. Hitting off the scent like a coachman, they went away again at score, and passing by Moorlinch Farm buildings, and threading the strip of plantation by Bexley Burn, he crossed Silverbury Green, leaving Longford Hutch to the right, and passing straight on by the gibbet at Harpen. Here, then, the gallant pack, breaking from scent to view, ran into their box in the open close upon Mountnessing Wood, evidently his point from the first, and into which a few more strides would have carried him. It was as fine a run as ever was seen, and the grunting of the hounds was the admiration of all who heard it. The distance could not have been less than ten miles as a cow goes. The justly popular owner of this most celebrated pack, though riding good fourteen stones, led the Walters on his famous chestnut horse Tappy Lappey. After this truly brilliant affair, Mr. Puffington, like a thorough sportsman, and one who never thrashes his hounds unnecessarily— unlike some masters who never know when to leave off—returned to Hanby House, where a distinguished party of noblemen and gentlemen partook of his splendid hospitality.

And the considerate Bloomer added of her own accord,

We hope we shall have to record many such runs in the imperishable columns of our paper.

XLI

A Dinner and a Deal

Another grand dinner, on a more extensive scale than its predecessor, marked the day of this glorious run.

'There's goin' to be a great blow-out,' observed Mr. Spraggon to Mr. Sponge, as, crossing his hands and resting them on the crown of his head, he threw himself back in his easy-chair, to recruit after the exertion of concocting the description of the run.

'How d'ye know?' asked Sponge.

'Saw by the dinner table as we passed,' replied Jack, adding, 'it reaches nearly to the door.'

'Indeed,' said Sponge, 'I wonder who's coming?'

'Most likely Guano again; indeed, I know he is, for I asked his groom if he was going home, and he said no; and Lumpleg, you may be sure, and possibly old Blossomnose, Slapp, and, very likely, young Pacey.'

'Are they chaps with any "go" in them?—shake their elbows, or anything of that sort?' asked Sponge, working away as if he had the dice-box in his hand.

'I hardly know,' replied Jack thoughtfully. 'I hardly know. Young Pacey, I think, might be made summut on; but his uncle, Major Screw, looks uncommon sharp after him, and he's a minor.'

'Would he *pay*?' asked Sponge, who, keeping as he said, 'no books,' was not inclined to do business on 'tick.'

'Don't know,' replied Jack, squinting at half-cock; 'don't know—would depend a good deal, I should say, upon how it was done. It's a deuced unhandsome world this. If one wins a trifle of a youngster at cards, let it be ever so openly done, it's sure to say one's cheated him, just because one happens to be a little older, as if age had anything to do with making the cards come right.'

'It's an ungenerous world,' observed Sponge, 'and it's no use being abused for nothing. What sort of a genius is Pacey? Is he inclined to go the pace?'

'Oh, quite,' replied Jack; 'his great desire is to be thought a sportsman.'

'A sportsman or a sporting man?' asked Sponge.

'W-h-o-y! I should say p'raps a sportin' man more than the sportsman,' replied Jack. 'He's a great lumberin' lad, buttons his great stomach into a Newmarket cutaway, and carries a betting-book in his breast pocket.'

'Oh, he's a better, is he!' exclaimed Sponge, brightening up.

'He's a raw poult of a chap,' replied Jack; 'just ready for anything—in a small way, at least—a chap that's always offering two to one in half-crowns. He'll have money, though, and can't be far off age. His father was a great spectacle-maker. You have heard of Pacey's spectacles?'

'Can't say as how I have,' replied Sponge, adding, 'they are more in your line than mine.'

The further consideration of the youth was interrupted by the entrance of a footman with hot water, who announced that dinner would be ready in half an hour.

'Who's there coming?' asked Jack.

'Don't know 'xactly, sir,' replied the man; 'believe much the same party as yesterday, with the addition of Mr. Pacey; Mr. Miller, of Newton; Mr. Fogo, of Bellevue; Mr. Brown, of the Hill; and some others whose names I forget.'

'Is Major Screw coming?' asked Sponge.

'I rayther think not, sir. I think I heard Mr. Plummey, the butler, say he declined.'

'So much the better,' growled Jack, throwing off his purple-lapped coat in commencement of his toilette. As the two dressed they discussed the point how Pacey might be done.

When our friends got downstairs it was evident there was a great spread. Two red-plushed footmen stood on guard in the entrance, helping the arrivers out of their wraps, while a buzz of conversation sounded through the partially opened drawing-room door, as Mr. Plummey stood, handle in hand, to announce the names of the guests. Our friends, having the *entrée*, of course passed in as at home, and mingled with the comers and stayers. Guest after guest quickly followed, almost all making the same observation, namely, that it was a fine day for the time of year, and then each sidled off, rubbing his hands, to the fire. Captain Guano monopolized about one half of it, like a Colossus of Rhodes, with a coat-lap under each arm. He seemed to think that, being a stayer, he had more right to the fire than the mere diners.

Mr. Puffington moved briskly among the motley throng, now expatiating on the splendour of the run, now hoping a friend was hungry, asking a third after his wife, and apologizing to a fourth for not having called on his sister. Still, his real thoughts were in the kitchen, and he kept counting noses and looking anxiously at the timepiece. After the door had had a longer rest than usual, Blossomnose at last cast up: 'Now we're all here surely!' thought he, counting about; 'one, two, three, four, five, six, seven, eight, nine, ten, eleven, twelve, thirteen, thirteen, fourteen, myself fifteen—fifteen, fifteen, must be another—sixteen, eight couples asked. Oh, that Pacey's wanting; always comes late, won't wait'—so saying, or rather thinking, Mr. Puffington rang the bell and ordered dinner. Pacey then cast up.

He was just the sort of swaggering youth that Jack had described; a youth who thought money would do everything in the world—make him a gentleman, in short. He came rolling into the room, grinning as if he had done something fine in being late. He had both his great red hands in his tight trouser pockets, and drew the right one out to favour his friends with it 'all hot.'

'I'm late, I guess,' said he, grinning round at the assembled guests, now dispersed in the various attitudes of expectant eaters, some standing ready for a start, some half-sitting on tables and sofa ends, others resigning themselves complacently to their chairs, abusing Mr. Pacey and all dinner delayers.

'I'm late, I guess,' repeated he, as he now got navigated up to his host and held out his hand.

'Oh, never mind,' replied Puffington, accepting as little of the proffered paw as he could; 'never mind,' repeated he, adding, as he looked at the French clock on the mantelpiece now chiming a quarter past six, 'I dare say I told you we dined at half-past five.'

'Dare say you did, old boy,' replied Pacey, kicking out his legs, and giving Puffington what he meant for a friendly poke in the stomach, but which in reality nearly knocked his wind out; 'dare say you did, old boy, but so you did last time, if you remember, and deuce a bite did I get before six; so I thought I'd be quits with you this—*he—he—he—haw—haw—haw*,' grinning and staring about as if he had done something very clever.

Pacey was one of those deplorable beings—a country swell. Tomkins and Hopkins, the haberdashers of Swillingford, never exhibited an ugly out-of-the-way neckcloth or waistcoat with the words 'patronized by the Prince,' 'very fashionable,' or 'quite the go,' upon them, but he immediately adorned himself in one. On the present occasion, he was attired in a wide-stretching, lace-tipped, black Joinville, with recumbent gills, showing the heavy amplitude of his enormous jaws, while the extreme scooping out of a collarless, flashy-buttoned, chain-daubed, black silk waistcoat, with broad blue stripes, afforded an uninterrupted view of a costly embroidered shirt, the view extending, indeed, up to a portion of his white satin 'forget-me-not' embroidered braces. His coat was a broad-sterned, brass-buttoned blue, with pockets outside, and of course he wore a pair of creaking highly varnished boots. He was apparently, about twenty; just about the age when a youth thinks it fine to associate with men, and an age at which some men are not above taking advantage of a youth. Perhaps he looked rather older than he was, for he was stiff built and strong, with an ample crop of whiskers extending from his great red docken ears round his harvest moon of a face. He was lumpy, and clumsy, and heavy all over. Having now got inducted, he began to stare round the party, and first addressed our worthy friend, Mr. Spraggon.

'Well, Sprag, how are you?' asked he.

'Well, Specs' (alluding to his father's trade), 'how are you?' replied Jack, with a growl, to the evident satisfaction of the party, who seemed to regard Pacey as the common enemy.

Fortunately, just at the moment Mr. Plummey restored harmony by announcing dinner; and after the usual backing and retiring of mock modesty, Mr. Puffington said he would 'show them the way,' when there was as great a rush to get in, to avoid the bugbear of sitting with their backs to the fire, as there had been apparent disposition not to go at all.

Notwithstanding the unfavourable aspect of affairs, Mr. Spraggon placed himself next Mr. Pacey, who sat a good way down the table, while Mr. Sponge occupied the post of honour by our host.

In accordance with the usual tactics of these sort of gentlemen, Spraggon and Sponge essayed to be two—if not exactly strangers, at all events gentlemen with very little acquaintance. Spraggon took advantage of a dead silence to call up the table to *Mister* Sponge to take wine; a compliment that Sponge acknowledged the accordance of by a very low bow into his plate, and by-and-by Mister Sponge 'Mistered' Mr. Spraggon to return the compliment.

'Do you know much of that—that—that—*chap*?' (he would have said snob if he'd thought it would be safe) asked Pacey, as Sponge returned to still life after the first wine ceremony.

'No,' replied Spraggon, 'nor do I wish.'

'Great snob,' observed Pacey.

'Shocking,' assented Spraggon.

'He's got a good horse or two, though,' observed Pacey; 'I saw them on the road coming here the other day.' Pacey, like many youngsters, professed to be a judge of horses, and thought himself rather sharp at a deal.

'They are *good* horses,' replied Jack, with an emphasis on the good, adding, 'I'd be very glad to have one of them.'

Mr. Spraggon then asked Mr. Pacey to take champagne, as the commencement of a better understanding.

The wine flowed freely, and the guests, particularly the fresh infusion, did ample justice to it. The guests of the day before, having indulged somewhat freely, were more moderate at first, though they seemed well inclined to do their best after they got their stomachs a little restored. Spraggon could drink any given quantity at any time.

The conversation got brisker and brisker: and before the cloth was drawn there was a very general clamour, in which all sorts of subjects seemed to be mixed—each man addressing himself to his immediate neighbour; one talking of taxes—another of tares—a third, of hunting and the system of kennel—a fourth, of the corn-laws—old Blossomnose, about tithes—Slapp, about timber and water-jumping—Miller, about Collison's pills; and Guano, about anything that he could get a word edged in about. Great, indeed, was the hubbub. Gradually, however, as the evening advanced Pacey and Guano out-talked the rest, and at length Pacey got the noise pretty well to himself. When anything definite could be extracted from the mass of confusion, he was expatiating on steeple-chasing, hurdle-racing, weights for age, ons and offs clever—a sort of mixture of hunting, racing, and 'Alken.'

Sponge cocked his ear, and sat on the watch, occasionally hazarding an observation, while Jack, who was next Pacey, on the left, pretended to decry Sponge's judgement, asking *sotto voce*, with a whiff through his nose, what such a Cockney as that could know about horses? What between Jack's encouragement, and the inspiring influence of the bottle, aided by his own self-sufficiency, Pacey began to look upon Sponge with anything but admiration; and at last it occurred to him that he would be a very proper subject to, what he called, 'take the shine out of.'

'That isn't a bad-like nag, that chestnut of yours, for the wheeler of a coach, Mr. Sponge,' exclaimed he, at the instigation of Spraggon, to our friend, producing, of course, a loud guffaw from the party.

'No, he isn't,' replied Sponge coolly, adding, 'very like one, I should say.'

'Devilish *good* horse,' growled Jack in Pacey's ear.

'Oh, I dare say,' whispered Pacey, pretending to be scraping up the orange syrup in his plate, adding, 'I'm only chaffing the beggar.'

'He looks solitary without the coach at his tail,' continued Pacey, looking up, and again addressing Sponge up the table.

'He does,' affirmed Sponge, amidst the laughter of the party.

Pacey didn't know how to take this; whether as a 'sell' or a compliment to his own wit. He sat for a few seconds grinning and staring like a fool; at last after gulping down a bumper of claret, he again fixed his unmeaning green eyes upon Sponge, and exclaimed:

'I'll challenge your horse, Mr. Sponge.'

A burst of applause followed the announcement; for it was evident that amusement was in store.

'You'll w-h-a-w-t?' replied Sponge, staring, and pretending ignorance.

'I'll challenge your horse,' repeated Pacey with confidence, and in a tone that stopped the lingering murmur of conversation, and fixed the attention of the company on himself.

'I don't understand you,' replied Sponge, pretending astonishment.

'Lor bless us! why, where have you lived all your life?' asked Pacey.

'Oh, partly in one place, and partly in another,' was the answer.

'I should think so,' replied Pacey, with a look of compassion, adding, in an undertone, 'a good deal with your mother, I should think.'

'If you could get that horse at a moderate figure,' whispered Jack to his neighbour, and squinting his eyes inside out as he spoke, 'he's well worth having.'

'The beggar won't sell him,' muttered Pacey, who was fonder of talking about buying horses than of buying them.

'Oh, yes, he will,' replied Jack; 'he didn't understand what you meant. Mr. Sponge,' said he, addressing himself slowly and distinctly up the table to our hero—'Mr. Sponge, my friend Mr. Pacey here challenges your chestnut.'

Sponge still stared in well-feigned astonishment.

'It's a custom we have in this country,' continued Jack, looking, as he thought, at Sponge, but, in reality, squinting most frightfully at the sideboard.

'Do you mean he wants to buy him?' asked Sponge.

'Yes,' replied Jack confidently.

'No, I don't,' whispered Pacey, giving Jack a kick under the table. Pacey had not yet drunk sufficient wine to be rash.

'Yes, yes,' replied Jack tartly, 'you do,' adding, in an undertone, 'leave it to me, man, and I'll let you in for a good thing. Yes, Mr. Sponge,' continued he, addressing himself to our hero, 'Mr. Pacey fancies the chestnut and challenges him.'

'Why doesn't he ask the price?' replied Sponge, who was always ready for a deal.

'Ah, the price must be left to a third party,' said Jack. 'The principle of the thing is this,' continued he, enlisting the aid of his fingers to illustrate his position: 'Mr. Pacey, here,' said he, applying the forefinger of his right hand to the thumb of the left, looking earnestly at Sponge, but in reality squinting up at the chandelier—'Mr. Pacey here challenges your horse Multum-in-somethin'—I forget what you said you call him—but the nag I rode to-day. Well, then,' continued Jack, 'you' (demonstrating Sponge by pressing his two forefingers together, and holding them erect) 'accept the challenge, but can challenge anything Mr. Pacey has—a horse, dog, gun—anything; and, having fixed on somethin', then a third party' (who Jack represented by cocking up his thumb), 'any one you like to name, makes the award. Well, having agreed upon that party' (Jack still cocking up the thumb to represent the arbitrator), 'he says, "Give me money." The two then put, say half a crown or five shillin's each, into his hand, to which the arbitrator adds the same sum for himself. That being done, the arbitrator says, "Hands in pockets, gen'lemen."' (Jack diving his right hand up to the hilt in his own.) 'If this be an award, Mr. Pacey's horse gives Mr. Sponge's horse so much—draw.' (Jack suiting the action to the word, and laying his fist on the table.) 'If each person's hand contains money, it is an award—it is a deal; and the arbitrator gets the half-crowns, or whatever it is, for his trouble; so that, in course, he has a direct interest in makin' such an award as will lead to a deal. *Now*, do you understand?' continued Jack, addressing himself earnestly to Sponge.

'I think I do,' replied Sponge who had been at the game pretty often.

'Well, then,' continued Jack, reverting to his original position, 'my friend, Mr. Pacey here, challenges your chestnut.'

'No, never mind,' muttered Pacey peevishly, in an undertone, with a frown on his face, giving Jack a dig in the ribs with his elbow. 'Never mind,' repeated he; '*I* don't care about it—*I* don't want the horse.'

'But *I* do,' growled Jack, adding, in an undertone also, as he stooped for his napkin, 'don't spoil sport, man; he's as good a horse as ever stepped; and if you'll challenge him, I'll stand between you and danger.'

'But he may challenge something I don't want to part with,' observed Pacey.

'Then you've nothin' to do,' replied Jack, 'but bring up your hand without any money in it.'

'Ah! I forgot,' replied Pacey, who did not like not to appear what he called 'fly.' 'Well, then, I challenge your chestnut!' exclaimed he, perking up, and shouting up the table to Sponge.

'Good!' replied our friend. 'I challenge your watch and chain, then,' looking at Pacey's chain-daubed vest.

'Name *me* arbitrator,' muttered Jack, as he again stooped for his napkin.

'Who shall handicap us? Captain Guano, Mr. Lumpleg, or who?' asked Sponge.

'Suppose we say Spraggon?—he says he rode the horse to-day,' replied Pacey.

'Quite agreeable,' said Sponge.

'Now, Jack!' 'Now, Spraggon!' 'Now, old Solomon!' 'Now, Doctor Wiseman,' resounded from different parts of the table.

Jack looked solemn; and diving both hands into his breeches' pockets, stuck out his legs extensively before him.

'Give me money,' said he pompously. They each handed him half a crown; and Jack added a third for himself. 'Mr. Pacey challenges Mr. Sponge's chestnut horse, and Mr. Sponge challenges Mr. Pacey's gold watch,' observed Jack sententiously.

'Come, old Slowman, go on!' exclaimed Guano, adding, 'have you got no further than that?'

'Hurry no man's cattle,' replied Jack tartly, adding, 'you may keep a donkey yourself some day.'

'Mr. Pacey challenges Mr. Sponge's chestnut horse,' repeated Jack. 'How old is the chestnut, Mr. Sponge?' added he, addressing himself to our friend.

'Upon my word I hardly know,' replied Sponge, 'he's past mark of mouth; but I think a hunter's age has very little to do with his worth.'

'Who-y, that depends,' rejoined Jack, blowing out his cheeks, and looking as pompous as possible—'that depends a good deal upon how he's been used in his youth.'

'He's about nine, I should say,' observed Sponge, pretending to have been calculating, though, in reality, he knew nothing whatever about the horse's age. 'Say nine, or rising ten, and never did a day's work till he was six.'

'Indeed!' said Jack, with an important bow, adding, 'being easy with them at the beginnin' puts on a deal to the end. Perfect hunter, I s'pose?'

'Why, you can judge of that yourself,' replied Sponge.

'Perfect hunter, I should say,' rejoined Jack, 'and steady at his fences—don't know that I ever rode a better fencer. Well,' continued he, having apparently pondered all that over in his mind, 'I must trouble you to let me look at your ticker,' said he, turning short round on his neighbour.

'There,' said Mr. Pacey, producing a fine flash watch from his waistcoat-pocket, and holding it to Jack.

'The chain's included in the challenge, mind,' observed Sponge.

'In course,' said Jack; 'it's what the pawnbrokers call a watch with its appurts.' (Jack had his watch at his uncle's and knew the terms exactly.)

'It's a repeater, mind,' observed Pacey, taking off the chain.

'The chain's heavy,' said Jack, running it up in his hand; 'and here's a pistol-key and a beautiful pencil-case, with the Pacey crest and motto,' observed Jack, trying to decipher the latter. 'If it had been without the words, whatever they are,' said he, giving up the attempt, 'it would have been worth more, but the gold's fine, and a new stone can easily be put in.'

He then pulled an old hunting-card out of his pocket, and proceeded to make sundry calculations and estimates in pencil on the back.

'Well, now,' said he, at length, looking up, 'I should say, such a watch as that and appurts,' holding them up, 'couldn't be bought in a shop under eight-and-twenty pund.'

'It cost five-and-thirty,' observed Mr. Pacey.

'Did it!' rejoined Jack, adding, 'then you were done.'

Jack then proceeded to do a little more arithmetic, during which process Mr. Puffington passed the wine and gave as a toast—'Success to the handicap.'

'Well,' at length said Jack, having apparently struck a balance, 'hands in pocket, gen'lemen. If this is an award, Mr. Pacey's gold watch and appurts gives Mr. Sponge's chestnut horse seventy golden sovereigns. Show money,' whispered Jack to Pacey, adding, 'I'll stand the shot.'

'Stop!' roared Guano, 'do either of you sport your hand?'

'Yes, I do,' replied Mr. Pacey coolly.

'And I,' said Mr. Sponge.

'Hold hard, then, gen'lemen!' roared Jack, getting excited, and beginning to foam. 'Hold hard, gen'lemen!' repeated he, just as he was in the habit of roaring at the troublesome customers in Lord Scamperdale's field; 'Mr. Pacey and Mr. Sponge both sport their hands.'

'I'll lay a guinea Pacey doesn't hold money,' exclaimed Guano.

'Done!' exclaimed Parson Blossomnose.

'I'll bet it does,' observed Charley Slapp.

'I'll take you,' replied Mr. Miller.

Then the hubbub of betting commenced, and raged with fury for a short time; some betting sovereigns, some half-sovereigns, other half-crowns and shillings, as to whether the hands of one or both held money.

Givers and takers being at length accommodated, perfect silence at length reigned, and all eyes turned upon the double fists of the respective champions.

Jack having adjusted his great tortoiseshell-rimmed spectacles, and put on a most consequential air, inquired, like a gambling-house keeper, if they were 'All done'—had all 'made their game?' And 'Yes! yes! yes!' resounded from all quarters.

'Then, gen'lemen,' said Jack, addressing Pacey and Sponge, who still kept their closed hands on the table, '*show*!'

At the word, their hands opened, and each held money.

'A deal! a deal! a deal!' resounded through the room, accompanied with clapping of hands, thumping of the table, and dancing of glasses. 'You owe me a guinea,' exclaimed one. 'I want half a sovereign of you,' roared another. 'Here's my half-crown,' said a third, handing one across the table to the fortunate winner. A general settlement took place, in the midst of which the 'watch and appurts' were handed to Mr. Sponge.

'We'll drink Mr. Pacey's health,' said Mr. Puffington, helping himself to a bumper, and passing the lately replenished decanters. 'He's done the thing like a sportsman, and deserves to have luck with his deal. Your good health, Mr. Pacey!' continued he, addressing himself specifically to our friend, 'and luck to your horse.'

'Your good health, Mr. Pacey—your good health, Mr. Pacey—your good health, Mr. Pacey,' then followed in the various intonations that mark the feelings of the speaker towards the toastee, as the bottles passed round the table.

The excitement seemed to have given fresh zest to the wine, and those who had been shirking, or filling on heel-taps, now began filling bumpers, while those who always filled bumpers now took back hands.

There is something about horse-dealing that seems to interest every one. Conversation took a brisk turn, and nothing but the darkness of the night prevented their having the horse out and trying him. Pacey wanted him brought into the dining-room, *à la* Briggs, but Puff wouldn't stand that. The transfer seemed to have invested the animal with supernatural charms, and those who in general cared nothing about horses wanted to have a sight of him.

Toasting having commenced, as usual, it was proceeded with. Sponge's health followed that of Mr. Pacey's, Mr. Puffington availing himself of the opportunity afforded by proposing it, of expressing the gratification it afforded himself and all true sportsmen to see so distinguished a character in the country; and he concluded by hoping that the diminution of his stud would not interfere with the length of his visit—a toast that was drunk with great applause.

Mr. Sponge replied by saying, 'That he certainly had not intended parting with his horse, though one more or less was neither here nor there, especially in these railway times, when a man had nothing to do but take a half-guinea's worth of electric wire, and have another horse in less than no time; but Mr. Pacey having taken a fancy to the horse, he had been more accommodating to him than he had to his friend, Mr. Spraggon, if he would allow him to call him so (Jack squinted and bowed assent), who,' continued Mr. Sponge, 'had in vain attempted that morning to get him to put a price upon him.'

'Very true,' whispered Jack to Pacey, with a feel of the elbow in his ribs, adding, in an undertone, 'the beggar doesn't think I've got him in spite of him, though.'

'The horse,' Mr. Sponge continued, 'was an undeniable good 'un, and he wished Mr. Pacey joy of his bargain.'

This venture having been so successful, others attempted similar means, appointing Mr. Spraggon the arbitrator. Captain Guano challenged Mr. Fogo's phaeton, while Mr. Fogo retaliated upon the captain's chestnut horse; but the captain did not hold money to the award. Blossomnose challenged Mr. Miller's pig; but the latter could not be induced to claim anything of the worthy rector's for Mr. Spraggon to exercise his appraising talents upon. After an evening of much noise and confusion, the wine-heated party at last broke up—the staying company retiring to their couches, and the outlying ones finding their ways home as best they could.

XLII

THE MORNING'S
REFLECTIONS

WHEN YOUNG PACEY AWOKE IN the morning he had a very bad headache, and his temples throbbed as if the veins would burst their bounds. The first thing that recalled the actual position of affairs to his mind was feeling under the pillow for his watch: a fruitless search that ended in recalling something of the overnight's proceedings.

Pacey liked a cheap flash, and when elated with wine might be betrayed into indiscretions that his soberer moments were proof against. Indeed, among youths of his own age he was reckoned rather a sharp hand; and it was the vanity of associating with men, and wishing to appear a match for them, that occasionally brought him into trouble. In a general way, he was a very cautious hand.

He now lay tumbling and tossing about in bed, and little by little he laid together the outline of the evening's proceedings, beginning with his challenging Mr. Sponge's chestnut, and ending with the resignation of his watch and chain. He thought he was wrong to do anything of the sort. He didn't want the horse, not he. What should he do with him? he had one more than he wanted as it was. Then, paying for him seventy sovereigns! confound it, it would be very inconvenient—*most* inconvenient—indeed, he couldn't do it, so there was an end of it. The facilities of carrying out after-dinner transactions frequently vanish with the morning's sun. So it was with Mr. Pacey. Then he began to think how to get out of it. Should he tell Mr. Sponge candidly the state of his finances, and trust to his generosity for letting him off? Was Mr. Sponge a likely man to do it? He thought he was. But, then, would he blab? He thought he would, and that would blow him among those by whom he wished to be thought knowing, a man not to be done. Altogether he was very much perplexed: seventy pounds was a vast amount of money; and then there was his watch gone, too! a hundred and more altogether. He must have been drunk to do it—*very* drunk, he should say; and then he began to think whether he had not better treat it as an after-dinner frolic, and pretend to forget all about it. That seemed feasible.

All at once it occurred to Pacey that Mr. Spraggon was the purchaser, and that he was only a middle-man. His headache forsook him for the moment, and he felt a new man. It was clearly the case, and bit by bit he recollected all about it. How Jack had told him to challenge the horse, and he would stand to the bargain; how he had whispered to him (Pacey) to name him (Jack) arbitrator; and how he had done so, and Jack had made the award. Then he began to think that the horse must be a good one, as Jack would not set too high a price on him, seeing that he was the purchaser. Then he wondered that he had put enough on to induce Sponge to sell him: that rather puzzled him. He lay a long time tossing, and proing and coning, without being able to arrive at any satisfactory solution of the matter. At last he rang his bell, and finding it was eight o'clock he got up, and proceeded to dress himself; which operation being accomplished, he sought Jack's room, to have a little confidential conversation with him on the subject, and arrange about paying Sponge for the horse, without letting out who was the purchaser.

Jack was snoring, with his great mouth wide open, and his grizzly head enveloped in a white cotton nightcap. The noise of Pacey entering awoke him.

'Well, old boy' growled he, turning over as soon as he saw who it was, 'what are you up to?'

'Oh, nothing particular,' replied Mr. Pacey, in a careless sort of tone.

'Then make yourself scarce, or I'll baptize you in a way you won't like,' growled Jack, diving under the bedclothes.

'Oh, why I just wanted to have—have half a dozen words with you about our last night's' (ha—hem—haw!) 'handicap, you know—about the horse, you know.'

'About the w-h-a-w-t?' drawled Jack, as if perfectly ignorant of what Pacey was talking about.

'About the horse, you know—about Mr. Sponge's horse, you know—that you got me to challenge for you, you know,' stammered Pacey.

'Oh, dash it, the chap's drunk,' growled Jack aloud to himself, adding to Pacey, 'you shouldn't get up so soon, man—sleep the drink off.'

Pacey stood nonplussed.

'Don't you remember, Mr. Spraggon,' at last asked he, after watching the tassel of Jack's cap peeping above the bedclothes, 'what took place last night, you know? You asked me to get you Mr. Sponge's chestnut, and you know I did, you know.'

'Hout, lad, disperse!—get out of this!' exclaimed Jack, starting his great red face above the bedclothes and squinting frightfully at Pacey.

'Well, my dear friend, but you did,' observed Pacey, soothingly.

'Nonsense!' roared Jack, again ducking under.

Pacey stood agape.

'Come!' exclaimed Jack, again starting up, 'cut your stick!—be off!—make yourself scarce!—give your rags a gallop, in short!—don't be after disturbin' a gen'leman of fortin's rest in this way.'

'But, my dear Mr. Spraggon,' resumed Pacey, in the same gentle tone, 'you surely forget what you asked me to do.'

'I do,' replied Jack firmly.

'Well, but, my dear Mr. Spraggon, if you'll have the kindness to recollect—to consider—to reflect on what passed, you'll surely remember commissioning me to challenge Mr. Sponge's horse for you?'

'Me!' exclaimed Jack, bouncing up in bed, and sitting squinting furiously. 'Me!' repeated he; 'unpossible. How could I do such a thing? Why, I handicap'd him, man, for you, man?'

'You told me, for all that,' replied Mr. Pacey, with a jerk of the head.

'Oh, by Jove!' exclaimed Jack, taking his cap by the tassel, and twisting it off his head, 'that won't do!—downright impeachment of one's integrity. Oh, by Jingo! that won't do!' motioning as if he was going to bounce out of bed; 'can't stand that—impeach one's integrity, you know, better take one's life, you know. Life without honour's nothin', you know. Cock Pheasant at Weybridge, six o'clock i' the mornin'!'

'Oh, I assure you, I didn't mean anything of that sort,' exclaimed Mr. Pacey, frightened at Jack's vehemence, and the way in which he now foamed at the mouth, and flourished his nightcap about. 'Oh, I assure you, I didn't mean anything of that sort,' repeated he, 'only I thought p'raps you mightn't recollect all that had passed, p'raps; and if we were to talk matters quietly over, by putting that and that together, we might assist each other and—'

'Oh, by Jove!' interrupted Jack, dashing his nightcap against the bedpost, 'too late for anything of that sort, sir—*down*right impeachment of one's integrity, sir—must be settled another way, sir.'

'But, I assure you, you mistake!' exclaimed Pacey.

'Rot your mistakes!' interrupted Jack; 'there's no mistake in the matter. You've *reg*larly impeached my integrity—blood of the Spraggons won't stand that. "Death before Dishonour!"' shouted he, at the top of his voice, flourishing his nightcap over his head, and then dashing it on to the middle of the floor.

'What's the matter?—what's the matter?—what's the matter?' exclaimed Mr. Sponge, rushing through the connecting door. 'What's the matter?' repeated he, placing himself between the bed in which Jack still sat upright, squinting his eyes inside out, and where Mr. Pacey stood.

'Oh, Mr. Sponge!' exclaimed Jack, clasping his raised hands in thankfulness, 'I'm so glad you're here!—I'm so thankful you're come! I've been insulted!—oh, goodness, how I've been insulted!' added he, throwing himself back in the bed, as if thoroughly overcome with his feelings.

'Well, but what's the matter?—what is it all about?' asked Sponge coolly, having a pretty good guess what it was.

'Never was so insulted in my life!' ejaculated Jack, from under the bedclothes.

'Well, but what *is* it?' repeated Sponge, appealing to Pacey, who stood as pale as ashes.

'Oh! nothing,' replied he; 'quite a mistake; Mr. Spraggon misunderstood me altogether.'

'Mistake! There's no mistake in the matter!' exclaimed Jack, appearing again on the surface like an otter; 'you gave me the lie as plain as a pikestaff.'

'Indeed!' observed Mr. Sponge, drawing in his breath and raising his eyebrows right up into the roof of his head. 'Indeed!' repeated he.

'No; nothing of the sort, I assure you,' asserted Mr. Pacey.

'Must have satisfaction!' exclaimed Jack, again diving under the bedclothes.

'Well, but let us hear how matters stand,' said Mr. Sponge coolly, as Jack's grizzly head disappeared.

'You'll be my second,' growled Jack, from under the bedclothes.

'Oh! second be hanged,' retorted Sponge. 'You've nothing to fight about; Mr. Pacey says he didn't mean anything, that you misunderstood him, and what more can a man want?'

'Just so,' replied Mr. Pacey, 'just so. I assure you I never intended the slightest imputation on Mr. Spraggon.'

'I'm sure not,' replied Mr. Sponge.

'H-u-m-p-h,' grunted Jack from under the bedclothes, like a pig in the straw. Not showing any disposition to appear on the surface again, Mr. Sponge, after standing a second or two, gave a jerk of his head to Mr. Pacey, and forthwith conducted him into his own room, shutting the door between Mr. Spraggon and him.

Mr. Sponge then inquired into the matter, kindly sympathizing with Mr. Pacey, who he was certain never meant anything disrespectful to Mr. Spraggon, who, Mr. Sponge thought, seemed rather quick at taking offence; though, doubtless, as Mr. Sponge observed, 'a man was perfectly right in being tenacious of his integrity,' a position that he illustrated by a familiar passage from Shakespeare, about stealing a purse and stealing trash, &c.

Emboldened by his kindness, Mr. Pacey then got Mr. Sponge on to talk about the horse of which he had become the unwilling possessor—the renowned chestnut, Multum-in-Parvo.

Mr. Sponge spoke like a very prudent, conscientious man; said that really it was difficult to give an opinion about a horse; that what suited one man might not suit another—that *he* considered Multum-in-Parvo a very good horse; indeed, that he wouldn't have parted with him if he hadn't more than he wanted, and the cream of the season had passed without his meeting with any of those casualties that rendered the retention of an extra horse or two desirable. Altogether, he gave Mr. Pacey to understand that he held him to his bargain. Having thanked Sponge for his great kindness, and got an order on the groom (Mr. Leather) to have the horse out, Mr. Pacey took his departure to the stable, and Sponge having summoned his neighbour Mr. Spraggon from his bed, the two proceeded to a passage window that commanded a view of the stable-yard.

Mr. Pacey presently went swaggering across it, cracking his jockey whip against his leg, followed by Mr. Leather, with a saddle on his shoulder and a bridle in his hand.

'He'd better keep his whip quiet,' observed Mr. Sponge, with a shake of his head, as he watched Pacey's movements.

'The beggar thinks he can ride anything,' observed Jack.

'He'll find his mistake out just now,' replied Sponge.

Presently the stable-door opened, and the horse stepped slowly and quietly out, looking blooming and bright after his previous day's gallop. Pacey, running his eyes over his clean muscular legs and finely shaped form, thought he hadn't done so far amiss after all. Leather stood at the horse's head, whistling and soothing him, feeling anything but the easy confidence that Mr. Pacey exhibited. Putting his whip under his arm, Pacey just walked up to the horse, and, placing the point of his foot in the stirrup, hoisted himself on by the mane, without deigning to take hold of the reins. Having soused himself into the saddle, he then began feeling the stirrups.

'How are they for length, sir?' asked Leather, with a hitch of his hand to his forehead.

'They'll do,' replied Pacey, in a tone of indifference, gathering up the reins, and applying his left heel to the horse's side, while he gave him a touch of the whip on the other. The horse gave a wince, and a hitch up behind; as much as to say, 'If you do that again I'll kick in right earnest,' and then walked quietly out of the yard.

'I took the fiery edge off him yesterday, I think,' observed Jack, as he watched the horse's leisurely movements.

'Not so sure of that,' replied Sponge, adding, as he left the passage-window, 'He'll be trying him in the park; let's go and see him from my window.'

Accordingly, our friends placed themselves at Sponge's bedroom window, and presently the clash of a gate announced that Sponge was right in his speculation. In another second the horse and rider appeared in sight—the horse going much at his ease, but Mr. Pacey preparing himself for action. He began working the bridle and kicking his sides, to get him into a canter; an exertion that produced quite a contrary effect, for the animal slackened his pace as Pacey's efforts increased. When, however, he took his whip from under his arm, the horse darted right up into the air, and plunging down again, with one convulsive effort shot Mr. Pacey several yards over his head, knocking his head clean through his hat. The brute then began to graze, as if nothing particular had happened. This easy indifference, however, did not extend to the neighbourhood; for no sooner was Mr. Pacey floored than there was such a rush of grooms, and helpers, and footmen, and gardeners—to say nothing of women, from all parts of the grounds, as must have made it very agreeable to him to know how he had been watched. One picked him up—another his hat-crown—a third his whip—a fourth his gloves—while Margaret, the housemaid, rushed to the rescue with her private bottle of *sal volatile*—and John, the under-butler, began to extricate him from the new-fashioned neckcloth he had made of his hat.

Though our friend was a good deal shaken by the fall, the injury to his body was trifling compared to that done to his mind. Being kicked off a horse was an indignity he had never calculated upon. Moreover, it was done in such a masterly manner as clearly showed it could be repeated at pleasure. In addition to which everybody laughs at a man that is kicked off. All these considerations rushed to his mind, and made him determine not to brook the mirth of the guests as well as the servants.

Accordingly, he borrowed a hat and started off home, and seeking his guardian, Major Screw, confided to him the position of affairs. The major, who was a man of the world, forthwith commenced a negotiation with Mr. Sponge, who, after a good deal of haggling, and not until the horse had shot the major over his head, too, at length, as a great favour, consented to take fifty pounds to rescind the bargain, accompanying his kindness by telling the major to advise his ward never to dabble in horseflesh after dinner; a piece of advice that we also very respectfully tender to our juvenile readers.

And Sponge shortly after sent Spraggon a five pound note as his share of the transaction.

XLIII

ANOTHER SICK HOST

WHEN MR. PUFFINGTON READ MESSRS. Sponge and Spraggon's account of the run with his hounds, in the Swillingford paper, he was perfectly horrified; words cannot describe the disgust that he felt. It came upon him quite by surprise, for he expected to be immortalized in some paper or work of general circulation, in which the Lords Loosefish, Sir Toms, and Sir Harrys of former days might recognize the spirited doings of their early friend. He wanted the superiority of his establishment, the excellence of his horses, the stoutness of his hounds, and the polish of his field, proclaimed, with perhaps a quiet cut at the Flat-Hat gentry; instead of which he had a mixed medley sort of a mess, whose humdrum monotony was only relieved by the absurdities and errors with which it was crammed. At first, Mr. Puffington could not make out what it meant, whether it was a hoax for the purpose of turning run-writing into ridicule, or it had suffered mutilation at the hands of the printer. Calling a good scent an exquisite perfume looked suspicious of a hoax, but then seasonal fox for seasoned fox, scorning to cry for scoring to cry, bay fox for bag fox, grunting for hunting, thrashing for trashing, rests for casts, and other absurdities, looked more like accident than design.

These are the sort of errors that non-sporting compositors might easily make, one term being as much like English to them as the other, though amazingly different to the eye or the ear of a sportsman. Mr. Puffington was thoroughly disgusted. He was sick of hounds and horses, and Bragg, and hay and corn, and kennels and meal, and saddles and bridles; and now, this absurdity seemed to cap the whole thing. He was ill-prepared for such a shock. The exertion of successive dinner-giving—above all, of bachelor dinner-giving—and that too in the country, where men sit, talk, talk, talking, sip, sip, sipping, and 'just another bottle-ing'; more, we believe, from want of something else to do than from any natural inclination to exceed; the exertion, we say, of such parties had completely unstrung our fat friend, and ill-prepared his nerves for such a shock. Being a great man for his little comforts, he always breakfasted in his dressing-room, which he had fitted up in the most luxurious style, and where he had his newspapers (most carefully ironed out) laid with his letters. It was late on the morning following our last chapter ere he thought he had got rid of as much of his winey headache as fitful sleep would carry off, and enveloped himself in a blue and yellow-flowered silk dressing-gown and Turkish slippers. He looked at his letters, and knowing their outsides, left them for future perusal, and sousing himself into the depths of a many-cushioned easy-chair, proceeded to spell his *Morning Post*—Tattersall's advertisements—'Grosjean's Pale-tots'—'Mr. Albert Smith'—'Coals, best Stewart Hetton or Lambton's'—'Police Intelligence,' and such other light reading as does not require any great effort to connect or comprehend.

Then came his breakfast, for which he had very little appetite, though he relished his coffee, and also an anchovy. While dawdling over these, he heard sundry wheels grinding about below the window, and the bumping and thumping of boxes, indicative of 'goings away,' for which he couldn't say he felt sorry. He couldn't even be at the trouble of getting up and going to the window to see who it was that was off, so weary and head-achy was he. He rolled and lolled in his chair, now taking a sip of coffee, now a bite of anchovy toast, now considering whether he durst venture on an egg, and again having recourse to the *Post*. At last, having exhausted all the light reading in it, and scanned through the list of hunting appointments, he took up the Swillingford paper to see that they had got his 'meets' right for the next week. How astonished he was to find the previous day's run staring him in the face, headed 'SPLENDID RUN WITH MR. PUFFINGTON'S HOUNDS,' in the imposing type here displayed. 'Well, that's quick work, however,' said he, casting his eyes up to the ceiling in astonishment, and thinking how unlike it was the Swillingford papers, which were always a week, but generally a fortnight behindhand with information. 'Splendid run with Mr. Puffington's hounds,' read he again, wondering who had done it: Bardolph, the innkeeper; Allsop, the cabinet-maker; Tuggins, the doctor, were all out; so was Weatherhog, the butcher. Which of them could it be? Grimes, the editor, wasn't there; indeed, he couldn't ride, and the country was not adapted for a gig.

He then began to read it, and the further he got the more he was disgusted. At last, when he came to the 'seasonal fox, which some thought was a bay one,' his indignation knew no bounds, and crumpling the paper up in a heap, he threw it from him in disgust. Just then in came Plummey, the butler. Plummey saw at a glance what had happened; for Mr. Bragg, and the whips, and the grooms, and the helpers, and the feeder—the whole hunting establishment—were up in arms at the burlesque, and vowing vengeance against the author of it. Mr. Spraggon, on seeing what a mess had been made of his labours, availed himself of the offer of a seat in Captain Guano's dog-cart, and was clear of the premises; while Mr. Sponge determined to profit by Spraggon's absence, and lay the blame on him.

'Oh, Plummey!' exclaimed Mr. Puffington, as his servant entered, 'I'm deuced unwell—quite knocked up, in short,' clapping his hand on his forehead, adding, 'I shall not be able to dine downstairs to-day.'

''Deed, sir,' replied Mr. Plummey, in a tone of commiseration—''deed, sir; sorry to hear that, sir.'

'Are they all gone?' asked Mr. Puffington, dropping his boiled-gooseberry-looking eyes upon the fine-flowered carpet.

'All gone, sir—all gone,' replied Mr. Plummey; 'all except Mr. Sponge.'

'Oh, he's still here!' replied Mr. Puffington, shuddering with disgust at the recollection of the newspaper run. 'Is he going to-day?' asked he.

'No, sir—I dare say not, sir,' replied Mr. Plummey. 'His man—his groom—his—whatever he calls him, expects they'll be staying some time.'

'The deuce!' exclaimed Mr. Puffington, whose hospitality, like Jawleyford's, was greater in imagination than in reality.

'Shall I take these things away?' asked Plummey, after a pause.

'Couldn't you manage to get him to go?' asked Mr. Puffington, still harping on his remaining guest.

'Don't know, sir. I could try, sir—believe he's bad to move, sir,' replied Plummey, with a grin.

'Is he really?' replied Mr. Puffington, alarmed lest Sponge should fasten himself upon him for good.

'They say so,' replied Mr. Plummey, 'but I don't speak from any personal knowledge, for I know nothing of the man.'

'Well,' said Mr. Puffington, amused at his servant's exclusiveness, 'I wish you would try to get rid of him, bow him out civilly, you know—say I'm unwell—very unwell—deuced unwell—*ordered* to keep quiet—say it as if from yourself, you know—it mustn't appear as if it came from me, you know.'

'In course not,' replied Mr. Plummey, 'in course not,' adding, 'I'll do my best, sir—I'll do my best.' So saying, he took up the breakfast things and departed.

Mr. Sponge regaling himself with a cigar in the stables and shrubberies, it was some time before Mr. Plummey had an opportunity of trying his diplomacy upon him, it being contrary to Mr. Plummey's custom to go out of doors after any one. At last he saw Sponge coming lounging along the terrace-walk, looking like a man thoroughly disengaged, and, timing himself properly, encountered him in the entrance.

'Beg pardon, sir,' said Mr. Plummey, 'but cook, sir, wishes to know, sir, if you dine here to-day, sir?'

'Of course,' replied Mr. Sponge, 'where would you have me dine?'

'Oh, I don't know, sir—only Mr. Puffington, sir, is very poorly, sir, and I thought p'raps you'd be dining out.

'Poorly is he?' replied Mr. Sponge; 'sorry to hear that—what's the matter with him?'

'Bad bilious attack, I think,' replied Plummey—'very subject to them, at this time of year particklarly; was laid up, at least confined to his room, three weeks last year of a similar attack.'

'Indeed!' replied Mr. Sponge, not relishing the information.

'Then I must say you'll dine here?' said the butler.

'Yes; I must have my dinner, of course,' replied Mr. Sponge. 'I'm not ill, you know. No occasion to make a great spread for me, you know; but still I must have some victuals, you know.'

'Certainly, sir, certainly,' replied Mr. Plummey.

'I couldn't think of leaving Mr. Puffington when he's poorly,' observed Mr. Sponge, half to himself and half to the butler.

'Oh, master—that's to say, Mr. Puffington—always does best when left alone,' observed Mr. Plummey, catching at the sentence: 'indeed the medical men recommend perfect quiet and moderate living as the best thing.'

'Do they?' replied Sponge, taking out another cigar. Mr. Plummey then withdrew, and presently went upstairs to report progress, or rather want of progress, to the gentleman whom he sometimes condescended to call 'master.'

Mr. Puffington had been taking another spell at the paper, and we need hardly say that the more he read of the run the less he liked it.

'Ah, that's Mr. Sponge's handiwork,' observed Plummey, as with a sneer of disgust Mr. Puffington threw the paper from him as Plummey entered the room.

'How do you know?' asked Mr. Puffington.

'Saw it, sir—saw it in the letter-bag going to the post.'

'Indeed!' replied Mr. Puffington.

'Mr. Spraggon and he did it after they came in from hunting.'

'I thought as much,' replied Mr. Puffington, in disgust.

Mr. Plummey then related how unsuccessful had been his attempts to get rid of the now most unwelcome guest. Mr. Puffington listened with attention, determined to get rid of him somehow or other. Plummey was instructed to ply Sponge well with hints, all of which, however, Mr. Sponge skilfully parried. So, at last, Mr. Puffington scrawled a miserable-looking note, explaining how very ill he was, how he regretted being deprived of Mr. Sponge's agreeable society, but hoping that it would suit Mr. Sponge to return as soon as he was better and pay the remainder of his visit—a pretty intelligible notice to quit, and one which even the cool Mr. Sponge was rather at a loss how to parry.

He did not like the aspect of affairs. In addition to having to spend the evening by himself, the cook sent him a very moderate dinner, smoked soup, sodden fish, scraggy cutlets, and sour pudding. Mr. Plummey, too, seemed to have put all the company bottle-ends together for him. This would not do. If Sponge could have satisfied himself that his host would not be better in a day or two, he would have thought seriously of leaving; but as he could not bring himself to think that he would not, and, moreover, had no place to go to, had it not been for the concluding portion of Mr. Puffington's note, he would have made an effort to stay. That, however, put it rather out of his power, especially as it was done so politely, and hinted at a renewal of the visit. Mr. Sponge spent the evening in cogitating what he should do—thinking what sportsmen had held out the hand of good-fellowship, and hinted at hoping to have the pleasure of seeing him. Fyle, Fossick, Blossomnose, Capon, Dribble, Hook, and others, were all run through his mind, without his thinking it prudent to attempt to fix a volunteer visit upon any of them. Many people he knew could pen polite excuses, who yet could not hit them off at the moment, especially in that great arena of hospitality—the hunting-field. He went to bed very much perplexed.

XLIV

WANTED—
A RICH GOD-PAPA!

'WHEN ONE DOOR SHUTS ANOTHER opens,' say the saucy servants; and fortune was equally favourable to our friend Mr. Sponge. Though he could not think of any one to whom he could volunteer a visit, Dame Fortune provided him with an overture from a party who wanted him! But we will introduce his new host, or rather victim.

People hunt from various motives—some for the love of the thing—some for show—some for fashion—some for health—some for appetites—some for coffee-housing—some to say they have hunted—some because others hunt.

Mr. Jogglebury Crowdey did not hunt from any of these motives, and it would puzzle a conjurer to make out why he hunted; indeed, the members of the different hunts he patronized—for he was one of the run-about, non-subscribing sort—were long in finding out. It was observed that he generally affected countries abounding in large woods, such as Stretchaway Forest, Hazelbury Chase, and Oakington Banks, into which he would dive with the greatest avidity. At first people thought he was a very keen hand, anxious to see a fox handsomely found, if he could not see him handsomely finished, against which latter luxury his figure and activity, or want of activity, were somewhat opposed. Indeed, when we say that he went by the name of the Woolpack, our readers will be able to imagine the style of man he was: long-headed, short-necked, large-girthed, dumpling-legged little fellow, who, like most fat men, made himself dangerous by compressing a most unreasonable stomach into a circumscribed coat, each particular button of which looked as if it was ready to burst off, and knock out the eye of any one who might have the temerity to ride alongside of him. He was a puffy, wheezy, sententious little fellow, who accompanied his parables with a snort into a large finely plaited shirt-frill, reaching nearly up to his nose. His hunting-costume consisted of a black coat and waistcoat, with white moleskin breeches, much cracked and darned about the knees and other parts, as nether garments made of that treacherous stuff often are. His shapeless tops, made regardless of the refinements of 'right and left,' dangled at his horse's sides like a couple of stable-buckets; and he carried his heavy iron hammer-headed whip over his shoulder like a flail. But we are drawing his portrait instead of saying why he hunted. Well, then, having married Mrs. Springwheat's sister, who was always boasting to Mrs. Crowdey what a loving, doting husband Springey was after hunting, Mrs. Crowdey had induced Crowdey to try his hand, and though soon satisfied that he hadn't the slightest taste for the sport, but being a great man for what he called gibbey-sticks, he hunted for the purpose of finding them. As we said before, he generally appeared at large woodlands, into which he would ride with the hounds, plunging through the stiffest clay, and forcing his way through the strongest thickets, making observations all the while of the hazels, and the hollies, and the blackthorns, and, we are sorry to say, sometimes of the young oaks and ashes, that he thought would fashion into curious-handled walking-sticks; and these he would return for at a future day, getting them with as large clubs as possible, which he would cut into the heads of beasts, or birds, or fishes, or men. At the time of which we are writing, he had accumulated a vast quantity—thousands; the garret at the top of his house was quite full, so were most of the closets, while the rafters in the kitchen, and cellars, and out-houses, were crowded with others in a state of *déshabille*. He calculated his stock at immense worth, we don't know how many thousand pounds; and as he cut, and puffed, and wheezed, and modelled, with a volume of Buffon, or the picture of some eminent man before him, he chuckled, and thought how well he was providing for his family. He had been at it so long, and argued so stoutly, that Mrs. Jogglebury Crowdey, if not quite convinced of the accuracy of his calculations, nevertheless thought it well to encourage his hunting predilections, inasmuch as it brought him in contact with people he would not otherwise meet, who, she thought, might possibly be useful to their children. Accordingly, she got him his breakfast betimes on hunting-mornings, charged his pockets with currant-buns, and saw to the mending of his moleskins when he came home, after any of those casualties that occur as well in the chase as in gibbey-stick hunting.

A stranger being a marked man in a rural country, Mr. Sponge excited more curiosity in Mr. Jogglebury Crowdey's mind than Mr. Jogglebury Crowdey did in Mr. Sponge's. In truth, Jogglebury was one of those unsportsmanlike beings, that a regular fox-hunter would think it waste of words to inquire about, and if Mr. Sponge saw him, he did not recollect him; while, on the other hand, Mr. Jogglebury Crowdey went home very full of our friend. Now, Mrs. Jogglebury Crowdey was a fine, bustling, managing woman, with a large family, for whom she exerted all her energies to procure desirable god-papas and mammas; and, no sooner did she hear of this newcomer, than she longed to appropriate him for god-papa to their youngest son.

'Jog, my dear,' said she, to her spouse, as they sat at tea; 'it would be well to look after him.'

'What for, my dear?' asked Jog, who was staring a stick, with a half-finished head of Lord Brougham for a handle, out of countenance.

'What for, Jog? Why, can't you guess?'

'No,' replied Jog doggedly.

'No!' ejaculated his spouse. 'Why, Jog, you certainly are the stupidest man in existence.'

'Not necessarily!' replied Jog, with a jerk of his head and a puff into his shirt-frill that set it all in a flutter.

'Not necessarily!' replied Mrs. Jogglebury, who was what they call a 'spirited woman,' in the same rising tone as before. 'Not necessarily! but I say necessarily—yes, necessarily. Do you hear me, Mr. Jogglebury?'

'I hear you,' replied Jogglebury scornfully, with another jerk, and another puff into the frill.

The two then sat silent for some minutes, Jogglebury still contemplating the progressing head of Lord Brougham, and recalling the eye and features that some five-and-twenty years before had nearly withered him in a breach of promise action, 'Smiler v. Jogglebury,'[1] that being our friend's name before his uncle Crowdey left him his property.

Mrs. Jogglebury, having an object in view, and knowing that, though Jogglebury might lead, he would not drive, availed herself of the lull to trim her sail, to try and catch him on the other tack.

'Well, Mr. Jogglebury Crowdey,' said she, in a passive tone of regret, 'I certainly thought however indifferent you might be to me' (and here she applied her handkerchief—rather a coarse one—to her eyes) 'that still you had some regard for the interests of your (sob) children'; and here the waterfalls of her beady black eyes went off in a gush.

'Well, my dear,' replied Jogglebury, softened, 'I'm (puff) sure I'm (wheeze) anxious for my (puff) children. You don't s'pose if I wasn't (puff), I'd (wheeze) labour as I (puff—wheeze) do to leave them fortins?'—alluding to his exertions in the gibbey-stick line.

'Oh, Jog, I dare say you're very good and very industrious,' sobbed Mrs. Jogglebury, 'but I sometimes (sob) think that you might apply your (sob) energies to a better (sob) purpose.'

'Indeed, my dear (puff), I don't see that (wheeze),' replied Jogglebury, mildly.

'Why, now, if you were to try and get this rich Mr. Sponge for a god-papa for Gustavus James,' continued she, drying her eyes as she came to the point, '*that*, I should say, would be worthy of you.'

'But, my (puff) dear,' replied Jogglebury, 'I don't know Mr. (wheeze) Sponge, to begin with.'

'That's nothing,' replied Mrs. Jogglebury; 'he's a stranger, and you should call upon him.'

Mr. Jogglebury sat silent, still staring at Lord Brougham, thinking how he pitched into him, and how sick he was when the jury, without retiring from the box, gave five hundred pounds damages against him.

'He's a fox-hunter, too,' continued his wife; 'and you ought to be civil to him.'

'Well, but, my (puff) dear, he's as likely to (wheeze) these fifty years as any (puff, wheeze) man I ever looked at,' replied Jogglebury.

'Oh, nonsense,' replied Mrs. Jogglebury; 'there's no saying when a fox-hunter may break his neck. My word! but Mrs. Slooman tells me pretty stories of Sloo's doings with the harriers—jumping over hurdles, and everything that comes in the way, and galloping along the stony lanes as if the wind was a snail compared to his horse. I tell you, Jog, you should call on this gentleman—'

'Well,' replied Mr. Jogglebury.

'And ask him to come and stay here,' continued Mrs. Jogglebury.

'Perhaps he mightn't like it (puff),' replied Jogglebury. 'I don't know that we could (puff) entertain him as he's (wheeze) accustomed to be,' added he.

'Oh, nonsense,' replied Mrs. Jogglebury; 'we can entertain him well enough. You always say fox-hunters are not ceremonious. I tell you what, Jog, you don't think half enough of yourself. You are far too easily set aside. My word! but I know some people who would give themselves pretty airs if their husband was chairman of a board of guardians, and trustee of I don't know how many of Her Majesty's turnpike roads,' Mrs. Jog here thinking of her sister Mrs. Springwheat, who, she used to say, had married a mere farmer. 'I tell you, Jog, you're far too humble, you don't think half enough of yourself.'

'Well, but, my (puff) dear, you don't (puff) consider that all people ain't (puff) fond of (wheeze) children,' observed Jogglebury, after a pause. 'Indeed, I've (puff) observed that some (wheeze) don't like them.'

'Oh, but those will be nasty little brats, like Mrs. James Wakenshaw's, or Mrs. Tom Cheek's. But such children as ours! such charmers! such delights! there isn't a man in the county, from the Lord-Lieutenant downwards, who wouldn't be proud—who wouldn't think it a compliment—to be asked to be god-papa to such children. I tell you what, Mr. Jogglebury Crowdey, it would be far better to get them rich god-papas and god-mammas than to leave them a whole house full of sticks.'

'Well, but, my (puff) dear, the (wheeze) sticks will prove very (wheeze) hereafter,' replied Jogglebury, bridling up at the imputation on his hobby.

'I *hope* so,' replied Mrs. Jogglebury, in a tone of incredulity.

'Well, but, my (puff) dear, I (wheeze) you that they will be—indeed (puff), I may (wheeze) say that they (puff) are. It was only the other (puff) day that (wheeze) Patrick O'Fogo offered me five-and-twenty (wheeze) shillings for my (puff) blackthorn Daniel O'Connell, which is by no means so (puff) good as the (wheeze) wild-cherry one, or, indeed (puff), as the yew-tree one that I (wheeze) out of Spankerley Park.'

'I'd have taken it if I'd been you,' observed Mrs. Jogglebury.

'But he's (puff) worth far more,' retorted Jogglebury angrily; 'why (wheeze) Lumpleg offered me as much for Disraeli.'

'Well, I'd have taken it, too,' rejoined Mrs. Jogglebury.

'But I should have (wheeze) spoilt my (puff) set,' replied the gibbey-stick man. 'S'pose any (wheeze) body was to (puff) offer me five guineas a (puff) piece for the (puff) pick of my (puff) collection—my (puff) Wellingtons, my (wheeze) Napoleons, my (puff) Byrons, my (wheeze) Walter Scotts, my (puff) Lord Johns, d'ye think I'd take it?'

'I should hope so,' replied Mrs. Jogglebury.

'I should (puff) do no such thing,' snorted her husband into his frill. 'I should hope,' continued he, speaking slowly and solemnly, 'that a (puff) wise ministry will purchase the whole (puff) collection for a (wheeze) grateful nation, when the (wheeze)' something 'is no more (wheeze).' The concluding words being lost in the emotion of the speaker (as the reporters say).

'Well, but will you go and call on Mr. Sponge, dear?' asked Mrs. Jogglebury Crowdey, anxious as well to turn the subject as to make good her original point.

'Well, my dear, I've no objection,' replied Joggle, wiping a tear from the corner of his eye with his coat-cuff.

'That's a good soul!' exclaimed Mrs. Jogglebury soothingly. 'Go to-morrow, like a nice, sensible man.'

'Very well,' replied her now complacent spouse.

'And ask him to come here,' continued she.

'I can't (puff) ask him to (puff) come, my dear (wheeze), until he (puff—wheeze) returns my (puff) call.'

'Oh, fiddle,' replied his wife, 'you always say fox-hunters never stand upon ceremony; why should you stand upon any with him?'

Mr. Jogglebury was posed, and sat silent.

1. *Vide* 'Barnwell and Alderson's Reports.'

XLV

THE DISCOMFORTED
DIPLOMATIST

WELL, THEN, AS WE SAID before, when one door shuts another opens; and just as Mr. Puffington's door was closing on poor Mr. Sponge, who should cast up but our newly introduced friend, Mr. Jogglebury Crowdey. Mr. Sponge was sitting in solitary state in the fine drawing-room, studying his old friend *Mogg*, calculating what he could ride from Spur Street, Leicester Square, by Short's Gardens, and across Waterloo Bridge, to the Elephant and Castle for, when the grinding of a vehicle on the gravelled ring attracted his attention. Looking out of the window, he saw a horse's head in a faded-red, silk-fronted bridle, with the letters 'J.C.' on the winkers; not 'J.C.' writhing in the elegant contortions of modern science, but 'J.C.' in the good, plain, matter-of-fact characters we have depicted above.

'That'll be the doctor,' said Mr. Sponge to himself, as he resumed his reading and calculations, amidst a peal of the door-bell, well calculated to arouse the whole house. 'He's a good un to ring!' added he, looking up and wondering when the last lingering tinkle would cease.

Before the fact was ascertained, there was a hurried tramp of feet past the drawing-room door, and presently the entrance one opened and let in—a rush of wind.

'Is Mr. Sponge at home?' demanded a slow, pompous-speaking, deep-toned voice, evidently from the vehicle.

'Yez-ur,' was the immediate answer.

'Who can that be?' exclaimed Sponge, pocketing his *Mogg*.

Then there was a creaking of springs and a jingling against iron steps, and presently a high-blowing, heavy-stepping body was heard crossing the entrance-hall, while an out-stripping footman announced Mr. Jogglebury Crowdey, leaving the owner to follow his name at his leisure.

Mrs. Jogglebury had insisted on Jog putting on his new black frock—a very long coat, fitting like a sack, with the well-filled pockets bagging behind, like a poor man's dinner wallet. In *lieu* of the shrunk and darned white moleskins, receding in apparent disgust from the dingy tops, he had got his nether man enveloped in a pair of fine cinnamon-coloured tweeds, with broad blue stripes down the sides, and shaped out over the clumsy foot.

Puff, wheeze, puff, he now came waddling and labouring along, hat in hand, hurrying after the servant; puff, wheeze, puff, and he found himself in the room. 'Your servant, sir,' said he, sticking himself out behind, and addressing Mr. Sponge, making a ground sweep with his woolly hat.

'*Yours*,' said Mr. Sponge, with a similar bow.

'Fine day (puff—wheeze),' observed Mr. Jogglebury, blowing into his large frill.

'It is,' replied Mr. Sponge, adding, 'won't you be seated?'

'How's Puffington?' gasped our visitor, sousing himself upon one of the rosewood chairs in a way that threatened destruction to the slender fabric.

'Oh, he's pretty middling, *I* should say,' replied Sponge, now making up his mind that he was addressing the doctor.

'Pretty middlin' (puff),' repeated Jogglebury, blowing into his frill; 'pretty middlin' (wheeze); I s'pose that means he's got a (puff) gumboil. My third (wheeze) girl, Margaret Henrietta has one.'

'Do you want to see him?' asked Sponge, after a pause, which seemed to indicate that his friend's conversation had come to a period, or full stop.

'No,' replied Jogglebury unconcernedly. 'No; I'll leave a (puff) card for him (wheeze),' added he, fumbling in his wallet behind for his card-case. 'My (puff) object is to pay my (wheeze) respects to you,' observed he, drawing a great carved Indian case from his pocket, and pulling off the top with a noise like the drawing of a cork.

'Much obliged for the compliment,' observed Mr. Sponge, as Jogglebury fumbled and broke his nails in attempting to get a card out.

'Do you stay long in this part of the world?' asked he, as at last he succeeded, and commenced tapping the corners of the card on the table.

'I really don't know,' replied Mr. Sponge, as the particulars of his situation flashed across his mind. Could this pudding-headed man be a chap Puffington had got to come and sound him, thought he.

Jogglebury sat silent for a time, examining his feet attentively as if to see they were pairs, and scrutinizing the bags of his cinnamon-coloured trousers.

'I was going to say (hem—cough—hem),' at length observed he, looking up, 'that's to say, I was thinking (hem—wheeze—cough—hem), or rather I should say, Mrs. Jogglebury Crowdey sent me to say—I mean to say,' continued he, stamping one of his ponderous feet against the floor as if to force out his words, 'Mrs. Jogglebury Crowdey and I would be glad—happy, that's to say (hem)—if you would arrange (hem) to (wheeze) pay us a visit (hem).'

'Most happy, I'm sure!' exclaimed Mr. Sponge, jumping at the offer.

'Before you go (hem),' continued our visitor, taking up the sentence where Sponge had interrupted him; 'I (hem) live about nine miles (hem) from here (hem).'

'Are there any hounds in your neighbourhood?' asked Mr. Sponge.

'Oh yes,' replied Mr. Jogglebury slowly; 'Mr. Puffington here draws up to Greatacre Gorse within a few (puff—wheeze) miles—say, three (puff)—of my (wheeze) house; and Sir Harry Scattercash (puff) hunts all the (puff—wheeze) country below, right away down to the (puff—wheeze) sea.'

'Well, you're a devilish good fellow!' exclaimed Sponge; 'and I'll tell you what, as I'm sure you mean what you say, I'll take you at your word and go at once; and that'll give our friend here time to come round.'

'Oh, but (puff—wheeze—gasp),' started Mr. Jogglebury, the blood rushing to his great yellow, whiskerless cheeks, 'I'm not quite (gasp) sure that Mrs. (gasp) Jogglebury (puff) Crowdey would be (puff—wheeze—gasp) prepared.'

'Oh, *hang* preparation!' interrupted Mr. Sponge. 'I'll take you as you are. Never mind me. I hate being made company of. Just treat me like one of yourselves; toad-in-the-hole, dog-in-the-blanket, beef-steaks and oyster-sauce, rabbits and onions—anything; nothing comes amiss to me.'

So saying, and while Jogglebury sat purple and unable to articulate, Mr. Sponge applied his hand to the ivory bell-knob and sounded an imposing peal. Mr. Jogglebury sat wondering what was going to happen, and thinking what a wigging he would get from Mrs. J. if he didn't manage to shake off his friend. Above all, he recollected that they had nothing but haddocks and hashed mutton for dinner.

'Tell Leather I want him,' said Mr. Sponge, in a tone of authority, as the footman answered the summons; then, turning to his guest, as the man was leaving the room, he said, 'Won't you take something after your drive—cold meat, glass of sherry, soda-water, bottled porter—anything in that line?'

In an ordinary way, Jogglebury would have said, 'if you please,' at the sound of the words 'cold meat,' for he was a dead hand at luncheon; but the fix he was in completely took away his appetite, and he sat wheezing and thinking whether to make another effort, or to wait the arrival of Leather.

Presently Leather appeared, jean-jacketed and gaitered, smoothing his hair over his forehead, after the manner of the brotherhood.

'Leather,' said Mr. Sponge, in the same tone of importance, 'I'm going to this gentleman's'; for as yet he had not sufficiently mastered the name to be able to venture upon it in the owner's presence. 'Leather, I'm going to this gentleman's, and I want you to bring me a horse over in the morning; or stay,' said he, interrupting himself, and, turning to Jogglebury, he exclaimed, 'I dare say you could manage to put me up a couple of horses, couldn't you? and then we should be all cosy and jolly together, you know.'

''Pon my word,' gasped Jogglebury nearly choked by the proposal; ''pon my word, I can hardly (puff) say, I hardly (wheeze) know, but if you'll (puff—wheeze) allow me, I'll tell you what I'll do: I'll (puff—wheeze) home, and see what I can (puff) do in the way of entertainment for (puff—wheeze) man as well as for (puff—wheeze) horse.'

'Oh, *thank you*, my dear fellow!' exclaimed Sponge, seeing the intended dodge; '*thank you*, my dear fellow!' repeated he; 'but that's giving you too much trouble—*far* too much trouble!—couldn't think of such a thing—no, indeed, I couldn't. *I'll* tell you what we'll do—*I'll* tell you what we'll do. You shall drive me over in that shandrydan-rattle-trap thing of yours'—Sponge looking out of the window, as he spoke, at the queer-shaped, jumped-together, lack-lustre-looking vehicle, with a turnover seat behind, now in charge of a pepper-and-salt attired youth, with a shabby hat, looped up by a thin silver cord to an acorn on the crown, and baggy Berlin gloves—'and I'll just see what there is in the way of stabling; and if I think it will do, then I'll give a boy sixpence or a shilling to come over to Leather, here,' jerking his head towards his factotum; 'if it won't do, why then—'

'We shall want *three* stalls, sir—recollect, sir,' interrupted Leather, who did not wish to move his quarters.

'True, I forgot,' replied Sponge, with a frown at his servant's officiousness; 'however, if we can get two good stalls for the hunters,' said he, 'we'll manage the hack somehow or other.'

'Well,' replied Mr. Leather, in a tone of resignation, knowing how hopeless it was arguing with his master.

'I really think,' gasped Mr. Jogglebury Crowdey, encouraged by the apparent sympathy of the servant to make a last effort, 'I really think,' repeated he, as the hashed mutton and haddocks again flashed across his mind, 'that my (puff—wheeze) plan is the (puff) best; let me (puff—wheeze) home and see how all (puff—wheeze) things are, and then I'll write you a (puff—wheeze) line, or send a (puff—wheeze) servant over.'

'Oh, no,' replied Mr. Sponge, 'oh, no—that's far too much trouble. I'll just go over with you now and reconnoitre.'

'I'm afraid Mrs. (puff—wheeze) Crowdey will hardly be prepared for (puff—wheeze) visitors,' ejaculated our friend, recollecting it was washing-day, and that Mary Ann would be wanted in the laundry.

'Don't mention it!' exclaimed Mr. Sponge; 'don't mention it. I hate to be made company of. Just give me what you have yourselves—just give me what you have yourselves. Where two can dine, three can dine, you know.'

Mr. Jogglebury Crowdey was nonplussed.

'Well, now,' said Mr. Sponge, turning again to Leather; 'just go upstairs and help me to pack up my things; and,' addressing himself to our visitor, he said, 'perhaps you'll amuse yourself with the paper—the *Post*—or I'll lend you my *Mogg*,' continued he, offering the little gilt-lettered, purple-backed volume as he spoke.

'Thank'ee,' replied Mr. Jogglebury, who was still tapping away at the card, which he had now worked very soft.

Mr. Sponge then left him with the volume in his hand, and proceeded upstairs to his bedroom.

In less than twenty minutes, the vehicle was got under way, Mr. Jogglebury Crowdey and Mr. Sponge occupying the roomy seats in front, and Bartholomew Badger, the before-mentioned tiger, and Mr. Sponge's portmanteau and carpet-bag, being in the very diminutive turnover seat behind. The carriage was followed by the straining eyes of sundry Johns and Janes, who unanimously agreed that Mr. Sponge was the meanest, shabbiest gent they had ever had in *their* house. Mr. Leather was, therefore, roasted in the servants' hall, where the sins of the masters are oft visited upon the servants.

But to our travellers.

Little conversation passed between our friends for the first few miles, for, in addition to the road being rough, the driving-seat was so high, and the other so low, that Mr. Jogglebury Crowdey's parables broke against Mr. Sponge's hat-crown, instead of dropping into his ear; besides which, the unwilling host's mind was a good deal occupied with wishing that there had been three haddocks instead of two, and speculating whether Mrs. Crowdey would be more pleased at the success of his mission, or put out of her way by Mr. Sponge's unexpected coming. Above all, he had marked some very promising-looking sticks—two blackthorns and a holly—to cut on his way home, and he was intent on not missing them. So sudden was the jerk that announced his coming on the first one, as nearly to throw the old family horse on his knees, and almost to break Mr. Sponge's nose against the brass edge of the cocked-up splash-board. Ere Mr. Sponge recovered his equilibrium, the whip was in the case, the reins dangling about the old screw's heels, and Mr. Crowdey scrambling up a steep bank to where a very thick boundary-hedge shut out the view of the adjacent country. Presently, chop, chop, chop, was heard, from Mr. Crowdey's pocket axe, with a tug—wheeze—puff from himself; next a crash of separation; and then the purple-faced Mr. Crowdey came bearing down the bank dragging a great blackthorn bush after him.

'What have you got there?' inquired Mr. Sponge, with surprise.

'Got! (wheeze—puff—wheeze),' replied Mr. Crowdey, pulling up short, and mopping his perspiring brow with a great claret-coloured bandana. 'Got! I've (puff—wheeze) got what I (wheeze) think will (puff) into a most elaborate and (wheeze) valuable walking-stick. This I (puff) think,' continued he, eyeing the great ball with which he had got it up, 'will (wheeze) come in most valuably (puff) for my great (puff—wheeze—gasp) national undertaking—the (puff) Kings and (wheeze) Queens of Great Britain (gasp).'

'What are *they*?' asked Mr. Sponge, astonished at his vehemence.

'Oh! (puff—wheeze—gasp) haven't you heard?' exclaimed Mr. Jogglebury, taking off his great woolly hat, and giving his lank, dark hair, streaked with grey, a sweep round his low forehead with the bandana. 'Oh! (puff—gasp) haven't you heard?' repeated he, getting a little more breath. 'I'm (wheeze) undertaking a series of (gasp) sticks, representing—(gasp)—immortalizing, I may say (puff), all the (wheeze) crowned heads of England (puff).'

'Indeed!' replied Mr. Sponge.

'They'll be a most valuable collection (wheeze—puff),' continued Mr. Jogglebury, still eyeing the knob. 'This,' added he, 'shall be William the Fourth.' He then commenced lopping and docking the sides, making Bartholomew Badger bury them in a sand-pit hard by, observing, in a confidential wheeze to Mr. Sponge, 'that he had once been county-courted for a similar trespass before.' The top and lop being at length disposed of, Mr. Crowdey, grasping the club-end, struck the other forcibly against the ground, exclaiming, 'There!—there's a (puff) stick! Who knows what that (puff—wheeze) stick may be worth some day?'

He then bundled into his carriage and drove on.

Two more stoppages marked their arrival at the other sticks, which being duly captured and fastened within the straps of the carriage-apron, Mr. Crowdey drove on somewhat more at ease in his mind, at all events somewhat comforted at the thoughts of having increased his wealth. He did not become talkative—indeed that was not his forte, but he puffed into his shirt-frill, and made a few observations, which, if they did not possess much originality, at all events showed that he was not asleep.

'Those are draining-tiles,' said he, after a hearty stare at a cart-load. Then about five minutes after he blew again, and said, 'I don't think (puff) that (wheeze) draining without (gasp) manuring will constitute high farming (puff).'

So he jolted and wheezed, and jerked and jagged the old quadruped's mouth, occasionally hissing between his teeth, and stamping against the bottom of the carriage, when other persuasive efforts failed to induce it to keep up the semblance of a trot. At last the ill-supported hobble died out into a walk, and Mr. Crowdey, complacently dropping his fat hand on his fat knees, seemed to resign himself to his fate.

So they crawled along the up-and-downy piece of road below Poplarton plantations, Mr. Jogglebury keeping a sharp eye upon the underwood for sticks. After passing these, they commenced the gradual ascent of Roundington Hill, when a sudden sweep of the road brought them in view of the panorama of the rich Vale of Butterflower.

'There's a snug-looking box,' observed Sponge, as he at length espied a confused jumble of gable-ends and chimney-pots rising from amidst a clump of Scotch firs and other trees, looking less like a farmhouse than anything he had seen.

'That's my house (puff); that's Puddingpote Bower (wheeze),' replied Crowdey slowly and pompously, adding an 'e' to the syllable, to make it sound better, the haddocks, hashed mutton, and all the horrors of impromptu hospitality rushing upon his mind.

Things began to look worse the nearer he got home. He didn't care to aggravate the old animal into a trot. He again wondered whether Mrs. J. would be pleased at the success of his mission, or angry at the unexpected coming.

'Where are the stables?' asked Sponge, as he scanned the in-and-out irregularities of the building.

'Stables (wheeze), stables (puff),' repeated Crowdey—thinking of his troubles—of its being washing-day, and Mary Ann, or Murry Ann, as he called her, the under-butler, being engaged; of Bartholomew Badger having the horse and fe-a-ton to clean, &c.—'stables,' repeated he for the third time; 'stables are at the back, behind, in fact; you'll see a (puff) vane—a (wheeze) fox, on the top.'

'Ah, indeed!' replied Mr. Sponge, brightening up, thinking there would be old hay and corn.

They now came to a half-Swiss, half-Gothic little cottage of a lodge, and the old horse turned instinctively into the open white gate with pea-green bands.

'Here's Mrs. Crow—Crow—Crowdey!' gasped Jogglebury, convulsively, as a tall woman, in flare-up red and yellow stunner tartan, with a swarm of little children, similarly attired, suddenly appeared at an angle of the road, the lady handling a great alpaca umbrella-looking parasol in the stand-and-deliver style.

'What's kept you?' exclaimed she, as the vehicle got within ear-shot. 'What's kept you?' repeated she, in a sharper key, holding her parasol across the road, but taking no notice of our friend Sponge, who, in truth, she took for Edgebone, the butcher. 'Oh! you've been after your sticks, have you?' added she, as her spouse drew the vehicle up alongside of her, and she caught the contents of the apron-straps.

'My dear (puff)' gasped her husband, 'I've brought Mr. (wheeze) Sponge,' said he, winking his right eye, and jerking his head over his left shoulder, looking very frightened all the time. 'Mr. (puff) Sponge, Mrs. (gasp) Jogglebury (wheeze) Crowdey,' continued he, motioning with his hand.

Finding himself in the presence of his handsome hostess, Sponge made her one of his best bows, and offered to resign his seat in the carriage to her. This she declined, alleging that she had the children with her—looking round on the grinning, gaping group, the majority of them with their mouths smeared with lollipops. Crowdey, who was not so stupid as he looked, was nettled at Sponge's attempting to fix his wife upon him at such a critical moment, and immediately retaliated with, 'P'raps (puff) you'd like to (puff) out and (wheeze) walk.'

There was no help for this, and Sponge having alighted, Mr. Crowdey said, half to Mr. Sponge and half to his fine wife, 'Then (puff—wheeze) I'll just (puff) on and get Mr. (wheeze) Sponge's room ready.' So saying, he gave the old nag a hearty jerk with the bit, and two or three longitudinal cuts with the knotty-pointed whip, and jingled away with a bevy of children shouting, hanging on, and dragging behind, amidst exclamations from Mrs. Crowdey, of 'O Anna Maria! Juliana Jane! O Frederick James, you naughty boy! you'll spoil your new shoes! Archibald John, you'll be kilt! you'll be run over to a certainty. O Jogglebury, you inhuman man!' continued she, running and brandishing her alpaca parasol, 'you'll run over your children! you'll run over your children!'

'My (puff) dear,' replied Jogglebury, looking coolly over his shoulder,' how can they be (wheeze) run over behind?'

So saying Jogglebury ground away at his leisure.

XLVI

PUDDINGPOTE BOWER, THE SEAT OF JOGGLEBURY CROWDEY, ESQ.

'YOUR GOOD HUSBAND,' OBSERVED MR. Sponge as he now overtook his hostess and proceeded with her towards the house, 'has insisted upon bringing me over to spend a few days till my friend Puffington recovers. He's just got the gout. I said I was 'fraid it mightn't be quite convenient to you, but Mr. Crowdey assured me you were in the habit of receivin' fox-hunters at short notice; and so I have taken him at his word, you see, and come.'

Mrs. Jogglebury, who was still out of wind from her run after the carriage, assured him that she was extremely happy to see him, though she couldn't help thinking what a noodle Jog was to bring a stranger on a washing-day. That, however, was a point she would reserve for Jog.

Just then a loud outburst from the children announced the approach of the eighth wonder of the world, in the person of Gustavus James in the nurse's arms, with a curly blue feather nodding over his nose. Mrs. Jogglebury's black eyes brightened with delight as she ran forward to meet him; and in her mind's eye she saw him inheriting a splendid mansion, with a retinue of powdered footmen in pea-green liveries and broad gold-laced hats. Great—prospectively great, at least—as had been her successes in the sponsor line with her other children, she really thought, getting Mr. Sponge for a god-papa for Gustavus James eclipsed all her other doings.

Mr. Sponge, having been liberal in his admiration of the other children, of course could not refuse unbounded applause to the evident object of a mother's regards; and, chucking the young gentleman under his double chin, asked him how he was, and said something about something he had in his 'box,' alluding to a paper of cheap comfits he had bought at Sugarchalk's, the confectioner's, sale in Oxford Street, and which he carried about for contingencies like the present. This pleased Mrs. Crowdey—looking, as she thought, as if he had come predetermined to do what she wanted. Amidst praises and stories of the prodigy, they reached the house.

If a 'hall' means a house with an entrance-'hall,' Puddingpote Bower did not aspire to be one. A visitor dived, *in medias res*, into the passage at once. In it stood an oak-cased family clock, and a large glass-case, with an alarming-looking, stuffed tiger-like cat, on an imitation marble slab. Underneath the slab, indeed all about the passage, were scattered children's hats and caps, hoops, tops, spades, and mutilated toys—spotted horses without heads, soldiers without arms, windmills without sails, and wheelbarrows without wheels. In a corner were a bunch of 'gibbeys' in the rough, and alongside the weather-glass hung Jog's formidable flail of a hunting-whip.

Mr. Sponge found his portmanteau standing bolt upright in the passage, with the bag alongside of it, just as they had been chucked out of the phaeton by Bartholomew Badger, who, having got orders to put the horse right, and then to put himself right to wait at dinner, Mr. Jogglebury proceeded to vociferate:

'Murry Ann!—Murry Ann!' in such a way that Mary Ann thought either that the cat had got young Crowdey, or the house was on fire. 'Oh! Murry Ann!' exclaimed Mr. Jogglebury, as she came darting into the passage from the back settlements, up to the elbows in soap-suds; 'I want you to (puff) upstairs with me, and help to get my (wheeze) gibbey-sticks out of the best room; there's a (puff) gentleman coming to (wheeze) here.'

'Oh, indeed, sir,' replied Mary Ann, smiling, and dropping down her sleeves—glad to find it was no worse.

They then proceeded upstairs together.

All the gibbey-sticks were bundled out, both the finished ones, that were varnished and laid away carefully in the wardrobe, and those that were undergoing surgical treatment, in the way of twistings, and bendings, and tyings in the closets. As they routed them out of hole and corner, Jogglebury kept up a sort of running recommendation to mercy, mingled with an inquiry into the state of the household affairs.

'Now (puff), Murry Ann!' exclaimed he; 'take care you don't scratch that (puff) Franky Burdett,' handing her a highly varnished oak stick, with the head of Sir Francis for a handle; 'and how many (gasp) haddocks d'ye say there are in the house?'

'Three, sir,' replied Mary Ann.

'Three!' repeated he, with an emphasis. 'I thought your (gasp) missus told me there were but (puff) two; and, Murry Ann, you must put the new (puff) quilt on the (gasp) bed, and (puff) just look under it (gasp) and you'll find the (puff) old Truro rolled up in a dirty (puff) pocket hankercher; and, Murry Ann, d'ye think the new (wheeze) purtaters came that I bought of (puff) Billy Bloxom? If so, you'd better (puff) some for dinner, and get the best (wheeze) decanters out; and, Murry Ann, there are two gibbeys on the (puff) surbase at the back of the bed, which you may as well (puff) away. Ah! here he is,' added Mr. Jogglebury, as Mr. Sponge's voice rose now from the passage into the room above.

Things now looked pretty promising. Mr. Sponge's attentions to the children generally, and to Gustavus James in particular, coupled with his free-and-easy mode of introducing himself, made Mrs. Crowdey feel far more at her ease with regard to entertaining him than she would have done if her neighbour, Mr. Makepeace, or the Rev. Mr. Facey himself, had dropped in to take 'pot luck,' as they called it. With either of these she would have wished to appear as if their every-day form was more in accordance with their company style, whereas Jog and she wanted to get something out of Mr. Sponge, instead of electrifying him with their grandeur. That Gustavus James was destined for greatness she had not the least doubt. She began to think whether it might not be advisable to call him Gustavus James Sponge. Jog, too, was comforted at hearing there were three haddocks, for though hospitably inclined, he did not at all like the idea of being on short commons himself. He had sufficient confidence in Mrs. Jogglebury's management—especially as the guest was of her own seeking—to know that she would make up a tolerable dinner.

Nor was he out of his reckoning, for at half-past five Bartholomew announced dinner, when in sailed Mrs. Crowdey, fresh from the composition of it and from the becoming revision of her own dress.

Instead of the loose, flowing, gipsified, stunner tartan of the morning, she was attired in a close-fitting French grey silk, showing as well the fulness and whiteness of her exquisite bust, as the beautiful formation of her arms. Her raven hair was ably parted and flattened on either side of her well-shaped head. Sponge felt proud of the honour of having such a fine creature on his arm, and kicked about in his tights more than usual.

The dinner, though it might show symptoms of hurry, was yet plentiful and good of its kind; and if Bartholomew had not been always getting in Murry Ann's way, would have been well set on and served. Jog quaffed quantities of foaming bottled porter during the progress of it, and threw himself back in his chair at the end, as if thoroughly overcome with his exertions. Scarcely were the wine and dessert set on, ere a violent outbreak in the nursery caused Mrs. Crowdey to hurry away, leaving Mr. Sponge to enjoy the company of her husband.

'You'll drink (puff) fox-hunting, I s'pose,' observed Jog after a pause, helping himself to a bumper of port and passing the bottle to Sponge.

'With all my heart,' replied our hero, filling up.

'Fine (puff, wheeze) amusement,' observed Mr. Crowdey, with a yawn after another pause, and beating the devil's tattoo upon the table to keep himself awake.

'Very,' replied Mr. Sponge, wondering how such a thick-winded chap as Jog managed to partake of it.

'Fine (puff, wheeze) appetizer,' observed Jogglebury, after another pause.

'It is,' replied Mr. Sponge.

Presently Jog began to snore, and as the increasing melody of his nose gave little hopes of returning animation, Mr. Sponge had recourse to his old friend *Mogg* and amidst speculations as to time and distances, managed to finish the port. We will now pass to the next morning.

Whatever deficiency there might be at dinner was amply atoned for at breakfast, which was both good and abundant; bread and cake of all sorts, eggs, muffins, toast, honey, jellies, and preserves without end. On the side-table was a dish of hot kidneys and a magnificent red home-fed ham.

But a greater treat far, as Mrs. Jogglebury thought, was in the guests set around. There were arranged all her tulips in succession, beginning with that greatest of all wonders, Gustavus James, and running on with Anna Maria, Frederick John, Juliana Jane, Margaret Henrietta, Sarah Amelia, down to Peter William, the heir, who sat next his pa. These formed a close line on the side of the table opposite the fire, that side being left for Mr. Sponge. All the children had clean pinafores on, and their hairs plastered according to nursery regulation. Mr. Sponge's appearance was a signal for silence, and they all sat staring at him in mute astonishment. Baby, Gustavus James, did more; for after reconnoitring him through a sort of lattice window formed of his fingers, he whined out, 'Who's that ogl-e-y man, ma?' amidst the titter of the rest of the line.

'Hush! my dear,' exclaimed Mrs. Crowdey, hoping Mr. Sponge hadn't heard. But Gustavus James was not to be put down, and he renewed the charge as his mamma began pouring out the tea.

'Send that ogl-e-y man away, ma!' whined he, in a louder tone, at which all the children burst out a-laughing.

'Baby (puff), Gustavus! (wheeze),' exclaimed Jog, knocking with the handle of his knife against the table, and frowning at the prodigy.

'Well, pa, he *is* a ogl-e-y man,' replied the child, amid the ill-suppressed laughter of the rest.

'Ah, but what have *I* got!' exclaimed Mr. Sponge, producing a gaudily done-up paper of comfits from his pocket, opening and distributing the unwholesome contents along the line, stopping the orator's mouth first with a great, red-daubed, almond comfit.

Breakfast was then proceeded with without further difficulty. As it drew to a close, and Mr. Sponge began nibbling at the sweets instead of continuing his attack on the solids, Mrs. Jogglebury began eyeing and telegraphing her husband.

'Jog, my dear,' said she, looking significantly at him, and then at the egg-stand, which still contained three eggs.

'Well, my dear,' replied Jog, with a vacant stare, pretending not to understand.

'You'd better eat them,' said she, looking again at the eggs.

'I've (puff) breakfasted, my (wheeze) dear,' replied Jog pompously, wiping his mouth on his claret-coloured bandana.

'They'll be wasted if you don't,' replied Mrs. Jog.

'Well, but they'll be wasted if I eat them without (wheeze) wanting them,' rejoined he.

'Nonsense, Jog, you always say that,' retorted his wife. 'Nonsense (puff), nonsense (wheeze), I say they *will*.'

'I say they *won't!*' replied Mrs. Jog; 'now will they, Mr. Sponge?' continued she, appealing to our friend.

'Why, no, not so much as if they went out,' replied our friend, thinking Mrs. Jog was the one to side with.

'Then you'd better (puff, wheeze, gasp) eat them between you,' replied Jog, getting up and strutting out of the room.

Presently he appeared in front of the house, crowned in a pea-green wide-awake, with a half-finished gibbey in his hand; and as Mr. Sponge did not want to offend him, and moreover wanted to get his horses billeted on him, he presently made an excuse for joining him.

Although his horses were standing 'free gratis,' as he called it, at Mr. Puffington's, and though he would have thought nothing of making Mr. Leather come over with one each hunting morning, still he felt that if the hounds were much on the other side of Puddingpote Bower, it would not be so convenient as having them there. Despite the egg controversy, he thought a judicious application of soft sawder might accomplish what he wanted. At all events, he would try.

Jog had brought himself short up, and was standing glowering with his hands in his coat-pockets, as if he had never seen the place before.

'Pretty look-out you have here, Mr. Jogglebury,' observed Mr. Sponge, joining him.

'Very,' replied Jog, still cogitating the egg question, and thinking he wouldn't have so many boiled the next day.

'All yours?' asked Sponge, waving his hand as he spoke.

'My (puff) ter-ri-tory goes up to those (wheeze) firs in the grass-field on the hill,' replied Jogglebury, pompously.

'Indeed,' said Mr. Sponge, 'they are fine trees'; thinking what a finish they would make for a steeple-chase.

'My (puff) uncle, Crowdey, planted those (wheeze) trees,' observed Jog. 'I observe,' added he, 'that it is easier to cut down a (puff) tree than to make it (wheeze) again.' 'I believe you're right,' replied Mr. Sponge; 'that idea has struck me very often.'

'Has it?' replied Jog, puffing voluminously into his frill.

They then advanced a few paces, and, leaning on the iron hurdles, commenced staring at the cows.

'Where are the stables?' at last asked Sponge, seeing no inclination to move on the part of his host.

'Stables (wheeze)—stables (puff),' replied Jogglebury, recollecting Sponge's previous day's proposal—'stables (wheeze) are behind,' said he, 'at the back there (puff); nothin' to see at them (wheeze).'

'There'll be the horse you drove yesterday; won't you go to see how he is?' asked Mr. Sponge.

'Oh, sure to be well (puff); never nothing the matter with him (wheeze),' replied Jogglebury.

'May as well see,' rejoined Mr. Sponge, turning up a narrow walk that seemed to lead to the back.

Jog followed doggedly. He had a good deal of John Bull in him, and did not fancy being taken possession of in that sort of way; and thought, moreover, that Mr. Sponge had not behaved very well in the matter of the egg controversy.

The stables certainly were nothing to boast of. They were in an old rubble-stone, red-tiled building, without even the delicacy of a ceiling. Nevertheless, there was plenty of room even after Jogglebury had cut off one end for a cow-house.

'Why, you might hunt the country with all this stabling,' observed Mr. Sponge, as he entered the low door. 'One, two, three, four, five, six, seven, eight, nine. Nine stalls, I declare,' added he, after counting them.

'My (puff) uncle used to (wheeze) a good deal of his own (puff) land,' replied Jogglebury.

'Ah, well, I'll tell you what: these stables will be much better for being occupied,' observed Mr. Sponge. 'And I'll tell you what I'll do for you.'

'But they *are* occupied!' gasped Jogglebury, convulsively.

'Only half,' replied Mr. Sponge; 'or a quarter, I may say—not even that, indeed. I'll tell you what I'll do. I'll have my horses over here, and you shall find them in straw in return for the manure, and just charge me for hay and corn at market price, you know. That'll make it all square and fair, and no obligation, you know. I hate obligations,' added he, eyeing Jog's disconcerted face.

'Oh, but (puff, wheeze, gasp)—' exclaimed Jogglebury, reddening up—'I don't (puff) know that I can (gasp) that. I mean (puff) that this (wheeze) stable is all the (gasp) 'commodation I have; and if we had (puff) company, or (gasp) anything of that sort, I don't know where we should (wheeze) their horses,' continued he. 'Besides, I don't (puff, wheeze) know about the market price of (gasp) corn. My (wheeze) tenant, Tom Hayrick, at the (puff) farm on the (wheeze) hill yonder, supplies me with the (puff) quantity I (wheeze) want, and we just (puff, wheeze, gasp) settle once a (puff) half-year, or so.'

'Ah, I see,' replied Mr. Sponge; 'you mean to say you wouldn't know how to strike the average so as to say what I ought to pay.'

'Just so,' rejoined Mr. Jogglebury, jumping at the idea.

'Ah, well,' said Mr. Sponge, in a tone of indifference; 'it's no great odds—it's no great odds—more the name of the thing than anything else; one likes to be independent, you know—one likes to be independent; but as I shan't be with you long, I'll just put up with it for once—I'll just put up with it for once—and let you find me—and let you find me.' So saying, he walked away, leaving Jogglebury petrified at his impudence.

'That husband of yours is a monstrous good fellow,' observed Mr. Sponge to Mrs. Jogglebury, who he now met coming out with her tail: 'he *will* insist on my having my horses over here—most liberal, handsome thing of him, I'm sure; and that reminds me, can you manage to put up my servant?'

'I dare say we can,' replied Mrs. Jogglebury thoughtfully. 'He's not a very fine gentleman, is he?' asked she, knowing that servants were often more difficult to please than their masters. 'Oh, not at all,' replied Sponge; 'not at all—wouldn't suit me if he was—wouldn't suit me if he was.'

Just then up waddled Jogglebury, puffing and wheezing like a stranded grampus; the idea having just struck him that he might get off on the plea of not having room for the servant.

'It's very unfortunate (wheeze)—that's to say, it never occurred to me (puff), but I quite forgot (gasp) that we haven't (wheeze) room for your (puff) servant.'

'Ah, you are a good fellow,' replied Mr. Sponge—'a devilish good fellow. I was just telling Mrs. Jogglebury—wasn't I, Mrs. Jogglebury?— what an excellent fellow you are, and how kind you'd been about the horses and corn, and all that sort of thing, when it occurred to me that it mightn't be convenient, p'raps to put up a servant; but your wife assures me that it will; so that settles the matter, you know—that settles the matter and I'll now send for the horses forthwith.'

Jog was utterly disconcerted, and didn't know which way to turn for an excuse. Mrs. Jogglebury, though she would rather have been without the establishment, did not like to peril Gustavus James's prospects by appearing displeased; so she smilingly said she would see and do what they could.

Mr. Sponge then procured a messenger to take a note to Hanby House, for Mr. Leather, and having written it, amused himself for a time with his cigars and his *Mogg* in his bedroom, and then turned out to see the stable got ready, and pick up any information about the hounds, or anything else, from anybody he could lay hold of. As luck would have it, he fell in with a groom travelling a horse to hunt with Sir Harry Scattercash's hounds, which, he said, met at Snobston Green, some eight or nine miles off, the next day, and whither Mr. Sponge decided on going.

Mr. Jogglebury's equanimity returning at dinner time, Mr. Sponge was persuasive enough to induce him to accompany him, and it was finally arranged that Leather should go on with the horses, and Jog should drive Sponge to cover in the phe-*a*-ton.

XLVII

A FAMILY BREAKFAST ON A HUNTING MORNING

Mrs. Jogglebury Crowdey was a good deal disconcerted at Gustavus James's irreverence to his intended god-papa, and did her best, both by promises and entreaties, to bring him to a more becoming state of mind. She promised him abundance of good things if he would astonish Mr. Sponge with some of his wonderful stories, and expatiated on Mr. Sponge's goodness in bringing him the nice comfits, though Mrs. Jogglebury could not but in her heart blame them for some little internal inconvenience the wonder had experienced during the night. However, she brought him to breakfast in pretty good form, where he was cocked up in his high chair beside his mamma, the rest of the infantry occupying the position of the previous day, all under good-behaviour orders.

Unfortunately, Mr. Sponge, not having been able to get himself up to his satisfaction, was late in coming down; and when he did make his appearance, the unusual sight of a man in a red coat, a green tie, a blue vest, brown boots, &c., completely upset their propriety, and deranged the order of the young gentleman's performance. Mr. Sponge, too, conscious that he was late, was more eager for his breakfast than anxious to be astonished; so, what with repressing the demands of the youngster, watching that the others did not break loose, and getting Jog and Mr. Sponge what they wanted, Mrs. Crowdey had her hands full. At last, having got them set a-going, she took a lump of sugar out of the basin, and showing it to the wonder, laid it beside her plate, whispering 'Now, my beauty!' into his ear, as she adjusted him in his chair. The child, who had been wound up like a musical snuff-box, then went off as follows:

'Bah, bah, back sheep, have 'ou any 'ool? Ess, marry, have I, three bags full; Un for ye master, un for ye dame, Un for ye 'ittle boy 'ot 'uns about ye 'are.'

But unfortunately, Mr. Sponge was busy with his breakfast, and the prodigy wasted his sweetness on the desert air.

Mrs. Jogglebury, who had sat listening in ecstasies, saw the offended eye and pouting lip of the boy, and attempted to make up with exclamations of 'That *is* a clever fellow! That *is* a wonder!' at the same time showing him the sugar.

'A little more (puff) tea, my (wheeze) dear,' said Jogglebury, thrusting his great cup up the table.

'Hush! Jog, hush!' exclaimed Mrs. Crowdey, holding up her forefinger, and looking significantly first at him, and then at the urchin.

'Now, "Obin and Ichard," my darling,' continued she, addressing herself coaxingly to Gustavus James.

'No, *not* "Obin and Ichard,"' replied the child peevishly.

'Yes, my darling, *do*, that's a treasure.'

'Well, *my* (puff) darling, give me some (wheeze) tea,' interposed Jogglebury, knocking with his knuckles on the table.

'Oh, dear. Jog, you and your tea!—you're always wanting tea,' replied Mrs. Jogglebury snappishly.

'Well, but, my (puff) dear, you forget that Mr. (wheeze) Sponge and I have to be at (puff) Snobston Green at a (wheeze) quarter to eleven, and it's good twelve (gasp) miles off.'

'Well, but it'll not take you long to get there,' replied Mrs. Jogglebury; 'will it, Mr. Sponge?' continued she, again appealing to our friend.

'Sure I don't know,' replied Sponge, eating away; 'Mr. Crowdey finds conveyance—I only find company.'

Mrs. Jogglebury Crowdey then prepared to pour her husband out another cup of tea, and the musical snuff-box, being now left to itself, went off of its own accord with:

Diddle, diddle, doubt,
My candle's out.
My 'ittle dame's not at 'ome—
So saddle my hog, and bridle my dog
And bring my 'ittle dame, 'ome.'

A poem that in the original programme was intended to come in after 'Obin and Ichard,' which was to be the *chef-d'oeuvre.*

Mrs. Jog was delighted, and found herself pouring the tea into the sugar-basin instead of into Jog's cup.

Mr. Sponge, too, applauded. 'Well, that *was* very clever,' said he, filling his mouth with cold ham.

'"Saddle my dog, and bridle my hog"—I'll trouble you for another cup of tea,' addressing Mrs. Crowdey.

'No, not "saddle my dog," sil-l-e-y man!' drawled the child, making a pet lip: '"saddle my *hog.*"'

'Oh! "saddle my hog," was it?' replied Mr. Sponge, with apparent surprise; 'I thought it was "saddle my dog." I'll trouble you for the sugar, Mrs. Jogglebury'; adding, 'you have devilish good cream here; how many cows have you?'

'Cows (puff), cows (wheeze)?' replied Jogglebury; 'how many cows?' repeated he.

'Oh, *two,*' replied Mrs. Jogglebury tartly, vexed at the interruption.

'Pardon me (puff),' replied Jogglebury slowly and solemnly, with a full blow into his frill; 'pardon me, Mrs. (puff) Jogglebury (wheeze) Crowdey, but there are *three* (wheeze).'

'Not in milk, Jog—not in milk,' retorted Mrs. Crowdey.

'Three cows, Mrs. (puff) Jogglebury (wheeze) Crowdey, notwithstanding,' rejoined our host.

'Well; but when people talk of cream, and ask how many cows you have, they mean in milk, *Mister* Jogglebury Crowdey.'

'Not necessarily. Mistress Jogglebury Crowdey,' replied the pertinacious Jog, with another heavy snort. 'Ah, now you're coming your fine poor-law guardian knowledge,' rejoined his wife. Jog was chairman of the Stir-it-stiff Union.

While this was going on, young hopeful was sitting cocked up in his high chair, evidently mortified at the want of attention.

Mrs. Crowdey saw how things were going, and turning from the cow question, endeavoured to re-engage him in his recitations.

'Now, my angel!' exclaimed she, again showing him the sugar; 'tell us about "Obin and Ichard."'

'No—not "Obin and Ichard,"' pouted the child.

'Oh yes, my sweet, *do,* that's a good child; the gentleman in the pretty coat, who gives baby the nice things, wants to hear it.'

'Come, out with it, young man!' exclaimed Mr. Sponge, now putting a large piece of cold beef into his mouth.

'Not a 'ung man,' muttered the child, bursting out a-crying, and extending his little fat arms to his mamma.

'No, my angel, not a 'ung man yet,' replied Mrs. Jogglebury, taking him out of the chair, and hugging him to her bosom.

'He'll be a man before his mother for all that,' observed Mr. Sponge, nothing disconcerted by the noise.

Jog had now finished his breakfast, and having pocketed three buns and two pieces of toast, with a thick layer of cold ham between them, looked at his great warming-pan of a watch, and said to his guest, 'When you're (wheeze), I'm (puff).' So saying he got up, and gave his great legs one or two convulsive shakes, as if to see that they were on.

Mrs. Jogglebury looked reproachfully at him, as much as to say, 'How *can* you behave so?'

Mr. Sponge, as he eyed Jog's ill-made, queerly put on garments, wished that he had not desired Leather to go to the meet. It would have been better to have got the horses a little way off, and have shirked Jog, who did not look like a desirable introducer to a hunting field.

'I'll be with you directly,' replied Mr. Sponge, gulping down the remains of his tea; adding, 'I've just got to run upstairs and get a cigar.' So saying, he jumped up and disappeared.

Murry Ann, not approving of Sponge's smoking in his bedroom, had hid the cigar-case under the toilet cover, at the back of the glass, and it was some time before he found it.

Mrs. Jogglebury availed herself of the lapse of time, and his absence, to pacify her young Turk, and try to coax him into reciting the marvellous 'Obin and Ichard.'

As Mr. Sponge came clanking downstairs with the cigar-case in his hand, she met him (accidentally, of course) at the bottom, with the boy in her arms, and exclaimed, 'O, Mr. Sponge, here's Gustavus James wants to tell you a little story.'

Mr. Sponge stopped—inwardly hoping that it would not be a long one.

'Now, my darling,' said she, sticking the boy up straight to get him to begin.

'Now, then!' exclaimed Mr. Crowdey, in the true Jehu-like style, from the vehicle at the door, in which he had composed himself.

'Coming, Jog! coming!' replied Mrs. Crowdey, with a frown on her brow at the untimely interruption; then appealing again to the child, who was nestling in his mother's bosom, as if disinclined to show off, she said, 'Now, my darling, let the gentleman hear how nicely you'll say it.'

The child still slunk.

'That's a fine fellow, out with it!' said Mr. Sponge, taking up his hat to be off.

'Now, then!' exclaimed his host again.

'Coming!' replied Mr. Sponge.

As if to thwart him, the child then began, Mrs. Jogglebury holding up her forefinger as well in admiration as to keep silence:

Obin and Ichard, two pretty men,
Lay in bed till 'e clock struck ten;
Up starts Obin, and looks at the sky—'

And then the brat stopped.

'Very beautiful!' exclaimed Mr. Sponge; 'very beautiful! One of Moore's, isn't it? Thank you, my little dear, thank you,' added he, chucking him under the chin, and putting on his hat to be off.

'O, but stop, Mr. Sponge!' exclaimed Mrs. Jogglebury, 'you haven't heard it all—there's more yet.'

Then turning to the child, she thus attempted to give him the cue.

'O, ho! bother—'

'Now, then! time's hup!' again shouted Jogglebury into the passage.

'O, dear, Mr. Jogglebury, will you hold your stoopid tongue!' exclaimed she, adding, 'you certainly are the most tiresome man under the sun.' She then turned to the child with:

'O, ho! bother Ichard' again.

But the child was mute, and Mr. Sponge fearing, from some indistinct growling that proceeded from the carriage, that a storm was brewing, endeavoured to cut short the entertainment by exclaiming:

'Wonderful two-year-old! Pity he's not in the Darby. Dare say he'll tell me the rest when I come back.'

But this only added fuel to the fire of Mrs. Jogglebury's ardour, and made her more anxious that Sponge should not lose a word of it. Accordingly she gave the fat dumpling another jerk up on her arm, and repeated:

'O ho! bother Ichard, the—What's very high?' asked Mrs. Jogglebury coaxingly.

'Sun's very high,' replied the child.

'Yes, my darling!' exclaimed the delighted mamma. Mrs. Jogglebury then proceeded with:

MAMMA—'Ou go before—'

CHILD.—'With bottle and bag,'

MAMMA.—'And I'll follow after—'

CHILD.—'With 'ittle Jack Nag.'

'Well now, that *is* wonderful!' exclaimed Mr. Sponge, hurrying on his dog-skin gloves, and wishing both Obin and Ichard farther.

'Isn't it!' exclaimed Mrs. Jogglebury, in ecstasies; then addressing the child, she said, 'Now that *is* a good boy—that *is* a fine fellow. Now couldn't he say it all over by himself, doesn't he think?' Mrs. Jogglebury looking at Sponge, as if she was meditating the richest possible treat for him.

'Oh,' replied Mr. Sponge, quite tired of the detention, 'he'll tell me it when I return—he'll tell me it when I return,' at the same time giving the child another parting chuck under the chin. But the child was not to be put off in that way, and instead of crouching, and nestling, and hiding its face, it looked up quite boldly, and after a little hesitation went through 'Obin and Ichard,' to the delight of Mrs. Jogglebury, the mortification of Sponge, and the growling denunciations of old Jog, who still kept his place in the vehicle. Mr. Sponge could not but stay the poem out.

At last they got started, Jog driving. Sponge occupying the low seat, Jog's flail and Sponge's cane whip-stick stuck in the straps of the apron. Jog was very crusty at first, and did little but whip and flog the old horse, and puff and growl about being late, keeping people waiting, over-driving the horse, and so on.

'Have a cigar?' at last asked Sponge, opening the well-filled case, and tendering that olive branch to his companion.

'Cigar (wheeze), cigar (puff)?' replied Jog, eyeing the case; 'why, no, p'raps not, I think (wheeze), thank'e.'

'Do you never smoke?' asked Sponge.

'(Puff—wheeze) Not often,' replied Jogglebury, looking about him with an air of indifference. He did not like to say no, because Springwheat smoked, though Mrs. Springey highly disapproved of it.

'You'll find them very mild,' observed Sponge, taking one out for himself, and again tendering the case to his friend.

'Mild (wheeze), mild (puff), are they?' said Jog, thinking he would try one.

Mr. Sponge then struck a light, and, getting his own cigar well under way, lit one for his friend, and presented it to him. They then went puffing, and whipping, and smoking in silence. Jog spoke first. 'I'm going to be (puff) sick,' observed he, slowly and solemnly.

'Hope not,' replied Mr. Sponge, with a hearty whiff, up into the air.

'I *am* going to be (puff) sick,' observed Jog, after another pause.

'Be sick on your own side, then,' replied Sponge, with another hearty whiff.

'By the (puff) powers! I *am* (puff) sick!' exclaimed Jogglebury, after another pause, and throwing away the cigar. 'Oh, dear!' exclaimed he, 'you shouldn't have given me that nasty (puff) thing.'

'My dear fellow, I didn't know it would make you sick,' replied Mr. Sponge.

'Well, but (puff) if they (wheeze) other people sick, in all (puff) probability they'll (wheeze) me. There!' exclaimed he, pulling up again.

The delays occasioned by these catastrophes, together with the time lost by 'Obin and Ichard,' threw our sportsmen out considerably. When they reached Chalkerley Gate it wanted ten minutes to eleven, and they had still three miles to go.

'We shall be late,' observed Sponge inwardly denouncing 'Obin and Ichard.'

'Shouldn't wonder,' replied Jog, adding, with a puff into his frill, 'consequences of making me sick, you see.'

'My dear fellow, if you don't know your own stomach by this time, you did ought to do,' replied Mr. Sponge.

'I (puff) flatter myself I *do* (wheeze) my own stomach,' replied Jogglebury tartly.

They then rumbled on for some time in silence.

When they came within sight of Snobston Green, the coast was clear. Not a red coat, or hunting indication of any sort, was to be seen.

'I told you so (puff)!' growled Jog, blowing full into his frill, and pulling up short.

'They be gone to Hackberry Dean,' said an old man, breaking stones by the roadside.

'Hackberry Dean (puff)—Hackberry Dean (wheeze)!' replied Jog thoughtfully; 'then we must (puff) by Tollarton Mill, and through the (wheeze) village to Stewley?' 'Y-e-a-z,' drawled the man.

Jog then drove on a few paces, and turned up a lane to the left, whose finger-post directed the road 'to Tollarton.' He seemed less disconcerted than Sponge, who kept inwardly anathematizing, not only 'Obin and Ichard,' but 'Diddle, diddle, doubt'—'Bah, bah, black sheep'—the whole tribe of nursery ballads, in short.

The fact was, Jog wanted to be into Hackberry Dean, which was full of fine, straight hollies, fit either for gibbeys or whip-sticks, and the hounds being there gave him the entree. It was for helping himself there, without this excuse, that he had been 'county-courted,' and he did not care to renew his acquaintance with the judge. He now whipped and jagged the old nag, as if intent on catching the hounds. Mr. Sponge liberated his whip from the apron-straps, and lent a hand when Jog began to flag. So they rattled and jingled away at an amended pace. Still it seemed to Mr. Sponge as if they would never get there. Having passed through Tollarton, and cleared the village of Stewley, Mr. Sponge strained his eyes in every direction where there was a bit of wood, in hopes of seeing something of the hounds. Meanwhile Jog was shuffling his little axe from below the cushion of the driving-seat into the pocket of his great-coat. All of a sudden he pulled up, as they were passing a bank of wood (Hackberry Dean), and handing the reins to his companion, said:

'Just lay hold for a minute whilst I (puff) out.'

'What's happened?' asked Sponge. 'Not sick again, are you?'

'No (puff), not exactly (wheeze) sick, but I want to be out all the (puff) same.'

So saying, out he bundled, and, crushing through the fern-grown woodbiney fence, darted into the wood in a way that astonished our hero. Presently the chop, chop, chop of the axe revealed the mystery.

'By the powers, the fool's at his sticks!' exclaimed Sponge, disgusted at the *contretemps*. 'Mister Jogglebury!' roared he, 'Mister Jogglebury, we shall never catch up the hounds at this rate!'

But Jog was deaf—chop, chop, chop was all the answer Mr. Sponge got.

'Well, hang me if ever I saw such a fellow!' continued Sponge, thinking he would drive on if he only knew the way.

'Chop, chop, chop,' continued the axe.

'Mister Jogglebury! Mister Jogglebury Crowdey *a-hooi*!' roared Sponge, at the top of his voice.

The axe stopped. 'Anybody comin'?' resounded from the wood.

'*You come*,' replied Mr. Sponge.

'Presently,' was the answer; and the chop, chop, chopping was resumed.

'The man's mad,' muttered Mr. Sponge, throwing himself back in the seat. At length Jog appeared, brushing and tearing his way out of the wood, with two fine hollies under his arm. He was running down with perspiration, and looked anxiously up and down the road as he blundered through the fence to see if there was any one coming.

'I really think (puff) this will make a four-in-hander (wheeze),' exclaimed he, as he advanced towards the carriage, holding a holly so as to show its full length—'not that I (puff, wheeze, gasp) do much in that (puff, wheeze) line, but really it is such a (puff, wheeze) beauty that I couldn't (puff, wheeze, gasp) resist it.'

'Well, but I thought we were going to hunt,' observed Mr. Sponge dryly.

'Hunt (puff)! so we are (wheeze); but there are no hounds (gasp). My good (puff) man,' continued he, addressing a smock-frocked countryman, who now came up, 'have you seen anything of the (wheeze) hounds?'

'E-e-s,' replied the man. 'They be gone to Brookdale Plantin'.'

'Then we'd better (puff) after them,' said Jog, running the stick through the apron-straps, and bundling into the phaeton with the long one in his hand.

Away they rattled and jingled as before.

'How far is it?' asked Mr. Sponge, vexed at the detention.

'Oh (puff), close by (wheeze),' replied Jog.

'Close by,' as most of our sporting readers well know to their cost, is generally anything but close by. Nor was Jog's close by, close by on this occasion.

'There,' said Jog, after they had got crawled up Trampington Hill; 'that's it (puff) to the right, by the (wheeze) water there,' pointing to a plantation about a mile off, with a pond shining at the end.

Just as Mr. Sponge caught view of the water, the twang of a horn was heard, and the hounds came pouring, full cry, out of cover, followed by about twenty variously clad horsemen, and our friend had the satisfaction of seeing them run clean out of sight, over as fine a country as ever was crossed. Worst of all, he thought he saw Leather pounding away on the chestnut.

XLVIII

Hunting the Hounds

TRAMPTINTON HILL, WHOSE SUMMIT THEY had just reached as the hounds broke cover, commanded an extensive view over the adjoining vale, and, as Mr. Sponge sat shading his eyes with his hands from a bright wintry sun, he thought he saw them come to a check, and afterwards bend to the left.

'I really think,' said he, addressing his still perspiring companion, 'that if you were to make for that road on the left' (pointing one out as seen between the low hedge-rows in the distance), 'we might catch them up yet.'

'Left (puff), left (wheeze)?' replied Mr. Jogglebury Crowdey, staring about with anything but the quickness that marked his movements when he dived into Hackberry Dean.

'Don't you see,' asked Sponge tartly, 'there's a road by the corn-stacks yonder?' pointing them out.

'I see,' replied Jogglebury, blowing freely into his shirt-frill. 'I see,' repeated he, staring that way; 'but I think (puff) that's a mere (wheeze) occupation road, leading to (gasp) nowhere.'

'Never mind, let's try!' exclaimed Mr. Sponge, giving the rein a jerk, to get the horse into motion again; adding, 'it's no use sitting here, you know, like a couple of fools, when the hounds are running.'

'Couple of (puff)!' growled Jog, not liking the appellation, and wishing to be home with the long holly. 'I don't see anything (wheeze) foolish in the (puff) business.'

'There they are!' exclaimed Mr. Sponge, who had kept his eye on the spot he last viewed them, and now saw the horsemen titt-up-ing across a grass field in the easy way that distance makes very uneasy riding look. 'Cut along!' exclaimed he, laying into the horse's hind-quarters with his hunting-whip.

'Don't! the horse is (puff) tired,' retorted Jog angrily, holding the horse, instead of letting him go to Sponge's salute.

'Not a bit on't!' exclaimed Sponge; 'fresh as paint! Spring him a bit, that's a good fellow!' added he.

Jog didn't fancy being dictated to in this way, and just crawled along at his own pace, some six miles an hour, his dull phlegmatic face contrasting with the eager excitement of Mr. Sponge's countenance. If it had not been that Jog wanted to see that Leather did not play any tricks with his horse, he would not have gone a yard to please Mr. Sponge. Jog might, however, have been easy on that score, for Leather had just buckled the curb-rein of the horse's bridle round a tree in the plantations where they found, and the animal, being used to this sort of work, had fallen-to quite contentedly upon the grass within reach.

Bilkington Pike now appeared in view, and Jog drew in as he spied it. He knew the damage: sixpence for carriages, and he doubted that Sponge would pay it.

'It's no use going any (wheeze) farther,' observed he, drawing up into a walk, as he eyed the red-brick gable end of the toll-house, and the formidable white gate across the road.

Tom Coppers had heard the hounds, and, knowing the hurry sportsmen are often in, had taken the precaution to lock the gate.

'Just a *leetle* farther!' exclaimed Mr. Sponge soothingly, whose anxiety in looking after the hounds had prevented his seeing this formidable impediment. 'If you would just drive up to that farmhouse on the hill,' pointing to one about half a mile off, 'I think we should be able to decide whether it's worth going on or not.'

'Well (puff), well (wheeze), well (gasp),' pondered Jogglebury, still staring at the gate, 'if you (puff) think it's worth (wheeze) while going through the (gasp) gate,' nodding towards it as he spoke.

'Oh, never mind the gate,' replied Mr. Sponge, with an ostentatious dive into his breeches pocket, as if he was going to pay it.

He kept his hand in his pocket till he came close up to the gate, when, suddenly drawing it out, he said:

'Oh, hang it! I've left my purse at home! Never mind, drive on,' said he to his host; exclaiming to the man, 'it's Mr. Crowdey's carriage—Mr. Jogglebury Crowdey's carriage! Mr. Crowdey, the chairman of the Stir-it-stiff Poor-Law Union!'

'Sixpence!' shouted the man, following the phaeton with outstretched hand.

''Ord, hang it (puff)! I could have done that (wheeze),' growled Jogglebury, pulling up.

'You harn't got no ticket,' said Coppers, coming up, 'and ain't a-goin' to not never no meetin' o' trustees, are you?' asked he, seeing the importance of the person with whom he had to deal;—a trustee of that and other roads, and one who always availed himself of his privilege of going to the meetings toll-free.

'No,' replied Jog, pompously handing Sponge the whip and reins.

He then rose deliberately from his seat, and slowly unbuttoned each particular button of the brown great-coat he had over the tight black hunting one. He then unbuttoned the black, and next the right-hand pocket of the white moleskins, in which he carried his money. He then deliberately fished up his green-and-gold purse, a souvenir of Miss Smiler (the plaintiff in the breach-of-promise action, Smiler v. Jogglebury), and holding it with both hands before his eyes, to see which end contained the silver, he slowly drew the slide, and took out a shilling, though there were plenty of sixpences in.

This gave the man an errand into the toll-house to get one, and, by way of marking his attention, when he returned he said, in the negative way that country people put a question:

'You'll not need a ticket, will you?'

'Ticket (puff), ticket (wheeze)?' repeated Jog thoughtfully. 'Yes, I'll take a ticket,' said he.

'Oh! hang it, no,' replied Sponge; 'let's get on!' stamping against the bottom of the phaeton to set the horse a-going. 'Costs nothin',' observed Jog drily, drawing the reins, as the man again returned to the gate-house.

A considerable delay then took place; first, Pikey had to find his glasses, as he called his spectacles, to look out a one-horse-chaise ticket.

Then he had to look out the tickets, when he found he had all sorts except a one-horse-chaise one ready—waggons, hearses, mourning-coaches, saddle-horses, chaises and pair, mules, asses, every sort but the one that was wanted. Well, then he had to fill one up, and to do this he had, first, to find the ink-horn, and then a pen that would 'mark,' so that, altogether, a delay took place that would have been peculiarly edifying to a Kennington Common or Lambeth gate-keeper to witness.

But it was not all over yet. Having got the ticket Jog examined it minutely, to see that it was all right, then held it to his nose to smell it, and ultimately drew the purse slide, and deposited it among the sovereigns. He then restored that expensive trophy to his pocket, shook his leg, to send it down, then buttoned the pocket, and took the tight black coat with both hands and dragged it across his chest, so as to get his stomach in. He then gasped and held his breath, making himself as small as possible, while he coaxed the buttons into the holes; and that difficult process being at length accomplished, he stood still awhile to take breath after the exertion. Then he began to rebutton the easy, brown great-coat, going deliberately up the whole series, from the small button below, to keep the laps together, up to the one on the neck, or where the neck would have been if Jog had not been all stomach up to the chin. He then soused himself into his seat, and, snorting heavily through his nostrils, took the reins and whip and long holly from Mr. Sponge, and drove leisurely on. Sponge sat anathematizing his slowness.

When they reached the farmhouse on the hill the hounds were fairly in view. The huntsman was casting them, and the horsemen were grouped about as usual, while the laggers were stealing quietly up the lanes and by-roads, thinking nobody would see them. Save the whites or the greys, our friends in the 'chay' were not sufficiently near to descry the colours of the horses; but Mr. Sponge could not help thinking that he recognized the outline of the wicked chestnut, Multum-in-Parvo.

'By the powers, but if it is him,' muttered he to himself, clenching his fist and grinding his teeth as he spoke, 'but I'll—I'll—I'll make *sich* an example of you,' meaning of Leather.

Mr. Sponge could not exactly say what he would do, for it was by no means a settled point whether Leather or he were master. But to the hounds. If it had not been for Mr. Sponge's shabbiness at the turnpike gate, we really believe he might now have caught them up, for the road to them was down hill all the way, and the impetus of the vehicle would have sent the old screw along. That delay, however, was fatal. Before they had gone a quarter of the distance the hounds suddenly struck the scent at a hedge-row, and, with heads up and sterns down, went straight away at a pace that annihilated all hope. They were out of sight in a minute. It was clearly a case of kill.

'Well, there's a go!' exclaimed Mr. Sponge, folding his arms, and throwing himself back in the phaeton in disgust. 'I think I never saw such a mess as we've made this morning.'

And he looked at the stick in the apron, and the long holly between Jog's legs, and longed to lay them about his great back.

'Well (puff), I s'pose (wheeze) we may as well (puff) home now?' observed Jog, looking about him quite unconcernedly.

'I think so,' snapped Sponge, adding, 'we've done it for once, at all events.'

The observation, however, was lost upon Jog, whose mind was occupied with thinking how to get the phaeton round without upsetting. The road was narrow at best, and the newly laid stone-heaps had encroached upon its bounds. He first tried to back between two stone-heaps, but only succeeded in running a wheel into one; he then tried the forward tack, with no better success, till Mr. Sponge seeing matters were getting worse, just jumped out, and taking the old horse by the head, executed the manoeuvre that Mr. Jogglebury Crowdey first attempted. They then commenced retracing their steps, rather a long trail, even for people in an amiable mood, but a terribly long one for disagreeing ones.

Jog, to be sure, was pretty comfortable. He had got all he wanted—all he went out a-hunting for; and as he hissed and jerked the old horse along, he kept casting an eye at the contents of the apron, thinking what crowned, or great man's head, the now rough, club-headed knobs should be fashioned to represent; and indulged in speculations as to their prospective worth and possible destination. He had not the slightest doubt that a thousand sticks to each of his children would be as good as a couple of thousand pounds a-piece; sometimes he thought more, but never less. Mr. Sponge, on the other hand, brooded over the loss of the run; indulged in all sorts of speculations as to the splendour of the affair; pictured the figure he would have cut on the chestnut, and the price he might have got for him in the field. Then he thought of the bucketing Leather would give him; the way he would ram him at everything; how he would let him go with a slack rein in the deep—very likely making him over-reach—nay, there was no saying but he might stake him.

Then he thought over all the misfortunes and mishaps of the day. The unpropitious toilet; the aggravation of 'Obin and Ichard'; the delay caused by Jog being sick with his cigar; the divergence into Hackberry Dean; and the long protracted wait at the toll-bar. Reviewing all the circumstances fairly and dispassionately, Mr. Sponge came to the determination of having nothing more to do with Mr. Jogglebury Crowdey in the hunting way. These, or similar cogitations and resolutions were, at length, interrupted by their arriving at home, as denoted by an outburst of children rushing from the lodge to receive them—Gustavus James, in his nurse's arms, bringing up the rear, to whom our friend could hardly raise the semblance of a smile.

It was all that little brat! thought he.

XLIX

COUNTRY QUARTERS

Sᴉʀ Hᴀʀʀʏ Sᴄᴀᴛᴛᴇʀᴄᴀsʜ's ᴡᴇʀᴇ ᴏɴʟʏ an ill-supported pack of hounds; they were not kept upon any fixed principles. We do not mean to say that they had not plenty to eat, but their management was only of the scrimmaging order. Sir Harry was what is technically called 'going it.' Like our noble friend, Lord Hard-up, now Earl of Scamperdale, he had worked through the morning of life without knowing what it was to be troubled with money; but, unlike his lordship, now that he had unexpectedly come into some, he seemed bent upon trying how fast he could get through it. In this laudable endeavour he was ably assisted by Lady Scattercash, late the lovely and elegant Miss Spangles, of the 'Theatre Royal, Sadler's Wells.' Sir Harry had married her before his windfall made him a baronet, having, at the time, some intention of trying his luck on the stage, but he always declared that he never regretted his choice; on the contrary, he said, if he had gone among the 'duchesses,' he could not have suited himself better. Lady Scattercash could ride—indeed, she used to do scenes in the circle (two horses and a flag)—and she could drive, and smoke, and sing, and was possessed of many other accomplishments. Sir Harry would sometimes drink straight on end for a week, and then not taste wine again for a month; sometimes the hounds hunted, and sometimes they did not; sometimes they were advertised, and sometimes they were not; sometimes they went out on one day, and sometimes on another; sometimes they were fixed to be at such a place, and went to quite a different one. When Sir Harry was on a drinking-bout they were shut up altogether; and the huntsman, Tom Watchorn, late of the 'Camberwell and Balham Hill Union Harriers,' an early acquaintance of Miss Spangles—indeed, some said he was her uncle—used to go away on a drinking excursion too. Altogether, they were what the country people called a very 'promiscuous set.' The hounds were of all sorts and sizes; the horses of no particular stamp; and the men scamps and vagabonds of the first class.

With such a master and such an establishment, we need hardly say that no stranger ever came into the country for the purpose of hunting. Sir Harry's fields were entirely composed of his own choice 'set,' and a few farmers, and people whom he could abuse and do what he liked with. Mr. Jogglebury Crowdey, to be sure, had mentioned Sir Harry approvingly, when he went to Mr. Puffington's, to inveigle Mr. Sponge over to Puddingpote Bower; but what might suit Mr. Jogglebury, who went out to seek gibbey sticks, might not suit a person who went out for the purpose of hunting a fox in order to show off and sell his horses. In fact, Puddingpote Bower was an exceedingly bad hunting quarter, as things turned out. Sir Harry Scattercash, having had the run described in our two preceding chapters, and having just imported a few of the 'sock-and-buskin' sort from town, was not likely to be going out again for a time; while Mr. Puffington, finding where Mr. Sponge had taken refuge, determined not to meet within reach of Puddingpote Bower, if he could possibly help it; and Lord Scamperdale was almost always beyond distance, unless horse and rider lay out over-night—a proceeding always deprecated by prudent sportsmen. Mr. Sponge, therefore, got more of Mr. Jogglebury Crowdey's company than he wanted, and Mr. Crowdey got more of Mr. Sponge's than he desired. In vain Jog took him up into his attics and his closets, and his various holes and corners, and showed him his enormous stock of sticks—some tied in sheaves, like corn; some put up more sparingly; and others, again, wrapped in silver paper, with their valuable heads enveloped in old gloves. Jog would untie the strings of these, and placing the heads in the most favourable position before our friend, just as an artist would a portrait, question him as to whom he thought they were.

'There, now (puff),' said he, holding up one that he thought there could be no mistake about; 'who do you (wheeze) that is?'

'Deaf Burke,' replied Mr. Sponge, after a stare.

'*Deaf Burke*! (puff),' replied Jog indignantly.

'Who is it, then?' asked Mr. Sponge.

'Can't you see? (wheeze),' replied Jog tartly.

'No,' replied Sponge, after another examination. 'It's not Scroggins, is it?'

'Napoleon (puff) Bonaparte,' replied Jog, with great dignity, returning the head to the glove.

He showed several others, with little better success, Mr. Sponge seeming rather to take a pleasure in finding ridiculous likenesses, instead of helping his host out in his conceits. The stick-mania was a failure, as far as Mr. Sponge was concerned. Neither were the peregrinations about the farms, or ter-ri-to-ry, as Jog called his estate, more successful; a man's estate, like his children, being seldom of much interest to any but himself.

Jog and Sponge were soon most heartily sick of each other. Nor did Mrs. Jog's charms, nor the voluble enunciation of 'Obin and Ichard,' followed by 'Bah, bah, black sheep,' &c, from that wonderful boy, Gustavus James, mend matters; for the young rogue having been in Mr. Sponge's room while Murry Ann was doing it out, had torn the back off Sponge's *Mogg*, and made such a mess of his tooth-brush, by cleaning his shoes with it, as never was seen.

Mr. Sponge soon began to think it was not worth while staying at Puddingpote Bower for the mere sake of his keep, seeing there was no hunting to be had from it, and it did not do to keep hack hunters idle, especially in open weather. Leather and he, for once, were of the same opinion, and that worthy shook his head, and said Mr. Crowdey was 'awful mean,' at the same time pulling out a sample of bad ship oats, that he had got from a neighbouring ostler, to show the 'stuff' their 'osses' were a eatin' of. The fact was, Jog's beer was nothing like so strong as Mr. Puffington's; added to which, Mr. Crowdey carried the principles of the poor-law union into his own establishment, and dieted his servants upon certain rules. Sunday, roast beef, potatoes, and pudding under the meat; Monday, fried beef, and stick-jaw (as they profanely called a certain pudding); Wednesday, leg of mutton, and so on. The allowance of beer was a pint and a half *per diem* to Bartholomew, and a pint to each woman; and Mr. Crowdey used to observe from the head of the servants' dinner-table on the arrival of each cargo, 'Now this (puff) beer is to (wheeze) a month, and, if you choose to drink it in a (gasp) day, you'll go without any for the rest of the (wheeze) time'; an intimation

that had a very favourable effect upon the tap. Mr. Leather, however, did not like it. 'Puffington's servants,' he said, 'had beer whenever they chose,' and he thought it 'awful mean' restricting the quantity. Mr. Jog, however, was not to be moved. Thus time crawled heavily on.

Mr. and Mrs. Jog had a long confab one night on the expediency of getting rid of Mr. Sponge. Mrs. Jog wanted to keep him on till after the christening; while Jog combated her reasons by representing the improbability of its doing Gustavus James any good having him for a godpapa, seeing Sponge's age, and the probability of his marrying himself. Mrs. Jog, however, was very determined; rather too much so, indeed, for she awakened Jog's jealousy, who lay tossing and tumbling about all through the night.

He was up very early, and as Mrs. Jog was falling into a comfortable nap, she was aroused by his well-known voice hallooing as loud as he could in the middle of the entrance-passage.

'BARTHOLO-*me-e-w*!' the last syllable being pronounced or prolonged like a mew of a cat. 'BARTHOLO-*me-e-w*!' repeated he, not getting an answer to the first shout.

'MURRY ANN!' shouted he, after another pause.

'MURRY ANN!' exclaimed he, still louder.

Just then, the iron latch of a door at the top of the house opened, and a female voice exclaimed hurriedly over the banisters:

'Yes, sir! here, sir! comin' sir! comin'!'

'Oh, Murry Ann (puff), that's (wheeze) you, is it?' asked Jog, still speaking at the top of his voice.

'Yes, sir,' replied Mary Ann.

'Oh! then, Murry Ann, I wanted to (puff)—that you'd better get the (puff) breakfast ready early. I think Mr. (gasp)—Sponge will be (wheezing) away to-day.'

'Yes, sir,' replied Mary Ann.

All this was said in such a tone as could not fail to be heard all over the house; certainly into Mr. Sponge's room, which was midway between the speakers.

What prevented Mr. Sponge wheezing away, will appear in the next chapter.

L

SIR HARRY SCATTERCASH'S HOUNDS

THE REASON MR. SPONGE DID not take his departure, after the pretty intelligible hint given by his host, was that, as he was passing his shilling army razor over his soapy chin, he saw a stockingless lad, in a purply coat and faded hunting-cap, making his way up to the house, at a pace that betokened more than ordinary vagrancy. It was the kennel, stable, and servants' hall courier of Nonsuch House, come to say that Sir Harry hunted that day.

Presently Mr. Leather knocked at Mr. Sponge's bedroom door, and, being invited in, announced the fact.

'Sir 'Arry's 'ounds 'unt,' said he, twisting the door handle as he spoke.

'What time?' asked Mr. Sponge, with his half-shaven face turned towards him.

'Meet at eleven,' replied Leather.

'Where?' inquired Mr. Sponge.

'Nonsuch House, 'bout nine miles off.'

It was thirteen, but Mr. Leather heard the malt liquor was good and wanted to taste it.

'Take on the brown, then,' said Mr. Sponge, quite pompously; 'and tell Bartholomew to have the hack at the door at ten—or say a quarter to. Tell him, I'll lick him for every minute he's late; and, mind, don't let old Rory O'More here know,' meaning our friend Jog, 'or he may take a fancy to go, and we shall never get there,' alluding to their former excursion.

'No, no,' replied Mr. Leather, leaving the room.

Mr. Sponge then arrayed himself in his hunting costume—scarlet coat, green tie, blue vest, gosling-coloured cords, and brown tops; and was greeted with a round of applause from the little Jogs as he entered the breakfast-room. Gustavus James would handle him; and, considering that his paws were all over raspberry jam, our friend would as soon have dispensed with his attentions. Mrs. Jog was all smiles, and Jog all scowls.

A little after ten our friend, cigar in mouth, was in the saddle. Mrs. Jog, with Gustavus James in her arms, and all the children clustering about, stood in the passage to see him start, and watch the capers and caprioles of the piebald, as he ambled down the avenue.

'Nine miles—nine miles,' muttered Mr. Sponge to himself, as he passed through the Lodge and turned up the Quarryburn road; 'do it in an hour well enough,' said he, sticking spurs into the hack, and cantering away.

Having kept this pace up for about five miles, till he thought from the view he had taken of the map it was about time to be turning, he hailed a blacksmith in his shop, who, next to saddlers, are generally the most intelligent people about hounds, and asked how far it was to Sir Harry's?

'Eight miles,' replied the man, in a minute. 'Impossible!' exclaimed Mr. Sponge. 'It was only nine at starting, and I've come I don't know how many.'

The next person Mr. Sponge met told him it was ten miles; the third, after asking him where he had come from, said he was a stranger in the country, and had never heard of the place; and, what with Mr. Leather's original mis-statement, misdirections from other people, and mistakes of his own, it was more good luck than good management that got Mr. Sponge to Nonsuch House in time.

The fact was, the whole hunt was knocked up in a hurry. Sir Harry, and the choice spirits by whom he was surrounded, had not finished celebrating the triumphs of the Snobston Green day, and as it was not likely that the hounds would be out again soon, the people of the hunting establishment were taking their ease. Watchorn had gone to be entertained at a public supper, given by the poachers and fox-stealers of the village of Bark-shot, as a 'mark of respect for his abilities as a sportsman and his integrity as a man,' meaning his indifference to his master's interests; while the first-whip had gone to visit his aunt, and the groom was away negotiating the exchange of a cow. With things in this state, Wily Tom of Tinklerhatch, a noted fox-stealer in Lord Scamperdale's country, had arrived with a great thundering dog fox, stolen from his lordship's cover near the cross roads at Dallington Burn, which being communicated to our friends about midnight in the smoking-room at Nonsuch House, it was resolved to hunt him forthwith, especially as one of the guests, Mr. Orlando Bugles, of the Surrey Theatre, was obliged to return to town immediately, and, as he sometimes enacted the part of Squire Tallyho, it was thought a little of the reality might correct the Tom and Jerry style in which he did it. Accordingly, orders were issued for a hunt, notwithstanding the hounds were fed and the horses watered. Sir Harry didn't 'care a rap; let them go as fast as they could.'

All these circumstances conspired to make them late; added to which, when Watchorn, the huntsman, cast up, which he did on a higgler's horse, he found the only sound one in his stud had gone to the neighbouring town to get some fiddlers—her ladyship having determined to compliment Mr. Bugles' visit by a quadrille party. Bugles and she were old friends. When Mr. Sponge cast up at half-past eleven, things were still behindhand.

Sir Harry and party had had a wet night of it, and were all more or less drunk. They had kept up the excitement with a champagne breakfast and various liqueurs, to say nothing of cigars. They were a sad, debauched-looking set, some of them scarcely out of their teens, with pallid cheeks, trembling hands, sunken eyes, and all the symptoms of premature decay. Others—the sock-and-buskin ones—were a made-up, wigged, and padded set. Bugles was resplendent. He had on a dress scarlet coat, lined and faced with yellow satin (one of the properties, we believe, of the Victoria), a beautifully worked pink shirt-front, a pitch-plaster coloured waistcoat, white ducks, and jack-boots, with brass heel spurs. He carried his whip in the arm's-length-way of a circus master following a horse. Some dozen of these curiosities were staggering, and swaggering, and smoking in front of Nonsuch House, to the edification of a lot of gaping grooms and chawbacons, when Mr. Sponge cantered becomingly up on the piebald. Lady Scattercash, with several elegantly dressed females, all with cigars in their mouths, were conversing with them from the open drawing-room windows above, while sundry good-looking damsels ogled them from the attics above. Such was the *tableau* that presented itself to Mr. Sponge as he cantered round the turn that brought him in front of the Elizabethan mansion of Nonsuch House.

Sir Harry, who was still rather drunk, thinking that every person there must be either one of his party, or a friend of one of his party, or a neighbour, or some one that he had seen before, reeled up to our friend as he stopped, and, shaking him heartily by the hand, asked him to come in and have something to eat. This was a godsend to Mr. Sponge, who accepted the proffered hand most readily, shaking it in a way that quite satisfied Sir Harry he was right in some one or other of his conjectures. Bugles, and all the reeling, swaggering bucks, looked respectfully at the well-appointed man, and Bugles determined to have a pair of nut-brown tops as soon as ever he got back to town.

Sir Harry was a tall, wan, pale young man, with a strong tendency to *delirium tremens*; that, and consumption, appeared to be running a match for his person. He was a harum-scarum fellow, all strings, and tapes, and ends, and flue. He looked as if he slept in his clothes. His hat was fastened on with a ribbon, or rather a ribbon passed round near the band, in order to fasten it on, for it was seldom or ever applied to the purpose, and the ends generally went flying out behind like a Chinaman's tail. Then his flashy, many-coloured cravats, stared and straggled in all directions, while his untied waistcoat-strings protruded between the laps of his old short-waisted swallow-tailed scarlet, mixing in glorious confusion with those of his breeches behind. The knee-strings were generally also loose; the web straps of his boots were seldom in; and, what with one set of strings and another, he had acquired the name of Sixteen-string'd Jack. Mr. Sponge having dismounted, and given his hack to the now half-drunken Leather, followed Sir Harry through a foil and four-in-hand whip-hung hall to the deserted breakfast-room, where chairs stood in all directions, and crumpled napkins strewed the floor. The litter of eggs, and remnants of muffins, and diminished piles of toast, and broken bread and empty toast racks, and cups and saucers, and half-emptied glasses, and wholly emptied champagne bottles, were scattered up and down a disorderly table, further littered with newspapers, letter backs, county court summonses, mustard pots, anchovies, pickles—all the odds and ends of a most miscellaneous meal. The side-table exhibited cold joints, game, poultry, lukewarm hashed venison, and sundry lamp-lit dishes of savoury grills.

'Here you are!' exclaimed Sir Harry, taking his hunting-whip and sweeping the contents of one end of the table on to the floor with a crash that brought in the butler and some theatrical-looking servants.

'Take those filthy things away! (hiccup),' exclaimed Sir Harry, crushing the broken china smaller under his heels; 'and (hiccup) bring some red-herrings and soda-water. What the deuce does the (hiccup) cook mean by not (hiccuping) things as he ought? Now,' said he, addressing Mr. Sponge, and raking the plates and dishes up to him with the handle of his whip, just as a gaming-table keeper rakes up the stakes, 'now,' said he, 'make your (hiccup) game. There'll be some hot (hiccup) in directly.' He meant to say 'tea,' but the word failed him.

Mr. Sponge fell to with avidity. He was always ready to eat, and attacked first one thing and then another, as though he had not had any breakfast at Puddingpote Bower.

Sir Harry remained mute for some minutes, sitting cross-legged and backwards in his chair, with his throbbing temples resting upon the back, wondering where it was that he had met Mr. Sponge. He looked different without his hat; and, though he saw it was no one he knew particularly, he could not help thinking he had seen him before.

Indeed, he thought it was clear, from Mr. Sponge's manner, that they had met, and he was just going to ask him whether it was at Offley's or the Coal Hole, when a sudden move outside attracted his attention. It was the hounds.

The huntsman's horse having at length returned from the fiddler hunt, and being whisped over, and made tolerably decent, Mr. Watchorn, having exchanged the postilion saddle in which it had been ridden for a horn-cased hunting one, had mounted, and, opening the kennel-door, had liberated the pent-up pack, who came tearing out full cry and spread themselves over the country, regardless alike of the twang, twang, twang of the horn and the furious onslaught of a couple of stable lads in scarlet and caps, who, true to the title of 'whippers-in,' let drive at all they could get within reach of. The hounds had not been out, even to exercise, since the Snobston-Green day, and were as wild as hawks. They were ready to run anything. Furious and Furrier tackled with a cow. Bountiful ran a black cart-colt, and made him leap the haw-haw. Sempstress, Singwell, and Saladin (puppies), went after some crows. Mercury took after the stable cat, while old Thunderer and Come-by-

chance (supposed to be one of Lord Scamperdale's) joined in pursuit
of a cur. Watchorn, however, did not care for these little ebullitions of
spirit, and never having been accustomed to exercise the Camberwell
and Balham Hill Union Harriers, he did not see any occasion for
troubling the fox-hounds. 'They would soon settle,' he said, 'when they
got a scent.'

It was this riotous start that diverted Sixteen-string'd Jack's attention
from our friend, and, looking out of the window, Mr. Sponge saw all the
company preparing to be off. There was the elegant Bugles mounting
her ladyship's white Arab; the brothers Spangles climbing on to their
cream-colours; Mr. This getting on to the postman's pony, and Mr. That
on to the gamekeeper's. Mr. Sponge hurried out to get to the brown
ere his anger arose at being left behind, and provoked a scene. He only
just arrived in time; for the twang of the horn, the cracks of the whips,
the clamorous rates of the servants, the yelping of the hounds, and the
general commotion, had got up his courage, and he launched out in
such a way, when Mr. Sponge mounted, as would have shot a loose rider
into the air. As it was, Mr. Sponge grappled manfully with him, and,
letting the Latchfords into his sides, shoved him in front of the throng,
as if nothing had happened. Mr. Leather then slunk back to the stables,
to get out the hack to have a hunt in the distance.

The hounds, as we said before, were desperately wild; but at length,
by dint of coaxing and cracking, and whooping and hallooing, they got
some ten couples out of the five-and-twenty gathered together, and Mr.
Watchorn, putting himself at their head, trotted briskly on, blowing most
lustily, in the hopes that the rest would follow. So he clattered along
the avenue, formed between rows of sombre-headed firs and sweeping
spruce, out of which whirred clouds of pheasants, and scuttling rabbits,
and stupid hares kept crossing and recrossing, to the derangement of Mr.
Watchorn's temper, and the detriment of the unsteady pack. Squeak,
squeak, squeal sounded right and left, followed sometimes by the heavy
retributive hand of Justice on the offenders' hides, and sometimes by
the snarl, snap, and worry of a couple of hounds contending for the
prey. Twang, twang, twang, still went the horn; and when the huntsman
reached the unicorn-crested gates, between tea-caddy looking lodges,
he found himself in possession of a clear majority of his unsizable pack.
Some were rather bloody to be sure, and a few carried scraps of game,

which fastidious masters would as soon have seen them without; but neither Sir Harry nor his huntsman cared about appearances.

On clearing the lodges, and passing about a quarter of a mile on the Hardington road, hedgerows ceased, and they came upon Farleyfair Downs, across which Mr. Watchorn now struck, making for a square plantation, near the first hill-top, where it had been arranged the bag-fox should be shook. It was a fine day, rather brighter perhaps, than sportsmen like, and there was a crispness in the air indicative of frost, but then there is generally a burning scent just before one. So thought Mr. Watchorn, as he turned his feverish face up to the bright, blue sky, imbibing the fine fresh air of the wide-extending downs, instead of the stale tobacco smoke of the fetid beer-shop. As he trotted over the springy sward, up the gently rising ground, he rose in his stirrups; and, laying hold of his horse's mane, turned to survey the long-drawn, lagging field behind.

'You'll have to look sharp, my hearties,' said he to himself, as he ran them over in his eye, and thought there might be twenty or five-and-twenty horsemen; 'you'll have to look sharp, my hearties,' said he, 'if you mean to get away, for Wily Tom has his hat on the ground, which shows he has put him down, and if he's the sort of gem'man I expect he'll not be long in cover.'

So saying, he resumed his seat in the saddle, and easing his horse, endeavoured, by sundry dog noises—such as, 'Yooi doit, Ravager!' 'Gently, Paragon!' 'Here again. Mercury!'—to restrain the ardour of the leading hounds, so as to let the rebellious tail ones up and go into cover with something like a body. This was rather a difficult task to accomplish, for those with him being light, and consequently anxious to be doing and ready for riot, were difficult to restrain from dashing forward; while those that had taken their diversion and refreshment among the game, were easy whether they did anything more or not.

While Watchorn was thus manoeuvring his forces Wily Tom beckoned him on, and old Cruiser and Marmion, who had often been at the game before, and knew what Wily Tom's hat on the ground meant, flew to him full cry, drawing all their companions after them.

'I think he's away to the west,' said Tom in an undertone, resting his hand on Watchorn's horse's shoulder; 'back home,' added he, jerking his head with a knowing leer of his roguish eye. 'They're on him!' exclaimed he after a pause, as the outburst of melody proclaimed that the hounds had crossed his line. Then there was such racing and striving among the field to get up, and such squeezing and crowding, and 'Mind, my horse kicks!' at the little white hunting wicket leading into cover. 'Knock down the wall!' exclaimed one. 'Get out of the way; I'll ride over it!' roared another. 'We shall be here all day!' vociferated a third. 'That's a header!' cried another, as a clatter of stones was followed by a pair of white breeches summerseting in the air with a horse underneath. 'It's Tom Sawbones, the doctor!' exclaimed one, 'and he can mend himself.' 'By Jove! but he's killed!' shrieked another. 'Not a bit of it,' added a third, as the dead man rose and ran after his horse. 'Let Mr. Bugles through,' cried Sir Harry, seeing his friend, or rather his wife's friend, was fretting the Arab.

Meanwhile, the melody of hounds increased, and each man, as he got through the little gate, rose in his stirrups and hustled his horse along the green ride to catch up those on before. The plantation was about twenty acres, rather thick and briary at the bottom; and master Reynard, finding it was pretty safe, and, moreover, having attempted to break just by where some chawbacons were ploughing, had headed short back, so that, when the excited field rushed through the parallel gate on the far side of the plantation, expecting to see the pack streaming away over the downs, they found most of the hounds with their heads in the air, some looking for halloos, others watching their companions trying to carry the scent over the fallow.

Watchorn galloped up in the frantic state half-witted huntsmen generally are, and one of the impromptu whips being in attendance, got quickly round the hounds, and commenced a series of assaults upon them that very soon sent them scuttling to Mr. Watchorn for safety. If they had been at the hares again, or even worrying sheep, he could not have rated or flogged more severely.

'MARKSMAN! MARKSMAN! *ough, ye old Divil, get to him*!' roared the whip, aiming a stinging cut with his heavy knotty-pointed whip, at a venerable sage who still snuffed down a furrow to satisfy himself the fox was not on before he returned to cover—an exertion that overbalanced the whip, and would have landed him on the ground, had not he caught by the spur in the old mare's flank. Then he went on scrambling and rating after Marksman, the field exclaiming, as the Edmonton people did, by Johnny Gilpin:

He's on! no, he's off, he hangs by the mane!

At last he got shuffled back into the saddle, and the cry of hounds in cover attracting the outsiders back, the scene quickly changed, and the horsemen were again overhead in wood. They now swept up the grass ride to the exposed part of the higher ground, the trees gradually diminishing in size, till, on reaching the top, they did not come much above a horse's shoulder. This point commanded a fine view over the adjacent country. Behind was the rich vale of Dairylow, with its villages and spires, and trees and enclosures, while in front was nothing but the undulating, wide-stretching downs, reaching to the soft grey hills in the distance. There was not, however, much time for contemplating scenery; for Wily Tom, who had stolen to this point immediately the hounds took up the scent, now viewed the fox stealing over a gap in the wall, and, the field catching sight, there was such a hullabaloo as would have made a more composed and orderly minded fox think it better to break instead of running the outside of the wall as this one intended to do. What wind there was swept over the downs; and putting himself straight to catch it, he went away whisking his brush in the air, as if he was fresh out of his kennel instead of a sack. Then what a commotion there was! Such jumpings off to lead down, such huggings and holdings, and wooaings of those that sat on, such slidings and scramblings, and loosenings and rollings of stones. Then the frantic horses began to bound, and the frightened riders to exclaim:

'Do get out of my way, sir.'

'Mind, sir! I'm a-top of you!'

'Give him his head and let him go!' exclaimed the still drunken brother Bob Spangles, sliding his horse down with a slack rein.

'That's your sort!' roared Sir Harry, and just as he said it, his horse dropped on his hind-quarters like a rabbit, landing Sir Harry comfortably on his feet, amid the roars of the foot-people, and the mirth of such of the horsemen as were not too frightened to laugh.

'I think I'll stay where I am,' observed Mr. Bugles, preparing for a bird's-eye view where he was. 'This hunting,' said he, getting off the fidgety Arab, 'seems dangerous.'

The parties who accomplished the descent had now some fine plain sailing for their trouble. The line lay across the open downs, composed of sound, springy, racing-like turf, extremely well adapted for trying

the pace either of horses or hounds. And very soon it did try the pace
of them, for they had not gone above a mile before there was very
considerable tailing with both. To be sure, they had never been very well
together, but still the line lengthened instead of contracting. Horses that
could hardly be held downhill, and that applied themselves to the turf,
on landing, as if they could never have enough of it, now began to bear
upon the rein and hang back to those behind; while the hounds came
straggling along like a flock of wild geese, with full half a mile between
the leader and the last. However, they all threw their tongues, and each
man flattered himself that the hound he was with was the first. In vain
the galloping Watchorn looked back and tootled his horn; in vain he
worked with his cap; in vain the whips rode at the tail hounds, cursing
and swearing, and vowing they would cut them in two.

There was no getting them together. Every now and then the fox
might be seen, looking about the size of a marble, as he rounded some
distant hill, each succeeding view making him less, till, at last, he seemed
no bigger than a pea.

Five-and-twenty minutes best pace over downs is calculated to try
the mettle of anything; and, long before the leading hounds reached
Cockthropple Dean, the field was choked by the pace. Sir Harry had
long been tailed off; both the brothers Spangles had dropped astern; the
horse of one had dropped too; Sawbones, the doctor's, had got a stiff
neck; Willing, the road surveyor, and Mr. Lavender, the grocer, pulled up
together. Muddyman, the farmer's four-year-old, had enough at the end
of ten minutes; both the whips tired theirs in a quarter of an hour; and
in less than twenty minutes Watchorn and Sponge were alone in their
glory, or rather Sponge was in his glory, for Watchorn's horse was beat.

'Lend me your horn!' exclaimed Sponge, as he heard by the hammer
and pincering of Watchorn's horse, it was all U P with him.

The horse stopped as if shot; and getting the horn, Mr. Sponge went
on, the brown laying himself out as if still full of running. Cockthropple
Dean was now close at hand, and in all probability the fox would not
leave it. So thought Mr. Sponge as he dived into it, astonished at the
chorus and echo of the hounds.

'Tally ho!' shouted a countryman on the opposite side; and the road
Sponge had taken being favourable to the point, he made for it at a
hand-gallop, horn in hand, to blow as soon as he got there.

'He's away!' cried the man as soon as our friend appeared; 'reet 'cross tornops!' added he, pointing with his hoe.

Mr. Sponge then put his horse's head that way, and blew a long shrill reverberating blast. As he paused to take breath and listen, he heard the sound of horses' hoofs, and presently a stentorian voice, half frantic with rage, exclaimed from behind:

'WHO THE DICKENS ARE YOU?'

'Who the Dickens are you?' retorted Mr. Sponge, without looking round.

'They commonly call me the EARL OF SCAMPERDALE,' roared the same sweet voice, 'and those are my hounds.'

'They're not your hounds!' snapped Mr. Sponge, now looking round on his big-spectacled, flat-hatted lordship, who was closely followed by his double, Mr. Spraggon.

'Not my hounds!' screeched his lordship. 'Oh, ye barber's apprentice! Oh, ye draper's assistant! Oh, ye unmitigated Mahomedon! Sing out, Jack! sing out! For Heaven's sake, sing out!' added he, throwing out his arms in perfect despair.

'Not his lordship's hounds!' roared Jack, now rising in his stirrups and brandishing his big whip. 'Not his lordship's hounds! Tell me *that*, when they cost him five-and-twenty 'underd—two thousand five 'underd a year! Oh, by Jingo, but that's a pretty go! If they're not his lordship's hounds, I should like to know whose they are?' and thereupon Jack wiped the foam from his mouth on his sleeve.

'Sir Harry's!' exclaimed Mr. Sponge, again putting the horn to his lips, and blowing another shrill blast.

'Sir Harry's!' screeched his lordship in disgust, for he hated the very sound of his name—'Sir Harry's! Oh, you rusty-booted ruffian! Tell me that to my very face!'

'Sir Harry's!' repeated Jack, again standing erect in his stirrups. 'What! impeach his lordship's integrity—oh, by Jove, there's an end of everything! Death before dishonour! Slugs in a saw-pit! Pistols and coffee for two! Cock Pheasant at Weybridge, six o'clock i' the mornin'!' And Jack, sinking exhausted on his saddle, again wiped the foam from his mouth.

His lordship then went at Sponge again.

'Oh, you sanctified, putrified, pestilential, perpendicular, gingerbread-booted, counter-skippin' snob, you think because I'm a lord, and can't swear or use coarse language, that you may do what you like; but I'll let you see the contrary,' said he, brandishing his brother to Jack's whip. 'Mark you, sir, I'll fight you, sir, any non-huntin' day you like, sir, 'cept Sunday.'

Just then the clatter and blowing of horses was heard, and Frostyface emerged from the wood followed by the hounds, who, swinging themselves 'forrard' over the turnips, hit off the scent and went away full cry, followed by his lordship and Jack, leaving Mr. Sponge transfixed with astonishment.

'Changed foxes,' at length said Sponge, with a shake of his head; and just then the cry of hounds on the opposite bank confirmed his conjecture, and he got to Sir Harry's in time to take up his lordship's fox.

His lordship's hounds ran into Sir Harry's fox about two miles farther on, but the hounds would not break him up; and, on examining him, he was found to have been aniseeded; and, worst of all, by the mark on his ear to be one that they had turned down themselves the season before, being one of a litter that Sly had stolen from Sir Harry's cover at Seedeygorse—a beautiful instance of retributive justice.

LI

FARMER PEASTRAW'S DINE-MATINÉE

THERE ARE PLEASANTER SITUATIONS THAN being left alone with twenty couple of even the best-mannered fox-hounds; far pleasanter situations than being left alone with such a tearing, frantic lot as composed Sir Harry Scattercash's pack. Sportsmen are so used (with some hounds at least) to see foxes 'in hand' that they never think there is any difficulty in getting them there; and it is only a single-handed combat with the pack that shows them that the hound does not bring the fox up in his mouth like a retriever. A tyro's first *tête-à-tête* with a half-killed fox, with the baying pack circling round, must leave as pleasing a souvenir on the memory as Mr. Gordon Cumming would derive from his first interview with a lion.

Our friend Mr. Sponge was now engaged with a game of 'pull devil, pull baker' with the hounds for the fox, the difficulty of his situation being heightened by having to contend with the impetuous temper of a high-couraged, dangerous horse. To be sure, the gallant Hercules was a good deal subdued by the distance and severity of the pace, but there are few horses that get to the end of a run that have not sufficient kick left in them to do mischief to hounds, especially when raised or frightened by the smell of blood; nevertheless, there was no help for it. Mr. Sponge knew that unless he carried off some trophy, it would never be believed he had killed the fox. Considering all this, and also that there was no one to tell what damage he did, he just rode slap into the middle of the pack, as Marksman, Furious, Thunderer, and Bountiful were in the act of despatching the fox. Singwell and Saladin (puppies) having been sent away howling, the one bit through the jowl, the other through the foot.

'Ah! leave him—leave him—leave him!' screeched Mr. Sponge, trampling over Warrior and Tempest, the brown horse lashing out furiously at Melody and Lapwing. 'Ah, leave him! leave him!' repeated he, throwing himself off his horse by the fox, and clearing a circle with his whip, aided by the hoofs of the animal. There lay the fox before him killed, but as yet little broken by the pack. He was a noble fellow; bright and brown, in the full vigour of life and condition, with a gameness, even in death, that no other animal shows. Mr. Sponge put his foot on the body, and quickly whipped off his brush. Before he had time to pocket it, the repulsed pack broke in upon him and carried off the carcass.

'Ah! dash ye, you may have *that*,' said he, cutting at them with his whip as they clustered upon it like a swarm of bees. They had not had a wild fox for five weeks.

'Who-hoop!' cried Mr. Sponge, in the hopes of attracting some of the field. 'WHO-HOOP!' repeated he, as loud as he could halloo. 'Where can they all be, I wonder?' said he, looking around; and echo answered—where?

The hounds had now crunched their fox, or as much of him as they wanted. Old Marksman ran about with his head, and Warrior with a haunch.

'Drop it, you old beggar!' cried Mr. Sponge, cutting at Marksman with his whip, and Mr. Sponge being too near to make a trial of speed prudent, the old dog did as he was bid, and slunk away.

Our friend then appended this proud trophy to his saddle-flap by a piece of whipcord, and, mounting the now tractable Hercules, began to cast about in search of a landmark. Like most down countries, this one was somewhat deceptive; there were plenty of landmarks, but they were all the same sort—clumps of trees on hill-tops, and plantations on hill-sides, but nothing of a distinguishing character, nothing that a stranger could say, 'I remember seeing that as I came'; or, 'I remember passing that in the run.' The landscape seemed all alike: north, south, east, and west, equally indifferent.

'Curse the thing,' said Mr. Sponge, adjusting himself in his saddle, and looking about; 'I haven't the *slightest* idea where I am. I'll blow the horn, and see if that will bring any one.'

So saying, he applied the horn to his lips, and blew a keen, shrill blast, that spread over the surrounding country, and was echoed back by the distant hills. A few lost hounds cast up from various quarters, in the unexpected way that hounds do come to a horn. Among them were a few branded with S,[1] who did not at all set off the beauty of the rest.

"Ord rot you, you belong to that old ruffian, do you?' said Mr. Sponge, riding and cutting at one with his whip, exclaiming, 'Get away to him, ye beggar, or I'll tuck you up short.'

He now, for the first time, saw them together in anything like numbers, and was struck with the queerness and inequality of the whole. They were of all sorts and sizes, from the solemn towering calf-like fox-hound down to the little wriggling harrier. They seemed, too, to be troubled with various complaints and infirmities. Some had the mange; some had blear eyes; some had but one; many were out at the elbows; and not a few down at the toes. However, they had killed a fox, and 'Handsome is that handsome does,' said Mr. Sponge, as, with his horse surrounded by them, he moved on in quest of his way home.

At first, he thought to retrace his steps by the marks of his horse's hoofs, and succeeded in getting back to the dean, where Sir Harry's hounds changed foxes with Lord Scamperdale's; but he got confused with the imprints of the other horses, and very soon had to trust entirely to chance. Chance, we are sorry to say, did not befriend him; for, after wandering over the wide-extending downs, he came upon the little hamlet of Tinkler Hatch, and was informed that he had been riding in a semicircle.

He there got some gruel for his horse, and, with day closing in, now set off, as directed, on the Ribchester road, with the assurance that he 'couldn't miss his way.' Some of the hounds here declined following him any farther, and slunk into cottages and outhouses as they passed along. Mr. Sponge, however, did not care for their company.

Having travelled musingly along two or three miles of road, now thinking over the glorious run—now of the gallant way in which Hercules had carried him—now of the pity it was that there was nobody there to see—now of the encounter with Lord Scamperdale, just as he passed a well-filled stackyard, that had shut out the view of a flaming red brick house with a pea-green door and windows, an outburst of 'hoo-rays!' followed by one cheer more—'hoo-ray!' made the remaining wild hounds prick up their ears, and our friend rein in his horse, to hear what was 'up.' A bright fire in a room on the right of the door overpowered the clouds of tobacco-smoke with which the room was enveloped, and revealed sundry scarlet coats in the full glow of joyous hilarity. It was Sir Harry and friends recruiting at Fanner Peastraw's after their exertions; for, though they could not make much of hunting, they were always ready to drink. They were having a rare set-to—rashers of bacon, wedges of cheese, with oceans of malt-liquor. It was the appearance of a magnificent cold round of home-fed beef, red with saltpetre and flaky with white fat, borne on high by their host, that elicited the applause and the one cheer more that broke on Mr. Sponge's ear as he was passing— applause that was renewed as they caught a glimpse of his red coat, not on account of his safety or that of the hounds, but simply because being in the cheering mood, they were ready to cheer anything.

'Hil-loo! there's Mr. What's-his-name!' exclaimed brother Bob Spangles, as he caught view of Sponge and the hounds passing the window.

'So there is!' roared another; 'Hoo-ray!'

'Hoo-ray!' yelled two or three more.

'Stop him!' cried another.

'Call him in,' roared Sir Harry, 'and let's liquor him.'

'Hilloo! Mister What's-your-name!' exclaimed the other Spangles, throwing up the window. 'Hilloo, won't you come in and have some refreshment?'

'Who's there?' asked Mr. Sponge, reining in the brown.

'Oh, we're all here,' shouted brother Bob Spangles, holding up a tumbler of hot brandy-and-water; 'we're all here—Sir Harry and all,' added he.

'But what shall I do with the hounds?' asked Mr. Sponge, looking down upon the confused pack, now crowding about his horse's head.

'Oh, let the beef-eaters—the scene-shifters—I meant to say the servants—those fellows, you know, in scarlet and black caps, look after them,' replied brother Bob Spangles.

'But there are none of them here,' exclaimed Mr. Sponge, looking back on the deserted road.

'None of them here!' hiccuped Sir Harry, who had now got reeled to the window. 'None of them here,' repeated he, staring vacantly at the uneven pack. 'Oh (hiccup) I'll tell you what do—(hiccup) them into a barn or a stable, or a (hiccup) of any sort, and we'll send for them when we want to (hiccup) again.' 'Then just you call them to you,' replied Sponge, thinking they would go to their master. 'Just you call them,' repeated he, 'and I'll put them to you.'

'(Hiccup) call to them?' replied Harry. 'I can't (hiccup).'

'Oh, yes!' rejoined Mr. Sponge; 'call one or two by their names, and the rest will follow.'

'Names! (hiccup) I don't know any of their nasty names,' replied Sir Harry, staring wildly.

'Towler! Towler! Towler! here, good dog—hoop!—here's your liquor!' cried brother Bob Spangles, holding the smoking tumbler of brandy-and-water out of the window, as if to tempt any hound that chose to answer to the name of Towler.

There didn't seem to be a Towler in the pack; at least, none of them qualified for the brandy-and-water.

'Oh, I'll (hiccup) you what we'll do,' exclaimed Sir Harry: 'I'll (hiccup) you what we'll do. 'We'll just give them a (hiccup) kick a-piece and send them (hiccuping) home,' Sir Harry reeling back into the room to the black horse-hair sofa, where his whip was.

He presently appeared at the door, and, going into the midst of the hounds, commenced laying about him, rating, and cutting, and kicking, and shouting.

'Geete away home with ye, ye brutes; what are you all (hiccup)ing here about? Ah! cut off his tail!' cried he, staggering after a venerable blear-eyed sage, who dropped his stern and took off.

'Be off! Does your mother know you're out?' cried Bob Spangles, out of the window, to old Marksman, who stood wondering what to do.

The old hound took the hint also.

'Now, then, old feller,' cried Sir Harry, staggering up to Mr. Sponge, who still sat on his horse, in mute astonishment at Sir Harry's mode of dealing with his hounds. 'Now, then, old feller,' said he, seizing Mr. Sponge by the hand, 'get rid of your quadruped, and (hiccup) in, and make yourself "o'er all the (hiccups) of life victorious," as Bob Spangles says, when he (hiccups) it neat. This is old (hiccup) Peastraw's, a (hiccup) tenant of mine, and he'll be most (hiccup) to see you.'

'But what must I do with my horse?' asked Mr. Sponge, rubbing some of the dried sweat off the brown's shoulder as he spoke; adding, 'I should like to get him a feed of corn.'

'Give him some ale, and a (hiccup) of sherry in it,' replied Sir Harry; 'it'll do him far more good—make his mane grow,' smoothing the horse's thin, silky mane as he spoke.

'Well, I'll put him up,' replied Mr. Sponge, 'and then come to you,' throwing himself, jockey fashion, off the horse as he spoke.

'That's a (hiccup) feller,' said Sir Harry; adding, 'here's old Pea himself come to see after you.'

So saying, Sir Harry reeled back to his comrades in the house, leaving Mr. Sponge in the care of the farmer.

'This way, sir; this way,' said the burly Mr. Peastraw, leading the way into his farmyard, where a line of hunters stood shivering under a long cart-shed.

'But I can't put my horse in here,' observed Mr. Sponge, looking at the unfortunate brutes.

'No, sir, no,' replied Mr. Peastraw; 'put yours in a stable, sir; put yours in a stable'; adding, 'these young gents don't care much about their horses.'

'Does anybody know the chap's name?' asked Sir Harry, reeling back into the room.

'Know his name!' exclaimed Bob Spangles; 'why, don't you?'

'No,' replied Sir Harry, with a vacant stare.

'Why, you went up and shook hands with him, as if you were as thick as thieves,' replied Bob.

'Did I?' hiccuped Sir Harry. 'Well, I thought I knew him. At least, I thought it was somebody I had (hiccup)ed before; and at one's own (hiccup) house, you know, one's 'bliged to be (hiccup) feller well (hiccup) with everybody that comes. But surely, some of you know his (hiccup) name,' added he, looking about at the company.

'I think I know his (hiccup) face,' replied Bob Spangles, imitating his brother-in-law.

'I've seen him somewhere,' observed the other Spangles, through a mouthful of beef.

'So have I,' exclaimed some one else, 'but where I can't say.'

'Most likely at church,' observed brother Bob Spangles.

'Well, I don't think he'll corrupt me,' observed Captain Quod, speaking between the fumes of a cigar.

'He'll not borrow much of me,' observed Captain Seedeybuck, producing a much tarnished green purse, and exhibiting two fourpenny-pieces at one end, and three-halfpence at the other.

'Oh, I dare say he's a good feller,' observed Sir Harry; 'I make no doubt he's one of the right sort.'

Just then in came the man himself, hat and whip in hand, waving the brush proudly over his head.

'Ah, that's (hiccup) right, old feller,' exclaimed Sir Harry, again advancing with extended hand to meet him, adding, 'you'd (hiccup) all you wanted for your (hiccup) horse: mutton broth—I mean barley-water, foot-bath, everything right. Let me introduce my (hiccup) brother-in-law, Bob Spangles, my (hiccup) friend Captain Ladofwax, Captain Quod, Captain (hiccup) Bouncey, Captain (hiccup) Seedeybuck, and my (hiccup) brother-in-law, Mr. Spangles, as lushy a cove as ever was seen; ar'n't you, old boy?' added he, grasping the latter by the arm.

All these gentlemen severally bobbed their heads as Sir Harry called them over, and then resumed their respective occupations—eating, drinking, and smoking.

These were some of the debauched gentlemen Mr. Sponge had seen before Nonsuch House in the morning. They were all captains, or captains by courtesy. Ladofwax had been a painter and glazier in the Borough, where he made the acquaintance of Captain Quod, while that gentleman was an inmate of Captain Hudson's strong house. Captain Bouncey was the too well-known betting-office keeper; and Seedeybuck was such a constant customer of Mr. Commissioner Fonblanque's court, that that worthy legal luminary, on discharging him for the fifth time, said to him, with a very significant shake of the head, 'You'd better not come here again, sir.' Seedeybuck, being of the same opinion, had since fastened himself on to Sir Harry Scattercash, who found him in meat, drink, washing, and lodging. They were all attired in red coats, of one sort or another, though some of which were of a very antediluvian, and others of a very dressing-gown cut. Bouncey's had a hare on the button, and Seedeybuck's coat sat on him like a sack. Still a scarlet coat is a scarlet coat in the eyes of some, and the coats were not a bit more unsportsmanlike than the men. To Mr. Sponge's astonishment, instead of breaking out in inquiries as to where they had run to, the time, the distance, who was up, who was down, and so on, they began recommending the victuals and drink; and this, notwithstanding Mr. Sponge kept flourishing the brush.

'We've had a rare run,' said he, addressing himself to Sir Harry.

'Have you (hiccup)? I'm glad of it (hiccup). Pray have something to (hiccup) after it; you *must* be (hiccup).'

'Let me help you to some of this cold round of beef?' exclaimed Captain Bouncey, brandishing the great broad-bladed carving knife.

'Have a slice of 'ot 'am,' suggested Captain Quod.

'The finest run I ever rode!' observed Mr. Sponge, still endeavouring to get a hearing.

'Dare say it would,' replied Sir Harry;' those (hiccup) hounds of mine are uncommon (hiccup).' He didn't know what they were, and the hiccup came very opportunely.

'The pace was terrific!' exclaimed Sponge.

'Dare say it would,' replied Sir Harry; 'and that's what makes me (hiccup) you're so (hiccup). Pea, here, has some rare old October—(hiccup) bushels to the (hiccup) hogshead.' 'It's capital!' exclaimed Captain Seedeybuck, frothing himself a tumblerful out of the tall brown jug.

'So is this,' rejoined Captain Quod, pouring himself out a liberal allowance of gin.

'That horse of mine carried me MAG*nificently*!' observed Mr. Sponge, with a commanding emphasis on the MAG.

'Dare say he would,' replied Sir Harry;'he looked like a (hiccup)er—a white 'un, wasn't he?'

'No; a *brown*,' replied Mr. Sponge, disgusted at the mistake.

'Ah, well; but there *was* somebody on a white,' replied Sir Harry. 'Oh—ah—yes—it was old Bugles on my lady's horse. By the (hiccup) way (hiccup), gentlemen, what's got Mr. Orlando (hiccup) Bugles?' asked Sir Harry, staring wildly round.

'Oh! old Bugles! old Pad-the-Hoof! old Mr. Funker! the horse frightened him so, that he went home crying,' replied Bob Spangles.

'Hope he didn't lose him?' asked Sir Harry.

'Oh, no,' replied Bob; 'he gave a lad a shilling to lead him, and they trudged away very quietly together.'

'The old (hiccup)!' exclaimed Sir Harry; 'he told me he was a member of the Surrey something.'

'The Sorry Union,' replied Captain Quod. 'He *was* out with them once, and fell off on his head and knocked his hat-crown out.'

'Well, but I was telling you about the run,' interposed Mr. Sponge, again endeavouring to enlist an audience. 'I was telling you about the run,' repeated he.

'Don't trouble yourself, my dear sir,' interrupted Captain Bouncey; 'we know all about it—found—checked—killed, killed—found—checked.'

'You *can't* know all about it!' snapped Mr. Sponge; 'for there wasn't a soul there but myself, much to my horror, for I had a reg'lar row with old Scamperdale, and never a soul to back me.'

'What! you fell in with that mealy-mouthed gentleman, who can't (hiccup) swear because he's a (hiccup) lord, did you?' asked Sir Harry, his attention being now drawn to our friend.

'*I did*,' replied Mr. Sponge; 'and a pretty passage of politeness we had of it.'

'Indeed! (hiccup),' exclaimed Sir Harry. 'Tell us (hiccup) all about it.'

'Well,' said Mr. Sponge, laying the brush lengthways before him on the table, as if he was going to demonstrate upon it. 'Well, you see we had a devil of a run—I don't know how many miles, as hard as ever we could lay legs to the ground; one by one the field all dropped astern, except the huntsman and myself. At last he gave in, or rather his horse did, and I was left alone in my glory. Well, we went over the downs at a pace that nothing but blood could live with, and, though my horse has never been beat, and is as thorough-bred as Eclipse—a horse that I have refused three hundred guineas for over and over again, I really did begin to think I might get to the bottom of him, when all of a sudden we came to a dean.'

'Ah! Cockthropple that would be,' observed Sir Harry.

'Dare say,' replied Mr. Sponge; 'Cock-anything-you-like-to-call-it for me. Well, when we got there, I thought we should have some breathing time, for the fox would be sure to hug it. But no; no sooner had I got there than a countryman hallooed him away on the far side. I got to the halloo as quick as I could, and just as I was blowing the horn,' producing Watchorn's from his pocket as he spoke; 'for I must tell you,' said he, 'that when I saw the huntsman's horse was beat, I took this from him—a horn to a foot huntsman being of no more use, you know, than a side-pocket to a cow, or a frilled shirt to a pig. Well, as I was tootleing the horn for hard life, who should turn out of the wood but old mealy-mouth himself, as you call him, and a pretty volley of abuse he let drive at me.'

'No doubt,' hiccuped Sir Harry; 'but what was *he* doing there?'

'Oh! I should tell you,' replied Mr. Sponge, 'his hounds had run a fox into it, and were on him full cry when I got there.'

'I'll be bund,' cried Sir Harry, 'it was all sham—that he just (hiccup) and excuse for getting into that cover. The old (hiccup) beggar is always at some trick, (hiccup)-ing my foxes or disturbing my covers or something,' Sir Harry being just enough of a master of hounds to be jealous of the neighbouring ones.

'Well, however, there he was,' continued Mr. Sponge; 'and the first intimation I had of the fact was a great, gruff voice, exclaiming, "Who the Dickens are you?"

'"Who the Dickens are you?" replied I.'

'Bravo!' shouted Sir Harry.

'Capital!' exclaimed Seedeybuck.

'Go it, you cripples! Newgate's on fire!' shouted Captain Quod.

'Well, what said he?' asked Sir Harry.

'"They commonly call me the Earl of Scamperdale," roared he, "and those are MY HOUNDS."

'"They're *not* your hounds," replied I.

'"Whose are they, then?" asked he.

'"Sir Harry Scattercash's, a devilish deal better fellow," replied I.

'"Oh, by Jove!" roared he, "there's an end of everything, Jack," shouted he to old Spraggon, "this gentleman says these are not my hounds!"

'"I'll tell you what it is, my lord," said I, gathering my whip and riding close up as if I was goin' to pitch into him, "I'll tell you what it is; you think, because you're a lord, you may abuse people as you like, but by Jingo you've mistaken your man. I'll not put up with any of your nonsense. The Sponges are as old a family as the Scamperdales, and I'll fight you any non-hunting day you like with pistols, broadswords, fists or blunder-busses."'

'Well done you! Bravo! that's your sort!' with loud thumping of tables and clapping of hands, resounded from all parts.

'By Jove, fill him up a stiff'un! he deserves a good drink after that!' exclaimed Sir Harry, pouring Mr. Sponge out a beaker, equal parts brandy and water.

Mr. Sponge immediately became a hero, and was freely admitted into their circle. He was clearly a choice spirit—a trump of the first water—and they only wanted his name to be uncommonly thick with him. As it was, they plied him with victuals and drink, all seeming anxious to bring him up to the same happy state of inebriety as themselves. They talked and they chattered, and they abused Old Scamperdale and Jack Spraggon, and lauded Mr. Sponge up to the skies.

Thus day closed in, with Farmer Peastraw's bright fire shedding its cheering glow over the now encircling group. One would have thought that, with their hearts mellow, and their bodies comfortable, their minds would have turned to that sport in whose honour they sported the scarlet; but no, hunting was never mentioned. They were quite as genteel as Nimrod's swell friends at Melton, who cut it altogether. They rambled from subject to subject, chiefly on indoor and London topics; billiards, betting-offices, Coal Holes, Cremorne, Cider Cellars, Judge and Jury Courts, there being an evident confusion in their minds between the characters of sportsmen and sporting men, or gents as they are called. Mr. Sponge tried hard to get them on the right tack, were it only for the sake of singing the praises of the horse for which he had so often refused three hundred guineas, but he never succeeded in retaining an hearing. Talkers were far more plentiful than listeners.

At last they got to singing, and when men begin to sing, it is a sign that they are either drunk, or have had enough of each other's company. Sir Harry's hiccup, from which he was never wholly free, increased tenfold, and he hiccuped and spluttered at almost every word. His hand, which shook so at starting that it was odds whether he got his glass to his mouth or his ear, was now steadied, but his glazed eye and green haggard countenance showed at what a fearful sacrifice the temporary steadiness had been obtained. At last his jaw dropped on his chest, his left arm hung listlessly over the back of the chair, and he fell asleep. Captain Quod, too, was overcome, and threw himself full-length on the sofa. Captain Seedeybuck began to talk thick.

Just as they were all about brought to a standstill, the trampling of horses, the rumbling of wheels, and the shrill twang, twang, twang of the now almost forgotten mail horn, roused them from their reveries. It was Sir Harry's drag scouring the country in search of our party. It had been to all the public-houses and beer-shops within a radius of some miles of Nonsuch House, and was now taking a speculative blow through the centre of the circle.

It was a clear frosty night, and the horses' hoofs rang, and the wheels rolled soundly over the hard road, cracking the thin ice, yet hardly sufficiently frozen to prevent a slight upshot from the wheels.

Twang, twang, twang, went the horn full upon Farmer Peastraw's house, causing the sleepers to start, and the waking ones to make for the window.

'COACH-A-HOY!' cried Bob Spangles, smashing a pane in a vain attempt to get the window up. The coachman pulled up at the sound.

'Here we are. Sir Harry!' cried Bob Spangles, into his brother-in-law's ear, but Sir Harry was too far gone; he could not 'come to time.' Presently a footman entered with furred coats, and shawls, and checkered rugs, in which those who were sufficiently sober enveloped themselves, and those who were too far gone were huddled by Peastraw and the man; and amid much hurry and confusion, and jostling for inside seats, the party freighted the coach, and whisked away before Mr. Sponge knew where he was.

When they arrived at Nonsuch House, they found Mr. Bugles exercising the fiddlers by dancing the ladies in turns.

1.   'S,' for Scamperdale, showing they were his lordship's.

LII

A MOONLIGHT RIDE

THE POSITION, THEN, OF MR. Sponge was this. He was left on a frosty, moonlight night at the door of a strange farmhouse, staring after a receding coach, containing all his recent companions.

'You'll not be goin' wi' 'em, then?' observed Mr. Peastraw, who stood beside him, listening to the shrill notes of the horn dying out in the distance.

'No,' replied Mr. Sponge.

'Rummy lot,' observed Mr. Peastraw, with a shake of the head.

'Are they?' asked Mr. Sponge.

'Very!' replied Mr. Peastraw. 'Be the death of Sir Harry among 'em.'

'Who are they all?' asked Mr. Sponge.

'Rubbish!' replied Peastraw with a sneer, diving his hands into the depths of his pockets. 'Well, we'd better go in,' added he, pulling his hands out and rubbing them, to betoken that he felt cold.

Mr. Sponge, not being much of a drinker, was more overcome with what he had taken than a seasoned cask would have been; added to which the keen night air striking upon his heated frame soon sent the liquor into his head. He began to feel queer.

'Well,' said he to his host, 'I think I'd better be going.'

'Where are you bound for?' asked Mr. Peastraw.

'To Puddingpote Bower,' replied Mr. Sponge.

'S-o-o,' observed Mr. Peastraw thoughtfully; 'Mr. Crowdey's—Mr. Jogglebury that was?'

'Yes,' replied Mr. Sponge.

'He is a deuce of a man, that, for breaking people's hedges,' observed

Mr. Peastraw; after a pause, 'he can't see a straight stick of no sort, but he's sure to be at it.'

'He's a great man for walking-sticks,' replied Mr. Sponge, staggering in the direction of the stable in which he put his horse.

The house clock then struck ten.

'She's fast,' observed Mr. Peastraw, fearing his guest might be wanting to stay all night.

'How far will Puddingpote Bower be from here?' asked Mr. Sponge.

'Oh, no distance, sir, no distance,' replied Mr. Peastraw, now leading out the horse. 'Can't miss your way, sir—can't miss your way. First turn on the right takes you to Collins' Green; then keep by the side of the church, next the pond; then go straight forward for about a mile and a half, or two miles, till you come to a small village called Lea Green; turn short at the finger-post as you enter, and keep right along by the side of the hills till you come to the Winslow Woods; leave them to the left, and pass by Mr. Roby's farm, at Runton—you'll know Mr. Roby?'

'Not I,' replied Mr. Sponge, hoisting himself into the saddle, and holding out a hand to take leave of his host.

'Good night, sir; good night!' exclaimed Mr. Peastraw, shaking it; 'and have the goodness to tell Mr. Crowdey from me that the next time he comes here a bush-rangin', I'll thank him to shut the gates after him. He set all my young stock wrong the last time he was here.'

'I will,' replied Mr. Sponge, riding off.

Mr. Peastraw's directions were well calculated to confuse a clearer head than Mr. Sponge then carried; and the reader will not be surprised to learn that, long before he reached the Winslow Woods, he was regularly bewildered. Indeed, there is no surer way of losing oneself than trying to follow a long train of directions in a strange country. It is far better to establish one's own landmarks, and make for them as the natural course of the country seems to direct. Our forefathers had a wonderful knack of getting to points with as little circumlocution as possible. Mr. Sponge, however, knew no points, and was quite at sea; indeed, even if he had, they would have been of little use, for a fitful and frequently obscured moon threw such bewildering lights and shades around, that a native would have had some difficulty in recognizing the country. The frost grew more intense, the stars shone clear and bright, and the cold took our friend by the nape of the neck, shooting across his shoulder-blades and right down his back. Mr. Sponge wished and wished he was anywhere but where he was—flattening his nose against the coffee-room window of the Bantam, tooling in a hansom as hard as he could go, squaring along Oxford Street criticizing horses—nay, he wouldn't care to be undergoing Gustavus James himself—anything, rather than rambling about a strange country in a cold winter's night, with nothing but the hooting of owls and the occasional bark of shepherds' dogs to enliven his solitude. The houses were few and far between. The lights in the cottages had long been extinguished, and the occupiers of such of the farmhouses as would come to his knocks were gruff in their answers, and short in their directions. At length, after riding, and riding, and riding, more with a view of keeping himself awake than in the expectation of finding his way, just as he was preparing to arouse the inmates of a cottage by the roadside, a sudden gleam of moonlight fell upon the building, revealing the half-Swiss, half-Gothic lodge of Puddingpote Bower.

LIII

PUDDINGPOTE BOWER

WE MUST NOW BACK THE train a little, and have a look at Jog and Co.

Mr. and Mrs. Jog had had another squabble after Mr. Sponge's departure in the morning, Mr. Jog reproving Mrs. Jog for the interest she seemed to take in Mr. Sponge, as shown by her going to the door to see him amble away on the piebald hack. Mrs. Jog justified herself on the score of Gustavus James, with whom she was quite sure Mr. Sponge was much struck, and to whom, she made no doubt, he would leave his ample fortune. Jog, on the other hand, wheezed and puffed into his frill, and reasserted that Mr. Sponge was as likely to live as Gustavus James, and to marry and to have a bushel of children of his own; while Mrs. Jog rejoined that he was 'sure to break his neck'—breaking their necks being, as she conceived, the inevitable end of fox-hunters. Jog, who had not prosecuted the sport of hunting long enough to be able to gainsay her assertion, though he took especial care to defer the operation of breaking his own neck as long as he could, fell back upon the expense and inconvenience of keeping Mr. Sponge and his three horses, and his saucy servant, who had taught their domestics to turn up their noses at his diet table; above all, at his stick-jaw and undeniable small-beer. So they went fighting and squabbling on, till at last the scene ended, as usual, by Mrs. Jogglebury bursting into tears, and declaring that Jog didn't care a farthing either for her or her children. Jog then bundled off, to try and fashion a most incorrigible-looking, knotty blackthorn into a head of Lord Chancellor Lyndhurst. He afterwards took a turn at a hazel that he thought would make a Joe Hume. Having occupied himself with these till the children's dinner-hour, he took a wandering, snatching sort of meal, and then put on his paletot, with a little hatchet in the pocket, and went off in search of the raw material in his own and the neighbouring hedges.

Evening came, and with it came Jog, laden, as usual, with an armful of gibbeys, but the shades of night followed evening ere there was any tidings of the sporting inmates of his house. At length, just as Jog was taking his last stroll prior to going in for good, he espied a pair of vacillating white breeches coming up the avenue with a clearly drunken man inside them. Jog stood straining his eyes watching their movements, wondering whether they would keep the saddle or come off—whenever the breeches seemed irrevocably gone, they invariably recovered themselves with a jerk or a lurch—Jog now saw it was Leather on the piebald, and though he had no fancy for the man, he stood to let him come up, thinking to hear something of Sponge. Leather in due time saw the great looming outline of our friend and came staring and shaking his head, endeavouring to identify it. He thought at first it was the Squire—next he thought it wasn't—then he was sure it wasn't.

'Oh! it's you, old boy, is it?' at last exclaimed he, pulling up beside the large holly against which our friend had placed himself, 'It's you, old boy, is it?' repeated he, extending his right hand and nearly overbalancing himself, adding as he recovered his equilibrium, 'I thought it was the old Woolpack at first,' nodding his head towards the house. 'Well,' spluttered he, pulling up, and sitting, as he thought, quite straight in the saddle, 'we've had the finest day's sport and the most equitable drink I've enjoyed for many a long day. 'Ord bless us, what a gent that Sir 'Arry is! He's the sort of man that should have money. I'm blowed, if I were queen, but I'd melt all the great blubber-headed fellows like this 'ere Crowdey down, and make one sich man as Sir 'Arry out of the 'ole on 'em. Beer! they don't know wot beer is there! nothin' but the werry strongest hale, instead of the puzzon one gets at this awful mean place, that looks like nothin' but the weshin' o' brewers' haprons. Oh! I 'umbly begs pardon,' exclaimed he, dropping from his horse on to his knees on discovering that he was addressing Mr. Crowdey—'I thought it was Robins, the mole-ketcher.'

'Thought it was Robins, the mole-catcher,' growled Jog; 'what have you to do with (puff) Robins, the (wheeze) mole-catcher?'

Jog boiled over with indignation. At first he thought of kicking
Leather, a feat that his suppliant position made extremely convenient,
if not tempting. Prudence, however, suggested that Leather might have
him up for the assault. So he stood puffing and wheezing and eyeing the
blear-eyed, brandy-nosed old drunkard with, as he thought, a withering
look of contempt; and then, though the man was drunk and the night
was dark, he waddled off, leaving Mr. Leather on his once white
breeches' knees. If Jog had had reasonable time, say an hour or an hour
and twenty minutes, to improvise it in, he would have said something
uncommonly sharp; as it was he left him with the pertinent inquiry we
have recorded—'What have you to do with Robins, the mole-catcher?'
We need hardly say that this little incident did not at all ingratiate Mr.
Sponge with his host, who re-entered his house in a worse humour than
ever. It was insulting a gentleman on his own ter-ri-tory—bearding an
Englishman in his own castle. 'Not to be borne (puff),' said Jog.

It was now nearly five o'clock, Jog's dinner hour, and still no Mr.
Sponge. Mrs. Jog proposed waiting half an hour, indeed, she had told
Susan, the cook, to keep the dinner back a little, to give Mr. Sponge
a chance, who could not possibly change his tight hunting things for
his evening tights in the short space of time that Jog could drop off his
loose-flowing garments, wash his hands, and run the comb through his
lank, candle-like hair.

Five o'clock struck, and Jog was just applying his hand to the fat
red-and-black worsted bell-pull, when Mrs. Jog announced what she
had done.

'Put off the dinner (wheeze)! put off the dinner (puff)!' repeated he,
blowing furiously into his clean shirt-frill, which stuck up under his
nose like a hand-saw; 'put off the dinner (wheeze)! put off the dinner
(puff), I wish you wouldn't do such (wheeze) things without consulting
(gasp) me.'

'Well, but, my dear, you couldn't possibly sit down without him,'
observed Mrs. Jog mildly.

'Possibly! (puff), possibly! (wheeze),' repeated Jog. 'There's no possibly
in the matter,' retorted he, blowing more furiously into the frill.

Mrs. Jog was silent.

'A man should conform to the (puff) hours of the (wheeze) house,'
observed Jog, after a pause.

'Well, but, my dear, you know hunters are always allowed a little law,' observed Mrs. Jog.

'Law! (puff), law! (wheeze),' retorted Jog. 'I never want any law,' thinking of Smiler *v.* Jogglebury.

Half-past five o'clock came, and still no Sponge; and Mrs. Jog, thinking it would be better to arrange to have something hot for him when he came, than to do further battle with her husband, gave the bell the double ring indicative of 'bring dinner.'

'Nay (puff), nay (wheeze); when you have (gasp)ed so long,' growled Jog, taking the other tack, 'you might as well have (wheez)ed a little longer'—snorting into his frill as he spoke.

Mrs. Jogglebury said nothing, but slipped quietly out, as if after her keys, to tell Susan to keep so-and-so in the meat-screen, and have a few potatoes ready to boil against Mr. Sponge arrived. She then sidled back quietly into the room. Jog and she presently proceeded to that all-important meal, Jog blowing out the company candles on the side-table as he passed.

Jog munched away with a capital appetite; but Mrs. Jog, who took the bulk of her lading in at the children's dinner, sat trifling with the contents of her plate, listening alternately for the sound of horses' hoofs outside, and for nursery squalls in.

Dinner passed over, and the fruity port and sugary sherry soon usurped the places that stick-jaw pudding and cheese had occupied.

'Mr. (puff) Sponge must be (wheeze), I think,' observed Jog, hauling his great silver watch out, like a bucket, from his fob, on seeing that it only wanted ten minutes to seven.

'Oh, Jog!' exclaimed Mrs. Jog, clasping her beautiful hands, and casting her bright beady eyes up to the low ceiling.

'Oh, Jog! What's the matter now? (puff—wheeze—gasp),' exclaimed our friend, reddening up, and fixing his stupid eyes intently on his wife.

'Oh, nothing,' replied Mrs. Jog, unclasping her hands, and bringing down her eyes.

'Oh, nothin'!' retorted Jog. 'Nothin'!' repeated he. 'Ladies don't get into such tantrums for nothin'.'

'Well, then, Jog, I was thinking if anything should have ha—ha—happened Mr. Sponge, how Gustavus Ja—Ja—James will have lost

his chance.' And thereupon she dived for her lace-fringed pocket-handkerchief, and hurried out of the room.

But Mrs. Jog had said quite enough to make the caldron of Jog's jealousy boil over, and he sat staring into the fire, imagining all sorts of horrible devices in the coals and cinders, and conjuring up all sorts of evils, until he felt himself possessed of a hundred and twenty thousand devils.

'I'll get shot of this chap at last,' said he, with a knowing jerk of his head and a puff into his frill, as he drew his thick legs under his chair, and made a semi-circle to get at the bottle. 'I'll get shot of this chap,' repeated he, pouring himself out a bumper of the syrupy port, and eyeing it at the composite candle. He drained off the glass, and immediately filled another. That, too, went down; then he took another, and another, and another; and seeing the bottle get low, he thought he might as well finish it. He felt better after it. Not that he was a bit more reconciled to our friend Mr. Sponge, but he felt more equal to cope with him—he even felt as if he could fight him. There did not, however, seem to be much likelihood of his having to perform that ceremony, for nine o'clock struck and no Mr. Sponge, and at half-past Mr. Crowdey stumped off to bed.

Mrs. Crowdey, having given Bartholomew and Susan a dirty pack of cards to play with to keep them awake till Mr. Sponge arrived, went to bed, too, and the house was presently tranquil.

It, however, happened that that amazing prodigy, Gustavus James, having been out on a sort of eleemosynary excursion among the neighbouring farmers and people, exhibiting as well his fine blue-feathered hat, as his astonishing proficiency in 'Bah! bah! black sheep,' and 'Obin and Ichard,' getting seed-cake from one, sponge cake from another, and toffy from a third, was troubled with a very bad stomach-ache during the night, of which he soon made the house sensible by his screams and his cries. Jog and his wife were presently at him; and, as Jog sat in his white cotton nightcap and flowing flannel dressing-gown in an easy chair in the nursery, he heard the crack of the whip, and the prolonged *yeea-yu-u-p* of Mr. Sponge's arrival. Presently the trampling of a horse was heard passing round to the stable. The clock then struck one.

'Pretty hour for a man to come home to a strange house!' observed Mr. Jog, for the nurse, or Murry Ann, or Mrs. Jog, or any one that liked, to take up.

Mrs. Jog was busy with the rhubarb and magnesia, and the others said nothing. After the lapse of a few minutes, the clank, clank, clank of Mr. Sponge's spurs was heard as he passed round to the front, and Mr. Jog stole out on to the landing to hear how he would get in.

Thump! thump! thump! went Mr. Sponge at the door; rap—tap—tap he went at it with his whip.

'Comin', sir! comin'!' exclaimed Bartholomew from the inside.

Presently the shooting of bolts, the withdrawal of bands, and the opening of doors, were heard.

'Not gone to bed yet, old boy?' said Mr. Sponge, as he entered.

'No, thir!' snuffled the boy, who had a bad cold, 'been thitten up for you.'

'Old puff-and-blow gone?' asked Mr. Sponge, depositing his hat and whip on a chair.

The boy gave no answer.

'Is old bellows-to-mend gone to bed?' asked Mr. Sponge in a louder voice.

'The charman's gone,' replied the boy, who looked upon his master—the chairman of the Stir-it-stiff Union—as the impersonification of all earthly greatness.

'Dash your impittance,' growled Jog, slinking back into the nursery; 'I'll pay you off! (puff),' added he, with a jerk of his white night-capped head, 'I'll bellows-to-mend you! (wheeze).'

LIV

FAMILY JARS

GUSTAVUS JAMES'S INTERNAL QUALMS BEING at length appeased, Mr. Jogglebury Crowdey returned to bed, but not to sleep—sleep there was none for him. He was full of indignation and jealousy, and felt suspicious of the very bolster itself. He had been insulted—grossly insulted. Three such names—the 'Woolpack,' 'Old puff-and-blow,' and 'Bellows-to-mend'—no gentleman, surely, ever was called before by a guest, in his own house. Called, too, before his own servant. What veneration, what respect, could a servant feel for a master whom he heard called 'Old bellows-to-mend'? It damaged the respect inspired by the chairmanship of the Stir-it-stiff Union, to say nothing of the trusteeship of the Sloppyhocks, Tolpuddle, and other turnpike-roads. It annihilated everything. So he fumed, and fretted, and snorted, and snored. Worst of all, he had no one to whom he could unburden his grievance. He could not make the partner of his bosom a partner in his woes, because—and he bounced about so that he almost shot the clothes off the bed, at the thoughts of the 'why.'

Thus he lay tumbling and tossing, and fuming and wheezing and puffing, now vowing vengeance against Leather, who he recollected had called him the 'Woolpack,' and determining to have him turned off in the morning for his impudence—now devising schemes for getting rid of Mr. Sponge and him together. Oh, could he but see them off! could he but see the portmanteau and carpet-bag again standing in the passage, he would gladly lend his phaeton to carry them anywhere. He would drive it himself for the pleasure of knowing and feeling he was clear of them. He wouldn't haggle about the pikes; nay, he would even give Sponge a gibbey, any he liked—the pick of the whole—Wellington, Napoleon Bonaparte, a crowned head even, though it would damage the set. So he lay, rolling and restless, hearing every clock strike; now trying to divert his thoughts, by making a rough calculation what all his gibbeys put together were worth; now considering whether he had forgotten to go for any he had marked in the course of his peregrinations; now wishing he had laid one about old Leather, when he fell on his knees after calling him the 'Woolpack'; then wondering whether Leather would have had him before the County Court for damages, or taken him before Justice Slowcoach for the assault. As morning advanced, his thoughts again turned upon the best mode of getting rid of his most unwelcome guests, and he arose and dressed, with the full determination of trying what he could do.

Having tried the effects of an upstairs shout the morning before, he decided to see what a down one would do; accordingly, he mounted the stairs and climbed the sort of companion-ladder that led to the servants' attics, where he kept a stock of gibbeys in the rafters. Having reached this, he cleared his throat, laid his head over the banisters, and putting an open hand on each side of his mouth to direct the sound, exclaimed with a loud and audible voice:

'BARTHOLO—*m*—*e*—*w*!'

'BAR—THO—LO—*m*—*e*—*e*—*w*!' repeated he, after a pause, with a full separation of the syllables and a prolonged intonation of the *m*—*e*—*w*.

No Bartholomew answered.

'MURRAY ANN!' then hallooed Jog, in a sharper, quicker key. 'MURRAY ANN!' repeated he, still louder, after a pause.

'Yes, sir! here, sir!' exclaimed that invaluable servant, tidying her pink-ribboned cap as she hurried into the passage below. Looking up, she caught sight of her master's great sallow chaps hanging like a flitch of bacon over the garret banister.

'Oh, Murry Ann,' bellowed Mr. Jog, at the top of his voice, still holding his hands to his mouth, as soon as he saw her, 'Oh, Murry Ann, you'd better get the (puff) breakfast ready; I think the (gasp) Mr. Sponge will be (wheezing) away to-day.'

'Yes, sir,' replied Mary Ann.

'And tell Bartholomew to get his washin' bills in.'

'He harn't had no washin' done,' replied Mary Ann, raising her voice to correspond with that of her master.

'Then his bill for postage,' replied Mr. Jog, in the same tone.

'He harn't had no letters neither,' replied Mary Ann.

'Oh, then, just get the breakfast ready,' rejoined Jog, adding, 'he'll be (wheezing) away as soon as he gets it, I (puff) expect.'

'Will he?' said Mr. Sponge to himself, as, with throbbing head, he lay tumbling about in bed, alleviating the recollections of the previous day's debauch with an occasional dive into his old friend *Mogg*. Corporeally, he was in bed at Puddingpote Bower, but mentally, he was at the door of the Goose and Gridiron, in St. Paul's Churchyard, waiting for the three o'clock bus, coming from the Bank to take him to Isleworth Gate.

Jog's bellow to 'Bartholo—*m*—*e*—*w*' interrupted the journey, just as in imagination Mr. Sponge was putting his foot on the wheel and hallooing to the driver to hand him the strap to help him on to the box.

'Will he?' said Mr. Sponge to himself, as he heard Jog's reiterated assertion that he would be wheezing away that day. 'Wish you may get it, old boy,' added he, tucking the now backless *Mogg* under his pillow, and turning over for a snooze.

When he got down, he found the party ranged at breakfast, minus the interesting prodigy, Gustavus James, whom Sponge proceeded to inquire after as soon as he had made his obeisance to his host and hostess, and distributed a round of daubed comfits to the rest of the juvenile party.

'But where's my little friend, Augustus James?' asked he, on arriving at the wonder's high chair by the side of mamma. 'Where's my little friend, Augustus James?' asked he, with an air of concern.

'Oh, *Gustavus* James,' replied Mrs. Jog, with an emphasis on Gustavus; '*Gustavus* James is not very well this morning; had a little indigestion during the night.'

'Poor little hound,' observed Mr. Sponge, filling his mouth with hot kidney, glad to be rid for a time of the prodigy. 'I thought I heard a row when I came home, which was rather late for an early man like me, but the fact was, nothing would serve Sir Harry but I should go with him to get some refreshment at a tenant's of his; and we got on talking, first about one thing, and then about another, and the time slipped away so quickly, that day was gone before I knew where I was; and though Sir Harry was most anxious—indeed, would hardly take a refusal—for me to go home with him, I felt that, being a guest here, I couldn't do it—at least, not then; so I got my horse, and tried to find my way with such directions as the farmer gave me, and soon lost my way, for the moon was uncertain, and the country all strange both to me and my horse.'

'What farmer was it?' asked Jog, with the butter streaming down the gutters of his chin from a mouthful of thick toast. 'Farmer—farmer—farmer—let me see, what farmer it was,' replied Mr. Sponge thoughtfully, again attacking the kidneys. 'Oh, farmer Beanstraw, I should say.'

'*Pea*straw, p'raps?' suggested Jog, colouring up, and staring intently at Mr. Sponge.

'Pea—Peastraw was the name,' replied Mr. Sponge.

'I know him,' said Jog; 'Peastraw of Stoke.'

'Ah, he said he knew you.' replied Mr. Sponge.

'Did he?' asked Jog eagerly. 'What did he say?'

'Say—let me see what he said,' replied he, pretending to recollect.' He said "you are a deuced good feller," and I'd to make his compliments to you, and to say that there were some nice young ash saplings on his farm that you were welcome to cut.'

'Did he?' exclaimed Jog; 'I'm sure that's very (puff) polite of him. I'll (wheeze) over there the first opportunity.'

'And what did you make of Sir Harry?' asked Mrs. Jog.

'Did you (puff) say you were going to (wheeze) over to him?' asked Jog eagerly.

'I told him I'd go to him before I left the country,' replied Mr. Sponge, carelessly; adding, 'Sir Harry is rather too fast a man for me.'

'Too fast for himself, I should think,' observed Mrs. Jog.

'Fine (puff—wheeze) young man,' growled Jog into the bottom of his cup.

'Have you known him long?' asked Mrs. Jogglebury.

'Oh, we fox-hunters all know each other,' replied Mr. Sponge evasively.

'Well, now that's what I tell Mr. Jogglebury,' exclaimed she. 'Mr. Jog's so shy, that there's no getting him to do what he ought,' added the lady. 'No one, to hear him, would think he's the great man he is.'

'Ought (puff)—ought (wheeze),' retorted Jog, puffing furiously into his capacious shirt-frill. 'It's one (puff) thing to know (puff) people out with the (wheeze) hounds, and another to go calling upon them at their (gasp) houses.' 'Well, but, my dear, that's the way people make acquaintance,' replied his wife. 'Isn't it, Mr. Sponge?' continued she, appealing to our friend.

'Oh, certainly,' replied Mr. Sponge, 'certainly; all men are equal out hunting.'

'So I say,' exclaimed Mrs. Jogglebury; 'and yet I can't get Jog to call on Sir George Stiff, though he meets him frequently out hunting.'

'Well, but then I can't (puff) upon him out hunting (wheeze), and then we're not all equal (gasp) when we go home.'

So saying, our friend rose from his chair, and after giving each leg its usual shake, and banging his pockets behind to feel that he had his keys safe, he strutted consequentially up to the window to see how the day looked.

Mr. Sponge, not being desirous of continuing the 'calling' controversy, especially as it might lead to inquiries relative to his acquaintance with Sir Harry, finished the contents of his plate quickly, drank up his tea, and was presently alongside of his host, asking him whether he 'was good for a ride, a walk, or what?'

'A (puff) ride, a (wheeze) walk, or a (gasp) what?' repeated Jog thoughtfully. 'No, I (puff) think I'll stay at (puff) home,' thinking that would be the safest plan.

''Ord, hang it, you'll never lie at earth such a day as this!' exclaimed Sponge, looking out on the bright, sunny landscape.

'Got a great deal to do,' retorted Jog, who, like all thoroughly idle men, was always dreadfully busy. He then dived into a bundle of rough sticks, and proceeded to select one to fashion into the head of Mr. Hume. Sponge, being unable to make anything of him, was obliged to exhaust the day in the stable, and in sauntering about the country. It was clear Jog was determined to be rid of him, and he was sadly puzzled what to do. Dinner found his host in no better humour, and after a sort of Quakers' meeting of an evening, they parted, heartily sick of each other.

LV

THE TRIGGER

JOG SLEPT BADLY AGAIN, AND arose next morning full of projects for getting rid of his impudent, unceremonious, free-and-easy guest.

Having tried both an up and a downstairs shout, he now went out and planted himself immediately under Mr. Sponge's bedroom window, and, clearing his voice, commenced his usual vociferations.

'Bartholo—*m*—*e*—*w*!' whined he. '*Bartholo*—*m*—*e*—*w*!' repeated he, somewhat louder. 'BAR—THOLO—*m*—*e*—*w*!' roared he, in a voice of thunder.

Bartholomew did not answer.

'Murry Ann!' exclaimed Jog, after a pause. '*Murry Ann*!' repeated he, still louder. 'MURRAY ANN!' roared he, at the top of his voice.

'Comin', sir! comin'!' exclaimed Mary Ann, peeping down upon him from the garret-window.

'Oh, Murry Ann,' cried Mr. Jog, looking up, and catching the ends of her blue ribbons streaming past the window-frame, as she changed her nightcap for a day one, 'oh, Murry Ann, you'd better be (puff)in' forrard with the (gasp) breakfast; Mr. Sponge'll most likely be (wheeze)in' away to-day.'

'Yes, sir,' replied Mary Ann, adjusting the cap becomingly.

'Confounded, puffing, wheezing, gasping, broken-winded old blockhead it is!' growled Mr. Sponge, wishing he could get to his former earth at Puffington's, or anywhere else. When he got down he found Jog in a very roomy, bright, green-plush shooting-jacket, with pockets innumerable, and a whistle suspended to a button-hole. His nether man was encased in a pair of most dilapidated white moleskins, that had been degraded from hunting into shooting ones, and whose cracks and darns showed the perils to which their wearer had been exposed. Below these were drab, horn-buttoned gaiters, and hob-nailed shoes.

'Going a-gunning, are you?' asked Mr. Sponge, after the morning salutation, which Jog returned most gruffly.

'I'll go with you,' said Mr. Sponge, at once dispelling the delusion of his wheezing away.

'Only going to frighten the (puff) rooks off the (gasp) wheat,' replied Jog carelessly, not wishing to let Sponge see what a numb hand he was with a gun.

'I thought you told me you were going to get me a hare,' observed Mrs. Jog; adding, 'I'm sure shooting is a much more rational amusement than tearing your clothes going after the hounds,' eyeing the much dilapidated moleskins as she spoke.

Mrs. Jog found shooting more useful than hunting.

'Oh, if a (puff) hare comes in my (gasp) way, I'll turn her over,' replied Jog carelessly, as if turning them over was quite a matter of course with him; adding, 'but I'm not (wheezing) out for the express purpose of shooting one.'

'Ah, well,' observed Sponge, 'I'll go with you, all the same.'

'But I've only got one gun,' gasped Jog, thinking it would be worse to have Sponge laughing at his shooting than even leaving him at home.

'Then, we'll shoot turn and turn about,' replied the pertinacious guest.

Jog did his best to dissuade him, observing that the birds were (puff) scarce and (wheeze) wild, and the (gasp) hares much troubled with poachers; but Mr. Sponge wanted a walk, and moreover had a fancy for seeing Jog handle his gun.

Having cut himself some extremely substantial sandwiches, and filled his 'monkey' full of sherry, our friend Jog slipped out the back way to loosen old Ponto, who acted the triple part of pointer, house-dog, and horse to Gustavus James. He was a great fat, black-and-white brute, with a head like a hat-box, a tail like a clothes-peg, and a back as broad as a well-fed sheep's. The old brute was so frantic at the sight of his master in his green coat, and wide-awake to match, that he jumped and bounced, and barked, and rattled his chain, and set up such yells, that his noise sounded all over the house, and soon brought Mr. Sponge to the scene of action, where stood our friend, loading his gun and looking as consequential as possible.

'I shall only just take a (puff) stroll over moy (wheeze) ter-ri-to-ry,' observed Jog, as Mr. Sponge emerged at the back door.

Jog's pace was about two miles and a half an hour, stoppages included, and he thought it advisable to prepare Mr. Sponge for the trial. He then shouldered his gun and waddled away, first over the stile into Farmer Stiffland's stubble, round which Ponto ranged in the most riotous, independent way, regardless of Jog's whistles and rates and the crack of his little knotty whip. Jog then crossed the old pasture into Mr. Lowland's turnips, into which Ponto dashed in the same energetic way, but these impediments to travelling soon told on his great buttermilk carcass, and brought him to a more subdued pace; still, the dog had a good deal more energy than his master. Round he went, sniffing and hunting, then dashing right through the middle of the field, as if he was out on his own account alone, and had nothing whatever to do with a master.

'Why, your dog'll spring all the birds out of shot,' observed Mr. Sponge; and, just as he spoke, whirr! rose a covey of partridges, eleven in number, quite at an impossible distance, but Jog blazed away all the same.

''Ord rot it, man! if you'd only held your (something) tongue,' growled Jog, as he shaded the sun from his eyes to mark them down, 'I'd have (wheezed) half of them over.'

'Nonsense, man!' replied Mr. Sponge. 'They were a mile out of shot.'

'I think I should know my (puff) gun better than (wheeze) you,' replied Jog, bringing it down to load.

'They're down!' exclaimed Mr. Sponge, who, having watched them till they began to skim in their flight, saw them stop, flap their wings, and drop among some straggling gorse on the hill before them. 'Let's break the covey; we shall bag them better singly.'

'Take time (puff),' replied Jog, snorting into his frill, and measuring out his powder most leisurely. 'Take time (wheeze),' repeated he; 'they're just on the bounds of moy ter-ri-to-ry.'

Jog had had many a game at romps with these birds, and knew their haunts and habits to a nicety. The covey consisted of thirteen at first, but by repeated blazings into the 'brown of 'em,' he had succeeded in knocking down two. Jog was not one of your conceited shots, who never fired but when he was sure of killing; on the contrary, he always let drive far or near;

and even if he shot a hare, which he sometimes did, with the first barrel, he always popped the second into her, to make sure. The chairman's shooting afforded amusement to the neighbourhood. On one occasion a party of reapers, having watched him miss twelve shots in succession, gave him three cheers on coming to the thirteenth—but to our day. Jog had now got his gun reloaded with mischief, the cap put on, and all ready for a fresh start. Ponto, meanwhile, had been ranging, Jog thinking it better to let him take the edge off his ardour than conform to the strict rules of lying down or coming to heel. 'Now, let's on,' cried Mr. Sponge, stepping out quickly.

'Take time (puff), take time (wheeze),' gasped Jog, waddling along; 'better let 'em settle a little (puff). Better let 'em settle a little (gasp),' added he, labouring on.

'Oh, no, keep them moving,' replied Mr. Sponge, 'keep them moving. Only get at 'em on the hill, and drive 'em into the fields below, and we shall have rare fun.'

'But the (puff) fields below are not mine,' gasped Jog.

'Whose are they?' asked Mr. Sponge.

'Oh (puff), Mrs. Moses's,' gasped Jog. 'My stoopid old uncle,' continued he, stopping, and laying hold of Mr. Sponge's arm, as if to illustrate his position, but in reality to get breath, 'my stoopid old uncle (puff) missed buying that (wheeze) land when old Harry Griperton died. I only wanted that to make moy (wheeze) ter-ri-to-ry extend all the (gasp) way up to Cockwhistle Park there,' continued he, climbing on to a stile they now approached, and setting aside the top stone. 'That's Cockwhistle Park, up there—just where you see the (puff) windmill—then (puff) moy (wheeze) ter-ri-to-ry comes up to the (wheeze) fallow you see all yellow with runch; and if my old (puff) uncle (wheeze) Crowdey had had the sense of a (gasp) goose, he'd have (wheezed) that when it was sold. Moy (puff) name was (wheeze) Jogglebury,' added he, 'before my (gasp) uncle died.'

'Well, never mind about that,' replied Mr. Sponge; 'let us go on after these birds.'

'Oh, we'll (puff) up to them presently,' observed Jog, labouring away, with half a ton of clay at each foot, the sun having dispelled the frost where it struck, and made the land carry.

'*Presently!*' retorted Mr. Sponge. 'But you should make haste, man.'

'Well, but let me go my own (puff) pace,' snapped Jog, labouring away.

'Pace!' exclaimed Mr. Sponge, 'your own crawl, you should say.'

'Indeed!' growled Jog, with an angry snort.

They now got through a well-established cattle-gap into a very rushy, squashy, gorse-grown pasture, at the bottom of the rising ground on which Mr. Sponge had marked the birds. Ponto, whose energetic exertions had been gradually relaxing, until he had settled down to a leisurely hunting-dog, suddenly stood transfixed, with the right foot up, and his gaze settled on a rushy tuft.

'P-o-o-n-to!' ejaculated Jog, expecting every minute to see him dash at it. 'P-o-o-n-to!' repeated he, raising his hand.

Mr. Sponge stood on the tip-toe of expectation; Jog raised his wide-awake hat from his eyes and advanced cautiously with the engine of destruction cocked. Up started a great hare; bang! went the gun, with the hare none the worse. Bang! went the other barrel, which the hare acknowledged by two or three stotting bounds and an increase of pace.

'Well missed!' exclaimed Mr. Sponge.

Away went Ponto in pursuit.

'P-o-o-n-to!' shrieked Jog, stamping with rage.

'I could have wiped your nose,' exclaimed Mr. Sponge, covering the hare with a hedge-stake placed to his shoulder like a gun.

'Could you?' growled Jog; ''spose you wipe your own,' added he, not understanding the meaning of the term.

Meanwhile, old Ponto went rolling away most energetically, the farther he went the farther he was left behind, till the hare having scuttled out of sight, he wheeled about and came leisurely back, as if he was doing all right.

Jog was very wroth, and vented his anger on the dog, which, he declared, had caused him to miss, vowing, as he rammed away at the charge, that he never missed such a shot before. Mr. Sponge stood eyeing him with a look of incredulity, thinking that a man who could miss such a shot could miss anything. They were now all ready for a fresh start, and Ponto, having pocketed his objurgation, dashed forward again up the rising ground over which the covey had dropped.

Jog's thick wind was a serious impediment to the expeditious mounting of the hill, and the dog seemed aware of his infirmity, and to take pleasure in aggravating him.

'P-o-o-n-to!' gasped Jog, as he slipped, and scrambled, and toiled, sorely impeded by the encumbrance of his gun.

But P-o-o-n-to heeded him not. He knew his master couldn't catch him, and if he did, that he durstn't flog him.

'P-o-o-n-to!' gasped Jog again, still louder, catching at a bush to prevent his slipping back. 'T-o-o-h-o-o! P-o-o-n-to!' wheezed he; but the dog just rolled his great stern, and bustled about more actively than ever.

'Hang ye! but I'd cut you in two if I had you!' exclaimed Mr. Sponge, eyeing his independent proceedings.

'He's not a bad (puff) dog,' observed Jog, mopping the perspiration from his brow.

'He's not a good 'un,' retorted Mr. Sponge.

'D'ye think not (wheeze)?' asked Jog.

'Sure of it,' replied Sponge.

'Serves me,' growled Jog, labouring up the hill.

'Easy served,' replied Mr. Sponge, whistling, and eyeing the independent animal.

'T-o-o-h-o-o! P-o-o-n-t-o!' gasped Jog, as he dashed forward on reaching level ground more eagerly than ever.

'P-o-o-n-to! T-o-o-h-o-o!' repeated he, in a still louder tone, with the same success.

'You'd better get up to him,' observed Mr. Sponge, 'or he'll spring all the birds.'

Jog, however, blundered on at his own pace, growling:

'Most (puff) haste, least (wheeze) speed.'

The dog was now fast drawing upon where the birds lit; and Mr. Sponge and Jog having reached the top of the hill, Mr. Sponge stood still to watch the result.

Up whirred four birds out of a patch of gorse behind the dog, all presenting most beautiful shots. Jog blazed a barrel at them without touching a feather, and the report of the gun immediately raised three brace more into the thick of which he fired with similar success. They all skimmed away unhurt.

'Well missed!' exclaimed Mr. Sponge again. 'You're what they call a good shooter but a bad hitter.'

'You're what they call a (wheeze) fellow,' growled Jog.

He meant to say 'saucy,' but the word wouldn't rise. He then commenced reloading his gun, and lecturing P-o-o-n-to, who still continued his exertions, and inwardly anathematizing Mr. Sponge. He wished he had left him at home. Then recollecting Mrs. Jog, he thought perhaps he was as well where he was. Still his presence made him shoot worse than usual, and there was no occasion for that.

'Let *me* have a shot now,' said Mr. Sponge.

'Shot (puff)—shot (wheeze); well, take a shot if you choose,' replied he.

Just as Mr. Sponge got the gun, up rose the eleventh bird, and he knocked it over.

'*That's* the way to do it!' exclaimed Mr. Sponge, as the bird fell dead before Ponto.

The excited dog, unused to such descents, snatched it up and ran off. Just as he was getting out of shot, Mr. Sponge fired the other barrel at him, causing him to drop the bird and run yelping and howling away. Jog was furious. He stamped, and gasped, and fumed, and wheezed, and seemed like to burst with anger and indignation. Though the dog ran away as hard as he could lick, Jog insisted that he was mortally wounded, and would die. 'He never saw so (wheeze) a thing done. He wouldn't have taken twenty pounds for the dog. No, he wouldn't have taken thirty. Forty wouldn't have bought him. He was worth fifty of anybody's money,' and so he went on, fuming and advancing his value as he spoke.

Mr. Sponge stole away to where the dog had dropped the bird; and Mr. Jog, availing himself of his absence, retraced his steps down the hill, and struck off home at a much faster pace than he came. Arrived there, he found the dog in the kitchen, somewhat sore from the visitation of the shot, but not sufficiently injured to prevent his enjoying a most liberal plate of stick-jaw pudding supplied by a general contribution of the servants. Jog's wrath was then turned in another direction, and he blew up for the waste and extravagance of the act, hinting pretty freely that he knew who it was that had set them against it. Altogether he was full of troubles, vexations, and annoyances; and after spending another most disagreeable evening with our friend Sponge, went to bed more determined than ever to get rid of him.

LVI

Nonsuch House Again

Poor Jog again varied his hints the next morning. After sundry prefatory 'Murry Anns!' and 'Bar-tho-lo-*mews*!' he at length got the latter to answer, when, raising his voice so as to fill the whole house, he desired him to go to the stable, and let Mr. Sponge's man know his master would be (wheezing) away.

'You're wrong there, old buck,' growled Leather, as he heard the foregoing; 'he's half-way to Sir 'Arry's by this time.'

And sure enough, Mr. Sponge was, as none knew better than Leather, who had got him his horse, the hack being indisposed—that is to say, having been out all night with Mr. Leather on a drinking excursion, Leather having just got home in time to receive the purple-coated, bare-footed runner of Nonsuch House, who dropped in, *en passant*, to see if there was anything to stow away in his roomy trouser-pockets, and leave word that Sir Harry was going to hunt, and would meet before the house.

Leather, though somewhat muzzy, was sufficiently sober to be able to deliver this message, and acquaint Mr. Sponge with the impossibility of his 'ridin' the 'ack.' Indeed, he truly said that he had 'been hup with him all night, and at one time thought it was all hover with him,' the all-overishness consisting of Mr. Leather being nearly all over the hack's head, in consequence of the animal shying at another drunken man lying across the road.

Mr. Sponge listened to the recital with the indifference of a man who rides hack-horses, and coolly observed that Leather must take on the chestnut, and he would ride the brown to cover.

'Couldn't, sir, couldn't,' replied Leather, with a shake of the head and a twinkle of his roguish, watery grey eyes.

'Why not?' asked Mr. Sponge, who never saw any difficulty.

'Oh, sur,' replied Leather, in a tone of despondency, 'it would be quite unpossible. Consider wot a day the last one was; why, he didn't get to rest till three the next mornin'.'

'It'll only be walking exercise,' observed Mr. Sponge; 'do him good.'

'Better valk the chestnut,' replied Mr. Leather; 'Multum-in-Parvo hasn't 'ad a good day this I don't know wen, and will be all the better of a bucketin'.'

'But I hate crawling to cover on my horse,' replied Mr. Sponge, who liked cantering along with a flourish.

'You'll have to crawl if you ride 'Ercles,' observed Leather, 'if not walk. Bless you! I've been a-nussin' of him and the 'ack most the 'ole night.'

'Indeed!' replied Mr. Sponge, who began to be alarmed lest his hunting might be brought to an abrupt termination.

'True as I'm 'ere,' rejoined Leather. 'He's just as much off his grub as he vos when he com'd in; never see'd an 'oss more reg'larly dished—more—'

'Well, well,' said Mr. Sponge, interrupting the catalogue of grievances; 'I s'pose I must do as you say—I s'pose I must do as you say: what sort of a day is it?'

'Vy, the day's not a bad day; at least that's to say, it's not a wery haggrivatin' day. I've seen a betterer day, in course; but I've also seen many a much worser day, and days at this time of year, you know, are apt to change—sometimes, in course, for the betterer—sometimes, in course, for the worser.'

'Is it a frost?' snapped Mr. Sponge, tired of his loquacity.

'Is it a frost?' repeated Mr. Leather thoughtfully; 'is it a frost? Vy, no; I should say it isn't a frost—at least, not a frost to 'urt; there may be a little rind on the ground and a little rawness in the hair, but the general concatenation—'

'Hout, tout!' exclaimed Mr. Sponge, 'let's have none of your dictionary words.'

Mr. Leather stood silent, twisting his hat about.

The consequence of all this was, that Mr. Sponge determined to ride over to Nonsuch House to breakfast, which would give his horse half an hour in the stable to eat a feed of corn. Accordingly, he desired Leather to bring him his shaving-water, and have the horse ready in the stable

in half an hour, whither, in due time, Mr. Sponge emerged by the back
door, without encountering any of the family. The ambling piebald
looked so crestfallen and woebegone in all the swaddling-clothes in
which Leather had got him enveloped, that Mr. Sponge did not care to
look at the gallant Hercules, who occupied a temporary loose-box at the
far end of the dark stable, lest he might look worse. He, therefore, just
mounted Multum-in-Parvo as Leather led him out at the door, and set
off without a word.

'Well, hang me, but you are a good judge of weather,' exclaimed
Sponge to himself, as he got into the field at the back of the house, and
found the horse made little impression on the grass. '*No frost!*' repeated
he, breathing into the air; 'why it's freezing now, out of the sun.'

On getting into Marygold Lane, our friend drew rein, and was for
turning back, but the resolute chestnut took the bit between his teeth
and shook his head, as if determined to go on.

'Oh, you brute!' growled Mr. Sponge, letting the spurs into his sides
with a hearty goodwill, which caused the animal to kick, as if he meant
to stand on his head. 'Ah, you *will*, will ye?' exclaimed Mr. Sponge, letting
the spurs in again as the animal replaced his legs on the ground. Up they
went again, if possible higher than before.

The brute was clearly full of mischief, and even if the hounds did
not throw off, which there was little prospect of their doing from
the appearance of the weather, Mr. Sponge felt that it would be well
to get some of the nonsense taken out of him; and, moreover, going
to Nonsuch House would give him a chance of establishing a billet
there—a chance that he had been deprived of by Sir Harry's abrupt
departure from Farmer Peastraw's. So saying, our friend gathered his
horse together, and settling himself in his saddle, made his sound hoofs
ring upon the hard road.

'He *may* hunt,' thought Mr. Sponge, as he rattled along; 'such a rum
beggar as Sir Harry may think it fun to go out in a frost. It's hard, too,'
said he, as he saw the poor turnip-pullers enveloped in their thick shawls,
and watched them thumping their arms against their sides to drive the
cold from their finger-ends.

Multum-in-Parvo was a good, sound-constitutioned horse, hard and
firm as a cricket-ball, a horse that would not turn a hair for a trifle even
on a hunting morning, let alone on such a thorough chiller as this one

was; and Mr. Sponge, after going along at a good round pace, and getting over the ground much quicker than he did when the road was all new to him, and he had to ask his way, at length drew in to see what o'clock it was. It was only half-past nine, and already in the far distance he saw the encircling woods of Nonsuch House.

'Shall be early,' said Mr. Sponge, returning his watch to his waistcoat-pocket, and diving into his cutty coat-pocket for the cigar-case. Having struck a light, he now laid the rein on the horse's neck and proceeded leisurely along, the animal stepping gaily and throwing its head about as if he was the quietest, most trustworthy nag in the world. If he got there at half-past ten, Mr. Sponge calculated he would have plenty of time to see after his horse, get his own breakfast, and see how the land lay for a billet.

It would be impossible to hunt before twelve; so he went smoking and sauntering along, now wondering whether he would be able to establish a billet, now thinking how he would like to sell Sir Harry a horse, then considering whether he would be likely to pay for him, and enlivening the general reflections by ringing his spurs against his stirrup-irons.

Having passed the lodges at the end of the avenue, he cocked his hat, twiddled his hair, felt his tie, and arranged for a becoming appearance. The sudden turn of the road brought him full upon the house. How changed the scene! Instead of the scarlet-coated youths thronging the gravelled ring, flourishing their scented kerchiefs and hunting-whips—instead of buxom Abigails and handsome mistresses hanging out of the windows, flirting and chatting and ogling, the door was shut, the blinds were down, the shutters closed, and the whole house had the appearance of mourning.

Mr. Sponge reined up involuntarily, startled at the change of scene. What could have happened! Could Sir Harry be dead? Could my lady have eloped? 'Oh, that horrid Bugles!' thought he; 'he looked like a gay deceiver.' And Mr. Sponge felt as if he had sustained a personal injury.

Just as these thoughts were passing in his mind, a drowsy, slatternly charwoman, in an old black straw bonnet and grey bed-gown, opened one of the shutters, and throwing up the sash of the window by where Mr. Sponge sat, disclosed the contents of the apartment. The last waxlight was just dying out in the centre of a splendid candelabra on the middle of a table scattered about with claret-jugs, glasses, decanters, pine-apple tops, grape-dishes, cakes, anchovy-toast plates, devilled biscuit-racks—all the concomitants of a sumptuous entertainment.

'Sir Harry at home?' asked Mr. Sponge, making the woman sensible of his presence, by cracking his whip close to her ear. 'No,' replied the dame gruffly, commencing an assault upon the nearest chair with a duster.

'Where is he?' asked our friend.

'Bed, to be sure,' replied the woman, in the same tone.

'Bed, to be sure,' repeated Mr. Sponge. 'I don't think there's any 'sure' in the case. Do you know what o'clock it is?' asked he.

'No,' replied the woman, flopping away at another chair, and arranging the crimson velvet curtains on the holders.

Mr. Sponge was rather nonplussed. His red coat did not command the respect that a red coat generally does. The fact was, they had such queer people in red coats at Nonsuch House, that a red coat was rather an object of suspicion than otherwise.

'Well, but, my good woman,' continued Mr. Sponge, softening his tone, 'can you tell me where I shall find anybody who can tell me anything about the hounds?'

'No,' growled the woman, still flopping, and whisking, and knocking the furniture about.

'I'll remember you for your trouble,' observed Mr. Sponge, diving his right hand into his breeches' pocket.

'Mr. Bottleends be gone to bed,' observed the woman, now ceasing her evolutions, and parting her grisly, disordered tresses, as she advanced and stood staring, with her arms akimbo, out of the window. She was the under-housemaid's deputy; all the servants at Nonsuch House doing the rough of their work by deputy. Lady Scattercash was a *real* lady, and liked to have the credit of the house maintained, which of course can only be done by letting the upper servants do nothing. 'Mr. Bottleends be gone to bed,' observed the woman.

'Mr. Bottleends?' repeated Mr. Sponge; 'who's he?'

'The butler, to be sure,' replied she, astonished that any person should have to ask who such an important personage was.

'Can't you call him?' asked Mr. Sponge, still fumbling in his pocket.

'Couldn't, if it was ever so,' replied the dame, smoothing her dirty blue-checked apron with her still dirtier hand.

'Why not?' asked Mr. Sponge.

'Why not?' repeated the woman; 'why, 'cause Mr. Bottleends won't be disturbed by no one. He said when he went to bed that he hadn't to be called till to-morrow.'

'Not called till to-morrow!' exclaimed Mr. Sponge; 'then is Sir Harry from home?'

'From home, no; what should put that i' your head?' sneered the woman.

'Why, if the butler's in bed, one may suppose the master's away.'

'Hout!' snapped the woman; 'Sir Harry's i' bed—Captin Seedeybuck's i' bed—Captin Quod's i' bed—Captin Spangle's i' bed—Captin Bouncey's i' bed—Captin Cutitfat's i' bed—they're all i' bed 'cept me, and I've got the house to clean and right, and high time it was cleaned and righted, for they've not been i' bed these three nights any on 'em.' So saying, she flourished her duster as if about to set-to again.

'Well, but tell me,' exclaimed Mr. Sponge, 'can I see the footman, or the huntsman, or the groom, or a helper, or anybody?'

'Deary knows,' replied the woman thoughtfully, resting her chin on her hand. 'I dare say they'll be all i' bed too.'

'But they are going to hunt, aren't they?' asked our friend.

'*Hunt!*' exclaimed the woman; 'what should put that i' your head.'

'Why, they sent me word they were.'

'It'll be i' bed, then,' observed she, again giving symptoms of a desire to return to her dusting.

Mr. Sponge, who still kept his hand in his pocket, sat on his horse in a state of stupid bewilderment. He had never seen a case of this sort before—a house shut up, and a master of hounds in bed when the hounds were to meet before the door. It couldn't be the case: the woman must be dreaming, or drunk, or both.

'Well, but, my good woman,' exclaimed he, as she gave a punishing cut at the chair, as if to make up for lost time; 'well, but, my good woman, I wish you would try and find somebody who can tell me something about the hounds. I'm sure they must be going to hunt. I'll remember you for your trouble, if you will,' added he, again diving his hand up to the wrist in his pocket.

'I tell you,' replied the woman slowly and deliberately, 'there'll be no huntin' to-day. Huntin'!' exclaimed she; 'how can they hunt when they've all had to be carried to bed?'

'Carried to bed! had they?' exclaimed Mr. Sponge; 'what, were they drunk?'

'Drunk! aye, to be sure. What would you have them be?' replied the crone, who seemed to think that drinking was a necessary concomitant of hunting.

'Well, but I can see the footman or somebody, surely,' observed Mr. Sponge, fearing that his chance was out for a billet, and recollecting old Jog's 'Bartholo-*m-e-ws*!' and 'Murry Anns!' and intimations for him to start.

''Deed you can't,' replied the dame—'ye can see nebody but me,' added she, fixing her twinkling eyes intently upon him as she spoke.

'Well, that's a pretty go,' observed Mr. Sponge aloud to himself, ringing his spurs against his stirrup-irons.

'Pretty go or ugly go,' snapped the woman, thinking it was a reflection on herself, 'it's all you'll get'; and thereupon she gave the back of the chair a hearty bastinadoing as if in exemplification of the way she would like to serve Mr. Sponge out for the observation.

'I came here thinking to get some breakfast,' observed Mr. Sponge, casting an eye upon the disordered table, and reconnoitring the bottles and the remains of the dessert.

'Did you?' said the woman; 'I wish you may get it.'

'I wish I may,' replied he. 'If you would manage that for me, just some coffee and a mutton chop or two, I'd remember you,' said he, still tantalizing her with the sound of the silver in his pocket.

'Me manish it!' exclaimed the woman, her hopes again rising at the sound; 'me manish it! how d'ye think I'm to manish sich things?' asked she.

'Why, get at the cook, or the housekeeper, or somebody,' replied Mr. Sponge.

'Cook or housekeeper!' exclaimed she. 'There'll be no cook or housekeeper astir here these many hours yet; I question,' added she, 'they get up to-day.'

'What! they've been put to bed too, have they?' asked he.

'W-h-y no—not zactly that,' drawled the woman; 'but when sarvants are kept up three nights out of four, they must make up for lost time when they can.'

'Well,' mused Mr. Sponge, 'this is a bother, at all events; get no breakfast, lose my hunt, and perhaps a billet into the bargain. Well, there's sixpence for you, my good woman,' said he at length, drawing his hand out of his pocket and handing her the contents through the window; adding, 'don't make a beast of yourself with it.'

'It's nabbut *fourpence*,' observed the woman, holding it out on the palm of her hand.

'Ah, well, you're welcome to it whatever it is,' replied our friend, turning his horse to go away. A thought then struck him. 'Could you get me a pen and ink, think you?' asked he; 'I want to write a line to Sir Harry.'

'Pen and ink!' replied the woman, who had pocketed the groat and resumed her dusting; 'I don't know where they keep no such things as penses and inkses.'

'Most likely in the drawing-room or the sitting-room, or perhaps in the butler's pantry,' observed Mr. Sponge.

'Well, you can come in and see,' replied the woman, thinking there was no occasion to give herself any more trouble for the fourpenny-piece.

Our worthy friend sat on his horse a few seconds staring intently into the dining-room window, thinking that lapse of time might cause the fourpenny-piece to be sufficiently respected to procure him something like directions how to proceed as well to get rid of his horse, as to procure access to the house, the door of which stood frowningly shut. In this, however, he was mistaken, for no sooner had the woman uttered the words, 'Well, you can come in and see,' than she flaunted into the interior of the room, and commenced a regular series of assaults upon the furniture, throwing the hearth-rug over one chair back, depositing the fire-irons in another, rearing the steel fender up against the Carrara marble chimney-piece, and knocking things about in the independent way that servants treat unoffending furniture, when master and mistress are comfortably ensconced in bed. 'Flop' went the duster again; 'bang' went the furniture; 'knock' this chair went against that, and she seemed bent upon putting all things into that happy state of sixes and sevens that characterizes a sale of household furniture, when chairs mount tables, and the whole system of domestic economy is revolutionized. Seeing that he was not going to get anything more for his money, our friend at length turned his horse and found his way to the stables by the unerring drag of carriage-wheels. All things there being as matters were in the house, he put the redoubtable nag into a stall, and helped him to a liberal measure of oats out of the well-stored unlocked corn-bin. He then sought the back of the house by the worn flagged-way that connected it with the stables. The back yard was in the admired confusion that might be expected from the woman's account. Empty casks and hampers were piled and stowed away in all directions, while regiments of champagne and other bottles stood and lay about among blacking bottles, Seltzer-water bottles, boot-trees, bath-bricks, old brushes, and stumpt-up besoms. Several pair of dirty top-boots, most of them with the spurs on, were chucked into the shoe-house just as they had been taken off. The kitchen, into which our friend now entered, was in the same disorderly state. Numerous copper pans stood simmering on the charcoal stoves, and the jointless jack still revolved on the spit. A dirty slip-shod girl sat sleeping, with her apron thrown over her head, which rested on the end of a table. The open door of the servants' hall hard by disclosed a pile of dress and other clothes, which, after mopping up the ale and other slops, would be carefully folded and taken back to the rooms of their respective owners.

'Halloo!' cried Mr. Sponge, shaking the sleeping girl by the shoulder, which caused her to start up, stare, and rub her eyes in wild affright. 'Halloo!' repeated he, 'what's happened to you?'

'Oh, beg pardon, sir!' exclaimed she; 'beg pardon,' continued she, clasping her hands; 'I'll never do so again, sir; no, sir, I'll never do so again, indeed I won't.'

She had just stolen a shape of blancmange, and thought she was caught.

'Then show me where I'll find pen and ink and paper,' replied our friend.

'Oh, sir, I don't know nothin' about them,' replied the girl; 'indeed, sir, I don't'; thinking it was some other petty larceny he was inquiring about.

'Well, but you can tell me where to find a sheet of paper, surely?' rejoined he.

'Oh, indeed, sir, I can't,' replied she; 'I know nothin' about nothin' of the sort.' Servants never do.

'What sort?' asked Mr. Sponge, wondering at her vehemence.

'Well, sir, about what you said,' sobbed the girl, applying the corner of her dirty apron to her eyes.

'Hang it, the girl's mad,' rejoined our friend, brushing by, and making for the passage beyond. This brought him past the still-room, the steward's room, the housekeeper's room, and the butler's pantry. All were in most glorious confusion; in the latter, Captain Cutitfat's lacquer-toed, lavender-coloured dress-boots were reposing in the silver soup tureen, and Captain Bouncey's varnished pumps were stuffed into a wine-cooler. The last detachment of empty bottles stood or lay about the floor, commingling with boot-jacks, knife-trays, bath-bricks, coat-brushes, candle-end boxes, plates, lanterns, lamp-glasses, oil bottles, corkscrews, wine-strainers—the usual miscellaneous appendages of a butler's pantry. All was still and quiet; not a sound, save the loud ticking of a timepiece, or the occasional creak of a jarring door, disturbed the solemn silence of the house. A nimble-handed mugger or tramp might have carried off whatever he liked.

Passing onward, Mr. Sponge came to a red-baized, brass-nailed door, which, opening freely on a patent spring, revealed the fine proportions of a light picture-gallery with which the bright mahogany doors of the entertaining rooms communicated. Opening the first door he came to, our friend found himself in the elegant drawing-room, on whose round bird's-eye-maple table, in the centre, were huddled all the unequal-lengthed candles of the previous night's illumination. It was a handsome apartment, fitted up in the most costly style; with rose-colour brocaded satin damask, the curtains trimmed with silk tassel fringe, and ornamented with massive bullion tassels on cornices, Cupids supporting wreaths under an arch, with open carved-work and enrichments in burnished gold. The room, save the muster of the candles, was just as it had been left; and the richly gilt sofa still retained the indentations of the sitters, with the luxurious down pillows, left as they had been supporting their backs.

The room reeked of tobacco, and the ends and ashes of cigars dotted the tables and white marble chimney-piece, and the gilt slabs and the finely flowered Tournay carpet, just as the fires of gipsies dot and disfigure the fair face of a country. Costly china and nick-nacks of all sorts were scattered about in profusion. Altogether, it was a beautiful room.

'No want of money here,' said Mr. Sponge to himself, as he eyed it, and thought what havoc Gustavus James would make among the ornaments if he had a chance.

He then looked about for pen, ink, and paper. These were distributed so wide apart as to show the little request they were in. Having at length succeeded in getting what he wanted gathered together, Mr. Sponge sat down on the luxurious sofa, considering how he should address his host, as he hoped. Mr. Sponge was not a shy man, but, considering the circumstances under which he made Sir Harry Scattercash's acquaintance, together with his design upon his hospitality—above all, considering the crew by whom Sir Harry was surrounded—it required some little tact to pave the way without raising the present inmates of the house against him. There are no people so anxious to protect others from robbery as those who are robbing them themselves. Mr. Sponge thought, and thought, and thought. At last he resolved to write on the subject of the hounds. After sundry attempts on pink, blue, and green-tinted paper, he at last succeeded in hitting off the following, on yellow:

Nonsuch House.

DEAR SIR HARRY,—I rode over this morning, hearing you were to hunt, and am sorry to find you indisposed. I wish you would drop me a line to Mr. Crowdey's, Puddingpote Bower, saying when next you go out, as I should much like to have another look at your splendid pack before I leave this country, which I fear will have to be soon.—Yours in haste,

H. SPONGE.

P.S.—I hope you all got safe home the other night from Mr. Peastraw's.

Having put this into a richly gilt and embossed envelope, our friend directed it conspicuously to Sir Harry Scattercash, Bart., and stuck it in the centre of the mantelpiece. He then retraced his steps through the back regions, informing the sleeping beauty he had before disturbed, and who was now busy scouring a pan, that he had left a letter in the drawing-room for Sir Harry, and if she would see that he got it, he (Mr. Sponge) would remember her the next time he came, which he inwardly hoped would be soon. He then made for the stable, and got his horse, to go home, sauntering more leisurely along than one would expect of a man who had not got his breakfast, especially one riding a hack hunter.

The truth was, Mr. Sponge did not much like the aspect of affairs. Sir Harry's was evidently a desperately 'fast' house; added to which, the guests by whom he was surrounded were clearly of the wide-awake order, who could not spare any pickings for a stranger. Indeed, Mr. Sponge felt that they rather cold-shouldered him at Farmer Peastraw's, and were in a greater hurry to be off when the drag came, than the mere difference between inside and outside seats required. He much questioned whether he got into Sir Harry's at all. If it came to a vote, he thought he should not. Then, what was he to do? Old Jog was clearly tired of him; and he had nowhere else to go to. The thought made him stick spurs into the chestnut, and hurry home to Puddingpote Bower, where he endeavoured to soothe his host by more than insinuating that he was going on a visit to Nonsuch House. Jog inwardly prayed that he might.

LVII

THE DEBATE

IT WAS JUST AS MR. Sponge predicted with regard to his admission to Nonsuch House. The first person who spied his note to Sir Harry Scattercash was Captain Seedeybuck, who, going into the drawing-room, the day after Mr. Sponge's visit, to look for the top of his cigar-case, saw it occupying the centre of the mantelpiece. Having mastered its contents, the Captain refolded and placed it where he found it, with the simple observation to himself of—'That cock won't fight.'

Captain Quod saw it next, then Captain Bouncey, who told Captain Cutitfat what was in it, who agreed with Bouncey that it wouldn't do to have Mr. Sponge there.

Indeed, it seemed agreed on all hands that their party rather wanted weeding than increasing.

Thus, in due time, everybody in the house knew the contents of the note save Sir Harry, though none of them thought it worth while telling him of it. On the third morning, however, as the party were assembling for breakfast, he came into the room reading it.

'This (hiccup) note ought to have been delivered before,' observed he, holding it up.

'Indeed, my dear,' replied Lady Scattercash, who was sitting gloriously fine and very beautiful at the head of the table, 'I don't know anything about it.'

'Who is it from?' asked brother Bob Spangles.

'Mr. (hiccup) Sponge,' replied Sir Harry.

'What a name!' exclaimed Captain Seedeybuck.

'Who is he?' asked Captain Quod.

'Don't know,' replied Sir Harry; 'he writes to (hiccup) about the hounds.' 'Oh, it'll be that brown-booted buffer,' observed Captain Bouncey, 'that we left at old Peastraw's.'

'No doubt,' assented Captain Cutitfat, adding, 'what business has he with the hounds?'

'He wants to know when we are going to (hiccup) again,' observed Sir Harry.

'Does he?' replied Captain Seedeybuck. 'That, I suppose, will depend upon Watchorn.'

The party now got settled to breakfast, and as soon as the first burst of appetite was appeased, the conversation again turned upon our friend Mr. Sponge.

'Who *is* this Mr. Sponge?' asked Captain Bouncey, the billiard-marker, with the air of a thorough exclusive.

Nobody answered.

'Who's your friend?' asked he of Sir Harry direct.

'Don't know,' replied Sir Harry, from between the mouthfuls of a highly cayenned grill.

'P'raps a bolting betting-office keeper,' suggested Captain Ladofwax, who hated Captain Bouncey.

'He looks more like a glazier, I think,' retorted Captain Bouncey, with a look of defiance at the speaker.

'Lucky if he is one,' retorted Captain Ladofwax, reddening up to the eyes; 'he may have a chance of repairing somebody's daylights.' The captain raising his saucer, to discharge it at his opponent's head.

'Gently with the cheney!' exclaimed Lady Scattercash, who was too much used to such scenes to care about the belligerents. Bob Spangles caught Ladofwax's arm at the nick of time, and saved the saucer.

'Hout! you (hiccup) fellows are always (hiccup)ing,' exclaimed Sir Harry. 'I declare I'll have you both (hiccup)ed over to keep the peace.'

They then broke out into wordy recrimination and abuse, each declaring that he wouldn't stay a day longer in the house if the other remained; but as they had often said so before, and still gave no symptoms of going, their assertion produced little effect upon anybody. Sir Harry would not have cared if all his guests had gone together. Peace and order being at length restored, the conversation again turned upon Mr. Sponge.

'I suppose we must have another (hiccup) hunt soon,' observed Sir Harry.

'In course,' replied Bob Spangles; 'it's no use keeping the hungry brutes unless you work them.'

'You'll have a bagman, I presume,' observed Captain Seedeybuck, who did not like the trouble of travelling about the country to draw for a fox.

'Oh, yes,' replied Sir Harry; 'Watchorn will manage all that. He's always (hiccup) in that line. We'd better have a hunt soon, and then, Mr. (hiccup) Bugles, you can see it.' Sir Harry addressing himself to a gentleman he was as anxious to get rid of as Mr. Jogglebury Crowdey was to get rid of Mr. Sponge.'

'No; Mr. Bugles won't go out any more,' replied Lady Scattercash peremptorily. 'He was nearly killed last time'; her ladyship casting an angry glance at her husband, and a very loving one on the object of her solicitude.

'Oh, nought's never in danger!' observed Bob Spangles.

'Then *you* can go, Bob,' snapped his sister.

'I intend,' replied Bob.

'Then (hiccup), gentlemen, I think I'll just write this Mr. (hiccup) What's-his-name to (hiccup) over here,' observed Sir Harry, 'and then he'll be ready for the (hiccup) hunt whenever we choose to (hiccup) one.'

The proposition fell still-born among the party.

'Don't you think we can do without him?' at last suggested Captain Seedeybuck.

'*I* think so,' observed the elder Spangles, without looking up from his plate.

'Who is it?' asked Lady Scattercash.

'The man that was here the other morning—the man in the queer chestnut-coloured boots,' replied Mr. Orlando Bugles.

'Oh, I think he's rather good-looking; I vote we have him,' replied her ladyship.

That was rather a damper for Sir Harry; but upon reflection, he thought he could not be worse off with Mr. Sponge and Mr. Bugles than he was with Mr. Bugles alone; so, having finished a poor appetiteless breakfast, he repaired to what he called his 'study,' and with a feeble, shaky hand, scrawled an invitation to Mr. Sponge to come over to Nonsuch House, and take his chance of a run with his hounds. He then sealed and posted the letter without further to do.

LVIII

FACEY ROMFORD

FOUR DAYS HAD NOW ELAPSED since Mr. Sponge penned his overture to Sir Harry, and each succeeding day satisfied him more of the utter impossibility of holding on much longer in his then billet at Puddingpote Bower. Not only was Jog coarse and incessant in his hints to him to be off, but Jawleyford-like he had lowered the standard of entertainment so greatly, that if it hadn't been that Mr. Sponge had his servant and horses kept also, he might as well have been living at his own expense. The company lights were all extinguished; great, strong-smelling, cauliflower-headed moulds, that were always wanting snuffing, usurped the place of Belmont wax; napkins were withdrawn; second-hand table-cloths introduced; marsala did duty for sherry; and the stick-jaw pudding assumed a consistency that was almost incompatible with articulation.

In the course of this time Sponge wrote to Puffington, saying if he was better he would return and finish his visit; but the wary Puff sent a messenger off express with a note, lamenting that he was ordered to Handley Cross for his health, but 'pop'lar man' like, hoping that the pleasure of Sponge's company was only deferred for another season. Jawleyford, even Sponge thought hopeless; and, altogether, he was very much perplexed. He had made a little money certainly, with his horses; but a permanent investment of his elegant person, such as he had long been on the look-out for, seemed as far off as ever. On the afternoon of the fifth day, as he was taking a solitary stroll about the country, having about made up his mind to be off to town, just as he was crossing Jog's buttercup meadow on his way to the stable, a rapid bang! bang! caused him to start, and, looking over the hedge, he saw a brawny-looking sportsman in brown reloading his gun, with a brace of liver-and-white setters crouching like statues in the stubble.

'Seek dead!' presently said the shooter, with a slight wave of his hand; and in an instant each dog was picking up his bird.

'I'll have a word with you,' said Sponge, 'on and off-ing' the hedge, his beat causing the shooter to start and look as if inclined for a run; second thoughts said Sponge was too near, and he'd better brave it.

'What sport?' asked Sponge, striding towards him.

'Oh, pretty middling,' replied the shooter, a great red-headed, freckly faced fellow, with backward-lying whiskers, crowned in a drab rustic. 'Oh, pretty middling,' repeated he, not knowing whether to act on the friendly or defensive.

'Fine day!' said Sponge, eyeing his fox-maskey whiskers and stout, muscular frame.

'It is,' replied the shooter; adding, 'just followed my birds over the boundary. No 'fence, I s'pose—no 'fence.'

'Oh, no,' said Mr. Sponge. 'Jog, I dessay, 'll be very glad to see you.'

'Oh, you'll be Mr. Sponge?' observed the stranger, jumping to a conclusion.

'I am,' replied our hero; adding, 'may I ask who I have the honour of addressing?'

'My name's Romford—Charley Romford; everybody knows me. Very glad to make your 'quaintance,' tendering Sponge a great, rough, heavy hand. 'I was goin' to call upon you,' observed the stranger, as he ceased swinging Sponge's arm to and fro like a pump-handle; 'I was goin' to call upon you, to see if you'd come over to Washingforde, and have some shootin' at me Oncle's—Oncle Gilroy's, at Queercove Hill.'

'Most happy!' exclaimed Sponge, thinking it was the very thing he wanted.

'Get a day with the harriers, too, if you like,' continued the shooter, increasing the temptation.

'Better still!' thought Sponge.

'I've only bachelor 'commodation to offer you; but p'raps you'll not mind roughing it a bit?' observed Romford.

'Oh, faith, not I!' replied Sponge, thinking of the luxuries of Puffington's bachelor habitation. 'What sort of stables have you?' asked our friend.

'Capital stables—excellent stables!' replied the shooter; 'stalls six feet in the clear, by twelve dip (deep), iron racks, oak stall-posts covered with zinc, beautiful oats, capital beans, splendacious hay—won without a shower!'

'Bravo!' exclaimed Sponge, thinking he had lit on his legs, and might snap his fingers at Jog and his hints. He'd take the high hand, and give Jog up.

'I'm your man!' said Sponge, in high glee.

'When will you come?' asked Romford.

'To-morrow!' replied Sponge firmly.

'So be it,' rejoined his proffered host; and, with another hearty swing of the arm, the newly made friends parted.

Charley Romford, or Facey, as he was commonly called, from his being the admitted most impudent man in the country, was a great, round-faced, coarse-featured, prize-fighting sort of fellow, who lived chiefly by his wits, which he exercised in all the legitimate lines of industry—poaching, betting, boxing, horse-dealing, cards, quoits—anything that came uppermost. That he was a man of enterprise, we need hardly add, when he had formed a scheme for doing our Sponge—a man that we do not think any of our readers would trouble themselves to try a 'plant' upon.

This impudent Facey, as if in contradiction of terms, was originally intended for a civil engineer; but having early in life voted himself heir to his uncle, Mr. Gilroy, of Queercove Hill, a great cattle-jobber, with a 'small independence of his own'—three hundred a year, perhaps, which a kind world called six—Facey thought he would just hang about until his uncle was done with his shoes, and then be lord of Queercove Hill.

Now, 'me Oncle Gilroy,' of whom Facey was constantly talking, had a left-handed wife and promising family in the sylvan retirement of St. John's Wood, whither he used to retire after his business in 'Smi'fiel'' was over; so that Facey, for once, was out in his calculations. Gilroy, however, being as knowing as 'his nevvey,' as he called him, just encouraged Facey in his shooting, fishing, and idle propensities generally, doubtless finding it more convenient to have his fish and game for nothing than to pay for them.

Facey, having the apparently inexhaustible sum of a thousand pounds, began life as a fox-hunter—in a very small way, to be sure—more for the purpose of selling horses than anything else; but, having succeeded in 'doing' all the do-able gentlemen, both with the 'Tip and Go' and Cranerfield hounds, his occupation was gone, it requiring an extended field—such as our friend Sponge roamed—to carry on cheating in horses for any length of time. Facey was soon blown, his name in connexion with a horse being enough to prevent any one looking at him. Indeed, we question that there is any less desirable mode of making, or trying to make money, than by cheating or even dealing in horses. Many people fancy themselves cheated, whatever they get; while the man who is really cheated never forgets it, and proclaims it to the end of time. Moreover, no one can go on cheating in horses for any length of time, without putting himself in the power of his groom; and let those who have seen how servants lord it over each other say how they would like to subject themselves to similar treatment.—But to our story.

Facey Romford had now a splendid milk-white horse, well-known in Mr. Nobbington's and Lord Leader's hunts as Mr. Hobler, but who Facey kindly rechristened the 'Nonpareil,' which the now rising price of oats, and falling state of his finances, made him particularly anxious to get rid of, ere the horse performed the equestrian feat of 'eating its head off.' He was a very hunter-like looking horse, but his misfortune consisted in having such shocking seedy toes, that he couldn't keep his shoes on. If he got through the first field with them on, they were sure to be off at the fence. This horse Facey voted to be the very thing for Mr. Sponge, and hearing that he had come into the country to hunt, it occurred to him that it would be a capital thing if he could get him to take Mother Overend's spare bed and lodge with him, twelve shillings a week being more than Facey liked paying for his rooms. Not that he paid twelve shillings for the rooms alone; on the contrary, he had a two-stalled stable, with a sort of kennel for his pointers, and a sty for his pig into the bargain. This pig, which was eaten many times in anticipation, had at length fallen a victim to the butcher, and Facey's larder was uncommonly well-found in black-puddings, sausages, spare ribs, and the other component parts of a pig: so that he was in very hospitable circumstances—at least, in his rough and ready idea of what hospitality ought to be. Indeed, whether he had or not, he'd have risked it, being quite as good at carrying things off with a high hand as Mr. Sponge himself.

The invitation came most opportunely; for, worn out with jealousy and watching, Jog had made up his mind to cut to Australia, and when Sponge returned after meeting Facey, Jog was in the act of combing out an advertisement, offering all that desirable sporting residence called Puddingpote Bower, with the coach-house, stables, and offices thereunto belonging, to let, and announcing that the whole of the valuable household furniture, comprising mahogany, dining, loo, card, and Pembroke tables; sofa, couch, and chairs in hair seating; cheffonier, with plate glass; book-case; flower-stands; pianoforte, by Collard and Collard; music-stool and Canterbury; chimney and pier-glasses; mirror; ormolu time-piece; alabaster and wax figures and shades; china; Brussels carpets and rugs; fenders and fire-irons; curtains and cornices; Venetian blinds; mahogany four-post, French, and camp bedsteads; feather beds; hair mattresses; mahogany chests of drawers; dressing-glasses; wash and dressing-tables; patent shower-bath; bed and table-linen; dinner and tea-ware; warming-pans, &c., would be exposed to immediate and unreserved sale.

How gratefully Sponge's inquiry if he knew Mr. Romford fell on his ear, as they sat moodily together after dinner over some very low-priced port.

'Oh yes (puff)—oh yes (wheeze)—oh yes (gasp)! Know Charley Romford—Facey, as they call him. He's (puff, wheeze, gasp) heir to old Mr. Gilroy, of Queercove Hill.'

'Just so,' rejoined Sponge, 'just so; that's the man—stout, square-built fellow, with backward-growing whiskers. I'm going to stay with him to shoot at old Gil's. Where does Charley live?'

'Live!' exclaimed Jog, almost choked with delight at the information; 'live! live!' repeated he, for the third time; 'lives at (puff, wheeze, gasp, cough) Washingforde—yes, at Washingforde; 'bout ten miles from (puff, wheeze) here. When d'ye go?'

'To-morrow,' replied Sponge, with an air of offended dignity.

Jog was so rejoiced that he could hardly sit on his chair.

Mrs. Jog, when she heard it, felt that Gustavus James's chance of independence was gone; for well she knew that Jog would never let Sponge come back to the Bower.

We need scarcely say that Jog was up betimes in the morning, most anxious to forward Mr. Sponge's departure. He offered to allow

Bartholomew to convey him and his 'traps' in the phaeton—an offer that Mr. Sponge availed himself of as far as his 'traps' were concerned, though he preferred cantering over on his piebald to trailing along in Jog's jingling chay. So matters were arranged, and Mr. Sponge forthwith proceeded to put his brown boots, his substantial cords, his superfine tights, his cuttey scarlet, his dress blue saxony, his clean linen, his heavy spurs, and though last, not least in importance, his now backless *Mogg*, into his solid leather portmanteau, sweeping the surplus of his wardrobe into a capacious carpet-bag. While the guest was thus busy upstairs, the host wandered about restlessly, now stirring up this person, now hurrying that, in the full enjoyment of the much-coveted departure. His pleasure was, perhaps, rather damped by a running commentary he overheard through the lattice-window of the stable, from Leather, as he stripped his horses and tried to roll up their clothing in a moderate compass.

''Ord rot your great carcass!' exclaimed he, giving the roll a hearty kick in its bulging-out stomach, on finding that he had not got it as small as he wanted. ''Ord rot your great carcass,' repeated he, scratching his head and eyeing it as it lay; 'this is all the consequence of your nasty brewers' hapron weshins—blowin' of one out, like a bladder!' and, thereupon, he placed his hand on his stomach to feel how his own was. 'Never see'd sich a house, or sich an awful mean man!' continued he, stooping and pommelling the package with his fists. It was of no use, he could not get it as small as he wished—'Must have my jacket out on you, I do believe,' added he, seeing where the impediment was; 'sticks in your gizzard just like a lump of old Puff-and-blow's puddin''; and then he thrust his hand into the folds of the clothing, and pulled out the greasy garment. 'Now,' said he, stooping again, 'I think we may manish ye'; and he took the roll in his arms and hoisted it on to Hercules, whom he meant to make the led horse, observing aloud, as he adjusted it on the saddle, and whacked it well with his hands to make it lie right, 'I wish it was old Jog—wouldn't I sarve him out!' He then turned his horses round in their stalls, tucked his greasy jacket under the flap of the saddle-bags, took his ash-stick from the crook, and led them out of the capacious door. Jog looked at him with mingled feelings of disgust and delight. Leather just gave his old hat a rap with his forefinger as he passed with the horses—a salute that Jog did not condescend to return.

Having eyed the receding horses with great satisfaction, Jog re-entered the house by the kitchens, to have the pleasure of seeing Mr. Sponge off. He found the portmanteau and carpet-bag standing in the passage, and just at the moment the sound of the phaeton wheels fell on his ear, as Bartholomew drove round from the coach-house to the door. Mr. Sponge was already in the parlour, making his adieus to Mrs. Jog and the children, who were all assembled for the purpose.

'What, are you goin'?' (puff) asked Jog, with an air of surprise.

'Yes,' replied Mr. Sponge; adding, as he tendered his hand, 'the best friends must part, you know.'

'Well (puff), but you'd better have your (wheeze) horse round,' observed Jog, anxious to avoid any overture for a return.

'Thankee,' replied Mr. Sponge, making a parting bow; 'I'll get him at the stable.'

'I'll go with you,' said Jog, leading the way.

Leather had saddled, and bridled, and turned him round in the stall, with one of Mr. Jog's blanket-rugs on, which Mr. Sponge just swept over his tail into the manger, and led the horse out.

'Adieu!' said he, offering his hand to his host.

'Good-bye!—good (puff) sport to you,' said Jog, shaking it heartily.

Mr. Sponge then mounted his hack, and cocking out his toe, rode off at a canter.

At the same moment, Bartholomew drove away from the front door; and Jog, having stood watching the phaeton over the rise of Pennypound Hill, scraped his feet, re-entered his house, and rubbing them heartily on the mat as he closed the sash-door, observed aloud to himself, with a jerk of his head:

'Well, now, that's the most (puff) impittent feller I ever saw in my life! Catch me (gasp) godpapa-hunting again.'

LIX

THE ADJOURNED DEBATE

THE FATAL INVITATION TO MR. Sponge having been sent, the question that now occupied the minds of the assembled sharpers at Nonsuch House, was, whether he was a pigeon or one of themselves. That point occupied their very deep and serious consideration. If he was a 'pigeon,' they could clearly accommodate him, but if, on the other hand, he was one of themselves, it was painfully apparent that there were far too many of them there already. Of course, the subject was not discussed in full and open conclave—they were all highly honourable men in the gross—and it was only in the small and secret groups of those accustomed to hunt together and unburden their minds, that the real truth was elicited.

'What an ass Sir Harry is, to ask this Mr. Sponge,' observed Captain Quod to Captain Seedeybuck, as (cigar in mouth) they paced backwards and forwards under the flagged veranda on the west side of the house, on the morning that Sir Harry had announced his intention of asking him.

'Confounded ass,' assented Seedeybuck, from between the whiffs of his cigar.

'Dash it! one would think he had more money than he knew what to do with,' observed the first speaker, 'instead of not knowing where to lay hands on a halfpenny.'

'Soon be who-hoop,' here observed Quod, with a shake of the head.

'Fear so,' replied Seedeybuck. 'Have you heard anything fresh?'

'Nothing particular. The County Court bailiff was here with some summonses, which, of course, he put in the fire.'

'Ah! that's what he always does. He got tired of papering the smoking-room with them,' replied Seedeybuck.

'Well, it's a pity,' observed Quod, spitting as he spoke; 'but what can you expect, eaten up as he is by such a set of rubbish.'

'Shockin',' replied Seedeybuck, thinking how long he and his friend might have fattened there together.

'Do you know anything of this Mr. Sponge?' asked Captain Quod, after a pause.

'Nothin',' replied Seedeybuck, 'except what we saw of him here; but I'm sure he won't do.'

'Well, I think not either,' replied Quod; 'I didn't like his looks—he seems quite one of the free-and-easy sort.'

'Quite,' observed Seedeybuck, determined to make a set against him, instead of cultivating his acquaintance.

'This Mr. Sponge won't be any great addition to our party, I think,' muttered Captain Bouncey to Captain Cutitfat, as they stood within the bay of the library window, in apparent contemplation of the cows, but in reality conning the Sponge matter over in their minds.

'I think not,' replied Captain Cutitfat, with an emphasis.

'Wonder what made Sir Harry ask him!' whispered Bouncey, adding, aloud, for the bystanders to hear, 'That's a fine cow, isn't it?'

'Very,' replied Cutitfat, in the same key, adding, in a whisper, with a shrug of his shoulders, 'Wonder what made him ask half the people that are here!'

'The black and white one isn't a bad un,' observed Bouncey, nodding his head towards the cows, adding in an undertone, 'Most of them asked themselves, I should think.'

'Admiring the cows, Captain Bouncey?' asked the beautiful and tolerably virtuous Miss Glitters, of the Astley's Royal Amphitheatre, who had come down to spend a few days with her old friend, Lady Scattercash. 'Admiring the cows, Captain Bouncey?' asked she, sidling her elegant figure between our friends in the bay.

'We were just saying how nice it would be to have two or three pretty girls, and a sillabub, under those cedars,' replied Captain Bouncey.

'Oh, charming!' exclaimed Miss Glitters, her dark eyes sparkling as she spoke. 'Harriet!' exclaimed she, addressing herself to a young lady, who called herself Howard, but whose real name was Brown—Jane

Brown—'Harriet!' exclaimed she, 'Captain Bouncey is going to give a *fête champetre* under those lovely cedars.'

'Oh, how nice!' exclaimed Harriet, clapping her hands in ecstasies—theatrical ecstasies at least.

'It must be Sir Harry,' replied the billiard-table man, not fancying being 'let in' for anything.

'Oh! Sir Harry will let us have anything we like, I'm sure,' rejoined Miss Glitters.

'What is it (hiccup)?' asked Sir Harry, who, hearing his name, now joined the party.

'Oh, we want you to give us a dance under those charming cedars,' replied the lady, looking lovingly at him.

'Cedars!' hiccuped Sir Harry, 'where do you see any cedars?'

'Why, there,' replied Miss Glitters, nodding towards a clump of evergreens.

'Those are (hiccup) hollies,' replied Sir Harry.

'Well, under the hollies,' rejoined Miss Glitters; adding, 'it was Captain Bouncey who said they were cedars.'

'Ah, I meant those beyond,' observed the captain, nodding in another direction.

'Those are (hiccup) Scotch firs,' rejoined Sir Harry.

'Well, never mind what they are,' resumed the lady; 'let us have a dance under them.'

'Certainly,' replied Sir Harry, who was always ready for anything. 'We shall have plenty of partners,' observed Miss Howard, recollecting how many men there were in the house.

'And another coming,' observed Captain Cutitfat, still fretting at the idea.

'Indeed!' exclaimed Miss Howard, raising her hands and eyebrows in delight; 'and who is he?' asked she, with unfeigned glee.

'Oh, such a (hiccup) swell,' replied Sir Harry; 'reg'lar Leicestershire man. A (hiccup) Quornite, in fact.'

'We'll not have the dance till he comes, then,' observed Miss Glitters.

'No more we will,' said Miss Howard, withdrawing from the group.

LX

FACEY ROMFORD AT HOME

WE WILL NOW SUPPOSE OUR distinguished Sponge entering the village, or what the natives call the town of Washingforde, towards the close of a short December day, on his arrival from Mr. Jog's.

'What sort of stables are there?' asked he, reining up his hack, as he encountered the brandy-nosed Leather airing himself on the main street.

'Stables be good enough—forage, too,' replied the stud groom—'*per*-wided you likes the sittivation.'

'Oh, the sittivation 'll be good enough,' retorted Sponge, thinking that, groom-like, Leather was grumbling because he hadn't got the best stables.

'Well, sir, as you please,' replied the man.

'Why, where are they?' asked Sponge, seeing there was more in Leather's manner than met the eye.

'*Rose and Crown!*' replied Leather, with an emphasis.

'Rose and Crown!' exclaimed Sponge, starting in his saddle; 'Rose and Crown! Why, I'm going to stay with Mr. Romford!'

'So he said.' replied Leather; 'so he said. I met him as I com'd in with the osses, and said he to me, said he, "You'll find captle quarters at the Crown!"' 'The deuce!' exclaimed Mr. Sponge, dropping the reins on his hack's neck; 'the deuce!' repeated he with a look of disgust. 'Why, where does he live?'

'"Bove the saddler's, thonder,' replied Leather, nodding to a small bow-windowed white house a little lower down, with the gilt-lettered words:

OVEREND, SADDLER AND HARNESS-MAKER TO THE
QUEEN,

above a very meagrely stocked shop.

'The devil!' replied Mr. Sponge, boiling up as he eyed the cottage-like dimensions of the place.

The dialogue was interrupted by a sledge-hammer-like blow on Sponge's back, followed by such a proffered hand as could proceed from none but his host.

'Glad to see ye!' exclaimed Facey, swinging Sponge's arm to and fro. 'Get off!' continued he, half dragging him down, 'and let's go in; for it's beastly cold, and dinner'll be ready in no time!'

So saying, he led the captive Sponge down street, like a prisoner, by the arm, and, opening the thin house-door, pushed him up a very straight staircase into a little low cabin-like room, hung with boxing-gloves, foils, and pictures of fighters and ballet girls.

'Glad to see ye!' again said Facey, poking the diminutive fire. 'Axed Nosey Nickel and Gutty Weazel to meet you,' continued he, looking at the little 'dinner-for-two' table; 'but Nosey's gone wrong in a tooth, and Gutty's away sweetheartin'. However, we'll be very cosy and jolly together; and if you want to wash your hands, or anything afore dinner, I'll show you your bedroom,' continued he, backing Sponge across the staircase landing to where a couple of little black doors opened into rooms, formed by dividing what had been the duplicate of the sitting-room into two.

'There!' exclaimed Facey, pointing to Sponge's portmanteau and bag, standing midway between the window and door: 'There! there are your traps. Yonder's the washhand-stand. You can put your shavin'-things on the chair below the lookin'-glass 'gainst the wall,' pointing to a fragment of glass nailed against the stencilled wall, all of which Sponge stood eyeing with a mingled air of resignation and contempt; but when Facey pointed to:

> The chest, contrived a double debt to pay
> A bed by night, a chest of drawers by day

and said that was where Sponge would have to curl himself up, our friend shook his head, and declared he could not.

'Oh, fiddle!' replied Facey, 'Jack Weatherley slept in it for months, and he's half a hand higher than you—sixteen hands, if he's an inch.' And Sponge jerked his head and bit his lips, thinking he was 'done' for once.

'W-h-o-y, ar thought you'd been a fox-hunter,' observed Facey, seeing his guest's disconcerted look.

'Well, but bein' a fox-hunter won't enable one to sleep in a band-box, or to shut oneself up like a telescope,' retorted the indignant Sponge.

''Ord hang it, man! you're so nasty partickler,' rejoined Facey; 'you're so nasty partickler. You'll never do to go out duck-shootin' i' your shirt. Dash it, man! Oncle Gilroy would disinherit me if ar was such a chap. However, look sharp,' continued he, 'if you are goin' to clean yourself; for dinner 'll be ready in no time, indeed, I hear Mrs. End dishin' it up.' So saying, Facey rolled out of the room, and Sponge presently heard him pulling off his clogs of shoes in the adjoining one. Dinner spoke for itself, for the house reeked with the smell of fried onions and roast pork.

Now, Sponge didn't like pork; and there was nothing but pork, or pig in one shape or another. Spare ribs, liver and bacon, sausages, black puddings, &c.—all very good in their way, but which came with a bad grace after the comforts of Jog's, the elegance of Puffington's, and the early splendour of Jawleyford's. Our hero was a good deal put out, and felt as if he was imposed upon. What business had a man like this to ask him to stay with him—a man who dined by daylight, and ladled his meat with a great two-pronged fork?

Facey, though he saw Mr. Sponge wasn't pleased, praised and pressed everything in succession down to a very strong cheese; and as the slip-shod girl whisked away crumbs and all in the coarse tablecloth, he exclaimed in a most open-hearted air, 'Well, now, what shall we have to drink?' adding, 'You smoke, of course—shall it be gin, rum, or Hollands—Hollands, rum, or gin?'

Sponge was half-inclined to propose wine, but recollecting what sloe-juice sort of stuff it was sure to be, and that Facey, in all probability, would make him finish it, he just replied, 'Oh, I don't care; 'spose we say gin?'

'Gin be it,' said Facey, rising from his seat, and making for a little closet in the wall, he produced a bottle labelled 'Fine London Spirit'; and, hallooing to the girl to get a few 'Captins' out of the box under his bed, he scattered a lot of glasses about the table, and placed a green dessert-dish for the biscuits against they came.

Night had now closed in—a keen, boisterous, wintry night, making the pocketful of coals that ornamented the grate peculiarly acceptable.

'B-o-y Jove, what a night!' exclaimed Facey, as a blash of sleet dashed across the window as if someone had thrown a handful of pebbles against it. 'B-o-y Jove, what a night!' repeated he, rising and closing the shutters, and letting down the little scanty red curtain. 'Let us draw in and have a hot brew,' continued he, stirring the fire under the kettle, and handing a lot of cigars out of the table-drawer. They then sat smoking and sipping, and smoking and sipping, each making a mental estimate of the other.

'Shall we have a game at cards? or what shall we do to pass the evenin'?' at length asked our host. 'Better have a game at cards, p'raps,' continued he.

'Thank'ee, no; thank'ee, no. I've a book in my pocket,' replied Sponge, diving into his jacket-pocket; adding, as he fished up his *Mogg*, 'always carry a book of light reading about with me.'

'What, you're a literary cove, are you?' asked Facey, in a tone of surprise.

'Not exactly that,' replied Sponge; 'but I like to improve my mind.' He then opened the valuable work, taking a dip into the Omnibus Guide—'Brentford, 7 from Hyde Park Corner—European Coffee House, near the Bank, daily,' and so worked his way on through the 'Brighton Railway Station, Brixton, Bromley both in Kent and Middlesex, Bushey Heath, Camberwell, Camden Town, and Carshalton,' right into Cheam, when Facey, who had been eyeing him intently, not at all relishing his style of proceeding and wishing to be doing, suddenly exclaimed, as he darted up:

'B-o-y Jove! You've not heard me play the flute! No more you have. Dash it, how remiss!' continued he, making for the little bookshelf on which it lay; adding, as he blew into it and sucked the joints, 'you're musical, of course?'

'Oh, I can stand music,' muttered Sponge, with a jerk of his head, as if a tune was neither here nor there with him.

'By Jingo! you should see me Oncle Gilroy when a'rm playin'! The old man act'ly sheds tears of delight—he's so pleased.'

'Indeed,' replied Sponge, now passing on into *Mogg's Cab Fares*—'Aldersgate Street, Hare Court, to or from Bagnigge Wells,' and so on, when Facey struck up the most squeaking, discordant, broken-winded:

Jump Jim Crow

that ever was heard, making the sensitive Sponge shudder, and setting all his teeth on edge.

'Hang me, but that flute of yours wants nitre, or a dose of physic, or something most dreadful!' at length exclaimed he, squeezing up his face as if in the greatest agony, as the laboured:

Jump about and wheel about

completely threw Sponge over in his calculation as to what he could ride from Aldgate Pump to the Pied Bull at Islington for.

'Oh no!' replied Facey, with an air of indifference, as he took off the end and jerked out the steam. 'Oh, no—only wants work—only wants work,' added he, putting it together again, exclaiming, as he looked at the now sulky Sponge, 'Well, what shall it be?'

'Whatever you please,' replied our friend, dipping frantically into his *Mogg*.

'Well, then, I'll play you me oncle's favourite tune, "The Merry Swiss Boy,"' whereupon Facey set to most vigorously with that once most popular air. It, however, came off as rustily as 'Jim Crow,' for whose feats Facey evidently had a partiality; for no sooner did he get squeaked through 'me oncle's' tune than he returned to the nigger melody with redoubled zeal, and puffed and blew Sponge's calculations as to what he could ride from 'Mother Redcap's at Camden Town down Liquorpond Street, up Snow Hill, and so on, to the 'Angel' in Ratcliff Highway for, clean out of his head. Nor did there seem any prospect of relief, for no sooner did Facey get through one tune than he at the other again.

'Rot it!' at length exclaimed Sponge, throwing his *Mogg* from him in despair, 'you'll deafen me with that abominable noise.' 'Bless my heart!' exclaimed Facey, in well-feigned surprise, 'Bless my heart! Why, I thought you liked music, my dear feller!' adding, 'I was playin' to please you.'

'The deuce you were!' snapped Mr. Sponge. 'I wish I'd known sooner: I'd have saved you a deal of wind.'

'Why, my dear feller,' replied Facey, 'I wished to entertain you the best in my power. One must do somethin', you know.'

'I'd rather do anything than undergo that horrid noise,' replied Sponge, ringing his left ear with his forefinger.

'Let's have a game at cards, then,' rejoined Facey soothingly, seeing he had sufficiently agonized Sponge.

'Cards,' replied Mr. Sponge. 'Cards,' repeated he thoughtfully, stroking his hairy chin. 'Cards,' added he, for the third time, as he conned Facey's rotund visage, and wondered if he was a sharper. If the cards were fair, Sponge didn't care trying his luck. It all depended upon that. 'Well,' said he, in a tone of indifference, as he picked up his *Mogg*, thinking he wouldn't pay if he lost, 'I'll give you a turn. What shall it be?'

'Oh—w-h-o-y—s'pose we say *écarté*?' replied Facey, in an off-hand sort of way.

'Well,' drawled Sponge, pocketing his *Mogg*, preparatory to action.

'You haven't a clean pack, have you?' asked Sponge, as Facey, diving into a drawer, produced a very dirty, thumb-marked set.

'W-h-o-y, no, I haven't,' replied Facey. 'W-h-o-y, no, I haven't: but, honour bright, these are all right and fair. Wouldn't cheat a man, if it was ever so.'

'Sure you wouldn't,' replied Sponge, nothing comforted by the assertion.

They then resumed their seats opposite each other at the little table, with the hot water and sugar, and 'Fine London Spirit' bottle equitably placed between them.

At first Mr. Sponge was the victor, and by nine o'clock had scored eight-and-twenty shillings against his host, when he was inclined to leave off, alleging that he was an early man, and would go to bed—an arrangement that Facey seemed to come into, only pressing Sponge to accompany the gin he was now helping himself to with another cigar. This seemed all fair and reasonable; and as Sponge conned matters over, through the benign influence of the "baccy,' he really thought Facey mightn't be such a bad beggar after all.

'Well, then,' said he, as he finished cigar and glass together, 'if you'll give me eight-and-twenty bob, I'll be off to Bedfordshire.'

'You'll give me my revenge surely!' exclaimed Facey, in pretended astonishment.

'To-morrow night,' replied Sponge firmly, thinking it would have to go hard with him if he remained there to give it.

'Nay, *now*!' rejoined Facey, adding, 'it's quite early. Me Oncle Gilroy and I always play much later at Queercove Hill.'

Sponge hesitated. If he had got the money, he would have refused point-blank; as it was, he thought, perhaps the only chance of getting it was to go on. With no small reluctance and misgivings he mixed himself another tumbler of gin and water, and, changing seats, resumed the game. Nor was our discreet friend far wrong in his calculations, for luck now changed, and Facey seemed to have the king quite at command. In less than an hour he had not only wiped off the eight-and-twenty shillings, but had scored three pound fifteen against his guest. Facey would now leave off. Sponge, on the other hand, wanted to go on. Facey, however, was firm. 'I'll cut you double or quits, then,' cried Sponge, in rash despair. Facey accommodated him and doubled the debt.

'Again!' exclaimed Sponge, with desperate energy.

'No! no more, thank ye,' replied Facey coolly. 'Fair play's a jewel.'

'So it is,' assented Mr. Sponge, thinking he hadn't had it.

'Now,' continued Facey, poking into the table-drawer and producing a dirty scrap of paper, with a little pocket ink-case, 'if you'll give me an "I.O.U.," we'll shut up shop.'

'An "I.O.U.!"' retorted Sponge, looking virtuously indignant. 'An "I.O.U.!" I'll give you your money i' the mornin'.'

'I know you will,' replied Facey coolly, putting himself in boxing attitude, exclaiming, as he measured out a distance, 'just feel the biceps muscle of my arm—do believe I could fell an ox. However, never mind,' continued he, seeing Sponge declined the feel. 'Life's uncertain: so you give me an "I.O.U." and we'll be all right and square. Short reckonin's make long friends, you know,' added he, pointing peremptorily to the paper.

'I'd better give you a cheque at once,' retorted Sponge, looking the very essence of chivalry.

'*Money*, if you please,' replied Facey; muttering, with a jerk of his head, 'don't like paper.'

The renowned Sponge, for once, was posed. He had the money, but he didn't like to part with it. So he gave the 'I.O.U.' and, lighting a twelve-to-the-pound candle, sulked off to undress and crawl into the little impossibility of a bed.

Night, however, brought no relief to our distinguished friend; for, little though the bed was, it was large enough to admit lodgers, and poor Sponge was nearly worried by the half-famished vermin, who seemed bent on making up for the long fast they had endured since the sixteen-hands-man left. Worst of all, as day dawned, the eternal 'Jim Crow' recommenced his saltations, varied only with the:

> Come, arouse ye, arouse ye, my merry Swiss boy
> of me Oncle Gilroy.

'Well, dash my buttons!' groaned Sponge, as the discordant noise shot through his aching head, 'but this is the worst spec I ever made in my life. Fed on pork, fluted deaf, bit with bugs, and robbed at cards—fairly, downrightly robbed. Never was a more reg'ler plant put on a man. Thank goodness, however, I haven't paid him—never will, either. Such a confounded, disreputable scoundrel deserves to be punished—big, bad, blackguard-looking fellow! How the deuce I could ever be taken in by such a fellow! Believe he's nothing but a great poaching blackleg. Hasn't the faintest outlines of a gentleman about him—not the slightest particle—not the remotest glimmerin'.'

These and similar reflections were interrupted by a great thump against the thin lath-and-plaster wall that separated their rooms, or rather closets, accompanied by an exclamation of:

'HALLOO, OLD BOY! HOW GOES IT?'—an inquiry to which our friend deigned no answer.

''Ord rot ye! you're awake,' muttered Facey to himself, well knowing that no one could sleep after such a 'Jim-Crow-ing' and 'Swiss-boy-ing' as he had given him. He therefore resumed his battery, thumping as though he would knock the partition in.

'HALLOO!' at last exclaimed Mr. Sponge, 'who's there?'

'Well, old Sivin-Pund-Ten, how goes it?' asked Facey, in a tone of the keenest irony.

'You be——!' growled Mr. Sponge, in disgust.

'Breakfast in half an hour!' resumed Facey. 'Pigs'-puddin's and sarsingers—all 'ot—pipin' 'ot!' continued our host.

'Wish you were pipin' 'ot,' growled Mr. Sponge, as he jerked himself out of his little berth.

Though Facey pumped him pretty hard during this second pig repast, he could make nothing out of Sponge with regard to his movements— our friend parrying all his inquiries with his *Mogg*, and assurances that he could amuse himself. In vain Facey represented that his Oncle Gilroy would be expecting them; that Mr. Hobler was ready for him to ride over on; Sponge wasn't inclined to shoot, but begged Facey wouldn't stay at home on his account. The fact was, Sponge meditated a bolt, and was in close confab with Leather, in the Rose and Crown stables, arranging matters, when the sound of his name in the yard caused him to look out, when—oh, welcome sight!—a Puddingpote Bower messenger put Sir Harry's note in his hand, which had at length arrived at Jog's through their very miscellaneous transit, called a post. Sponge, in the joy of his heart, actually gave the lad a shilling! He now felt like a new man. He didn't care a rap for Facey, and, ordering Leather to give him the hack and follow with the hunters, he presently cantered out of town as sprucely as if all was on the square.

When, however, Facey found how matters stood, he determined to stop Sponge's things, which Leather resisted; and, Facey showing fight, Leather butted him with his head, sending him backwards downstairs and putting his shoulder out. Leather than marched off with the kit, amid the honours of war.

LXI

NONSUCH HOUSE AGAIN

THE GALLANT INMATES OF NONSUCH House had resolved themselves into a committee of speculation, as to whether Mr. Sponge was coming or not; indeed, they had been betting upon it, the odds at first being a hundred to one that he came, though they had fallen a point or two on the arrival of the post without an answer.

'Well, I say Mr. What-d'ye-call-him—Sponge—doesn't come!' exclaimed Captain Seedeybuck, as he lay full length, with his shaggy greasy head on the fine rose-coloured satin sofa, and his legs cocked over the cushion.

'Why not?' asked Miss Glitters, who was beguiling the twilight half-hour before candles with knitting.

'Don't know,' replied Seedeybuck, twirling his moustache, 'don't know—have a presentiment he won't.'

'Sure to come!' exclaimed Captain Bouncey, knocking the ashes off his cigar on to the fine Tournay carpet.

'I'll lay ten to one—ten fifties to one—he does,—a thousand to ten if you like.' If all the purses in the house had been clubbed together, we don't believe they would have raised fifty pounds.

'What sort of a looking man is he?' asked Miss Glitters, now counting her loops.

'Oh—whoy—ha—hem—haw—he's just an ordinary sort of lookin' man—nothin' 'tickler any way,' drawled Captain Seedeybuck, now wetting and twirling his moustache.

'Two legs, a head, a back, and so on, I presume,' observed the lady.

'Just so,' assented Captain Seedeybuck.

'He's a horsey-lookin' sort o' man, I should say,' observed Captain Bouncey, 'walks as if he ought to be ridin'—wears vinegar tops.'

'Hate vinegar tops,' growled Seedeybuck.

Just then, in came Lady Scattercash, attended by Mr. Orlando Bugles, the ladies' attractions having caused that distinguished performer to forfeit his engagement at the Surrey Theatre. Captain Cutitfat, Bob Spangles, and Sir Harry quickly followed, and the Sponge question was presently renewed.

'Who says old brown boots comes?' exclaimed Seedeybuck from the sofa.

'Who's that with his nasty nob on my fine satin sofa?' asked the lady.

'Bob Spangles,' replied Seedeybuck.

'Nothing of the sort,' rejoined the lady; 'and I'll trouble you to get off.'

'Can't—I've got a bone in my leg,' rejoined the captain.

'I'll soon make you,' replied her ladyship, seizing the squab, and pulling it on to the floor.

As the captain was scrambling up, in came Peter—one of the wageless footmen—with candles, which having distributed equitably about the room, he approached Lady Scattercash, and asked, in an independent sort of way, what room Mr. Soapsuds was to have.

'Soapsuds!—Soapsuds!—that's not his name,' exclaimed her ladyship.

'*Sponge*, you fool! Soapey Sponge,' exclaimed Cutitfat, who had ferreted out Sponge's *nomme de Londres*.

'He's not come, has he?' asked Miss Glitters eagerly.

'Yes, my lady—that's to say, miss,' replied Peter.

'Come, has he!' chorused three or four voices.

'Well, he must have a (hiccup) room,' observed Sir Harry. 'The green—the one above the billiard-room will do,' added he.

'But *I* have that, Sir Harry,' exclaimed Miss Howard.

'Oh, it'll hold two well enough,' observed Miss Glitters.

'Then *you* can be the second,' replied Miss Howard, with a toss of her head.

'Indeed!' sneered Miss Glitters, bridling up. 'I like that.'

'Well, but where's the (hiccup) man to be put?' asked Sir Harry.

'There's Ladofwax's room,' suggested her ladyship.

'The captain's locked the door and taken the key with him,' replied the footman; 'he said he'd be back in a day or two.'

'Back in a (hiccup) or two!' observed Sir Harry. 'Where is he gone?'
The man smiled.

'*Borrowed*,' observed Captain Quod, with an emphasis.

'Indeed!' exclaimed Sir Harry, adding, 'well, I thought that was
Nabbum's gig with the old grey.'

'He'll not be back in a hurry,' observed Bouncey. 'He'll be like the
Boulogne gents, who are always going to England, but never do.'

'Poor Wax!' observed Quod; 'he's a big fool, to give him his due.'

'If you give him his due it's more than he gives other people, it seems.'
observed Miss Howard.

'Oh, fie, Miss H.!' exclaimed Captain Seedeybuck.

'Well, but the (hiccup) man must have a (hiccup) bed somewhere,'
observed Sir Harry; adding to the footman, 'you'd better (hiccup) the
door open, you know.'

'Perhaps you'd better try what one of yours will do,' observed Bob
Spangles, to the convulsion of the company.

In the midst of their mirth Mr. Bottleends was seen piloting Mr.
Sponge up to her ladyship.

'Mr. Sponge, my lady,' said he in as low and deferential a tone as if he
got his wages punctually every quarter-day.

'How do you do, Mr. Sponge?' said her ladyship, tendering him her
hand with an elegant curtsey.

'How are you, Mr. (hiccup) Sponge?' asked Sir Harry, offering his;
'I believe you know the (hiccup) company?' continued he, waving his
hand around; 'Miss (hiccup) Glitters, Captain (hiccup) Quod, Captain
Bouncey, Mr. (hiccup) Bugles, Captain (hiccup) Seedeybuck, and so on';
whereupon Miss Glitters curtsied, the gentlemen bobbed their heads and
drew near our hero, who had now stationed himself before the fire.

'Coldish to-night,' said he, stooping, and placing both hands to the
bars. 'Coldish,' repeated he, rubbing his hands and looking around.

'It generally is about this time of year, I think,' observed Miss Glitters,
who was quite ready to enter for our friend.

'Hope it won't stop hunting,' said Mr. Sponge.

'Hope not,' replied Sir Harry; 'would be a bore if it did.'

'I wonder you gentlemen don't prefer hunting in a frost,' observed
Miss Howard; 'one would think it would be just the time you'd want a
good warming.'

'I don't agree with you, there,' replied Mr. Sponge, looking at her, and thinking she was not nearly so pretty as Miss Glitters.

'Do you hunt to-morrow?' asked he of Sir Harry, not having been able to obtain any information at the stables.

'(Hiccup) to-morrow? Oh, I dare say we shall,' replied Sir Harry, who kept his hounds as he did his carriages, to be used when wanted. 'Dare say we shall,' repeated he.

But though Sir Harry spoke thus encouragingly of their prospects, he took no steps, as far as Mr. Sponge could learn, to carry out the design. Indeed, the subject of hunting was never once mentioned, the conversation after dinner, instead of being about the Quorn, or the Pytchley, or Jack Thompson with the Atherstone, turning upon the elegance and lighting of the Casinos in the Adelaide Gallery and Windmill Street, and the relative merits of those establishments over the Casino de Venise in High Holborn. Nor did morning produce any change for the better, for Sir Harry and all the captains came down in their usual flashy broken-down player-looking attire, their whole thoughts being absorbed in arranging for a pool at billiards, in which the ladies took part. So with billiards, brandy, and 'baccy,—'baccy, brandy, and billiards, varied with an occasional stroll about the grounds, the non-sporting inmates of Nonsuch House beguiled the time, much to Mr. Sponge's disgust, whose soul was on fire and eager for the fray. The reader's perhaps being the same, we will skip Christmas and pass on to New Year's Day.

LXII

A FAMILY BREAKFAST

'TWERE ALMOST SUPERFLUOUS TO SAY that NEW YEAR'S DAY is always a great holiday. It is a day on which custom commands people to be happy and idle, whether they have the means of being happy and idle or not. It is a day for which happiness and idleness are 'booked,' and parties are planned and arranged long beforehand. Some go to the town, some to the country; some take rail; some take steam; some take greyhounds; some take gigs; while others take guns and pop at all the little dicky-birds that come in their way. The rural population generally incline to a hunt. They are not very particular as to style, so long as there are a certain number of hounds, and some men in scarlet, to blow their horns, halloo, and crack their whips.

The population, especially the rising population about Nonsuch House, all inclined that way. A New Year's Day's hunt with Sir Harry had long been looked forward to by the little Raws, and the little Spooneys, and the big and little Cheeks, and we don't know how many others. Nay, it had been talked of by the elder boys at their respective schools—we beg pardon, academies—Dr. Switchington's, Mr. Latherington's, Mrs. Skelper's, and a liberal allowance of boasting indulged in, as to how they would show each other the way over the hedges and ditches. The thing had long been talked of. Old Johnny Raw had asked Sir Harry to arrange the day so long ago that Sir Harry had forgotten all about it. Sir Harry was one of those good-natured souls who can't say 'No' to any one. If anybody had asked if they might set fire to his house, he would have said:

'Oh (hiccup) certainly, my dear (hiccup) fellow, if it will give you any (hiccup) pleasure.'

Now, for the hiccup day.

It is generally a frost on New Year's Day. However wet and sloppy the weather may be up to the end of the year, it generally turns over a new leaf on that day. New Year's Day is generally a bright, bitter, sunshiny day, with starry ice, and a most decided anti-hunting feeling about it—light, airy, ringy, anything but cheery for hunting.

Thus it was in Sir Harry Scattercash's county. Having smoked and drunk the old year out, the captains and company retired to their couches without thinking about hunting. Mr. Sponge, indeed, was about tired of asking when the hounds would be going out. It was otherwise, however, with the rising generation, who were up betimes, and began pouring in upon Nonsuch House in every species of garb, on every description of steed, by every line and avenue of approach.

'Halloo! what's up now?' exclaimed Lady Scattercash, as she caught view of the first batch rounding the corner to the front of the house.

'Who have we here?' asked Miss Glitters, as a ponderous, parti-coloured clown, on a great, curly-coated cart-horse, brought up the rear.

'Early callers,' observed Captain Seedeybuck, eating away complacently.

'Friends of Mr. Sponge's, most likely,' suggested Captain Quod.

'Some of the little Sponges come to see their pa, p'raps,' lisped Miss Howard, pretending to be shocked after she had said it.

'Bravo, Miss Howard!' exclaimed Captain Cutitfat, clapping his hands.

'*I* said nothing, Captain,' observed the young lady with becoming prudery.

'Here we are again!' exclaimed Captain Quod, as a troop of various-sized urchins, in pea-jackets, with blue noses and red comforters, on very shaggy ponies, the two youngest swinging in panniers over an ass, drew up alongside of the first comers.

'Whose sliding-scale of innocence is that, I wonder!' exclaimed Miss Howard, contemplating the variously sized chubby faces through the window.

'He, he, he! ho, ho, ho!' giggled the guests.

Another batch of innocence now hove in sight.

'Oh, those are the little (hiccup) Raws,' observed Sir Harry, catching sight of the sky-blue collar of the servant's long drab coat. 'Good chap, old Johnny Raw; ask them to (hiccup) in,' continued he, 'and give them some (hiccup) cherry brandy'; and thereupon Sir Harry began nodding and smiling, and making signs to them to come in. The youngsters, however, maintained their position.

'The little stupexes!' exclaimed Miss Howard, going to the window, and throwing up the sash. 'Come in, young gents!' cried she, in a commanding tone, addressing herself to the last comers. 'Come in, and have some toffy and lollypops! D'ye hear?' continued she, in a still louder voice, and motioning her head towards the door.

The boys sat mute.

'You little stupid monkeys,' muttered she in an undertone, as the cold air struck upon her head. 'Come in, like good boys,' added she in a louder key, pointing with her finger towards the door.

'Nor, thenk ye!' at last drawled the elder of the boys.

'Nor, thenk ye!' repeated Miss Howard, imitating the drawl. 'Why not?' asked she sharply.

The boy stared stupidly.

'Why won't you come in?' asked she, again addressing him.

'Don't know!' replied the boy, staring vacantly at his younger brother, as he rubbed a pearl off his nose on the back of his hand.

'Don't know!' ejaculated Miss Howard, stamping her little foot on the Turkey carpet.

'Mar said we hadn't,' whined the younger boy, coming to the rescue of his brother.

'Mar said we hadn't!' retorted the fair interrogator. 'Why not?'

'Don't know,' replied the elder.

'Don't know! you little stupid animal,' snapped Miss Howard, the cold air increasing the warmth of her temper. 'I wonder what you *do* know. Why did your ma say you were not to come in?' continued she, addressing the younger one.

'Because—because,' hesitated he, 'she said the house was full of trumpets.'

'Trumpets, you little scamp!' exclaimed the lady, reddening up; 'I'll get a whip and cut your jacket into ribbons on your back.' And thereupon she banged down the window and closed the conversation.

LXIII

THE RISING GENERATION

THE LULL THAT PREVAILED IN the breakfast-room on Miss Howard's return from the window was speedily interrupted by fresh arrivals before the door. The three Master Baskets in coats and lay-over collars, Master Shutter in a jacket and trousers, the two Master Bulgeys in woollen overalls with very large hunting whips, Master Brick in a velveteen shooting-jacket, and the two Cheeks with their tweed trousers thrust into fiddle-case boots, on all sorts of ponies and family horses, began pawing and disordering the gravel in front of Nonsuch House.

George Cheek was the head boy at Mr. Latherington's classical and commercial academy, at Flagellation Hall (late the Crown and Sceptre Hotel and Posting House, on the Bankstone road), where, for forty pounds a year, eighty young gentlemen were fitted for the pulpit, the senate, the bar, the counting-house, or anything else their fond parents fancied them fit for.

George was a tall stripling, out at the elbows, in at the knees, with his red knuckled hands thrust a long way through his tight coat. He was just of that awkward age when boys fancy themselves men, and men are not prepared to lower themselves to their level. Ladies get on better with them than men: either the ladies are more tolerant of twaddle, or their discerning eyes see in the gawky youth the germ of future usefulness. George was on capital terms with himself. He was the oracle of Mr. Latherington's school, where he was not only head boy and head swell, but a considerable authority on sporting matters. He took in *Bell's Life*, which he read from beginning to end, and 'noted its contents,' as they say in the city.

'I'll tell you what all these little (hiccup) animals will be wanting,' observed Sir Harry, as he cayenne-peppered a turkey's leg; 'they'll be come for a (hiccup) hunt.'

'Wish they may get it,' observed Captain Seedeybuck; adding, 'why, the ground's as hard as iron.'

'There's a big boy,' observed Miss Howard, eyeing George Cheek through the window.

'Let's have him in, and see what he's got to say for himself,' said Miss Glitters.

'*You* ask him, then,' rejoined Miss Howard, who didn't care to risk another rub.

'Peter,' said Lady Scattercash to the footman, who had been loitering about, listening to the conversation,—'Peter, go and ask that tall boy with the blue neckerchief and the riband round his hat to come in.'

'Yes, my lady,' replied Peter.

'And the (hiccup) Spooneys, and the (hiccup) Bulgeys, and the (hiccup) Raws, and all the little (hiccup) rascals,' added Sir Harry.

'The Raws won't come. Sir H.,' observed Miss Howard soberly.

'Bigger fools they,' replied Sir Harry.

Presently Peter returned with a tail, headed by George Cheek, who came striding and slouching up the room, and stuck himself down on Lady Scattercash's right. The small boys squeezed themselves in as they could, one by Captain Seedeybuck, another by Captain Bouncey, one by Miss Glitters, a fourth by Miss Howard, and so on. They all fell ravenously upon the provisions.

Gobble, gobble, gobble was the order of the day.

'Well, and how often have you been flogged this half?' asked Lady Scattercash of George Cheek, as she gave him a cup of coffee.

Her ladyship hadn't much liking for youths of his age, and would just as soon vex them as not.

'Well, and how often have you been flogged this half?' asked she again, not getting an answer to her first inquiry.

'Not at all,' growled Cheek, reddening up.

'Oh, flogged!' exclaimed Miss Glitters. 'You wouldn't have a young man like him flogged; it's only the little boys that get that—is it, Mister Cheek?'

'To be sure not,' assented the youth.

'Mister Cheek's a man,' observed Miss Glitters, eyeing him archly, as he sat stuffing his mouth with currant-loaf plentifully besmeared with raspberry-jam. 'He'll be wanting a wife soon,' added she, smiling across the table at Captain Seedeybuck.

'I question but he's got one,' observed the captain.

'No, ar haven't,' replied Cheek, pleased at the imputation.

'Then there's a chance for you, Miss G.,' retorted the captain. 'Mrs. George Cheek would look well on a glazed card with gilt edges.'

'What a cub!' exclaimed Miss Howard, in disgust.

'You're another,' replied Master Cheek, amidst a roar of laughter from the party.

'Well, but you ask your master if you mayn't have a wife next half, and we'll see if we can't arrange matters,' observed Miss Glitters.

'Noo, ar sharn't,' replied George, stuffing his mouth full of preserved apricot.

'Why not?' asked Miss Howard, 'Because—because—ar'll have somethin' younger,' replied George.

'Bravo, young Chesterfield!' exclaimed Miss Howard; adding, 'what it is to be thick with Lord John Manners!'

'Ar'm not,' growled the boy, amidst the mirth of the company.

'Well, but what must we do with these little (hiccup)?' asked Sir Harry, at last rising from the breakfast-table, and looking listlessly round the company for an answer.

'Oh! liquor them well, and send them home to their mammas,' suggested Captain Bouncey, who was all for the drink.

'But they won't take their (hiccup),' replied Sir Harry, holding up a Curacao bottle to show how little had disappeared.

'Try them with cherry brandy,' suggested Captain Seedeybuck; adding, 'it's sweeter. Now, young man,' continued he, addressing George Cheek, as he poured him out a wineglassful, 'this is the real Daffy's elixir that you read of in the papers. It's the finest compound that ever was known. It will make your hair curl, your whiskers grow, and you a man before your mother.'

'N-o-a, n-o-ar, don't want any more,' growled the young gentleman, turning away in disgust. 'Ar won't drink any more.'

'Well, but be sociable,' observed Miss Howard, helping herself to a glass.

'N-o-a, no, ar don't want to be sociable,' growled he, diving into his trouser-pockets, and wriggling about on his chair.

'Well, then, what *will* you do?' asked Miss Howard.

'Hunt,' replied the youth.

'Hunt!' exclaimed Bob Spangles; 'why, the ground's as hard as bricks.'

'N-o-a, it's not,' replied the youth.

'What a whelp!' exclaimed Miss Howard, rising from the table in disgust.

'My Uncle Jellyboy wouldn't let such a frost stop him, I know,' observed the boy.

'Who's your Uncle Jellyboy?' asked Miss Glitters.

'He's a farmer, and keeps a few harriers at Scutley,' observed Bob Spangles, *sotto voce*.

'And is that your extraordinary horse with all the legs?' asked Miss Howard, putting her glass to her eye, and scrutinizing a lank, woolly-coated weed, getting led about by a blue-aproned gardener. 'Is that your extraordinary horse, with all the legs?' repeated she, following the animal about with her glass.

'Hoots, it hasn't more legs than other people's,' growled George.

'It's got ten, at all events,' replied Miss Howard, to the astonishment of the juveniles.

'Nor, it hasn't,' replied George.

'Yes, it has,' rejoined the lady.

'Nor, it hasn't,' repeated George.

'Come and see,' said the lady; adding, 'perhaps it's put out some since you got off.'

George slouched up to where she stood at the window.

'Now,' said he, as the gardener turned the horse round, and he saw it had but four, 'how many has it?'

'Ten!' replied Miss Howard.

'Hoots,' replied George, 'you think it's April Fool's Day, I dare say.'

'No, I don't,' replied Miss Howard; 'but I maintain your horse has ten legs. See, now!' continued she, 'what do you call these coming here?'

'His two forelegs,' replied George.

'Well, two fours—twice four's eight, eh? and his two hind ones make ten.'

'Hoots,' growled George, amidst the mirth of his comrades, 'you're makin' a fool o' one.'

'Well, but what must I do with all these little (hiccup) creatures?' asked Sir Harry again, seeing the plot still thickening outside.

'Turn them out a bagman?' suggested Mr. Sponge, in an undertone; adding, 'Watchorn has a three-legged 'un, I know, in the hay-loft.'

'Oh, Watchorn wouldn't (hiccup) on such a day as this,' replied Sir Harry. 'New Year's Day, too—most likely away, seeing his young hounds at walk.'

'We might see, at all events,' observed Mr. Sponge.

'Well,' assented Sir Harry, ringing the bell. 'Peter,' said he, as the servant answered the summons, 'I wish you would (hiccup) to Mr. Watchorn's, and ask if he'll have the kindness to (hiccup) down here.' Sir Harry was obliged to be polite, for Watchorn, too, was on the 'free' list as Miss Glitters called it.

'Yes, Sir Harry,' replied Peter, leaving the room.

Presently Peter's white legs were seen wending their way among the laurels and evergreens, in the direction of Mr. Watchorn's house; he having a house and grass for six cows, all whose milk, he declared, went to the puppies and young hounds. Luckily, or unluckily perhaps, Mr. Watchorn was at home, and was in the act of shaving as Peter entered. He was a square-built dark-faced, dark-haired, good-looking, ill-looking fellow who cultivated his face on the four-course system of husbandry. First, he had a bare fallow—we mean a clean shave; that of course was followed by a full crop of hair all over, except on his upper lip; then he had a soldier's shave, off by the ear; which in turn was followed by a Newgate frill. The latter was his present style. He had now no whiskers, but an immense protuberance of bristly black hair, rising like a wave above his kerchief. Though he cared no more about hunting than his master, he was very fond of his red coat, which he wore on all occasions, substituting a hat for a cap when 'off duty,' as he called it. Having attired himself in his best scarlet, of which he claimed three a year—one for wet days, one for dry days, another for high days—very natty kerseymere shorts and gaiters, with a small-striped, standing-collar, toilenette waistcoat, he proceeded to obey the summons.

'Watchorn,' said Sir Harry, as the important gentleman appeared at the breakfast-room door—'Watchorn, these young (hiccup) gentlemen want a (hiccup) hunt.'

'Oh! want must be their master, Sir 'Arry,' replied Watchorn, with a broad grin on his flushed face, for he had been drinking all night, and was half drunk then.

'Can't you manage it?' asked Sir Harry, mildly.

''Ow is't possible. Sir 'Arry,' asked the huntsman, "ow is't possible? No man's fonder of 'untin' than I am, but to turn out on sich a day as this would be a daring—a desperate violation of all the laws of registered propriety. The Pope's bull would be nothin' to it!'

'How so?' asked Sir Harry, puzzled with the jumble.

'How so?' repeated Watchorn; 'how so? Why, in the fust place, it's a mortal 'ard frost, 'arder nor hiron; in the second place, I've got no arrangements made—you can't turn out a pack of 'igh-bred fox-'ounds as you would a lot of "staggers" or "muggers"; and, in the third place, you'll knock all your nags to bits, and they are a deal better in their wind than they are on their legs, as it is. No, Sir 'Arry—no,' continued he, slowly and thoughtfully. 'No, Sir 'Arry, no. Be Cardinal Wiseman, for once. Sir 'Arry; be Cardinal Wiseman for once, and don't *think* of it.'

'Well,' replied Sir Harry, looking at George Cheek, 'I suppose there's no help for it.'

'It was quite a thaw where I came from,' observed Cheek, half to Sir Harry and half to the huntsman.

''Deed, sir, 'deed,' replied Mr. Watchorn, with a chuck of his fringed chin, 'it generally is a thaw everywhere but where hounds meet.'

'My Uncle Jollyboy wouldn't be stopped by such a frost as this,' observed Cheek.

''Deed, sir, 'deed,' replied Watchorn, 'your Uncle Jellyboy's a very fine feller, I dare say—very fine feller; no such conjurers in these parts as he is. What man dare, I dare; he who dares more, is no man,' added Watchorn, giving his fat thigh a hearty slap.

'Well done, old Talliho!' exclaimed Miss Glitters. 'We'll have you on the stage next.'

'What will you wet your whistle with after your fine speech?' asked Lady Scattercash.

'Take a tumbler of chumpine, if there is any,' replied Watchorn, looking about for a long-necked bottle.

'Fear you'll come on badly,' observed Captain Seedeybuck, holding up an empty one, 'for Bouncey and I have just finished the last'; the captain chucking the bottle sideways on to the floor, and rolling it towards its companion in the corner.

'Have a fresh bottle,' suggested Lady Scattercash, drawing the bell-string at her chair.

'Champagne,' said her ladyship, as the footman answered the summons.

'Two on 'em!' exclaimed Captain Bouncey.

'Three!' shouted Sir Harry.

'We'll have a regular set-to,' observed Miss Howard, who was fond of champagne.

'New Year's Day,' replied Bouncey, 'and ought to be properly observed.'

Presently, Fiz—z,—pop,—bang! Fiz—z,—pop,—bang! went the bottles; and, as the hissing beverage foamed over the bottle-necks, glasses were sought and held out to catch the creaming contents.

'Here's a (hiccup) happy new year to us all!' exclaimed Sir Harry, drinking off his wine. 'H-o-o-ray!' exclaimed the company in irregular order, as they drank off theirs.

'We'll drink Mr. Watchorn and the Nonsuch hounds!' exclaimed Bob Spangles, as Watchorn, having drained off his tumbler, replaced it on the sideboard.

'With all the honours!' exclaimed Captain Cutitfat, filling his glass and rising to give the time; 'Watchorn, your good health!' 'Watchorn, your good health!' sounded from all parts, which Watchorn kept acknowledging, and looking about for the means to return the compliment, his friends being more intent upon drinking his health than upon supplying him with wine. At last he caught the third of a bottle of 'chumpine,' and, emptying it into his tumbler, held it up while he thus addressed them:

'Gen'lemen all!' said he, 'I thank you most 'ticklarly for this mark of your 'tention (applause); it's most gratifying to my feelins to be thus remembered (applause). I could say a great deal more, but the liquor won't wait.' So saying, he drained off his glass while the wine effervesced.

'Well, and what d'ye (hiccup) of the weather now?' asked Sir Harry, as his huntsman again deposited his tumbler on the sideboard.

''Pon my soul! Sir 'Arry,' replied Watchorn, quite briskly, 'I really think we *might* 'unt—we might try, at all events. The day seems changed,

some'ow,' added he, staring vacantly out of the window on the bright
sunny landscape, with the leafless trees dancing before his eyes.

'*I* think so,' said Sir Harry. 'What do you think, Mr. Sponge?' added
he, appealing to our hero.

'Half an hour may make a great difference,' observed Mr. Sponge. 'The
sun will then be at its best.'

'We'll try, at all events,' observed Sir Harry.

'That's right,' exclaimed George Cheek, waving a scarlet bandana over
his head.

'I shall expect you to ride up to the 'ounds, young gent,' observed
Watchorn, darting an angry look at the speaker.

'Won't I, old boy!' exclaimed George; 'ride over you, if you don't get
out of the way.'

''Deed,' sneered the huntsman, whisking about to leave the room;
muttering, as he passed behind the large Indian screen at the door,
something about 'jawing jackanapes, well called Cheek.'

''Unt in 'alf an hour!' exclaimed Watchorn, from the steps of the front
door; an announcement that was received by the little Raws, and little
Spooneys, and little Baskets, and little Bulgeys, and little Bricks, and little
others, with rapturous applause.

All was now commotion and hurry-scurry inside and out; glasses were
drained, lips wiped, and napkins thrown hastily away, while ladies and
gentlemen began grouping and talking about hats and habits, and what
they should ride.

'You go with me, Orlando,' said Lady Scattercash to our friend Bugles,
recollecting the quantity of diachylon plaster it had taken to repair
the damage of his former equestrian performance. 'You go with me,
Orlando,' said she, 'in the phaeton; and I'll lend Lucy,' nodding towards
Miss Glitters, 'my habit and horse.'

'Who can lend me a coat?' asked Captain Seedeybuck, examining the
skirts of a much frayed invisible-green surtout.

'A coat!' replied Captain Quod; 'I can lend you a Joinville, if that will
do as well,' the captain feeling his own extensive one as he spoke.

'Hardly,' said Seedeybuck, turning about to ask Sir Harry.

'What!—you are going to give Watchorn a tussle, are you?' asked
Captain Cutitfat of George Cheek, as the latter began adjusting the fox-
toothed riband about his hat.

'I believe you,' replied George, with a knowing jerk of his head; adding, 'it won't take much to beat him.'

'What! he's a slow 'un, is he?' asked Cutitfat, in an undertone.

'Slowest coach I ever saw,' growled George.

'Won't ride, won't he?' asked the Captain.

'Not if he can help it,' replied George, adding, 'but he's such a shocking huntsman—never saw such a huntsman in all my life.'

George's experience lay between his Uncle Jellyboy, who rode eighteen stone and a half, Tom Scramble, the pedestrian huntsman of the Slowfoot hounds, near Mr. Latherington's, and Mr. Watchorn. But critics, especially hunting ones, are all ready made, as Lord Byron said.

'Well, we'd better disperse and get ready,' observed Bob Spangles, making for the door; whereupon the tide of population flowed that way, and the room was presently cleared.

George Cheek and the juveniles then returned to their friends in the front; and George got up pony races among the Johnny Raws, the Baskets, the Bulgeys, and the Spooneys, thrice round the carriage ring and a distance, to the detriment of the gravel and the discomfiture of the flower-bed in the centre.

LXIV

THE KENNEL AND THE STUD

W E WILL NOW ACCOMPANY MR. Watchorn to the stable, whither his resolute legs carried him as soon as the champagne wrought the wonderful change in his opinion of the weather, though, as he every now and then crossed a spangled piece of ground upon which the sun had not struck, or stopped to crack a piece of ice with his toe, he shook his heated head and doubted whether *he* was Cardinal Wiseman for making the attempt. Nothing but the fact of his considering it perfectly immaterial whether he was with his hounds or not encouraged him in the undertaking. 'Dash them!' said he, 'they must just take care of themselves.' With which laudable resolution, and an inward anathema at George Cheek, he left off trying the ground and tapping the ice.

Watchorn's hurried, excited appearance produced little satisfaction among the grooms and helpers at the stables, who were congratulating themselves on the opportune arrival of the frost, and arranging how they should spend their New Year's Day.

'Look sharp, lads! look sharp!' exclaimed he, clapping his hands as he ran up the yard. 'Look sharp, lads! look sharp!' repeated he, as the astonished helpers showed their bare arms and dirty shirts at the partially opened doors, responsive to the sound. 'Send Snaffle here, send Brown here, send Green here, send Snooks here,' exclaimed he, with the air of a man in authority.

Now Snaffle was the stud-groom, a personage altogether independent of the huntsman, and, in the ordinary course of nature, Snaffle had just as much right to send for Watchorn as Watchorn had to send for him; but Watchorn being, as we said before, some way connected with Lady

Scattercash, he just did as he liked among the whole of them, and they were too good judges to rebel.

'Snaffle,' said he, as the portly, well-put-on personage waddled up to him; 'Snaffle,' said he, 'how many sound 'osses have you?'

'*None*, sir,' replied Snaffle confidently.

'How many three-legged 'uns have you that can go, then?'

'Oh! a good many,' replied Snaffle, raising his hands to tell them off on his fingers. 'There's Hop-the-twig, and Hannah Bell (Hannibal), and Ugly Jade, and Sir-danapalis—the Baronet as we calls him—and Harkaway, and Hit-me-hard, and Single-peeper, and Jack's-alive, and Groggytoes, and Greedyboy, and Puff-and-blow; that's to say *two* and three-legged 'uns, at least,' observed Snaffle, qualifying his original assertion.

'Ah, well!' said Watchorn, 'that'll do—two legs are too many for some of the rips they'll have to carry—Let me see,' continued he thoughtfully, 'I'll ride 'Arkaway.'

'Yes, sir,' said Snaffle.

'Sir 'Arry, 'It-me-'ard.'

'Won't you put him on Sir-danapalis?' asked Snaffle.

'No,' replied Watchorn, 'no; I wants to save the Bart.—I wants to save the Bart. Sir 'Arry must ride 'It-me-'ard.'

'Is her ladyship going?' asked Snaffle.

'Her ladyship drives,' replied Watchorn. 'And you, Snooks,' addressing a bare-armed helper, 'tell Mr. Traces to turn her out a pony phaeton and pair, with fresh rosettes and all complete, you know.'

'Yes, sir,' said Snooks, with a touch of his forelock.

'And you'd better tell Mr. Leather to have a horse for his master,' observed Watchorn to Snaffle, 'unless as how you wish to put him on one of yours.'

'Not I,' exclaimed Snaffle; 'have enough to mount without him. D'ye know how many'll be goin'?' asked he.

'No,' replied Watchorn, hurrying off; adding, as he went, 'oh, hang 'em, just saddle 'em all, and let 'em scramble for 'em.'

The scene then changed. Instead of hissing helpers pursuing their vocations in stable or saddle-room, they began bustling about with saddles on their heads and bridles in their hands, the day of expected ease being changed into one of unusual trouble. Mr. Leather declared, as he swept the clothes over Multum-in-Parvo's tail, that it was the most unconscionable proceeding he had ever witnessed; and muttered something about the quiet comforts he had left at Mr. Jogglebury Crowdey's, hinting his regret at having come to Sir Harry's, in a sort of dialogue with himself as he saddled the horse. The beauties of the last place always come out strong when a servant gets to another. But we must accompany Mr. Watchorn.

Though his early career with the Camberwell and Balham Hill Union harriers had not initiated him much into the delicacies of the chase, yet, recollecting the presence of Mr. Sponge, he felt suddenly seized with a desire of 'doing things as they should be'; and he went muttering to the kennel, thinking how he would leave Dinnerbell and Prosperous at home, and how the pack would look quite as well without Frantic running half a field ahead, or old Stormer and Stunner bringing up the rear with long protracted howls. He doubted, indeed, whether he would take Desperate, who was an incorrigible skirter; but as she was not much worse in this respect than Chatterer or Harmony, who was also an inveterate babbler, and the pack would look rather short without them, he reserved the point for further consideration, as the judges say.

His speculations were interrupted by arriving at the kennel, and finding the door fast, he looked under the slate, and above the frame, and inside the window, and on the wall, for the key; and his shake, and kick, and clatter were only answered by a full chorus from the excited company within.

'Hang the feller! what's got 'im!' exclaimed he, meaning Joe Haggish, the feeder, whom he expected to find there.

Joe, however, was absent; not holiday-making, but on a diplomatic visit to Mr. Greystones, the miller, at Splashford, who had positively refused to supply any more meal, until his 'little bill' (£430) for the three previous years was settled; and flesh being very scarce in the country, the hounds were quite light and fit to go. Joe had gone to try and coax Greystones out of a ton or two of meal, on the strength of its being New Year's Day.

'Dash the feller! wot's got'im?' exclaimed Watchorn, seizing the latch, and rattling it furiously. The melody of the hungry pack increased. ''Ord rot the door!' exclaimed the infuriated huntsman, setting his back against it; at the first push, open it flew. Watchorn fell back, and the astonished pack poured over his prostrate body, regardless alike of his holiday coat, his tidy tie, and toilenette vest. What a scrimmage! What a kick-up was there! Away the hounds scampered, towling and howling, some up to the fleshwheel, to see if there was any meat; some to the bone heap, to see if there was any there; others down to the dairy, to try and effect an entrance in it; while Launcher, and Lightsome, and Burster, rushed to the backyard of Nonsuch House, and were presently over ears in the pig-pail.

'Get me my horn! get me my whop!—get me my cap!—get me my bouts!' exclaimed Watchorn, as he recovered his legs, and saw his wife eyeing the scene from the door. 'Get me my bouts!—get me my cap!—get me my whop!—get me my horn, woman!' continued he, reversing the order of things, and rubbing the hounds' feetmarks off his clothes as he spoke.

Mrs. Watchorn was too well drilled to dwell upon orders, and she met her lord and master in the passage with the enumerated articles in her hand. Watchorn having deposited himself on an entrance-hall chair—for it was a roomy, well-furnished house, having been the steward's while there was anything to take care of—Mrs. Watchorn proceeded to strip off his gaiters while he drew on his boots and crowned himself with his cap. Mrs. Watchorn then buckled on his spurs, and he hurried off, horn in hand, desiring her to have him a basin of turtle-soup ready against he came in; adding, 'She knew where to get it.' The frosty air then resounded with the twang, twang, twang of his horn, and hounds began drawing up from all quarters, just as sportsmen cast up at a meet from no one knows where.

'He-here, hounds—he-here, good dogs!' cried he, coaxing and making much of the first-comers: 'he-here. Galloper, old boy!' continued he, diving into his coat-pocket, and throwing him a bit of biscuit. The appearance of food had a very encouraging effect, for forthwith there was a general rush towards Watchorn, and it was only by rating and swinging his 'whop' about that he prevented the pack from pawing, and perhaps downing him. At length, having got them somewhat tranquillized, he set off on his return to the stables, coaxing the shy hounds, and rating and rapping those that seemed inclined to break away. Thus he managed to march into the stable-yard in pretty good order, just as the house party arrived in the opposite direction, attired

ROBERT S. SURTEES

in the most extraordinary and incongruous habiliments. There was Bob Spangles, in a swallow-tailed, mulberry-coloured scarlet, that looked like an old pen-wiper, white duck trousers, and lack-lustre Napoleon boots; Captain Cutitfat, in a smart new 'Moses and Son's' straight-cut scarlet, with bloodhound heads on the buttons, yellow-ochre leathers, and Wellington boots with drab knee-caps; little Bouncey in a tremendously baggy long-backed scarlet, whose gaping outside-pockets showed that they had carried its late owner's hands as well as his handkerchief; the clumsy device on the tarnished buttons looking quite as much like sheep's-heads as foxes'. Bouncey's tight tweed trousers were thrust into a pair of wide fisherman's boots, which, but for his little roundabout stomach, would have swallowed him up bodily. Captain Quod appeared in a venerable dresscoat of the Melton Hunt, made in the popular reign of Mr. Errington, whose much-stained and smeared silk facings bore testimony to the good cheer it had seen. As if in contrast to the light airiness of this garment, Quod had on a tremendously large shaggy brown waistcoat, with horn buttons, a double tier of pockets, and a nick out in front. With an unfair partiality his nether man was attired in a pair of shabby old black, or rather brown, dress trousers, thrust into long Wellington boots with brass heel spurs. Captain Seedeybuck had on a spruce swallow-tailed green coat of Sir Harry's, a pair of old tweed trousers of his own, thrust into long chamois-leather opera-boots, with red morocco tops, giving the whole a very unique and novel appearance. Mr. Orlando Bugles, though going to drive with my lady, thought it incumbent to put on his jack-boots, and appeared in kerseymere shorts, and a highly frogged and furred blue frock-coat, with the corner of a musked cambric kerchief acting the part of a star on his breast.

"Here comes old sixteen-string'd Jack!" exclaimed Bob Spangles, as his brother-in-law, Sir Harry, came hitching and limping along, all strings, and tapes, and ends, as usual, followed by Mr. Sponge in the strict and severe order of sporting costume; double-stitched, back-stitched, sleeve-strapped, pull-devil, pull-baker coat, broad corduroy vest with fox-teeth buttons, still broader corded breeches, and the redoubtable vinegar tops. "Now we're all ready!" exclaimed Bob, working his arms as if anxious to be off, and giving a shrill shilling-gallery whistle with his fingers, causing the stable-doors to fly open, and the variously tackled steeds to emerge from their stalls.

"A horse! a horse! my kingdom for a horse!" exclaimed Miss Glitters, running up as fast as her long habit, or rather Lady Scattercash's long habit, would allow her. "A horse! a horse! my kingdom for a horse!" repeated she, diving into the throng.

'White Surrey is saddled for the field,' replied Mr. Orlando Bugles, drawing himself up pompously, and waving his right hand gracefully towards her ladyship's Arab palfrey, inwardly congratulating himself that Miss Glitters was going to be bumped upon it instead of him.

'Give us a leg up, Seedey!' exclaimed Lucy Glitters to the 'gent' of the green coat, fearing that Miss Howard, who was a little behind, might claim the horse.

Captain Seedeybuck seized her pretty little uplifted foot and vaulted her into the saddle as light as a cork. Taking the horse gently by the mouth, she gave him the slightest possible touch with the whip, and moved him about at will, instead of fretting and fighting him as the clumsy, heavy-handed Bugles had done. She looked beautiful on horseback, and for a time riveted the attention of our sportsmen. At length they began to think of themselves, and then there were such climbings on, and clutchings, and catchings, and clingings, and gently-ings, and who-ho-ings, and who-ah-ings, and questionings if 'such a horse was quiet?' if another 'could leap well?' if a third 'had a good mouth?' and whether a fourth 'ever ran away?'

'Take my port-stirrup up two 'oles!' exclaimed Captain Bouncey from the top of high Hop-the-twig, sticking out a leg to let the groom do it.

The captain had affected the sea instead of the land service, while a betting-list keeper, and found the bluff sailor character very taking.

'Avast there!' exclaimed he, as the groom ran the buckle up to the desired hole. 'Now,' said he, gathering up the reins in a bunch, 'how many knots an hour can this 'orse go?'

'Twenty,' replied the man, thinking he meant miles.

'Let her go, then!' exclaimed the captain, kicking the horse's sides with his spurless heels.

Mr. Watchorn now mounted Harkaway; Sir Harry scrambled on to Hit-me-hard; Miss Howard was hoisted on to Groggytoes, and all the rest being 'fit' with horses of some sort or other, and the races in the front being over the juveniles poured into the yard. Lady Scattercash's pony-phaeton turned out, and our friends were at length ready for a start.

LXV

THE HUNT

WHILE THE FOREGOING ARRANGEMENTS WERE in progress, Mr. Watchorn had desired Slarkey, the knife-boy, to go into the old hay-loft and take the three-legged fox he would find, and put him down among the laurels by the summer-house, where he would draw up to him all 'reg'lar' like. Accordingly, Slarkey went, but the old cripple having mounted the rafters, Slarkey didn't see him, or rather seeing but one fox, he clutched him, with a greater regard to his not biting him than to seeing how many legs he had; consequently he bagged an uncommonly fine old dog fox, that Wiley Tom had just stolen from Lord Scamperdale's new cover at Faggotfurze; and it was not until Slarkey put him down among the bushes, and saw how lively he went, that he found out his mistake. However, there was no help for it, and he had just time to pocket the bag when Watchorn's half-drunken cheer, and the reverberating cracks of ponderous whips on either side of the Dean, announced the approach of the pack.

'He-leu in there!' cried Watchorn to the hounds. ''Ord, dommee, but it's slippy,' said he to himself. 'Have at him. Plunderer, good dog! I wish I may be Cardinal Wiseman for comin',' added he, seeing how his breath showed on the air. 'Ho-o-i-icks! pash 'im hup! I'll be dashed if I shan't be down!' exclaimed he, as his horse slid a long slide. 'He-leu, in! Conqueror, old boy!' continued he, exclaiming loud enough for Mr. Sponge who was drawing near to hear, 'find us a fox that'll give us five and forty minnits!' the speaker inwardly hoping they might chop their bagman in cover. 'Y-o-o-icks! rout him out!' continued he, getting more energetic. 'Y-o-o-icks! wind him! Y-o-o-icks! stir us hup a teaser!'

'No go, I think,' observed George Cheek, ambling up on his leggy weed.

'No go, ye young infidel,' growled Watchorn, 'who taught you to talk about go's, I wonder? ought to be at school larnin' to cipher, or ridin' the globes,' Mr. Watchorn not exactly knowing what the term 'use of the globes,' meant. 'D'ye call that *nothin*'!' exclaimed he, taking off his cap as he viewed the fox stealing along the gravel walk; adding to himself, as he saw his even action, and full, well-tagged brush, ''Ord rot him, he's got hold of the wrong 'un!'

It was, however, no time for thought. In an instant the welkin rang with the outburst of the pack and the clamour of the field. 'Talli ho!' 'Talli ho!' 'Talli ho!' 'Hoop!' 'Hoop!' 'Hoop!' cried a score of voices, and 'Twang! twang! twang!' went the shrill horn of the huntsman. The whips, too, stood in their stirrups, cracking their ponderous thongs, which sounded like guns upon the frosty air, and contributed their 'Get together! get together, hounds!' 'Hark away!' 'Hark away!' 'Hark away!' 'Hark' to the general uproar. Oh, what a row, what a riot, what a racket! Watchorn being 'in' for it, and recollecting how many saw a start who never thought of seeing a finish, immediately got his horse by the head, and singled himself out from the crowd now pressing at his horse's heels, determining, if the hounds didn't run into their fox in the park, to ride them off the scent at the very first opportunity. The 'chumpine' being still alive within him, in the excitement of the moment he leaped the hand-gate leading out of the shrubberies into the park; the noise the horse made in taking off resembling the trampling on wood-pavement.

'Cuss it, but it's 'ard!' exclaimed he, as the horse slid two or three yards as he alighted on the frozen field.

George Cheek followed him; and Multum-in-Parvo, taking the bit deliberately between his teeth, just walked through the gate, as if it had been made of paper.

'Ah, ye brute!' groaned Mr. Sponge, in disgust, digging the Latchfords into his sides, as if he intended to make them meet in the middle. 'Ah, ye brute!' repeated he, giving him a hearty cropper as he put up his head after trying to kick him off.

'Thank you!' exclaimed Miss Glitters, cantering up; adding, 'you cleared the way nicely for me.'

Nicely he had cleared it for them all; and the pent-up tide of equestrianism now poured over the park like the flood of an irrigated water meadow. Such ponies! such horses! such hugging! such kicking! such scrambling! and so little progress with many!

The park being extensive—three hundred acres or more—there was ample space for the aspiring ones to single themselves out; and as Lady Scattercash and Orlando sat in the pony-phaeton, on the rising ground by the keeper's house, they saw a dark-clad horseman (George Cheek), Old Gingerbread Boots, as they called Mr. Sponge, with Lucy Glitters alongside of him, gradually stealing away from the crowd, and creeping up to Mr. Watchorn, who was sailing away with the hounds.

'What a scrimmage!' exclaimed her ladyship, standing up in the carriage, and eyeing the strange confusion in the vale below.

'There's Bob in his old purple,' said she, eyeing her brother hustling along; 'and there's "Fat" in his new Moses and Son; and Bouncey in poor Wax's coat; and there's Harry all legs and wings, as usual,' added she, as her husband was seen flibberty-gibbertying it along.

'And there's Lucy; and where's Miss Howard, I wonder?' observed Orlando, straining his eyes after the scrambling field.

Nothing but the inspiriting aid of 'chumpine,' and the hope that the thing would soon terminate, sustained Mr. Watchorn under the infliction in which he so unexpectedly found himself; for nothing would have tempted him to brave such a frost with the burning scent of a game four-legged fox. The park being spacious, and enclosed by a high plank paling, he hoped the fox would have the manners to confine himself within it; and so long as his threadings and windings favoured the supposition, our huntsman bustled along, yelling and screaming in apparent ecstasy at the top of his voice. The hounds, to be sure, wanted keeping together, for Frantic as usual had shot ahead, while the gorged pigpailers could never extricate themselves from the ponies.

'F-o-o-o-r-r-a-r-d! f-o-o-o-r-r-a-r-d! f-o-o-o-r-r-a-r-d!' elongated Watchorn, rising in his stirrups, and looking back with a grin at George Cheek, who was plying his weed with the whip, exclaiming, 'Ah, you confounded young warmint, I'll give you a warmin'! I'll teach you to jaw about 'untin'!'

As he turned his head straight to look at his hounds, he was shocked to see Frantic falling backwards from a first attempt to leap the park-palings, and just as she gathered herself for a second effort, Desperate, Chatterer, and Galloper, charged in line and got over. Then came the general rush of the pack, attended with the usual success—some over, some back, some a-top of others.

'Oh, the devil!' exclaimed Watchorn, pulling up short in a perfect agony of despair. 'Oh, the devil!' repeated he in a lower tone, as Mr. Sponge approached.

'Where's there a gate?' roared our friend, skating up.

'Gate! there's never a gate within a mile, and that's locked,' replied Watchorn sulkily.

'Then here goes!' replied Mr. Sponge, gathering the chestnut together to give him an opportunity of purging himself of his previous *faux pas*. 'Here goes!' repeated he, thrusting his hard hat firmly on his head. Taking his horse back a few paces, Mr. Sponge crammed him manfully at the palings, and got over with a rap.

'Well done you!' exclaimed Miss Glitters in delight; adding to Watchorn, 'Now, old Beardey, you go next.'

Beardey was irresolute. He pretended to be anxious to get the tail hounds over.

'Clear the way, then!' exclaimed Miss Glitters, putting her horse back, her bright eyes flashing as she spoke. She took him back as far as Mr. Sponge had done, touched him with the whip, and in an instant she was high in the air, landing safely on the far side.

'Hoo-ray!' exclaimed Captains Quod and Cutitfat, who now came panting up.

'Now, Mr. Watchorn!' cried Captain Seedeybuck, adding, 'You're a huntsman!'

'Yooi over, Prosperous! Yooi over, Buster!' cheered Watchorn, still pretending anxiety about his hounds.

'Let *me* have a shy,' squeaked George Cheek, backing his giraffe, as he had seen Mr. Sponge and Miss Glitters do.

George took his screw by the head, and, giving him a hearty rib-roasting with his whip, ran him full tilt at the palings, and carried away half a rood.

'Hoo-ray!' cried the liberated field.

'*I* knew how it would be,' exclaimed Mr. Watchorn, in well-feigned disgust as he rode through the gap; adding, '*con*-founded young

waggabone! Deserves to be well *chaste*-tized for breakin' people's palin's in that way—lettin' in all the rubbishin' tail.'

The scene then changed. In *lieu* of the green, though hard, sward of the undulating park, our friends now found themselves on large frozen fallows, upon whose uneven surface the heaviest horses made no impression while the shuffling rats of ponies toiled and floundered about, almost receding in their progress. Mr. Sponge was just topping the fence out of the first one, and Miss Glitters was gathering her horse to ride at it, as Watchorn and Co. emerged from the park. Rounding the turnip-hill beyond, the leading hounds were racing with a breast-high scent, followed by the pack in long-drawn file.

'What a mess!' said Watchorn to himself, shading the sun from his eyes with his hand; when, remembering his *role*, he exclaimed, 'Y-o-o-n-d-e-r they go!' as if in ecstasies at the sight. Seeing a gate at the bottom of the field, he got his horse by the head, and rattled him across the fallow, blowing his horn more in hopes of stopping the pack than with a view of bringing up the tail-hounds. He might have saved his breath, for the music of the pack completely drowned the noise of the horn. 'Dash it!' said he, thumping the broad end against his thigh; 'I wish I was quietly back in my parlour. Hold up, horse!' roared he, as Harkaway nearly came on his haunches in pulling up at the gate. 'I know who's *not* Cardinal Wiseman,' continued he, stooping to open it.

The gate was fast, and he had to alight and lift it off its hinges. Just as he had done so, and had got it sufficiently open for a horse to pass, George Cheek came up from behind, and slipped through before him.

'Oh, you unrighteous young renegade! Did ever mortal see sich an uncivilized trick?' roared Watchorn; adding, as he climbed on to his horse again, and went spluttering through the frozen turnips after the offender, 'You've no 'quaintance with Lord John Manners, I think!'

'Oh dear!—oh dear!' exclaimed he, as his horse nearly came on his head, 'but this is the most punishin' affair I ever was in at. Puseyism's nothin' to it.' And thereupon he indulged in no end of anathemas at Slarkey for bringing the wrong fox.

'About time to take soundings, and cast anchor, isn't it?' gasped Captain Bouncey, toiling up red-hot on his pulling horse in a state of utter exhaustion, as Watchorn stood craneing and looking at a rasper through which Mr. Sponge and Miss Glitters had passed, without disturbing a twig.

'C—a—s—t anchor!' exclaimed Watchorn, in a tone of derision—
'not this half-hour yet, I hope!—not this forty minnits yet, I hope;—not
this hour and twenty minnits yet, I hope!' continued he, putting his
horse irresolutely at the fence. The horse blundered through it, barking
Watchorn's nose with a branch.

''Ord rot it, cut off my nose!' exclaimed he, muffling it up in his hand.
'Cut off my nose clean by my face, I do believe,' continued he, venturing
to look into his hand for it. 'Well,' said he, eyeing the slight stain of blood
on his glove, 'this will be a lesson to me as long as I live. If ever I 'unt
again in a frost, may I be———. Thank goodness! they've checked at last!'
exclaimed he, as the music suddenly ceased, and Mr. Sponge and Miss
Glitters sat motionless together on their panting, smoking steeds.

Watchorn then stuck spurs to his horse, and being now on a flat rushy
pasture, with a bridle-gate into the field where the hounds were casting,
he hustled across, preparing his horn for a blow as soon as he got there.

'Twang—twang—twang—twang,' he went, riding up the hedgerow
in the contrary direction to what the hounds leant. 'Twang—twang—
twang,' he continued, inwardly congratulating himself that the fox would
never face the troop of urchins he saw coming down with their guns.

'Hang him!—he's never that way!' observed Mr. Sponge, *sotto voce*, to
Miss Glitters. 'He's never that way,' repeated he, seeing how Frantic flung
to the right.

'Twang—twang—twang,' went the horn, but the hounds regarded it
not.

'Do, Mr. Sponge, put the hounds to me!' roared Mr. Watchorn,
dreading lest they might hit off the scent.

Mr. Sponge answered the appeal by turning his horse the way the
hounds were feathering, and giving them a slight cheer.

''Ord rot it!' roared Watchorn, '*do* let 'em alone! that's a *fresh* fox! ours
is over the 'ill,' pointing towards Bonnyfield Hill.

'Hoop!' hallooed Mr. Sponge, taking off his hat, as Frantic hit off the
scent to the right, and Galloper, and Melody, and all the rest scored to
cry.

'Oh, you confounded brown-bouted beggar!' exclaimed Mr. Watchorn,
returning his horn to its case, and eyeing Mr. Sponge and Miss Glitters
sailing away with the again breast-high-scent pack. 'Oh, you exorbitant
usurer!' continued he, gathering his horse to skate after them. 'Well now,

that's the most disgraceful proceedin' I ever saw in the whole course of my life. Hang me, if I'll stand such work! Dash me, but I'll 'quaint the Queen!—I'll tell Sir George Grey! I'll write to Mr. Walpole! Fo-orrard! fo-orrard!' hallooed he, as Bob Spangles and Bouncey popped upon him unexpectedly from behind, exclaiming with well-feigned glee, as he pointed to the streaming pack with his whip, ''Ord dash it, but we're in for a good thing!'

Little Bouncey's horse was still yawning and star-gazing, and Bouncey, being quite unequal to riding him and well-nigh exhausted, 'downed' him against a rubbing-post in the middle of a field, making a 'cannon' with his own and his horse's head, and was immediately the centre of attraction for the panting tail. Bouncey got near a pint of sherry from among them before he recovered from the shock. So anxious were they about him, that not one of them thought of resuming the chase. Even the lagging whips couldn't leave him. George Cheek was presently *hors de combat* in a hedge, and Watchorn seeing him 'see-sawing,' exclaimed, as he slipped through a gate:

'I'll send your mar to you, you young 'umbug.'

Watchorn would gladly have stopped too, for the fumes of the champagne were dead within him, and the riding was becoming every minute more dangerous. He trotted on, hoping each jump of brown boots would be the last, and inwardly wishing the wearer at the devil. Thus he passed through a considerable extent of country, over Harrowdale Lordship, or reputed Lordship, past Roundington Tower, down Sloppyside Banks, and on to Cheeseington Green; the severity of his affliction being alone mitigated by the intervention of accommodating roads and lines of field gates. These, however, Mr. Sponge generally declined, and went crashing on, now over high places, now over low, just as they came in his way, closely followed by the fair Lucy Glitters.

'Well, I never see'd sich a man as that!' exclaimed Watchorn, eyeing Mr. Sponge clearing a stiff flight of rails, with a gap near at hand. 'Nor woman nouther!' added he, as Miss Glitters did the like. 'Well, I'm dashed if it arn't dangerous!' continued he, thumping his hand against his thick thigh, as the white nearly slipped upon landing. 'F-o-r-r-ard! for-rard! hoop!' screeched he, as he saw Miss Glitters looking back to see where he was. 'F-o-r-r-ard! for-rard!' repeated he; adding, in apparent delight, 'My eyes, but we're in for a stinger! Hold up, horse!' roared he, as his horse now went starring up to the knees through a long sheet of ice, squirting the clayey water into his rider's face. 'Hold up!' repeated he, adding, 'I'm dashed if one mightn't as well be crashin' over the Christial Palace as ridin' over a country froze in this way! 'Ord rot it, how cold it is!' continued he, blowing on his finger-ends; 'I declare my 'ands are quite numb. Well done, old brown bouts!' exclaimed he, as a crash on the right attracted his attention; 'well done, old brown bouts!—broke every bar i' the gate!' adding, 'but I'll let Mr. Buckram know the way his beautiful horses are 'bused. Well,' continued he, after a long skate down the grassy side of Ditchburn Lane, 'there's no fun in this—none whatever. Who the deuce would be a huntsman that could be anything else? Dash it! I'd rayther be a hosier—I'd rayther be a 'atter—I'd rayther be an undertaker—I'd rayther be a Pusseyite parson—I'd rayther be a pig-jobber—I'd rayther be a besom-maker—I'd rayther be a dog's-meat man—I'd rayther be a cat's-meat man—I'd rayther go about a sellin' of chick-weed and sparrow-grass!' added he, as his horse nearly slipped up on his haunches.

'Thank 'eavens there's relief at last!' exclaimed he, as on rising Gimmerhog Hill he saw Farmer Saintfoin's southdowns wheeling and clustering, indicative of the fox having passed; 'thank 'eavens, there's relief at last!' repeated he, reining up his horse to see the hounds charge them.

Mr. Sponge and Miss Glitters were now in the bottom below, fighting their way across a broad mill-course with a very stiff fence on the taking-off side.

'Hold up!' roared Mr. Sponge, as, having bored a hole through the fence, he found himself on the margin of the water-race. The horse did hold up, and landed him—not without a scramble—on the far side. 'Run him at it, Lucy!' exclaimed Mr. Sponge, turning his horse half round to his fair companion. 'Run him at it, Lucy!' repeated he; and Lucy fortunately hitting the gap, skimmed o'er the water like a swallow on a summer's eve.

'Well done! you're a trump!' exclaimed Mr. Sponge, standing in his stirrups, and holding on by the mane as his horse rose the opposing hill.

He just got up in time to save the muttons; another second and the hounds would have been into them. Holding up his hand to beckon Lucy to stop, he sat eyeing them intently. Many of them had their heads up, and not a few were casting sheep's eyes at the sheep. Some few of the line hunters were persevering with the scent over the greasy ground. It was a critical moment. They cast to the right, then to the left, and again took a wider sweep in advance, returning however towards the sheep, as if they thought them the best spec after all.

'Put 'em to me,' said Mr. Sponge, giving Miss Glitters his whip; 'put 'em to me!' said he, hallooing, 'Yor-geot, hounds!—yor-geot!'—which, being interpreted, means, 'here again, hounds!—here again!'

'Oh, the conceited beggar!' exclaimed Mr. Watchorn to himself, as, disappointed of his finish, he sat feeling his nose, mopping his face, and watching the proceedings. 'Oh, the conceited beggar!' repeated he, adding, 'old 'hogany bouts is *absolutely* a goin' to kest them.'

Cast them, however, he did, proceeding very cautiously in the direction the hounds seemed to lean. They were on a piece of cold scenting ground, across which they could hardly own the scent.

'Don't hurry 'em!' cried Mr. Sponge to Miss Glitters, who was acting whipper-in with rather unnecessary vigour.

As they got under the lee of the hedge, the scent improved a little, and, from an occasional feathering stern, a hound or two indulged in a whimper, until at length they fairly broke out in a cry. 'I'll lose a shoe,' said Watchorn to himself, looking first at the formidable leap before him, and then to see if there was any one coming up behind. 'I'll lose a shoe,' said he. 'No notion of lippin' of a navigable river—a downright arm of the sea,' added he, getting off.

'Forward! forward!' screeched Mr. Sponge, capping the hounds on, when away they went, heads up and sterns down as before.

'Ay, for-rard! for-rard!' mimicked Mr. Watchorn; adding, 'you're for-rard enough, at all events.'

After running about three-quarters of a mile at best pace, Mr. Sponge viewed the fox crossing a large grass field with all the steam up he could raise, a few hundred yards ahead of the pack, who were streaming along most beautifully, not viewing, but gradually gaining upon him. At last they broke from scent to view, and presently rolled him over and over among them.

'WHO-HOOP!' screamed Mr. Sponge, throwing himself off his horse and rushing in amongst them. 'WHO-HOOP!' repeated he, still louder, holding the fox up in grim death above the baying pack.

'Who-hoop!' exclaimed Miss Glitters, reining up in delight alongside the chestnut. 'Who-hoop!' repeated she, diving into the saddle-pocket for her lace-fringed handkerchief.

'Throw me my whip!' cried Mr. Sponge, repelling the attacks of the hounds from behind with his heels. Having got it, he threw the fox on the ground, and clearing a circle, he off with his brush in an instant. 'Tear him and eat him!' cried he, as the pack broke in on the carcass. 'Tear him and eat him!' repeated he, as he made his way up to Miss Glitters with the brush, exclaiming, 'We'll put this in your hat, alongside the cock's feathers.'

The fair lady leant towards him, and as he adjusted it becomingly in her hat, looking at her bewitching eyes, her lovely face, and feeling the sweet fragrance of her breath, a something shot through Mr. Sponge's pull-devil, pull-baker coat, his corduroy waistcoat, his Eureka shirt, Angola vest, and penetrated the very cockles of his heart. He gave her such a series of smacking kisses as startled her horse and astonished a poacher who happened to be hid in the adjoining hedge.

Sponge was never so happy in his life. He could have stood on his head, or been guilty of any sort of extravagance, short of wasting his money. Oh, he was happy! Oh, he was joyous! He was intoxicated with pleasure. As he eyed his angelic charmer, her lustrous eyes, her glowing cheeks, her pearly teeth, the bewitching fulness of her elegant *tournure*, and thought of the masterly way she rode the run—above all, of the dashing style in which she charged the mill-race—he felt a something quite different to anything he had experienced with any of the buxom widows or lackadaisical misses whom he could just love or not, according to circumstances, among whom his previous experience had lain. Miss Glitters, he knew, had nothing, and yet he felt he could not do without her; the puzzlement of his mind was, how the deuce they should manage matters—'make tongue and buckle meet,' as he elegantly phrased it.

It is pleasant to hear a bachelor's pros and cons on the subject of matrimony; how the difficulties of the gentleman out of love vanish or change into advantages with the one in—'Oh, I would never think of marrying without a couple of thousand a year at the *very least!*' exclaims young Fastly. '*I* can't do without four hunters and a hack. *I* can't do without a valet. *I* can't do without a brougham. *I* must belong to half-a-dozen clubs. *I'll* not marry any woman who can't keep me comfortable—bachelors can live upon nothing—bachelors are welcome everywhere—very different thing with a wife. Frightful things milliners' bills—fifty guineas for a dress, twenty for a bonnet—ladies' maids are the very devil—never satisfied—far worse to please than their mistresses.' And between the whiffs of a cigar he hums the old saw—

'Needles and pins, needles and pins, When a man marries his sorrow begins.'

Now take him on the other tack—Fast is smitten.

''Ord hang it! a married man can live on very little,' soliloquizes our friend. A nice lovely creature to keep one at home. Hunting's all humbug; it's only the flash of the thing that makes one follow it. Then the danger far more than counterbalances the pleasure. Awful places one has to ride over, to be sure, or submit to be called "slow." Horrible thing to set up for a horseman, and then have to ride to maintain one's reputation. Will be thankful to give it up altogether. The bays will make capital carriage-horses, and one can often pick up a second-hand carriage as good as new. Shall save no end of money by not having to put "B" to my name in the assessed tax-payer. One club's as good as a dozen—will give up the Polyanthus and the Sunflower, and the Refuse and the Rag. Ladies' dresses are cheap enough. Saw a beautiful gown t'other day for a guinea. Will start Master Bergamotte. Does nothing for his wages; will scarce clean my boots. Can get a chap for half what I give him, who'll do double the work. Will make Beans into coachman. What a convenience to have one's wife's maid to sew on one's buttons, and keep one's toes in one's stocking-feet! Declare I lose half my things at the washing for want of marking. Hanged if I won't marry and be respectable—marriage is an honourable state!' And thereupon Tom grows a couple of inches taller in his own conceit.

Though Mr. Sponge's thoughts did not travel in quite such a luxurious first-class train as the foregoing, he, Mr. Sponge, being more of a two-shirts-and-a-dicky sort of man, yet still the future ways and means weighed upon his mind, and calmed the transports of his present joy. Lucy was an angel! about that there was no dispute. He would make her Mrs. Sponge at all events. Touring about was very expensive. He could only counterbalance the extravagance of inns by the rigid rule of giving nothing to servants at private houses. He thought a nice airy lodging in the suburbs of London would answer every purpose, while

his accurate knowledge of cab-fares would enable Lucy to continue her engagement at the Royal Amphitheatre without incurring the serious overcharges the inexperienced are exposed to. 'Where one can dine, two can dine,' mused Mr. Sponge; 'and I make no doubt we'll manage matters somehow.'

'Twopence for your thoughts!' cried Lucy, trotting up, and touching him gently on the back with her light silver-mounted riding-whip. 'Twopence for your thoughts!' repeated she, as Mr. Sponge sauntered leisurely along, regardless of the bitter cold, followed by such of the hounds as chose to accompany him.

'Ah!' replied he, brightening up; 'I was just thinking what a deuced good run we'd had.'

'Indeed!' pouted the fair lady.

'No, my darling; I was thinking what a very pretty girl you are,' rejoined he, sidling his horse up, and encircling her neat waist with his arm.

A sweet smile dimpled her plump cheeks, and chased the recollection of the former answer away.

It would not be pretty—indeed, we could not pretend to give even the outline of the conversation that followed. It was carried on in such broken and disjointed sentences, eyes and squeezes doing so much more work than words, that even a reporter would have had to draw largely upon his imagination for the substance. Suffice it to say that, though the thermometer was below zero, they never moved out of a foot's pace; the very hounds growing tired of the trail, and slinking off one by one as the opportunity occurred.

A dazzling sun was going down with a blood-red glare, and the partially softened ground was fast resuming its fretwork of frost, as our hero and heroine were seen sauntering up the western avenue to Nonsuch House, as slowly and quietly as if it had been the hottest evening in summer.

'Here's old Coppertops!' exclaimed Captain Seedeybuck, as, turning round in the billiard-room to chalk his cue, he espied them crawling along. 'And Lucy!' added he as he stood watching them.

'How slowly they come!' observed Bob Spangles, going to the window.

'Must have tired their horses,' suggested Captain Quod.

'Just the sort of man to tire a horse,' rejoined Bob Spangles.

'Hate that Sponge,' observed Captain Cutitfat.

'So do I,' replied Captain Quod.

'Well, never mind the beggar! It's you to play!' exclaimed Bob Spangles to Captain Seedeybuck.

But Lady Scattercash, who was observing our friends from her boudoir window, saw with a woman's eye that there was something more than a mere case of tired horses; and, tripping downstairs, she arrived at the front door just as the fair Lucy dropped smilingly from her horse into Mr. Sponge's extended arms. Hurrying up into the boudoir, Lucy gave her ladyship one of Mr. Sponge's modified kisses, revealing the truth more eloquently than words could convey.

'Oh,' Lady Scattercash was 'so glad!' 'so delighted!' 'so charmed!'

Mr. Sponge was such a nice man, and so rich. She was sure he was rich—couldn't hunt if he wasn't. Would advise Lucy to have a good settlement, in case he broke his neck. And pin-money! pin-money was most useful! no husband ever let his wife have enough money. Must forget all about Harry Dacre and Charley Brown, and the swell in the Blues. Must be prudent for the future. Mr. Sponge would never know anything of the past. Then she reverted to the interesting subject of settlements. 'What had Mr. Sponge got, and what would he do?' This Lucy couldn't tell. 'What! hadn't he told her where is estates were?—'No.' 'Well, was his dad dead?' This Lucy didn't know either. They had got no further than the tender prop. 'Ah! well; would get it all out of him by degrees.' And with the reiteration of her 'so glads,' and the repayment of the kiss Lucy had advanced, her ladyship advised her to get off her habit and make herself comfortable while she ran downstairs to communicate the astonishing intelligence to the party below.

'What d'ye think?' exclaimed she, bursting into the billiard-room, where the party were still engaged in a game at pool, all our sportsmen, except Captain Cutitfat, who still sported his new Moses and Son's scarlet, having divested themselves of their hunting-gear—'What d'ye think?' exclaimed she, darting into the middle of them.

'That Bob don't cannon?' observed Captain Bouncey from below the bandage that encircled his broken head, nodding towards Bob Spangles, who was just going to make a stroke.

'That Wax is out of limbo?' suggested Captain Seedeybuck, in the same breath.

'No. Guess again!' exclaimed Lady Scattercash, rubbing her hands in high glee.

'That the Pope's got a son?' observed Captain Quod.

'No. Guess again!' exclaimed her ladyship, laughing.

'I give it up,' replied Captain Bouncey.

'So do I,' added Captain Seedeybuck.

'*That Mr. Sponge is going to be married*,' enunciated her ladyship, slowly and emphatically, waving her arms.

'Ho-o-ray! Only think of that!' exclaimed Captain Quod. 'Old 'hogany-tops goin' to be spliced!'

'Did you ever?' asked Bob Spangles.

'No, I *never*,' replied Captain Bouncey.

'He should be called Spooney Sponge, not Soapey Sponge,' observed Captain Seedeybuck.

'Well, but to whom?' asked Captain Bouncey.

'Ah, to whom indeed! That's the question,' rejoined her ladyship archly.

'I know,' observed Bob Spangles.

'No, you don't.'

'Yes, I do.'

'Who is it, then?' demanded her ladyship.

'Lucy Glitters, to be sure,' replied Bob, who hadn't had his stare out of the billiard-room window for nothing.

'Pity her,' observed Bouncey, sprawling along the billiard-table to play for a cannon.

'Why?' asked Lady Scattercash.

'Reg'lar scamp,' replied Bouncey, vexed at missing his stroke.

'Dare say you know nothing about him,' snapped her ladyship.

'Don't I?' replied Bouncey complacently; adding, 'that's all you know.'

'He'll whop her, to a certainty,' observed Seedeybuck.

'What makes you think that?' asked her ladyship.

'Oh—ha—hem—haw—why, because he whopped his poor horse—whopped him over the ears. Whop his horse, whop his wife; whop his wife, whop his horse. Reg'lar Rule-of-three sum.'

'Make her a bad husband, I dare say,' observed Bob Spangles, who was rather smitten with Lucy himself.

'Never mind; a bad husband's a deal better than none, Bob,' replied Lady Scattercash, determined not to be put out of conceit of her man.

'He, he, he!—haw, haw, haw!—ho, ho, ho! Well done you!' laughed several.

'She'll have to keep him,' observed Captain Cutitfat, whose turn it now was to play.

'What makes you think that?' asked Lady Scattercash, coming again to the charge.

'He has nothing,' replied Fat, coolly.

''Deed, but he has—a very good property, too,' replied her ladyship.

'In *Air*shire, I should think,' rejoined Fat.

'No, in Englandshire,' retorted her ladyship: 'and great expectations from an uncle,' added she.

'Ah—he looks like a man to be on good terms with his uncle,' sneered Captain Bouncey.

'Make no doubt he pays him many a visit,' observed Seedeybuck.

'Indeed! that's all you know,' snapped Lady Scattercash.

'It's not all I know,' replied Seedeybuck.

'Well, then, what else do you know?' asked she.

'I know he has nothing,' replied Seedey.

'How do you know it?'

'I *know*,' said Seedey, with an emphasis, now settling to his stroke.

'Well, never mind,' retorted her ladyship; 'if he has nothing, she has nothing, and nothing can be nicer.'

So saying, she hurried out of the room.

LXVI

MR. SPONGE AT HOME

SPONGE WAS MOST WARMLY CONGRATULATED by Sir Harry and all the assembled captains, who inwardly hoped his marriage would have the effect of 'snuffing him out,' as they said, and they had a most glorious jollification on the strength of it. They drank Lucy's and his health nine times over, with nine times nine each time. The consequence was, that the footmen and shutter were in earlier requisition than usual to carry them to their respective apartments. Sponge's head throbbed a good deal the next morning; nor was the pulsation abated by the recollection of his matrimonial engagement, and his total inability to keep the angel who had ridden herself into his affections. However, like all untried men, he was strong in the confidence of his own ability, and the sight of his smiling charmer chased away all prudential considerations as quickly as they arose. He made no doubt there would something turn up.

Meanwhile, he was in good quarters, and Lady Scattercash having warmly espoused his cause, he assumed a considerable standing in the establishment. Old Beardey having ventured to complain of his interference in the kennel, my lady curtly told him he might 'make himself scarce if he liked'; a step that Beardey was quite ready to take, having heard of a desirable public-house at Newington Butts, provided Sir Harry paid him his wages. This not being quite convenient, Sir Harry gave him an order on 'Cabbage and Co.' for three suits of clothes, and acquiesced in his taking a massive silver soup-tureen, on which, beneath the many quartered Scattercash arms, Mr. Watchorn placed an inscription, stating that it was presented to him by Sir Harry Scattercash,

Baronet, and the noblemen and gentlemen of his hunt, in admiration of his talents as a huntsman and his character as a man.

Mr. Sponge then became still more at home. It was very soon 'my hounds,' and 'my horses,' and 'my whips'; and he wrote to Jawleyford, and Puffington, and Guano, and Lumpleg, and Washball, and Spraggon, offering to make meets to suit their convenience, and even to mount them if required. His *Mogg* was quite neglected in favour of Lucy; and it says much for the influence of female charms that, before they had been engaged a fortnight, he, who had been a perfect oracle in cab fares, would have been puzzled to tell the most ordinary fare on the most frequented route. He had forgotten all about them. Nevertheless, Lucy and he went out hunting as often as they could raise hounds, and when they had a good run and killed, he saluted her; and when they didn't kill, why—he just did the same. He headed and tailed the stringing pack, drafted the skirters and babblers (which he sent to Lord Scamperdale, with his compliments), and presently had the uneven kennel in something like shape.

Nor was this the only way in which he made himself useful, for Nonsuch House being now supported almost entirely by voluntary contributions—that is to say, by the gullibility of tradesmen—his street and shop knowledge was valuable in determining who to 'do.' With the Post Office Directory and Mr. Sponge at his elbow, Mr. Bottleends, the butler—'delirius tremendous,' as Bottleends called it, having quite incapacitated Sir Harry—wrote off for champagne from this man, sherry from that, turtle from a third, turbot from a fourth, tea from a fifth, truffles from a sixth, wax-lights from one, sperm from another; and down came the things with such alacrity, such thanks for the past and hopes for the future, as we poor devils of the untitled world are quite unacquainted with. Nay, not content with giving him the goods, many of the poor demented creatures actually paraded their folly at their doors in new deal packing-cases, flourishingly directed 'To SIR HARRY SCATTERCASH, BART., NONSUCH HOUSE, &c. *By Express Train*.' In some cases they even paid the carriage.

And here, in the midst of love, luxury, and fox-hunting, let us for a time leave our enterprising friend, Mr. Sponge, while we take a look at a species of cruelty that some people call 'sport.' For this purpose we will begin a fresh chapter.

LXVII

How They Got Up the 'Grand Aristocratic Steeplechase'

THERE IS NO SAYING WHAT advantages railway communication may confer upon a country. But for the Granddiddle Junction,——shire never would have had a steeplechase—an 'Aristocratic,' at least—for it is observable that the more snobbish a thing is, the more certain they are to call it aristocratic. When it is too bad for anything, they call it 'Grand.' Well, as we said before, but for the Granddiddle Junction,——shire would never have had a 'Grand Aristocratic Steeple-Chase.' A few friends or farmers might have got up a quiet thing among themselves, but it would never have seen a regular trade transaction, with its swell mob, sham captains, and all the paraphernalia of odd laying, 'secret tips,' and market rigging. Who will deny the benefit that must accrue to any locality by the infusion of all the loose fish of the kingdom?

Formerly the prize-fights were the perquisite of the publicans. They it was who arranged for Shaggy Tom to pound Harry Billy's nob upon So-and-so's land, the preference being given to the locality that subscribed the most money to the fight. Since the decline of 'the ring,' steeple-chasing, and that still smaller grade of gambling—coursing—have come to their aid. Nine-tenths of the steeple-chasing and coursing-matches are got up by inn-keepers, for the good of their houses. Some of the town publicans, indeed, seem to think that the country was just made for their matches to come off in, and scarcely condescend to ask the leave of the landowners.

We saw an advertisement the other day, where a low publican, in a manufacturing town, assured the subscribers to his coursing-club that he would take care to select open ground, with 'plenty of stout hares,' as if all the estates in the neighbourhood were at his command. Another advertised a steeplechase in the centre of a good hunting country—'amateur and gentleman riders'—with a half-crown ordinary at the end! Fancy the respectability of a steeplechase, with a half-crown ordinary at the end!

Our 'Aristocratic' was got up on the good-of-the-house principle. Whatever benefit the Granddiddle Junction conferred upon the country at large, it had a very prejudicial effect upon the Old Duke of Cumberland Hotel and Posting House, which it left, high and dry, at an angle sufficiently near to be tantalized by the whirr and the whistle of the trains, and yet too far off to be benefited by the parties they brought. This once well-accustomed hostelry was kept by one Mr. Viney, a former butler in the Scattercash family, and who still retained the usual 'old and faithful servant' *entrée* of Nonsuch House, having his beefsteak and bottle of wine in the steward's room whenever he chose to call. Viney had done good at the Old Duke of Cumberland; and no one, seeing him 'full fig,' would recognize, in the solemn grandeur of his stately person, the dirty knife-boy who had filled the place now occupied by the still dirtier Slarkey. But the days of road travelling departed, and Viney, who, beneath the Grecian-columned portico of his country-house-looking hotel, modulated the ovations of his cauliflower head to every description of traveller—from the lordly occupant of the barouche-and-four, down to the humble sitter in a gig—was cut off by one fell swoop from all further traffic. He was extinguished like a gaslight, and the pipe was laid on a fresh line.

Fortunately, Mr. Viney was pretty warm; he had done pretty well; and having enjoyed the intimacy of the great 'Jeames' of railway times, had got a hint not to engage the hotel beyond the opening of the line. Consequently, he now had the great house for a mere nothing until such times as the owner could convert it into that last refuge for deserted houses—an academy, or a 'young ladies' seminary.' Mr. Viney now, having plenty of leisure, frequently drove his 'missis' (once a lady's maid in a quality family) up to Nonsuch House, as well for the sake of the airing— for the road was pleasant and picturesque—as to see if he could get the 'little trifle' Sir Harry owed him for post-horses, bottles of soda-water, and such trifles as country gentlemen run up scores for at their posting-houses—scores that seldom get smaller by standing. In these excursions, Mr. Viney made the acquaintance of Mr. Watchorn; and a huntsman being a character with whom even the landlord of an inn—we beg pardon, hotel and posting-house—may associate without degradation, Viney and Watchorn became intimate. Watchorn sympathized with Viney, and never failed to take a glass in passing, either at exercise or out hunting, to deplore that such a nice-looking house, so 'near the station, too,' should be ruined as an inn. It was after a more than usual libation that Watchorn, trotting merrily along with the hounds, having accomplished three blank days in succession, asked himself, as he looked upon the surrounding vale from the rising ground of Hammercock Hill, with the cream-coloured station and the rose-coloured hotel peeping through the trees, whether something might not be done to give the latter a lift. At first he thought of a pigeon match—a sweepstake open to all England—fifty members say, at two pound ten each, seven pigeons, seven sparrows, twenty-one yards rise, two ounces of shot, and so on. But then, again, he thought there would be a difficulty in getting guns. A coursing match—how would that do? Answer: 'No hares.' The farmers had made such an outcry about the game, that the landowners had shot them all off, and now the farmers were grumbling that they couldn't get a course.

'Dash my buttons!' exclaimed Watchorn; 'it would be the very thing for a steeplechase! There's old Puff's hounds, and old Scamp's hounds, and these hounds,' looking down on the ill-sorted lot around him; 'and the deuce is in it if we couldn't give the thing such a start as would bring down the lads of the "village," and a vast amount of good business might be done. I'm dashed if it isn't the very country for a steeple-chase!' continued Watchorn, casting his eye over Cloverly Park, round the enclosure of Langworth Grange, and up the rising ground of Lark Lodge.

The more Watchorn thought of it, the more he was satisfied of its feasibility, and he trotted over, the next day, to the Old Duke of Cumberland, to see his friend on the subject. Viney, like most victuallers, was more given to games of skill—billiards, shuttlecock, skittles, dominoes, and so on—than to the rude out-of-door chances of flood and field, and at first he doubted his ability to grapple with the details; but on Mr. Watchorn's assurance that he would keep him straight, he gave Mrs. Viney a key, desiring her to go into the inner cellar, and bring out a bottle of the green seal. This was ninety-shilling sherry—very good stuff to take; and, by the time they got into the second bottle, they had got into the middle of the scheme too. Viney was cautious and thoughtful. He had a high opinion of Watchorn's sagacity, and so long as Watchorn confined himself to weights, and stakes, and forfeits, and so on, he was content to leave himself in the hands of the huntsman; but when Watchorn came to talk of 'stewards,' putting this person and that together, Viney's experience came in aid. Viney knew a good deal. He had not stood twisting a napkin negligently before a plate-loaded sideboard without picking up a good many waifs and strays in the shape of those ins and outs, those likings and dislikings, those hatreds and jealousies, that foolish people let fall so freely before servants, as if for all the world the servants were sideboards themselves; and he had kept up his stock of service-gained knowledge by a liberal, though not a dignity-compromising intercourse—for there is no greater aristocrat than your out-of-livery servant—among the upper servants of all the families in the neighbourhood, so that he knew to a nicety who would pull together, and who wouldn't, whose name it would not do to mention to this person, and who it would not do to apply to before that.

Neither Watchorn nor Viney being sportsmen, they thought they had nothing to do but apply to two friends who were; and after thinking over who hunted in couples, they were unfortunate enough to select our Flat Hat friends, Fyle and Fossick. Fyle was indignant beyond measure at being asked to be steward to a steeplechase, and thrust the application into the fire; while Fossick just wrote below, 'I'll see you hanged first,' and sent it back without putting even a fresh head on the envelope. Nothing daunted, however, they returned to the charge, and without troubling the reader with unnecessary detail, we think it will be generally admitted that they at length made an excellent selection in Mr. Puffington, Guano, and Tom Washball.

Fortune favoured them also in getting a locality to run in, for Timothy Scourgefield, of Broom Hill, whose farm commanded a good circular three miles of country, with every variety of obstacle, having thrown up his lease for a thirty-per-cent reduction—a giving up that had been most unhandsomely accepted by his landlord—Timothy was most anxious to pay him off by doing every conceivable injury to the farm, than which nothing can be more promising than having a steeple-chase run over it. Scourgefield, therefore, readily agreed to let Viney and Watchorn do whatever they liked, on condition that he received entrance-money at the gate.

The name occupied their attention some time, for it did not begin as the 'Aristocratic.' The 'Great National,' the 'Grand Naval and Military,' the 'Sports-man,' the 'Talli-ho,' the 'Out-and-Outer,' the 'Swell,' were all considered and canvassed, and its being called the 'Aristocratic' at length turned upon whether they got Lord Scamperdale to subscribe or not. This was accomplished by a deferential call by Mr. Viney upon Mr. Spraggon, with a little bill for three pound odd, which he presented, with the most urgent request that Jack wouldn't think of it then—any time that was most convenient to Mr. Spraggon—and then the introduction of the neatly-headed sheet-list. It was lucky that Viney was so easily satisfied, for poor Jack had only thirty shillings, of which he owed his washerwoman eight, and he was very glad to stuff Viney's bill into his stunner jacket-pocket, and apply himself exclusively to the contemplated steeplechase.

Like most of us, Jack had no objection to make a little money; and as he squinted his frightful eyes inside out at the paper, he thought over what horses they had in the stable that were like the thing; and then he sounded Viney as to whether he would put him one up for nothing, if he could induce his lordship to send. This, of course, Viney readily assented to, and again requesting Jack not to *think* of his little bill till it was *perfectly* convenient to him—a favour that Jack was pretty sure to accord him—Mr. Viney took his departure, Jack undertaking to write him the result. The next day's post brought Viney the document—unpaid, of course—with a great 'Scamperdale' scrawled across the top; and forthwith it was decided that the steeple-chase should be called the 'Grand Aristocratic.' Other names quickly followed, and it soon assumed an importance. Advertisements appeared in all the sporting and would-be sporting papers, headed with the imposing names of the stewards, secretary, and clerk of the course, Mr. Viney. The 'Grand Aristocratic Stakes,' of 20 sovs. each, half-forfeit, and £5 only if declared, &c. The winner to give two dozen of champagne to the ordinary, and the second horse to save his stake. Gentlemen riders (titled ones to be allowed 3 lb.). Over about three miles of fine hunting country, under the usual steeplechase conditions.

Then the game of the 'Peeping Toms,' and 'Sly Sams,' and 'Infallible Joes,' and 'Wideawake Jems,' with their tips and distribution of prints began; Tom counselling his numerous and daily increasing clients to get well on to No. 9, Sardanapalus (the Bart., as Watchorn called him), while 'Infallible Joe' recommended his friends and patrons to be sweet on No. 6 (Hercules), and 'Wide-awake Jem' was all for something else. A gentleman who took the trouble of getting tips from half a dozen of them, found that no two of them agreed in any particular. What information to make books upon!

'But what good,' as our excellent friend Thackeray eloquently asks, 'ever came out of, or went into, a betting book? If I could be CALIPH OMAR for a week,' says he, 'I would pitch every one of those despicable manuscripts into the flames; from my-lord's, who is "in" with Jack Snaffle's stable, and is overreaching worse-informed rogues, and swindling greenhorns, down to Sam's, the butcher's boy, who books eighteen-penny odds in the tap-room, and stands to win five-and-twenty bob.' We say ditto to that, and are not sure that we wouldn't hang a 'leg' or a 'list' man or two into the bargain.

Watchorn had a prophet of his own, one Enoch Wriggle, who, having tried his hand unsuccessfully first at tailoring, next as an accountant, then in the watercress, afterwards in the buy "at-box, bonnet-box,' and lastly in the stale lobster and periwinkle line, had set up as an oracle on turf matters, forwarding the most accurate and infallible information to flats in exchange for half-crowns, heading his advertisements, 'If it be a sin to covet honour, I am the most offending soul alive!' Enoch did a considerable stroke of business, and couched his advice in such dubious terms, as generally to be able to claim a victory whichever way the thing went. So the 'offending soul' prospered; and from scarcely having shoes to his feet, he very soon set up a gig.

LXVIII

How the 'Grand Aristocratic' Came Off

STEEPLECHASES ARE GENERALLY CRUDE, ILL-arranged things. Few sportsmen will act as stewards a second time; while the victim to the popular delusion of patronizing our 'national sports' considers—like gentlemen who have served the office of sheriff, or church-warden—that once in a lifetime is enough; hence, there is always the air of amateur actorship about them. There is always something wanting or forgotten. Either they forget the ropes, or they forget the scales, or they forget the weights, or they forget the bell, or—more commonly still—some of the parties forget themselves. Farmers, too, are easily satisfied with the benefits of an irresponsible mob careering over their farms, even though some of them are attired in the miscellaneous garb of hunting and racing costume. Indeed, it is just this mixture of two sports that spoils both; steeple-chasing being neither hunting nor racing. It has not the wild excitement of the one, nor the accurate calculating qualities of the other. The very horses have a peculiar air about them—neither hunters nor hacks, nor yet exactly race-horses. Some of them, doubtless, are fine, good-looking, well-conditioned animals; but the majority are lean, lathy, sunken-eyed, woe-begone, iron-marked, desperately-abused brutes, lacking all the lively energy that characterizes the movements of the up-to-the-mark hunter. In the early days of steeple-chasing, a popular fiction existed that the horses were hunters; and grooms and fellows used to come nicking and grinning up to masters of hounds at checks and critical times, requesting them to note that they were out, in order to ask for certificates of the horses having been 'regularly hunted'—a species of regularity than which nothing could be more irregular. That nuisance, thank goodness, is abated. A steeplechaser now generally stands on his own merits; a change for which sportsmen may be thankful.

But to our story.

The whole country was in a commotion about this 'Aristocratic'. The unsophisticated looked upon it as a grand *reunion* of the aristocracy; and smart bonnets and cloaks, and jackets and parasols were ordered with the liberality incident to a distant view of Christmas. As Viney sipped his sherry-cobler of an evening, he laughed at the idea of a son-of-a-day-labourer like himself raising such a dust. Letters came pouring in to the clerk of the course from all quarters; some asking about beds; some about breakfasts; some about stakes; some about stables; some about this thing, some about that. Every room in the Old Duke of Cumberland was speedily bespoke. Post-horses rose in price, and Dobbin and Smiler, and Jumper and Cappy, and Jessy and Tumbler were jobbed from the neighbouring farmers, and converted for the occasion into posters. At last came the great and important day—day big with the fate of thousands of pounds; for the betting-list vermin had been plying their trade briskly throughout the kingdom, and all sorts of rumours had been raised relative to the qualities and conditions of the horses.

Who doesn't know the chilling feel of an English spring, or rather of a day at the turn of the year before there is any spring? Our gala-day was a perfect specimen of the order—a white frost succeeded by a bright sun, with an east wind, warming one side of the face and starving the other. It was neither a day for fishing, nor hunting, nor coursing, nor anything but farming. The country, save where there were a few lingering patches of turnips, was all one dingy drab, with abundant scalds on the undrained fallows. The grass was more like hemp than anything else. The very rushes were yellow and sickly.

Long before midday the whole country was in commotion. The same sort of people commingled that one would expect to see if there was a balloon to go up, and a man to go down, or be hung at the same place. Fine ladies in all the colours of the rainbow; and swarthy, beady-eyed dames, with their stalwart, big-calved, basket-carrying comrades; gentle young people from behind the counter; Dandy Candy merchants from behind the hedge; rough-coated dandies with their silver-mounted whips; and Shaggyford roughs, in their baggy, poacher-like coats, and formidable clubs; carriages and four, and carriages and pairs; and gigs and dog-carts, and Whitechapels, and Newport Pagnels, and long carts, and short carts, and donkey carts, converged from all quarters upon the point of attraction at Broom Hill.

If Farmer Scourgefield had made a mob, he could not have got one that would be more likely to do damage to his farm than this steeple-chase one. Nor was the assemblage confined to the people of the country, for the Granddiddle Junction, by its connection with the great network of railways, enabled all patrons of this truly national sport to sweep down upon the spot like flocks of wolves; and train after train disgorged a generous mixture of sharps and flats, commingling with coatless, baggy-breeched vagabonds, the emissaries most likely of the Peeping Toms and Infallible Joes, if not the worthies themselves.

'Dear, but it's a noble sight!' exclaimed Viney to Watchorn as they sat on their horses, below a rickety green-baize-covered scaffold, labelled, 'GRAND STAND; admission, Two-and-sixpence,' raised against Scourgefield's stack-yard wall, eyeing the population pouring in from all parts. 'Dear, but it's a noble sight!' said he, shading the sun from his eyes, and endeavouring to identify the different vehicles in the distance. 'Yonder's the 'bus comin' again,' said he, looking towards the station, 'loaded like a market-gardener's turnip-waggon. That'll pay,' added he, with a knowing leer at the landlord of the Hen Angel, Newington Butts. 'And who have we here, with the four horses and sky-blue flunkeys? Jawleyford, as I live!' added he, answering himself; adding, 'The beggar had better pay me what he owes.'

How great Mr. Viney was! Some people, who have never had anything to do with horses, think it incumbent upon them, when they have, to sport top-boots, and accordingly, for the first time in his life, Viney appears in a pair of remarkably hard, tight, country-made boots, above which are a pair of baggy white cords, with the dirty finger-marks of the tailor still upon them. He sports a single-breasted green cutaway coat, with basket-buttons, a black satin roll-collared waistcoat, and a new white silk hat, that shines in the bright sun like a fish-kettle. His blue-striped kerchief is secured by a butterfly brooch. Who ever saw an innkeeper that could resist a brooch?

He is riding a miserable rat of a badly clipped, mouse-coloured pony that looks like a velocipede under him.

His companion, Mr. Watchorn, is very great, and hardly condescends to know the country people who claim his acquaintance as a huntsman. He is a Hotel Keeper—master of the Hen Angel, Newington Butts. Enoch Wriggle stands beside them, dressed in the imposing style of a cockney sportsman. He has been puffing 'Sir Danapalus (the Bart.)' in public, and taking all the odds he can get against him in private. Watchorn knows that it is easier to make a horse lose than win. The restless-looking, lynx-eyed caitiff, in the dirty green shawl, with his hands stuffed into the front pockets of the brown tarriar coat, is their jockey, the renowned Captain Hangallows; he answers to the name of Sam Slick in Mr. Spavin the horse-dealer's yard in Oxford Street, when not in the country on similar excursions to the present. And now in the throng on the principal line are two conspicuous horses—a piebald and a white—carrying Mr. Sponge and Lucy Glitters. Lucy appears as she did on the frosty-day hunt, glowing with health and beauty, and rather straining the seams of Lady Scattercash's habit with the additional *embonpoint* she has acquired by early hours in the country. She has made Mr. Sponge a white silk jacket to ride in, which he has on under his grey tarriar coat, and a cap of the same colour is in his hard hat. He has discarded the gosling-green cords for cream-coloured leathers, and, to please Lucy, has actually substituted a pair of rose-tinted tops for the 'hogany bouts'. Altogether he is a great swell, and very like the bridegroom.

But hark—what a crash! The leaders of Sir Harry Scattercash's drag start at a blind fiddler's dog stationed at the gate leading into the fields, a wheel catches the post, and in an instant the sham captains are scattered about the road: Bouncey on his head, Seedeyhuck across the wheelers, Quod on his back, and Sir Harry astride the gate. Meanwhile, the old fiddler, regardless of the shouts of the men and the shrieks of the ladies, scrapes away with the appropriate tune of 'The Devil among the Tailors!' A rush to the horses' heads arrests further mischief, the dislodged captains are at length righted, the nerves of the ladies composed, and Sir Harry once more essays to drive them up the hill to the stand. That feat being accomplished, then came the unloading, and consternation, and huddling of the tight-laced occupants at the idea of these female *women* coming amongst them, and the usual peeping and spying, and eyeing of the '*creatures*.' 'What impudence!' 'Well, I think!' ''Pon my word!' 'What next!'—exclamations that were pretty well lost upon the fair objects of them amid the noise and flutter and confusion of the scene. But hark again! What's up now?

'Hooray!' 'hooray!' 'h-o-o-o-ray!' 'Three cheers for the Squire! H-o-o-o-ray!' Old Puff as we live! The 'amazin' instance of a pop'lar man' greeted by the Swillingford snobs. The old frost-bitten dandy is flattered by the cheers, and bows condescendingly ere he alights from the well-appointed mail phaeton. See how graciously the ladies receive him, as, having ascended the stairs, he appears among them. 'A man is never too old to marry' is their maxim.

The cry is still, 'They come! they come!' See at a hand-gallop, with his bay pony in a white lather, rides Pacey, grinning from ear to ear, with his red-backed betting-book peeping out of the breast pocket of his brown cutaway. He is staring and gaping to see who is looking at him.

Pacey has made such a book as none but a wooden-headed boy like himself could make. He has been surfeited with tips. Peeping Tom had advised him to back Daddy Longlegs; and, *nullus error*, Sneaking Joe has counselled him that the 'Baronet' will be 'California without cholera, and gold without danger'; while Jemmy something, the jockey, who advertises that his 'tongue is not for falsehood framed,' though we should think it was framed for nothing else, has urged him to back Parvo to half the amount of the national debt.

Altogether, Pacey has made such a mess that he cannot possibly win, and may lose almost any sum from a thousand pounds down to a hundred and eighty. Mr. Sponge has got well on with him, through the medium of Jack Spraggon.

Pacey is now going to what he calls 'compare'—see that he has got his bets booked right; and, throwing his right leg over his cob's neck, he blobs on to the ground; and, leaving the pony to take care of itself, disappears in the crowd.

What a hubbub! what roarings, and shoutings, and recognizings! 'Bless my heart! who'd have thought of seeing you?' and, 'By jingo! what's sent *you* here?'

'My dear Waffles,' cries Jawleyford, rushing up to our Laverick Wells friend (who is looking very debauched), 'I'm overjoyed to see you. Do come upstairs and see Mrs. Jawleyford and the dear girls. It was only last night we were talking about you.' And so Jawleyford hurries Mr. Waffles off, just as Waffles is *in extremis* about his horse.

Looking around the scene there seems to be everybody that we have had the pleasure of introducing to the reader in the course of Mr. Sponge's Tour. Mr. and Mrs. Springwheat in their dog-cart, Mrs. Springey's figure looking as though 'wheat had got above forty, my lord'; old Jog and his handsome wife in the ugly old phaeton, well-garnished with children, and a couple of sticks in the rough, peeping out of the apron, Gustavus James held up in his mother's arms, with the curly blue feather nodding over his nose. There is also Farmer Peastraw, and faces that a patient inspection enables us to appropriate to Dribble, and Hook, and Capon, and Calcot, and Lumpleg, and Crane of Crane Hall, and Charley Slapp of red-coat times—people look so different in plain clothes to what they do in hunting ones. Here, too, is George Cheek, running down with perspiration, having run over from Dr. Latherington's, for which he will most likely 'catch it' when he gets back; and oh, wonder of wonders, here's Robert Foozle himself!

'Well, Robert, you've come to the steeplechase?'

'Yes, I've come to the steeplechase.'

'Are you fond of steeplechases?'

'Yes, I'm fond of steeplechases.'

'I dare say you never were at one before,' observes his mother.

'No, I never was at one before,' replies Robert.

And though last not least, here's Facey Romford, with his arm in a sling, on Mr. Hobler, come to look after that sivin-p'und-ten, which we wish he may get.

Hark! there's a row below the stand, and Viney is seen in a state of excitement inquiring for Mr. Washball. Pacey has objected to a gentleman rider, and Guano and Puffington have differed on the point. A nice, slim, well-put-on lad (Buckram's rough rider) has come to the scales and claimed to be allowed 3 lb. as the Honourable Captain Boville. Finding the point questioned, he abandons the 'handle', and sinks into plain Captain Boville. Pacey now objects to him altogether. 'S-c-e-u-s-e me, sir; s-c-e-u-s-e me, sir,' simpers our friend Dick Bragg, sidling up to the objector with a sort of tendency of his turn-back-wristed hand to his hat. 'S-c-e-u-s-e me, sir; s-c-e-u-s-e me,' repeats he, 'but I think you was wrong, sir, in objecting to Captain Boville, sir, as a gen'l'man rider, sir.'

'Why?' demands Pacey, in the full flush of victory.

'Oh, sir—because, sir—in fact, sir—he *is* a gen'l'man, sir.'

'*Is* a gentleman! How do *you* know?' demands Pacey, in the same tone as before.

'Oh, sir, he's a gen'l'man—an undoubted gen'l'man. Everything about him shows that. Does nothing—breeches by Anderson—boots by Bartley; besides which, he drinks wine every day, and has a whole box of cigars in his bedroom. But don't take my word for it, pray,' continued Bragg, seeing Pacey was wavering; 'don't take my word for it, pray. There's a gen'l'man, a countryman of his, somewhere about,' added he, looking anxiously into the surrounding crowd—there's a gen'l'man, a countryman of his, somewhere about, if we could but find him,' Bragg standing on his tiptoes, and exclaiming, 'Mr. Buckram! Mr. Buckram! Has anybody seen anything of Mr. Buckram!'

'Here!' replied a meek voice from behind; upon which there was an elbowing through the crowd, and presently a most respectable, rosy-gilled, grey-haired, hawbuck-looking man, attired in a new brown cutaway, with bright buttons and a velvet collar, with a buff waistcoat, came twirling an ash-stick in one hand, and fumbling the silver in his drab trousers' pocket with the other, in front of the bystanders.

'Oh! 'ere he is!' exclaimed Bragg, appealing to the stranger with a hasty '*You* know Captain Boville, don't you?'

'Why, now, as to the matter of that,' replied the gentleman, gathering all the loose silver up into his hand and speaking very slowly, just as a country gentleman, who has all the live-long day to do nothing in, may be supposed to speak—'Why, now, as to the matter of that,' said he, eyeing Pacey intently, and beginning to drop the silver slowly as he spoke, 'I can't say that I've any very 'ticklar 'quaintance with the captin. I knows him, in course, just as one knows a neighbour's son. The captin's a good deal younger nor me,' continued he, raising his new eight-and-sixpenny Parisian, as if to show his sandy grey hair. 'I'm a'most sixty; and he, I dare say, is little more nor twenty,' dropping a half-crown as he said it. 'But the captin's a nice young gent—a nice young gent, without any blandishment, I should say; and that's more nor one can say of all young gents nowadays,' said Buckram, looking at Pacey as he spoke, and dropping two consecutive half-crowns.

'Why, but you live near him, don't you?' interrupted Bragg.

'Near him,' repeated Buckram, feeling his well-shaven chin thoughtfully. 'Why, yes—that's to say, near his dad. The fact is,' continued he, 'I've a little independence of my own,' dropping a heavy five-shilling piece as he said it, 'and his father—old Bo, as I call him—adjoins me; and if either of us 'appen to have a *battue*, or a 'aunch of wenzun, and a few friends, we inwite each other, and wicey wersey, you know,' letting off a lot of shillings and sixpences. And just at the moment the blind fiddler struck up 'The Devil among the Tailors,' when the shouts and laughter of the mob closed the scene.

And now gentlemen, who heretofore have shown no more of the jockey than Cinderella's feet in the early part of the pantomime disclose of her ball attire, suddenly cast off the pea-jackets and bearskin wraps, and shawls and overcoats of winter, and shine forth in all the silken flutter of summer heat.

We know of no more humiliating sight than misshapen gentlemen playing at jockeys. Playing at soldiers is bad enough, but playing at jockeys is infinitely worse—above all, playing at steeple-chase jockeys, combining, as they generally do, all the worst features of the hunting-field and racecourse—unsympathizing boots and breeches, dirty jackets that never fit, and caps that won't keep on. What a farce to see the great bulky fellows go to scale with their saddles strapped to their backs, as if to illustrate the impossibility of putting a round of beef upon a pudding plate!

But the weighed-in ones are mounting. See, there's Jack Spraggon getting a hoist on to Daddy Longlegs! Did ever mortal see such a man for a jockey? He has cut off the laps of a stunner tartan jacket, and looks like a great backgammon-board. He has got his head into an old gold-banded military foraging-cap, which comes down almost on to the rims of his great tortoise-shell spectacles. Lord Scamperdale stands with his hand on the horse's mane, talking earnestly to Jack, doubtless giving him his final instructions. Other jockeys emerge from various parts of the farm-buildings; some out of stables; some out of cow-houses; others from beneath cart-sheds. The scene becomes enlivened with the varied colours of the riders—red, yellow, green, blue, violet, and stripes without end. Then comes the usual difficulty of identifying the parties, many of whose mothers wouldn't know them.

'That's Captain Tongs,' observes Miss Simperley, 'in the blue. I remember dancing with him at Bath, and he did nothing but talk about steeple-chasing.'

'And who's that in yellow?' asks Miss Hardy.

'That's Captain Gander,' replies the gentleman on her left.

'Well, I think he'll win,' replies the lady.

'I'll bet you a pair of gloves he doesn't,' snaps Miss Moore, who fancies Captain Pusher, in the pink.

'What a squat little jockey!' exclaims Miss Hamilton, as a little dumpling of a man in Lincoln green is led past the stand on a fine bay horse, some one recognizing the rider as our old friend Caingey Thornton.

'And look who comes here?' whispers Miss Jawleyford to her sister, as Mr. Sponge, having accomplished a mount without derangement of temper, rides Hercules quietly past the stand, his whip-hand resting on his thigh, and his head turned to his fair companion on the white.

'Oh, the wretch!' sneers Miss Amelia; and the fair sisters look at Lucy and then at him with the utmost disgust.

Mr. Sponge may now be doubled up by half a dozen falls ere either of them would suggest the propriety of having him bled.

Lucy's cheeks are rather blanched with the 'pale cast of thought,' for she is not sufficiently initiated in the mysteries of steeple-chasing to know that it is often quite as good for a man to lose as to win, which it had just been quietly arranged between Sponge and Buckram should be the case on this occasion, Buckram having got uncommonly 'well on' to the losing tune. Perhaps, however, Lucy was thinking of the peril, not the profit of the thing.

The young ladies on the stand eye her with mingled feelings of pity and disdain, while the elderly ones shake their heads, call her a bold hussy—declare she's not so pretty—adding that they 'wouldn't have come if they'd known,' &c. &c.

But it is half-past two (an hour and a half after time), and there is at last a disposition evinced by some of the parties to go to the post. Broad-backed parti-coloured jockeys are seen converging that way, and the betting-men close in, getting more and more clamorous for odds. What a hubbub! How they bellow! How they roar! A universal deafness seems to have come over the whole of them. 'Seven to one 'gain the Bart.!'

screams one—'I'll take eight!' roars another. 'Five to one agen Herc'les!'
cries a third—'Done!' roars a fourth. 'Twice over!' rejoins the other—
'Done!' replies the taker. 'Ar'll take five to one agin the Daddy!'—'I'll lay
six!' 'What'll any one lay 'gin Parvo?' And so they raise such an uproar
that the squeak, squeak, squeak of the

    Devil among the tailors

is hardly heard.

Then, in a partial lull, the voice of Lord Scamperdale rises, exclaiming,
'Oh, you hideous Hobgoblin, bull-and-mouth of a boy! you think,
because I'm a lord, and can't swear, or use coarse language—' And again
the hubbub, led on by the

    Devil among the tailors,

drowns the exclamations of the speaker. It's that Pacey again; he's
accusing the virtuous Mr. Spraggon of handing his extra weight to Lord
Scamperdale; and Jack, in the full consciousness of injured guilt, intimates
that the blood of the Spraggons won't stand that—that there's 'only *one*
way of settling it, and he'll be ready for Pacey half an hour after the race.'

At length the horses are all out—one, two, three, four, five, six, seven,
eight, nine, ten, eleven, twelve, thirteen, fourteen, fifteen—fifteen of
them, moving about in all directions: some taking an up-gallop, others
a down; some a spicy trot, others walking to and fro; while one has still
his muzzle on, lest he should unship his rider and eat him; and another's
groom follows, imploring the mob to keep off his heels if they don't
want their heads in their hands. The noisy bell at length summons the
scattered forces to the post, and the variegated riders form into as good a
line as circumstances will allow. Just as Mr. Sponge turns his horse's head
Lucy hands him her little silver sherry-flask, which our friend drains to
the dregs. As he returns it, with a warm pressure of her soft hand, a pent-
up flood of tears burst their bounds, and suffuse her lustrous eyes. She
turns away to hide her emotion; at the same instant a wild shout rends
the air—'W-h-i-r-r! They're off!'

Thirteen get away, one turns tail, and our friend in the Lincoln green
is left performing a *pas seul*, asking the rearing horse, with an oath, if he

thinks 'he stole him'? while the mob shout and roar; and one wicked wag, in coaching parlance, advises him to pay the difference, and get inside.

But what a display of horsemanship is exhibited by the flyers! Tongs comes off at the first fence, the horse making straight for a pond, while the rest rattle on in a mass. The second fence is small, but there's a ditch on the far side, and Pusher and Gander severally measure their lengths on the rushy pasture beyond. Still there are ten left, and nobody ever reckoned upon these getting to the far end.

'Master wins, for a 'undr'd!' exclaims Leather, as, getting into the third field, Mr. Sponge takes a decided lead; and Lucy, encouraged by the sound, looks up, and sees her 'white jacket' throwing the dry fallow in the faces of the field.

'Oh, how I hope he will!' exclaims she, clasping her hands, with upturned eyes; but when she ventures on another look, she sees old Spraggon drawing upon him, Hangallows's flaming red jacket not far off, and several others nearer than she liked. Still the tail was beginning to form. Another fence, and that a big one, draws it out. A striped jacket is down, and the horse, after a vain effort to rise, sinks lifeless on the ground. On they go all the same!

Loud yells of exciting betting burst from the spectators, and Buckram gets well on for the cross.

There are now five in front—Sponge, Spraggon, Hangallows, Boville, and another; and already the pace begins to tell. It wasn't possible to run it at the rate they started. Spraggon makes a desperate effort to get the lead; and Sponge, seeing Boville handy, pulls his horse, and lets the light-weight make play over a rough, heavy fallow with the chestnut. Jack spurs and flogs, and grins and foams at the mouth. Thus they get half round the oval course. They are now directly in front of the hill, and the spectators gaze with intense anxiety;—now vociferating the name of this horse, now of that; now shouting 'Red jacket!' now 'White!' while the blind fiddler perseveres with the old melody of—

The Devil among the Tailors.

'Now they come to the brook!' exclaims Leather, who has been over the ground; and as he speaks, Lucy distinctly sees Mr. Sponge's gather an effort to clear it; and—oh, horror!—the horse falls—he's down—no, he's up!—and her lover's in his seat again; and she flatters herself it was her sherry that saved him. Splash!—a horse and rider duck under; three get over; two go in; now another clears it, and the rest turn tail.

What splashing and screaming, and whipping and spurring, and how hopeless the chance of any of them to recover their lost ground. The race is now clearly between five. Now for the wall! It's five feet high, built of heavy blocks, and strong in the staked-out part. As he nears it, Jack sits well back, getting Daddy Longlegs well by the head, and giving him a refresher with the whip. It is Jack's last move! His horse comes, neck and croup over, rolling Jack up like a ball of worsted on the far side. At the same moment, Multum-in-Parvo goes at it full tilt; and, not rising an inch, sends Captain Boville flying one way, his saddle another, himself a third, and the stones all ways. Mr. Sponge then slips through, closely followed by Hangallows and a jockey in yellow, with a tail of three after them. They then put on all the steam they can raise over the twenty-acre pasture that follows.

The white!—the red!—the yaller! The red!—the white!—the yaller! and anybody's race! A sheet would cover them!—crack! whack! crack! how they flog! Hercules springs at the sound.

Many of the excited spectators begin hallooing, and straddling, and working their arms as if their gestures and vociferations would assist the race. Lord Scamperdale stands transfixed. He is staring through his silver spectacles at the awkwardly lying ball that represents poor Spraggon.

'By Heavens!' exclaims he, in an undertone to himself, 'I believe he's killed!' And thereupon he swung down the stand-stairs, rushed to his horse, and, clapping spurs to his sides, struck across the country to the spot.

Long before he got there the increased uproar of the spectators announced the final struggle; and looking over his shoulder, he saw white jacket hugging his horse home, closely followed by red, and shooting past the winning-post.

'Dash that Mr. Sponge!' growled his lordship, as the cheers of the winners closed the scene.

'The brute's won, in spite of him!' gasped Buckram, turning deadly pale at the sight.

LXIX

HOW OTHER THINGS
CAME OFF

'TWERE HARD TO SAY WHETHER Lucy's joy at Sponge's safety, or Lord Scamperdale's grief at poor Spraggon's death, was most overpowering. Each found relief in a copious flood of tears. Lucy sobbed and laughed, and sobbed and laughed again; and seemed as if her little heart would burst its bounds. The mob, ever open to sentiment—especially the sentiment of beauty—cheered and shouted as she rode with her lover from the winning to the weighing-post.

'A', she's a bonny un!' exclaimed a countryman, looking intently up in her face.

'She is that!' cried another, doing the same.

'Three cheers for the lady!' shouted a tall Shaggyford rough, taking off his woolly cap, and waving it.

'Hoo-ray! hoo-ray! hoo-ray!' shouted a group of flannel-clad navvies.

'Three for white jacket!' then roared a blue-coated butcher, who had won as many half-crowns on the race.—Three cheers were given for the unwilling winner.

'Oh, my poor dear Jack!' exclaimed his lordship, throwing himself off his horse, and wringing his hands in despair, as a select party of thimble-riggers, who had gone to Jack's assistance, raised him up, and turned his ghastly face, with his eyes squinting inside out, and the foam still on his mouth, full upon him. 'Oh, my poor dear Jack!' repeated his lordship, sinking on his knees beside him, and grasping his stiffening hand as he spoke. His lordship sank overpowered upon the body.

The thimble-riggers then availed themselves of the opportunity to ease his lordship and Jack of their watches and the few shillings they had about them, and departed.

When a lord is in distress, consolation is never long in coming; and Lord Scamperdale had hardly got over the first paroxysms of grief, and gathered up Jack's cap, and the fragments of his spectacles, ere Jawleyford, who had noticed his abrupt departure from the stand and scurry across the country, arrived at the spot. His lordship was still in the full agony of woe; still grasping and bedewing Jack's cold hand with his tears.

'Oh, my dear Jack! Oh, my dear Jawleyford! Oh, my dear Jack!' sobbed he, as he mopped the fast-chasing tears from his grizzly cheeks with a red cotton kerchief. 'Oh, my dear Jack! Oh, my dear Jawleyford! Oh, my dear Jack!' repeated he, as a fresh flood spread o'er the rugged surface. 'Oh, what a tr-reasure, what a tr—tr—trump he was. Shall never get such another. Nobody could s—s—lang a fi—fi—field as he could; no hu—hu—humbug 'bout him—never was su—su—such a fine natural bl—bl—blackguard'; and then his feelings wholly choked his utterance as he recollected how easily Jack was satisfied; how he could dine off tripe and cow-heel, mop up fat porridge for breakfast, and never grumbled at being put on a bad horse.

The news of a man being killed soon reached the hill, and drew the attention of the mob from our hero and heroine, causing such a spread of population over the farm as must have been highly gratifying to Scourgefield, who stood watching the crashing of the fences and the demolition of the gates, thinking how he was paying his landlord off.

Seeing the rude, unmannerly character of the mob, Jawleyford got his lordship by the arm, and led him away towards the hill, his lordship reeling, rather than walking, and indulging in all sorts of wild, incoherent cries and lamentations.

'Sing out, Jack! sing out!' he would exclaim, as if in the agony of having his hounds ridden over; then, checking himself, he would shake his head and say, 'Ah, poor Jack, poor Jack! shall never look upon his like again—shall never get such a man to read the riot act, and keep all square.' And then a fresh gush of tears suffused his grizzly face.

The minor casualties of those few butchering spasmodic moments may be briefly dismissed, though they were more numerous than most sportsmen see out hunting in a lifetime.

One horse broke his back, another was drowned, Multum-in-Parvo was cut all to pieces, his rider had two ribs and a thumb broken, while Farmer Slyfield's stackyard was fired by some of the itinerant tribe, and all its uninsured contents destroyed—so that his landlord was not the only person who suffered by the grand occasion.

Nor was this all, for Mr. Numboy, the coroner, hearing of Jack's death, held an inquest on the body; and, having empanelled a matter-of-fact jury—men who did not see the advantage of steeple-chasing, either in a political, commercial, agricultural, or national point of view, and who, having surveyed the line, and found nearly every fence dangerous, and the wall and brook doubly so, returned a verdict of manslaughter against Mr. Viney for setting it out, who was forthwith committed to the county gaol of Limbo Castle for trial at the ensuing assizes, from whence let us join the benevolent clerk of arraigns in wishing him a good deliverance.

Many of the hardy 'tips' sounded the loud trump of victory, proclaiming that their innumerable friends had feathered their nests through their agency; but Peeping Tom and Infallible Joe, and Enoch Wriggle, 'the offending soul,' &c, found it convenient to bolt from their respective establishments, carrying with them their large fire-screens, camp-stools, and boards for posting up their lists, and setting up in new names in other quarters; while the Hen Angel was shortly afterwards closed, and the presentation-tureen made into 'white soup.'

So much for the 'small deer.' We will now devote a concluding chapter to the 'great guns' of our story.

LXX

How Lord Scamperdale and Co. Came Off

Our noble master's nerves were so dreadfully shattered by the lamentable catastrophe to poor Jack, that he stepped, or rather was pushed, into Jawleyford's carriage almost insensibly, and driven from the course to Jawleyford Court.

There he remained sufficiently long for Mrs. Jawleyford to persuade him that he would be far better married, and that either of her amiable daughters would make him a most excellent wife. His lordship, after very mature consideration, and many most scrutinizing stares at both of them through his formidable spectacles, wondering which would be the least likely to ruin him—at length decided upon taking Miss Emily, the youngest, though for a long time the victory was doubtful, and Amelia practised her 'Scamperdale' singing with unabated ardour and confidence up to the last. We believe, if the truth were known, it was a slight touch of rouge, that Amelia thought would clench the matter, that decided his lordship against her. Emily, we are happy to say, makes him an excellent wife, and has not got her head turned by becoming a countess. She has improved his lordship amazingly, got him smart new clothes, and persuaded him to grow bushy whiskers right down under his chin, and is now feeling her way to a pair of moustaches.

Woodmansterne is quite another place. She has marshalled a proper establishment, and got him coaxed into the long put-a-way company rooms. Though he still indulges in his former cow-heel and other delicacies, they do not appear upon table; while he sports his silver-mounted specs on all occasions. The fruit and venison are freely distributed, and we have come in for a haunch in return for our attentions.

Best of all, Lady Scamperdale has got his lordship to erect a handsome marble monument to poor Jack, instead of the cheap country stone he intended. The inscription states that it was erected by Samuel, Eighth Earl of Scamperdale, and Viscount Hardup, in the Peerage of Ireland, to the Memory of John Spraggon, Esquire, the best of Sportsmen, and the firmest of Friends. Who or what Jack was, nobody ever knew, and as he only left a hat and eighteen pence behind him, no next of kin has as yet cast up.

Jawleyford has not stood the honour of the Scamperdale alliance quite so well as his daughter; and when our 'amaazin' instance of a pop'lar man,' instigated perhaps by the desire to have old Scamp for a brother-in-law, offered to Amelia, Jaw got throaty and consequential, hemmed and hawed, and pretended to be stiff about it. Puff, however, produced such weighty testimonials, as soon exercised their wonted influence. In due time Puff very magnanimously proposed uniting his pack with Lord Scamperdale's, dividing the expense of one establishment between them, to which his lordship readily assented, advising Puff to get rid of Bragg by giving him the hounds, which he did; and that great sporting luminary may be seen 's-c-e-u-s-e'-ing himself, and offering his service to masters of hounds any Monday at Tattersall's—though he still prefers a 'quality place.'

Benjamin Buckram, the gentleman with the small independence of his own, we are sorry to say has gone to the 'bad.' Aggravated by the loss he sustained by his horse winning the steeple-chase, he made an ill-advised onslaught on the cash-box of the London and Westminster Bank; and at three score years and ten this distinguished 'turfite,' who had participated with impunity in nearly all the great robberies of the last forty years, was doomed to transportation. And yet we have seen this cracksman captain—for he, too, was a captain at times—jostling and bellowing for odds among some of the highest and noblest of the land!

Leather has descended to the cab-stand, of which he promises to be a distinguished ornament. He haunts the Piccadilly stands, and has what he calls "'stablish'd a raw' on Mr. Sponge to the extent of three-and-six-pence a week, under threats of exposing the robbery Sponge committed on our friend Mr. Waffles. That volatile genius, we are happy to add, is quite well, and open to the attentions of any young lady who thinks she can tame a wild young man. His financial affairs are not irretrievable.

And now for the hero and heroine of our tale. The Sponges—for our friend married Lucy shortly after the steeple-chase—stayed at Nonsuch House until the bailiffs walked in. Sir Harry then bolted to Boulogne, where he shortly afterwards died, and Bugles very properly married my lady. They are now living at Wandsworth; Mr. Bugles and Lady Scattercash, very 'much thought of'—as Bugles says.

Although Mr. Sponge did not gain as much by winning the steeple-chase as he would have done had Hercules allowed him to lose it, he still did pretty well; and being at length starved out of Nonsuch House, he arrived at his old quarters, the Bantam, in Bond Street, where he turned his attention very seriously to providing for Lucy and the little Sponge, who had now issued its prospectus. He thought over all the ways and means of making money without capital, rejecting Australia and California as unfit for sportsmen and men fond of their *Moggs*. Professional steeple-chasing Lucy decried, declaring she would rather return to her flag-exercises at Astley's, as soon as she was able, than have her dear Sponge risking his neck that way. Our friend at length began to fear fortune-making was not so easy as he thought—indeed, he was soon sure of it.

One day as he was staring vacantly out of the Bantam coffee-room window, between the gilt labels, 'Hot Soups' and 'Dinners,' he was suddenly seized with a fit of virtuous indignation at the disreputable frauds practised by unprincipled adventurers on the unwary public, in the way of betting offices, and resolved that he would be the St. George to slay this great dragon of abuse. Accordingly, after due consultation with Lucy, he invested his all in fitting up and decorating the splendid establishment in Jermyn Street, St. James's, now known as the SPONGE AND CIGAR BETTING ROOMS, whose richness neither pen nor pencil can do justice to.

We must, therefore, entreat our readers to visit this emporium of honesty, where, in addition to finding lists posted on all the great events of the day, they can have the use of a *Mogg* while they indulge in one of Lucy's unrivalled cigars; and noblemen, gentlemen, and officers in the household troops may be accommodated with loans on their personal security to any amount. We see by Mr. Sponge's last advertisements that he has £116,300 to lend at three and a half per cent.!

'What a farce,' we fancy we hear some enterprising youngster exclaim—'what a farce, to suppose that such a needy scamp as Mr. Sponge, who has been cheating everybody, has any money to lend, or to pay bets with if he loses!' Right, young gentleman, right; but not a bit greater farce than to suppose that any of the plausible money-lenders, or infallible 'tips' with whom you, perhaps, have had connection have any either, in case it's called for. Nay, bad as he is, we'll back old Soapey to be better than any of them,—with which encomium we most heartily bid him ADIEU.

THE END

For forthcoming titles and sales information see
www.nonsuch-publishing.com